Jack Rosenbaum
1019 Park Valley Road
Baltimore, MD 21208

March 1979

Books by Herman Wouk

───────

Novels

AURORA DAWN

THE CITY BOY

THE CAINE MUTINY

MARJORIE MORNINGSTAR

YOUNGBLOOD HAWKE

DON'T STOP THE CARNIVAL

THE WINDS OF WAR

WAR AND REMEMBRANCE

Plays

THE TRAITOR

THE CAINE MUTINY COURT-MARTIAL

NATURE'S WAY

Nonfiction

THIS IS MY GOD

WAR
AND
REMEMBRANCE

WAR AND

a novel by

Little, Brown and Company

REMEMBRANCE

Herman Wouk

VOLUME TWO

BOSTON TORONTO

A limited edition of this book has been
privately printed.

ACKNOWLEDGMENTS

The author is grateful to the following publishers for permission to reprint excerpts from selected material as noted below.

Chappell Music Company for "Hut-Sut Song" by Leo V. Killion, Ted McMichael and Jack Owens. Copyright © 1941 by Schumann Music Co. Copyright renewed, assigned to Unichappell Music, Inc. (Belinda Music, publisher). International copyright secured. All rights reserved. Used by permission.

Edward B. Marks Music Corporation and Chappell Music Company for "Lili Marlene" by Norbert Schultze. All rights for the United States © Copyright: Edward B. Marks Music Corporation. Used by permission. All rights for Canada and the Philippines Copyright © Chappell Music Co., Inc. International copyright secured. All rights reserved. Used by permission.

Southern Music Publishing Company, Inc. for "Der Fuehrer's Face" by Oliver Wallace. Copyright 1942 by Southern Music Publishing Company, Inc. Copyright renewed. Used by permission.

United Artists Music Publishing Group, Inc. and West's Ltd. for "Three O'Clock In The Morning" by Dorothy Terriss and Julian Robledo. Copyright © 1921, 1922. Renewed 1949, 1950 West's Ltd. All rights for North America administered by Leo Feist, Inc. All rights reserved. Used by permission.

Published simultaneously in Canada
by Little, Brown & Company (Canada) Limited

50

I N September 1941, Victor Henry had left a country at peace, but
with isolationists and interventionists in a screechy squabble, the
production of munitions a trickle, despite all the "arsenal of democracy" rhetoric; the military services shuddering over Congress's renewal of the draft by one vote; a land without rationing, with business
booming from defense spending, with lights blazing at night from coast
to coast, with the usual cataracts of automobiles on the highways and
the city streets.

Now as he returned, San Francisco from the air spelled War: shadowy lampless bridges under a full moon, pale ribbons of deserted highways, dimmed-out residential hills, black tall downtown buildings. In
the dark quiet streets and in the glare of the hotel lobby the swarms of
uniforms astounded him. Hitler's Berlin had looked no more martial.

Newspapers and magazines that he read next day on the eastbound
flight mirrored the change. In the advertisements, all was bellicose pa-
triotism. Where heroic-looking riveters, miners, or soldiers and their
sweethearts were not featured in the ads, a toothy Jap hyena, or a snake
with a Hitler mustache, or a bloated scowling Mussolini-like pig took
comic beatings. The news columns and year-end summaries surged with
buoyant confidence that at Stalingrad and in North Africa the tide of
the war had turned. The Pacific was getting short treatment. Sketchy
references to Midway and Guadalcanal, perhaps through the fault of
the closemouthed Navy, miserably missed the scope of these battles. As
for the sinking of the *Northampton,* Pug saw that if released the story
would have been ignored. This calamity in his life, this loss of a great
ship of war, would have been a dark flyspeck on a golden picture of optimism.

And it was all mighty sudden! Island-hopping across the Pacific in
recent days, he had been reading in airplanes and waiting rooms scuffed
periodicals of the past months. With one voice they had bemoaned the
dilatory Allied war effort, the deep German advances into the Caucasus, the pro-Axis unrest in India, South America, and the Arab lands,
and Japan's march across Burma and the Southwest Pacific. Now with
one voice the same journals were hailing the inevitable downfall of

Adolf Hitler and his partners in crime. This civilian change of mood struck Pug as frivolous. If the strategic turn was at hand, the main carnage in the field was yet to come. Americans had only begun to die. To military families, if not to military columnists, this was no small thing. He had called Rhoda from San Francisco, and she had told him that there was no news of Byron. In wartime, no news, especially about a son in submarines, was not necessarily good news.

His orders to BuPers and the talk with Spruance were much on his mind as the plane bounced and tossed through the wintry gray skies. The key man at the Bureau for four-striper assignments was Digger Brown, his old Academy chum. Pug had drilled the ambitious Brown, who couldn't learn languages, through three years of German, boosting him to top grades which had raised Brown's class standing and helped his whole career. Pug expected to be ordered back to Cincpac without trouble, for nobody in the Navy swung much more weight right now than Nimitz and Spruance; still, if there were any bureaucratic shuffling about it, he meant to look Digger Brown in the eye and tell him what he wanted. The man could not refuse him.

What about Rhoda? What could he say in the first moments? How should he act? He had been puzzling over this while he flew halfway around the globe, and the quandary was still with him.

In the dark marble-tiled foyer of the big Foxhall Road house, she wept in his arms. His bulky bridge coat was flecked with snow, his embrace was awkward, but she clung to him against the cold wet blue cloth and the bumpy brass buttons, exclaiming through sobs, "I'm sorry, oh, I'm sorry, Pug. I didn't mean to cry, truly I didn't. I'm so glad to see you I could DIE. Sorry, darling! Sorry I'm such a crybaby."

"It's all right, Rho. Everything's all right."

And in this first tender moment he really thought everything might turn out all right. Her body felt soft and sweet in his embrace. In all their long marriage he had seen his wife in tears only a few times; for all her frothy ways she had a streak of stoical self-control. She clutched him like a child seeking comfort, and her wet eyes were large and bright. "Oh, damn, *damn,* I was going to carry this off with a smile and a martini. The martini is probably still a SCRUMPTIOUS idea, isn't it?"

"At high noon? Well, maybe, at that." He tossed his coat and cap on a bench. She led him hand in hand into the living room, where flames leaped in the fireplace, and ornaments glittered on a large Christmas tree that filled the room with a smell of childhood, of family joy.

He took both her hands. "Let's have a good look at you."

"Madeline's coming here for Christmas, you know," she chattered, "and not having a maid and all, I thought I'd just buy a tree early and trim the darn thing up, and—well, well, SAY something!" She shakily laughed, freeing her hands. "This captain's inspection is giving me the WIM-WAMS. What do you think of the old hulk?"

It was almost like sizing up another man's wife. Rhoda's skin was soft, clear, scarcely lined. In the clinging jersey dress her figure was as seductive as ever; if anything, a shade thin. Her hip bones jutted. Her movements and gestures were lithe, fetching, feminine. Her comic waggle of ten spread fingers at him when she said "WIM-WAMS" brought back her roguish charm in their first dates.

"You look marvelous."

The admiring tone brought instant radiance to her face. She spoke huskily, her voice catching, "You would say that. And you look so smart! A bit grayer, old thing, but it's attractive."

He walked to the fire, holding out his hands. "This feels good."

"Oh, I'm being ever so patriotic. Also practical. Oil's a problem. I keep the thermostat down, close off most of the rooms, and burn a lot of wood. Now, you WRETCH! Why didn't you call me from the airport? I've been pacing the house like a LEOPARD."

"The booths were jammed."

"Well, I've been FALLING on the phone for an hour. It kept ringing. That fellow Slote called from the State Department. He's back from Switzerland."

"Slote! Any news of Natalie? Or of Byron?"

"He was in a terrific hurry. He's going to call again. Natalie seems to be in Lourdes, and—"

"What? Lourdes? France? How'd she get to Lourdes?"

"She's with our interned diplomats and journalists. That's all he said about her. Byron was in Lisbon, trying to get transportation back, last Slote heard. He's got orders to new construction."

"Well! And the baby?"

"Slote didn't say. I asked him to dinner. And do you remember Sime Anderson? He called, too. The phone never stopped ringing."

"The midshipman? The one who ran me all over the tennis court while Madeline giggled and clapped?"

"He's a lieutenant commander! How about that, Pug? I declare, these days if you've been WEANED you're a lieutenant commander. He wanted Madeline's phone number in New York."

Staring into the fire, Pug said, "She's back with that monkey Cleveland, isn't she?"

"Dear, I got to know Mr. Cleveland in Hollywood. He's not a bad fellow." At her husband's ugly look she faltered, "Besides, she's having such fun! And the MONEY the child makes!" The firelight was casting harsh shadows on Victor Henry's face. She came to him. "Darling, how about that drink? I'm frankly all of a QUIVER."

His arm went round her waist, and he kissed her cheek. "Sure. Just let me ring Digger Brown first, and find out why in hell I'm here on Class One priority."

"Oh, Pug, he'll only tell you to call the White House. Let's just pretend your plane's late and—why, what on EARTH is wrong, sweetie?"

"The White House?"

"Well, sure." She clapped a hand to her lips. "Oh, LORDY. Lucy Brown will have my HEAD. She swore me to secrecy, but I just assumed you knew."

"Knew *what?*" His tone changed. He might have been talking to a quartermaster. "Rhoda, tell me exactly what Lucy Brown told you, and when."

"Dear me! Well—it seems the White House ordered BuPers to get you back here, p.d.q. This was early in November, before, well, before you lost the *Northampton,* Pug. That's all I know. That's all even Digger knows."

Pug was at a telephone, dialling. "Go ahead and make that drink."

"Dear, just don't let on to Digger that Lucy told me. He'll ROAST her over a slow fire."

The Navy Department switchboard was long in answering. Victor Henry stood alone in the big living room, recovering from his surprise. *The White House* was still for him, as for any American, a magic expression, but he had come to know the sour aftertaste of serving a President. Franklin Roosevelt had used him like a borrowed pencil, and in the same way had dropped him; paying off, politician fashion, with the command of the unlucky *California.* Victor Henry bore the President no grudge. Near or far, he still regarded the masterful old cripple with awe. But he was resolved to fight off, at any cost, further presidential assignments. Those sterile shorebound exercises as flunky to the great had all but wrecked his professional life. He had to get back to the Pacific.

Digger was out. Pug went over to the fireplace and stood with his back to the blaze. He did not feel at home, yet in Janice's cramped cottage he had. Why was that? Before going to Moscow he had spent less than three months in this house. How huge it was! What had they been thinking of, to buy such a mansion? Once again he had allowed her to chip in some of her own trust money, because she wanted to live in a style beyond his means. Wrong, wrong. There had been talk of putting up lots of grandchildren. What a bitter memory! And what were the summer slipcovers doing on the furniture in chill December, in a room smelling of Christmas? He had never liked this garish flower pattern on green chintz. Though he could feel the fire heat on his jacket, the chill in the house seemed to pierce to his marrow. Maybe it was true that serving in the tropics thinned the blood. But he could not remember feeling so cold before, on returning from Pacific duty.

"Martinis," Rhoda announced, marching in with a clinking tray. "What about Digger?"

"Not there."

The first sip made a fiery streak down Pug's throat. He had not tasted alcohol in months; not since a spell of heavy self-numbing after Warren's death. "Good," he said, but he regretted agreeing to the martini. He might need all his wits at BuPers. Rhoda offered him a plate of open-face sandwiches, and he commented with assumed heartiness, "Hey, caviar! Really cosseting me, aren't you?"

"You don't remember?" Her smile was archly flirtatious. "You sent it from Moscow. An Army colonel brought me six tins, with this note from you."

"For when we meet again," the scrawl on shoddy Russian paper read. *"Martinis, caviar, a fire, AND . . . especially AND . . . ! Love, Pug."*

It all came back to him now: the boisterous afternoon when the Harriman party had shopped in the one tourist store still functioning, in the National Hotel, months before Pearl Harbor. Pamela had vetoed all the shawls and blouses; an elegant woman like Rhoda, she had said, wouldn't be caught dead in these tacky things. The fur hats had seemed made for giantesses. So he had bought the caviar and scrawled this silly note.

"Well, it's damn good caviar, at that."

Rhoda's warm glance was inviting a pass. That much, Victor Henry had often pictured: the sea captain home from the wars, Odysseus and Penelope heading for the couch. Her voice was dulcet. "You look as though you haven't slept for days."

"Not all that much." He put both palms to his eyes and rubbed. "I've come a long way."

"Haven't you ever! How does the good old U.S.A. look to you, Pug?"

"Peculiar, especially from the air at night. Solid blackout on the West Coast. Inland you begin to see lights. Peaceful blaze in Chicago. Past Cleveland they start dimming down again, and Washington's dark."

"Oh, that's so typical! No consistency. This ungodly mess with shortages! All the talk about rationing! Off again, on again! You never know where you're at. And the HOARDING that's going on, Pug. Why, people BOAST about how clever they've been, piling up tires, and meat, and sugar, and heating oil, and I don't know what all. I tell you, we're a nation of spoiled HOGS."

"Rhoda, it's a good idea not to expect too much of human nature."

The remark cut his wife short. A doubtful look, a silent moment. She put her hand on his. "Darling, do you feel like talking about the *Northampton?*"

"We got torpedoed and sank."

"Lucy says most of the officers and crew were saved."

"Jim Grigg did a good job. Still, we lost too many men."

"Did you have a close call yourself?"

Her face was eager, expectant. In lieu of some affectionate move, for which he felt no impulse, he began to talk about the loss of his ship. He rose and paced, the words running free after a while, the emotions of the terrible night reviving. Rhoda listened shiny-eyed. When the telephone rang he halted in his tracks, staring like a wakened sleepwalker. "I guess that's Digger."

Captain Brown boomed heartily, "Well, well, Pug. Made it, did you? Great."

"Digger, did you get a dispatch from Cincpac about me?"

"Look, let's not do any business over the phone, Pug. Why don't you and Rhoda just take it easy and enjoy yourselves today? It's been a long time, and so on and so forth. Heh heh! We'll talk tomorrow. Give me a ring about nine in the morning."

"Are you tied up today? Suppose I come down right now?"

"Well, if that's what you want." Pug heard his old friend sigh. "But you do sound tired."

"I'm coming, Digger." Pug hung up, strode to his wife, and kissed her cheek. "I'd better find out what's doing."

"Okay." She cupped his face in her hands, and gave his mouth a lingering kiss. "Take the Oldsmobile."

"It still runs? Fine."

"Maybe you'll get to be the President's naval aide. That's Lucy's guess. Then at least we'd see something of each other for a while, Pug."

She walked to a little desk and took out car keys. The unselfconscious pathos of Rhoda's words got to him more than all the flirting. Alone in a cold house, bereaved of her firstborn son—whom they still hadn't mentioned, whose picture smiled from the piano top; her husband home after more than a year away, rushing out about his business; she was being very good about all this. This sway of her slender hips was beguiling. Pug wondered at his own lack of desire for her. He had an impulse to throw off the bridge coat he was donning, and to seize her. But Digger Brown was expecting him, and she was dropping the keys into his hand with an arch little flip. "Anyway, we'll dine at home, won't we? Just the two of us?"

"Sure we'll dine at home, just the two of us. With wine, I trust, and—" he hesitated, then forced a ribald lift of the eyebrows, "especially *and.*"

The flash in her eyes leaped across the gulf between them. "On your way, sailor boy."

Outside it was the same old Navy Building, the long dismal "temporary" structure from the last war still disfiguring Constitution Avenue, but inside it had a new air: a hurrying pace, a general buzz, crowds of Waves and callow-looking staff officers in the corridors. Lurid combat paintings that hardly seemed dry hung on the dusty walls: dogfights over carriers, night gun battles, bombardments of tropic islands. During most of Pug's career, the decor had been mementos of the Spanish-American War, and of Atlantic action in 1918.

Digger Brown looked every bit the king of the hill that he was: tall, massive, healthy, with a thatch of grizzled hair, with a year of battleship command under his belt (Atlantic service, but good enough), and now this top post in BuPers. Digger had flag rank in the bag. Pug wondered how he must seem to Brown. He had never been overawed by his fast-moving old friend, nor was he now. Much passed unspoken as they shook hands and scanned each other's faces. The fact was, Pug Henry made Captain Brown think of an oak tree in his own back yard, blasted by lightning yet still vigorous, and putting forth green shoots each spring from charred branches.

"That's hell about Warren," Brown said.

Henry made an elaborate business of lighting a cigarette. Brown had to get the rest spoken. "And the *California,* and then the *Northampton.* Christ!" He gripped Pug's shoulder in awkward sympathy. "Sit you down."

Pug said, "Well, sometimes I tell myself I didn't volunteer to be born, Digger, I got drafted. I'm all right."

"And Rhoda? How'd you find her?"

"Splendid."

"What about Byron?"

"Coming back from Gib to new construction, or so I hear." Pug cocked his head at his old friend, squinting through smoke. "You're riding high."

"I've yet to hear a gun go off in anger."

"There's plenty of war left out there."

"Pug, it may be a reprehensible sentiment, but I hope you're right."

Captain Brown put on horn-rimmed glasses, thumbed through dispatches on a clipboard, and handed one to Pug. "You asked me about this, I believe?"

FROM: CINCPAC
TO: BUPERS
DESIRE ASSIGNMENT STAFF DUTY THIS COMMAND VICTOR (NONE) HENRY CAPTAIN USN SERIAL 4329 EX CO NORTHAMPTON X NIMITZ

Pug nodded.

Brown unwrapped a stick of chewing gum. "I'm supposed to quit smoking. Blood pressure. It's got me climbing the walls."

"Come on, Digger, are my orders to Cincpac set?"

"Pug, did you wangle this on the trip home?"

"I didn't wangle it. Spruance sprang it on me. I was amazed. I thought I'd catch hell for losing my ship."

"Why? You went down fighting." Under Pug's hard inquiring look, Digger Brown chewed and chewed. The big body shifted in the swivel chair. "Pug, you ducked Cincpac staff duty last year, according to Jocko Larkin."

"That was then."

"Why do you suppose you were recalled with Class One air priority?"

"You tell me."

Slowly, with a portentous air, Brown said, *"The . . . Great . . . White . . . Father."* Then more lightly, "Yessir! The boss man himself. You're supposed to report in to him soonest, in full feathers and war paint." Brown laughed at his own humor.

"What's it about?"

"Oh, blast, give me a butt. Thanks." Brown dragged at the cigarette, his eyes popping. "You know Admiral Standley, I believe. The ambassador to Russia, that is."

"Sure. I went there with him last year on the Harriman mission."

"Exactly. He's back for consultations with the President. Even before the *Northampton* was lost, Rear Admiral Carton was telephoning us from the White House in a big sweat about you. Standley was inquiring about your availability. Hence the Class One priority."

Pug said, trying to keep the irritation out of his voice, "Nimitz should draw more water around here than Standley does."

"Pug, I have my instructions. You're to call Russ Carton for an appointment to see the President."

"Does Carton know about the Cincpac dispatch?"

"I haven't told him."

"Why not?"

"I wasn't asked."

"Okay, Digger. I'm asking you to notify Russ Carton about that Cincpac dispatch. Today."

A brief contest of cold stares. With a deep drag on the cigarette, Digger Brown said, "You're asking me to get out of line."

"Why? You're derelict in not telling the White House Cincpac wants me."

"Christ on a bicycle, Pug, don't give me that. When that man up on Pennsylvania Avenue snaps his fingers, we jump around here. Nothing else signifies."

"But this is just a whim of old Bill Standley's, you say."

"I'm not sure. Tell Russ Carton about Cincpac yourself when you see him."

"N.G. He must get the word from BuPers."

Captain Brown sullenly avoided his eyes. "Who says he must?"

Victor Henry intoned as in a language drill, *"Ich muss, du musst, er muss."*

An unhappy grin curled Brown's mouth and he picked up the chant, *"Wir müssen, ihr müsst, sie müsst."*

"Müssen, Digger."

"Müssen. I never could hack German, could I?" Brown pulled deeply on the cigarette and abruptly ground it out. "God, that tasted good. Pug, I *still* think you should find out first what the Great White Father wants." He hit a buzzer in an annoyed gesture. "But have it your way. I'll shoot a copy to Russ."

The house was warmer. Pug heard a man talking in the living room. "Hello there," he called, very loud.

"Oh, hi!" Rhoda's cheery voice. "Back so soon?"

A deeply tanned young officer was on his feet when Pug walked in. The mustache puzzled him, then he put together the blond hair and the bright new gold half-stripe of a lieutenant commander. "Hello there, Anderson."

Pouring tea at a table by the fire, Rhoda said, "Sime just stopped by to drop off Maddy's Christmas present."

"Something I picked up in Trinidad." Anderson gestured at the gaily wrapped box on the table.

"What were you doing in Trinidad?"

Rhoda gave the men tea and left, while Anderson was telling Pug about his destroyer duty in the Caribbean. U-boats had been having fat pickings off Venezuela and the Guianas, and in the Gulf of Mexico: oil tankers, bauxite carriers, freighters, and passenger liners. Emboldened by the easy pickings, the German skippers had even taken to surfacing and sinking ships with gunfire, so as to save torpedoes. The American and British navies had now worked up a combined convoy system to control the menace, and Anderson had been out on that convoy duty.

Pug was only vaguely aware of the Caribbean U-boat problem. Anderson's tale made him think of two large photographs in the Navy Building, showing Eskimos bundled in furs watching the loading of a Catalina flying boat in a snowstorm, and Polynesians naked but for G-strings staring at an identical Catalina moored in a palm-fringed lagoon. This war was a leprosy spreading all over the globe.

"Say, Anderson, weren't you working with Deak Parsons at BuOrd on the AA proximity fuse, advanced hush-hush stuff?"

"Yes, sir."

"Then why the Sam Hill were you shipped off to the Caribbean on an old four-piper?"

"Shortage of deck officers, sir."

"That fuse is fantastic, Sime."

The bright blue eyes glowed in the brown face. "Oh, has it gotten out to the fleet?"

"I saw a demonstration off Nouméa against drone planes. Sheer slaughter. Three out of three drones splashed in minutes. Downright spooky, those AA bursts opening up right by the planes every time."

"We worked pretty hard on it."

"How the devil did Deak Parsons get a whole radio signal set inside an AA shell? And how does it survive a jolt of muzzle velocity, and a spin in trajectory of five hundred times a second?"

"Well, sir, we figured out the specs. The industry fellows said, 'Can do,' and they did it. As a matter of fact, I'm going down to Anacostia now to see Captain Parsons."

Victor Henry had never liked any of Madeline's gosling suitors, but this one looked pretty good to him, especially by contrast with Hugh Cleveland. "Any chance you can come and have Christmas dinner with us? Madeline will be here."

"Yes, sir. Thank you. Mrs. Henry's been kind enough to invite me."

"She has? Well! Give Deak my regards. Tell him SoPac's buzzing about that fuse."

In the stuffy office of the Naval Research Laboratory, looking out over the mud flats to the river, Captain William Parsons complimented Anderson on his suntan, and nodded without comment at Pug Henry's message. He was a man in his forties with a wrinkled pale brow and receding hair, run-of-the-mill in appearance but the most hardworking and brilliant man Anderson had ever served under.

"Sime, what do you know about uranium?"

Anderson felt as though he had stepped on a third rail. "I've done no work in radioactivity, sir. Nor in neutron bombardment."

"You do know that there's something funny going on in uranium."

"Well, when I did my postgrad work at Cal Tech in 1939, there was a lot of talk about the fission results of the Germans."

"What sort of talk?"

"Wild talk, Captain, about superbombs, also about atomic-powered propulsion, all very theoretical."

"D'you suppose we've left it at that? Just a theoretical possibility? Just a promising freak of nature? With all the German scientists working around the clock for Hitler?"

"I hope not, sir."

"Come with me."

They went outside and hurried with heads down toward the main laboratory building, through a bitter wind blowing from the river. Even at a distance, an eerie hissing and whistling sounded from the lab. Inside, the noise was close to deafening. Steam was escaping from a forest of freestanding slender pipes reaching almost to the very high roof, giving the place the dank warmth of the Caribbean. Men in shirt-sleeves or coveralls were pottering at the pipes or at instrument panels.

"Thermal diffusion," Parsons shouted, "for separating U-235. Did you know Phil Abelson at Cal Tech?" Parsons pointed to a slender man in shirt-sleeves and tie, about Anderson's age, standing arms akimbo at a wall covered with dials.

"No, but I heard about him."

"Come and meet him. He's working with us in a civilian capacity."

Abelson gave the lieutenant commander a keen look when Parsons explained over the noise that Anderson had worked on the proximity fuse. "We've got a chemical engineering problem here," Abelson said, gesturing around at the pipes. "That your field?"

"Not exactly. Out of uniform I'm a physicist."

Abelson briefly smiled and turned back to his instrument panel.

"I just wanted you to see this setup," Parsons said. "Let's get out of here."

The air outside seemed arctic. Parsons buttoned his bridge coat to his chin, jammed his hands in his pockets, and strode toward the river, where nests of gray Navy ships rode to anchor.

"Sime, you know the principle of the Clusius tube, don't you?"

Anderson searched his memory. "That's the lab tube with the dough-nut-shaped cross-section?"

"Yes. That's what Abelson's got in there. Two pipes one inside the other, actually. You heat the inside pipe and chill the outside one, and if there's a liquid in the space between, the molecules of any lighter isotope will move toward the heat. Convection takes them to the top, and you skim them off. Abelson's put together a lot of giant Clusius tubes, a whole jungle of them in series. The U-235 gradually cooks out. It's damned slow, but he's already got measurable enrichment."

"What's his liquid?"

"That's his original achievement. Uranium hexafluoride. He developed the stuff and it's pretty touchy, but stable enough to work with. Now, this thing is getting pretty hot, and BuOrd wants to station a line officer here. I've recommended you. It's a shore billet again. You young fellows can always get sea duty if you prefer."

But Sime Anderson had no seafaring ambitions. He had gone to the Academy to get a superior free education. Annapolis had stamped him out in the standard mold, and on the bridge of a destroyer he was just another OOD; but inside this standard replacement part a first-class young physicist was imprisoned, and here was his chance to leap out. The proximity fuse had been an advance in ordnance, but not a thrust into a prime secret of nature. Abelson with his messy array of steam pipes was hunting big game.

At Cal Tech there had been speculation about a U-235 bomb that could wipe out a whole city, and of engines that could drive an ocean liner three times around the world on a few kilograms of uranium. Among Navy men the talk was of the ultimate submarine; power without the combustion that needed air. This was a grand frontier of applied human intelligence. A more mundane inducement occurred to young Anderson. Stationed in Anacostia, he could see a lot more of Madeline Henry than he had been doing. "Sir, if the Bureau considers me qualified, I've no objection."

"Okay. Now what I'm going to tell you next, Anderson, blows away on the wind." Parsons rested his elbows on an iron railing that fenced off a rocky drop to the river. "As I said, our interest is propulsion, but the Army's working on a bomb. We're excluded. Compartmentalized secrecy. Still, we know." Parsons glanced at the younger man, hurrying his words. "Our first objective and the Army's are the same, to produce pure U-235. For them the next step is making a weapon. A battery of theoreticians is already working on that. Maybe some fact of nature will prevent it. Nobody can say for sure yet."

"Does the Army know what we're doing?"

"Hell, yes. We gave them their uranium hexafluoride to start with. But the Army thinks thermal diffusion is for the birds. Too slow, and the enrichment is too low-grade. Their assignment is to beat Hitler to a bomb. A prudent notion, that. They're starting from the ground up, with untried designs and new concepts that are supposed to be short-cuts, and they're doing it on a colossal industrial scale. Nobel Prize heavyweights like Lawrence, Compton, and Fermi have been supplying the ideas. The size of the Army effort really staggers the mind, Anderson. They're commandeering power, water, land, and strategic materials till hell won't have it. Meantime we've got enriched U-235 in hand. Low enrichment, not bomb material as yet, but a first stage. The Army's got a lot of big ideas and big holes in the ground. Now if the Army falls on its face it'll be the biggest scientific and military bust of all time. And then—just conceivably, mind you—then it could be up to the Navy to beat the Germans to atomic bombs, right here in Anacostia."

"Wow."

Parsons wryly grinned. "Don't hold your breath. The Army's got the President's ear, and the world's greatest minds working on it, and they're outspending us a million dollars to one. They'll probably make a bomb, if nature was careless enough to leave that possibility open. Meantime we'll keep our little tinpot operation cooking. Just keep the other remote contingency in your mind, and pick up your orders at BuPers tomorrow."

"Aye aye, sir."

By candlelight Rhoda's face was like a young woman's. As they ate cherry tarts she had baked for dessert, Pug was telling her, through a fog of fatigue, about his stop in Nouméa on his way home. They were on their third bottle of wine, so his description of the somnolent French colony south of the equator, overrun by the carnival of American war-making, was not very coherent. He was trying to describe the comic scene in the officers' club in an old fusty French hotel, of men in uniform clustering four and five deep around a few Navy nurses and Frenchwomen, captains and commanders up close, junior officers hovering on the outer edges just to stare at the females. Pug was so weary that Rhoda's face seemed to be blurrily wavering between the candle flames.

"Darling," she interrupted quietly and hesitantly, "I'm afraid you're not making very good sense."

"What? Why not?"

"You just said you and Warren were watching all this, and Warren cracked a joke—"

Pug shuddered. He had indeed been drifting into a doze while he talked, fusing dreams with memory, picturing Warren alive in that jammed smoky Nouméa club long after Midway, holding a can of beer in his old way, and saying, *"Those gals are forgetting, Dad, that once the uniform comes off, the more stripes, the less action."* It was pure fantasy; in his lifetime Warren had never come to Nouméa.

"I'm sorry." He vigorously shook his head.

"Let's skip the coffee"—she looked concerned—"and put you to bed."

"Hell, no. I want my coffee. And brandy, too. I'm enjoying myself, Rhoda."

"Probably the fire's making you sleepy."

Most of the rooms in this old house had fireplaces. The carved wooden mantelpiece of this large dining room, in the flicker of light and shadow from the log fire, was oppressively elegant. Pug had grown unused to Rhoda's style of life, which had always been too rich for him. He stood up, feeling the wine in his head and in his knees. "Probably. I'll take the Chambertin inside. You deploy the coffee."

"Dear, I'll bring you the wine, too."

He dropped in a chair in the living room, by the fireplace heaped with gray ashes. The bright chandelier gave the trimmed Christmas tree a tawdry store-window look. It was warm all through the house now, and there was a smell of hot dusty radiators. She had put up the thermostat with the comment, "I've gotten used to a cool house. No wonder the British think we steam ourselves alive like SEAFOOD. But of course you've just come from the tropics."

Pug wondered at his macabre waking vision of Warren. How could his dreaming mind have invented that wisecrack? The voice had been so recognizable, so alive! *"Once the uniform comes off, Dad, the more stripes, the less action!"* Pure Warren; neither he himself nor Byron would ever have said that.

Rhoda set the bottle and glass at his elbow. "Coffee will be right along, honey."

Sipping at the wine, he felt he could fall into bed and sleep fourteen hours without moving. But Rhoda had gone to so much trouble, and the dinner had been so good: onion soup, rare roast beef, baked potatoes with sour cream, au gratin cauliflower; her new form-fitting red silk dress was a stunner, her hair was done up as for a dance, her whole manner was loving and willing. Penelope was more than ready for the returned wayfarer, and Pug didn't want to disappoint or humiliate his wife. Yet whether because he was aging, or weary, or because the Kirby business lay raw and unresolved, he sensed no stir of amorousness for her. None.

A shy touch on his face, and he opened his eyes to see her smiling down at him. "I don't think coffee'll help much, Pug."

"No. Most discouraging."

Getting ready for bed half-woke him. Coming from the bathroom, he found her, fully dressed, turning down his twin bed. He felt like a fool. He tried to embrace her. She fended him off with the laughing deftness of a coed. "Sweetie pie, I love you to little pieces, but I truly don't believe you'd make it. One good night's sleep, and the tiger will be back on the prowl."

Pug sank into bed with a sleepy groan. Softly she kissed him on the mouth. "It's good to have you back."

"Sorry about this," he murmured, as she turned out the light.

Not in the least put out, rather relieved than otherwise, Rhoda took off the red dress and donned an old housecoat. She went downstairs and cleaned up every trace of the dinner, and of the day gone by; emptied the living room ashtrays, shovelled the fireplace ashes into a scuttle, laid a new fire for the morning, and put out the ashes and the garbage. She enjoyed the moment's breath of icy air in the alley, the glimpse of glittering stars, and the crunch of snow under her slippers.

In her dressing room, with a glass of brandy at hand, she ran a hot bath and set about the dismantling job under glaring lights between large mirrors. Off came the rouge, the lipstick, the mascara, and the skin makeup which she wore down to her collar bone. The naked woman stepping into the vaporous tub was lean, almost stringy, after months of resolute starving. Her ribs unattractively showed; but her belly was straight, her hips slim, her breasts small and passably shaped. About the face, alas, there was nothing girlish. Still, Colonel Harrison Peters, she thought, would find her desirable.

To Rhoda's view desirability was nine-tenths in the man's mind, anyway; the woman's job was to foster the feeling, if she detected it and if it suited her purpose. Pug liked her thin, so she had damned well gotten thin for this reunion. Rhoda knew she was in trouble, but about her sexual allure for her husband she was not worried. Given Pug's dour fidelity, this was the rock on which their marriage stood.

The warm water enveloped and deliciously relaxed her. Despite her outer calm she had been taut as a scared cat all evening. In his gentleness, his absence of reproach, his courteous manner, and his lack of ardor, Pug had said it all. His silences disclosed more than other men's words. No doubt he had forgiven her (whatever that might mean) but he had not even begun to forget; though it seemed he was not going to bring up the anonymous letters. Adding it all up, she was not unhappy with this first day. It was over, and they were off the knife-edge, on a bearable footing. She had dreaded the first encounter in bed. It could so easily have gone wrong, and a few silly minutes might have exacerbated the estrangement. Sex as pleasure, at this point, mattered to her not at all. She had more serious concerns.

Rhoda was a woman of method, much given to lists, written and mental. The bath was her time for review. Item one tonight was nothing less than her marriage itself. Despite Pug's kind letters, and the wave of reconciling emotion after Warren's death—now that they had faced each other, was it salvageable? On the whole, she thought so. This had immediate practical consequences.

Colonel Harrison Peters was amazingly taken with her. He was coming to Saint John's Church on Sundays just to see more of her. At first she had wondered what he wanted of her, when (so she had heard) plenty of round-heeled Washington girls were his at a push. Now she knew, because he had told her. She was the military man's lady of his dreams: good-looking, true, decorous, churchgoing, elegant, and brave. He admired the way she was bearing the loss of her son. In their moments together—she was keeping them infrequent and public, having learned her lesson with Kirby—he had gotten her to talk about Warren, and sometimes had wiped away his own tears. The man was tough and important, doing some highly secret Army job; but when it came down to cases, he was just a lonesome bachelor in his mid-fifties, tired of fooling around, too old to start a family, but wistful to settle down. There the man was for the having.

But if she could hold on to Pug, that was what she wanted. He was her life. She had worked out with Palmer Kirby her romantic yearnings. Divorce and remarriage were messy at best. Her identity, her prestige, her self-respect, were bound up with remaining Mrs. Victor Henry. Moving to Hawaii had proven too difficult and complicated; but maybe it was just as well that time had passed before a reunion, and the newest wounds had somewhat healed. Pug was a real man. You could never count Pug Henry out. Why, here was the White House calling him again! He had had a rotten run of luck, including her own misconduct; but if ever a man had the stuff to weather it, he did. In her way Rhoda admired and even loved Pug. The death of Warren had enlarged her limited capacity for love. A broken heart sometimes stretches when it mends.

The way Rhoda now sized matters up, soaking in her tub, it appeared that after a touch-and-go reconciliation they would make it. After all, there was the Pamela Tudsbury business; she had something to forgive too, though she did not know just what. When they had talked of Tudsbury's death at dinner she had carefully watched Pug's face. "I wonder what Pamela will do now," she had ventured. "I saw them when they passed through Hollywood, you know. Did you get my letter? The poor man gave a BRILLIANT speech at the Hollywood Bowl."

"I know. You sent me the speech."

"Actually, Pug, she wrote it. So she told me."

"Yes, Pam was ghosting a lot for him toward the end. But he gave her the ideas." No surprising the old fox, tired or not; his tone was perfectly casual.

Not that it mattered. Rhoda had digested Pamela Tudsbury's astounding revelation in Hollywood more or less in this wise: if a passionate young beauty like that one—who by the look of her knew plenty about men—could not snag Pug right after poor Warren's death, when he was far from home, vulnerable, estranged by the Kirby affair, and no doubt drunk every night, then the marriage was probably safe. Colonel Harrison Peters, all handsome six feet three of him, could go hang if she could keep Pug. Harrison's admiration was like an accident insurance policy. She was glad she had it, and hoped she would never have to fall back on it.

In the dim glow of the bedroom nightlight, the grim lines of Pug's face were smoothed by sleep. An unwonted impulse came to Rhoda's mind: should she slip into his bed? She had seldom done this down the years; mostly a long time ago, after too much to drink or an evening of flirting with someone else's husband. Pug took her rare advances as great compliments. He looked handsome and sweet. Many a breach between them had quickly closed with lovemaking.

Yet she hesitated. It was one thing for the modest spouse to yield to a yen for her man back from the war. For her—on probation, seeking forgiveness—wasn't it something else; a bribing use of her body, a hint of coarsened appetite? None of this was articulated by Rhoda, naturally. It raced through her mind in a sort of female symbolic logic, and she got into her own bed.

Pug snapped awake, the alcohol wearing off and his nerves jangling an alarm. Rhoda, dead to the world, wore a wrinkly cap on her hair. No use turning over. He would have to drink more or take a pill. He found the warmest bathrobe in his closet, and went to the library where the movable bar was. On the antique desk lay a big leather-bound scrapbook, with Warren's photograph worked into the cover over gold-stamped lettering:

Lieutenant Warren Henry, USN

He mixed a stiff bourbon and water, staring at the album as at a spectre. He walked out of the room, snapping off the light; then he went back, groped to the desk, and lit the reading lamp. Standing drink in hand, he went through the scrapbook leaf by leaf. On the inside front cover, bordered in black, was Warren's baby picture; on the inside back cover, his obituary in the *Washington Post,* with a blurry photograph; and facing this, the citation for his posthumous Navy Cross, boldly signed in black ink by the Secretary of the Navy.

In this album Rhoda had marshalled their firstborn son's whole short life: the first attempt at lettering—MERRY CHRISTMAS—in red and green crayon on coarse kindergarten paper; the first report card in Grade One of a school in Norfolk—Effort A, Work A+, Conduct C; pictures of children's birthday parties, pictures at summer camps, honor certificates, athletic citations, programs of school plays, track meets, and graduations; sample letters, with penmanship and language improving from year to year; Academy documents and photographs, his commission, promotion letters, and transfer dispatches, interspersed with snapshots of him on ships and in the cockpits of airplanes; half a dozen pages devoted to pictures and mementos of his engagement and marriage to Janice Lacouture (an unexpected photograph of Natalie Jastrow in a black dress, standing beside the white-clad married pair in the sun, gave Pug a turn); and the last pages were full of war souvenirs—his squadron posing on the deck of the *Enterprise,* Warren in his cockpit on deck and in the air, a jocular cartoon of him in the ship's newspaper reporting his lecture on the invasion of Russia; and finally, centered on two pages, also bordered in black, his last letter to his mother, typed on *Enterprise* stationery. It was dated in March, three months before his death.

Shaken at finding these fresh words from his dead son, Pug avidly read them. Warren had always hated to write letters. He had filled the first page by recounting Vic's bright doings and sayings, and housekeeping problems in Hawaii. On the second page he had warmed up:

I fly dawn patrol, so I had better sign off, Mom. Sorry I haven't written more often. I usually manage to see Dad when we're in port. I assume he keeps you up to date. Also I can't write much about what I do.

But I'll say this. Every time I take off over the water, and every time I come in for a deck landing, I thank my stars that I made it through Pensacola. There are just a handful of naval aviators in this war. When Vic grows up and reads all about it, and he looks at the gray-headed old crock he calls Dad, I don't think he'll be ashamed of the part I played.

I certainly hope that by the time Vic's a man the world will be getting rid of war. This exercise used to be fun, and maybe even profitable for the victor, I don't know. But mine's the last generation that can get a kick out of combat, Mom, it's all getting too impersonal, and complicated, and costly, and deadly. People have to figure out a saner way to run this planet. Armed robbers like the Germans and the Japs create problems, but hereafter they'll have to be snuffed out before they get rolling.

So I almost hate to confess how much fun it's been. I hope my son never knows the fear and the glory of diving a plane into AA fire. It's a hell of a stupid way to make a living. But now that I'm doing it, I have to tell you I wouldn't have missed it for all the tea in China. I'd like to see Vic become a politician and work at straightening the world out. I may even have a shot at it myself when all this is over, and cut a trail for him. Meantime, dawn patrol.

Love,
Warren

Pug closed the album, tossed off his second drink, and passed his hand over the rough leather as over the cheek of a child. Turning off the lights, he trudged upstairs to the bedroom. Warren's mother was asleep as before, on her back, the pretty profile cut off by the grotesque hair bag. He stared at her as though she were a stranger. How could she have endured putting that album together? It was a wonderful job, like everything she did. He could not yet trust himself to speak his son's name aloud, and she had done all that: dug up the mementos, faced them, handled them, made a nice ornamental arrangement of them.

Pug got into bed, face buried in the pillow, to let the whiskey whirl him down into a few more hours of oblivion.

51

THE broad gold admiral's stripe on Russell Carton's sleeve was very shiny. His overheated little office in the west wing of the White House was crusted with many paint jobs, the latest oyster gray. This newly minted rear admiral was only two Academy classes senior to Pug. The face was jowlier, the body thicker than in the days when Carton had marched by on the Annapolis parade ground shouting orders to his battalion. He had been stiff then and he was stiff now. Seated at a metal desk under a large autographed picture of the President, he shook hands without rising, and made pointless chitchat, not mentioning the Nimitz request. So Pug decided to risk a probe. "Admiral, did BuPers notify you of a dispatch from Cincpac about me?"

"Well, yes." Guarded and grudging answer.

"Then the President knows that Admiral Nimitz wants me for his staff?"

"Henry, my advice to you is simply to go in there and listen when summoned," Carton said testily. "Admiral Standley is with the President now. Also Mr. Hopkins and Admiral Leahy." He pulled a basket of correspondence forward. "Now until we're buzzed, I do have these letters to get out."

Pug had his answer; the President did not know. The wait went by without another word from Carton while Pug reviewed his situation and planned his tactics. In over a year he had received no comment on his battlefront report to Harry Hopkins from Moscow, nor a reply to his letter to the President about the evidence of a Jewish massacre in Minsk. He had long since concluded that that letter had finished him with the White House, showing him up as a sentimental meddler in matters not his concern. That had not bothered him much. He had never sought the role of a minor presidential emissary, and had not relished it. Evidently old Admiral Standley was behind this White House summons. The countering tactic must be simple: disclose the Nimitz dispatch to nullify Standley, pull out and stay out of the President's field of force, and return to the Pacific.

The buzzer sounded twice. "That's us," said Carton. The White

House hallways and stairways appeared quiet and unchanged, the calm at the eye of the hurricane. Secretaries and uniformed orderlies moved softly at a peacetime pace. In the Oval Office the gadgets and ship models cluttering the big desk did not seem to have been moved in nearly two years. But Franklin Roosevelt was much altered: the gray hair thinner, the eyes filmy in purple pouches, the whole aspect strikingly aged. Harry Hopkins, slouching waxen-faced in an armchair, wearily waved at Pug. The two admirals emblazoned with gold and ribbons, sitting rigidly on a couch, barely glanced at him.

Roosevelt's tired big-jawed face took on lively pleasure as Victor Henry came in with Carton. "Well, Pug, old top!" The voice was rich, lordly, Harvardish, like all the boring radio comedians' imitations. "So the Japs made you swim for it, eh?"

"I'm afraid so, Mr. President."

"That's my favorite exercise, you know, swimming," Roosevelt said with a waggish grin. "It's good for my health. However, I like to pick my own time and place."

Nonplussed for a moment, Pug realized that the heavy pleasantry was intended as a kindness. Roosevelt's eyebrows were expectantly raised for his answer. He forced the lightest riposte he could think of. "Mr. President, I agree it was an ill-timed swim, but it was pretty good for my own health."

"Ha, ha!" Roosevelt threw back his head and laughed with gusto, whereupon the others also laughed a little. "Well put! Otherwise you wouldn't be here, would you?" He delivered this as though it were another joke, and the others laughed again. Russell Carton withdrew. The President's expressive face went grave. "Pug, I regret the loss of that grand ship, and of all those brave men. The *Northampton* gave a bully account of herself, I know that. I'm terribly glad you came away safe. You must know Admiral Leahy"—Roosevelt's lean, dry-looking chief of staff gave Pug a wooden nod suited to his four stripes and sunken ship—"and of course Bill Standley. Bill's been singing your praises ever since you went with him to Moscow."

"Hello, Henry," said Admiral Standley. Leathery, wizened, a bulky hearing aid in his ear, his thin lipless lower jaw thrust out over a corded, wattled neck, he looked a bit like an angry tortoise.

"You know, Admiral Standley grew so fond of the Russians on that Harriman mission, Pug"—Roosevelt signalled another joke with arched eyebrows—"that I had to send him back to Moscow as ambassador, just to keep him happy! And though he's been home on leave, he misses them so much he's hurrying back there tomorrow. Right, Bill?"

"Right as rain, Chief." The tone was coarsely sarcastic.

"How did you like the Russians, Pug?"

"I was impressed by them, Mr. President."

"Oh? Well, other people occasionally have been, too. What impressed you most about them?"

"Their numbers, sir, and their willingness to die."

Glances darted among the four men. Harry Hopkins spoke up in a weak hoarse voice, "Well, Pug, I guess at this point the Germans at Stalingrad might agree with you."

Standley gave Pug a peevish look. "The Russians are numerous and brave. Nobody disputes that. They're also impossible. That's the basic problem, and there's a basic answer. Firmness and clarity." Standley waved a bony finger at the tolerantly smiling President. "Words are wasted on them. It's like dealing with beings from another planet. They understand only the language of deeds. Even that they can get wrong. I don't think they understand Lend-Lease to this minute. It's available, so they simply demand and demand, and grab and grab, like kids at a party where the ice cream and cake are free."

Cocking his head, the President almost gaily replied, "Bill, did I ever tell you about my talk with Litvinov, way back in 1933? I was negotiating recognition of the Soviet Union with him. Well, I'd never dealt with such people before. Gracious, I got mad! It was over the issue of religious freedom for our nationals in Russia, as I recall. He was being slippery as an eel. I simply blew up at him. I've never forgotten his comeback, as cool as you please.

"He said, 'Mr. President, right after our revolution, your people and mine could hardly communicate. You were still one hundred percent capitalistic, and we had dropped to zero.'" Roosevelt spread his meaty hands vertically in the air, far apart. "'Since then we've come up to here, to about twenty, and you've come down to about eighty. In the years to come I believe we'll narrow it to sixty and forty.'" The President's hands converged. "'We may not get any closer,' he said, 'but across that gap we'll communicate quite well.' Now Bill, I see Litvinov's words coming true in this war."

"So do I," said Hopkins.

Standley fairly snapped at Hopkins, "You fellows don't stay long. Their company manners are fine with you vodka visitors. Working with them day to day is something else. Now, Mr. President, I know my time's up. Let me summarize, and I'll take my leave." He ticked off brisk pleas for stricter administration of Lend-Lease, for promotion of his attachés, and for direct control by the embassy of visiting VIPs. He mentioned Wendell Willkie with special abhorrence, and shot Hopkins a sour look. Nodding, smiling, Roosevelt promised Standley that it would all be done. As the two admirals went out, Standley gave Pug a pat on the shoulder and a crabbed grin.

Sighing, the President pressed a button. "Let's have some lunch. You too, Pug?"

"Sir, my wife just gave me a late breakfast of fresh trout."

"You don't say! Trout! Well, I call *that* a nice welcome! How is Rhoda? Such an elegant and pretty woman."

"She's well, Mr. President. She hoped you'd remember her."

"Oh, she's hard to forget." Taking off his pince-nez and rubbing his purple-rimmed eyes, Franklin Roosevelt said, "Pug, when I heard from SecNav about your boy, Warren, I felt terrible. That's the one I never met. Is Rhoda bearing up?"

The old politician's trick of remembering first names, and the sudden reference to his dead son, threw Pug off balance. "She's fine, sir."

"That was a remarkable victory at Midway, Pug. It was all due to brave youngsters like Warren. They saved our situation in the Pacific." The President abruptly changed his tone and manner from the warmest sympathy to straight business. "But see here, we've lost far too many warships around Guadalcanal in night actions. Haven't we? How is that? Are the Japs better night fighters than we are?"

"No, sir!" Pug felt the question as a personal jab. Glad to get off the subject of Warren, he answered crisply, "They started the war at a much higher level of training. They were geared up and ready to go. We weren't. Even so, we've stood them off. They've given up trying to reinforce Guadalcanal. We're going to win there. I admit we have to do better in night gun battles, and we will."

"I agree with all you say." The President's look was cold and penetrating. "But I was terribly worried for a while there, Pug. I thought we might have to pull out of Guadalcanal. Our people would have taken that very hard. The Australians would simply have panicked. Nimitz did just the right thing, putting Halsey in there. That Halsey's a tough bird." The President was fitting a cigarette into his holder. "He's done splendidly on a shoestring. Rescued the whole picture there. *One* operational carrier! Imagine! We'll not be in that fix much longer, our production is starting to roll. It's taken a year longer than it should have, Pug. But just as you say, they were plotting war, and I wasn't! No matter what some newspapers keep hinting. Ah, here we are."

The white-coated Negro steward wheeled in a servidor. Putting aside the cigarette holder, Roosevelt startled Pug by complaining, "Just *look* at this portion, will you? Three eggs, maybe four. Darn it all, Pug, you're going to have to divide this with me. Serve it for two!" he ordered the steward. "Go ahead and have your soup, Harry. Don't wait."

The steward, looking scared, slid out a shelf from a corner of the desk, pulled up a chair, and served Victor Henry eggs, toast, and coffee, while Hopkins listlessly spooned soup from a bowl on a tray in his lap.

"This is more like it," said Franklin Roosevelt, eagerly starting to eat. "Now you can tell your grandchildren, Pug, that you shared a Presidential lunch. And maybe the staff will get the idea, once for all, that I don't like wasteful portions. It's a constant battle." The loose lukewarm eggs lacked salt and pepper. Pug ate them down, feeling historically privileged if not at all hungry.

"Say, Pug," said Hopkins in a faded voice, "we ran into a heck of a shortage of landing craft for North Africa. There was talk of a crash program to turn them out, and your name came up. But now the invasion's a success, and the U-boat problem has gotten more acute. So destroyer escorts are the number one shipyard priority. Nevertheless, the landing craft problem won't go away, so—"

"Absolutely not," the President cut in, dropping his fork with a clunk. "It haunts every discussion of the invasion of France. I remember our talks way back in August '41, Pug, aboard the *Augusta* before I went to meet Churchill. You knew your stuff. One forceful man riding herd on the landing craft program for the Navy, with my full backing, is what I need. But here old Bill Standley has come along, quite by coincidence, and asked for you as a special military aide." Roosevelt glanced up over the rim of his coffee cup. "Do you have a preference?"

After weeks of wondering, here was a tumble of revelations for Victor Henry. So they had whisked him back from the Pacific to put him into landing craft production; an important but dreary BuShips job, a career dead end. The Standley request was just an unlucky complication. How to bring up the Nimitz dispatch at this point? Torpedo water!

"Well, Mr. President, this goes to my head a bit, being offered such a choice, and by you."

"Why, that's most of what I do, old fellow," the President chuckled. "I just sit here, a sort of traffic cop, trying to direct the right men to the right jobs."

Roosevelt said this with pleasantly flattering intimacy, as though he and Victor Henry were boyhood friends. Cornered though Pug was, he yet could admire the President. The whole war was on this aging cripple's mind; and he had to run the country, too, and wrestle with a fractious Congress at every point to get things done. Harry Hopkins was growing restless, Pug could see. Probably some major meeting was scheduled next in this office. Yet Roosevelt could chat on with an anonymous midget of a naval captain, and make him feel important to the war. It was Pug's way with a ship's crew; he tried to give every sailor a sense that he mattered to the ship. But this was leadership magnified to a superhuman dimension, under unimaginable pressure.

It was very hard to cope with. It took all the willpower Victor Henry had, to remain silent under the scrutiny of those wise, weary eyes, two astrally remote sparks in a mask of intimate good fellowship. Mentioning the Nimitz dispatch was beyond him. It meant undercutting Carton and in a sense turning Roosevelt down flat. Let the President sense his hesitation, at least.

Roosevelt broke the slight tension. "Well! You've got to take ten days' leave first, in any case. Show Rhoda a good time. Now that's an order! Then, get in touch with Russ Carton, and one way or another we'll put you to work. By the bye, how's your submariner?"

"He's doing well, sir."

"And his wife? That Jewish girl who was having difficulties in Italy?"

A drop in the President's tone, a shift of his eyes to Hopkins, told Pug he was now overstaying his time. He jumped up. "Thank you, Mr. President. She's all right. I'll report in ten days to Admiral Carton. Thank you for lunch, sir."

Franklin Roosevelt's mobile face settled into lines that looked carved on stone. "Your letter from Moscow about the Minsk Jews was appreciated. Also your eyewitness report from the front to Harry. I read it. You proved right in predicting that the Russians would hold. You and Harry. A lot of experts here were wrong about that. You have insight, Pug, and a knack for putting things clearly. Now, the Jewish situation is simply terrible. I'm at my wits' end about that. That Hitler is a sort of satanic person, really, and the Germans have gone berserk. The only answer is to smash Nazi Germany as fast as we can, and give the Germans a beating they'll remember for generations. We're trying." His handshake was brief. Chilled, Pug left.

"If you think I'm a bold hussy, that's too bad," said Rhoda. "I'm just not easily discouraged."

Logs were burning in the living room fireplace, and on the coffee table were gin, vermouth, the mixing jug, and a jar of olives; also a freshly opened tin of caviar, thin-cut squares of bread, and plates of minced onions and eggs. She wore a peach negligee. Her hair was done up, her face lightly touched with rouge.

"A beautiful sight, all this," said Pug, embarrassed and yet stimulated, too. "Incidentally, the President sent you his best."

"Oh yes, I'll bet."

"He did, Rho. He said you're an elegant and pretty woman, and not easy to forget."

Blushing to her eartips—she very rarely blushed, and it gave her a fleeting girlish glow—Rhoda said, "Well, how nice. But what happened? What's the news?"

Over the drinks he gave her a deliberately laconic report. All Rhoda could gather was that the President had a couple of jobs in mind for him, and meantime had ordered him to take ten days' leave.

"Ten whole days! Lovely! Will either job keep you in Washington?"

"One would."

"Then that's the job I hope you land. We've been separated enough. Too much."

When they had eaten a lot of caviar, and finished the martinis, Pug was in the mood, or thought he was. His first gestures were rusty, but this soon passed. Rhoda's body felt delicious and exciting in his arms. They went upstairs to the bedroom and drew the blinds—which nevertheless let through much subdued afternoon light—and laughing at each other and making little jokes as they undressed, they got into her bed together.

Rhoda swept ahead with her old pleasing passionate ways. But from the moment he saw his wife's naked body, for the first time in a year and a half—and it still seemed dazzlingly pretty to him—an awareness seized Victor Henry that this body had been penetrated by another man. It was not that he bore Rhoda a grudge; on the contrary, he thought he had forgiven her. At least now, of all times, he wanted to blot the fact out. Instead, with her every caress, her every murmured endearment, her every lovemaking move, he kept picturing her doing exactly this with the big engineer. It did not interfere with what was happening. In a way—in a pornographic way—that enjoyment even seemed to be enhanced, for the moment. But the end was faint disgust.

Not for Rhoda, though. She gave every evidence of ecstatic gratification, covering his face with kisses and babbling nonsense. After a while, yawning like an animal and laughing, she snuggled down and fell asleep. The sun coming through the crack in the curtains blazed a bar of gold on one wall. Victor Henry left her bed, shut out the sunlight, returned to his own bed, and lay staring at the ceiling. So he was staring when she awoke an hour later with a smile.

52

LESLIE SLOTE woke in his old Georgetown flat, put on old trousers and a tweed jacket hanging in a closet he had locked away from sub-tenant use, and made toast and coffee in the airless little kitchen as he had done a thousand times. Carrying the old portfolio swollen with papers as usual, he walked down to the State Department in common-place midwinter Washington weather; low gray clouds, cold wind, a threat of snow in the air.

It was like returning to normal life after a long illness. The sights and sounds and smells of upper Pennsylvania Avenue, in other times ordi-nary and dreary, were beautiful to him. The people who walked past him, Americans all, stared at his Russian fur hat, and this delighted him; in Moscow and in Bern nobody would have noticed. He was home. He was safe. Not since the start of the German march on Moscow, he now realized, had he drawn an easy breath. Even in Bern the pavement un-derfoot had seemed to quake to the near thump of German boots. But the Germans were no longer just beyond the Alps, they were an ocean away; and the Atlantic headwinds were roaring their icy throats out at other scared men.

The rash of small pillars all over the façade of the State Department building did not, this once, seem ugly to Slote, but quaint and naïve and homey; an American architectural abomination, and therefore charm-ing. Armed guards inside halted him and he had to draw a celluloid pass. This was his first brush with the war in Washington. He stopped in the office of the Vichy desk for a look at the confidential list of some two hundred fifty Americans, mostly diplomatic and consular personnel, confined in Lourdes.

Hammer, Frederick, Friends Refugee Committee
Henry, Mrs. Natalie, journalist
Holliston, Charles, vice consul
Jastrow, Dr. Aaron, journalist

Still there! He hoped the omission of the baby, as in the list at the Lon-don embassy, was an oversight.

"Well, here you are," said the Division Director for European Affairs, standing up and scrutinizing Slote with an oddly excited air. Ordinarily he was a phlegmatic professional who had stayed cool and quiet even when they had played squash together years ago. In his shirt-sleeves, shaking hands over the desk, he disclosed the beginnings of a pot belly. His handshake was sweaty and rather convulsive. "And here *it* is." He handed Slote a two-page typed document scarred with red-ink cuts.

December 15, 1942 (tentative)

JOINT UNITED NATIONS STATEMENT ON
GERMAN ATROCITIES AGAINST JEWS

"What on earth is this?"

"A keg of dynamite, that's what. Official, approved, ready to go. We've been at it day and night for a week. It's all set at this end, and we're waiting for confirming cables from Whitehall and the Russians. Then, simultaneous release follows in Moscow, London, and Washington. Maybe as soon as tomorrow."

"Jesus, Foxy, what a development!"

People at State had always called the director Foxy. It was his nickname from Yale days. Slote had first encountered him as an alumnus of his secret society. Then Foxy Davis had seemed a debonair, remotely superior, and glamorous personage, a career Foreign Service officer just returned from Paris. Now Foxy was one among many men grayish of hair, face, and character who strolled State's corridors in grayish suits.

"Yes, it's a hell of a breakthrough."

"Seems I've crossed the ocean for nothing."

"Not in the least. The fact that you were coming"—Foxy jabbed a thumb toward the portfolio Slote had laid on the desk—"with that stuff gave us a lot of leverage. We knew from Tuttle's memoranda what you were bringing. You served. And you're needed here. Read the thing, Leslie."

Slote sat down on a hard chair, lit a cigarette, and conned the sheets while Foxy worked on his mail, chewing his lower lip in his old way. Foxy for his part noticed Slote's unchanged habit of drumming fingers on the back of a document as he read it; also that Slote looked yellow, and that his forehead was wrinkling like an old man's.

The attention of His Majesty's Government in the United Kingdom, of the Soviet Government, and of the United States Government has been drawn to reports from Europe ~~which leave no room for doubt~~ that the German authorities, not content with denying to persons of Jewish race, in all the territories over which their barbarous rule has been extended, the most elementary human rights, are now carrying into effect

Hitler's oft-repeated intention to exterminate the Jewish people in Europe. From all the countries Jews are being transported, ~~irrespective of~~ ~~age and sex and~~ in conditions of appalling horror and brutality, to Eastern Europe. In Poland, which has been made the principal Nazi slaughterhouse, the ghettos are being systematically emptied of all Jews except a few highly skilled workers required for war industries. None of those taken away are ever heard of again. The ablebodied are slowly worked to death in labor camps. The infirm are left to die of exposure and starvation or are deliberately massacred in mass executions.

His Majesty's Government in the United Kingdom, the Soviet Government, and the United States Government condemn in the strongest possible terms this bestial policy of cold-blooded extermination. They declare that such events can only strengthen the resolve of all freedom-loving peoples to overthrow the barbarous Hitlerite tyranny. They reaffirm their solemn resolution to ensure, in common with the governments of the United Nations, that those responsible for these crimes shall not escape retribution, and to press on with the necessary practical measures to this end.

Dropping the document on the desk, Slote asked, "Who made those cuts?"

"Why?"

"They castrate the thing. Can't you get them put back?"

"Les, that's a very strong document as it stands."

"But those strikeouts are malevolent surgery. Reports *'which leave no room for doubt'* says that our government believes this. Why cut that? *'Irrespective of age and sex'* is crucial. Those Germans are exterminating women and children wholesale. Anybody can respond to that! Otherwise the thing's just about 'Jews.' Far-off bearded kikes. Who cares?"

Foxy grimaced. "Now *that's* an overwrought reaction. Look, you're tired, and I think slightly biased, and—"

"Come on, Foxy, who made those cuts? The British? The Russians? Can we still fight?"

"They came from the second floor here." A serious look passed between them. "I went to the mat on this, my friend. I headed off a lot of other cuts. This thing will make an explosion in the world press, Leslie. It's been torture getting three governments to agree on the wording, and what we've ended with is remarkable."

Slote gnawed on a bony knuckle. "All right. How do we back it up?" He tapped his portfolio. "Can I prepare a selection of this stuff to release with the statement? It's hard confirmation. I can pull together a devastating selection in a few hours."

"No, no, no." Foxy shook his head. "We'd have to put all that on the wires to London and Moscow. Weeks could go by in more arguments."

"Foxy, without documentation that release is just a propaganda broadside. Mere boiler plate. That's how the press will take it. Milktoast stuff anyway, compared to what Goebbels puts out."

The division director spread his hands. "But your material all comes from Geneva Zionists or London Poles, doesn't it? The British Foreign Office raises its hackles at any Zionist material, and the Soviets foam at the very mention of the Polish government-in-exile. You know all that. Be practical."

"No backup, then." Slote struck a fist on the desk in frustration. "Words. Just words. The best the civilized nations can do against this horrible massacre, with all the damning evidence in hand."

Foxy got up, slammed his door shut, and turned on Slote, thrusting out a stiff arm and forefinger.

"Now look here. My wife is Jewish, as you know"—Slote didn't know it—"just as Mr. Hull's is. I've given this thing agonized thought, sleepless nights. Don't wave off what we've accomplished here. It will make a hell of a difference. The Germans will think twice before proceeding with their barbarities. It's a signal to them that'll sink in."

"Will it? I think they'll ignore it or laugh it off."

"I see. You want a world howl, and a big rescue push by the Allied governments."

"Yes. Especially of Jews piled up in neutral countries."

"Okay. You'd better start thinking in Washington terms again." Foxy slumped in his chair, looking irritated and sad, but he took a cool even tone. "The Arabs and the Persians are already over on Hitler's side, as you well know. In Morocco and Algeria right now there's hell to pay about our so-called pro-Jewish policy, simply because our military authorities removed the Vichy anti-Semitic laws. The Moslems are up in arms. Eisenhower's got Moslems all around his armies and up ahead in Tunis. If a world howl leads to a popular push to open Palestine for the Jews, that will *really* kick over the crock in the whole Mediterranean and Middle East. It will, Leslie! What's more, it'll alienate Turkey. It's an unacceptable political hazard. Do you disagree?"

At Slote's scowling silence, Foxy sighed and talked on, ticking off points on his fingers. "Now. Did you follow the elections while you were over there? President Roosevelt almost lost control of Congress. He squeaked through in both houses, and that nominal Democratic majority is riddled with rebelliousness. There's a big reaction gathering force in this country, Les. The isolationists are feeling their oats again. There's a record defense budget coming up. Big Lend-Lease appropriations, especially for the Soviet Union, which aren't popular at all. Renewal of price controls, rationing, and the draft, vital things the President must have to fight the war. Start a cry in this country to let in more Jews, Les, and just watch the counterblast in Congress against the whole war effort!"

"Well delivered, Foxy," Slote all but sneered. "I know the line well. Do you believe a word of it?"

"I believe all of it. Those are the facts. Unfortunate but true. The President saw Woodrow Wilson frustrated and his peace plans blown to hell by a Congress that got out of control. I'm sure the spectre of Wilson haunts him. The Jewish question is right on the red line, Leslie, in this government's basic political and military policies. The working room is narrow, fearfully narrow. Within those cramped limits, the document's an achievement. The British drafted it. Most of what I did was fight to keep the substance. I think I succeeded."

Suppressing the old sense of hopelessness, Slote asked, "Okay, what do I do next?"

"You have an appointment at three with Assistant Secretary Breckinridge Long."

"Any idea what he has in mind for me?"

"Not a clue."

"Fill me in on him."

"Long? Well, what do you know about him?"

"Just what Bill Tuttle told me. Long recruited Tuttle to organize the Republicans for Roosevelt in California. They both raced thoroughbred horses, or something, and that's how they got acquainted. Also, I know Long was ambassador to Italy. So I guess he's rich."

"His wife's rich." Foxy hesitated, then gave a heavy sigh. "He's a man on a hot seat."

"In what way?"

Foxy Davis began to pace his small office. "All right, short *curriculum vitae* on Breckinridge Long. You'd better know these things. Gentleman-politician of the old school. Fine Southern family. Princeton. Lifelong Missouri Democrat. Third Assistant Secretary of State under Wilson. Flopped trying to run for the Senate. In electoral politics, a washout." Foxy halted, standing over Slote, and poked his shoulder. "BUT—Long's an old, old, *old* Roosevelt man. That's the key to Breckinridge Long. If you were for Roosevelt before 1932 you're in, *and* Long goes back to 1920, when FDR ran for Vice President. Long's been a floor manager for him at the conventions. Ever since Wilson's time he's been a big contributor to Democratic campaigns."

"I get the idea."

"Okay. Reward, the post in Italy. Record, so-so. Admired Mussolini. Got disillusioned. Got recalled. Ulcers was the story. Actually, I believe he behaved ineptly during the Ethiopian war. Came back and raced his thoroughbreds. But of course he wanted back in, and FDR takes care of his own. When the war came, he created a job for Long—Special Assistant Secretary of State for emergency war matters. Hence the hot seat. The refugee problem is smack in his lap, because the visa division is his baby. Delegations in an unending parade—labor leaders, rabbis, businessmen, even Christian clergy—keep urging him to do more for the Jews. He has to keep saying no, no, no, in polite doubletalk, and he's too thin-skinned for the abuse that's ensued. Especially in the liberal press." Foxy sat down at his desk. "That's the drill on Breck Long. Now, until you get set, if you want an office—"

"Foxy, is Breckinridge Long an anti-Semite?"

A heavy sigh; a prolonged stare, not at Slote but into vacancy. "I don't think he's an inhumane man. He detests the Nazis and the Fascists. He really does. Certainly he's not an isolationist, he's very strong for a new League of Nations. He's a complicated fellow. No genius, not a bad guy, but the attacks are hurting and stiffening him. He's touchy as a bear with a sore nose."

"You're ducking my question."

"Then I'll answer it. *No.* He's not an anti-Semite. I don't think so, though God knows he's being called that. He's in a rotten spot, and he's overburdened with other work. I'm sure he doesn't know half of what's going on. He's one of the busiest men in Washington, and personally one of the nicest. A gentleman. I hope you go to work for him. I think you can get him to eliminate some of the worst abuses in the visa division, at the very least."

"Good Lord, that's inducement enough."

Foxy was looking through papers on his desk. "Now. Do you know a Mrs. Selma Ascher Wurtweiler? Formerly of Bern?"

It took Slote a moment to remember. "Yes. Of course. What about her?"

"She'd like you to telephone her. Says it's urgent. Here's her number in Baltimore."

Heavily pregnant, Selma came waddling behind the headwaiter to Slote's table, followed by a short red-faced almost bald young man. Slote jumped out of his chair. She wore plain black, with one brooch of big diamonds. Her hand was as cold and damp as if she had been making snowballs. Despite the huge bulge of her abdomen, the resemblance to Natalie was still marked.

"This is my husband."

Julius Wurtweiler put warm force into the banal greeting, "It's a pleasure to meet *you!*" As soon as he sat down, Wurtweiler called the waiter and began ordering the drinks and the lunch. He had to see several congressmen and two senators, he said, so he would eat and run, if that was all right, leaving Slote and Selma to chat about old times. The drinks came, with tomato juice for Selma. Wurtweiler lifted his glass toward Slote. "Well, here's to that United Nations statement. When's it coming out? Tomorrow?"

"Ah, what statement would that be?"

"Why, the statement about the Nazi massacres. What else?" Wurtweiler's pride in his inside knowledge glowed on the healthy face.

Better let the man disclose his hand, such as it was, Slote quickly decided. "You have a private line to Cordell Hull, I gather."

Wurtweiler laughed. "How do you suppose that statement originated?"

"I'm actually not sure."

"The British Jewish leaders finally got to Churchill and to Eden with some incontrovertible evidence. Terrible stuff! Churchill's heart is in the right place, but he has to buck that damned Foreign Office, and this time he did it. Of course, we've been kept informed."

"We?"

"The Zionist Councils here."

Before the food came—it took a while, because the restaurant was packed—Wurtweiler did a lot of talking over the loud chatter all around them. His manner was forceful and pleasant, his accent faintly Southern. He served on several committees of protest and rescue. He had given scores of personal affidavits for refugees. He had twice been in Cordell Hull's office with delegations. Mr. Hull was a thorough gentleman, he said, but aging and rather out of things.

Wurtweiler was not in total despair about the massacres. The Nazi persecution would prove a turning point in Jewish history, he believed. It would create the Jewish homeland. The political line of the Jews and their friends, he said, now had to be strong and single: *Repeal the White Paper! Open Palestine to European Jewry!* His committee was thinking of following up the Allied statement with a massive popular descent on Washington, and he wanted Slote's opinion of this. It would be called the "March of the Million." Americans of all faiths would take part. It would present a petition to the White House, signed with a million names, demanding—as the price of continuing Lend-Lease to the British—that London repeal the White Paper. Many senators and congressmen were ready to support such a resolution.

"Tell me candidly what you think," Wurtweiler said, attacking a cheese omelette while Selma picked at a fruit salad and gave Slote what seemed a warning glance.

Slote put a few mild questions. Assuming the British yielded, how could the Jews in German-held Europe actually be moved to Palestine? No problem, retorted Wurtweiler; plenty of neutral shipping was available: Turkish, Spanish, Swedish. For that matter, empty Allied Lend-Lease ships could carry them under a flag of truce.

But would the Germans honor a flag of truce or release the Jews?

Well, Hitler did want to clear Europe of Jews, said Wurtweiler, and this plan would do it, so why shouldn't he cooperate? The Nazis would demand a big ransom, no doubt. All right, the Jews in the free countries would beggar themselves to save Hitler's captives. He would himself. So would his four brothers.

Slote found himself, to his surprise, thinking in Foxy's "Washington terms" about the matter, in a reaction to this man's naïve self-assurance. He pointed out that such a large transfer of foreign currency would enable the Nazis to buy a lot of scarce war materials. In effect, Hitler would be bartering Jewish lives for the means to kill Allied soldiers.

"I don't see that at all!" Wurtweiler's answer shaded into impatience. "That's weighing remote military conjectures against the certain deaths of innocent people. It's a plain question of rescue before it's too late."

Slote mentioned that Arab sabotage could close the Suez Canal overnight. Wurtweiler had a brisk answer to "that old chestnut." The threat to the canal was finished. Rommel was running away from Egypt. Eisenhower and Montgomery were closing a nutcracker on him. The Arabs veered with the winds of victory, and they wouldn't dare to touch the canal.

They were now talking over coffee. As pleasantly as he could, Slote cautioned Wurtweiler against the charm of this one big simple answer, the "March of the Million" to open Palestine. He did not think the British would do it, or that there was any way for Jews in Nazi Europe to go there if they did.

"You're a total pessimist, then. You think they must all die."

Not at all, Slote replied. There were two things to work for: in the long range to destroy Nazi Germany, and in the short range to frighten the Nazis into stopping the murders. In the Allied world there were many thousands of sparsely settled square miles. Five thousand Jews, to start with, admitted to twenty countries—perhaps even including Palestine—would add up to a hundred thousand rescued souls. There were more than that many piled up in neutral lands. A concerted Allied decision to give them haven at once would jolt the Germans. At the moment, the Nazis kept jeering at the outside world, "If you're so worried about the Jews, why don't you take them in?" The only answer was shamed silence. That had to end. If America would lead, twenty countries would follow. Once the Allies showed they really cared about the fate of the Jews, that might scare Hitler's executioners, and slow down or even stop the killing. Agitation to open Palestine was futile and therefore beside the point.

Wurtweiler listened, his brow furrowed, his eyes intent on Slote, who thought he was making some headway. "Well, I get your point," he said at last, "and I completely disagree with you. A hundred thousand Jews! With millions facing doom! Once we support such a program, with the little strength we've got, it'll mean the end for Palestine. Your twenty havens would back out at the last minute anyhow. And most Jews wouldn't want to go to them."

With the friendliest farewell, Wurtweiler left after paying the bill, kissing his wife, and urging Slote to come to dinner soon in Baltimore.

"I like your husband," Slote ventured, as the waiter poured them more coffee.

Selma had eaten almost nothing, and she had turned very pale. She burst out, "He has a wonderful heart, he's given a fortune to rescue work, but his Zionist solution is a dream. I don't argue any more. He and his friends are so full of plans, meetings, projects, demonstrations, marches, rallies, this, that! They mean so well! There are so many other committees with different plans, meetings, rallies! He thinks *they're* so misguided! These American Jews! They run in circles like poisoned mice, and it's all too late. I don't blame them. I don't blame the Congress, or even your own State Department people. They aren't bad or stupid, they just can't imagine this thing."

"Some of them are pretty bad and pretty stupid."

She held up a protesting hand. "The Germans, the Germans are the killers. And you can't even blame them, exactly. They've turned into wild animals driven by a maniac. It's all too hopeless and horrible. I'm sorry we spent our whole lunch discussing it. I'll have nightmares tonight." She put both hands to her temples, and forced a smile. "What's happened to the girl who looked like me? And her baby?"

Her expression hardened at his reply. "Lourdes! My God! Isn't she in terrible danger?"

"She's as safe as our own consular people are."

"Even though she's Jewish?"

Slote shrugged. "I believe so."

"I'll dream about her. I dream all the time that I'm back in Germany, that we never got out. I can't tell you what awful, awful dreams I have. My father is dead, my mother's sick, and here I am in a strange country. I dread the nights." She looked around the restaurant in a stunned way, and gathered up bag and gloves in some agitation. "But it's a sin to be ungrateful. I'm alive. I'd better get my shopping done. Will you accept Julius's invitation to come to dinner in Baltimore?"

"Of course," Slote said too politely.

Her look was skeptical and resigned. On the sidewalk outside she said, "Your idea about refugees is not bad. You should push it. The Germans are losing the war. Soon they'll start worrying about saving their individual necks. Germans are very good at that. If America and twenty other countries would really take in a hundred thousand Jews now, that could worry those SS monsters. They might start looking for excuses to save Jews, so they could show good records. It's very sensible, Leslie."

"If you think so, I'm encouraged."

"Is there any chance of it happening?"

"I'm going to find out."

"God bless you." She held out her hand. "Is it cold?"

"Ice."

"You see? America hasn't changed me so much. Good-bye. I hope that your friend and her baby will be saved."

Walking back to the State Department under a clearing blue sky, leaning into a frigid wind, Slote paused and stared through the White House fence across the snowy lawn, trying to imagine Franklin Roosevelt at work somewhere inside that big edifice. For all the fireside chats, speeches, newsreels, and millions of newspaper words about him, Franklin Roosevelt remained for Slote an elusive man. Wasn't there a trace of fraud about a politician who could seem to Europeans a great humanitarian deliverer, yet whose policies, if Foxy was right, were fully as cold and inhumane as Napoleon's?

Tolstoy's grand theme in *War and Peace*—so Slote thought, as he hurried on—was the sinking of Napoleon in Pierre Bezukhov's mind from liberal deliverer of Europe to bloodthirsty invader of Russia. In Tolstoy's dubious theory of war, Napoleon was a mere monkey riding an elephant; an impotent egomaniac swept along by time and history, mouthing orders he couldn't help giving, winning battles that were bound to be won, because of small battlefield events that he didn't know about and couldn't control; then later losing wars with the same "strokes of genius" that had brought him "victories," because the stream of history had changed course away from him, stranding him in failure.

If Foxy was accurately reflecting Roosevelt's policy on the Jews, if he wouldn't even risk a clash with Congress to halt this vast crime, then wasn't the President Tolstoy's monkey after all—an inconsequential man, inflated by history's strong breath into a grandiose figure, seeming to be winning the war only because the tides of industrial prowess were moving that way; time's puppet, less free in confronting the Hitler horror than a single frightened Jew escaping over the Pyrenees, because that Jew at least was lowering the toll of murder by one?

Slote did not want to believe any of that.

The sunlight streaming through the tall windows of Breckinridge Long's office was no more pleasant to the eye, or more warm and cheery, than the Assistant Secretary himself, as he strode across the room like a young man to shake hands. Long's patrician face, thinly chiselled mouth, neat curling iron-gray hair, and short athletic figure went with a well-tailored dark gray suit, manicured nails, gray silk tie, and white kerchief in breast pocket. He was the very model of an Assistant Secretary of State; and far from appearing harried, or bitter, or in any way on a hot seat, Breckinridge Long might have been welcoming an old friend to his country home.

"Well, Leslie Slote! We should have met long ago. How's your father?"

Slote blinked. "Why, he's very well, sir." This was a disconcerting start. Slote did not remember his father's ever mentioning Breckinridge Long.

"Haven't seen him since God knows when. Dear me! He and I just about ran Ivy Club, played tennis almost every day, sailed, got in hot water with the girls—" With a melancholy charming smile, he waved at a sofa. "Ah, well! You know, you look more like Timmy Slote than he himself does now, I daresay. Ha-ha."

With an embarrassed smile, Slote sat down, searching his memory. At Harvard Law School the father had developed a scornful regret for his "wasted" years at Princeton: a country club, he would say, for rich featherheads trying to avoid an education. He had strongly advised his son to go elsewhere, and had spoken little of his college experiences. But how strange not to mention to a son in the Foreign Service that he knew an ambassador, an Assistant Secretary of State!

Long offered him a cigarette from a silver case, and leaning back on the sofa, fingering the handkerchief in his breast pocket, he said jocularly, "How did you ever happen to go to a tinpot school like Yale? Why didn't Timmy put his foot down?" He chuckled, regarding Slote with a fatherly eye. "Still, despite that handicap, you've made an admirable Foreign Service officer. I know your record."

Was this heavy sarcasm?

"Well, sir, I've tried. I feel pretty helpless sometimes."

"How well I know the feeling! How's Bill Tuttle?"

"Thriving, sir."

"Bill's a sound man. I've had some distressing communications from him. He's in a sensitive spot there in Bern." Breckinridge Long's eyes drooped half-shut. "You've both handled matters prudently there. If we'd had a couple of these radical boys out in that mission, the stuff you've been turning up might have been smeared all over the world press."

"Mr. Assistant Secretary—"

"Great day, young fellow, you're Tim Slote's son. Call me Breck."

In a memory flash Slote now recalled his father's talking of a "Breck," in conversations with his mother long, long ago; a shadowy figure from his racketing youth. "Well, then, Breck—I consider that material I've brought authentic and appalling."

"Yes, so does Bill. He made that clear. All the more credit to both of you for sensing where your duty lies." Long fingered his breast-pocket handkerchief and smoothed his tie. "I wish some of these wild-eyed types we're getting in Washington were more like you, Leslie. At least you know that a man who eats the government's bread shouldn't embarrass his country. You learned that lesson from that little episode in Moscow. Quite understandable and forgivable. The Nazi oppression of the Jews horrifies me, too. It's repulsive and barbaric. I was condemning that policy back in 1935. My memoranda from those days are right here in the files. Now then, young fellow. Let me tell you what I have in mind for you."

It was a while before Slote found out. Long first spoke of the nineteen divisions he headed. Cordell Hull actually had him drawing up a plan for the new postwar League of Nations. *There* was a challenge! He was working nights and Sundays, his health was suffering, but that didn't matter. He had seen Woodrow Wilson destroyed by Congress's rejection of the League in 1919. That must not happen to his great old friend, Franklin Roosevelt, and his grand visions for world peace.

Also, Congress had to be kept in line, and the Secretary had delegated to him most dealings with the Hill. *There* was a backbreaker! If Congress balked at Lend-Lease aid to Russia, Stalin might make a treacherous separate peace overnight. This war would be touch and go till the last shot was fired. The British could not be trusted, either. They were already intriguing to put de Gaulle into North Africa, so that they could control the Mediterranean after the war. They were in this war strictly for themselves; the British never changed much.

After this global rambling, Breckinridge Long came to the point at last. Somebody in the Division of European Affairs should be disposing of Jewish matters, he said, not passing them up to him—all these delegations, petitions, correspondence, important individuals who had to be treated with kid gloves, and the like. The situation required just the right man to keep it on an even keel, and he thought Leslie was that man. Leslie's reputation as a sympathizer with the Jews was a wonderful asset. His discretion in Bern had demonstrated his soundness. He came from good stock, and he had bred true. He had a shining future in the Department. Here was a chance to take on a really prickly job, show his stuff, and earn brilliant advancement.

Slote was appalled by all this. Taking over as a buffer for Breckinridge Long, "*saying no, no, no, in polite doubletalk*" to Jewish petitioners, was a disgusting prospect. The end of his career seemed now no farther off than the door of Long's office, and he hardly cared.

"Sir—"

"Breck."

"Breck, I don't want to be placed in such a spot unless I can help the people who come to me."

"But that's exactly what I want you to do."

"But what do I do besides turn them down? Say 'No,' every devious way I can think of?"

Breckinridge Long sat up straight, giving Slote a stern righteous stare. "Why, when you can possibly help somebody, you're to say yes, not no."

"But the existing regulations make that almost impossible."

"How? Tell me," Breckinridge Long inquired, his manner very kindly. A muscle in his jaw worked, and he fingered first his handkerchief, then his tie.

Slote started to explain the preposterousness of requiring Jews to produce exit permits and good conduct certificates from the police of their native lands. Long interrupted, his brow wrinkled in puzzlement, "But, Leslie, those are standard rules devised to keep out criminals, illegal fugitives, and other riffraff. How can we bypass them? Nobody has a God-given right to enter the United States. People have to show evidence that if we let them in they'll become good Americans."

"Breck, Jews have to get such papers from the Gestapo. That's obviously an absurd and cruel requirement."

"Oh, the New York bleeding hearts have made that a scare word. *Gestapo* simply means federal Secret Service, *Geheime Staatspolizei.*

I've had dealings with the Gestapo. They're Germans like any others. I'm sure their methods are mighty tough, but we have a mighty tough Secret Service ourselves. Every country does. Besides, not all Jews come from Germany."

Battling a ragged-nerve impulse to walk out and seek another livelihood—because he did sense in Long a peculiar streak of honest if perverse reasonableness—Slote said, "Wherever the Jews come from, they've fled for their lives. How could they have stopped to apply for official documents?"

"But if we drop these regulations," said Long patiently, "what's to prevent saboteurs, spies, dynamiters, and all sorts of undesirables in the thousands from getting into the country, posing as poor refugees? Just answer me that. If I were in German intelligence, I wouldn't miss that bet."

"Require other evidence of good character. Investigation by the Quakers. Affidavits of personal histories. Endorsements by the local U.S. consul. Or by some reliable relief agency, like the Joint. There are ways, if we'll look for them."

Breckinridge Long sat with his hands clasped under his chin, thoughtfully regarding Slote. His reply was slow and cautious. "Yes. Yes, I can see merit in that. The regulations can be onerous for deserving individuals. I've had other things on my mind, like the structure of the postwar world. I'm not pigheaded and"—his smile now was rather harried—"I'm not an anti-Semite, despite all the smears in the press. I'm a servant of the government and of its laws. I try to be a good one. Would you prepare a memorandum on your ideas for me to give the visa division?"

Slote could scarcely believe he was moving Breckinridge Long, but the man spoke with warm sincerity. Emboldened, he asked, "May I offer another idea?"

"Go ahead, Leslie. I find this talk refreshing."

Slote described his plan for the admission of a hundred thousand Jews to twenty countries. Breckinridge Long listened carefully, fingers moving from his tie to his handkerchief, and back to his tie.

"Leslie, you're talking about a second Evian, a major international conference on refugees."

"I hope not. Evian was an exercise in futility. Another conference like that will consume a lot of time while people are being slaughtered."

"But the political refugees are a more acute problem now, Leslie, and there's no other way to get such a thing going. A major policy can't be developed on the departmental level." Long's eyes were narrowed almost shut. "No, *that* is an imaginative and substantial suggestion. Will you let me have a confidential paper on it? For my eyes only, now. Put in all the practical detail that occurs to you."

"Breck, are you really interested?"

"Whatever you've heard of me," the Assistant Secretary replied with a shade of weary tolerance, "I'm not given to wasting my time. Nor that of anyone who works with me. We're all carrying too heavy a load."

But the man might be brushing him off; *write me a memorandum* was a very old departmental dodge. "Sir, you know about the Joint Allied statement on the Jews, I suppose?"

Long silently nodded.

"Do you believe—as I do—that it's the plain truth? That the Germans are murdering millions of European Jews, and intend to murder them all?"

A smile came and went on the Assistant Secretary's face; an empty smile, a mere agitation of the mouth muscles.

"I happen to know quite a bit about that statement. Anthony Eden drew it up under pressure, and it's nothing but a sop to some prominent British citizens of that race. I think it will do more harm than good, just provoke the Nazis to harsher measures. But we can't pass judgment on that unfortunate race, we must help them if we can, within the law, in their time of agony. That's my whole policy, and that's why I want a memo on that conference idea right away. It sounds practical and constructive." Breckinridge Long stood up and held out his hand. "Now will you help me, Leslie? I need your help."

Getting to his feet and accepting the handshake, Slote took the plunge. "I'll try, Breck."

The four-page letter that Slote wrote that night to William Tuttle ended this way:

> So perhaps you were right, after all! It's almost too good to be true, this possibility that I can have some influence on the situation, root out the worst abuses, and enable thousands of innocent people to go on living, largely due to the accident that my father was Princeton '05, and Ivy Club. Sometimes things do work out that way in this Alice-in-Wonderland town. If I'm pitifully deceived, I'll know soon enough. Meantime, I'll give Breckinridge Long my full allegiance. Thanks for everything. I'll keep you informed.

53

S LOTE and Foxy Davis were reviewing the early press clippings about the United Nations statement for a first report to the Secretary on the national reaction, when Slote remembered that he was dining at the Henry home. "I'll take these with me," he said, stuffing the batch into his portfolio, "and draft the thing tonight."

"I don't envy you," said Foxy. "Bricks without straw."

"Well, all the returns aren't in."

Walking to the corner to catch a cab, Slote noticed a stack of the new *Time* magazines, still tied with string, on the sidewalk by a news-stand. He and Foxy had been hungering for a look at it, since a *Time* reporter had interviewed Foxy on the telephone for almost an hour about the evidence for the massacre. He bought a copy, and in the light of a streetlamp, despite a drizzle that made the pages limp and sticky, he thumbed the issue eagerly. Nothing in the news section; nothing under features; front to back, *nothing.* How could that be? The *New York Times* had at least run it on the front page; a disappointing single-column story, overshadowed by a right-hand streamer on the flight of Rommel, and a two-column story about a cut in gas rationing. Most of the other big papers had dropped it inside, the *Washington Post* on page ten, but they had all done something with it. How could *Time* utterly ignore such an event? He paged through the copy again.

Not one word.

In the *People* section the picture of Pamela and her father that he had seen in the *Montreal Gazette* caught his eye.

Pamela Tudsbury, fiancée of Air Vice Marshal Lord Duncan Burne-Wilke (*Time,* Feb. 16), will leave London for Washington next month, to carry on the work of her late father as a correspondent for the *London Observer*. Until a land mine at El Alamein ended Alistair Tudsbury's career (*Time,* Nov. 16), the future Lady Burne-Wilke, on leave from the WRAF corps, globetrotted with eloquent, corpulent Tudsbury, collaborated on many of his front-line dispatches, barely escaped Jap capture in Singapore and Java.

Well, he thought, this may just interest Captain Henry. The flicker of malice slightly assuaged his disappointment. Slote did not like Henry much. To him, military men by and large were grown-up boy scouts; hard-drinking time-servers at worst, efficient conformists at best, banal narrow-minded conservatives to a man. Captain Henry bothered Slote because he did not quite fit the pigeonhole. He had too incisive and agile a mind. On that memorable night in the Kremlin, Henry had talked up to the awesome Stalin quite well, and he had pulled off a feat in getting to the front outside Moscow. But the man had no conversation, and anyway he reminded Slote of his galling defeats with Natalie and Pamela. Slote had accepted the dinner invitation only because in all conscience he thought he ought to tell Byron's family what he knew.

Welcoming Slote at the door of the Foxhall Road house, Henry scarcely smiled. He looked much older and peculiarly diminished in a brown suit and red bow tie.

"Seen this?" Slote pulled the magazine from his overcoat, open to the photograph.

Henry glanced at the page as Slote hung up his damp coat. "No. Too bad about old Talky, isn't it? Come on in. I believe you know Rhoda, and this is our daughter, Madeline."

The living room was astonishingly large. Altogether, this establishment looked beyond a naval officer's means. The two women sat on a sofa near a trimmed Christmas tree, drinking cocktails. Captain Henry handed his wife the magazine. "You were wondering what Pamela would do next."

"Bless me! Coming here! Engaged to Lord Burne-Wilke!" Mrs. Henry gave her husband a sidewise glance and passed the magazine to Madeline. "Well, she's done all right for herself."

"Christ, she looks so old, so tacky," Madeline said. "I remember when I met her, she was wearing this mauve halter dress"—she waggled one little white hand at her own bosom—"all terribly terrific. Wasn't Lord Burne-Wilke there, too? A blond dreamboat with a beautiful accent?"

"He was indeed," said Rhoda. "It was my dinner party for the Bundles for Britain concert."

"Burne-Wilke's an outstanding man," Pug said.

Slote could detect no trace of emotion in the words, yet he was sure that in Moscow Pamela Tudsbury and this upright gentleman had been having a hot little time of it. Indeed, it had been his pique at Henry's success with Pamela that had impelled him to drop his professional caution, and slip the Minsk documents to a *New York Times* man, thus starting his slide to his present nadir. Pamela's reaction in London to the news about Henry had indicated that the romance was far from dead. If Victor Henry did not have the soul of a wooden Indian, he was very good at simulating it.

"Oh, his lordship's unforgettable," exclaimed Madeline. "In RAF blue, all campaign stars and ribbons, and so slender and straight and blond! Sort of a stern Leslie Howard. But isn't that a screwy match? He's as old as you, Dad, at least. She's about my age."

"Oh, she's older than that," said Rhoda.

"I saw her in London, briefly," Slote said. "She was rather broken up over her father."

"What news of Natalie?" Pug asked Slote abruptly.

"They're still in Lourdes, still safe. That's the nub of it. But there's a lot to tell."

"Madeline, dear, let's get the dinner on." Rhoda rose, carrying her drink. "We'll talk at the table."

The candle-lit dining room had fine sea paintings on the walls and a log fire flaming in the fireplace. The mother and daughter served the dinner. The roast beef seemed a luxurious splurge of money and red points, and the plate and china were far more elegant than Slote had expected. While they ate, he narrated Natalie's odyssey as he had gathered it from her early letters, some Swiss reports, the Zionist rumors in Geneva, and Byron's story. It was a sketchy version patched together with a lot of guesswork. Slote knew nothing of Werner Beck's pressure on Jastrow to broadcast. A German diplomat had befriended Natalie and her uncle, as he told it, and settled them safely in Siena. But they had illegally disappeared in July, escaping with some Zionist fugitives, and had popped up months later in Marseilles, where Byron had caught sight of them for a few hours. They had planned to join him in Lisbon, but the invasion of North Africa had brought the Germans into Marseilles and prevented their departure. Now they were in Lourdes with all the American diplomats and journalists caught in southern France. He passed over Natalie's refusal to go with her husband; let Byron tell that to the family, Slote thought.

"Why Lourdes?" Captain Henry asked. "Why are they interned there?"

"I don't really know. I'm sure Vichy put them exactly where the Germans wanted them."

Madeline said, "Well, then, can't the Germans take her from Lourdes whenever they feel like it, with her uncle and her baby, and ship them off to some camp? Maybe cook them into soap?"

"Madeline, for heaven's SAKE!" exclaimed Rhoda.

"Mom, those are the gruesome stories going around. You've heard them, too." Madeline turned on Slote. "Well, what about all that? My boss says it's a lot of baloney, just stale British propaganda from the last war. I just don't know what to believe. Does anybody?"

Slote contemplated with heavy eyes, across his half-eaten dinner and a centerpiece of scarlet poinsettias, this bright comely girl. For Madeline Henry, clearly, these were all happenings in the Land of Oz. "Does your boss read the *New York Times?* There was a front-page story about this day before yesterday. Eleven Allied governments have announced it as a fact that Germany is exterminating the Jews of Europe."

"In the *Times?* You're sure?" Madeline asked. "I always read it straight through. I saw no such story."

"You overlooked it, then."

"I didn't notice that story, and I read the *Times,* too," Victor Henry observed. "It wasn't in the *Washington Post,* either."

"It was in both papers."

Even a man like Victor Henry, Slote thought in despair, had unconsciously blocked out the story, slid his eyes unseeing past the disagreeable headlines.

"Well, then they are in a pickle. From what you say, their papers are phony," Madeline persisted. "Really, won't the Germans get wise and haul them off?"

"They're still in official French custody, Madeline, and their position's not like that of other Jews. They're interned, you see, not detained."

"I can't follow you," Madeline said, wrinkling her pretty face.

"Neither can I," said Rhoda.

"Sorry. In Bern the distinction became second nature to us. You're *interned,* Mrs. Henry, when war catches you in an enemy country. You've done nothing wrong, you see. You're just a victim of timing. Internees get traded off: newspapermen, Foreign Service officers, and the like. That's what we expect to happen with our Americans in Lourdes. Natalie and her uncle, too. But if you're *detained* when a war starts—that is, if you're arrested—for anything from passing a red light to suspicion of being a spy, it's just too bad. You have no rights. The Red Cross can't help you. That's the problem about the European Jews. The Red Cross can't get to them because the Germans assert that the Jews are in protective custody. *Detained,* not *interned.*"

"Christ Almighty, people's lives hanging on a couple of goddamned words!" Madeline expostulated. "How sickening!"

This one lethal technicality, Slote thought, had penetrated the girl's hard shell. "Well, the words do mean something, but on the whole I agree with you."

"When will she ever get home, then?" Rhoda asked plaintively.

"Hard to say. The negotiations for the exchange are well along, but—"

The doorbell rang. Madeline jumped up, giving Slote a charming smile. "This is all wildly interesting, but I'm going to the National Theatre, and my friend's here. Please forgive me."

"Of course."

The outer door opened and closed, letting cold air swirl through the room. Rhoda began to clear away the dinner, and Pug took Slote to the library. They sat down with brandy in facing armchairs. "My daughter is a knucklehead," Pug said.

"On the contrary," Slote held up a protesting hand, "she's very bright. Don't blame her for not being more upset about the Jews than the President is."

Victor Henry frowned. "He's upset."

"Is he losing sleep nights?"

"He can't afford to lose sleep."

Slote ran a hand through his hair. "But the evidence the State Department has in hand is monstrous. What gets up to the President, of course, I don't know, and I can't find out. It's like trying to catch a greased eel with oily hands in the dark."

"I report back to the White House next week. Can I do anything about Natalie?"

Slote sat up. "You *do*? Do you still have your contact with Harry Hopkins?"

"Well, he still calls me Pug."

"All right, then. There was no point in alarming you before." Slote leaned forward, clutching the big brandy glass so hard in both hands that Pug thought he might smash it. "Captain Henry, they won't remain in Lourdes."

"Why not?"

"The French are helpless. We're actually dealing with the Germans. They've caught some fresh American civilians, and they're squeezing that advantage. They want in exchange a swarm of agents from South America and North Africa. We've already had strong hints from the Swiss that the Lourdes people will soon be taken to Germany, to build up the bargaining pressure. That will enormously heighten Natalie's danger."

"Obviously, but what can the White House do?"

"Get Natalie and Aaron out of Lourdes before they're moved. It might be done through our people in Spain. The Spanish border isn't forty miles away. Informal, quiet deals can be made, sometimes indirectly even with the Gestapo. People like Franz Werfel and Stefan Zweig have been spirited across borders. I'm not saying it'll work. I'm saying you'd better try it."

"But how?"

"I could attempt it. I know whom to talk to at State. I know where the cables should go. A phone call from Mr. Hopkins would enable me to move. Do you know him that well?"

Victor Henry drank in silence.

Slote's voice tightened. "I don't want to sound frantic, but I urge you to try this. If the war goes on two more years, every Jew in Europe will be dead. Natalie's no journalist. Her documents are fraudulent. If they break down she'll be a goner. Her baby, too."

"Did this *New York Times* story say the German government plans to kill all the Jews they can lay their hands on?"

"Oh, the text was fudged, but the implication was to that effect, yes."

"Why hasn't such an announcement created more noise?"

With an almost insane jolly grin, Leslie Slote said, "You tell me, Captain Henry."

Leaning his chin on a hand and rubbing it hard, Henry gave Slote a long quizzical look. "What about the Pope? If such a thing is happening, he's bound to know."

"The Pope! This Pope has been a lifelong reactionary politician. A decent German priest I talked to in Bern said he prayed nightly for the Pope to drop dead. I'm a humanist, so I expect nothing of any Pope. But this one is destroying whatever was left of Christianity after Galileo —I see that offends you. Sorry. All I want to impress on you is, this is a time to cash whatever credit at the White House you have. *Try to get Natalie out of Lourdes.*"

"I'll think about it, and call you."

Slote nervously leaped to his feet. "Good. Sorry if I got worked up. Will Mrs. Henry think me rude if I leave? I've got a lot to do tonight."

"I'll give her your apologies." Pug stood up. "Incidentally, Slote, when is Pamela getting married? Did she tell you?"

Slote suppressed the grin of a huntsman who sees the fox break from cover. In his overwrought state, he took this almost as comic relief. "Well, you know, Captain, *la donna è mobile!* Pam once complained to me that his lordship's a slave driver, a snob, and a bore. Maybe it won't come off."

Pug saw him out the front door. He could hear Rhoda pottering in the kitchen. On the coffee table in the living room, the copy of *Time* lay. Pug opened it and sat hunched over the magazine.

He had lost the snapshot of Pamela in the *Northampton* sinking, but the image was fixed in his memory, a little icon of dead romance. This story of her marriage had hit him hard. Acting indifferent had been tough. She didn't look good at all in this chance shot; with her head down, her nose appeared long, her mouth prissily thin. The desert sun overhead put dark shadows around her eyes. Yet this small poor picture of a woman four thousand miles away could wake a storm in him; while toward his very attractive flesh-and-blood wife in the next room he was numb. A hell of a note! He trudged back to the library, and was sitting there reading *Time* and drinking brandy when Madeline and Sime Anderson returned from the theatre in a rollicking mood. "Is that spook from the State Department gone? Thank heavens," she said.

"How was the play? Shall I take your mother to see it?"

"Christ, yes, give the old girl some giggles, Pop. You'll enjoy it yourself, these four girls in a Washington apartment, popping in and out of closets in their scanties—"

Anderson said, grinning uncomfortably, "There's not much to it, sir."

"Oh, come on, you laughed yourself silly, Sime, and your eyes about fell out of your head." Madeline noticed the Warren album, and her manner sobered. "What's this?"

"Haven't you seen it yet? Your mother put it together."

"No," Madeline said. "Come here, Sime."

Their heads together, they went through the scrapbook, at first silently; then she began exclaiming over the pages. A gold medal reminded her of how Warren had been borne off the field on his schoolmates' shoulders after winning a track meet with a spectacular high jump. "Oh, my God, and his birthday party in San Francisco! Look at me, cross-eyed in a paper hat! There was this horrible boy, who crawled under the table and looked up girls' dresses. Warren dragged him out and almost murdered him. Honestly, the memories this brings back!"

"Your mother's done an outstanding job," said Anderson.

"Oh, Mom! System is her middle name. Lord, Lord, how *handsome* he was! How about this graduation picture, Sime? Other kids look so sappy at that age!"

Her father was watching and listening with a cold calm expression. As Madeline turned the pages, her comments died off. Her hand faltered, her mouth trembled; she crashed the album shut, dropped her head on her arms, and cried. Anderson awkwardly put an arm around her, with an embarrassed glance at Pug. After a few moments, Madeline dried her eyes, saying, "Sorry, Sime. You'd better go home." She went out with him and soon returned. She sat down, crossing shapely legs, quite self-possessed again. It still jarred Victor Henry to see her light up a cigarette with the automatic gestures of a boatswain's mate. "Say, Pop, a Caribbean sunburn does things for Sime Anderson, eh? You should talk to him. He tells wild tales about hunting the U-boats."

"I've always liked Sime."

"Well, he used to remind me of custard. You know? Sort of bland and blond and blah. He's matured, and—all right, all right, never mind the grin. I'm glad he's coming to Christmas dinner." She dragged deeply on the cigarette and gave her father a hangdog glance. "I'll tell you something. *The Happy Hour* is beginning to embarrass me. We tool from camp to camp, making money off the naïve antics of kids in uniform. These wise-guy scriptwriters I work with laugh up their sleeves at sailors and soldiers a lot better than they are. I get so goddamned mad."

"Why don't you chuck it, Madeline?"

"And do what?"

"You'd find work in Washington. You're an able girl. Here's this nice house, almost empty. Your mother's alone."

Her expression disturbed him—sad, timorous, with a touch of defiant mischief. She had looked like this at fourteen, bringing him a bad report card. "Well, frankly, that very thought crossed my mind tonight. The thing is, I'm pretty involved."

"They'll get someone else to handle that fol-de-rol."

"Oh, I like my work. I like the money. I like those numbers jumping up in my little brown bank book."

"Are you happy?"

"Why, I'm just fine, Pop. There's nothing I can't handle."

Victor Henry was seeing her on this visit for the first time in a year and a half. The letter he had received at Pearl Harbor, warning him that she might be named in a divorce action, was going unmentioned. Yet Madeline was flying distress signals, if he knew her at all.

"Maybe I should go and have a talk with this fellow Cleveland."

"What on earth about?"

"You."

Her laugh was artificial. "Funnily enough, he wants to talk to you. I was almost ashamed to mention it." She flicked ash from her skirt. "Tell me, how does the draft work? Do you know anything about it? It seems so cockeyed. There are young fellows I know, unmarried, healthy as horses, who haven't gotten their draft notices yet. And Hugh Cleveland's got his."

"Oh? Fine," Pug said. "Now we'll win the war."

"Don't be mean. The chairman of his draft board is one of these creeps who enjoy hounding a celebrity. Hugh thinks he'd better get into uniform. Volunteer, you understand, and just keep on with *The Happy Hour* and everything. Do you know anyone in Navy public relations?"

Victor Henry slowly, silently shook his head.

"Okay." Madeline sounded relieved. "I've done my duty, I've asked you. I said I would. It's his problem. But Hugh really shouldn't carry a gun, he's all thumbs. He'd be more of a menace to our side than to the enemy."

"Doesn't he have all kinds of military contacts?"

"You wouldn't believe how they fade away, once they know he's got his draft notice."

"Glad to hear that. You should get away from him yourself. He's nothing but trouble."

"I'm having no trouble with Mr. Cleveland." Madeline stood up, tossed her head exactly as she had done when she was five, and she kissed her father. "If anything, the shoe's on the other foot. Night, Pop."

A really grown-up woman, Pug thought as she left, could lie better than that. Undoubtedly she was in a wretched mess. But she was young, she had margins for error, and there was nothing he could do about it. Shut it from mind!

He picked up *Time* to look yet again at the little picture of Pamela and her dead father. "The future Lady Burne-Wilke," coming to Washington. Something else to shut from mind; and one excellent reason to duck the landing craft job and return to the Pacific. Rhoda had adroitly laid the true basis for salvaging their marriage in the scrapbook there on the table, in the pool of yellow lamplight, where Madeline had slammed it shut. They were linked by the past and by death. The least he could do was cause her no more pain. He might not make it through the war. If he did, they would be old. There would be five or ten years to live side by side in cool decay. She was pitifully contrite, she would surely not slip again, and there was nothing she could do about what had happened. Let time repair what it could. He tossed the magazine in a leather wastebasket, suppressing as kid stuff a notion to tear out the picture, and went off to his dressing room.

In her boudoir, Rhoda was thinking, too. Weary from kitchen work, she was more than ready for sleep. But should she tell Pug of her talk with Pamela? It was the old marital question: have something out, or let it lie? As a rule, Rhoda thought the less said the better, but this time might be the exception. She was getting tired of remorse. Were those nasty anonymous letters on his mind? Well, he had been no saint himself. It might clear the air if she put that truth before him. The news of Pam's engagement was an opening. The scene might be a rough one. Fred Kirby would come up, and possibly the letters. Still, she was wondering if even that might not be better than the dead thick heaviness of Pug's long silences. Their marriage was going out, like the candle under the glass jar in the high school experiment, for want of air. Even the lovemaking at night was making little difference. She had a horrid sense that her husband with some effort was being polite to her in bed. Rhoda put on a lace-trimmed black silk nightgown, brushed out her hair for looks instead of pinning it up for the pillow, and out she went, ready for peace or a sword. He was sitting up in bed with his old bedside Shakespeare in the cracked maroon binding.

"Hi, honey," she said.

He laid the book on the night table. "Say, Rhoda, this fellow Slote has an idea about helping Natalie."

"Oh?" She got in bed and listened, her back to the headboard, her brow furrowed.

Pug was honestly consulting her, by way of trying to grope back to their old footing. She heard him out, nodding and not interrupting. "Why not do it, Pug? What's there to lose?"

"Well, I don't want to make more trouble for the White House than they've got."

"I don't see that. Harry Hopkins may turn you down, for his own reasons. MOUNTAINS of such requests must come his way. But they're your family, and they're in danger. To me the real question is, suppose he's willing to try? Do you trust Slote that much?"

"Why not? It's his field."

"But he's so, I don't know, so OBSESSED. Pug, I'd worry about rocking that boat. You're far away. You can't know what's going on. By singling them out—I mean the WHITE House, honestly!—won't you throw a spotlight on them? And isn't their game to stay inconspicuous, just two more names in that batch of Americans, until they get exchanged? Besides, Natalie's a pretty woman with a baby. The worst fiends in the world would lean over backward for her. Maybe it's tempting fate to interfere."

He took her hand and squeezed it. "That's good thinking."

"Oh, I'm not sure I'm right. Just be very careful."

"Rhoda, Madeline is getting to like Sime Anderson. Has she talked to you? Isn't she in a mess in New York?"

Rhoda could not readily share with Pug her own suspicions, and misconduct was a high-voltage topic. "Madeline's a cool one, Pug. That radio crowd really isn't her kind. If she takes up with Sime, she'll be fine."

"She says the show's very dirty. I'll get us tickets down front."

"Well, how lovely." Rhoda laughed uncertainly. "You're an old RIP, and I always knew it." She was deciding, as she said it, to let the Pamela matter lie.

When she emptied the wastebaskets next day, she couldn't resist turning the pages of *Time* to the picture of Pamela Tudsbury. It was still there, of course. She felt like a fool. Not all that attractive a woman, at that; aging fast, and badly. Engaged to Lord Burne-Wilke, besides. Let it lie, she thought. Let it lie.

54

A Jew's Journey
(from Aaron Jastrow's manuscript)

CHRISTMAS DAY, 1942.
LOURDES.

I awoke this morning thinking of Oswiecim.

The Americans in all four hotels were permitted, just this once, to go to church together, to the midnight Mass at the basilica. As usual we were accompanied by our reasonably pleasant Sûreté shadows, and by the surly German soldiers who since last week have been following us on our walks, shopping trips, and visits to the doctor, dentist, or barber. The soldiers were clearly irked at drawing such disagreeable duty on Christmas Eve (it is very cold up here in the Pyrenees, and of course neither the basilica nor the hotel lobbies are heated) when they might have been greeting the birth of their Savior with drunken wassail, or perhaps with animal raptures on the bodies of the few poor French whores who service the conquerors here. Well, Natalie would not go to the Mass, but I did.

It is a very long time since I attended a Mass. In this pilgrimage town you get the real thing, with a crowd of real worshippers; and because of the shrine, those who come include the paralyzed, the crippled, the blind, the deformed, the dying, a terrible parade; a parade of God's cruel jokes or inept mistakes, if you seriously maintain that He heeds the sparrow's fall. Cold as it was in the basilica, the air was warm as May compared to the chill in my heart as the Mass proceeded; chants, bells, elevations, genuflections, and all. It would have been only courteous to kneel at the proper time, as all did, since I had voluntarily come; but for all the disapproving glances, I, the stiff-necked Jew, would not kneel. Nor would I go afterward to a Christmas party for our group at the Hôtel des Ambassadeurs, where, I was told, the black-market wine would flow free, and there would be black-market turkey and sausage. I returned to the Gallia, accompanied to the door of my room by a grumpy German with a hideous breath. I went to sleep, and I awoke thinking of Oswiecim.

It was in the yeshiva at Oswiecim that I first broke with my own religion. I remember it all as though it were yesterday. I can still feel my cheek stinging from the slap of the *mashgiakh,* the study hall supervisor, as I trudge in the snow on the town square in the purple evening, having been ordered out of the *bet midrash* for impudent heresy. I have not thought about all this for years, yet even now it rises in my mind as an intolerable outrage. Perhaps in a yeshiva in a larger city—say Cracow or Warsaw—the *mashgiakh* would have had the sense to smile at my effrontery, and pass it off. Then the whole course of my life might have been different. That slap was the twig that turned the torrent.

It was so utterly unfair! After all, I was a good boy; a "silken boy," as they would say in Yiddish. I excelled in expounding the abstruse legal distinctions that are the meat and the glory of the Talmud, the subtle ethical nuances that the foolish call "hair-splitting." These arguments have an austere, almost geometrical elegance for which one acquires not only a taste, but a thirst. I did have that thirst. I was a star Talmud student. I was brighter and quicker than the *mashgiakh.* Possibly he was glad of the chance, narrow thick-skulled black-capped bearded fool that he was, to take me down a peg; so he slapped my face, ordered me out of the study hall, and set my foot on the path to the Cross.

I remember the passage: page one hundred eleven, Tractate *Passover Offerings.* I remember the subject: demons, and how to avoid them, foil them, and conjure them away. I remember why I was slapped. I asked, "But Reb Laizar, are there really such things as demons?" I remember the bearded fool bawling at me, as I lay on the floor stunned, with a flaming cheek, "Get up! Get out! *Shaygetz!*" (nonbeliever, abomination!) And so I stumbled out into dreary snowy Oswiecim.

I was fifteen. To me, Oswiecim was still a big town. I had visited the grand metropolis of Cracow only once. Our village of Medzice, some ten kilometers up the Vistula, was all wooden houses and crooked muddy pathways. Even the Medzice church—which we children steered clear of as though it were a leprosarium—was built of wood. Oswiecim had straight paved streets, a large railroad station, brick and stone houses, shops with lighted glass windows, and several churches of stone.

I did not know the town well. We lived a strictly regimented life in the yeshiva, seldom venturing beyond the mews on which it faced, bounded by our little dormitory and the teachers' houses. But my rebellious anger that day carried me out of the mews into the town. I walked all over Oswiecim, seething at my ill-treatment, giving way at last to the suppressed doubts that had been plaguing me for years.

For I was no fool. I knew German and Polish, I read newspapers and

novels, and precisely because I was a bright Talmudist I could look beyond the *bet midrash* to the world outside; a world glittering with
strange dangers and evil temptations, but nevertheless a broader world
than one saw in the everlasting straight and narrow march down black
columns of Talmud, hemmed in by wise but wearying commentators,
who absorbed all one's young wit and energy in exhaustive microanal-
ysis of a main text fourteen centuries old. Between my eleventh year
and the moment of the slap, I had been even more painfully wrenched
between the natural yeshiva boy's ambition to become a world-famous
ilui (prodigy), and a wicked whisper in my soul that I was WASTING MY
TIME.

Thinking of all this as I trudged ankle-deep in snow, freed by the
mashgiakh's anger to wander like a homeless dog, I halted in front of
Oswiecim's largest church. Strange that I should have forgotten its
name! The one nearest the yeshiva was called *Calvaria;* that I recall.
This was another, and much more imposing, edifice on a main square.

My anger had not cooled. Rather, as the rebelliousness of four years
came bursting through the bounds of lifelong drilling and a very tender
religious conscience, I did something that a few hours earlier would
have been as unthinkable as cutting my wrists. I slipped into the
church. Wrapped against the cold, I did not look very different from a
Christian child, I suppose. In any case some sort of service was going
on, and everybody was looking to the front. Nobody paid attention to
me.

So long as I live, I shall not forget the shock of seeing a great bloody
naked Christ hanging from a cross on the front wall, where in a synagogue the Holy Ark would stand; nor the strange sweetish Gentile smell
of incense; nor the big painted saints on the side walls. I was stunned to
think that for the "outside" world (as I then regarded it), this was
religion, this was the way to God! Half-horrified, half-fascinated, I
stayed a long time. Never since have I felt so alien and alone, so dizzily
on the brink of a shattering irreversible change in my soul.

Never, that is, until last night.

Whether it was the cumulative effect of living for weeks in the appalling commercialism of Lourdes, which still garishly pervades the town,
even off-season, even in wartime; or whether it was the pathetic gathering of the maimed in the basilica; or whether, as once my rebelliousness
surfaced, so everything that has been happening to me and Natalie
broke through a suppressing instinct in my spirit—however all that may
be, the fact is that at midnight Mass last night, familiar as Christ on his
cross now is to me, and much as I have written about Christianity, and

much indeed as I have loved the religious art of Europe, I felt last night as alienated and alone as I did at fifteen in the Oswiecim church.

I woke this morning thinking of it. I am writing this note as I drink my morning coffee. It is not bad coffee. In France, in the depths of war, under the conqueror's heel, money can still buy everything. The illegal prices are not even very high in Lourdes. It is off-season.

I have neglected this diary ever since our arrival in Lourdes; hoping—to be honest—that I would resume it on a steamship bound for home. That hope is dimming. Our situation is probably worse than my niece and I admit to each other. I hope her good cheer is more real than mine. She knows less. The consul general wisely avoids upsetting her with the ins and outs of our problem, but he is fairly straight with me.

What has gone wrong is a matter far beyond anybody's control. It was of course the most ghastly misfortune that we failed by a few days to leave Vichy France legally. All was in order, the precious papers were in hand, but with the first news of the American landings all train schedules were suspended and the borders were closed. Jim Gaither acted with coolness and dispatch to protect us, by providing us with official journalists' documents predated to 1939, accrediting us to *Life* magazine, which has in fact published a couple of my essays on wartime Europe.

But he went further than that. In the consulate files which they were burning, they turned up some letters from *Life,* requesting courtesies for various writers and photographers. In Marseilles there is a most accomplished ring of document fakers for refugees, run by a remarkable Catholic priest. The consul general, despite everything else he had to do in the sudden crisis, obtained through his underground contacts forged letters on the *Life* letterhead, establishing both Natalie and myself as regularly employed correspondents; papers authentic-looking to the extent of being rubbed, folded, and faded as though they were several years old.

James Gaither did not anticipate that these concocted papers would have to shield us for any very long time, but he thought they would stand up until we got out. However, as time passes, the risk increases. At first he expected that our release would be a matter of days or weeks. After all, we are not at war with Vichy France. There is but a rupture of relations, and so Americans are not "enemies" and should not be "interned" at all. But the group here in Lourdes, about a hundred and sixty of us, most definitely is interned. We have been under strict French police surveillance from the start, unable to move about except under the eyes of a uniformed inspector. And a few days ago, Gestapo men took station around all four hotels where we Americans are sequestered. Ever since, we have been under German guard, as well as in official French police custody. The French act vaguely humiliated and embarrassed by all this, and in small ways try to make us more comfortable. But the Germans are there always, stolidly marching with us wherever we move, staring at us in the lobbies, and ordering us about severely if one of us happens to trespass on a Boche regulation.

Only gradually have I learned what the long delay is all about. For a while Gaither himself did not know. The American chargé d'affaires, who was brought here from Vichy with our entire embassy staff, lives in another hotel, and telephone communication is forbidden. The chargé, an able man named Tuck—a great admirer of my writings, though that is neither here nor there—is apparently allowed one telephone talk a day, of short duration, with the Swiss representative in Vichy. So we are virtually cut off, especially here at the Gallia, and are very much in the dark.

The snag turns out to be simple enough. The Vichy personnel in the United States who should have been swapped for us refused almost to a man to go back to France; understandably, since the Hun now occupies all of it. This has created great confusion, into which the Germans have stepped to seize an advantage. Thus far they still talk through their Vichy puppets, but it is plainly they who are bargaining over us.

We might have gotten away in the first week or two, if the French had simply sent us off the thirty miles to the Spanish border. That would have been a decent return for the food and medical supplies America has lavished on this government for years. But the Vichy men are a loathsome form of life—crawling, sycophantic, pretentious, lying, self-righteous, anti-Semitic, reactionary, feebly militaristic, and altogether base and unworthy of French culture—the very slimy dregs of the anti-Dreyfusards of old. In short, we didn't get out. Here we are, counters in German haggling for assorted Nazi agents being held abroad; and that they will drive a close and savage bargain goes without saying.

I woke thinking of Oswiecim for yet another reason.

During our long stay in the Mendelson apartment in Marseilles, a stream of refugees kept passing through, usually staying not more than one or two nights. In consequence, we heard a lot of the grisly talk that circulates in the European Jewish grapevine about the atrocities in the east, the mass shootings, the gassing in sealed vans, the camps where everybody who arrives is either murdered outright or starved and worked to death. I have never known how much credit to give to these reports and still don't, but one thing is sure: a place name that keeps recurring, and that is never uttered except in hushed terms of the most profound horror and dread, is Oswiecim; usually in its ugly Germanization that I remember well, *Auschwitz.*

If these rumors amount to more than mass paranoid fears brought on by suffering, then Oswiecim is the focal point of the whole horror; my Oswiecim, the place where I studied as a boy, where my father bought me a bicycle, where the whole family sometimes came to spend a Sabbath and hear a great traveling cantor or *maggid,* a revivalist Yiddish preacher; and where I first saw the inside of a church and a life-size Christ on the cross.

The ultimate menace that faces us, in that case, is transportation to the mysterious and frightful camp at Oswiecim. There would be a neat closing of the circle for me! But our random existence on this petty planet does not move in such artistic patterns—that thought really consoles me—and we are a continent away from Oswiecim, and only thirty miles from Spain and safety. I still have faith that we will end by going home. It is vital to keep up one's hopes in a time of danger; to remain alert, and ready to face down bureaucrats and brutes when one must. That takes spirit.

Natalie and the baby, who had a chance to escape, are trapped because at a crucial moment she lacked spirit. I wrote a decidedly intemperate journal entry on Byron's thunderbolt visit and its miserable outcome. My anger at Natalie was fueled by my guilt at having mired her and her baby in this ever-worsening predicament. She will never let me express it; invariably she cuts me off by saying that she is grown up, acted of her own free will, and bears me no grudge.

Now we have been shadowed and ordered about by Germans for a week; and while I still think she should have taken the chance and gone with Byron, I can sympathize more with her reluctance. It would be a fearful thing to fall into the hands of these hard uncouth men without legal papers. All policemen, in relation to those they guard, must seem more or less wooden, hostile, and cruel; for to carry out their orders they must suppress fellow feelings. There has been nothing attractive about the Italian and French police I've dealt with during the past two years, nor—for that matter—about certain American consuls.

But these Germans are different. Orders do not seem merely to guide their actions; orders, as it were, fill their souls, leaving no room for a human flicker in their faces or eyes. They are herdsmen, and we are cattle; or they are soldier ants, and we are aphids. The orders cut all ties between them and us. All. It is eerie. Truly, their cold empty expressions make my skin crawl. I understand that one or two of the

gher-ups are "decent sorts" (Gaither's words), but I have not met
em. I too once knew "decent sorts" who were German. Here one sees
ly the other face of the Teuton.

Natalie might well have chanced it with Byron; I know no more reso-
te or resourceful young man, and he had special diplomatic papers. It
as a question of a fast dash through the flames. If she had been the
d Natalie, she would have done it, but she balked because of the
aby. James Gaither still maintains (if with less assurance as the days
ass) that he advised her correctly, and that all will yet be well. I think
e's beginning to wonder. We talked the whole matter out again last
ight, Gaither and I, as we slogged through the snow to the midnight
lass. He insists that the Germans, wanting to recover as many of their
gents as possible in this swap, are not at any point going to examine
nybody's papers too closely. Natalie, Louis, and I are three warm bod-
s, exchangeable for perhaps fifteen Huns. They will be satisfied with
at, and will look no further.

He does think it is important that I remain inconspicuous. So far we
re dealing with very low-grade Frenchmen and Germans, none of
hom is likely to have read any books in years, let alone one of my
ooks. He says that my credentials as a journalist are holding, and that
one of the police officers has yet singled me out as a "celebrity" or
erson of consequence, nor as a Jew. For this reason he quashed a sug-
estion that I give a lecture to our hotel group. The United Press man is
rranging a lecture series here at the Gallia, to pass the time. The topic
e suggested to me was Jesus, naturally. This was a few days ago, and
ut for Jim Gaither's veto, I might have consented.

But since my experience at the midnight Mass, I would under no cir-
umstances—even back in the States, and offered a large fee—lecture
bout Jesus. Something has been happening to me that I have yet to
athom. In recent weeks I have found it harder and harder to work even
n Martin Luther. Last night that something began to surface. I have
till to focus on it and determine what it is. One of these days I shall
race in this journal the path from my first glimpse of Christ crucified in
)swiecim, to my brief conversion to Christianity in Boston, eight years
ater. Just now Natalie has come in from her bedroom with Louis, all
undled up for her morning walk. In the open doorway our surly Ger-
1an shadow glowers.

55

O N New Year's Eve Pug surprised Rhoda by suggesting that they go to the Army-Navy Club. She knew he detested the rigmarole of paperhats, noisemakers, and alcoholic kissing; but tonight, he said he wanted distraction. Rhoda loved the New Year's Eve nonsense, so she happily got herself up; and in the merry crowd of senior military men with their wives moving through the lobby, she felt that few women looked as pretty or glittery as she did in the silver lamé dress from the old Bundles for Britain days. She had an uneasy moment when, as she and Pug entered the dining room, Colonel Harrison Peters stood up and waved to them to join him. Her conduct with Peters had been snowily blameless, but might he not mention Palmer Kirby, or show too much warmth?

Arm in arm, feeling her hesitate, Pug gave her a questioning look. She decided she didn't give a damn. Let it come out at last! "Well, bless me! There's Colonel Peters. Let's join him, by all means," she said cheerily. "He's a fine man, I've met him at church. But where on earth did he get that CHORUS GIRL? Can I trust you at the same table with her?"

Peters towered a head and a half over Pug Henry, shaking hands with him. His blonde bosomy young companion, in a white Grecian-drapery sort of dress that showed much rosy skin, was a secretary at the British Purchasing Council. Rhoda mentioned that they knew Pamela Tudsbury. "Oh, really? The next Lady Burne-Wilke?" the girl trilled, and her accent stirred an ache in Victor Henry. "Dear Pam! You could have knocked us all over with a feather at the Council. Pamela used to be our office mutineer. Always muttering against the old slave driver! Now his lordship will pay for all that overtime, won't he just?"

The hour before midnight melted away in dull war talk over dull club food and very flat champagne. An Army Air Corps colonel with purple bulldog jowls, sitting at this table by chance with his highly rouged wispy wife, railed at the neglect of the "CBI" theatre from which he had just returned, by which he meant China, Burma, and India. Half the human race lived there, said the colonel; even Lenin had once called it the richest war prize in the world. If it fell to the Japs, the white man had better find himself another planet to live on, because Earth would soon be too hot for him. Nobody in Washington seemed to grasp that.

An Army brigadier general, with conspicuously more ribbons than either Peters or the CBI colonel, held forth on the assassination of Admiral Darlan; whom, he said, he had come to know very well in Algiers. "It's a great pity about Popeye. That's what we on Ike's staff all called Darlan, Popeye. The fellow looked like an insulted frog. Of course he was a plain pro-Nazi, but he was a realist, and once we nabbed him, he delivered the goods, saved a whole lot of American lives. This de Gaulle fellow, now, thinks he's Joan of Arc. We'll get nothing from him but rhetoric and grief. Try telling that to all these pinko typewriter strategists."

Rhoda might have spared herself any concern about Colonel Peters. He was scarcely looking her way, sizing up instead the squat husband with the forbidding tired face. Pug was saying nothing at all. Peters at last asked how he thought the war was going.

"Where?" asked Pug.

"All over. How does the Navy see it?"

"Depends, Colonel, on where you sit in the Navy."

"From where you sit, then."

Puzzled by the idle probing of this big good-looking Army man, Pug answered, "I see plenty of hell behind and plenty ahead."

"Concur," said Peters, as the lights in the noisy dining room blinked and darkened, "and that's a better year-end summary than I've read in all the newspapers. Well, five minutes to midnight, ladies and gentlemen. Allow me, Mrs. Henry." She was sitting beside him, and in an oddly gentle and pleasing way, to which she felt Pug couldn't possibly take exception, he placed on her head a paper shepherdess's bonnet, then tilted a gilt cardboard helmet on his own handsome gray hair. Not everybody at the table put on paper hats, but to Rhoda's astonishment her husband did. Not since the children's early birthday parties had she seen that happen. On Victor Henry's head a pink hat with gold frills, far from looking playful or funny, brought out a terrible sadness in his face.

"Oh, Pug! No."

"Happy New Year, Rhoda."

Champagne glasses in hand, the guests stood up to kiss all around and sing *"Auld Lang Syne"* in candlelight. Pug gave his wife an absent kiss, and yielded her to a polite buss from Colonel Peters. His mind was drifting back over 1942. He was thinking of Warren leaning in the doorway of the cabin on the *Northampton,* with one hand on the overhead, saying, *"Hi, Dad. If you're too busy for me, say so";* and of the officers and men lying entombed in the sunken hull of the *Northampton,* in the black waters off Guadalcanal. And he was thinking, in the depths of bitter sorrow, that he would ask Hopkins to try to get Natalie and her baby out of Lourdes, after all. She at least was alive.

Harry Hopkins's bedroom in the White House was at one end of a long dark gloomy hall, a few doors down from the Oval Office. In a gray suit that hung on him like a scarecrow's rags, he stood looking out toward the sunlit Washington Monument. "Hello there, Pug. Happy New Year."

He kept skinny hands clasped behind his back as he turned. This stooped, shabby, emaciated, yellow-faced civilian made a sharp contrast to the beefy Rear Admiral Carton, red of cheek and straight as a pole, standing near him in tailored blue and gold with a golden froth of shoulder cords. In newspaper accounts Hopkins sometimes seemed a Dumas figure, a sort of shadowy gliding Mazarin in the presidential back rooms; but face to face he looked to Pug more like a debauched playboy, by the glint in his eye and his fatigued grin still hoping for fun. At a glance Pug took in the dark Lincoln painting and the plaque saying the Emancipation Proclamation had been signed here; also the homey touches of a rumpled red dressing gown flung over the unmade four-poster bed, a frilly negligee beside it, pink mules on the floor, and bottles of medicines lined up on the bedside table.

"Thank you for seeing me, sir."

"Always a pleasure. Sit you down." Carton left, and Hopkins faced Pug on a wine-colored couch seedily worn at the arms. "So! Cincpac wants you, too. Popular fella, aren't you?" Caught by surprise, Pug made no comment. "I suppose that would be your choice?"

"I naturally prefer combat operations."

"What about the Soviet Union?"

"I'm not interested, sir."

Hopkins crossed bone-thin legs and rubbed a hand over his long curving jaw. "Do you remember a General Yevlenko?"

"Yes. Big burly gent. I met him on my trip to the Moscow front."

"Just so. He's now Russia's top dog on Lend-Lease. Admiral Standley thinks you could help a lot in that area. Yevlenko has mentioned you to Standley. Also Alistair Tudsbury's daughter, who I gather went along on that trip."

"Yes, she did."

"Well, you both made quite an impression on him. You know, Pug, your report about the Moscow front last December was a big help. I was a lonely voice around here, maintaining that the Russians would hold. The Army's intelligence estimate was all wrong. Your paper impressed the President. He thinks you have horse sense, which is always in short supply around these parts."

"I thought I'd queered myself by my gratuitous letter about the Minsk Jews."

"Not at all." Hopkins casually waved away Pug's words. "Between you and me, Pug, the whole Jewish situation is a fearsome headache. The President has to keep dodging delegations of rabbis. The State Department tries to deflect them, but some do get through. It's all terribly pitiful, but what can he tell them? They just go over and over the same depressing ground. Invading France and breaking up that insane Nazi system is the only way to keep faith with the Russians, save the Jews, and end this damned war. And the key to *that* is landing craft, my friend." Hopkins leaned back on the couch with a shrewd look at Pug.

Trying to stave off that tricky topic, Pug asked, "Sir, why don't we take in a lot more refugees?"

"Modify the immigration laws, you mean," Hopkins replied briskly. "That's a tough one." He picked a blue book off a side table, and handed it to Pug. The title was *America's Ju-Deal.* "Ever see this?"

"No, sir." Pug made a disgusted face and dropped it. "Nazi propaganda?"

"Possibly. The FBI says it's been widely circulated for years. It came in the mail, and should have gone into the wastebasket, but it reached my desk, and Louise saw it. It sickened her. My wife and I get a flood of hate mail, Pug. Half of it in various filthy ways calls us Jews, which would be funny if it weren't tragic. It's hit a peak since the Baruch dinner."

Victor Henry looked puzzled.

"Were you still abroad? Barney Baruch threw a sort of belated—and frankly, ill-advised—wedding dinner for us. Some reporter got hold of the menu. You can imagine, Pug, a Baruch blowout! Pâté de foie gras, champagne, caviar, the works. With all the discontent about rationing and shortages, I took my lumps again. That, plus the damned lie that Beaverbrook gave Louise an emerald necklace worth half a million as a wedding present, really made things rough around here. I've got a rhinoceros hide, but I've exposed Louise to all this by marrying her. It's terrible." He made a gesture of loathing at the book. "Well, try to pass a new immigration law, and that poison will boil up all over the land. We'd probably get beaten on the Hill. Certainly the war effort would suffer. And in the end what good would it do? We can't pry the Jews out of the German clutches." He gave Victor Henry an inquisitive glance. "Where's your daughter-in-law now?"

"Sir, that's why I asked to see you."

Pug described Natalie's predicament, and Slote's idea for getting her out of Lourdes. Asking a favor came hard to him, and he somewhat fumbled his words. Hopkins listened with his thin mouth pursed. His reaction was quick and hard. "That's negotiating with the enemy. It would have to go to the President, and he'd bump it over to Welles. Lourdes, eh? Who's this fellow at State, again?" He penciled Leslie Slote's name and telephone number on a bit of paper fished from his pocket. "Let me look into this."

"I'm very grateful, sir." Pug made a move to rise.

"Sit where you are. The President will call me soon. He has a cold and he's sleeping late." With a grin Hopkins unfolded a yellow sheet from his breast pocket. "Just an average basket of crabs for him today. Like to hear it? *One. Chinese calling home their military mission.* Now, there's a bad business, Pug. Their demands for aid are just moonshine, in view of what we need in Europe. On the other hand, the Chinese front is a running sore for Japan. They've been fighting this war longer than any of us, and we have to keep them placated.

"*Two. Heating oil crisis in New England.* God, what a flap! The weather's fooled us, it's been a much colder winter than predicted. Everybody's freezing from New Jersey to Maine. The Big Inch pipeline has fallen behind half a year. More controls, more trouble."

Thus he read off and commented dourly on a list of topics:

3. *Snag over the Siberian route for Lend-Lease.*
4. *Sudden acute shortage of molybdenum.*
5. *Pessimistic revised report on rubber.*
6. *Another rash of U-boat sinkings in the Atlantic.*
7. *German reinforcements in Tunisia throwing back Eisenhower's advance, and famine in Morocco threatening his supply lines.*
8. *General MacArthur again, more troops and air power in New Guinea desperately needed.*
9. *Revision of the State of the Union speech.*
10. *Plans for a meeting with Churchill in North Africa.*

"Now that one's top secret, Pug." Hopkins rattled the paper at him. "We'll be going in about a week to Casablanca, Joint Chiefs of Staff and all. Stalin begged off because of the Stalingrad battle, but we'll keep him informed. We're going to settle strategy for the rest of the war. The President hasn't been in an airplane in nine years, not since he took office. What's more, no President has *ever* flown abroad. He's as excited as a boy."

Victor Henry was wondering at Hopkins's chatty expansiveness, but now came the explanation. Hopkins hunched forward and touched Pug's knee. "You know, Stalin's howling for a Channel crossing this year. That'll get thirty or forty German divisions off his back, and then he probably could throw the Germans out of Russia. He claims we welshed on a second front in '42. But we didn't have the landing craft, and we weren't ready in any respect. The British hate the whole idea of invading France. At Casablanca they're bound to plead the landing craft shortage again."

Drawn in despite himself, Pug asked, "What are the numbers now, sir?"

"Come here." Hopkins led Henry into another room, small, airless, full of dowdy old furniture, with one incongruous card table piled with files and papers. "Have a seat. The Monroe Room, they call this, Pug. He signed the Doctrine here—now, what the devil! I was just looking at those figures." He shuffled papers on the table, and some fell off. Hopkins ignored these, pulling out and brandishing an ordinary file card, while Pug marvelled at this slapdash casualness at the hub of the war. "Here you are. Figures as of December fifteenth. They're cloudy, Pug, because the losses in North Africa aren't firmed up yet."

Victor Henry knew by heart the landing craft projections he had brought to the Argentia conference, and he was shocked by the statistics on the card that Hopkins read off. "Mr. Hopkins, what in God's name has happened to production?"

Hopkins threw down the card. "A nightmare! We've lost a year! Not only in landing craft, but across the board. The trouble was priorities. Tugs of war between the Army, industry, the home economy, squabbles between this board and that board, jealous infighting among some fine men. All at each other's throats. Everybody was brandishing triple-A priorities, and nobody was getting anything delivered. We had a crazy sort of priority inflation, Pug. Priorities were getting meaningless as old German marks. The mess was beyond description. Then along came Victor Henry."

Hopkins laughed at Pug's astonished blink. "Not really you, of course. Your sort. Ferdie Eberstadt is his name. One of these fellows nobody hears about, who can get things done. You'll have to meet him. A stockbroker, would you believe it? A Princeton type straight out of Wall Street. Never in government. They got him down here on the War Production Board, and Ferdie worked out a brand-new priorities scheme. The *Controlled Materials Plan,* he calls it. It gears all production plans to the flow of three materials—steel, copper, and aluminum. That stuff's being allotted now in a vertical pattern, according to the thing that's being produced. Destroyer escort, long-range bomber, heavy truck for the Soviets, whatever it is, those materials get allotted to make every single component of the thing. Not horizontally, some here, some there, some to the armed forces, some to the factories"—Hopkins waved his long arms wildly about—"depending on who has the coziest inside track in Washington. Well, it's a miracle. Production figures are shooting up all over the country."

He was pacing as he talked, his lean clever face electrically alive. He dropped in a chair beside Henry's. "Pug, you can't imagine what was going on before Eberstadt did this. Piecemeal insanity! Waste to frighten the gods! Ten thousand tank tracks, and no tanks to put them on! A football field full of airplane frames, without engines or controls even being manufactured! A hundred LCIs docked and rusting away, for want of winches to drop and raise the ramps! That awful time is over, and we can get the landing craft we need, but the Navy has to run a coherent show. That means one good man, a Ferdie Eberstadt, in charge. I've talked to Secretary Forrestal and to Vice Admiral Patterson. They know your record. They're for you." Hopkins leaned back in his chair, spectacle frames to his mouth, his eyes twinkling. "Well, old top? Will you sign on the dotted line?"

The telephone on the card table rang. "Yes, Mr. President. Right away. As it happens, Pug Henry's here . . . Yes, sir. Of course." He hung up. "Pug, the boss will say hello to you."

They walked out into the dark book-lined hall and down a rubber-padded ramp toward the Oval Office. Hopkins took Pug's elbow. "What say? Shall I tell the President you're taking it on? There are a lot of Navy captains who can do Cincpac's staff work, you know that. There's only one Pug Henry who has a grasp of landing craft from A to Z."

Victor Henry had never before had a clash of wills with Hopkins. The great seal of the Presidency was in this man's pocket. Yet he was not the Commander-in-Chief, or he would be issuing orders, not cajoling. The affable insiders' talk, the flattery about Eberstadt, and now this arm-twisting were tactics of a powerful subordinate. Hopkins had taken it into his head to put him in landing craft, and the visit about Natalie had given him his opening. He probably did this sort of persuasion all the time. He was damned good at it, but Victor Henry meant to go to Cincpac. Hopkins's airy dismissal of that job was civilian talk. There were plenty of good men in the landing craft program, too.

They were walking past the Oval Office toward the open door of the President's bedroom. The President's rich resonant voice sounded hoarse today. Pug felt a touch of awe and affection at hearing Franklin Roosevelt's accents.

"Mr. Hopkins, this probably means the rest of my war service. Let me talk it over down at BuShips."

Harry Hopkins smiled. "Oke. I know they're all for it."

They entered the bedroom just as the President violently sneezed into a large white handkerchief. Rear Admiral McIntire, the President's physician, stood beside the bed in full uniform. He and several elderly civilians in the room chorused, "God bless you."

Pug recognized none of the civilians. They all stared at him, looking self-important, while McIntire, whom he had known in San Diego, gave him a slight nod. Wiping his reddened nose, the President glanced up blearily at Pug. He was sitting propped on cushions, wearing over wrinkled striped pajamas a royal blue cape, with *FDR* monogrammed on it in red. Picking pince-nez glasses off a breakfast tray, he said, "Well, Pug, how are you? Did you and Rhoda have a nice New Year?"

"Yes, thank you, Mr. President."

"Good. What were you and Harry cooking up just now? Where are you going next?"

It was an offhand polite question. The other men in the room were looking at Henry as at an interloper, like a Roosevelt grandchild who had wandered in. Despite the President's cold, which showed in his irritated nose and rheumy eyes, he had a gay air, a look of relish for the new day's business.

Victor Henry plunged, fearing Hopkins might overcommit him by speaking up first. "I'm not sure, Mr. President. Admiral Nimitz has requested my services as Deputy Chief of Staff for Operations."

"Oh, I see! Really!" The President arched his heavy brows at Hopkins. Clearly this was news to him. A shade of vexation flickered over Hopkins's face. "Well, then, that's where you'll go, I suppose. I certainly couldn't blame you for that. All the best."

Roosevelt rubbed his eyes with two fingers, and put on his glasses. This changed his aspect. He looked younger, more formidable, more the familiar President of the newspaper pictures, less an old man with mussed gray hair in bed with a cold. Obviously he was finished with Victor Henry, and ready to get on with his morning's work. He was turning toward the other men.

It was Pug who took the matter further, with a few words that haunted his memory always. There was a touch of disappointment in the President's reaction, a resigned acceptance of a naval officer's narrow human desire to promote his own career during a war, that stung him into saying, "Well, Mr. President, I'm always yours to command."

Roosevelt turned back to him with a surprised and charming smile. "Why, Pug, it's just that Admiral Standley really did feel he could use you in Moscow. I had another cable from him about you only yesterday. He has his hands full over there." The President's jaw lifted and stuck out. A formidable aspect came over him, as he straightened up under the cape. "We're fighting a very big war, you know, Pug. There's never been anything like it. The Russians are difficult allies, Heaven knows, perfectly awful to deal with sometimes, but they are tying down three and a half million German soldiers. If they go on doing that, we'll win this war. If for some reason they don't, we may lose it. So if you can help out in Russia, and my man on the spot seems to think so, why, maybe that's where you should be."

The faces of the other men were turned to Victor Henry with mild curiosity, but he was scarcely aware of them. There was only the sombre face of Roosevelt before him; the face of a man he had once known as a handsome Assistant Secretary of the Navy, scrambling up a destroyer's ladders like a boy; now the visible face of American history, the face of a worn old cripple.

"Aye aye, sir. In that case, I'll go from here to the Bureau of Personnel, and request those orders."

A pleased light came into the President's eyes. He held out his hand with a sweep of a long arm from under the cape, gesturing manly gratitude and admiration. It was all the reward Victor Henry ever got. When he thought about this scene in after years, it seemed enough. A love for President Roosevelt welled up in his heart as they shook hands. He tasted the acrid pleasure of sacrifice, and the pride of measuring up to the Commander-in-Chief's opinion of him.

"Good luck, Pug."

"Thank you, Mr. President."

A friendly nod and smile from Franklin Roosevelt, and Victor Henry was walking out of the bedroom, the course of his days turned and fixed. Hopkins, near the door, drily said, "So long, Pug." His eyes were narrow, his smile cool.

Rhoda jumped up as her husband walked into the living room. "Well? What's the verdict?"

He told her. At the way her face fell, Pug felt a passing throb of his old love for her, which only told him how nearly it was gone.

"Oh, dear, and I was so hoping for Washington. Was that what you wanted—Moscow again?"

"It's what the President wanted."

"That means a year. Maybe two years."

"It means a long time."

She took his hand, and twined her fingers in his. "Oh, well. We've had a lovely couple of weeks. When do you take off?"

"As a matter of fact, Rho"—Pug looked uncomfortable—"BuPers used some muscle and put me on the Clipper that leaves tomorrow."

"Tomorrow!"

"Dakar, Cairo, Tehran, Moscow. Admiral Standley really seems to want me there."

They drank their best wine at dinner, and fell into reminiscing about old times, about their many separations and reunions, retracing the years until they were back to the night when Pug proposed. Rhoda said, laughing, "Nobody can say you didn't warn me! Honestly, Pug, you talked on and on about how AWFUL it was to be a Navy wife. The separations, the poor pay, the periodic uprooting, the kowtowing to the wives of big brass, you reeled it all off. At one point, I SWEAR, I thought you were trying to talk me out of it. And I said to myself, 'Fat chance, mister! This was your idea, now you're HOOKED.'"

"I thought you should know what you were getting into."

"I've never regretted it." Rhoda sighed, and drank her wine. "It's such a pity. You'll miss Byron. That convoy should be getting here any day."

"I know. I don't like that much."

They were relaxed enough, and Rhoda was female enough, and it was near enough to the end, so that she couldn't resist adding, very casually, "And you'll miss Pamela Tudsbury."

He looked her straight in the eye. What they had never yet talked about suddenly lay, as it were, out on the table—his romance with Pamela, and her affair with Palmer Kirby, a name that had not crossed his lips, any more than Warren's had. "That's right. I'll miss Pamela."

Long seconds passed. Rhoda's eyes dropped.

"Well, if you can stand it, I've made an apple pie."

"Great. I won't get that in Moscow."

They went to bed early. The lovemaking was self-conscious and soon past, and Pug fell heavily asleep. After smoking a cigarette, Rhoda got up, put on a warm robe, and went downstairs to the living room. The album of records she pulled out from a low shelf was dusty. The record was scratched and slightly cracked, and the faded orange label was scrawled over with crayon, for at one point the kids had gotten at this album, and had played the records to death. The old recording was tinny and high-pitched, a ghostly voice from the distant past, coming weak and muffled through the worn surface:

> *It's three o'clock in the morning*
> *We've danced the whole night through*
> *And daylight soon will be dawning*
> *Just one more waltz with you . . .*

She was back in the officers' club in Annapolis. Ensign Pug Henry, the Navy football star, was taking her to some big dance. He was much too short for her, but very sweet and somehow different, and crazily in love with her. It showed in his every word and look. Not handsome, but virile, and promising, and sweet. Irresistible, really.

> *That melody so entrancing*
> *Seems to be made for us two*
> *I could just keep right on dancing*
> *Forever dear with you.*

The antique jazz band sounded so thin and old-fashioned; the record ran out so fast! The needle scratched round and round and round, and Rhoda sat there staring dry-eyed at the phonograph.

PART FIVE

Pug
and
Pamela

56

P UG didn't miss Byron by much.

Two days after the Clipper left for the Azores on the first leg of his circuitous flight to Moscow, the destroyer *Brown* came steaming up-channel into New York harbor. Happy sailors crowded the flying bridge, hands jammed in the pockets of their pea jackets, feet stamping, breath smoking in eager ribald talk about shore leave. Byron stood apart from them in a heavy blue bridge coat, white silk muffler, and white peaked cap, staring up at the Statue of Liberty as the green colossus slid past, starkly lit by a clear cold midwinter sunrise. The crew were wary of this passenger officer. Because the wardroom was short-handed he had stood deck watches under way; a cool shiphandler who spoke little and smiled less while on the bridge. Joining the watch list had made Byron feel that he was getting back in the war, and the officers of the *Brown,* relieved of a grinding one-in-three, had gratefully treated him as one of themselves.

As the convoy scattered, the merchant vessels heading for the New Jersey shore or the sunlit skyscrapers of Manhattan, the screening ships toward Brooklyn, Byron impatiently jingled in a coat pocket a fistful of sweaty quarters. When the *Brown* tied up at a fueling dock, he was the first man down the gangway and into the lone telephone booth on the wharf. A queue of sailors was lined up at the booth by the time his call got through the State Department switchboard.

"Byron! Where are you? When did you get back?" Leslie Slote sounded hoarse and harried.

"Brooklyn Navy Yard. Just docked. What about Natalie and the kid?"

"Well—" at Slote's hesitation, Byron immediately felt sick, "—they're all right, and that's the main thing, isn't it? The fact is, they've been moved to Baden-Baden with those other Americans who were in Lourdes. Just temporarily, you understand, before they're all exchanged, and—"

"*Baden-Baden?*" Byron broke in. "You mean Germany? Natalie's in *Germany?*"

"Well, yes, but—"

"GOD ALMIGHTY!"

"Look, there are reassuring aspects to this. They're in a superb hotel, getting A-one treatment. The Brenner's Park. They're still classed as journalists, still in with diplomats, newspapermen, Red Cross workers, and such. Our chargé d'affaires who was in Vichy, Pinkney Tuck, heads the group. He's a top man. A Swiss diplomat is at the hotel, looking out for their rights. Also a German Foreign Ministry man and a French official. We're holding plenty of Germans that their government wants back very badly. It'll just be a haggling process."

"Are there any other Jews in that group?"

"I don't know. Now, I happen to be busy as hell, Byron. Phone me at home tonight, if you like." Slote gave him the number and hung up.

As Byron's white forbidding face passed through the wardroom full of officers dressed for going ashore, the raillery died. Alone in his cabin, folding uniforms into his footlocker, he tried to plan his next move, but he could scarcely think straight. If one brush with Germans on a French train had been too grim a risk for Natalie to take, what about now? She was in Nazi Germany, over the line, over on the other side! It was beyond imagining; she must be scared out of her mind. In Lisbon Slote had told a bloodcurdling tale of what was happening to the Jews, even claiming that he was returning to Washington to deliver evidence to President Roosevelt. Byron found the story beyond belief, a hysterical exaggeration of what was probably going on in Germany in the fog of war. He did not fear that his wife and son really risked being caught in a continent-wide process of railroading Jews to secret camps in Poland, where they would be gassed to death and their bodies burned up. That was a fairy tale; even Germans could not do such things.

But he did fear that their diplomatic protection might fail. They were illegal fugitives from Fascist Italy, and their journalist credentials were phony. If the Germans turned ugly, they might be singled out first for harsh treatment, among those Americans trapped in Baden-Baden. Louis might sicken or die from mistreatment; he was such a little thing! Byron left the *Brown* sunk in wretchedness.

Trudging through the Navy Yard with his footlocker, amid laborers thronging off their jobs for lunch, he decided that if he could locate Madeline, he would stay in New York overnight; then go to Washington, and from there fly to San Francisco, or to Pearl Harbor if the *Moray* had departed. But how to get hold of Madeline? His mother had written that she was back working for Hugh Cleveland, and had sent him an address on Claremont Avenue, just off the Columbia campus.

He could drop his stuff at his old fraternity house, he figured, and spend the night there if he couldn't track her down. Since their parting in California, he had not heard from her.

The cab wound through Brooklyn, came out on the Williamsburg Bridge for another brilliant view of the skyscrapers, then plowed into the lower east side of Manhattan, where Jews in numbers were hustling along the sidewalks. His mind circled back to Natalie. She had struck him from the start as a sophisticated American, all the more alluring for a dusky spicy trace of Jewishness—to which she had never alluded in the old days except in self-mockery, or in contempt for Slote because he had allowed it to matter. Yet in Marseilles she had appeared overpowered, paralyzed, by her Jewishness. Byron could not understand. He took little account of race differences; he thought it was all bigoted nonsense, and his attitude toward the Nazi doctrines was one of incredulous contempt. He felt out of his depth in this thing, but the residue was anger and frustration at his stiff-necked wife, and scarcely endurable concern for his son.

The fraternity house had the same old dusty banners and trophies on the walls. The brick fireplace was piled as ever with cold wood ashes, fruit peelings, cigarette packages and butts, and over the mantel, the portrait of an early benefactor was much darkened by more years of wood smoke and tobacco fumes. As always, two collegians clicked away at the ping-pong table, watched as always by idlers on broken-down sofas; and as always blaring jazz shook the walls. Surprisingly callow and pimply high school boys seemed to have taken over the place. The spottiest of these introduced himself to Byron as the chapter president. He had obviously never heard of Byron, but the uniform impressed him.

"Hey," he bellowed up the stairs, "anybody using Jeff's room? Old grad here for overnight."

No answer. The spotty president ascended with Byron to a back bedroom where the same sepia picture of Marlene Dietrich hung, wrinkling and askew. The president explained that the occupant Jeff, about to flunk all his midterms, had abruptly joined the Marines. The wise-guy Columbia grin that went with this disclosure made Byron feel more at home.

One o'clock. No use trying to track down Madeline now, all those radio types would be out to lunch. Byron had stood the midwatch, and had stayed awake ever since. He set his alarm for three and stretched out on the dingy bed. The discordant crash and bleat of jazz did not keep him from falling fast asleep.

Cleveland, Hugh, Enterprises, Inc. 630 Fifth Avenue. The directory at the telephone under the staircase was a couple of years old, but he tried the number. A blithe girlish voice came on. "Program coordinator's office, Miss Blaine."

"Hello, I'm Madeline Henry's brother. Is she there?"

"You ARE? You're Byron, the submarine officer? Really?"

"That's right. I'm in New York."

"Oh, how terrif! She's at a meeting. Where can she reach you? She'll be back in an hour or so."

Byron gave her the number of the pay telephone, hunted up the spotty president through the smoke, and got his promise to take any message that came in. He escaped from the jazz din into the windy freezing street, where he heard very different music: the "Washington Post March." On South Field, blue-coated ranks of midshipmen were marching and countermarching with rifles. In Byron's time the only marching on South Field had been for anarchic antiwar rallies. These fellows might be a year getting out to sea, Byron thought, and then months would pass before they could stand watch under way. This marching mass of unblooded reservists made him feel pretty good about his combat record; then he wondered, in his low frame of mind, what was so praiseworthy about repeated exposure to getting killed.

Why not walk to the *Prairie State,* scene of his own reserve training? Nothing else to do. He strode up Broadway, and over to the river on 125th Street. There was the old decommissioned battleship, tied up and swarming with midshipmen. The smells from the Hudson, the piping and loudspeaker announcements, deepened his nostalgia. On the *Prairie State,* in the long bull sessions at night, there had been so much talk of the kind of wife one wanted! Hitler and the Nazis then had been ludicrous figures in the newsreels; and the Columbia demonstrators had been signing pledges right and left not to fight in any wars. Natalie's predicament seemed, in the familiar scene at the foot of 125th Street, a dim incredible nightmare.

It occurred to Byron that he could go back to the fraternity house through Claremont Avenue, and slip a note under Madeline's door telling her where he was staying. He found the house, and pressed the outside call bell beside her name. The door buzzed in reply; so she was in! He opened the door, leaped up two flights of stairs, and rang her bell.

It is almost never a good idea to walk in on a woman without warning her: not a sweetheart, not a wife, not a mother, and certainly not a sister. Madeline, in a fluffy blue negligee, with her black hair down to her shoulders, looked out at him. Her eyes rounded and popped, and she exclaimed "EEK!" exactly as though he had come upon her naked, or as though he were a rat or a snake.

Before Byron could say anything, a deep rich male voice rumbled from inside, "What is it, honey?" Hugh Cleveland came in sight, nude to the waist, and below that clad in a flopping flowery lava-lava, scratching his hairy chest.

"It's *Byron,*" Madeline gasped. "How are you, Byron? My God, when did you get back?"

Fully as disconcerted as she was, Byron asked, "Didn't you get my message?"

"What message? No, nothing. Well, Jesus Christ, now that you're here, come in."

"Hi, Byron," said Hugh Cleveland, with the charming smile that showed all his big white teeth.

"Say, are you two married already?" Byron said, walking into a well-furnished living room where an ice bucket, a bottle of Scotch, and soda bottles stood on a table.

Cleveland and Madeline exchanged a look, and Madeline said, "Sweetie, how long will you be here, anyway? Where are you staying? Jesus Christ, why didn't you write or telephone or something?"

A door was open to a bedroom, and Byron could see a big rumpled double bed. Though abstractly he accepted the possibility that his sister was misbehaving, he literally did not believe his eyes. He said to Madeline, with clumsy blundering bluntness, "Madeline, come on, are you married, or what?"

Hugh Cleveland might have been well-advised to keep quiet at this point. But he smiled a big white smile, spread his hands, and rumbled warmly, "Look, Byron, we're all adults, and this is the twentieth century. So if you'll—"

Byron swiftly drew back his arm despite the bulk of his bridge coat, and crashed a fist into Cleveland's smiling face.

Madeline gave another "EEK!" louder and shriller than before. Cleveland went down like a poled ox, but he was not really knocked out, because he landed on his hands and knees, crawled about, and got up. As he did so his lava-lava fell off, and he was standing stark naked, with a sizable white paunch protruding over his spindly legs and private parts. This unprepossessing sight was quite eclipsed by the astounding transformation of his face. He looked like Dracula. All his upper front teeth were filed to sharp little points, with slightly longer fangs at either end.

"Jesus CHRIST, Hugh," Madeline cried out, "your teeth! Look at your *teeth!*"

Hugh Cleveland stumbled to a wall mirror, grinned at himself, and uttered an eerie wail. "Jethuth Chritht, my bridge! My porthelain bridge. It cotht me fifteen hundred fucking dollarth! Where the hell ith it?" He glanced wildly around the floor, turned on Byron and lisped in great indignation, "Why the hell did you thock me? How ridiculouth can you get? Let'th find that bridge, and damned fatht!"

"Oh, Hugh," Madeline said nervously, "put something on, for Heaven's sake, will you? You're prancing around naked as a jaybird."

Cleveland blinked down at his bare body, snatched the lava-lava, and fastened it on as he strode around searching the floor for his bridge-work. Byron saw a white thing lying on the carpet under a chair. "Is this it?" he said, picking up the object and offering it to Cleveland. "Sorry I did that." Byron wasn't really very sorry, but the man was a pitifully idiotic sight with his sharpened-down tooth stumps, and the lava-lava carelessly dragging on his bulging belly.

"That'th it!" Cleveland went back to the mirror, and with two thumbs pressed the thing into his mouth. He turned around. "How's that, now?" He looked normal again, flashing the celebrated smile that Byron had seen in so many magazine advertisements of Cleveland's radio sponsor, a toothpaste company.

"Oh, heavens, that's better," said Madeline, "and Byron, you *apologize* to Hugh."

"I did," Byron said.

After grimacing at himself in the mirror and gnashing his teeth to test the fixity of the bridge, Cleveland turned to them. "Well, it's just a damned good thing it didn't break. I've got that U.S. Chamber of Commerce banquet tonight to toastmaster, and that reminds me, Mad, Arnold never did give me my thcript. What am I thuppothed to do if—oh, Chritht, there it goeth. It'th thlipping! I'm loothing it!" As he talked, Byron could indeed see the bridge come loose and drop out of his mouth. Cleveland lunged to catch it, stepped on the hem of the lava-lava, and fell on his face naked again, the flowery cloth pulling off and crumpling under him.

Madeline clapped her hand to her mouth and glanced at Byron, her wide eyes sparkling with their sense of fun shared since childhood. Hurrying to Cleveland, she spoke in tones of tender concern, "Are you hurt, honey?"

"Hurt? Thit, no." Cleveland got to his feet, the bridge clutched in his fingers, and strode to the bedroom, his plump white bottom waggling. "Thith ith damned theriouth, Mad. I'm calling my dentitht, and he better be in! I'm getting paid a thouthand buckth to be toathtmathter tonight. Thon of a bith!"

He slammed the door.

Picking up the lava-lava, Madeline snapped at Byron, "Oh, YOU! How could you be such an ANIMAL!"

Byron glanced around the room. "Honestly, what is this setup, Madeline? Does he live here with you?"

"What? How can he? He's got a family, stupid."

"Well, what are you doing then?" Pouting, she did not answer. "Mad, are you just having a toss now and then with this fat old guy? How is that possible?"

"Oh, you don't understand anything. Hugh is a friend, a dear good friend. You'll never know how good he's been to me, and what's more—"

"You're committing adultery, Mad."

A fleeting miserable look came and went on her face. Madeline flipped a hand, shook her head, and smiled a super-wise female smile. "Oh, you're so naïve. His marriage is better now than it was, MUCH better. And I'm a much better person. There's more than one way to live, Briny. You and I come from a family of fossils. I know Hugh would marry me if I pushed him, he's daffy about me, but—"

Half-dressed, Cleveland looked out of the bedroom and lisped loudly at Madeline that his dentist was driving in from Thcarthdale. "Call Tham right away. Tell him to get hith ath over here in ten minuteth. Chrith, what a meth!"

"Tham?" Byron said as Cleveland closed the door.

"Sam's his chauffeur," Madeline said, hurrying to a telephone and dialling. "Oh, Byron, are you disowning me? Can I cook you a dinner? Shall we get blind drunk tonight? Want to stay here? There's a spare room. When are you leaving? What's the news of Natalie?—Hello, hello, let me talk to Sam . . . Well, *find* him, Carol. Yes, yes, I KNOW my brother Byron's in town. Jesus Christ, do I know it . . . Never mind, just find Sam, and tell him to get the Cadillac over here in ten minutes flat."

She said as she hung up, "Byron, I've worked for Hugh for four years, and I didn't know he had bridgework."

"Live and learn, Mad."

"If the whole thing weren't so awful," she said, "and if you weren't such a disgusting neanderthal, it would be the funniest goddamned thing I've been through in my life." Her mouth was wrinkling, suppressing laughter. "I've nagged him for years to get rid of that horrible stomach. Look at you, now! Flat as a boy, just like Dad. Will you give your adulterous sister a kiss?"

"Lechery, lechery; still, wars and lechery; nothing else holds fashion," rails the sour Thersites. "A burning devil take them!"

Janice had some warning, so she was able to receive Byron in poised innocence; as Madeline could have done too, given half a chance.

When her father-in-law had passed through Honolulu, dissembling to him about her affair with Carter Aster had given her not a qualm. It was none of his business. No man could think like a woman about these things, least of all Captain Victor Henry, who wouldn't even play cards on Sunday. Frankness would have led only to embarrassment, and no possible useful purpose would have been served. But Byron's cable posed a problem to Janice.

Aster had told her that her brother-in-law would be reporting to the *Moray*. Byron was altogether a peculiar sort, fully as dashing as Warren, but with a sweetly idealistic attitude toward women which could prove a nuisance. His moral views seemed as narrow as his father's. His tale about the girl in Australia had been all but incredible, but Janice had believed it. What would have been the point of a lie that made him out a prudish simpleton?

Yet, when a war was on, when men were far from home and lonely, when everywhere there was great activity in what Aster robustly called "unauthorized ass"—a phrase that much amused Janice, though she pretended to bridle at it—why should Byron have denied himself a natural and beautiful relationship? The Aster affair had sprung up more or less accidentally. After Midway an attack of dengue fever had laid her low, and Carter Aster had visited her every day and had seen to her needs of food and medicine, and one thing had led to another.

She knew that Byron would be scandalized if he found out. Janice didn't understand that side of Byron; he was damned different from his brother. She regarded his prudishness as a quaint minor foible, and she certainly did not want to disillusion or estrange him. She considered herself a Henry, she liked that family better than her own, and she had always found Byron a very attractive man. It was wonderful to have him around.

So as Aster was getting dressed to return to the submarine late one night, Janice decided to take things in hand. She was smoking a cigarette in bed, nude under a sheet.

"Byron's due in the morning, honey."

"He is?" Aster paused in pulling on khaki trousers. "So soon? How do you know that?"

"He cabled me from San Francisco. He's getting a ride on NATS."

"Well, great! It's high time. We need him aboard."

It was past midnight. Aster never stayed till morning. He liked to be up and about on the submarine at reveille; also, he was tender of Janice's reputation, living as she did in a row of houses with early-rising neighbors. Janice loved Aster, or at least loved her hours with him, but she wanted nothing permanent with him. He had nothing like Warren's breadth, he read trash, and his talk was pure Navy. He reminded her of the many Pensacola pilots who had bored her before Warren had come along. Aster was an able naval engineer, with an urge to excel and to kill, born for submarining. And he was a considerate and satisfying lover; the perfect partner for unauthorized ass, so to say, but not much more. If Aster sensed her qualified regard for him, he wasn't complaining.

"The point is, dear," Janice said, "that hanky-panky has to be out for a while." He gave her a cool inquiring look, tucking in his shirt. "I mean, you know Byron. I love him dearly. I don't want him getting all upset and disapproving. I can't have it."

"Now let me understand you. Are you calling it off?"

"Oh, would you mind, all that much?"

"Hell, yes, I'd mind, Janice."

"Well, don't look so tragic. Smile."

"Why does Byron have to know?"

"When you're in port, he'll be spending nights here."

"He'll have the duty every other night."

"Yes, I suppose he will. All the same—"

Aster came to the bed, sat down, and gathered her in his arms.

After a breathless few kisses she murmured, "Well, we'll see, we'll see. One thing, Carter. Byron must never, *never* find out. Understand?"

"Sure," Aster said. "No need for it."

The morning he arrived Byron stayed only long enough to have breakfast, then went on to the submarine; but in that short time he unburdened with frank and deep bitterness of heart the gist of what had happened in Marseilles. The news that Natalie and her baby were caught in Germany horrified Janice. Automatically she defended what her sister-in-law had done, and tried to reassure Byron that it would all turn out well. But she feared Natalie was doomed. Watching him play with Vic in the garden before he left, she had to exert willpower not to cry. The instant mutual magnetism between the uncle and the child was poignant to behold. When Byron said he had to go, Victor clung to him with arms and legs as he had never done with Warren.

The *Moray* stayed around Pearl Harbor for several more weeks, most of the time out at sea in the training areas. When the submarine came into port Byron spent every other night at Janice's cottage. The first time he remained aboard, Aster telephoned. Janice did not know what to do. She told him to come over, but not until after little Vic was asleep in bed. His visit was a failure. She was uneasy, Aster quickly discerned it, and after a couple of drinks he left without touching her. She saw him only once after that before the *Moray* left on patrol. When Byron told her that they were sailing in the morning, she said, "Oh! Well, why don't you ask Carter to come to dinner, then? He's been awfully kind to me and Vic."

"That's nice of you, Jan. Can he bring a girl?"

"If he wants to, sure."

Aster brought no girl. The three of them dined by candlelight, drinking a lot of wine and working up to a jolly mood. Byron's spirits were improving with his return to submarine duty. Aster's correct mixture of informality and aloofness won Janice's gratitude. At one point they turned on the radio for the war news, and heard that the Germans had at last surrendered at Stalingrad. They opened another bottle of wine on that.

"There go the Krauts," Byron said, lifting his glass, "and none too soon." To his wine-flushed mind, this news signalled the early deliverance of his family.

"Damn right. Now we get the Japs," said Aster.

When the evening was over and Janice was left alone, her head reeled with wine, and she was feeling in delighted girlish confusion that the death of her husband was behind her, and that she truly loved two men.

*   *   *

57

𝔊lobal 𝔚aterloo
4: 𝔖talingrad

(from *World Holocaust* by Armin von Roon)

TRANSLATOR'S NOTE: *General von Roon's discussion of Stalingrad con-cludes the strategic analysis section of* World Holocaust. *The original book sketches all campaigns and battles to the end of the war. But as it happens, his subsequent ground is covered briefly, and with much more anecdotal interest, in the epilogue to Roon's magnum opus: a personal memoir of his dealings with Adolf Hitler called "Hitler as Military Leader." This gives inter-esting glimpses of the Führer in decay during the mounting collapse of Ger-many on all fronts. My translation continues with excerpts from the mem-oirs, adding only Roon's essay on the Battle of Leyte Gulf.*

I have taken some liberties with Roon's writing on Stalingrad. Seen in isolation, the battle was a senseless five-month grinding of whole German armies to hamburger in a remote industrial town on the Volga. One needs the context of the 1942 summer campaign to grasp what happened there. But Roon's Case Blue analysis is so fogged with names of Russian cities and rivers, and with German army movements, that American readers cannot get through it. So I have inserted some passages of "Hitler as Military Leader" to illuminate the picture, employing only the words of Armin von Roon, and I have tried to cut out as many confusing technical and geo-graphical references as possible.—V.H.

Stalingrad fulfilled on the battlefield Spengler's prophetic vision of the decline of the West. It was the Singapore of Christian culture.

The true tragedy of Stalingrad is that it need not have happened. The West had the strength to prevent it. It was not like the fall of Rome, or of Constantinople, or even of Singapore: not a world-historical crushing of a weak culture by a stronger one. On the contrary! We of the Christian West had we but been united, could readily have repulsed the barbaric Scythian out of the steppes in their new guise of Marxist predators. We could have pacified Russia for a century and changed its essential menacing nature.

But this was not to be. Franklin Delano Roosevelt's one war aim was to destroy Germany so as to win unimpeded rule of the world for American monopoly capital. Rightly he perceived that England was finished. As for the menace of Bolshevism he was either blind to it, or saw no way to eradicate it, and decided that Germany was the competitor he could destroy.

The great Hegel has taught us that it is irrelevant to challenge the morality of world-historical individuals. Morally, if one values the Christian civilization now being swamped by Marxist barbarism, Franklin Roosevelt was unquestionably one of mankind's archcriminals. But in military history, one regards only how well the political aim of a war leader was achieved. However shortsighted Roosevelt's aim, he certainly achieved the destruction of Germany.

Sunset Glow

Our second great assault on the Soviet Union, called "Case Blue,"* led to Stalingrad. It was an insightful concept, it was mainly Hitler's, and it came close to success. Hitler himself ruined it.

The contrast of Franklin Delano Roosevelt and Adolf Hitler in their warmaking is altogether Plutarchian. Spidery calculation versus all-out gambling; steadfast planning versus impulsive improvising; careful use of limited armed strength versus prodigal dissipation of overwhelming strength; prudent reliance on generals versus reckless overruling of them; anxious concern for troops versus impetuous outpouring of their lives; a timid dip of a toe in combat versus total war with the last reserves thrown in; such was the contrast between the two world opponents as they at last came to grips in 1942, nine years after they both took power.

In retrospect the world sees Hitler as the disgusting 1945 figure in the bunker: Roosevelt's trapped victim, a disintegrating, trembling, unrepentant horror lost in dreams, maintaining his grip on a prostrate Reich by sheer terror. But this was not the Hitler of July 1942. Then he was still our all-masterful FÜHRER: a remote, demanding, difficult warlord, but the ruler of an empire unmatched by those of Alexander, Caesar, Charlemagne, and Napoleon. The glow of German victory lit the planet. Only in retrospect do we see that it was a sunset glow.

* The code name was altered to *Braunschweig* (Brunswick) during the campaign. This translation retains "Blue" throughout.—V.H.

Case Blue

Case Blue was a summer drive to end the war in the east.

Our great 1941 drive, Barbarossa, had aimed to destroy the Red Army and shatter the Bolshevik state in one grand three-pronged summer campaign. We had tried to do too much at once. We had hurt the enemy, but the Russian is a stolid fatalist, with an animal ability to resist and endure. The Japanese unwillingness to attack Siberia—duly reported to Stalin by his spy Sorge from our embassy in Tokyo—had enabled the Red dictator to denude his Asian front and hurl fresh divisions of hardy brutish Mongol troops at us. These winter counterattacks, though halting us in the snows outside Moscow, had petered out. When the spring thaw came we still held an area of the Soviet Union roughly analogous to the entire U.S.A. east of the Mississippi. Who can doubt that under such an occupation the flighty Americans would have collapsed? But the Russians are a different breed, and they needed one more convincing blow.

Case Blue carried forward Barbarossa in its southern phase. The aim was to seize southern Russia for its agricultural, industrial, and mineral wealth. The theme was limited and clear: *Hold in the north and center, win in the south.* Granted that Hitler's continental mentality could not grasp the Mediterranean strategy, it was the next best thing to do. We were in it, and we had to attack. Moreover, it did not appear that we could fight the war to a finish without the Caucasus oil.

Under all the muddled political verbiage of Hitler's famous Directive Number 41, rewritten by his own hand from Jodl's professional draft, the governing concepts of Case Blue were:

1. Straighten out the winter penetrations;
2. Hold fast, north and center, on the Leningrad–Moscow–Orel line;
3. Conquer the south to the Turkish and Iranian borders;
4. Take Leningrad, and possibly Moscow;
5. The main objectives in Russia thus achieved, if the enemy still fights on, fortify the eastern line from the Gulf of Finland to the Caspian Sea, and go on the defensive against an emasculated foe.

Essentially then, the original Barbarossa goal now shifted to a slanting Great Wall of fortified positions from the Gulf of Finland to the great Baku oil fields on the Caspian, sealing off our "Slavic India." Other vital benefits, if the campaign succeeded, would be cutting off Lend-Lease via the Persian Gulf, tilting Turkey to our side, and denying our enemies Persian oil. An advance to India might even be in the offing, if all went well, or a northward sweep east of the Volga to take Moscow from the rear. Admittedly, this was adventurous policy. We had failed once, and were trying again with weaker forces. But Russia was weakened, too. The whole grandiose drive of the German people under Hitler for world empire was only a pyramiding of gambles.

If only we could change the war balance by seizing Russia's wheat and oil, and then stabilize the eastern front, two political solutions of the war could open up: an Anglo-Saxon change of heart at the prospect of facing our full fury, or a realistic peace by Stalin. Roosevelt's fear of such a separate eastern peace governed all his war-making. And Stalin remained suspicious to the end that the plutocracies were planning to leave him in the lurch. It was uncertain right up to our surrender whether the bizarre alliance of our foes would not fall apart.

Why in fact did the Americans and British never grasp that only by letting us win against Russia could the world flood of Bolshevism be stemmed? Churchill at least wanted to land in the Balkans to forestall Stalin in middle Europe. If this was bad strategy, because we were too strong and the terrain too difficult, it was at least alert politics. Roosevelt would have none of it. Since he could not annihilate us, he wanted to help the Bolsheviks to do it. So he sacrificed Christian Europe to American monopoly capital for a brief gluttonous feast, at the price of a new dark age now fast falling on the world.

Answers to Critics of Blue

After every war, the armchair strategists and the history professors have their pallid fun, telling those who bled in battle how they should have done it. Certain shallow criticisms of Case Blue have been repeated until they have taken on a false aura of fact. Stalingrad was a great and fatal turn in world history, and the record leading up to it should be clear.

Strategically, Blue was a good plan.

Tactically, Blue went awry, because of Hitler's day-to-day interference.

Critics carp that the one acceptable objective of a major campaign is the destruction of the enemy's armed forces. In the summer of 1942 Stalin had concentrated his armies around Moscow, assuming we would try to end the war by smashing the bulk of his forces and occupying the capital. Our critics assert we should have done so. This would indeed have been orthodox strategy. By striking south we achieved massive surprise. That too is orthodox strategy.

TRANSLATOR'S NOTE: *Russian sources bear out Roon. Stalin was so positive that the attack in the south was a feint to draw off Moscow's defenses* and he hung on to this idea so long, that only Hitler's botch of the tactics saved Stalingrad, and possibly the Soviet Union.—V.H.

We are also told that the strategic aim of Case Blue was *economic,* and therefore wrong. One must destroy the enemy's armed force, then one can do as one pleases with his wealth; so the banal admonition goes. These critics miss the whole point of Blue. It was a plan to enforce a *gigantic land blockade of the poor but governing north rump of the Soviet Union,* by depriving it of food, fuel, and heavy industry. Blockade, if one can enforce it, is a tedious but tested way to humble an enemy. When Blue was planned, the Japanese were running wild in the Pacific and in Southeast Asia. We assumed that they would neutralize the United States for a year or more. Alas, the stunning early turnabouts at Midway and Guadalcanal freed Roosevelt to flood Lend-Lease aid to the Russians in 1942, past our blockade. That made a powerful difference.

Finally, critics contend that Blue's double objective, Stalingrad and the Caucasus, required a stretching out of the southern front far beyond the capacity of the Wehrmacht to hold it, so that the outcome of the campaign was foredoomed.

But Stalingrad was not an objective of Case Blue. It became Hitler's objective when he lost control of himself in September.

Strategy of Case Blue

Near Stalingrad, the rivers Don and Volga converge in a very striking way. The two great bends point their V's at each other over a forty-mile space of dry land. The first phase of Blue called for capture of this strategic land bridge, so as to block attacks from the north on our southern invasion forces; also, to cut the Volga as a supply route of fuel and food to the north.

At the V of the Volga, a medium-sized industrial town straggled along the bluffs of the west bank: *Stalingrad.* We did not need to occupy it, we needed merely to neutralize it with bombardment in order to dominate the bottleneck. Our general plan was to thrust two heavy fast-moving pincers along the two arms of the enormous V of the Don, thus trapping and destroying most of the Soviet forces defending south Russia. The first pincer, the Volga Force—jumping off first, since it had the longer distance to go—would march down the upper arm of the Don. The second, the Caucasus Force, would advance along the lower arm. They would meet between the rivers, near Stalingrad. After defeating and mopping up the trapped forces, these two great army groups would divide responsibilities for the second or conquest phase. The Caucasus Force would wheel south, cross the Don, and drive down to the Black Sea, to the Caspian, and through the high passes to the borders of Turkey and Iran. The Volga Force would defend the dangerous flank opened up all along the Don, which would be manned during our advance by three satellite armies: Hungarian, Italian, and Rumanian.

Here was the weak link in Blue, and we knew it. But we had already lost nearly a million men in the war, and we were near the limit of German man power. We had to use these auxiliaries on the flanks while the Wehrmacht struck ahead. But we did not plan that they should man the Don against a full assault by the Red Army. That happened only because the Führer lost his head, and disrupted the timetable of the campaign.

TRANSLATOR'S NOTE: *In editing Roon, I have omitted Manstein's conquest of the Crimea and Sevastopol, and the failure of Timoshenko's May attack against Kharkov. These big German victories weakened Russia in the south, making Blue a much more promising operation. I have called "Army Group A" Caucasus Force, and "Army Group B" Volga Force. The technical Wehrmacht designations are hard to follow, especially as regroupings occurred in mid-campaign.—V.H.*

. . .

(From "Hitler as Military Leader")

What Went Wrong

. . . Supreme Headquarters is an edgy place during a campaign. One waits in a map room for developments, day after day. The war seems to drag and drag. Out in the field is reality: hundreds of thousands of men marching over fields and through cities, moving masses of equipment, coming under fire. In Headquarters one sees the same faces, the same walls, the same maps, one eats in the same place with the same elderly tired men in uniform. The atmosphere is strained and quiet, the air stale. There is a remoteness and abstraction about this nerve center of the war. The perpetual tension of deferred hope gnaws at the heart.

At our advance headquarters at Vinnitsa in the Ukraine all this was doubly true. "Werewolf," as Hitler named the installation, was a crude compound of log cabins and wooden huts in the open pine country near the southern River Bug. Socially, there was no relief. Physically, we could go splash in the slow muddy river, if we cared to expose our naked skins to clouds of stinging insects. The weather was blazing hot and sticky, too much so for Hitler even to walk his dog, his only exercise.

We moved there in mid-July, at the height of the campaign. Hitler did not take the heat well, strong sunlight bothered him, and altogether it was an uncomfortable situation. His digestion was worse than ever, his flatulence a trial for everybody in a room with him. Even the dog, Blondi, was out of sorts and whiny.

But even before that, while we were still in our cooler and more comfortable compound in the East Prussian woods, he had already shown signs of strain and instability, by his drastic change of plan for the Caucasus Force and for the Fourth Panzer Army. . . .

• • •

(From *World Holocaust*)

The faltering of Blue can be dated precisely to the thirteenth of July.

Hitler's anxiety had been mounting day by day. He could not understand why we were not hauling in the hordes of prisoners that our great enveloping movements had yielded in 1941. Whether Stalin had learned at last not to order his troops to stand fast and be captured; or whether the southern armies were fading away before us in undisciplined rout; or whether the front was just weakly manned; or whether, finally, the Russians were resorting to their classic tactic of trading space for time, the fact was we were capturing Russians in the tens of thousands, instead of the hundreds of thousands.

On July 13, Hitler suddenly decided to divert the *entire eastward campaign away from the Stalingrad land bridge, southwest toward Rostov!* Thus he hoped, by a tighter enveloping move, to bag a supposed enormous Red Army force in the Don bend. The whole Caucasus Force wheeled off on this mission. He even peeled off the Volga Force's panzer army, the doughty Fourth, and sent it clanking toward Rostov, too, although Halder bitterly opposed piling so much armor against one minor objective. The Volga Force slowed to a standstill, very low on gasoline, for the main supplies had to go to this adventure of catching Russians.

The huge power thrust captured Rostov and netted some forty thousand prisoners. But precious time had been lost, and the whole Blue plan was in disarray. The Caucasus Force and the Fourth Army were milling around Rostov, choking the transit arteries, and creating unimaginable difficulties in improvised organization and supply.

At this critical point Adolf Hitler sprang on our stupefied Headquarters his notorious and catastrophic Directive Number 45, perhaps the worst military orders ever issued. It abrogated the Blue plan altogether. A responsible General Staff would have analyzed, war-gamed, and organized such an operation for months, or even for a year. Hitler airily scrawled it all out in a day or two, and so far as I know, all by himself. If Jodl helped him with it, he never boasted of it!

In essence, Directive Number 45 consisted of three points:

1. A mere *assertion* (contrary to known fact) that the first aim of the campaign had been achieved: i.e., that the Red Army in the south had been "largely destroyed."
2. The Volga Force was to resume the drive toward Stalingrad, with the Fourth Panzer Army rejoining it.
3. The Caucasus Force under List was to proceed southward at once, with additions to its original difficult task, such as securing the entire Black Sea coast.

This was Hitler's last attack directive. It was at this point that we at Supreme Headquarters began to lose heart, though in the field things still looked rosy. Halder, the Army Chief of Staff, was scandalized. He noted in his diary—and he said baldly to me—that these orders no longer bore any resemblance to military realities.

The *conditions* for carrying out our summer campaign in any reasonable form had now melted away. Neither the upper bend of the Don, nor the crucial land bridge, had been secured. The Caucasus Force, the lower pincer of the Don phase, had been scheduled to move south *only* when the Don flank stretching to Stalingrad was secure. Now the two great forces were to separate and operate in different directions with unsecured flanks—leaving a constantly widening gap between them as they pursued diverse missions!

Moreover, the Blue plan had called for Manstein's Eleventh Army, which had conquered the Crimea and captured Sevastopol, to cross to the Caucasus and support List in his drive. But Hitler, in his glee at the capture of Rostov, had decided that things were going too well in the south to waste Manstein there; and *he had ordered Manstein to take most of his army eleven hundred miles north to attack Leningrad!*

Hitler's numbered directives end with Number 51, dated late in 1943; but in fact, after this fatal Number 45, they trail off in defensive measures. This was his final wielding of the initiative. Lack of experience, and the strain of arrogating to himself all the political and military authority of Germany, had told at last on a high-strung temperament, a very adept mind, and a fearsome will. The order was madness. Yet only in our innermost HQ councils was the picture clear in all its folly. The Wehrmacht obeyed, and marched off into the remotest depths of southern Russia on two separate roads to its sombre fate.

Arrival at Stalingrad

With awesome inevitability, the tragedy now began to unfold.

The Caucasus Force performed wonders, marching across vast steppes blazing with midsummer heat, climbing to the peaks of snowcapped mountain ranges, investing the Black Sea coast, and actually sending patrols as far as the Caspian Sea. But it fell short of its objectives. What Hitler had ordered was beyond its manpower, its firepower, and its logistical support. The force stood still for as much as ten days at a time, for want of gasoline, and of supply trucks to bring up the fuel. At one point, with true Greek irony, gasoline was even being brought to the Caucasus Force on the backs of camels! List's great armies stalled in the mountains, harried by elusive tough Red units, and unable to advance.

Meanwhile, on August 23 the Volga Force, driving on toward Stalingrad, reached the riverbank north of the city, and the neutralization phase began with heavy air and artillery bombardment. Resistance was at first meager. For a day or two it looked as though Stalingrad might fall to a *coup de main*. But it did not happen. We were at a far stretch ourselves, and Stalingrad held against the first shock.

TRANSLATOR'S NOTE: *These dry words of Roon scarcely convey the reality as the Russians saw it.*

The advance of the Sixth Army on Stalingrad was apparently the most terrifying event of what the Russians call the Great Patriotic War. The army commanders, the populace, and Stalin himself were astounded at this renewed powerful thrust of the Germans into the vitals of their country. The August twenty-third bombardment was one of the most horrible ordeals by fire the Russians ever endured. Some forty thousand civilians were killed. The flaming streets of the town literally "ran with blood." All communication with Moscow was cut off. For several hours Josef Stalin believed that Stalingrad had fallen. But though the city was to undergo one of the worst punishments in the history of warfare thereafter, that was the low point.

Most military writers conclude that if Hitler had not interfered with the Blue plan, the Volga Force would have reached the river weeks earlier, while Stalin was still under the delusion that the southern attack was a feint. Stalingrad would have fallen, a fruit of the massive initial surprise, and the whole war might have gone differently. Hitler disembowelled the Blue campaign by the diversion to Rostov.—V.H.

Catastrophe at Stalingrad

As previously stated, the capture of Stalingrad was *not* a military necessity.

Our aim was to take the land bridge between the rivers, and to deny the Soviets the use of the Volga as a supply route. Now we were at the Volga. All we had to do was invest the city and bombard it to rubble. After all, we invested Leningrad for more than two years. About a million Russians fell in Leningrad streets from starvation, and for all intents and purposes of the war, the city was a withered corpse. There was no *military* reason not to treat Stalingrad the same way.

But there was increasing *political* reason. For as the Caucasus Force came to a halt in the wild mountain passes despite all Hitler's savage urging; as Rommel stalled at El Alamein, failed in two assaults, and at last underwent the grinding assault of the British; as the RAF increased its barbaric fire raids on our cities, slaughtering thousands of innocent women and children and pulverizing important factories; as our U-boat losses suddenly and alarmingly shot up; as the Americans landed in North Africa with world-shaking political effect; as all these chickens came home to roost, and Adolf Hitler's great summer flush of triumph waned, and the first cracks in his gigantic imperium appeared, the embattled Führer felt a more and more desperate need for a prestige victory to turn all this around.

STALINGRAD!

STALINGRAD, bearing the name of his strongest foe! STALINGRAD, symbol of the Bolshevism he had fought all his life! STALINGRAD, a city appearing more and more in world headlines as a pivot of the war!

The capture of Stalingrad became for Adolf Hitler an unbelievably violent obsession. His orders in the ensuing weeks were madness compounded and recompounded. The Sixth Army, which with its mobile striking power had won an unbroken string of victories in Poland, France, and Russia, was fed division by division into the meat grinder of Stalingrad's ruined streets, where mobile tactics were impossible. Slav snipers mowed down the veterans of the great Sixth in a house-to-house "rat war." The Russian General Staff poured in defenders across the Volga to keep up this annihilation, while methodically preparing a stupendous counterstroke against the weak satellite armies on the Don flank. For Josef Stalin had finally grasped that Hitler, with his obsessive cramming of his finest divisions into the Moloch maw of Stalingrad, was giving him a glorious opportunity.

Late in November the blow fell. The Red Army hurtled across the Don into the Rumanian army, guarding the flank of the Volga Force, northwest of Stalingrad. These unwarlike auxiliaries gave way like cheese to a knife. A similar attack routed the Rumanian flank corps in our Fourth Panzer Army on the southern flank. As the attack developed into December, the Russians smashed into our lines all along the Don where Italians and Hungarians were protecting the Sixth Army's rear; and a steel trap closed on three hundred thousand German soldiers, the flower of the Wehrmacht.

•   •   •

(From "Hitler as Military Leader")

Transformation of Hitler

. . . As it happened, I was away from Supreme Headquarters during much of this trying period, on a long inspection tour. When I left late in August, all was going well enough in Russia. Both forces were advancing rapidly on their diverging fronts; the Red Army still seemed to be fading away, taking no advantage of the great gap opening up in our line; and Hitler, though understandably tense and nervous, and suffering dreadfully from the heat, seemed in good spirits.

I returned to find a shocking change at Werewolf. Halder was gone, fired. Nobody had relieved him. General List of the Caucasus Force had been fired. Nobody had relieved him, either. Hitler had assumed both posts!

Adolf Hitler was now not only head of the German State, head of the Nazi Party, and Supreme Commander of the armed forces; he was now his own Army Chief of Staff, and he was in direct command of the Caucasus Force, stymied six hundred miles away in the mountains. And this was not a nightmare; it was all really happening.

Hitler was not speaking to Jodl, his erstwhile pet and confidant. He was not speaking to anybody. He was taking his meals alone, spending most of his time in a darkened room, brooding. At his formal meetings with the staff, secretaries came and went in relays, writing down every word; and it was with these secretaries and nobody else that Hitler was conversing. The break with the army was complete.

Gradually I pieced together what had happened. Halder's objections to Hitler's senseless pressing of the Stalingrad attack had at last resulted in his summary dismissal in September; and so the last level head among us, the one senior staff officer who for years would talk up to Hitler, was gone.

As for the pliable Jodl, the Führer had sent him by plane to the Caucasus Force, to urge General List to resume the advance at all cost. But Jodl had come back and, for once in his life, had told Hitler the truth—that List could not advance until logistics improved. Hitler had turned nasty; Jodl, in an amazing burst of spirit, had rounded on his master, reeling off all Hitler's orders which had led to this impasse. The two men had ended screeching at each other like washerwomen, and thereafter Jodl had been barred from the great man's presence.

It was several days before I was summoned to appear at a briefing. I was quite prepared, even at the cost of my head, to give my report on the bad state of Rommel's supply. As it happened, Hitler did not call on me to speak. But I will never forget the glance he fixed on me when I first entered the room. Gray-faced, red-eyed, slumped in his chair with his head sunk between his shoulders, holding one trembling hand with the other, he was searching my face for the nature of my news, for a ray of optimism or hope. What he saw displeased him. He gave me a menacing glare, uncovering his teeth, and turned away. I was looking at a cornered animal. I realized that he knew in his heart that he had botched the Blue campaign, thrown away Germany's last chance, and lost the war; and that from all quarters of the globe, the hangmen were approaching with the rope.

But it was not in his nature to admit mistakes. All we heard, in the dreadful weeks that dragged on until the Sixth Army surrendered—and indeed until he shot himself in the bunker in 1945—was how we generals had failed him; how Bock's delay at Voronezh had lost Stalingrad; how incompetent List was; how battle nerves had incapacitated Rommel; and so on without end. Even when the Stalingrad pocket, cut to pieces, began surrendering piecemeal, all he could think of was to promote Paulus to Field Marshal; and when Paulus failed to kill himself rather than surrender, he threw one of his worst fits of rage. That ninety thousand of his best soldiers were going into captivity; that more than two hundred thousand more had been hideously lost for his sake; all that meant nothing to the man. Paulus had failed to show proper gratitude for promotion, by blowing his brains out. That upset Hitler.

· · ·

(From *World Holocaust*)

Post Mortem

Hitler would never allow the Sixth Army its one chance, which was to fight its way out to the west; either early in the entrapment, when it might have broken out by itself, or in December, when Manstein at the head of the newly formed Don Force battled his way through the snow to within thirty-five miles of a join-up. Not once would he give Paulus permission to break out. The screeching refrain that echoed through Headquarters until Paulus surrendered was, "*I won't leave the Volga!*"

He kept prating of "Fortress Stalingrad," but there was no "fortress," only a surrounded and shrinking army. He boasted in a national broadcast, late in October, that he had actually captured Stalingrad, and was reducing pockets of resistance at leisure because "he did not want another Verdun," and time was of no consequence. Thus he burned his public bridges, condemning the Sixth Army to stand and die.

Some military analysts now lay the disaster to Göring, who promised to supply the trapped Sixth Army at a rate of seven hundred tons of supplies a day. The Luftwaffe effort never reached two hundred tons, and Göring blamed the bad weather. Of course Göring's promise was just a jig to his master's tune. They were old comrades-in-arms. He knew what Hitler wanted him to say, so he said it, and condemned large numbers of Luftwaffe pilots to useless deaths. Hitler never reproached Göring for this. He wanted to stay at the Volga until tragedy befell, and Göring's transparent lie helped him to do it.

Jodl testified at Nuremberg that as early as November Hitler privately admitted to him that the Sixth Army was done for; still it had to be sacrificed to protect the retreat of the armies in the Caucasus. What balderdash! A fighting retreat from Stalingrad would have made far more sense. But the propagandist in Hitler sensed that a heartrending drama of a lost army might rally the people to him, whereas an ignominious swallowing of his boasts with a retreat would sully his prestige. On some such reasoning, he sacrificed a superb striking arm of battle-hardened veterans which could never be replaced.

Roosevelt Triumphant

Franklin Roosevelt's proclamation at this time of the slogan "Unconditional Surrender," at the Casablanca conference in January, was in every way a masterstroke. Critics of the slogan—including the august General Eisenhower—fail to understand what Roosevelt accomplished with this thunderous stroke; which, with his usual guile, he passed off as a casual remark at a press conference.

In the first place, he drove home to the entire world, and above all to the German people, the fundamental fact that we were now losing the war. The entire Global Waterloo turnabout was crystallized in those two simple words. This was in itself a stunning propaganda success.

Secondly, he publicly signalled to Stalin an Anglo-American pledge against a negotiated peace in the west. No doubt Stalin remained skeptical, but it was as loud and powerful a commitment as Roosevelt could give him.

Third, Roosevelt reassured the wavering nations like Turkey and Spain, and the subject peoples all over Europe, and the ever-veering Arabs, that the Western powers would not relax at the turn of the tide in Russia, and allow Bolshevism to sweep the continent and the Middle East.

Fourth, he gave his own spoiled and soft nation, in its first moment of success against us, a clear and simple war aim, which appealed to its naïve psychology, and discouraged notions of a short war or a compromise peace.

It is objected that the German people were stiffened to resist to the last under Hitler's leadership; that Roosevelt should have appealed over his head to them and to the army to topple the Nazi regime and make an honorable peace. This objection shows fatuous ignorance of what the Third Reich really was.

Hitler had made Germany over in the only form he ever wanted; a system of headless structures, including the army, with all power concentrated in himself. *There was nobody to topple the Nazis. There was nobody to appeal to.* Our national destiny was bound up with this man. This had been the one aim of all his actions since attaining power, and this he achieved.

He was Germany. The armed forces were pledged to him with their sacred honor. The assassination attempt that failed in July 1944 was witless and traitorous. I took no part in it, and I have never regretted that decision. It should have been plain to every general, as it was to me, that to order men to die in the field for a Leader, and then to murder this same Leader (however unsatisfactory he might be) was a betrayal of principle.

More than once, at bad moments in Headquarters, I thought of how relatively easy it would be for one of us to shoot Hitler. But he knew he could rely on two pillars in the German character: Honor and Duty.

The German people were in a tragic trap of history, condemned to fight for two and a half more fearful years, simply to keep alive the Head of State who had led them to destruction. Too late did we learn the fatal mistake of the *Führerprinzip*. A monarch can sue for peace and preserve his nation's honor and stability in defeat, as the Japanese emperor did. A dictator who fails in war is only a beleaguered usurper, who must fight on to the last like Shakespeare's Macbeth, wading ever deeper in blood.

Hitler could not step down; and none of the Nazis could step down. Their secret massacres of the Jews had rendered that impossible. "Unconditional Surrender" made not the slightest difference either to them or to the German people. Nothing could now sunder Hitler and the Germans, and put an end to the war, but *Götterdämmerung*.

———

TRANSLATOR'S NOTE: *General von Roon's operational sketch of the fate of the Caucasus Force, which follows the Stalingrad account, he calls "Epic Anabasis of Army Group A." It is the longest essay in* World Holocaust. *I do not believe the American reader would be as interested in it as Roon's German readers are. Essentially, once Paulus's army surrendered at Stalingrad, the Caucasus Force faced a complete cutoff of their line of retreat. After con-*

siderable dithering, Hitler put the very able General von Manstein in charge of the northern and most threatened of these luckless armies, to pull him out of the mess. This Manstein did, with some brilliant maneuvering under the worst winter conditions. Another general, Kleist, led the retreat of the southern forces to a bridgehead on the Black Sea. In the end the Caucasus Force got out in good order, inflicting strong blows on the Red Army as it retreated; and the Germans found themselves more or less back on the jumping-off line of Case Blue. It was a stupendously futile military exercise, thanks to Germany's supreme "intuitive" genius who ordered it and then messed it up. A bitter name for the campaign gained currency in the Wehrmacht: "the Caucasus round trip."

I had occasion to meet Hitler, so I know how plausible and even amiable he could be, like a gangster boss; he had all the forcefulness and cunning of a master criminal. But that is not greatness in my book. Hitler's early "successes" were only the startling depredations of a resolute felon become a head of state and turned loose with the power of a great nation to back him up.

Why the Germans committed themselves to him remains a historical puzzle. They knew what they were getting. He had spelled it all out in advance, in Mein Kampf. He and his National Socialist cohorts were from the start a gang of recognizable and very dangerous thugs, but the Germans by and large adored and believed in these monsters right up to the rude Stalingrad awakening, and even long afterward.—V.H.

*   *   *

58

A Jew's Journey
(*from Aaron Jastrow's manuscript*)

FEBRUARY 20, 1943.
BADEN-BADEN.

. . . I shall never forget the moment when the train passed through opened barrier gates over which a large red swastika flag fluttered, and signs in German began appearing along the track. We were in the dining car, eating an abominable lunch of salt fish and rotten potatoes. The American faces all around us were a study. I could hardly bear to look at my niece. She has since told me that she was already in such shock that she scarcely noticed the crossing of the border. So she says now. I saw then on her face the terror of a person being swept over Niagara Falls.

For me it was not quite such a plunge. My memories of pre-Hitler Germany were pleasant enough; and during my brief reluctant trip to the 1936 Olympics to write a magazine piece, when swastikas were flying wherever the eye turned, I had encountered no problems beyond my own uneasiness. I knew some Jews who travelled in Hitler's Germany on business, and a thick-skinned few for perverse pleasure. Nor were they at much risk. The German moves on tracks; that is at once his virtue and his menace. The travelling Jews were on the track of tourism, as I was on the track of journalism, and therefore safe. I am counting much on this Teutonic trait. Even if the worst stories of German brutality prove true, we are on the diplomatic track. I cannot see anti-Semitism jumping its track and harming us on this one, especially since we are being bargained off for Nazi agents, probably at a rate of four or five to one.

All the same, in our first days here I did not draw a quiet breath. Natalie did not sleep or eat for a week. The defiant haunted gleam in her eyes when she held her son on her lap seemed not quite sane. But after a while we both calmed down. It is the old story, nothing is as terrifying as the unknown. The thing you have most feared, once it is upon you, is seldom as bad as imagined. Life here in Brenner's Park Hotel is dismal enough, but we are used to it now and mainly bored to death with it. If ever asked whether fear or boredom oppressed me more in Baden-Baden, I shall have to reply, "Boredom, by a wide margin."

We are quarantined off from the local inhabitants. Our shortwave radios have been confiscated, and we hear no news except the Berlin broadcasts. Our only newspapers and magazines are Nazi publications, and a couple of French papers full of the crudest German lies, set forth in the language of Molière, Voltaire, Lamartine, and Hugo. It is a prostitution worse than any poor French whore's submission to the pumping and thumping of a hairy Hun. If I were a French journalist, they would have to shoot me before I would so stain my own honor, and the honor of my elegant language. At least I hope that is true.

With so little to read, and no news, and nothing to do, all the Americans immured in Baden-Baden are deteriorating, myself perhaps more than others. In five weeks I have not written in this journal. I, who once prided myself on my work habits; I, who produced words as unfailingly as Anthony Trollope; I, who have nothing else to do, and worlds to tell; I have let this record slide like a schoolgirl who starts a diary, then slacks off and lets the almost empty notebook molder in a desk, to be found and giggled over by her own schoolgirl daughter twenty years later.

But sound the trumpets! The first Red Cross food packages came in yesterday, and everybody has snapped out of the doldrums. *Canned ham! Corned beef! Cheese! Canned salmon! Canned sardines! Canned pineapple! Canned peaches! Powdered eggs! Instant coffee! Sugar! Margarine!* I love just writing down the words. These American staples are beautiful to our eyes, exquisite to our palates, reviving to our fading physiques.

How on earth do the Germans fight a war on their everlasting black bread and potatoes and spoiled vegetables? No doubt the soldiers get whatever good food there is; but the civilians! Our ration, we are told, is fifty percent more than the average German's. One can fill up on starch and cellulose, but eating such food a dog could not thrive. I say nothing of the disgusting cookery in this famous hotel. The Swiss representative assures us that we are not being mistreated, that hotel food all over Germany nowadays is worse than ours. Another time I shall describe what we have been eating, the strange dining room arrangements, the wretched wine, the black-market potato schnapps, the whole way we live under our German "hosts." It is all worth recording. But first I want to make up lost ground.

It is eleven in the morning, and very cold. I am out on the balcony in pale sunshine, well wrapped up as I write. Those Red Cross proteins and vitamins are coursing through my system, and I am myself again, craving the sun, the fresh air, and the moving pen. Thank God!

My digestion has been poor since we left Marseilles. In Lourdes I thought it was only nervous tension. But I was taken terribly ill on the train after that awful lunch, and my bowels have been in grave disorder ever since. Yet today I feel fit as a boy. I have had (ridiculous to set down, but true) a gloriously normal stool, over which I felt inclined to crow like a hen over her egg. It is not just the nourishment, I am sure, that has worked such healing magic. There is something psychic to it; my stomach recognizes American food. I could congratulate it on its sensitive politics.

About Louis.

He is the pet of the hotel. He grows in dexterity, vocabulary, and charm from week to week. He began to cast his spell over the group on the train. In Lourdes nobody had seen much of him; but at the station someone gave him a fine toy monkey that squeaked, and he went toddling up and down the train, keeping his balance admirably as our car swayed, offering his monkey to people to squeeze. He was having such fun that Natalie let him roam. He quite broke up the glumness in the car. He even brought the monkey to our uniformed Gestapo man, who hesitated, then took the monkey and unsmilingly made it go *Squeak!*

It would require another treatise like Meredith's on the comic spirit to explain why it was that everyone in the car burst out laughing. The Gestapo man looked around in embarrassment, then he laughed, too; and the horrible absurdity of the war seemed to strike us all, even him, for just that moment. The incident was talked about all over the train, and the little boy with the monkey became our first celebrity at the Brenner's Park Hotel.

I have given more space to a trivial incident than it perhaps warrants, to suggest the beguiling nature of the child. In my bouts of illness in recent weeks (some have been severe) one cardinal thought has kept me from sinking into apathy. I cannot and will not go under until Natalie and Louis are safe. I will guard them to the death, if I must, and I will fight depression and illness to be able to protect them. Our flimsy journalists' credentials rest on my few magazine pieces. The special treatment we are getting—this two-room suite on a high floor with a balcony, overlooking the hotel garden and a public park—can only be due to my literary standing, such as it is. Our lives in the end may hang on my jump, with a book-club selection, from academic obscurity to a name of sorts.

There are many children in the group, but Louis stands out. He is a privileged imp, getting more and better food than the others from a master scrounger, the naval attaché. When this man found out Natalie was a Navy wife, he was enslaved. They are quite close in an intimacy of (I am certain) antiseptic purity. He brings milk, eggs, and even meat for Louis. He brought a forbidden electric hot plate too, and Natalie cooks on the balcony to dissipate the odors. Now he is coaxing her to take the role of Eliza in *Pygmalion,* which he wants to put on with the dramatic group. She is actually considering it. Often the three of us play card games or anagrams. All in all, considering that we are on the soil of Hitler's Germany, Natalie and I are living a strangely banal existence, like people on an endless cruise aboard a third-rate ship, forever seeking ways to kill time. Boredom is the repeating bass note of our days, fear an intermittent piccolo shriek.

Our Jewish identity is known. The German Foreign Ministry man stationed here in the Brenner's Park has made a point of complimenting me on *A Jew's Jesus.* In fact, he talked rather intelligently about it. At first I was appalled, but granted the thoroughness of the Germans, it now seems naïve to have hoped that I would pass unnoticed. I am listed in *The International Who's Who,* the *Writers Directory,* and various academic reference tomes. So far my Jewishness has made no difference, and my semi-celebrity has helped. Germans respect writers and professors.

This must account for the assiduous medical attention I have been receiving. Our American doctor, a Red Cross man, was inclined to shrug off my gastric troubles as "detentionitis," his own facetious term for the malaise that afflicts our group. But in the third week I became so violently ill that he requested my hospitalization. So it was that at the Baden-Baden Municipal Hospital I met Dr. R——. I will not write down his real name even in this bothersome Yiddish-letter cipher. I must draw a portrait of Dr. R—— when I have more time. Natalie is calling me to lunch. We have given some of our precious Red Cross food to the hotel kitchen, which has promised to cook it up in style. We are to have corned beef hash; at last, at last, a way to doctor up those infernal potatoes.

FEBRUARY 21.
BADEN-BADEN.

I was very ill last night, and I am far from recovered today. However, I am determined to keep writing this record, now that I have started again. Moving a pen across a page makes me feel alive.

The hotel kitchen's execrable bungling of the corned beef hash upset me. Anger no doubt triggered the indigestion. How could a dish be simpler to prepare? But it was burned, lumpy, cold, greasy, altogether odious. We have learned our lesson. Natalie, the attaché, and I will pool our Red Cross food, and cook and eat it in our rooms, and to hell with the Boches. Others are doing it; the aroma drifts in the corridors.

The latest rumor is that the exchange and release will take place at Easter time, to show Germany's civilized respect for religion. Pinkney Tuck himself has told me this is sheer wishful fantasy, but the rumor mill grinds on. The psychology of this group is fascinating. A novel as good as *The Magic Mountain* could be made of it; pity I have no atom of creativity in me. If Louis were older he could well be our Thomas Mann, and possibly his acute little mind is recording more than we can discern.

The mention of Easter reminds me that in my Lourdes entry I started the topic of my abortive conversion to Catholicism. It is an old sad dreary story, a stirring up of cold ashes. Still, since these pages, if they survive me, may be the last testament of my brief and insignificant passage through the world, let me scrawl out the main facts. They should take but a paragraph or two. I have already described my alienation from the Oswiecim yeshiva, the key to it all.

I could not tell my father about that. Respect for parents was too deep in the grain for us Polish Jews. He was a lovable man, a dealer in farm implements, with a lively trade in bicycles. We were well-to-do, and he was pious and learned in an unquestioning way. It would have shattered him to know that I had become an *epikoros,* an unbeliever. So I went on being a star Talmud pupil, while laughing up my sleeve at Reb Laizar and the conforming young noddies around me.

Our family doctor was a Yiddishist agnostic. In those days Jewish doctors often returned from the university smelling of pork. One day on impulse I went and asked him to lend me Darwin's book. *Dar-veen,* the yeshiva whisper went, was the very Satan of modern godlessness. Well, "Dar-veen" was hard going in German; but I devoured *The Origin of Species* on the sly by candlelight, or away from the house by day. The first actual Sabbath violation of my life was carrying the Darwin book in my pocket down to the meadow by the river. Sabbath law forbids the bearing of burdens in "the public domain," and a book counts as a burden. Strange to say, though in spirit I was already far from the faith, the physical deed of carrying that book out of my father's house on Saturday was a terribly hard thing to do.

Next, the doctor loaned me Haeckel, Spinoza, Schopenhauer, and Nietzsche. I raced through those books as adolescents do through pornography, with mixed feelings of appetite and shame, thumbing eagerly for the irreligious parts: sneers at miracles and at God, attacks on the Bible, and the like. Two books I shall never forget, cheap German anthologies in green paper covers: *Introduction to Science,* and *Great Modern Thinkers.* Galileo, Copernicus, Newton, Voltaire, Hobbes, Hume, Rousseau, Kant, the whole radiant company burst on me, a fifteen-year-old Jewish boy lying alone on the grass by the Vistula. In a couple of weeks of feverish reading, my world and the world of my father fell in ruins: demolished, devastated, crumbled to dust, no more to be restored than the works of Ozymandias.

So my mind opened up.

When my family came to the United States, I was the precocious wonder of a Brooklyn high school. I learned English as though it were the multiplication table, sped through the school in two years, and won a full scholarship to Harvard. By then my parents had seen me turn Yankee Doodle in speech, dress, and manners. They were proud of the Harvard scholarship, but fearful, too. Yet how could they stop me? Away I went.

At Harvard I was a prodigy. The professors and their wives made much of me, and I was invited to wealthy people's homes, where my yeshiva-accented English was a piquant novelty. I took all the petting as my due. I was a good-looking young man then, with something of Louis Henry's unforced charm, and a great gift for conversation. I could make the Brahmins feel my own excitement in discovering western culture. I loved America; I read prodigiously in American literature and history; I knew most of Mark Twain by heart. My yeshiva-trained memory retained everything I read. I talked with a fluency of ideas and richness of allusion that the Bostonians found dazzling. I could spice my talk with Talmudic lore, too. In that way I stumbled on the perception that later made my name; to wit, that Christians are fascinated when one presents Judaism to them, with dignity and a touch of irony, as a neglected part of their own background. Thirty years later I wrote my *Talmudic Themes in Early Christianity,* which metamorphosed into a best-seller with a catchier title, *A Jew's Jesus.*

I am not proud of what happened next, and I shall be brief. Anyway, how repetitious life is! What story is more threadbare than an infatuation between a wealthy girl and a poor tutor? Comic operas, novels, tragedies, films abound on that simple plot. I lived it. She was a Catholic girl of a prominent Boston family. In one's early twenties one is not wise, and in love one is not honest, not with others or with oneself. My own fluency of ideas and argumentation, turned in upon myself, persuaded me that Christ had come into my heart. The rest was simple. Catholicism was the true tradition, the treasure house of Christian art and philosophy; and it was a strongly elaborated ritual system, the only sort of faith I really understood. I went through a conversion.

It was a shallow dream. The awakening was ghastly, and I pass over it in silence. At heart, through all the instruction I remained—as I still remain—the Oswiecim yeshiva boy, who came into a church out of the snow, and was shocked to his soul at seeing on the far wall the image of the crucified Christ, where in a synagogue the Holy Ark would be. If her family had not thrown me out, and if she had stood by me instead of liquefying in tears like a candy figure in the rain, I should still have lapsed. My essential condition for admiring, pitying, loving, and endlessly studying and writing about Jesus of Nazareth, as I have done, has been that I cannot believe in him.

According to the Nuremberg Laws, since all this happened before 1933 and I never did anything about "de-converting," I may be technically safe from persecution as a Jew. The exemption, as I understand it, applies to German half-Jews, and as an American I might well get the benefit, too, if it came to that. When my passport problems grew sticky in 1941, a good friend in the Vatican procured for me photocopies of the Boston documents that recorded my conversion. I still have those dark blurry papers. I have never yet officially produced them, because I might in some way become separated from Natalie. That must not happen. If I can help her with them, I will.

As for saving my own life—well, I have lived most of it. I shall not return to the Martin Luther book. I meant to round out, with this Reformation figure, my picture of Christ moving through history. But the coarse strident Teutonism of my hero was giving me greater and greater pause, quite aside from his diatribes against the Jews, indistinguishable from the bawlings of Dr. Goebbels. That he was a religious genius I do not doubt. But he was a German genius, therefore a destroying angel. Luther's best brilliance goes to smashing the Papacy and the Church. His eye for weaknesses is terrifying, his eloquence explosive. His bold irreverent hatred of old institutions and structures sounds the true German note, the harsh bellow out of the Teutoburg Forest, the ring of the hammer of Thor. We shall hear it again in Marx, the Jew turned German and combining the fanatic elements of each; we shall hear it in Wagner's music and writings; and it will shake the earth in Hitler.

Let other pens tell of what was great in Luther. I should like to write next some dialogues in the Platonic manner, ranging in the casual fashion of my Harvard conversations over the philosophical and political problems of this catastrophic century. I could contribute nothing new; but writing as I do with a light hand, I might charm a few readers into pausing, in their heedless hurry after pleasure and money, for a look at the things that matter.

———

Another rambling entry! But I have done my six pages. I have been writing in great abdominal pain, clenching my teeth to get the words down. I shall find it hard to rise from this chair, I feel so weak and poorly. There is something gravely wrong with me. These are not psychosomatic spasms. Alarm thrills through my system. I shall certainly see the doctor again.

FEBRUARY 26, 1943.
BADEN-BADEN.

I am feeling a little better than I did in the hospital. Actually, it was a relief to get away for three days from the boredom of Brenner's Park Hotel and the smell of the bad food. The hospital jellies and custards went down well, though I am sure they were distilled by German inventive genius out of petroleum waste or old tires. I was put through every possible gastrointestinal test. I still await the diagnosis. The hospital time passed quickly because I talked a lot with Dr. R———.

He wants me to bear witness, when I return to the United States, that the "other Germany" lives on, shamed, silenced, and horrified by the Hitler regime; the Germany of the great poets and philosophers, of Goethe and Beethoven, of the scientific pioneers, of the advanced social legislators of Weimar, of the progressive labor movement that Hitler destroyed, of the good-hearted common people who in the last free election voted by an increased majority against the Nazis; only to be betrayed by the old-line politicians like Papen and the senile Hindenburg who took Hitler into the government when he had passed his peak, and brought on the great disaster.

As for what ensued, he asks me to picture the Ku Klux Klan seizing power in the United States. That is what has happened to Germany, he says. The Nazi Party is an enormous German Ku Klux Klan. He points to the dramatic use of fire rituals at night, the anti-Semitism, the bizarre uniforms, the bellicose know-nothing hatred of liberal ideas and of foreigners and so forth. I rejoined that the Klan is a mere lunatic splinter group, not a major party capable of governing the nation. Then he cited the Klan of Reconstruction days, a respectable widespread movement which many of the leading Southerners joined; also the role of the modern Klan in the Democratic politics of the twenties.

Extremism, he says, is the universal tuberculosis of modern society: a world infection of resentment and hatred generated by rapid change and the breakdown of old values. In the stabler nations the tubercles are sealed off in scar tissue, and these are the harmless lunatic movements. In times of social disorder, depression, war, or revolution, the germs can break forth and infect the nation. This has happened in Germany. It could happen anywhere, even in the United States.

Germany is sick unto death of the infection, the doctor says. Millions of Germans know it and are grieved by it. He himself is a Social Democrat. One day Germany will return to that path, the only road to the future and to freedom. German culture, and the German people as a whole, must never be condemned for producing Hitler, and for what he is doing to the Jews. The greatest misfortune of the Hitler era has befallen the Germans themselves. There is Dr. R———'s thesis.

What of Hitler's popularity with the Germans? Well, he argues that terror, and total control of the press and radio, produce a mere simulacrum of popularity. But I wrote magazine pieces on Hitler. I know facts and figures. I know how the universities in a body went over to Hitler, how eagerly Germany's best minds began touting this great man of destiny, how readily and enthusiastically the civil service, the business world, the judiciary, and the army swore allegiance to him. I said to the doctor that in future study of this insane era, the chief phenomenon to explain will be the almost general spiritual surrender to Hitler of the German nation. If you call his movement a Ku Klux Klan, then all Germany overnight either turned Klansmen or cheered the Klan, as though liberalism, humanism, and democracy had never existed on this soil.

His retort: the American mind cannot comprehend the Germans' predicament. They are imprisoned on a narrow patch of central Europe's poorest earth, living for centuries under the pressure of the Russian threat, with France harrying them at their back. Their two great cultural foci, Prussia and Austria, were trodden under the boots of Napoleon's armies. England intrigued with czarist Russia for a century to keep the German people weak. This led to the ascendancy of Bismarck; and because of his stubborn preservation of absolutism when all of Europe was swept by liberalism, the German people remained politically immature. When the amorphous Weimar "system-time" began to fall apart in the Depression, and Hitler's clear strong voice of command rang out, there was a reflex of energy and enthusiasm. Hitler played upon the best qualities of the nation to bring about an economic recovery much like Roosevelt's New Deal. Unfortunately his military successes, to a nation hungry for self-respect, swamped resistance to his evil tendencies. Were not the Americans themselves worshippers of success?

On my bed lay a copy of the Propaganda Ministry's foreign-language magazine, *Signal,* with a long obfuscated account in French of the Stalingrad surrender. The story made it sound almost like a victory. Of course here in Baden-Baden one cannot learn much about Stalingrad, but obviously it was a towering defeat, possibly the pivot of the war. Yet *Signal* declares it all went according to plan; the sacrifice of the Sixth Army strengthened the eastern battle line and foiled the Bolsheviks' campaign. Did Dr. R—— think the German people would swallow that, I asked, or would resistance to Hitler grow now?

He commented that my very impressive historical insight did not extend to current military expertise. In point of fact the Stalingrad operation *had* stabilized the eastern front. His own son, an army officer, had written him to this effect. It was in any case irrelevant to the discussion of the nature and culture of the German people. It was very important to him, he said, that a man of my standing should grasp these ideas, for a time was coming when the world should be told them by a powerful literary voice.

It has occurred to me that the doctor may be a Gestapo agent, but he does not strike me as such. His manner is immensely earnest and sincere. He is a big blond chap with thick glasses, and small eyes that peer with eager seriousness as he makes his points. He speaks in low tones, unconsciously looking over his shoulder now and then at the blank wall of my room. I think he has approached me in all ingenuousness to convince me that the "other Germany" survives. No doubt it does, and I believe he is part of it. Pity it counts for so little.

FEBRUARY 27.

The tentative diagnosis is diverticulitis. The treatment: a special diet, bed rest, and continuous medication. Ulcers and similar digestive ailments have afflicted several other members of our group. One of the U.P. correspondents, a heavy drinker, was taken to Frankfurt last week under Gestapo guard for an operation. If my condition greatly worsens, I also could be sent to Frankfurt for surgery. Would this mean separation from Natalie? I shall take that up with Pinkney Tuck. It must not happen, if I have to die here.

59

SINCE the day Miriam Castelnuovo arrived at the children's home outside Toulouse, she has been a favorite of the director. In happier times long ago Madame Rosen—not married, not pretty, not hopeful—spent her vacations in Italy, loved Italian art and music, and once almost married a nice Italian Jewish man, who was too ill with heart trouble to go through with it. Miriam's clear Tuscan speech brings back those golden days, and Miriam's disposition is so sweet that Madame Rosen, who tries not to play favorites—the home was built for three hundred children, and more than eight hundred are jammed in now—despite herself rather dotes on this newcomer.

It is the free play period before bedtime. Madame Rosen knows where Miriam probably is. The girl has a favorite herself, a little French orphan named Jean Halphan, barely a year and a half old. Jean resembles Louis Henry, above all in the way his large blue eyes light up when he smiles. While Miriam was still with her parents she never stopped talking about Louis. She soon ceased asking questions, because she saw that they saddened her mother and irritated her father. But she endlessly reminisced, reliving her time with him, displaying a memory like a film library. Now that her parents are gone, and she has nobody, she has fastened on Jean. The little boy adores her, and when she is with him she is happy.

Madame Rosen finds them on the floor of Jean's big dormitory room, carefully building blocks amid milling children. She chides Miriam for sitting on the cold floor, though both children are bundled up as though they were outside in the snow. The home has not yet received its meager fuel ration this month. What little coal is left must be used to keep the water pipes from freezing, and to cook the meals. Miriam wears the fringed red shawl Madame Rosen gave her. It is so big it quite hides her face, but it is very warm. Miriam and Jean perch on a cot, and Madame Rosen talks to the girl in Italian. Miriam always likes that; she holds Jean on her lap, playing with his hands, and making him repeat Italian words. This visit of Madame Rosen's does not last long. She returns to the office, warmed and cheered to face her problems.

They are the old administrative ones, many times magnified: overcrowding, shortages, staffing difficulties, lack of funds. Now that the small Toulouse Jewish community is almost gone, she is all but overwhelmed. Happily, the mayor of Toulouse is a kindly man. When matters get desperate, as they are now regarding fuel, medicine, bed linen, and the milk supply, she appeals to him. She sits at her desk to resume writing her letter, this time with dimmed expectations. The French friends of the Jewish children have become very wary of showing their sympathy. This wizened yellow-faced little woman in her late fifties, wrapped in a faded coat and a torn shawl, weeps as she writes. The situation seems hopeless when she puts it down on paper. But she must do something, or what will become of the children?

Worse yet, warnings have been chilling the remaining Jews in the area for a week: *another action impending.* Madame Rosen feels safe herself. She has an official position, and clear papers of native French citizenship. So far, only foreign Jews have been taken, though in the last action some of the deportees were naturalized citizens. Her concern is for the children. Nearly all the newcomers are foreigners. Hundreds of them! For about a third she has no papers at all. They were dumped on her by the police; the French government separates children from parents being deported to the east, and puts them anywhere. The Jewish orphanages are becoming swamped. The regulation seems humanely intended, despite the anguish for the torn-apart families, for horrible stories circulate about the east; but why is so little provision made for the children?

And now supposing that in this new action, the police come and ask for the foreign tots? Dare she claim she has no records of any child's origin? Or since that is so farfetched in bureaucratic France, can she plead that she burned her records in panic when the Allies landed in North Africa? Shall she actually burn the records now? Will that save the foreign waifs, or merely condemn the French-born children to be taken off with them?

Madame Rosen has no reason to believe that the Germans are collecting foreign children. She has not yet heard of such a thing, and the fact that they have been dumped on her argues that they are meant to be spared deportation. But the anxiety haunts her. It is about midnight, bitter cold, and she is folding the letter up with numbed fingers in the candlelight (the electricity has long since gone off) when she hears crashing knocks at the street door.

Her office is close to the street. The knocks startle her out of the chair. Crash! Crash! Crash! My God, all the children will wake up! They will be frightened to death!

"*Ouvrez! Ouvrez!*" Loud coarse male shouts. "*Ouvrez!*"

SS Obersturmführer Nagel has a problem too.

A tremendous flap is going on: a quota unfilled, and a partly empty train scheduled to pass through Toulouse in the morning. The top SS man in Jewish affairs in Paris is in a gigantic rage, but there just aren't that many Jews left in this prefecture. They have melted into the countryside, or fled to the Italian-occupied zone. There is just no way to fill three entire freight cars. The Toulouse action so far has collected five hundred. The demanded count from Paris is fifteen hundred.

Fortunately, the Toulouse police records show that the children and the staff here add up to nine hundred and seven Jews. Nagel has obtained permission from Paris to pick them up, while a squad combs Toulouse for the balance needed; any Jews, no protection applicable. So the SS lieutenant sits in a car across the street from the children's home, watching the French policemen knocking at the door. Given half a chance, those fellows would report back with some lame excuse and no results. He will sit here until the police chief comes out and reports to him.

The story Nagel has given the chief to tell is a good one. The occupation authority needs the building as a convalescent home for wounded German soldiers. Therefore the children and staff will be moved to a ski resort in the Tyrol, where all the hotels have been converted into an enormous special care center for children, with a school, a hospital, and many playgrounds; and where thousands of children from the bigger camps near Paris are already settled. In transporting Jews, standard procedure requires giving them some kind of reassuring story. Secret circulated instructions from Berlin emphasize that the Jews are very trusting, and eagerly believe any kind of flimsy official information. This greatly facilitates the processing of the Jews.

The door opens, the police disappear inside. Lieutenant Nagel waits. He is on his third cigarette, very chilled despite his warm new greatcoat and wool-lined service boots, and he is nervously thinking of going over there himself, though the uniform may scare the Jew staffers, when the door opens again, and out comes the police chief.

That fellow manages to stay nice and fat on French rations; plenty of black-market fat on that belly. He comes to the car, and reports with very garlicky breath that it is all arranged. The staff people will pack their belongings, and the central records of the institution. Nagel emphasized that touch about taking the records; it makes the story more plausible. The children will be wakened at three, dressed, and given a hot meal. The police vans and the trucks will come for them at five. They will all be on the railroad station platform at six. The Frenchman's fat face in the pallid moonlight is expressionless, and when Lieutenant Nagel says, *"Bon,"* the drooping mustache lifts in a nasty sad smile.

So all is well. The train is due at a quarter to seven, and at that hour most people of the town won't be up and about. That is a bit of luck, Nagel thinks, as he drives back to his apartment to catch a few winks before the morning's business. Orders are to avoid arousing sympathy in the population when transports leave. Repeated bulletins from Berlin caution that there can be unpleasant episodes, especially if children are moved about by day in populous places.

In fact, it turns out to be a gloomy morning, and when the train pulls in it is still almost dark. The Jews are shadowy figures, climbing into the cars. The station lights have to be turned on to speed up the loading of the children. They march quietly up the wooden ramps into the freight cars, two abreast, hand in hand as they have been told to do, the staff women carrying the youngest ones. Miriam Castelnuovo is walking with little Jean. She has been moved several times in this fashion, so she is used to it. This is not as bad as when they took her from her parents. Jean's hand in hers makes her happy. Madame Rosen walks behind her carrying a baby, and that too is reassuring.

Lieutenant Nagel wonders at the last minute whether there is any point in shoving those twelve big cartons of records into the freight car. They will just be a nuisance, and they may puzzle the fellows at the other end. But he sees the white terrorized face of Madame Rosen, who is staring out of the freight car at the cartons, as if her life hung on what happened to them. Why panic her? She's the one to keep the children quiet all the way to the end. He gestures with his stick at the cartons. The SS men load them into the car, and shut the big sliding doors on the children. Black gloved hands seize the frigid iron levers, rotate them, lock the doors in place.

The train starts with no whistle sound, only the chuffing of the locomotive.

60

P UG HENRY had made a fast departure for the Soviet Union. However, he was awhile getting there.

As the Clipper slapped and pounded clear of Baltimore harbor and roared up into low gray January murk, he pulled from his dispatch case two letters which he had had no time to read. He opened the bulky White House envelope first to skim the typewritten pages, a lengthy harangue by Hopkins on Lend-Lease.

"I'm taking breakfast orders, sir." A white-coated steward touched his elbow. Pug ordered ham and eggs and pancakes, though his uniform was tight after two weeks of Rhoda's food and wine. One should fatten up for Soviet Union duty, he thought, like a bear for the winter sleep. His career was damned well going into hibernation, he was damned well hungry, and he would damned well eat. And Harry Hopkins's disquisition could damned well wait while he found out what was on Pamela Tudsbury's mind. The spiky handwriting on the airmail envelope from London was obviously hers, and Pug tore it open with more eagerness than he wanted to feel.

December 20th, 1942

Dear Victor,

This is a mere quick scrawl, I'm just off to Scotland to do a story on American ferry pilots. You surely know that my father's gone, killed by a land mine at El Alamein. The *Observer* has generously given me a chance at carrying on as a correspondent. No use writing about Talky. I've pulled myself together, though for a while I felt that I had died too, or might as well have.

Did my long letter from Egypt ever reach you, before you lost your ship? That news horrified me, but luckily hard upon it I learned that you were safe and en route to Washington, where I myself will shortly be heading. I said in that letter, among other things, that Duncan Burne-Wilke wanted to marry me. In effect, I guess, I asked for your blessing. I received no answer. We have since become engaged, and he's off to India as Auchinleck's new deputy chief of staff for air.

I may not stay in Washington long. The great crunch at Stalingrad has given my editor the notion of sending me back to the Soviet Union.

But I've run into mysterious visa problems which the *Observer* is working on, and meantime here I come. If I can't ever return to Moscow, for inscrutable Marxist reasons, my usefulness will dim; and I may then just pack it up and join Duncan for a tour of duty as memsahib. We'll see.

No doubt you know that Rhoda and I met in Hollywood, and that I told her about us. I just wanted to take myself out of the picture, and I trust you're not angry at me. Now I'm engaged to a darling man, with my future all settled, so that's that. I'll be at the Wardman Park Hotel on or about January 15th. Will you give me a ring? I can't tell how Rhoda would feel about my telephoning you, though obviously I'm no threat to her. About meeting you of course I want to be open and aboveboard. I just don't propose to pretend you don't exist.

Love,
Pamela

So, Pug thought—astonished, amused, impressed—Rhoda knew all along and said nothing. Good tactics; good girl. Perhaps she had noticed the London postmark, too, when she handed him the letters. About the disclosure, he felt sheepish; innocent, but sheepish. Rhoda was quite a woman, take her for all in all. Pamela's letter was proper, calm, friendly; in the situation, well put. He ate the large breakfast very cheerily, despite grim clouds tumbling past the window of the bumping Clipper, because of the slight chance that he might see the future Lady Burne-Wilke in the Soviet Union.

Then he read the Hopkins letter.

THE WHITE HOUSE

Jan. 12

Dear Pug,

You pleased the Boss greatly the other morning, and he'll remember it. The landing craft problem won't go away. You might still tackle it, depending on how long Ambassador Standley wants you. The special request about your daughter-in-law went through, but the Germans queered the effort by moving those people to Baden-Baden. Welles says they're in no hazard, and that negotiations for exchanging the whole crowd are well along.

Now to business:

Admiral Standley came back to Washington at his own request because he thinks we're mishandling Lend-Lease. But there are only two ways to handle Lend-Lease: unconditional aid, or aid on a quid pro quo basis. It burns up the old admiral that we give, give, give, asking for no accounting, no justification of requests, no trade-offs. That's our policy, all right. Standley's a wise and salty old bird, but the President as usual is miles ahead of him.

The President's overall policy toward the Russians is three-pronged, and very simple. Remember it, Pug:

(1) Keep the Red Army fighting Germany
(2) Bring the Red Army in against Japan
(3) Create a stronger postwar League of Nations with the Soviet Union in it.

Lenin walked out of World War I in 1917, you know, by making a deal with the Kaiser. Stalin opted out of this war in 1939 by making a deal with Hitler. He'd still be out of it if Hitler hadn't attacked him. The President doesn't forget those things.

Stalin's rhetoric notwithstanding, I doubt that Hitlerism is such a great evil to him. He too is a dictator running a police state, and he got cozily into bed with Hitler for two whole years. Now Russia's been invaded, so he has to fight. He's a total pragmatist, and our intelligence is that they've been exchanging peace feelers over there. A separate peace on that front is always possible, if Germany makes a substantial offer.

That may not be in the cards just yet. Hitler would have to show his people some territorial gains for all the German blood he's spilled. The more we strengthen the Russians, the less likely it is that Stalin will make such a deal. We want him to throw the Germans clear out of Russia, and not stop there, but drive on to Berlin. This will save millions of American lives, because our war aim is to eradicate Nazism, and we won't quit till we do.

So, it's a confusion of objectives to look for quid pro quos from Lend-Lease. The quid pro quo is that the Russians are killing large numbers of German soldiers who won't oppose us one day in France.

We have not exactly lived up to our commitments on Lend-Lease. We're at about 70 percent. We've tried, and our aid is massive, but the U-boats have taken a big toll, the Japanese war is a drain, and we had to cannibalize Lend-Lease to mount the North African landings. Nor have we lived up to our promise of a second front in Europe, not yet. So we are in no position to get tough with the Russians.

Even if we were, it would be bad war-making. We need them more than they need us. Stalin can't be fooled about such a fundamental reality. He is a very complicated figure, very difficult to deal with, a sort of Red Ivan the Terrible, but I'm damn glad we've got him and his people in the war on our side. I'm candid about that in public, and take a lot of lumps for it.

Admiral Standley will want you to try to obtain quid pro quos. He has a high opinion of your ability to handle Russians. It's true that they could loosen up a lot on air transport routes, military intelligence, shuttle bases for our bombers, release of our airmen downed in Siberia, and so on. Perhaps you'll make Standley happy by succeeding where others have failed. But on the basic issue, General Marshall has told the President that nothing the Russians can give us as a Lend-Lease trade-off would change our strategy or tactics in this war. He approves of unconditional aid.

The President wants you to know all this, and to resume sending him informal reports, as you did from Germany. He mentioned again your prediction of the Hitler-Stalin pact in 1939, and he requested (not wholly humorously) that if your crystal ball warns you of any moves toward a separate peace over there, to let him know fast.

Harry H.

Scarcely an encouraging letter; Pug was on his way to serve under a former CNO, and here was an order right at the start to bypass the old admiral with "informal reports" to the Commander-in-Chief. This new post promised to be nothing but a quagmire. Pug took from his dispatch case a sheaf of intelligence documents on the Soviet Union, and dug into them. Work was the best refuge from such thoughts.

The Clipper was diverted to Bermuda; no explanation. As the passengers were lunching in a beach hotel they could see, through the dining room windows, their flying boat heavily lifting away into the rain. They remained in Bermuda for weeks. In time they learned that the aircraft had been recalled to take Franklin Roosevelt to the Casablanca Conference. The conference by then was the great news on the radio and in the press, sharing the headlines with the growing German collapse at Stalingrad.

Pug did not mind the delay. He was in no great hurry to get to Russia. This little green isle far out in the Atlantic, in peacetime a quiet flowery Eden without automobiles, was now an American naval outpost. Jeeps, trucks, and bulldozers boiled around in clouds of exhaust and coral dust; patrol bombers buzzed overhead, gray warships crowded the sound, and sailors jammed the shops and the narrow town streets. The idle rich in the big pink houses seemed to have gone underground, waiting for the Americans to sink all the bothersome U-boats, win the war, and go away; the black populace looked prosperous and happy, for all the fumes and noise.

The commandant put up Pug in his handsome newly built quarters, complete with tennis court. Besides playing occasional tennis or cards with the admiral, Pug passed the time reading up on the Soviet Union. The intelligence papers he had brought were thin stuff. Poking around in Bermuda's library and bookstores, he came on erudite British books highly favorable to the Soviets, written by George Bernard Shaw, and a man named Laski, and a couple named Beatrice and Sidney Webb. He ground sedulously through these long stylish paeans to Russian social-ism, but came on little substance that a military man could use.

He found harshly negative books, too, by various defectors and de-bunkers; lurid accounts of fake trials, mass murders, gigantic famines engineered by the government, and secret concentration camps all over the communist paradise, where millions of people were being worked to death. The crimes ascribed to Stalin in these books seemed worse even than Hitler's reputed malefactions. Where did the truth lie? This blank wall of contradiction brought back vividly to Victor Henry his last trip to the Soviet Union, with the Harriman mission; the sense of baffled isolation there, the frustration of dealing with people who looked and acted like ordinary human beings, who even projected a hearty if shy charm, and yet who could suddenly start behaving like Martians, for sheer inability to communicate, and for icy remote hostility.

When his flight was rescheduled, he bought a three-volume paper-bound history of the Russian Revolution by Leon Trotsky to read on the way. Pug knew of Trotsky as a Jew who had organized the Red Army, the number two man under Lenin during the revolution; he knew too that on Lenin's death Stalin had outmaneuvered Trotsky for power, had driven him into exile in Mexico, and—at least according to the unfriendly books—had sent assassins who had brained him there. He was surprised at the literary brilliance of the work, and appalled by its contents. The six days of his trip across the Atlantic, over North Africa, and up through the Middle East to Tehran passed easily; for when clouds shut off the magnificent geography unreeling far below, or he was waiting for a connection, or spending a night in a dismal Quonset hut on an air base, he had Trotsky to turn to.

This intermingling of a flight across much of the globe with a flaring epic of czardom's fall was quite an experience. Trotsky wrote of sordid plots and counterplots by squalid formidable men to seize power, which gripped like a novel; but there were long passages of stupefying Marxist verbiage which defeated Victor Henry's earnest efforts to get through them. He did dimly grasp that a volcanic social force had broken loose in Russia in 1917, reaching for a grand utopian dream; but it seemed to him that on Trotsky's own testimony—and the book was intended to celebrate the revolution—the thing had foundered in a sea of sanguinary horror.

Except for hopping from one hot dusty base to another, Pug saw little of the war in North Africa, where, from radio reports, Rommel was giving the invaders a bad time. Green jungles slipped by, empty deserts, rugged mountains, day after day. The Pyramids and the Sphinx at last drifted past far below, and the Nile, glittering in its band of greenery. A alf-day delay in Palestine enabled him to drive to old Jerusalem, and alk the crooked streets where Jesus Christ had borne his cross; then e was back in an aircraft high above the earth, reading about plots, nprisonments, tortures, poisonings, shootings, all in the name of the ocialist brotherhood of man, inevitable under Marxism. When he got ɔ Tehran he was just beginning the third volume, and he left the nfinished book on the plane. At his next stop, Trotsky was not a welome import.

"The whole point, Henry," said Admiral Standley, "is to get through ɔ this General Yevlenko. If anyone can do it, you can."

"What's Yevlenko's official position, Admiral?"

Standley made a frustrated gesture with gnarled hands. "If I knew nd I told you, you'd be no better off. He's Mister Big on Lend-Lease, hat's all. He's a hero, I gather. Lost a hand in the battle for Moscow. Vears a fake hand in a leather glove."

They were at the long dinner table in Spaso House, just the two of hem. Arrived from Kuibyshev scarcely an hour earlier, Pug would have een glad to forgo dinner, take a bath, and turn in for the night. But it vas not to be. The little old admiral, who looked lost in this grand and pacious embassy, formerly the mansion of a czarist sugar merchant, ad developed a great head of steam about Lend-Lease, and with Pug's rrival the safety valve popped.

In Washington, said Standley, he had gotten the President's promise hat the Lend-Lease mission would be subordinated to him. The orders ad gone out, but the head of the mission, one General Faymonville, 'as blandly ignoring the President. Growing red in the face, hardly ɔuching his boiled chicken, Standley struck the table with a fist over nd over, declaring that Harry Hopkins must be at the bottom of this, ɪust have told Faymonville that the order didn't mean anything, that he prodigal handouts should continue. But he, Standley, had come out f retirement to take this post at the President's request. He was going ɔ fight for America's best interests come hell or Harry Hopkins.

"Say, incidentally, Pug," said Standley with a sudden glare, "when 've talked to this General Yevlenko socially, he's referred to you more han once as Harry Hopkins's military aide. Hey? How's that?"

Pug answered cautiously, "Admiral, when we came over with Hariman in 1941, the President wanted an eyewitness report from the front. Ir. Hopkins designated me to go, because I'd taken a crash course in Russian. I met Yevlenko out in the forward area, and maybe the Nark ɪan who accompanied me put that idea into his head."

"Hm. Is that so?" The ambassador's glare slowly metamorphosed into a cunning wrinkled grin. "I see! Well, in that case, land's sakes don't ever disabuse the fellow. If he really thinks you're *Garry Gopkins*'s boy, you may get some action out of him. *Garry Gopkins* is Father Christmas around here."

Pug could remember first meeting William Standley ten years ago when as Chief of Naval Operations he had visited the *West Virginia;* a straight austere little four-star admiral in white and gold, number one man in the Navy, saying a kind word to the lowly Lieutenant Commander Henry about the battleship's gunnery record. Standley was still full of fire, but what a change! During that dinner it seemed to Victor Henry that he had relinquished the post at Cincpac in order to help a tetchy old man cannonade at gnats. On and on the grievances poured out. The gifts of the Russian Relief Society, which Standley's own wife had worked hard for, weren't being acknowledged. The American Red Cross aid wasn't getting enough thankful publicity in the Soviet Union. The Russians weren't giving any quid pro quos for Lend-Lease. Bone-weary after the elaboration of these gripes for perhaps an hour and a half, Pug ventured to ask Standley over coffee what the purpose would be in seeking out General Yevlenko.

"That's business," said the ambassador. "We'll get to it in the morning. You look a bit bushed. Get some sleep."

Possibly because the sun shone brightly into the ambassador's library, or because he was at his best in morning hours, their next meeting went better. There was in fact a touch of the CNO about Standley.

Congress was debating the extension of the Lend-Lease act, he explained, and the State Department wanted a report from the Soviets on how Lend-Lease supplies had helped them on the battlefield. Molotov had agreed "in principle"—a fatal Russian phrase, which meant an indefinite stall. Molotov had referred the request to Yevlenko's Lend-Lease section. Standley had been hounding Faymonville to keep after Yevlenko, and Faymonville claimed he was doing his best, but nothing was happening.

Worse than nothing, actually. In Stalin's latest Order of the Day, the dictator had stated that the Red Army was bearing the whole weight of the war alone, with no help from its allies! Now, how would *that* go down with Congress? These damned Russians, said Standley coolly, just didn't comprehend the depth of anti-Bolshevik feeling in America. He admired their fighting spirit. He just had to save them from themselves. One way or another he had to get that statement about the battlefield benefits of Lend-Lease. Otherwise, come June there might be no more Lend-Lease. The whole alliance might collapse, and the whole damned war might be lost. Pug did not argue, though he thought Standley was exaggerating. No doubt the Russians were being boorish, and his first thankless task was to hunt down General Yevlenko, force him to face that fact, and try to get something done about it.

It took him two days of trudging through the Moscow streets ridged with black unremoved ice, amid crowds of shabby pedestrians, from one official structure to another in the government's uncharted maze, just to find out where General Yevlenko's office was. He could not obtain a telephone number, not even an accurate address. The British air attaché, whom he had known in Berlin, finally took him in hand and pointed out the building where Yevlenko had not long ago given him a red-hot dressing-down, over the diversion of forty Lend-Lease Aircobra fighters to the British forces in the North African landings. But when Pug tried to enter the building, a silent burly red-cheeked young sentry put a bayonetted rifle athwart his chest, and was deaf to his protests in sputtering Russian. Pug went back to his office, dictated a long letter, and brought it to the building. Another sentry accepted it, but days passed without an answer.

Meantime, Pug met General Faymonville, an affable Army man not much like the monster Standley had described. Faymonville said that he understood Yevlenko was in Leningrad; and that, in any case, Americans never saw Yevlenko on business. One dealt with him through his liaison officer, a general with a jawbreaker of a name. But Standley's attachés had already warned Pug that General Jawbreaker was a waste of time, a dead end; his sole job was to absorb questions and demands like a feather pillow with no comeback, and he was matchless at it.

After about a week of this frustration, Pug awoke in his bedroom in Spaso House and found a note under his door.

Henry—
Some American correspondents are returning from a tour of the southern front; and I'm seeing them this morning at 0900 in the library. Be there at 0845.

He found Standley alone at his desk, dark red in the face and glaring dangerously. The admiral slung a pack of Chesterfield cigarettes across the desk at him. Pug picked it up. Stamped in bright purple ink on the package were these words: FROM THE FELLOW WORKERS PARTY, NEW YORK.

"Those are Red Cross *or* Lend-Lease cigarettes!" The admiral could barely choke out the words. "Can't be anything else. We're giving them by the millions to the Red Army. Yet I got that from a Czech last night. The fellow said a Red Army officer gave it to him, and told him that the generous communist comrades in New York are keeping the whole army supplied."

Victor Henry could only shake his head in disgust.

"Those reporters will be here in ten minutes," grated Standley, "and they'll get an earful."

"Admiral, the new Lend-Lease act comes to a vote this week. Is this a time to blow the whistle?"

"It's the only time. Give these scoundrels a jolt. Show 'em what ingratitude can lead to, when you deal with the American people."

Pug pointed at the cigarette package. "Sir, this is a bit of knavery on a very low level. I wouldn't magnify it."

"That? I quite agree. Not worth discussing."

The reporters came in, a bored lot obviously disappointed in their trip. As usual, they said, they had gotten nowhere near the front. In the chat over coffee Standley asked whether they had seen any American equipment out in the countryside. They had not. One reporter inquired whether the ambassador thought the new Lend-Lease act would pass in Congress.

"I wouldn't venture to say." Standley glanced at Victor Henry, and laid all ten bony fingers straight before him on the desk, like a main battery trained for a broadside. "You know, boys, ever since I've been here, I've been looking for evidence that the Russians are getting help from the British and us. Not only Lend-Lease, but also Red Cross and Russian Relief. I've yet to find any such evidence."

The reporters looked at each other and at the ambassador.

"That's right," he went on, drumming the fingers before him. "I've also tried to obtain evidence that our military supplies are actually in use by the Russians on the battlefield. I haven't succeeded. The Russian authorities seem to want to cover up the fact that they're receiving outside help. Apparently they want their people to believe that the Red Army is fighting this war alone."

"This is off the record, of course, Mr. Ambassador," said a reporter, though they were all pulling out pads and pencils.

"No, *use* it." Standley spoke on very slowly, virtually dictating. The drumming of his fingers quickened. In his pauses, the scribbling was an angry hiss. *"The Soviet authorities apparently are trying to create the impression at home and abroad that they are fighting the war alone, and with their own resources. I see no reason why you should not use my remarks if you care to."*

The reporters asked a few more excited questions, then bolted from the room.

Next morning, as Pug walked through the snow-heaped streets from the National Hotel to Spaso House, he was wondering whether he would find that the ambassador had already been recalled. Breakfasting with the reporters at the hotel, he had been told that Standley's statement had hit the front pages all over the United States and England, that the State Department had refused comment, that the President had cancelled a scheduled press conference, and that Congress was in an uproar. The whole world was asking whether Standley had spoken for himself or for Roosevelt. One rumor had it that the Russian censors who had allowed the statement out had been arrested.

In these wide quiet Moscow streets drifted high with fresh snow, amid the hundreds of Russians slogging past and the usual truckloads of soldiers coming and going, the whole fuss seemed petty and far-off. Still, Standley had done an incredible thing; on an explosively delicate issue between the United States and the Soviet Union, he had publicly vented his personal irritation. How could he survive?

In the small room assigned to him as a temporary office, he found a note on the desk from the telephone operator: *Call 0743.* He placed the call, heard the usual cracklings, poppings, and random noises of the Moscow telephone system, and then a harsh bass voice, *"Slushayu!"*

"Govorit Kapitan Victor Genry."

"Yasno. Yevlenko."

This time the sentry stiffly saluted and let the American naval officer pass without the exchange of a word. In the large marbled lobby an unsmiling army man at a desk looked up, pressing a button. *"Kapitan Genry?"*

"Da."

An unsmiling girl in uniform came down a broad curved staircase, and spoke prim stiff English. "How do you do? Well, General Yevlenko's office is on the second floor. If you please to come with me."

Ornate iron balustrades, marble stairs, marble pillars, high arched ceilings: another czarist mansion, brought up-to-date by red marble busts of Lenin and Stalin. Large thick patches of peeling old paint gave the edifice the general wartime look of neglect. Typewriters clattered behind closed doors all down the bare long corridor to Yevlenko's office. Pug remembered him as a giant of a man, but as he stood up unsmiling, holding out his left hand across the desk, he did not look so big; possibly because the desk and the room were enormous, and the photograph of Lenin behind him was many times life-size. Pictures on other walls were black and white reproductions of old czarist generals' portraits. Tall dusty red curtains shut out the gray midwinter Moscow daylight. In a high curlicued brass chandelier naked electric bulbs glared.

The awkward clasp of Yevlenko's left hand was strong. The big jowly face looked even wearier and sadder than it had on the Moscow front with the Germans breaking through. He wore many decorations, including the red and yellow wound stripe, and his trim greenish-brown uniform was festooned with new gold braid. They exchanged greetings in Russian, and Yevlenko gestured at the girl. "Well, shall we have the translator?"

She woodenly returned Pug's glance: pretty face, heavy blonde hair, a charming red mouth, a fine bosom, blank cool eyes. Since leaving Washington, Pug had been drilling two hours a day on vocabulary and grammar, and his Russian was again about as good as it had been after the crash course in 1941. On instinct he replied, *"Nyet."* Like a clockwork figure the girl turned and walked out. Pug assumed that microphones would still record everything he said, but he had no reason to be cautious, and Yevlenko no doubt could look after himself. "One less pair of eyes and ears," he said.

General Yevlenko smiled. Pug at once thought of the evening of drinking and dancing in the cottage near the front, and Yevlenko clodhopping around with Pamela, smiling in that big-toothed way. Yevlenko waved toward a sofa and a low table with the artificial right hand, shocking to see, projecting from his sleeve in a stiff brown leather glove. On the table were platters of cakes, fish slices, and paper-wrapped candy, bottles of soft drinks and mineral water, a bottle of vodka, and large and small glasses. Though Pug didn't want anything, he took a cake and a soft drink. Yevlenko took exactly what he did, and said, puffing at a cigarette clipped in a metal ring on his fake hand, "I received your letter. I have been very busy, so forgive my delay in answering. I thought it would be better to talk than to write."

"I agree."

"You asked for information about the use of Lend-Lease matériel on battlefields. Of course we have made very good use of Lend-Lease matériel on battlefields." He was slowing his speech and using simple words, so that Pug had no trouble understanding him. The deep rough voice brought timbres of the combat zone into the office. "Still, the Hitlerites would be very grateful to know the exact quantity, quality, and battlefield performance of Lend-Lease matériel used against them. As is known, they have access to the *New York Times,* the Columbia Broadcasting System, and so forth. The enemy's long nose must be reckoned with."

"Then don't disclose anything the Germans can use. A general state-

ent will suffice. Lend-Lease is very costly, you see, and our President
eeds popular support if it is to continue."

"But haven't victories like Stalingrad gained enough American public
upport for Lend-Lease?" Yevlenko passed his good hand over his
early bald close-barbered head. "We have smashed several German
my groups. We have turned the tide of the war. When you open your
ng-delayed second front in Europe, your soldiers will face greatly
eakened opposition, and will take far smaller losses than we have. The
merican people are clever. They understand these plain facts. There-
re they will support Lend-Lease. Not because of some 'general state-
ent.'"

Since this was exactly what Pug thought, he found it hard to respond.
rotten job, shooting at Standley's gnats! He poured his soft drink and
pped the sickly-sweet red concoction. General Yevlenko went to his
esk, brought back a thick file folder, and opened it on the table. With
s good hand, he riffled gray clippings glued to sheets of paper. "Be-
des, are your Moscow correspondents asleep? Here are just a few re-
ent articles from *Pravda, Trud,* and *Red Star.* Here are general state-
ents. Read them yourself." He took a final puff at the clipped stub,
nd ground it out in practiced motions of the lifeless hand.

"General, in Mr. Stalin's recent Order of the Day, he said the Red
rmy is bearing the brunt of the war, with no help from its allies."

"He was speaking after Stalingrad." The retort came sharp and un-
bashed. "Wasn't he telling the truth? The Hitlerites stripped the Atlan-
c coast to throw everything they had against us. Still, Churchill would
ot move. Even your great President could not budge him. We had to
in all by ourselves."

This was getting nowhere, and a riposte about North Africa would
ot help. Since Pug would have to report back to Standley, he decided
e might as well fire at all gnats. "It's not just a question of Lend-
ease. The Red Cross and the Russian Relief Society have made gener-
us contributions to the Soviet people, which have not been acknowl-
dged."

Grimacing incredulously, Yevlenko said, "Are you talking about a
w million dollars in gifts? We are a grateful people, and we show it by
ghting. What else would you have us do?"

"My ambassador feels that there has been insufficient publicity for
e gifts here."

"Your ambassador? Surely he is speaking for your government, not
r himself?"

Less and less comfortable, Pug replied, "The request for a statement on battlefield use of Lend-Lease comes from the State Department. Renewal of Lend-Lease is before Congress, you know."

Yevlenko inserted another cigarette into the clip. His lighter failed, and he muttered till he struck a flame. "But our Washington embassy has told us that Lend-Lease renewal will pass Congress easily. Therefore Admiral Standley's outburst is most disturbing. Does it signal a shift in Mr. Roosevelt's policy?"

"I can't speak for President Roosevelt."

"And what about Mr. Hopkins?" Yevlenko gave him a hard wise look through wreathing smoke.

"Harry Hopkins is a great friend of the Soviet Union."

"We know that. In fact," said Yevlenko, reaching for the vodka and turning very jolly all at once, "I would like to drink to Harry Hopkins's health with you. Will you join me?"

Here we go, Pug thought. He nodded. The vodka streaked down inside him, leaving a warm tingling trail. Yevlenko smacked thick lips and startled Pug by winking. "What is your rank, may I ask?"

Pointing to the shoulder bars on his bridge coat—the room was cold and he still wore it—Pug said, "Four stripes. Captain, U.S. Navy."

Yevlenko knowingly smiled. "Yes. That I see. I'll tell you a true story. When your country first recognized the USSR in 1933, we sent as military attachés an admiral and a vice admiral. Your government complained that their high rank created protocol difficulties. Next day they were reduced in rank to captain and commander, and everything was fine."

"I'm nothing but a captain."

"Yet Harry Hopkins, next to your President, is the most powerful man in your country."

"Not at all. In any case, that has nothing to do with me."

"Your embassy is already fully staffed with military attachés, isn't it? Then what is your position, may I ask? Aren't you representing Harry Hopkins?"

"No." Pug figured there was no harm, and there might be some good, in adding, "As a matter of fact, I'm here by direct personal order of President Roosevelt. Nevertheless I'm just a Navy captain, I assure you."

General Yevlenko gravely stared at him. Pug endured the stare with a solemn face. Let the Russians try to figure us out for a change, he thought. "I see. Well, since you are an emissary of the President, please clarify his misgivings on Lend-Lease," said Yevlenko, "which led to your ambassador's disturbing outburst."

"I have no authority to do that."

"Captain Henry, as a courtesy granted to Harry Hopkins, you toured the Moscow front at a bad moment in 1941. Also at your request, a British journalist and his daughter, who acted as his secretary, accompanied you."

"Yes, and I remember well your hospitality within sound of the guns."

"Well, by a pleasant coincidence, I can offer you another such trip. I am about to leave Moscow to inspect the Lend-Lease situation in the field. I will visit active fronts. I won't enter any zones of fire"—briefly the big-toothed grin—"not intentionally, but there may be hazards. If you wish to accompany me and render an eyewitness report to Mr. Hopkins and to your President on battlefield usage of Lend-Lease, that can be arranged. And perhaps we can then agree on a 'general statement' as well."

"I accept. When will we start?" Though surprised, Pug seized the chance. Let Standley veto it, if he had some objection.

"So? American style." Yevlenko stood up and offered his left hand. "I'll let you know. We'll probably go first to Leningrad, where—I may say—no correspondent, and I believe no foreigner, has been for over a year. It is still under siege, as you know, but the blockade has been broken. There are ways through that are not too dangerous. It is my birthplace, so I welcome a chance to go there. I have not been there since my mother died in the siege."

"I'm sorry," Pug said awkwardly. "Was she killed in the bombardment?"

"No. She starved."

61

STARVED.

It may have been the worst siege in the history of the world. It was a siege of Biblical horror; a siege like the siege of Jerusalem, when, as the Book of Lamentations tells, women boiled and ate their children. When the war began, Leningrad was a city of close to three million. By the time Victor Henry visited it, there were about six hundred thousand people left. Half of those who were gone had been evacuated; the other half had died. Gruesome tales persist that not a few were eaten. But at the time there was little outside awareness of the siege and the famine, and to this day much of the story remains untold, the records sealed in the Soviet archives or destroyed. Probably nobody knows, within a hundred thousand people, how many died of hunger, or the diseases of hunger, in Leningrad. The figure falls between a million and a million and a half.

Soviet historians are caught in an embarrassment over Leningrad. On the one hand, in the city's successful three-year resistance lie the makings of a world epic. On the other hand, the Germans rolled over the Red Army and arrived at the city in a matter of weeks, thus setting the stage for the drama. How does the infallible Communist Party explain that? And how explain that this great water-locked city was not mobilized for siege by rapid evacuation of the useless mouths, and by stockpiling of necessities for the garrison facing huge powerful armies drawing near?

Western historians are free and quick to blame their leaders and their governments for defeats and disasters. The Soviet Union, however, is governed by a party which has the invariably correct approach to all situations. This creates a certain awkwardness for its historians. The Party alone decides the allotment of paper for the printing of histories. The siege of Leningrad is something of a bone in the throat of Soviet historians who want to see their work in print. Thus a magnificent Russian feat of heroism goes half-told in its grim and great truth.

Lately, these historians have in gingerly fashion touched things that went wrong in the Great Patriotic War, including the total surprise of he Red Army in 1941, its near-collapse, and its failure for nearly three ears to free half of Russia from the Germans, a much smaller people t war on other fronts as well. The explanation is that blunders were nade by Stalin. Yet this too is a hazy business. As the years pass, and obscure shifts in high Soviet policy come and go, Stalin's stock as a wartime leader falls and rises again. He has yet to be blamed directly or what happened at Leningrad. The Party is by dogma blameless.

What is undeniable is that the Germans of Army Group North, some four hundred thousand strong, drove to the outskirts of the city in a quick summer campaign, and cut it off by land from the "Great Earth," the unconquered Soviet mainland. Hitler decided against an immediate grand assault. His orders were to blockade the city into submission, starve the defenders or wipe them out, and level it stone by stone to an extinct waste.

The people of Leningrad knew they could expect little more than that. Declaring it an open city like Paris, as showers of enemy leaflets kept urging, was out of the question. As winter drew on, the people started bringing in supplies under the German guns, across the frozen surface of Lake Ladoga. The invaders tried to smash the ice with artillery shells, but ice seven feet thick is tough stuff. Convoys kept running on the ice road through the winter, through darkness, blizzards, and artillery barrages; and Leningrad did not fall. As food came in, useless mouths departed on the empty trucks. By the time the ice melted in the spring there was something like a balance between mouths and food.

In January 1943, shortly before Victor Henry's visit, Red Army units defending Leningrad pushed back the German lines a short distance, at terrible cost, and freed a key railroad junction. This broke the blockade. Under the invaders' artillery pounding, rail supply resumed along a strip of roadbed called the "corridor of death," cut by the German shelling over and over, and always reopened. Most cargoes and travellers got through safely, and that was how Victor Henry entered the city. General Yevlenko's ski plane landed near the freed rail depot, where Pug saw immense stacks of food cartons, with U.S.A. stencillings; also arrays of American jeeps and Army trucks marked with red stars. They took the train into Leningrad at night in an absolute blackout. Outside the train windows on the left, German guns flared and muttered.

The breakfast in the chilly barracks was black bread, powdered eggs, and reconstituted milk. Yevlenko and Pug ate with a crowd of young soldiers at long metal tables. Gesturing at the eggs, Yevlenko said, "Lend-Lease."

"I recognize the stuff." Pug had eaten a lot of it aboard the *Northampton* when the cold-storage eggs ran out.

The artificial hand waved around at the soldiers. "Also the uniforms and boots of this battalion."

"Do they know what they're wearing?"

Yevlenko asked the soldier beside him, "Is that a new uniform?"

"Yes, General." Quick reply, the young ruddy face alert and serious. "American-made. Good material, good uniform, General."

Yevlenko glanced at Pug, who nodded his satisfaction.

"Russian body," observed Yevlenko, eliciting a rueful laugh from Pug.

Outside it was growing light. A Studebaker command car drove up, its massive tires showering snow, and the driver saluted. "Well, we will see what has happened to my hometown," said Yevlenko, turning up the collar of his long brown greatcoat and securing his fur cap.

Victor Henry did not know what to expect: another dreary Moscow, perhaps, only burned, battered, and scarred like London. The reality struck him dumb.

Except for silvery barrage balloons serenely floating in the still air, Leningrad scarcely seemed to be inhabited. Clean untracked snow covered the avenues lined with imposing old buildings. No people and no vehicles were moving. It was like Sunday morning back home, but in his life Pug had never seen a Sabbath peace like this. An eerie blue silence reigned; blue rather than white, the blue of the brightening sky caught and reflected by the pristine snow. Pug had not known of the charming canals and bridges; he had not imagined magnificent cathedrals, or splendid wide thoroughfares rivalling the Champs-Elysées, white-mantled in crystalline air; or noble houses ranged along granite embankments of a frozen river grander than the Seine. All the breadth, strength, history, and glory of Russia seemed to burst on him at a glance when the command car drove out on the stupendous square before the façade of the Winter Palace, a sight more extravagantly majestic than Versailles. Pug remembered this square from films of the revolution, roaring with mobs and czarist horse guards. It was deserted. There was not one track in the acres of snow.

The car halted.

"Quiet," said Yevlenko, speaking for the first time in a quarter of an hour.

"This is the most beautiful city I have ever seen," said Pug.

"Paris is more beautiful, they say. And Washington."

"No place is more beautiful." Impulsively Pug added, "Moscow is a village."

Yevlenko gave him a very peculiar look.

"Is that an offensive remark? I just said what I think."

"Very undiplomatic," Yevlenko growled. The growl came out rather like a purr.

As the day went on Pug saw much shell damage: broken buildings, barricaded streets, hundreds of windows patched with scrap wood. The sun rose, making a blinding dazzle of the thoroughfares. The city came to life, especially in the southern sector nearer the German lines, where the factories were. Here the artillery scars were worse; whole blocks were burned out. Pedestrians trudged in the cleared streets, an occasional trolley car bumped by, and there was heavy traffic of army trucks and personnel vehicles. Pug heard the intermittent thump of German guns, and saw stencilled on buildings, CITIZENS! DURING ARTILLERY SHELLING, THIS SIDE OF THE STREET IS MORE DANGEROUS. Yet the sense of an almost empty, almost peaceful great city persisted even here; and these later and more mundane impressions did not erase—nothing ever erased—Pug Henry's vivid morning vision of wartime Leningrad as a sleeping beauty, an enchanted blue frosty metropolis of the dead.

Even the Kirov Works, which Yevlenko said would be very busy, had a desolate air. In one big bombed-out building, half-assembled tanks stood in rows under the burned rubble from the cave-in, and dozens of shawled women were patiently clearing away the debris. One place was very busy: an immense open-air depot of trucks under an elaborate camouflage netting that stretched for blocks. Here maintenance work was proceeding at a hot pace in a tumult of clanking tools and shouting workmen, and here was Lend-Lease come to life: an outpouring from Detroit, seven thousand miles away beyond the U-boat gauntlet; uncountable American trucks showing heavy wear. Yevlenko said most of these had been running on the ice road through the winter. Now the ice was getting soft, the rail line was open, and that route was probably finished. After reconditioning, the trucks would go to the central and southern fronts, where great counterattacks were beating back the Germans. Yevlenko then took him to an airdrome ringed with antiaircraft batteries that looked like U.S. Navy stuff. Russian Yak fighters and Russian-marked Aircobras were dispersed under camouflage all over the bomb-plowed field.

"My son flies this airplane," said Yevlenko, slapping the cowl of an Aircobra. "It is a good airplane. You will meet him when we go to Kharkov."

Near sundown they picked up Yevlenko's daughter-in-law, a volunteer nurse coming off duty at a hospital. The car wound through silent streets that looked as though a tornado had swept them clean of houses, leaving block after block of shallow foundations and no rubble. All the wooden houses here, Yevlenko explained, had been pulled down and burned as fuel. At a flat waste where rows of tombstones stuck out of the snow, the car stopped. Much of the graveyard was randomly marked with bits of debris—a piece of broken pipe, a stick, a slat from a chair—or crude crosses of wood or tin. Yevlenko and his daughter-in-law left the car, and searched among the crosses. Far off, the general knelt in the snow.

"Well, she was almost eighty," he said to Pug, as the car drove away from the cemetery. His face was calm, his mouth a bitter line. "She had a hard life. Before the revolution she was a parlor maid. She was not very educated. Still, she wrote poetry, nice poetry. Vera has some poems she wrote just before she died. We can go back to the barracks now, but Vera invites us to her apartment. What do you say? The food will be better at the barracks. The soldiers get the best we have."

"The food doesn't matter," said Pug. An invitation to a Russian home was an extraordinary thing.

"Well, then, you'll see how a Leningrader lives nowadays."

Vera smiled at Pug, and despite poor teeth she all at once seemed less ugly. Her eyes were a pretty green-blue, and charming warmth brightened her face, which might once have been plump. The skin hung in folds, the nose was very sharp, and the eye sockets were dark holes.

In an almost undamaged neighborhood they entered a gloomy hallway smelling of clogged toilets and frying oil, and went up four narrow flights of a black-dark staircase. A key grated in a lock. Vera lit an oil lamp, and by the greenish glow, Pug saw one tiny room jammed with a bed, a table, two chairs, and a pile of broken wood around a tiled stove, with a tin flue wandering to a boarded-up window. It was colder here than outside, where the sun had just gone down. Vera lit the stove, broke a skin of ice in a pail, and poured water into a kettle. The general set out a bottle of vodka from a canvas bag he had carried up the stairs. Frozen through, despite heavy underwear and bulky boots, gloves, and a sweater, Pug was glad to toss off several glassfuls with the general.

Yevlenko pointed to the bed where he sat. "Here she died, and lay for two weeks. Vera couldn't get her a coffin. There were no coffins. No wood. Vera would not put her in the ground like a dog. It was very cold, much below zero, so it was not a health problem. Still, you would think it was horrible. But Vera says she just looked asleep and peaceful all that long time. Naturally the old people went first, they didn't have the stamina."

The room was rapidly warming. Frying pancakes at the stove, Vera took off her shawl and fur coat, disclosing a ragged sweater, and a skirt over thick leggings and boots. "People ate strange things," she said calmly. "Leather straps. Glue off the wallpaper. Even dogs and cats, and rats and mice and sparrows. Not me, none of that. But I heard of such things. In the hospital we heard awful stories." She pointed at the pancakes starting to sizzle on the stove. "I've made these with sawdust and petroleum jelly. Terrible, you got very sick, but it filled your stomach. There was a small ration of bread. I gave it all to Mama, but after a while she stopped eating. Apathetic."

"Tell him about the coffin," said Yevlenko.

"A poet lives downstairs," Vera said, turning the sputtering cakes. "Lyzukov, very well-known in Leningrad. He broke up his desk and made Mama a coffin. He still has no desk."

"And about the cleanup," said the general.

The daughter-in-law snapped with sudden peevishness, "Captain Henry doesn't want to hear of these sad things."

Pug said haltingly, "If it makes you sad, that's different, but I am interested."

"Well, later, maybe. Now let us eat."

She began setting the table. Yevlenko took from the wall a photograph of a young man in uniform. "This is my son."

The lamplight showed a good Slavic face: curly hair, broad brow, high cheekbones, a naïve clever expression. Pug said, "Handsome."

"I believe you told me you have an aviator son."

"I had. He was killed in the Battle of Midway."

Yevlenko stared, then gripped Pug's shoulder with his good hand. Vera was setting a bottle of red wine on the table from the canvas bag. Yevlenko uncorked the bottle. "His name?"

"Warren."

The general got to his feet, filling three glasses. Pug stood up, too. "*Varren Viktorovich Genry,*" said Yevlenko. As Pug drank down the thin sour wine, in this wretched lamplit room growing stuffy from the stove heat, he felt—for the first time—something about Warren's death that was not pure agony. However briefly, the death bridged a gulf between alien worlds. Yevlenko set down his drained glass. "We know about the Battle of Midway. It was an important United States Navy victory which reversed the tide in the Pacific."

Pug could not speak. He nodded.

With the pancakes there were sausages and American canned fruit salad from the general's bag. They rapidly emptied the bottle of wine and opened another. Vera began to talk about the siege. The worst thing, she said, had been when the snow had started to melt last spring, late in March. Bodies had begun to appear everywhere, bodies frozen and unburied for months, people who had just fallen down in the streets and died. The garbage, the rubble, and the wreckage, emerging with the thousands of bodies, had created a ghastly situation, a sickening smell everywhere, a big threat of an epidemic. But the authorities had severely organized the people, and a gigantic cleanup had saved the city. Bodies had been dumped in enormous mass graves, some identified, many not.

"You see, whole families had starved," Vera said. "Or only one would be left, sick or apathetic. People wouldn't be missed. Oh, you could tell when a person was getting ready to die. It was the apathy. If you could get them to a hospital, or put them to bed and try to feed them, it might help. But they would say they were all right, and insist on going out to work. Then they would sit or lie down on the sidewalk, and die in the snow." She glanced at Yevlenko and her voice dropped. "And often their ration cards would be stolen. Some people became like wolves."

Yevlenko drank wine and thudded his glass on the table. "Well, enough about it. Big blunders were made. Crude stupid unforgivable blunders."

They had been drinking enough so that Pug was emboldened to say, "By whom?"

Immediately he thought he had committed a fatal offense. General Yevlenko gave him a nasty glare, showing his big yellow teeth. "A million old people, children, and others who weren't ablebodied should have been evacuated. With the Germans a hundred miles away, and bombers coming around the clock, food stores shouldn't have been left in old wooden warehouses. Six months' rations for the whole city burned up in one night. Tons of sugar melted and ran into the ground. The people ate that dirt."

"I ate it," said Vera. "I paid a good price for it."

"People ate worse than that." Yevlenko stood up. "But the Germans did not take Leningrad, and they will not. Moscow gave the orders, but Leningrad saved itself." His speech was growing muffled and he was putting on his greatcoat with his back to Pug, who thought he heard him add, "Despite the orders." He turned around and said, "Well, starting tomorrow, *Kapitan,* you will see some places that the Germans took."

Yevlenko travelled at a gruelling pace. Place names melted into each other—Tikhvin, Rzhev, Mozhaisk, Vyazma, Tula, Livny—like American midwestern cities, they were all settlements on a broad flat plain under a big sky, one much resembling another; not in peaceful and banal sameness, as in the American repetition of filling stations, diners, and motels, but in horror. As they flew on and on for hundreds of miles, descending to visit an army in the field, or a headquarters in a village, or a depot of tanks and motor transport, or an operating airfield, Pug got a picture of the Russian front colossal in scale and numbing in wreckage and death.

The retreating Germans had executed a scorched-earth policy in reverse. Whatever was worth stealing, they had carried off; what would burn, they had burned; what would not, they had dynamited. For thousands and thousands of square miles they had ravaged the land like locusts. Where they had been gone for a while, buildings were rising again. Where they had recently been pushed out, shabby haggard Russians with shocked eyes were poking in the ruins or burying their dead; or they were being fed by army field kitchens in queues, under the open sky on the flat snowy plain.

Here was the problem of a separate peace, written plain across the devastated land. That the Russians loathed and despised the Germans as a form of invading vermin was obvious. Each village or city had its horror stories, its dossier of atrocity photographs of beatings, of shootings, of rapes, of heaps of bodies. The pictures numbed and bored by their grisly repetition. That the Russians wanted vengeance was equally obvious. But if after a few more bloody defeats like Stalingrad, the hated invaders would agree to leave the Soviet earth, stop torturing these people, and pay for the damage they had wrought, could the Russians be blamed for making peace?

Pug saw vast quantities of Lend-Lease matériel in use. Above all, there were the trucks, the trucks everywhere. Once Yevlenko said to him, at a depot in the south where olive-painted trucks, not yet marked with Russian lettering and red stars, stretched literally out of sight in parallel rows, "You have put us on wheels. It is making a difference. Now Fritz's wheels are wearing out. He is going back to horses. One day he will eat the horses, and run out of Russia on foot."

In an army HQ in a large badly shattered river town called Voronezh, they were eating an all-Russian supper: cabbage soup, canned fish, and some kind of fried grits. The aides were at another table. Yevlenko and Pug sat alone. "*Kapitan Genry,* we will not be going to Kharkov after all," the general said in a formal tone. "The Germans are counterattacking."

"Don't alter your itinerary on my account."

Yevlenko gave him the unsettling glare he had flashed in Leningrad. "Well, it's quite a counterattack. So instead we will go to Stalingrad."

"I'm sorry to miss your son."

"His air wing is in action, so we would not see him. He is not a bad young fellow. Maybe some other time you will meet him."

From the air, the approaches to Stalingrad were a moonscape. Giant bomb craters, pustular rings by the thousands, scarred a snowy earth littered with machines. Stalingrad itself, straggling along a black broad river flecked with floating ice, had the roofless broken look of a dug-up ancient city. As Yevlenko and his aides stared down at the ruins, Pug recalled his own dismaying airplane arrival over Pearl Harbor. But Honolulu had been untouched; only the fleet had been hit. No city on American soil had known such destruction. In the Soviet Union it was everywhere, and worst in this scene below.

Yet as they drove into the city past burned-out huts and buildings, tumbled masonry, and piles of wrecked machines, all in a vile stink of destruction, the crowds of workers clearing away the debris looked healthful and high-spirited. Merry children were playing around the ruins. There were many traces of the vanished Germans: street signs in their heavy black lettering, smashed tanks, guns, and trucks piled about or jammed in the rubble, a soldiers' cemetery in a crater-pocked park, with painted wooden grave markers topped by simulated iron crosses. High on one broken wall, Pug noticed a half-scraped-off propaganda poster: a school-age German girl in blonde braids, cowering before a slavering ape in a Red Army uniform, reaching hairy talons for her breasts.

The jeep pulled up before a bullet-riddled building, on a broad central square where all the other structures were entirely bombed out. Inside, Soviet bureaucracy was regenerating itself, complete with file cabinets, noisy typewriters, pasty men at rough desks, and women carrying tea. Yevlenko said, "I will be very busy today. I will turn you over to Gondin. During the battle Gondin was secretary to the Central Committee. He did not sleep for six months. Now he is quite sick."

A big very tough-looking gray-headed man in uniform, his face graven with deep lines of fatigue, sat behind a plank desk under a photograph of Stalin. Resting a large hairy fist on the desk, he looked pugnaciously at the stranger in the blue bridge coat. Yevlenko introduced Victor Henry. Gondin sized the newcomer up with a lengthy stare, thrust out a heavy jaw, and sardonically inquired, *"Sprechen Sie Deutsch?"*

"Govaryu po-russki nemnogo" ("I speak a little Russian"), Pug mildly returned.

The official raised thick eyebrows at Yevlenko, who put his good hand on Victor Henry's shoulder. *"Nash,"* he said. ("Ours.")

Pug never forgot that, and never understood what had prompted Yevlenko to say it. At any rate, *"Nash"* worked on Gondin like magic. For two hours he walked and rode with Pug around the wrecked city, out into the hills, down into the ravines that sloped to the river, and along the waterfront. Pug could scarcely follow his rapid Russian talk about the battle, spate of commanders' names, unit numbers, dates, and maneuvers, all poured out with mounting excitement. Gondin was reliving the battle, glorying in it, and Victor Henry did get the general idea: the defenders backed up against the Volga, surviving on supplies and reinforcements ferried across the broad river or brought across the ice; the fighting slogan, *There is no land east of the Volga;* the long horror of Germans on the hills in plain view, on rooftops of captured sections, or rumbling in tanks down the streets; the bloody deafening house-by-house, cellar-by-cellar fighting, sometimes in rain and in blizzards, the unceasing artillery and air bombardment, week upon week, month upon month. In the outskirts of the city, the German defeat was written in the snow, in long trails winding westward of smashed tanks, self-propelled guns, howitzers, trucks, half-tracks, and most of all in gray-clad bodies by the thousands, still strewn like garbage over the quiet cratered fields, miles upon miles. "It's a tremendous job," said Gondin. "I suppose in the end we'll have to pile up and burn these dead rats. We're still taking care of our own. They won't be back to bury theirs."

That night, in a cellar, Pug found himself at the sort of feast the Russians seemingly could produce in any place, under any circumstances: many varieties of fish, some meat, black and white bread, red and white wine, and endless vodka, served up on plank tables. The feasters were army officers, city officials, Party officials, about fifteen men; the introductions went fast, and obviously didn't matter. It was Yevlenko's party, and three themes ran through the boisterous talk, singing, and toasts: the Stalingrad victory, gratitude for American Lend-Lease, and the imperative need of a second front. Pug gathered that his presence was the excuse for some relaxation by these big shots. He too bore a heavy burden of emotion and tension. He let go, and ate and drank as though there were no tomorrow.

Next morning when an aide woke him in the frigid darkness, a blurry recollection made him shake his aching head. If it was not a dream, he and Yevlenko had staggered down a corridor together, and Yevlenko had said as they parted, "The Germans have retaken Kharkov."

After Pug's swift passage through wartorn Russia, Moscow appeared to him about as untouched, peaceful, well-kept, and cheery as San Francisco, despite the unfinished buildings abandoned and deteriorating, the sparseness of traffic, the difficulty of getting around, the dirty humps and ridges of ice, and the whole look of wartime neglect.

He found the ambassador ebullient. *Pravda* had printed every word of the Stettinius Report on Lend-Lease, leading off with it on the front page! A rash of stories on Lend-Lease was breaking out in the Soviet press! Moscow Radio was broadcasting Lend-Lease items almost every day!

Back home the Senate had passed the renewal of Lend-Lease unanimously, the House with only a few dissenting votes. Standley was snowed under with congratulations for speaking out. American and British newspapers had officially but gently disowned him. The President had passed it all off with an ambiguous joke to reporters about the tendency of admirals to talk too little or too much. "By God, Pug, maybe my head will roll yet for what I did, but by God, it worked! They'll think twice before kicking us around anymore."

Thus Standley, in the warm pleasant library at Spaso House, over excellent American coffee and white rolls and butter; his wrinkled eyes bright, his corded neck and face red with pleasure. He got all this out before Victor Henry said anything about his trip. Pug's account was brief. He would at once write up his observations, he said, and submit them to Standley.

"Fine, Pug. Well! Leningrad, Rzhev, Voronezh, Stalingrad, hey? By God, you covered ground. Won't this ever put Faymonville's nose out of joint! Here he sits on his ditty box, the grand high mucky-muck of Lend-Lease, never gets a look-see at what's really happening and here you come along, and go right out and get the dope. Outstanding, Pug."

"Admiral, I'm the beneficiary of a delusion around here that I'm somebody."

"By God, you are somebody. Let me see that report soonest. Say, how about the Germans retaking Kharkov? That confounded maniac Hitler has nine lives. Lot of down-in-the-mouth Russkis at the Swedish embassy last night."

Among the letters piled on Pug's desk, a State Department envelope caught his eye with *Leslie Slote* handwritten in red ink on a corner. He first read a letter from Rhoda. The change in tone from her former false-breezy notes was marked.

"I did my best to make you happy while you were here, Pug darling. I was very happy, God knows. But I honestly don't know how I rate with you anymore." That was the key sentence in a couple of subdued pages. Byron had passed through, and had told her about Natalie's removal to Baden-Baden. *"I'm sorry you missed Byron. He's a man, every inch of him. You'd be proud. Like you, though, he's capable of*

scary silent anger. Even if Natalie gets home safe with that child, as Mr. Slote assures me she will, I'm not sure she can ever make it up to him. He's in an agony of worry over the baby, and he feels she let him down."

Slote's letter was written on long yellow sheets. The red ink, unexplained, made the contents seem more sensational than they perhaps were.

March 1, 1943

Dear Captain Henry:

The pouch is a handy thing. I have some news for you and a request.

The request first. Pam Tudsbury is here, as you know, working for the *London Observer*. She wants to go to Moscow, where indeed all the major war stories are to be found these days. She applied for a visa some time ago. No soap. Pam sees her journalist's career going glimmering, whereas she's developed an interest in her work and wants to keep at it.

Quite simply, can you, and will you, do something about this? When I suggested to Pam that she write you, she turned colors and said not a chance, she wouldn't dream of pestering you. But having observed you in action in Moscow, I had a notion that you might pull it off. I told Pamela that I would write you about her, and she turned more flamboyant colors and said, "Leslie, don't you dare! I won't hear of it." I took that as British female doubletalk for "Oh, please, please do."

One can never be sure why the Narkomindel turns deaf or sulky. If you want to have a go at this, the problem may be a matter of some forty Lend-Lease Aircobras. These planes were earmarked for the Soviet Union, but the British managed to divert them for the invasion of North Africa. Lord Burne-Wilke had a hand in this. Of course that may not turn out to be the hitch at all. I mention it because Pam did.

I come to my news. The attempt to get Natalie and her uncle out of Lourdes fell through, because the Germans moved the whole group to Baden-Baden, quite against international law. A month or so ago Dr. Jastrow fell dangerously ill with an intestinal ailment requiring surgery. Operating facilities in Baden-Baden evidently were limited. A Frankfurt surgeon came and looked him over, and recommended that he be moved to Paris. The best man in Europe for such surgery is in the American Hospital there, we're told.

The Swiss Foreign Office has handled this very smoothly. Natalie, Dr. Jastrow and the baby are in Paris now. The Germans were quite decent about allowing them to remain together. Apparently his life was in some danger, because there were complications. He was operated on twice, and he is slowly recuperating.

Paris must be far pleasanter for Natalie than Baden-Baden. She is under Swiss protection, and we are not at war with France. There are other Americans living in Paris under such special circumstances, awaiting the grand Baden-Baden swap, in which they will be lumped. They have to report to the police and so forth, but they are warmly treated by the French. The Germans keep hands off so long as the legalities are observed. If Aaron and Natalie can stay in Paris until the swap comes off, they'll probably be the envy of the Baden-Baden crowd. There is the problem of their Jewish identity, and I can't pretend it isn't worrisome. But that existed in Baden-Baden too, perhaps more acutely. In short, I remain concerned, but with a little luck all should go well. The Lourdes thing was worth a try, and I regret it didn't come off. I'm very impressed at the water you draw with Harry Hopkins.

I saw Byron as he whistled through Washington. For the first time I noticed a physical resemblance to you. He used to look like an adolescent movie actor. And I had a long phone talk with your wife about Natalie, which calmed her somewhat. Natalie's mother calls me every week, poor lady.

About myself there is little to tell, none of it good, so I will pass that by. I hope you can do something for Pamela. She does yearn to go to Moscow.

Yours,
Leslie Slote

General Yevlenko did not rise or shake hands, but nodded a welcome, waving off his aide and motioning Pug to a chair with the dead hand. There were no refreshments in sight.

"Thank you for agreeing to see me."

A nod.

"I'm looking forward to the Lend-Lease statistical summary you said you'd let me have."

"It is not ready. I told you that on the telephone."

"That is not why I am here. You mentioned last week the correspondent who came to the Moscow front with me, Alistair Tudsbury."

"Yes?"

"He was killed in North Africa by a land mine. His daughter is carrying on his work as a correspondent. She is having difficulties obtaining a journalist's visa to the Soviet Union."

With a cold incredulous little smile, Yevlenko said, *"Kapitan Genry,* that is something to take up at the visa section of the Narkomindel."

Pug rode over this predictable brush-off. "I would like to help her."

"She is a *particular* friend of yours?" A man-to-man insinuating note on the Russian word *osobaya.*

"Yes."

"Perhaps I am mistaken, then. I have heard from British correspondents here that she is engaged to be married to the Air Vice Marshal, Lord Duncan Burne-Wilke."

"She is. Still, we are good friends."

The general laid his living hand over the artificial one on his desk. He was wearing what Pug thought of as his "official" face: no smile, eyes half-closed, heavy mouth pulled down. It was his usual aspect, and a truculent one. "Well. As I say, visas are not my concern. I am sorry. Is there something else?"

"Have you heard from your son on the Kharkov front?"

"Not as yet. Thank you for inquiring," Yevlenko replied in a final tone, standing up. "Tell me, does your ambassador still feel we are suppressing the facts of Lend-Lease?"

"He is gratified by recent Soviet press and radio coverage."

"Good. Of course some facts are best suppressed, as, for example, when the United States breaks a pledge to send Lend-Lease Aircobras urgently needed by our squadrons, and allows the British to divert the planes instead to themselves. To publicize such facts would only delight our enemies. Nevertheless, wouldn't you say such bad faith between allies is a very serious matter?"

"I have no information on such an occurrence."

"Really? Yet Lend-Lease seems to be your sphere of duty. Our British friends are afraid, of course, to let the Soviet Union become too strong. They are thinking, what about after the war? That is very far-sighted." Yevlenko was standing with both hands on the desk, grating out sarcastic words. "Winston Churchill tried to stamp out our socialist revolution in 1919. No doubt he has not changed his low opinion of our form of government. That is most regrettable. But meantime, what about the war against Hitler? Even Churchill wants to win that war. Unfortunately, the only way to do that is to kill German soldiers. As you have now seen with your own eyes, we are killing our share of German soldiers. But the British are very reluctant to fight German soldiers. Those Aircobras were diverted by Lord Duncan Burne-Wilke, as it happens, for the landings in French North Africa, where there are no German soldiers."

In this tirade, Yevlenko's intonation on each repetition of *nemetskie soldati,* "German soldiers," was intolerably coarse and sneering.

"I said I know nothing about this." Pug reacted in a quick hard fashion. He had his answer on Pamela's visa, but the thing was going much beyond that. "If my government broke a pledge, that is a grave matter. As for Prime Minister Churchill, the British under his leadership fought against Germany for a whole year alone, while the Soviet Union was supplying Hitler. At El Alamein and elsewhere they have killed their share of German soldiers. Their thousand-bomber raids on Germany are causing great damage and tying down a great force of antiair defenders. Any misunderstanding like this Aircobra affair certainly should not be publicized, but corrected among ourselves. Lend-Lease must go on despite such things, and despite our heavy losses. One of our Lend-Lease convoys has just suffered the worse U-boat onslaught yet in this war. Twenty-one ships sunk by a wolf pack, thousands of American and British sailors drowned in icy waters so that Lend-Lease can reach you."

Yevlenko's tone slightly moderated. "Have you reported yet to Harry Hopkins on your tour with us?"

"I have not completed my report. I shall include this complaint on Aircobras. Your statistical summary will go with it."

"You will have that on Monday."

"Thank you."

"In return, may I have a copy of your report to Mr. Hopkins?"

"I will deliver a copy to you myself."

Yevlenko offered his left hand.

Pug wrote a twenty-page report. Admiral Standley, delighted with this cornucopia of Lend-Lease intelligence, ordered it mimeographed for a large political distribution list back home, including the President.

Pug also wrote a letter by hand to Harry Hopkins. He sat up late one night scrawling it, fueled by sips of vodka, and he intended to put it in the pouch an hour before the courier departed. Such surreptitious bypassing of Standley was distasteful, but it was his job, if in this formless assignment anything was his job.

27 March 1943

Dear Mr. Hopkins:

Ambassador Standley is forwarding to you and to others my intelligence report on a recent eight-day observer trip through the Soviet Union with General Yuri Yevlenko. All my facts are in that document. I add, at your request, some "crystal ball" footnotes.

As to Lend-Lease: the trip convinced me that the President's policy of freehanded giving, without demanding any quid pro quo, is the only sane one. Congress did itself proud by showing how well it understood that. Even if the Russians weren't slaughtering great numbers of our foes, it would be churlish to tie strings to our help. This war will end, and we will have to live with the Soviet Union. If we now start bargaining about the price of a lifeline, before we throw it to a man struggling in deep waters, he may pay anything, but he'll remember.

As I see it, the Russians are starting to break the backbone of Hitlerism, but at terrible cost. I keep picturing the Japs rampaging ashore on our Pacific Coast and sweeping halfway across the country, killing or capturing maybe twenty million Americans, ravaging all the foodstuffs, taking over the factories, sending a few million people back to Nippon as slave labor, and spreading destruction and atrocities everywhere. That's roughly what the Russians have been going through. That they've hung on and come back is amazing. No doubt Lend-Lease has helped, but it wouldn't have helped a gutless country. General Yevlenko showed me some soldiers in new Lend-Lease uniforms, and he dryly remarked, "Russian bodies." So far as I'm concerned, that's the first and last word on Lend-Lease.

Just as amazing, however, is the German war effort. We see these things on maps and read about them, but it is another thing to fly along a battlefront for more than a thousand miles and view the reality. Considering that Hitler is also maintaining large forces in western Europe from Norway to the Pyrenees, and conducting massive operations in North Africa and a ferocious large-scale U-boat campaign—and that I didn't visit the Caucasus at all, which has been another huge front in itself—this sustained onslaught on a country ten times as big as Germany, twice as populous, and highly industrialized and militarized, boggles the mind. It may be history's most remarkable (and odious) military feat. Could we and the British stamp out this monstrous predatory force without Russia? I wonder. Again, the President's policy of keeping the Soviet Union fighting at all costs is the only sane one.

This raises the question of a separate peace, on which you have specifically asked for a judgment. Unfortunately the Soviet Union baffles me; the people, the government, the social philosophy, everything about it. Of course I'm not alone in that.

I don't feel that the Russians love or even like their Communist government. I think they're stuck with it by the accidents of a revolution that went wrong. Despite the blanket of propaganda, I think they sense too that Stalin and his brutal gang bungled the start of the war and almost lost it. Maybe one day this great patient people will have a reckoning with the regime, as they did with the Romanoffs. Meantime Stalin remains in the saddle, providing harsh driving leadership. He'll make the separate peace decision, one way or the other. The people will obey. Nobody's going to rebel against Stalin, not after the way the Germans have behaved here.

At this point such a peace would be perfidious, and when I'm among Russians I don't sense or fear perfidy. War-weariness is something else. The German resilience as shown in the recapture of Kharkov is ominous. I ask myself, why did the Russian authorities permit me to go on this unusual trip? And why did General Yevlenko invite me to the squalid flat of his daughter-in-law in Leningrad, and prod her to tell me horror stories of the siege? Possibly to make our complaints of Russian ingratitude seem shameful. Possibly to drive home to me—for as described in my main report, I've been treated as your unofficial aide—that there may be limits even to Russian endurance. The hints here, sometimes subtle but usually very crude, about a second front in Europe are interminable.

I've been through some cruel warfare in the Pacific, but that's mainly a war of professionals. This one is all-out—two entire nations at each other's jugulars. The Russians don't mean to do us a favor by fighting for their lives, but it's working that way. Lend-Lease is an inspired and historic policy. But bloodshed on the battlefield remains the decisive thing in wars, and people can stand only so much of it without hope of relief.

My "crystal ball" says therefore something very obvious: if we can convince the Russians that we're serious about a second front in Europe soon, we can forget about a separate peace. Otherwise it's a risk.

> Sincerely,
> Victor Henry

"The matter of the Aircobras," Pug said, "is discussed on pages seventeen and eighteen."

A weekend had passed. He and Yevlenko were exchanging papers: a copy of his report to Yevlenko, a thick-bound document to him. Riffling through Yevlenko's summary, Pug saw pages on pages of figures, graphs, and tables, with long pages of solid text in Russian.

"Well, of course I cannot read your report myself." Yevlenko's tone was chatty but hurried. He slipped the report into his travelling portfolio, which lay on the desk; his fur-lined greatcoat and a valise were on the sofa. "I am off to the southern front, and my aide will translate at sight on the plane."

"General, I have also written a personal letter to Harry Hopkins." Pug pulled more papers from his portfolio. "I have translated it myself into Russian for you, though I had to use a dictionary and a grammar."

"But why? We have excellent translators."

"So have we. I don't want to leave a copy with you. If you care to read it and hand it back to me, that is what I prepared it for."

Yevlenko looked puzzled and suspicious, then gave him a slow patronizing smile. "Well! That is the sort of cautious secrecy we Russians are often accused of."

Pug said, "Possibly it's infectious."

"Unfortunately, I have very little time just now, *Kapitan Genry.*"

"In that case, when you return, I'll be at your service."

Yevlenko took the telephone and growled quick words; hung up, and held out his hand. Pug gave him the translated letter. Inserting a cigarette in the clip, still wryly smiling, Yevlenko began to read. The smile faded. A couple of times he shot at Pug the nasty glare he had first flashed in the Leningrad apartment. Turning over the last page, he sat staring at the letter, then handed it back to Pug. His face was expressionless. "You have to work on your Russian verbs."

"If you have any comment, I will transmit it to Harry Hopkins."

"You might not like what I would say."

"That doesn't matter."

"Your political understanding of the Soviet Union is very superficial, very prejudiced, and very uninformed. Now I must go." Yevlenko stood up. "You asked about my son on the Kharkov front. We have heard from him. He is all right."

"I'm absolutely delighted to hear it."

Yevlenko barked an order into the telephone and began putting on his coat, dead hand first. An aide entered and gathered up his luggage. "As for Miss Pamela Tudsbury, her visa has been issued. Your driver will return you to your flat. Good-bye."

"Good-bye," Pug said, too startled to react about Pamela. He thought Yevlenko was offering him the live hand, but it went up to his shoulder for a brief almost painful squeeze. Then Yevlenko left.

62

No locomotive will ride the steel tracks that Berel Jastrow, Sammy Mutterperl, and the other Jews of Kommando 1005 are handling, nor will the heavy wooden ties piled nearby support the weight of rolling trains. The rails and ties are for railroad bed repair, but Standartenführer Blobel has found another use for them.

Since first light the kommando has been out at the job, setting up the steel frame. The frame is the secret of the 1005 operation. For a professional architect like Paul Blobel it was a simple thing to design, build, and put into use, but the thick heads at Auschwitz and the other camps still cannot grasp the advantage of it. Blobel has offered copies of the drawings to the camp commandants. So far, they have shown little interest, though that fellow Hoess at Auschwitz has indicated he will give it a try. The frame is the answer to the disposal problem about which he whines and makes so many excuses, and which in fact is a serious health problem. But the fellow obviously did not grasp the idea when Blobel described it, and was afraid to admit his stupidity, so he nodded and smiled and passed the thing off. Just an old concentration camp hand, no culture or imagination.

This morning Standartenführer Blobel is at the site when work begins. That is unusual. The procedure is cut-and-dried, and this latest squad from Auschwitz—a sturdy gang of Jews at last, hardworking physical specimens with smart work leaders—has caught on fast. Usually at this hour Blobel is in his van or at quarters in town if the section is not too far out in the sticks, quaffing schnapps to chase off the morning chill. This duty is lonely, repetitious, boring, and very hard on the nervous system. The SS men get their schnapps ration at night; during work hours they have to keep an eye on the Jews. The escape rate is very bad, worse than Blobel reports to Berlin. Rank has its privileges, and SS Colonel Blobel likes to start the day with a few shots, but this morning is special. He is cold sober.

The pit was opened yesterday. Fortunately, the snowfall at night wasn't much. There are the bodies in rows, lightly snowed over. A medium-sized job, maybe two thousand. The smell as usual is awful, but the cold and the snow keep it down some, and the frame stands to windward, which helps. Blobel is pleased to observe how quickly the frame takes form. The Jew work leader "Sammy" had a good idea, cutting numbers into the rails for sorting and matching. It is up, bolted, braced, and ready to go in less than half an hour—a long narrow sturdy structure of rails held together with steel crossbeams, like a section of track on stilts. Next will come the pileup: a layer of wooden ties, a layer of bodies and fuel-soaked rags, wood, bodies, wood, bodies, with a row or two of heavy steel rails to hold the mass down, until you have all the bodies out of the hole, or until the pyre is toppling-high.

What Blobel has come to watch is the new search procedure. The looting has been getting out of hand. These are all early graves around the Minsk district, from the 1941 executions. Nobody had any know-how then. Jews were taken out by the hundreds of thousands, and shot and buried with their clothes on, without even being searched. Rings, watches, gold coins, old paper money (plenty of American dollars, too) stiff with black blood but still good, are all over White Russia in these mass graves. Up the assholes and in the cunts of these cheesy bodies you are apt to find valuable gems, no fun to make the search, but worth it! Here and there the local population has already been robbing the graves; to discourage the practice Blobel has had to shoot a few kids, who tend to be adept at such ghoulishness. Germany needs all the wealth it can acquire to carry on its world-historical struggle. They are collecting pots and pans back home for the Führer, and here is real buried treasure, amid all this rotting garbage that now has to be burned up.

Until today the treasure has been picked over randomly, a lot of it carelessly given to the flames, some going into the pockets of the SS underlings; and some Jews have even become so bold in their Yiddish greed that they have been caught with loot. Blobel suspects that escapees may have bribed their way past the guards with looted jewels and money; on this duty SS morale and training tend to break down. He has had to make an example and shoot seven perfectly healthy Jews, who will be missed in the work force.

He observes the new system go into action. Excellent! Jewish body-searchers, Jewish loot-collectors, Jewish inventory-writers, Jews with pliers for the gold teeth, all under close SS supervision, go to work on the corpses as they are handed up and laid out on the snow in rows. Untersturmführer Greiser is in charge. From now on that young fellow will do nothing else but attend to the "economic processing," as Blobel has termed it, so long as Kommando 1005 is obliterating the 1941 graves. Greiser is a good-looking idealistic rookie from Breslau, a fine

SS type with whom Blobel enjoys philosophical discussions. Formerly an accountant with a university degree, he can be relied upon to handle this business. Kommando 1005 will be remitting plenty of stuff to the central bank depository in Berlin, and Blobel's promotion file will duly record this.

The search adds some time to the whole process, but less than he expected. It goes fast. Most of the people were poor and had nothing on them. The thing is, you never know when you'll come on a loaded one. The Standartenführer's orders are, *"Search them all, even the kids!"* It's an old Yid trick to hide valuables on the children.

Well, something accomplished!

It is finished. The rifled bodies are all piled up with the railroad ties and rails. As the Jews climb their ladders to pour waste oil and gasoline over the pyre, Blobel waves to his chauffeur. Gasoline for the pyre is getting to be a real problem. The Wehrmacht is becoming stingier all the time about this, just as it won't ever provide enough soldiers to cordon off a work area. Without gasoline the blaze just doesn't get going. You can have a terrible smoldering mess for days. But today there is plenty. In a moment, as it seems, the pile of more than a thousand long-dead Jews bursts into towering flame. Blobel has to recoil a bit from the blast of heat.

He is driven back to his van. Downing many glasses of schnapps, he drafts a report to Berlin on his procedure. It pays to get these things on the record. Nobody else can claim credit for the frame; he wrote a long report on it, pointing out that the great problem in the combustion of corpses, especially old ones, was getting enough oxygen to the conflagration. Those open pits in Auschwitz—well, he has used open pits, too: slow, visible far and wide at night, soaking up four times as much oil and gasoline as the frame does because oxygen can't get down in there. The pits at Chelmno burned cherry-red for three days, and there was still a big problem with bones. All he can say for a pit is it beats a crematorium.

He has argued in vain against the Auschwitz crematoriums, and given up. He knows more about this business than anyone, but to hell with it. The gas-chamber concept is fine, it does a quiet smooth job with large numbers; but the damned fools who designed the installation gave it a gassing capacity four times the burning capacity. The overload in peak periods must end in a tremendous mess. Well, let those wiseacres in Berlin spend money and waste scarce material and machinery. Let them find out for themselves that no chimney linings will hold up against the heat of combustion of hundreds of thousands of human bodies, dead meat burning by the hundreds of metric tons on a twenty-four-our basis. Those big complicated structures will give nothing but trouble. The height of foolishness; amateur architecture, amateur disposal techniques! Bureaucrats a thousand miles from the job dreaming up fancy installations when all they ever needed was plenty of God's open air and Paul Blobel's frame.

Depending on the wind, the burning time on the frame can be two to ten hours. Some Jews tend the crackling pyre with iron forks. Others, including Jastrow and Mutterperl, are down in the long narrow pit, passing up more bodies. It is starting to snow again. Black smoke and red flames climb into the white snowfall, a beautiful sight if any eye here can see beauty. But the forty-odd SS men surrounding the job, guns in hand, are bored and numb, waiting for their reliefs; and the Jews—those who are sane enough to notice things—are all driven and busy.

Many of these Jews are now quite harmless madmen. They work because they will be fed if they do, and starved and beaten if they don't. Uncovering and descending into hideously foul mass graves; handling desiccated rotted corpses that can come apart in one's leather-gloved hands, that drip fat worms; piling up one's murdered fellow Jews and setting them afire, day in and day out; these things have been too great a strain. Minds and spirits have given way, fallen apart like old corpses. These docile lunatic automatons are no more trouble to their guards than cattle; which is how the SS men handle the squad, with shouts and with dogs.

But not all minds and spirits are gone. There are tough-willed fellows among them who mean to survive. They too obey the SS, but with eyes and ears alert for self-protection. For Jastrow and Mutterperl, working down in the graves has advantages, once one is steeled to handling gap-mouthed limp skeletal bodies all day. The SS allows you to wear a cloth over nose and mouth, and the guards, having no great zest for the sight and smell of the bodies, stand well clear of the holes. Slave workers can be shot to death without warning for talking on the job, but Jastrow and Mutterperl carry on long free conversations behind their masks.

Today they are rehashing an old argument. Berel Jastrow is against trying a getaway here. True, he knows the forests, he knows partisan pathways and hiding places, and he even recalls old passwords. That is Sammy Mutterperl's argument; this is Jastrow's territory, and it's a good place to make the try.

But Berel is thinking ahead. It is not a question of taking to the woods to save their skins. Their mission is to bring the photographs and documents of Auschwitz to Prague, where the organized Resistance can

get the material to the outside world, above all to the Americans. Bu
Kommando 1005 has been moving farther and farther from Prague. Es
caping here, they will have to traverse all of Poland through the wood
behind German lines. Some of the Poles are all right, but many of thei
partisan bands in the forests are unfriendly enough to Jews to kill then
and the Polish villagers cannot be trusted not to turn Jews in. Berel ha
heard talk among the SS officers about an impending transfer of Kom
mando 1005 to the Ukraine. That is many hundreds of miles closer t
Prague.

Mutterperl doesn't want to rely on SS gossip. The transfer may n
happen. He wants to act. He does most of the talking as they work thei
way down the row, lifting each maggoty body with what reverence the
can, and passing it up to waiting hands above; signalling, when th
corpse is a loose disintegrating one, for a canvas sling to hold it to
gether.

While he does this work, Berel Jastrow recites psalms for the dead
He knows the psaltery by heart. Several times each day he goes throug
all hundred and fifty *t'hilim*. The dead hold no terrors for Berel. In th
old days, as an officer of the burial society, the *hevra kadisha,* h
washed and prepared for interment many bodies. Here the terribl
odor, the disgusting condition of these long-buried corpses, cannot ma
his deep affection for them. They cannot help the way they died, thes
pitiful Jews, many still streaked with black blood from visible bulle
holes.

For Berel Jastrow these rotten remains possess all the sad sacre
sweetness of the dead: poor cold silent mechanisms, once warm happ
creatures sparkling with life, now dumb and motionless without th
spark of God in them, but destined one day in His good time to ris
again. So the Jewish faith teaches. He goes about this gruesome tas
with love, murmuring psalms. He cannot give these dead the orthodo
purification by water, but fire purifies too, and the psalms will comfo
their souls. The Hebrew verses are so graven in his memory that he ca
listen to Mutterperl, or even break off to argue, without missing a wor
of a psalm.

Mutterperl is beginning to alarm Berel Jastrow. Sammy's health i
good; the man is burly, and Kommando 1005 feeds its exhumers wel
before (as they all realize) their turn comes to be shot and burned o
the frame. Until recently Sammy has seemed to be retaining his har
sanity, but he is talking really wildly now. The idea of crossing Polan
through the forests is not enough for him today. He wants to organiz
the strongest Jews in the kommando and make a break in a body; *seiz*

ɔme guards' guns, and kill as many SS men as they can before plung-
ɩg into the forest.*

Sammy is talking so vehemently that his breath makes risky telltale
ɱoke through the cloth mask. This situation is nothing like Auschwitz,
ɛ argues. There are no electrified wire fences. The SS men are a stu-
ɪd, lazy, drunken, altogether careless gang. The cordon of soldiers is
ɪr off, and alerted only to keep the peasants away from the grave.
'hey could kill a dozen Germans before getting away—maybe twice as
ɩany—if they could seize two or three machine guns.

Berel replies that if organizing an uprising and killing a dozen Ger-
ɩans will help a getaway, fine, but how can it? The chances of being in-
ɔrmed on and caught will increase with every Jew they approach. A si-
ɛnt escape always has the best chance of succeeding. Killing Germans
'ill raise a hue and cry and start the whole military police force in
yelorussia after the fugitives. Why do it?

Sammy Mutterperl is handing up out of the grave a little girl in a
lac dress. Her face is a peering grinning skull patched with shreds of
ɼeenish skin, but her dark streaming hair is feminine and pretty. "For
ɛr," he says, as a Jew above takes the girl. The wide-eyed glittery look
ɛ gives Berel Jastrow above his mask is more horrible than the dead
ɪrl's face.

Berel does not answer. He heaves up body after body—they are light,
ɪese long-dead Jews, one seizes a body by the waist and twitches it
ɛadily into the air, into the waiting hands above—and goes on murmur-
ɩg psalms. This is how Berel Jastrow holds on to his sanity. He is
ɔing *hevra kadisha* work; his religious structure can contain and sup-
ort even this heavy horror. Why such strange death has befallen so
ɩany Jews he cannot fathom. God will have much to answer for! Yet
ɿod did not do this, the Germans did it. Why did God not pass a mira-
le and stop the Germans? It may be that the generation did not de-
ɛrve a miracle. So things went naturally, and the Germans broke loose
ll over Europe, murdering Jews. In this narrow squirrel-cage of ques-
ɪon and answer Jastrow's mind runs when he allows himself such vain
ɪoughts. He does his best to suppress them.

Mutterperl says after a long silence, "I intend to talk to Goodkind
ɩd Finkelstein tonight, to start with."

He is serious, then!

What can one say to him? Mutterperl knows as well as Jastrow that
ɛyond this grave where living Jews in a long file are handing up dead
ɛws, beyond the pyre which is now burning down to glowing ash, the
ɩng of SS men stands always with tommy guns at the ready, with
ɛashed dogs that if released will kill any moving prisoner. There are

different ways that this work changes men. There are the crazy ones Berel understands them. There are the ones who have been robbing the bodies, and—usually the same ones—sucking up to the SS, informing on other Jews, doing anything to get more food, more comfort, more assurance of surviving. He even understands them. God did not make human nature strong enough to stand what the Germans are doing.

The bullying Jewish kapos in Auschwitz, the *Judenrat* officials in Warsaw and the other cities who picked people to go on the trains, and protected their relatives and friends, are all a product of the German cruelty. He can understand them. The mysterious crazy ferocity of the Germans is too much to endure; it turns normal people into treacherous animals. The hundreds of thousands of Jews that now lie in these graves meekly marched out to the pits and stood on the brink to let themselves be shot, with their wives, children, old parents, and all. Why? Because the Germans were acting beyond human nature. The surprise was too numbing. It could not be happening. People didn't do such things for no reason. On the brink of the hole, with the Germans or their Latvian or Ukrainian shooters pointing the guns at them, these Jews, clothed or naked, probably thought that it was all a mistake, or a hoax, or a dream.

Now Mutterperl wants to fight. Good, maybe that is the way, but with sense, not crazily! When Berel was with the partisans they killed some Germans. But what Mutterperl is talking about is a suicide rush; the work has gotten to him, and he really wants to die, whether he knows it or not; and this is wrong. They do not have the right to the surcease of death. They have to get to Prague.

"There he is," Mutterperl says with hoarse hate. *"Ut iz er."*

An SS man with gun tucked under an arm has come to the edge of the hole. He looks down, yawning, then takes out a pale penis and urinates over the bodies. This same fellow does this every day, usually several times. It is either his idea of humor, or a special way he has to show contempt for Jews. He is not a bad-looking young German, with a long narrow face, thick blond hair, and bright blue eyes. They know nothing else about him; they call him the Pisser. Marching to and from the work sites he is like the other SS men, tough and harsh, but not one of the sadists who look for excuses to beat a Jew. It is just his fancy to piss on the dead.

Mutterperl says, "Him, I want to kill."

Later, when both men are on the bone-disposal detail, raking warm fragments or whole collarbones, thighs, and skulls out of the smoking ash heap and feeding them into the bone-crushing mill, Mutterperl pokes Jastrow with an elbow.

"Ut iz er."

At the pit, the SS man is urinating again, picking a spot where the odies still lie.

Mutterperl repeats, *"Him,* I want to kill."

The sun has gone down. It is almost dark, and bitter cold. The last re of the day is flickering low all along the frame, lighting up the faces nd arms of the Jews who are raking the fallen ashes for bones. The rucks have arrived. This grave is too far out from town to march the ommando there and back; not that one has to coddle Jews, but time is mportant. Blobel has even taken criticism for "taxiing" Jews with pre-ious gasoline, as one critical SS inspector put it; but he has a tough ide and he runs his show as he pleases. Only he knows the true magni-ude and urgency of the job. He knows more about it than the great Iimmler, who assigned it to him, because he is the man on the spot, nd he has all the maps and reports of the execution squads.

So the Jews will ride back to the cow barns at an abandoned dairy in Minsk. There are of course no cattle or horses in occupied Russia. The Sermans have long since taken them off. Blobel's far-roaming Kom-mando 1005 has no trouble quartering its Jews in one animal stall or nother, and its SS contingent merely turns out of their homes as many Russians as may be necessary. Food for the field kitchens is a chronic roblem, because the Wehrmacht is so stingy about it, but Blobel's fficers are now old hands at smelling out and requisitioning victuals rom the local people. Even in this scrubby and devastated part of the Soviet Union there is food. People must eat. One has to know how to ay hands on their stores, that is all.

By the last light of the fire, Untersturmführer Greiser is himself lock-ng up the valuables collected from the corpses, in heavy canvas bags ised for transporting secret SS correspondence.

More of this disagreeable work tomorrow; a pretty deep grave, after ll, two layers of bodies left. Half a day's work to clean them up, shovel n the ashes, level off the pit with dirt and scatter grass seed. By next pring it will be hard to find the place. In two years brush will cover it; n five years the woods will obliterate it with new growth, and that will e that.

Standartenführer Blobel's car drives up. In the dim firelight, the hauffeur gets out and salutes. Untersturmführer Greiser is to report to he Standartenführer at once, and the car has come for him. Greiser is urprised and concerned. The Standartenführer seems to like him, but ny summons from a superior can be bad news. Probably the boss vants a report on the economic processing. Greiser puts his master ser-

geant in charge of the sacks, keeping the keys himself. The car drive
off with him toward Minsk.

How Greiser would love a bath before he makes his report! It's n
use keeping clear of the pit, the bodies, the smoke; the smell infects th
air all around a work area. It haunts the nerves of your nose. You'r
still smelling it even after a bath, when you sit down to try to enjo
your dinner. Rough duty!

Untersturmführer Greiser reported to Kommando 1005 with a hig
rating for loyalty and intelligence. His father is an old National So
cialist, a top official in the post office. Greiser was brought up in th
Hitler movement. The special treatment of Jews was a hard concept t
swallow when he first heard of it in a secret SS training program. Bu
now he understands it. Still, he has had trouble with the Komman
1005 mission. Why conceal and obliterate the graves? On the contrary
once the New Order triumphs these places should all have monumenta
markers to show where the enemies of mankind perished, at the hand
of the German people, Western civilization's rescuers. He once ven
tured to say this to the Standartenführer. Blobel explained that once th
new day dawns for mankind, all these evildoers and the world war
they caused must simply be forgotten, so that innocent children ca
grow up in a happy Jew-free world, without even a memory of the ba
past.

But, Greiser objected, what will the world think happened t
Europe's eleven million Jews, that they just vanished into thin air
Blobel, with an indulgent smile, advised the young man to read *Mei
Kampf* again, on the stupidity and short memory of the masses.

Standartenführer Blobel, well along in his evening boozing, is porin
over his SS maps of the Ukraine while he waits for Greiser to arrive. H
finds the loyal naïveté of the young officer very engaging. Blobel coul
not tell him the truth about the 1005 operation, which he himself ha
surmised but has never breathed to a soul; and which is, that Heinric
Himmler now thinks Germany may lose the war, and is taking steps t
preserve Germany's reputation. Blobel thinks the Reichsführer is ver
wise. One can hope the Führer will still pull it off, in spite of all th
odds, and in spite of the hard Stalingrad blow. But now is the time t
prepare for an unfavorable result of the war.

Whatever happens, doing away with the Jews will remain Germany'
historic achievement. For two thousand years the European nation
tried converting them, or isolating them, or driving them out. Yet whe
the Führer took power there they were still. Only the leader of Kom
mando 1005 can appreciate the true grandeur of Adolf Hitler to th
fullest. As Himmler said, "We will never talk about this to the world.

Even the mute evidence of the corpses must not exist. For otherwise the decadent democracies will pretend holy horror at Germany's special measures against the Jews, should they find out, though they have no use for the Jews themselves; and the Bolsheviks of course will make crude distorted propaganda of anything that can be turned to the Reich's discredit.

In short, Kommando 1005 has become the custodian of the great and sacred Reich secret; indeed, of Germany's national honor. He, Paul Blobel, is in the last analysis as great a guardian of that honor as the most famous general in the war; but the difficult work he must do will never get the praise it merits. He is a German hero who must go unsung. Drunk or sober, this is what Paul Blobel truly thinks. He is, in his own mind, no common concentration camp plug-ugly; nothing like it. He is a cultivated professional man, in peacetime an independent architect, a loyal German who understands German world-philosophy and is serving heart and soul in a very demanding war job. One honestly needs nerves of iron.

Greiser learns, on arriving at the house in Minsk which the Standartenführer is occupying, that Blobel is not interested in a report on the economic process. There is big news. Kommando 1005 is going to the Ukraine! The Standartenführer has been nagging Berlin for a month to issue these orders. He is in a jovial mood, and presses a large glass of schnapps on the young officer, who is glad enough to get it. Down in the Ukraine things will hum, because that is his own territory, Blobel says. He was a leading officer of *Einsatzgruppe* C, and he insisted from the start on keeping decent maps and accurate body-count reports. As a result the Ukraine sweep can be done with system. All this groping around for grave sites wastes precious time, and the ground in the north is still frozen, and the whole thing is stupid. While they are cleaning out the Ukraine, he will send an officer detail back to Berlin to make a thorough review of all the confused records, maps, and reports of *Einsatzgruppen* A and B. That detail will then return and search out and mark every northern grave site *in advance*.

Hope stirs in Greiser that he is being detailed back to Berlin, but that is not it. Blobel has another mission for him. The graves in the Ukraine are enormous, much bigger than any Greiser has seen. One frame will not do down there, they will have to work with three for best results. Greiser is to proceed at once to Kiev with a detachment of a hundred Jews from the section, a suitable number of SS guards, and report to the office of the Reich commissar for the Ukraine. Blobel will issue to him the necessary top-priority authorizations for steel rails and the use of a foundry. The Jew work leader "Sammy" is a construction man, and Greiser will have no trouble manufacturing the frames in a week or so. Blobel wants them finished and ready for use when Section 1005 arrives in Kiev. Meanwhile, it will clean out one more small grave to the west of Minsk, which was found today.

Greiser diffidently asks about the economic processing of the new grave. Very little to do, says Blobel; the bodies in that grave are naked.

But Standartenführer Blobel's plan for the move to the Ukraine is delayed at the outset by a grave accident at the Minsk railroad station.

At about nine o'clock in the morning, when the train has already failed to show up for two hours, and the Jews in striped suits are drooping sleepily on their feet in two long lines that stretch the length of the platform, and the SS guards are grouped in desultory talk to kill time, a burly figure bursts from the Jews, grabs a machine gun from one of the guards, and begins shooting! It is never known whose gun he snatched, because several guards fall and their guns go clattering over the platform. But no other Jews have time to snatch up the fallen guns and make real trouble. From both ends of the platform SS men come running, pumping bullets into Sammy Mutterperl. He topples, still holding the machine gun, blood flowing over his striped suit. The surviving guards surround him in rage and riddle his body with bullets; possibly a hundred slugs enter his already lifeless body. They boot and stamp and kick the corpse all around the platform, kicking and kicking at his face until it is a mere pulp of blood and broken bone, as a hundred Jews look on in dumb paralyzed fear. Yet they do not quite kick off the wrecked face the contours of a grin.

Four SS men are sprawled dead on the platform; one crawls around wounded, trailing blood, crying like a woman. It is the Pisser; and after a few moments he lies still across the track, dead as any corpse he ever pissed on, his blood spurting on the steel rails and the wooden ties.

In his report Greiser fixes the blame on the SS noncom in charge of the armed guards, who drifted together instead of holding spaced positions along the double line of Jews as regulations require. The Jew work leader "Sammy" was a privileged character who got special food rations. The incident demonstrates again that the subhuman Jews are totally unpredictable. Therefore the harshest and most vigilant severity, as with wild animals, is the only safe method of handling them.

The detachment marches back from the station carrying the bodies. The dead SS men are left in Minsk, to receive honored burial in a German military cemetery. Mutterperl's blood-soaked and bullet-riddled remains go on the truck with the Jews to the grave site, to be burned on

e frame with the day's corpses. Berel Jastrow sees the body, hears the
hispered story down in the pit, and makes the blessing on evil news,
lessed be the true judge. He places himself at the frame when the pyre
as burned down, and himself rakes out what he believes are Mutterperl's
one fragments. As he shoves them into the crusher, he murmurs the
d burial service:

*"Lord, full of mercy, dweller on high, grant true rest, under the
ings of the Presence among the holy and pure ones, to the soul of
amuel, son of Nahum Mendel, who has gone to his eternity. . . .
lessed is the Lord who created you justly, fed and sustained you justly,
ve you death justly, and in the future will resurrect you justly . . ."*

So the faith teaches. But what resurrection can there be for these
urned atomized remains? Well, the Talmud takes up the question of
odies destroyed by fire. It teaches that in each Jew there is one small
one that no fire can consume, that nothing can shatter; and that out of
is minute indestructible bone, the resurrected body will grow and rise.

"Go in peace, Sammy," Berel says when it is finished.

Now it is up to him to get to Prague.

63

A MERICAN torpedoes were still failing when the *Moray* set forth on its first war patrol. The two problems that haunted SubPac were dud torpedoes and dud captains. The service was secretive about both alarming deficiencies, but the submariners themselves all knew about the unreliable magnetic exploders of the Mark Fourteen torpedo, and about the captains who either had to be beached for overcaution or, on the Branch Hoban pattern, fell apart under attack. Aces like Captain Aster who combined cold courage with skill and luck in battle were few. Such men of picturesque sobriquets—Mush Morton, Fearless Freddie Warder, Lady Aster, Red Coe—were setting the pace in SubPac, inspiring the rest of the skippers despite the damnable torpedo failures. Within broad limits, they could get away with murder.

A large sign over Admiral Halsey's advance headquarters in the Solomons read:

KILL JAPS
KILL JAPS
KILL MORE JAPS

A photograph of this sign hung on the bulkhead of Captain Aster's cabin in the *Moray.*

. . .

April 19, 1943; one more day of war; a day burned into Byron Henry's memory. For others elsewhere it was also a fateful day.

On April 19 the International Bermuda Conference was opening after much delay, to decide on ways and means of helping "war refugees," and Leslie Slote was there in the American delegation. And on that selfsame April 19, Passover Eve, the Jews in the Warsaw Ghetto were rising in revolt, having been warned that the Germans were about to wipe the ghetto out—a few underground fighters taking on the Wehrmacht, seeking only the death of a Sammy Mutterperl in fighting and killing Germans.

On April 19 sorrowing Japanese were cremating Admiral Yamamoto. The Japanese still could not grasp that their codes were being broken, and so the plan for Yamamoto's risky air tour of forward bases had been broadcast in code. American fighter planes ambushed him in the sky, shot their way past escorting Zeroes, and gunned down the bomber he rode in. The search party groping in the Bougainville jungle came on Yamamoto's scorched corpse in full-dress inspection uniform, still gripping his sword. So perished the best man Japan had.

On April 19 the American and British forces in North Africa were closing the ring around Rommel's armies in Tunis, a German defeat as big as Stalingrad.

And on April 19 the Soviet government was reaching the point of breaking relations with the Polish government-in-exile. Nazi propagandists had been trumpeting the discovery of some ten thousand corpses in the uniforms of Polish army officers, buried in the Katyn woods in territory that the Russians had occupied from 1941 onward. Expressing righteous horror at this Soviet atrocity, the Germans were inviting neutral delegations to come and view the terrible mass graves. Since Stalin had openly shot multitudes of his own Red Army officers, the charge was at least plausible, and the Polish politicians in London had joined in suggesting an investigation. The fury of the Russian government at this idea was volcanic, and on April 19 the sensation was cresting.

So things were happening; yet in general, on the worldwide fronts the war simply went on, sluggishly here, actively there. No great turning point occurred on April 19. But nobody aboard the *Moray* was likely to forget that day.

* * *

It started with the down-the-throat shot.

"Open the doors forward," Aster said.

Goose pimples rose all over Byron's body. Submariners talked a lot about down-the-throat shots; usually in the calm safety of bars on dry land, or in wardrooms late at night. Aster had often said that in extremis he might try it; and in the training of his new vessel off Honolulu, he had taken many practice shots at a destroyer charging straight for him. Even those dummy runs had been hair-raising. Only a few skippers had ever tried it against the enemy and returned to tell the story.

Aster took the microphone. His voice was quiet, yet vibrant with controlled rage. "All hands hear this. He's heading for us along our torpedo wakes. I'm going to shoot him down the throat. We've been tracking this convoy for three days, and I'm not about to lose it because of those torpedo failures. Our fish ran straight, but they were duds again.

We've still got twelve torpedoes on board, and there are major targets up there, a troop transport and two big freighters. He's the only escort, and if he drives us down and works us over they'll escape. So I'm going to shoot him with contact exploders on a shallow setting. Look alive."

The periscope stayed up. The executive officer reeled off ranges, bearings, target angles, his voice tightening and steadying; Pete Betmann, a man of thirty, bald as an egg, taciturn and quick-witted. Hastily Byron cranked the data into the computer, giving the destroyer an estimated flank speed of forty knots. It was a weird problem, evolving with unbelievable rapidity. No down-the-throat exercise in the attack trainer, or at sea off Honolulu, had gone this fast.

"Range twelve hundred yards. Bearing zero one zero, drifting to port."

"Fire one!"

Thump of the escaping torpedo; jolt of the deck underfoot. Byron had no confidence in his small gyro angle. Luck would decide this one.

"The wake is missing to starboard, Captain," said Betmann.

"Hell!"

"Range nine hundred yards . . . Range eight hundred fifty yards . . ."

Aster's choices were melting like a handful of snow in a fire. He could still order, *"Go deep—use negative,"* and plunge, or he could make a radical turn, probably take a terrific blast from a pinpointed depth-charging, and then hope to go deep and survive. Or he could fire again. Either way the *Moray* was already on the brink.

"Range eight hundred yards."

Could a torpedo still work? It shot out of the tube locked on safety. At eight hundred yards and closing so fast, it might not arm before it struck . . .

"Fire two! Fire three! Fire four!"

Byron's heart was beating so hard, and seemed to have swelled so huge in his chest, that he had to gasp for air. The closing speed of the destroyer and torpedo must be seventy knots! Propellers approaching, *ker-da-TRUMM, ker-da-TRUMM, ker-da-TRUMM—*

BLAMMM!

The exec in a scream: "HIT! My God, Captain, *you blew his bow off!* He's in two pieces!"

Thunderous rumbling shakes the hull.

"HIT! Oh, Captain, he's a shambles! His magazines must be going up! There's a gun mount flying through the air! And wreckage, and bodies, and his motor whaleboat, end over end—"

"Let me have a look," Aster snapped. The exec stepped away from the periscope, his face red and distorted, his naked scalp glistening.

Aster swung the periscope about, droning, "Kay, the two freighters are hightailing it away, but the transport is turning *toward* us. That captain must be demented or in panic. Very good. Down scope!"

Folding up the handles, stepping away from the smoothly plunging shaft of the periscope, Aster bit out clear level words over the microphone. "Now all hands. The U.S.S. *Moray* has scored its first victory. That Jap destroyer is sinking in two sections. Well done. And our prime target, the transport, is heading this way. He's a ten-thousand-tonner, full of soldiers. So here's a big chance. We'll shoot him, then pursue the freighters on the surface. Let's get them all this time, and make up for the convoy we lost and for all those dud fish. Clean sweep!"

Eager yells echoed through the ship. Aster, curt and loud: "Knock it off! Celebrate when we've got 'em. Make ready the bow tubes."

The attack developed like a blackboard drill. Betmann exposed the periscope time after time, crisply rattling off data. The Jap came plodding into position. Perhaps because he was heading away from the sinking pieces of the destroyer he thought he was on an escape course.

"Open the outer doors."

The attack diagram was clear and perfect in Byron's mind, the eternal moving triangle of submarining: the transport steaming along in the sunshine at twenty knots, the *Moray* half a mile on its beam and some sixty feet under water, slinking toward it at four knots, and the torpedoes in the open flooded stern tubes, ready to race from the one to the other at forty-five knots. Only malfunction, massive malfunction of American machinery, could save the Jap now.

"Final bearing and shoot."

"Up periscope! Mark. Bearing zero zero three. Down scope!"

Aster fired a spread of three torpedoes. Within seconds explosions rocked the conning tower, and heavy shocking detonations rang along the hull. Whoops, cheers, rebel yells, laughter, whistles, shouts broke out all over the submarine. In the crowded tower sailors punched each other and capered.

The exec shouted, "Captain, two sure *hits*. On the quarter, and amidships. I see *flames*. She's afire, smoking, listing to starboard, down by the bow."

"Surface and man all guns."

The rush of fresh air at the cracking of the hatch, the shaft of sunlight, the drip of sparkling seawater, the healthy growl of the diesels starting up, touched off in Byron a surge of exhilaration. He seemed to float up the ladder to the bridge.

"God in heaven, what a sight!" said Betmann, coming beside him.

It was a beautiful day: clear blue sky with a few high puffy clouds, gently swelling blue sea, blinding white sun. The equatorial air was humid and very hot. Close by, the transport steeply listed under a cloud of smoke, its red bottom showing. A strident alarm siren was wailing, and yelling men in life jackets were climbing over the side and down cargo nets. A couple of miles away the forecastle of the destroyer still floated, with forlorn figures clinging to it and crowded boats tossing close by.

"Let's circle this fellow," said Captain Aster, chewing on his cigar, "and see where the freighters have got off to."

His tone was debonair, but as he took the cigar from his mouth Byron could see his hand shake. The patrol was a success right now, but by the look of Carter Aster he was ravening for more; tightened grinning mouth, coldly shining eyes. For thirty-seven days, sharpened by the torpedo failure, this greed for action had been building up in him. Until a quarter of an hour ago, a goose-egg first patrol threatened him. No more.

As they rounded the stern, passing the huge brass propeller lifted clear out of the water, a wild sight burst on them. The transport was disgorging its troops on this side. In covered launches, in open landing craft and motorboats, on wide gray rafts, Jap soldiers crowded in the thousands. Hundreds more were swarming on the deck and fleeing down the dangling cargo nets and rope ladders. "Like ants off a hot plate," Aster gaily observed. The blue sea was half-gray with troops bobbing in kapok life vests.

"Good Lord," Betmann said, "how many of them does it hold?"

Aster said absently, peering through binoculars at the two distant freighters, "Oh, these Japs are cattle. They just pack 'em in. What's the range to those freighters, Pete?"

Betmann looked through a dripping alidade. A burst of machine gun fire drowned out his reply, as smoke and flame spurted from a covered launch jammed with soldiers.

"I'll be damned," said Aster, smiling, "he's trying to put a hole in us! He just might, too." Cupping his hands, he shouted, "Number two gun, sink him."

The forty-millimeters opened up, and the Japanese began leaping off the launch. Pieces flew from its hull, but it went on firing for a few seconds, and then the silent smoking little wreck sank. Many inert bodies in green uniforms and gray life vests floated off it.

Aster turned to Betmann. "What's that range, now?"

"Seven thousand, Captain."

"Okay. We'll circle, charge our batteries, and get our pictures of this transport." Aster glanced at his watch and at the sun. "We can overtake those other two monkeys before dusk, easy. Meantime let's sink these boats and rafts, and send all the floaters to join their honorable ancestors."

Byron was more sickened than surprised, but what the exec did surprised him. Betmann firmly put his hand on Aster's forearm as the captain was lifting the bridge microphone to his mouth. "Captain, don't do it." It was said *sotto voce*. Byron, at Aster's elbow, barely heard it.

"Why not?" Aster was just as quiet.

"It's butchery."

"What are we out here for? Those are combat troops. If they're picked up, they'll be in action against our guys on New Guinea in a week."

"It's like shooting prisoners."

"Come on, Pete. What about the guys on Bataan? What about the guys still inside the hull of the *Arizona?*" Aster shook off Betmann's hand. His voice rang out over the deck. "Now gun crews, hear this. All these boats, barges, and rafts are legitimate targets of war, and so are the men in the water. If we don't kill them, they'll live to kill Americans. *Fire at will.*"

On the instant every gun barrel on the *Moray* was spitting yellow fire and white smoke.

"All ahead slow," Aster called down the tube. "Maximum charge on the batteries." He turned to Byron. "Call away the quartermaster. Let's get pictures of that tin can while he's still afloat, and of this fat boy."

"Aye aye, sir." Byron passed the order on his telephone.

The Japanese were leaping frantically off the boats and rafts. The four-inch gun was methodically picking off boats, and at this point-blank range they were flying apart one by one. Soon the rafts and launches were empty, the troops were all in the water, and some were shucking their life jackets to dive deep. Machine gun bullets were drilling rows of white spurts in the water. Byron saw heads bursting redly open like dropped melons.

"Captain," Betmann said, "I am going below."

"Very well, Pete." Aster was lighting a fresh cigar. "Go ahead."

By the time the transport reared its stern up and sank, uncountable lifeless Japanese floated all around the *Moray* on the bloodstained water. A few still swam here and there like porpoises harried by a shark.

"Well, I guess that's that," Carter Aster said. "Time's a-wasting, Byron. We'd better catch those freighters. Secure the gun crews. Set cruising watch. All ahead full."

The sun was low when the *Moray,* overhauling the freighters in an end run at long range, submerged. The unprotected ships were making only eleven knots. Lieutenant Betmann came back on the periscope, good-humored and accurate as though the events of the morning had made no difference to him. But among the crew, they had made a difference. During the daylong chase, whenever Byron had come on a group of sailors, he had been met with silence and odd looks, as though he were interrupting talk not meant for an officer's ears. They were a new crew, just working in together, and they should have been buoyant and noisy over the victories, but they were not.

Lieutenant Betmann was a hard one for Byron to figure out. He had come to the *Moray* from BuOrd; he was a Christian Scientist, and he had initiated voluntary (and ill-attended) Sunday services on the submarine. Whatever his scruples about the morning slaughter, he was now all crisp aggressiveness once more.

Aster gambled three of his remaining five torpedoes on an overlapping shot at the two ships steaming close together. Betmann reported one hit flaring up in the night; the explosion rumbled through the *Moray*'s hull.

"Surface!"

The light in the conning tower was dim and red to protect night vision, but Byron could see the disappointed grimace on Carter Aster's face. The *Moray* came up in moonlight on a choppy sea. The undamaged ship was turning away from its stricken companion, dark smoke pouring out of its funnel and obscuring the stars.

"All ahead full!"

Both freighters began firing wildly at the black shape cutting the swells in phosphorescent spray. Judging by the muzzle flames, they were armed not only with machine guns but also with three-inch cannon; a solid hit from one of these could sink a submarine. But Aster bore on through the red tracers and whirring shells as though they were the ticker tape of a hero's parade, and pulled abreast of the fleeing freighter, which swelled big as an ocean liner and blazed with gunfire.

"Left full rudder. Open the stern tubes." The submarine swung around under a fusillade of crimson tracers and high-whining bullets. The lookouts were cowering behind their bullet shields. So was Byron. Aster, erect and staring astern, fired one torpedo. The night burst into thundering red day. The freighter flamed up amidships.

"Dive, dive, dive!"

Byron, shaking in his shoes, had to admire this. With both targets hit and halted, Aster was taking no more gunfire.

"Okay, after torpedo room," Aster said into the microphone, as the submarine slanted down into the sea, "we got him. Now comes our last torpedo. Our last shot of the patrol. It's the freighter we hit before, and he's a sitting duck. He needs one more punch. So, no foul-ups. Let's sink him and head for the barn."

Aster crept up on the cripple, reversed the submarine, and made his shot at six hundred yards. The *Moray* rocked in the very close underwater explosion, and the crew cheered.

"Surface! Surface! Surface! And I'm so proud of the whole lot of you, I could damn near cry." Indeed, Aster's voice was choking with unabashed emotion. "You're the greatest submarine crew in the Navy. And let me tell you something, the *Moray* has only BEGUN to kill Japs."

Whatever the roiled emotions of the day, the crew was with him again. The cheering and whooping and hugging and handshaking went on and on until the quartermaster cracked the hatch, the diesels coughed and roared, and moonlit seawater dripped down the ladder.

Coming out into the hot night, Byron saw both vessels dead in the water and burning. There was no gunfire. One freighter sank fast, its flame going out like a spent candle. But the other burned on, its broken hulk staying obstinately afloat, until Aster with a yawn told Betmann to finish it off with the four-inch gun. Peppered with blazing hits, it still took a long time to sink. At last the sea went dark, except for the yellow path of a low half-moon.

"Now hear this, gentlemen of the U.S.S. *Moray*," Aster announced, "we will come to zero six seven, the course for Pearl Harbor. When we pass channel buoy number one, ten days from now, we'll tie a broom to the periscope. All engines ahead standard, and God bless you all, you marvelous gang of fighting fools."

Such was the April 19th of Byron Henry.

The broom was up there when they entered Pearl Harbor. On a long streamer behind the broom, four small Japanese flags fluttered. Sirens, foghorns, steam whistles, serenaded the *Moray* all the way up-channel. On the dock at the sub base, a stunning surprise: Admiral Nimitz, in dress whites, stood amid the entire khaki-clad staff of SubPac. When the gangplank went over, Aster called the men to quarters. Nimitz marched aboard alone. "Captain, I want to shake the hand of every officer and man on this ship." He did, passing along the forecastle with his wrinkled eyes agleam; then the SubPac staff came crowding on deck. Somebody brought a *Honolulu Advertiser*. The lead headline was

CLEAN SWEEP ON FIRST PATROL

Sub Wipes Out Convoy and Escort
"One-boat Wolf Pack"—Lockwood

The picture of Aster, grinning in strong sunlight, was recent, but the newspaper had dug up Betmann's Academy graduation photograph, and he looked decidedly odd with all that hair.

Dry land felt good underfoot. Byron made slow progress to the Com-SubPac building. The word was spreading fast about the killing of the Jap troops in the water, and the long walk became a sort of straw poll on Aster's deed. Officers kept stopping him to talk about it, and reactions ranged from nauseated disapproval to bloodthirsty enthusiasm. The vote seemed to go against Aster, though not by much.

Later in the day, Janice flung herself at Byron when he arrived with a wild kiss that dizzied, thrilled, and shot fire through him.

"Holy smoke," he gasped. "*Janice!*"

"Oh, hell, I love you, Briny. Don't you know that? But don't be afraid of me, I won't eat you." She broke loose, eyes glowing, yellow hair tumbled this way and that. Her thin satiny pink dress swished as she darted to a table and brandished the *Advertiser*. "Seen this?"

"Oh, sure."

"And did you get my message? Is Carter coming for dinner?"

"He's coming."

Aster showed up far from sober, wearing several leis that had been piled on him at the officers' club. He draped one flowery wreath on Byron and another on Janice, who gave him a decorous kiss. They washed down a feast of shrimps, steak, baked potatoes, and apple pie à la mode, with four bottles of California champagne, joking randomly and laughing themselves helpless. Afterward Janice donned an apron and ordered them to let her clear up herself. "Conquering heroes," she said a bit thickly, "stay the hell out of my kitchen. Go out on the lanai. No mosquitoes tonight, offshore wind."

On the dark porch facing the canal, as they sank into wicker chairs with the wine bottle between them, Aster said in a flat sober tone, "Pete Betmann has asked to be transferred."

After a silence Byron said, "And? What do we do for an exec?"

"I told the admiral I wanted you."

"Me?" Byron's head was spinning from the wine. He tried to collect himself. "That's impossible."

"Why?"

"I'm too junior. I'm a reserve. Battle stations, sure, I'd love the periscope, but I'm a zilch administrator."

"The roster shows you qualified, and you are. The admiral's considering it. You'd only be the third reserve exec in SubPac, but he's inclined to give me what I want. The other two guys are senior to you, they've been on active duty since '39. But you've done a lot of combat patrolling."

"I had all that dead time in the Med."

"Maintenance at an advance base isn't dead time."

Byron poured for both of them. They drank in darkness. Over the clinking and splashing in the kitchen they could hear Janice singing "Lovely Hula Hands."

After a while Aster said, "Or do you agree with Pete Betmann? Don't you want to sail with me again? That can be arranged, too."

In the long voyage back to base there had been very little talk in the wardroom about the slaughter episode. Byron hesitated, then said, "I haven't asked off."

"We go out there to kill Japs, don't we?"

"They didn't have a fighting chance in the water."

"Horseshit." The word had harsh force because Aster tended to avoid obscenities. "We're in a war. The way to end it, to win it, and to save lives in the long run, is to kill large numbers of the enemy. Right? Or wrong?" No answer from Byron. "Well?"

"Lady, you loved it."

"I didn't mind doing a job on the bastards, no. I admit that. The war was their idea."

Silence in the dark.

"They killed your brother."

"I said I haven't asked off. Drop it, Captain."

Janice sat up talking with Byron long after Aster left, about the patrol, and then about Warren, reminiscing affectionately as they had never done before. He said nothing about Natalie, except that he meant to call the State Department in the morning. When he went off to bed he held out his arms and gave her a passionate kiss. Surprised, moved, she looked into his eyes. "That's for Natalie, isn't it?"

"No. 'Night."

Before she left she looked into his room and listened to his quiet breathing. The Military Government pass on her car eliminated the curfew problem, and she drove through the blackout to the small hotel Aster now stayed at for their meetings. She slipped back into her house a few hours later, weary, spent, aglow with the transient rapture of unauthorized ass. Again she listened to Byron's breathing; heavy, regular, no change. Janice went to bed blissful in body and soul, yet with an irrational wisp of guilty feeling, almost as though she had committed adultery.

The controversy over Aster's killing of the Jap troops went on for a long time within SubPac. It never spilled over to the newspapers, or even to the rest of the Navy. The submariners kept it a family secret. Long after the war, when all patrol reports were declassified, it came out at last. Carter Aster's report described the killing in candid detail, and ComSubPac's endorsement was one of unqualified high praise. The draft endorsement by the chief of staff was also declassified. He had written a long paragraph disapproving of the slaughter of helpless swimmers. The admiral had struck it out with an angry scratch of the pen; the ink splatters still stain the page moldering in the Navy's war files.

"If I had ten more aggressive killers like Aster in this command," the admiral said to the chief of staff at the time, "the war would end a year sooner. I will not criticize Lieutenant Commander Aster for killing Japs. This was a great patrol, and I will recommend him for his second Navy Cross."

64

ARLY in July, the minister of the American legation in Bern heard from Leslie Slote after a very long silence. Ordinary mail from the United States had been cut off since the German seizure of southern France, and there were no official pouches anymore. But the pouches of neutral diplomats were an irregular recourse for getting letters and reports back and forth. One of Slote's old friends in the Swiss Foreign Ministry brought Tuttle the thick envelope—handing it to him, after a meeting on another matter, without a word as he left.

June 3, 1943

Dear Bill,

I'll start by apologizing for the illegibility of my enclosed memorandum on the Bermuda Conference. I'm writing in bed, nursing a sprained ankle. I've resigned from the Foreign Service, so I have no office or secretary.

My sprained ankle is due to a parachute jump. An altered Leslie Slote scrawls these lines! I have always been—to put it charitably—a timid sort. But on quitting the Department I landed in the Office of Strategic Services. I've been on the run ever since, with no notion of where I'll fetch up, but with a novel if somewhat alarmed sense of euphoria, such as a man might have upon falling out of an airplane and finding himself enjoying—however briefly—the panoramic view and cold breeze of the plunge. Images of falling come to me readily, after my parachute jump yesterday: an utter nightmare, yet in a blood-curdling way quite exhilarating.

Of course you know about the OSS. As I recall, General "Wild Bill" Donovan rather ruffled your feathers when he whirled through Bern last year. It is an improvised intelligence outfit, bizarre in the extreme. Obviously I can tell you very little about what I'm doing. *But I am doing something;* and that, after the State Department, is a good feeling. I've been through a professional catastrophe, but things have been moving too fast for me to give much time to self-pity.

Bill, the State Department is a seraglio from which the beauties have all been kidnapped, leaving behind a drove of squeaking eunuchs with nothing to do. Mr. Roosevelt and Mr. Hopkins between them preempt most of foreign policy; General Donovan's outfit is moving in on the rest; and the castratos at State impotently continue to pass papers around which might as well be toilet tissue.

If all this sounds bitter, remember that I've destroyed my career, relinquished ten years of precious seniority, because I think it's the truth. What the State Department did at the Bermuda Conference finished me off, though it was probably only a question of time before I'd have quit anyway. The Jewish problem had grown for me into a cancerous obsession, and Breckinridge Long was aggravating my condition to dementia. Now I am *out*, and recovering.

Long drafted me into the Division of European Affairs, as you know, to handle Jewish problems. He was then under very heavy pressure to break the visa logjam facing refugees from Hitler, and also to do something about the Jews being railroaded to extermination. He's a beset man who has taken to clutching at straws. I guess he wanted one plausible figure in the division with a "pro-Jewish" reputation, who could speak sympathetically to Jews without having any power to help them. And I guess he counted on me, as a good loyal State Department hack, to follow his policies no matter how they went against my grain. The real question is why I accepted the job. The answer is, I don't know. I suppose I hoped that Long meant what he said, and that I could be a loosening, liberalizing, moderating voice on Jewish matters.

If so, I was self-deceived. From the first, and until I left the Bermuda Conference in mid-session, I ran into a blank wall. On the whole, I now feel sorry for Breckinridge Long. I don't even regard him as the villain of the piece. He can't help being what he is. He sent me to Bermuda to be a sort of Gentile Sol Bloom, a support diplomat with demonstrable pro-Jewish sympathies, to be cited at future congressional investigations, if any. My resignation is not going to look very good on the record, but of course I have no interest now in keeping up the State Department façade.

And what a façade it was! How carefully it was stage-managed by our Department and the British Foreign Office to screen out pressure, challenge, and controversy! Newspapermen couldn't get there. Labor leaders, Jewish leaders, protest marchers—the broad ocean protected the conference from all that. Bermuda was lovely with spring flowers, and we met in charming hotels far from the new military bases, with plenty of time off to swim in the pools and drink the island's rum concoctions. In the social evenings amid Bermuda's smart set one could almost forget there was a war on.

Poor Dr. Harold Dodds—the president of Princeton, dragooned for the chairmanship of our delegation—beseeched me to stay on, but by the third day I had had enough. I told him that I was either going to raise the question of the Jews threatened with extermination (*these Jews were a forbidden topic at the conference!*) or I was going to fly back to Washington and resign from the Foreign Service. Dodds was helpless. He couldn't authorize me to go against the policies that bound him. So I left, and at least I brought away a small shred of my self-respect.

The proceedings of the conference haven't yet been published. The Department is now frenziedly pleading a need for secrecy "to protect the measures to aid political refugees." What Messrs. Hull and Long really hope is that interest in the conference will die out, and they'll never have to come clean. But it will not. The pressure for disclosure will build, and there is going to be a hell of an explosion when the truth is uncovered.

My memorandum will give you an inkling of what really happened at Bermuda. You remember that horrible document I received in the Bern movie theatre, describing the Wannsee Conference? I could not authenticate it, but events have since done so with a vengeance. Unless President Roosevelt acts quickly, history will say that the Jews of Europe were destroyed between the hammer of the Wannsee Conference and the anvil of the Bermuda Conference. The American people under Roosevelt will be blamed, equally with the Germans under Hitler, for the massacre! That is a cruel distortion, but it is exactly what Breck Long is bringing about.

You know President Roosevelt well. I send you this memorandum, to do with what you will. It is a clear and true warning of what impends after Bermuda, not only for the European Jews, but for the historical reputation of Franklin Delano Roosevelt, and certainly for the postwar moral position of America in the world. Please read it carefully, and consider whether—in any form you choose to revise or amplify it—it should go to the President.

Hurricanes never find people prepared, Bill, and by the time improvised safety measures are taken, the storm has wreaked its worst. The German massacre of the Jews is a hurricane. There has never been anything like it. It is going on behind the smokescreen of a world war, in a rogue nation cut off from civilized society. It could not be happening otherwise. Recognition of it has been slow, measures to deal with it laggard. But all these mitigating facts will be lost in later years. Seen in retrospect, the Bermuda Conference will be perceived as a ruthless, heartless farce, perpetrated by America and England to avoid taking any action while millions of innocent people were being slaughtered.

So long as the responsibility is not taken from Breck Long this distortion will deepen and harden, yet the final disgrace will not rest with him, for he will be a forgotten small man. If the Bermuda Conference remains the Allies' last word on the Nazi barbarity, Franklin Roosevelt will go down as the great American President who led his country out of depression and into world triumph; but who, with full knowledge of this horrendous massacre, failed the Jews. Don't let it happen, Bill. Warn the President.

For the sake of my own sanity, with this memorandum I sever my accidental involvement in the most terrible crime in the history of the world. The burden was never mine, except in the sense that it is every man's. The world so far refuses to shoulder it. I have tried and failed, because I am nobody and powerless. This memorandum written in blood—the Jews', and mine—is my legacy of the experience.

Sincerely,
Leslie Slote

William Tuttle could readily see in the enclosed memorandum, scrawled on legal-length yellow sheets, the exasperated outpouring of a subordinate quitting his job in anger. The style was hurried, the tone intemperate. That this careful and timorous man had taken a job involving parachutist training sufficiently showed how shaken up he was.

Nevertheless, the memorandum disturbed Tuttle. He had been wondering about the Bermuda Conference. He did not sleep well for a couple of nights, wondering what to do about all this. Breck Long had always seemed to him a sound enough person; a polished self-assured gentleman, very much an insider, a good judge of horseflesh, and all in all anything but a villain.

But Tuttle still resented the recent orders that had come from the State Department to stop transmitting through Department codes the Jewish reports out of Geneva about the exterminations; and he was well aware that all the information he had sent to the Division of European Affairs had vanished into silence. He himself did not like to dwell on the Jewish horror, and he had let the lack of response pass as bureaucratic delay and inattention. But if Long was at the bottom of it, and doing it purposefully, the President perhaps ought to know. How to tell him?

In the end he heavily cut Slote's memorandum, toning down the bitter diatribes against Breckinridge Long. He sent the typed revision to Washington via the Swiss pouch, with a handwritten covering letter marked *Personal and Urgent, for the President.*

August 5, 1943

Dear Mr. President:

   The author of the enclosed document served at the Bermuda Conference and resigned from the Foreign Service in protest. He is a Rhodes Scholar who worked with me here in Bern. I found him a man of rare intelligence, always thoroughly reliable.

   I hesitate to add to your grave burdens, but a twofold concern compels me to do so: firstly, for the terrible fate of the European Jews; secondly, for your own place in history. This report may help fill in for you a true picture of what happened at the Bermuda Conference, behind the official reports. I am afraid I tend to believe Leslie Slote.

   With deepest respect and admiration,

Sincerely,
Bill

CONFIDENTIAL MEMORANDUM

The Bermuda Conference: American and British Complicity in the Extermination of the European Jews

1. *Historical Background*

Since early 1941 the German government has been engaged in a secret systematic operation to murder Europe's Jews. This stark fact goes so far beyond all previous human experience that no social machinery exists to cope with it.

Because of the war the German government is an international outlaw, answerable only to the German people. By police state terror the Nazi regime has reduced them to docile compliance in its savage acts. Yet the sad truth is, popular resistance to the Nazi policy against Jewry has been minimal since Hitler took power.

The roots of the massacre lie in a broad and deep German cultural strain, a sort of desperate romantic nationalism, an extreme reaction to the humane liberalism of the West. This body of thought extols a brutish self-glorification of warlike German "Kultur," and implies, where it does not openly express, virulent anti-Semitism. This is a complex and dark subject. The philosopher Croce traces this uncivilized strain to an event in Roman times, the victory of Arminius in the Teutoburg Forest, which cut off the German tribes from the meliorating influence of Roman law and manners. Whatever the origin, Adolf Hitler's rise and popularity indicate how that strain persists.

2. *Embarrassments of the Allies*

The Bermuda Conference took place because the secret of the massacre leaked out. On December 17, 1942, the governments of the United Nations publicly and jointly warned that its perpetrators would be punished. This official disclosure sparked a strong public demand in the United States and Great Britain for action.

Unfortunately, in his Jewish policy Adolf Hitler struck at the Achilles' heel of Western liberalism.

Quite aside from the Jews, the call for action has come from press, church, progressive politicians, intellectuals, and the like. But other forces, glacially silent and immovable, have prevented action.

What the Jews want from England is the opening of Palestine to unrestricted Jewish immigration, an obvious step to relieve the Nazi pressure. But the British Foreign Office believes it cannot risk Arab opposition, at this stage of the war, to such a step. An equally obvious move for the United States would be emergency legislation to admit the threatened victims of Hitler. But our drastic restrictive laws are the will of Congress, which is against changing the "racial composition" of our country.

If Allied liberalism were government policy, rather than something between an ideal and a myth, these steps would be taken. As realities stand, Adolf Hitler has put the Allies on the spot.

Hence, the Bermuda Conference. It was launched with fanfare as the Allied response to the Nazi horrors. The Conference produced an appearance of action, to placate the demand; and the fact of inaction, to conform to policy. It was a mockery. The diplomatic menials went through the motions with very bad consciences, to which they adjusted with bravado, mendacity, or ulcers.

In all this there was not so much villainy as a pathetic inability to come to grips with history's most monstrous villainy.

That is the heart of the matter. The Nazi massacre of the Jews is still far-fetched newspaper talk to most people, obscured by big battle stories. The German action is so savage, so incomprehensible, so far from the mild dislike of Jews which is an old story everywhere, that public opinion shuts it out of mind. The glare of war makes that easy.

3. *The Conference*

The agreed purpose of the Conference was *"to deal with the problem of political refugees."* Great emphasis was placed on the avoidance of the word "Jews" in the agenda. Moreover, the only "political refugees" that could be discussed were those in neutral countries; that is, people whose lives were already safe! These rules were secret. No word of them ever got out to the press.

Someday the minutes will have to come to light. They will show nothing but a dreary sham, a repulsive exercise in diplomatic dodging, shadowboxing, and double-talking. Every attempt to expand the agenda is beaten down; every suggestion for real action—even to relieve the pileup of refugees in neutral countries—is frustrated. There are no funds; or there is no shipping; or there is no place to send people; or they pose too great a security problem, because of possible spies and saboteurs among them; or the action in question might "interfere with the war effort."

A game of buck-passing goes on and on. The Americans push for North Africa and the Near East as a place to dump refugees. The British insist on an opening up of the western hemisphere. In the end they cordially agree on negative conclusions; and to produce the illusion of action, they agree to revive the moribund Committee on Refugees established by the Evian Conference, a similar fiasco perpetrated in 1938.

It is easy to condemn the delegates who had to go through this contemptible charade. But they were puppets, acting out the policies of their governments, and ultimately the public will of their nations.

4. *The Need for Further Steps*

After the disaster of the Conference, what can still be done?

At best, very little can be done. The Germans are bent on their savage deed. They have most of Europe's Jews in their grip. Only Allied victory can prevent their carrying out their purpose. But *if we will but do with vigor what little we can do, we will be absolved of complicity in the Nazi crime.* As things stand now, the Bermuda Conference has made the United States government a passive bystander at murder.

Some sixteen months from now, there will be a presidential election. The massacre of the European Jews may by then be almost an accomplished fact. The American people will have had another year and a half to overcome their lag in awareness of this incredible horror. Evidence will have mounted to a flood. Conceivably Europe will have been invaded, and some murder camps captured. The American public is a humane one. Though today it does not want to "admit all those Jews," by the end of 1944 it will be looking for somebody to blame for letting the thing happen. The blame will fall squarely on those in power now.

The author of this memorandum knows the President to be a true humanitarian, who would like to help the Jews. But in this vast global war, the problem is a low-priority one. Since so little can be done, and since the subject is so ghastly, Mr. Roosevelt can hardly be blamed for attending to other things.

The agitation to open Palestine or to change the immigration laws seems hopeless. Extravagant mass ransom schemes, and proposals to bomb nonmilitary targets like concentration camps, run afoul of major war-making policies. Still, some things can be done, and must be done.

5. *Short-term Steps*

The single most urgent and useful thing that President Roosevelt can do at once is *to take the entire refugee problem out of the State Department,* and above all away from Mr. Breckinridge Long.

He is now in charge of this problem, and he is a disaster. This unfortunate man, forced out on a limb of negativism, is resolved to do as little as possible; to prevent anybody else from doing any more; and to move heaven and earth to prove that he is right and has always been right, and that nobody could be a better friend of the Jews. At heart he still seems to think that talk of the Nazi massacre is mostly a clever trick to get around the immigration laws.

State personnel have had this viewpoint drummed into them. Too many share his rigid restrictionist convictions. The Department's morale, and its capacity to perform in humanitarian matters, are low. An executive agency must be created, empowered to explore any possibility to save Jewish lives, and to act with speed. Commonsense adjustment of visa rules in itself can at once rescue a large number of Jews *eligible to enter the United States under existing quotas*. They will be no financial burden. Relief funds in almost any magnitude will be procurable from the Jewish community.

Latin America's restrictionism is based on our own. Once the new agency projects to Latin American countries the changed attitude of the United States, some of those countries will follow suit.

The new agency should at once move as many refugees as possible from the four neutral European havens—Switzerland, Sweden, Spain, and Portugal—to relieve the strain on them, and change their present attitude of "the lifeboat is full" to one of welcome to those hunted Jews who can still reach their borders.

The new agency should work on congressional leaders for the temporary admission of perhaps twenty thousand refugees. If ten other countries around the world will follow such a lead, this will be a loud and clear signal to the slaughterers themselves, and to the satellite governments which have not yet handed over their Jewish citizens to the Germans, that the Allies mean business.

For as the tide of war shifts, the murders are bound to slow, and at last stop. Sooner or later, the murderers and their accomplices will take fright. That turning point can come when ninety-nine percent of the Jews are gone, or when sixty or seventy percent are gone. No better figure can probably be hoped for; but even that much would be a historic achievement.

Leslie Slote

• • •

William Tuttle received no acknowledgment of his letter to the President, and never found out whether it had reached him. As a matter of history, the public reaction gradually swelled to a roar during 1943, as the facts of the Bermuda Conference came out. On January 22, 1944, an Executive Order from the White House took the refugee problem out of the State Department's hands. It created the War Refugee Board, an executive agency empowered to deal with "Nazi plans to exterminate all the Jews." A new policy of forceful American rescue action began. By then the hurricane had long been blowing its worst.

65

THE Swiss diplomat who walked into the hospital alongside Jastrow's wheelchair brought a letter from the German ambassador to the director, Comte Aldebert de Chambrun. "You know, of course," said the Swiss casually, "Monsieur's masterpiece, *Le Jésu d'un Juif.*"

Comte de Chambrun was a retired general, a financier, an old-line aristocrat, and an in-law of Premier Laval, all of which made him fairly imperturbable, even in these disordered times. He nodded as he glanced over the letter, which called for the finest possible treatment for the "distinguished author." Since the abrupt departure of most of the staff after Pearl Harbor, the comte had taken on the directorship of the American Hospital. The few Americans left in Paris came there for treatment, but Jastrow was the first from the Baden-Baden group. The comte did not keep up with current American literature and wasn't sure he had ever heard of Jastrow. *A Jew's Jesus!* Strange letter, in the circumstances.

"You will note," went on the Swiss, as though reading his mind, "that the occupying authority considers racial origin irrelevant."

"Just so," replied the comte. "Prejudice cannot pass the doorway of a hospital."

The Swiss received this sentiment with a face twitch, and left. Within the hour the German embassy telephoned to inquire about Jastrow's condition and accommodations. That settled it. When Jastrow began to mend, after difficult two-stage surgery and a few bad days, the director placed him in a sunny room and had him nursed around the clock.

Comte de Chambrun discussed this odd German solicitude for Jastrow with his wife, a very positive American woman with a quick answer for everything. The comtesse was a *grande dame:* a Longworth, related by marriage to the Roosevelts, sister of the former Speaker of the House. She was whiling away the war by managing the American Library, and pursuing her Shakespearean studies. Their son was married to the daughter of Pierre Laval. The comtesse had long since taken on French citizenship, but in talk and manner she remained pungently American, with a patina of rabid French old-nobility snobbishness; a walking anomaly of seventy, begging for the pen of a Proust.

There was nothing in the least odd about the thing, the comtesse briskly told her husband. She had read *A Jew's Jesus,* and didn't think much of it, but the man did have a name. He would soon be going home. What he had to say about his treatment would be widely quoted in American newspapers and magazines. Here was a chance for the Boches to counter the unfavorable propaganda about their Jewish policy; she was surprised only at the good sense they were showing, for she regarded the Germans as a coarse and thickheaded lot.

General de Chambrun also told her about Jastrow's niece. Chatting with her in visiting hours, he had been struck by her haggard sad beauty, perfect French, and quick intelligence. The young lady might work at the library, he suggested, since Jastrow's convalescence would take time. The comtesse perked up at that. The library was far behind in sorting and cataloguing piles of books left behind in 1940 by hastily departing Americans. The Boches might veto the idea; then again, the American niece of a famous author, wife of a submarine officer, might be quite all right, even if she was Jewish. The comtesse consulted the German official who supervised libraries and museums, and he readily gave her permission to employ Mrs. Henry.

Thereupon she lost no time. Natalie was visiting Aaron at the hospital when the comtesse barged into the room and introduced herself. She liked the look of Natalie at once; quite chic for a refugee, pleasantly American, with a dark beauty that might easily be of Italian or even French origin. The old Jew in the bed looked more dead than alive; gray-bearded, big-nosed, with large melancholy brown eyes feverishly bright in a waxy sunken face.

"Your uncle seems to be very sick indeed," said the comtesse in the director's office, where she invited Natalie for a cup of "verbena tea" which tasted like, and perhaps was, boiled grass.

"He almost died of internal hemorrhaging," said Natalie.

"My husband says he can't return to Baden-Baden for a while. When he's well enough he'll be moved to our convalescent home. Now then, Mrs. Henry, the general tells me that you're Radcliffe, with a Sorbonne graduate degree. *Pas mal.* How would you like to do something useful?"

She walked with Natalie to her boardinghouse; declared the place unfit for an American to be caught dead in; cooed, or rather croaked, over Louis; and undertook to move them to decent lodgings. Marching Natalie to an old mansion near the hospital, converted to flats occupied by hospital staff, she then and there arranged room and board for her and the baby. By nightfall she had moved them to the new place, executed the necessary papers at the prefecture, and checked them in with the German administrator of the Neuilly suburb. When she left, she promised to return in the morning and take Natalie to the library by Métro. She would arrange, she said, for someone to look after Louis.

Natalie was quite overborne by this crabbed old fairy godmother materializing out of nowhere. Her transportation into Germany had put her into a state of mild persisting shock. In the Baden-Baden hotel with its unfriendly German staff, incessant German talk, German menus and signs, Gestapo men in the lobby and the corridors, and glum American internees, her nervous system had half-shut down, narrowing her awareness to herself and Louis, to their day-to-day needs, and to possible dangers. The opportunity to go to Paris had seemed like a pardon from jail, once the Swiss representative had assured her that several special-case Americans dwelled freely in German-occupied Paris, and that she would be under Swiss protective surveillance there, just as in Baden-Baden. But before the comtesse burst upon her, she had seen little of Paris. She had cowered in her room, playing with Louis or reading old novels. Mornings and evenings she had scurried to the hospital to visit her uncle and scurried back again, fearing police challenge and having no confidence in her papers.

A new time began with her employment at the library. She had work, the best of anodynes. She was moving about. The first scary check of her papers in the Métro went off without trouble. After all, Paris was almost as familiar to her as New York, and not much changed. The crushing crowds in the Métro, including many young German soldiers, were a disagreeable novelty, but there was no other way to get around Paris now except for bicycles, decrepit old horse carriages, and queer bicycle-taxis like rickshaws. The library task was simple, and the comtesse was enchanted with her speed and ready grasp.

Natalie had mixed feelings about the strange old woman. Her literary talk was bright, her run of anecdotes about famous people tartly amusing; and she was an impressive Shakespeare scholar. Her political and social opinions, however, were hard to take. France had lost the war, she averred, for three reasons; Herbert Hoover's moratorium on German war reparations, the weakening of France by the socialist Front Populaire, and the treachery of the British in running away at Dunkirk. France had been misled by the English and her own stupid politicians into attacking Germany (Natalie wondered whether to believe her ears at that remark). Still, if the French army had only listened to her husband and massed its tank forces in armored divisions, instead of scattering them piecemeal among the infantry, an armored counterstroke in Belgium could have cut off the panzer columns in their dash to the sea, and won the war then and there.

She never troubled to coordinate or justify her opinions and judgments; she just let them off like firecrackers. Pierre Laval was the misunderstood savior of France. Charles de Gaulle was a posturing charlatan, and his statement, "France has lost a battle, not a war," was irresponsible rubbish. The Resistance was a riffraff of communists and bohemians, preying on their fellow Frenchmen and bringing reprisals on them without hurting the Germans. As to the occupation, despite its austerities, there was something to be said for it. The theatre was much more wholesome now, offering classics and clean comedies, not the sexy farces and depraved boulevardier dramas of other days; and the concerts were more enjoyable without all the horrid modern dissonance which nobody really understood.

Anything Natalie said touched off a monologue. Once as they worked together on cartons of books left by an American movie producer, Natalie remarked that life in Paris seemed curiously close to normal.

"My dear child, normal? It's ghastly. Of course the Boche wants to make Paris *seem* normal, even charming. Paris is the showpiece, don't you see, of the 'New Order.' " She uttered the phrase with acid sarcasm. "That's why the theatres, the opera, and the concerts are encouraged and even subsidized. That's why our poor little library is staying open. Dear me, the poor Boches do try so hard to act civilized, but they're such animals, really. Of course, they're a lot better than the Bolsheviks. Actually, if Hitler had just had the common sense not to invade France, just to finish off the Soviet Union, which he obviously could have done in 1940, he'd be a world hero today and there'd be peace. Now we must wait for America to rescue us."

Natalie saw her first yellow star while walking to lunch with the comtesse along a busy boulevard. Two women in smart tailored suits passed them, one talking vivaciously, the other laughing. On both women's suits, over the left breast, the star glared. The comtesse took no notice whatever. As time passed Natalie saw a few more; not many, just an occasional yellow star worn in the same matter-of-fact way. Rabinovitz had told her of a tremendous public roundup of Jews in Paris a year ago; either most of them had been swept away by that, or they were staying out of sight. The placards barring Jews from restaurants and public telephone booths were curling and dusty. Every day, the casually ferocious anti-Semitism in familiar papers like *Paris-Soir* and *Le Matin* startled her, for the front pages looked no different than in peacetime, and some of the columnists were the same.

Occupied Paris did have its peculiarly charming aspect: quiet clean streets free of honking taxicabs and jammed-up automobiles, clear fumeless air, brightly dressed children playing in uncrowded flowery parks, horse carriages bearing women in striking Parisian finery, all as in old paintings of the city. But the leprous trace of occupation was everywhere: large black-lettered signs like CONCORDE-PLATZ and SOLDATEN KINO; yellow wall posters with long lists of executed saboteurs; crimson swastika flags fluttering on official buildings and monuments, on the Arc de Triomphe, on the Eiffel Tower; chalked menus in German outside restaurants, German army machines driving down the wide empty boulevards, and off-duty Wehrmacht soldiers in their green-gray uniforms sloppily strolling the sidewalks with cameras. Once Natalie came on a fife and drum corps leading a goose-stepping guard up the Champs-Elysées toward the Arc de Triomphe with rat-tat-tat and shrill martial music, swastika banners streaming; the occupation was summed up in that one strange glimpse.

The adaptability of the human spirit is its saving. So long as Natalie was buried in work at the library, or spending the evening with Louis, or strolling after lunch along the Seine looking at the bookstalls, she was all right. Once a week she checked in at the Swiss legation. On a day when Louis was ill and she stayed home, a tall well-dressed young Swiss diplomat came calling, to make certain all was well. That was reassuring. Paris seemed less frightening than Marseilles; the people looked less hunted and better fed, and the police acted more civilized.

After three weeks Aaron was moved to the convalescent home and given a room overlooking the garden. Weak and lethargic still, hardly able to talk, he appeared to take the luxurious treatment quite for granted. But it puzzled Natalie. She had accepted the move to Paris as innocuous, since the doctor in Baden-Baden had explained that the American Hospital had an excellent staff, and that her uncle would be better off there than in Frankfurt. Paris itself was incomparably pleasanter than Baden-Baden. Nevertheless, a shadowy dread never quite left her, a dread like that of a child's about the mystery of a locked room, a dread of the unknown; an uneasy sense that the gracious treatment of her uncle and her own freedom in a German-occupied city were not bits of good luck, but a riddle. When the answer came at last at the American Library it was less a surprise than the fright of opening the dark locked room.

The comtesse called from the outer office, "Natalie! We have a visitor. An old friend of yours."

She was squatting amid piles of books in a back room, writing up lists. Pushing the hair away from her face, she hurried out to the office. There Werner Beck stood, bowing, clicking his heels, wrinkling his eyes shut in an amiable smile.

"The minister of the German embassy," said the comtesse. "Why didn't you tell me you knew Werner?"

She had not dressed in formal clothes since leaving Siena; where, despite the casual Italian house arrest, she had sometimes put on a faded long dress for an evening out. By now living out of suitcases, alternating the same few travelling clothes, had become her way of life. In Natalie's shocked and frightened frame of mind that evening, putting on the Cinderella finery which the comtesse had obtained for her seemed a grotesque mockery, a morbid last farewell to her femininity before getting hanged. The stuff fitted; the comtesse's cousin was just her size. Drawing smooth pearly silk stockings on her legs and up her thighs to the garters gave Natalie a very queer feeling. Where did even a rich Parisienne get such stockings nowadays? What would it be like to dress like this for an evening out with Byron in peacetime, instead of for this chilling nightmare?

She did her best to paint herself to match the high-fashion gray crepe silk dress, but she had only rudimentary cosmetics, dry and cracking with disuse: a rouge pot, a lipstick, the stub of an eyebrow pencil, and a little mascara. Louis watched her making up with wide wondering eyes, as though she were setting fire to herself. She was still at this task when the gray-headed baby-sitter looked in. "Madame, your gentleman is here in his car downstairs—oh, madame, but you are ravishing!"

There had been no alternative to accepting Beck's staggering invitation; and had there been, she would have been too frightened to try. To the comtesse's wry comment when he left the library—"Well! The German minister, and *The Marriage of Figaro! Pas mal*"—Natalie had blurted, "But how can he possibly do this? Aside from my being an enemy alien, he knows I'm Jewish."

With a curving grin of her thin wrinkled old mouth—they had never referred to this topic before—the comtesse replied, "My dear, the Germans please themselves, *ils sont les vainqueurs*. The thing is, what will you wear?"

Not a question about Natalie's relation with Beck, not a catty remark; just a brisk getting down to the business of equipping a fellow female for a fashionable night out in Paris. The comtesse's cousin, a dark bucktoothed young woman, was quite buffaloed by the comtesse's sudden appearance at her flat with the American girl. Without many words, if also without visible joy, she meekly produced the finery demanded of her. The comtesse passed judgment on every item, even insisting on a bottle of good scent. Whether the comtesse was doing this out of kindness, or to curry favor with the German minister, Natalie had no way of discerning. She just did it, quickmarch.

Louis stared in a hurt way when his mother left without kissing him. Her lips felt thick and greasy, and she was afraid to smear him up, and herself, too. Down the stairs she went in a wine-colored velvet cowled cloak, feeling after all the womanly excitement of dressing up. She did look beautiful, he was a man, and she was under Swiss protection. This was the scariest thing that had happened to her yet in these endless months of trouble, but she had survived much, and she felt ready for a desperate defense.

The Mercedes stood there in the blue streetlight and the light of a full moon. Murmuring compliments, he stepped out and opened the door for her. The night was warm, and smelled of flowering trees in the railed front garden of the old house.

Natalie said as he started the car, "This may be a tactless question, but how can you be seen with a Jewess?"

His serious face, dimly lit by the glow of the dashboard dials, relaxed in a smile. "The ambassador knows that you and your uncle are in Paris. The Gestapo of course knows, too. They also know I am taking you to the opera tonight. Who you are is nobody else's business. Are you uneasy?"

"Horribly."

"What can I do to reassure you? Or would you rather not go? The last thing I want to do is force a disagreeable evening on you. I thought you might enjoy this. I intended it as a friendly, or at least reconciling, gesture."

Natalie had to find out what this man was up to, if she possibly could. "Well, I'm dressed up now. It's very kind of you."

"You do like Mozart?"

"Of course. I haven't heard *The Marriage of Figaro* in years."

"I'm happy I've hit on a pleasant amusement."

"How long have you known that we were in Paris?"

"Mrs. Henry, I knew that you were in Lourdes." He was driving slowly down the empty black streets. "Winston Churchill, you know, paid General Rommel a handsome compliment during the Africa campaign. 'Across the gulf of war,' he said, 'I salute a great general.' Your uncle is a brilliant scholar, Mrs. Henry, but he isn't a strong or practical man. Getting from Siena to Marseilles surely was your doing. Your escape caused me terrific embarrassment. However, 'across the gulf of war' I salute you. You have courage."

Left hand on the wheel, Beck offered Natalie his pudgy right hand. Natalie could do nothing but shake it. It felt damp and cold.

"How did you find out we were in Lourdes?" Involuntarily she wiped her hand on the cloak, then hoped he didn't notice.

"Through the effort to get you released. The French brought it to our attention at once, naturally, and—"

"What? What effort? We didn't know about any such effort."

"You're sure?" His head turned in surprise.

"It's complete news to me."

"That is interesting." He nodded several times. "Well, there was an approach from Washington to let you cross quietly into Spain. My reaction when you turned up was one of relief. I feared you had come to harm."

Natalie was stunned. Who had tried to get them released? What bearing did it have on their predicament now? "So that betrayed our presence to you?"

"Oh, I was bound to find out. At the embassy we've kept close watch on your group right along. Quite a mixture, eh? Diplomats, journalists, Quakers, wives, babies, whatnot! By the way, the doctor at the Victoria Home informed me today that your uncle is much on the mend."

Natalie said nothing, and after a while Beck spoke again. "Don't you find the Comtesse de Chambrun an interesting woman? Very cultured?"

"A character, certainly."

"Yes, that's an apt word for her."

That ended the chitchat. Walking out of the blackout into the blaze of the opera foyer dazzled Natalie. A time machine, as it were, hurtled her back to the Paris of 1937. Nothing was different from her opera-going evenings with Leslie Slote, except the scattering of German uniforms. Here was the essence of the Paris she remembered, this grandiose lobby with its marble columns, magnificent staircase, and rich statuary; the hairy students in raincoats with their short-skirted girl friends, crowding amid working people toward the entrances to the cheap seats; the middle-class comfortable-looking couples heading for the orchestra; and the thin glittery stream of the beau monde threading through the crowd. The noise was animated and very French, the faces —perhaps a shade more pinched and pallid than in the old days—were mostly French, and the smart few were pure French top to toe; especially the women, the eternal elegant Parisiennes, beautifully coiffed and made up, displaying in every flash of eye, turn of bare arm, quick laughter, the arts of shining and pleasing. Some were with Frenchmen in dinner jackets, some with German officers. In the commoner crowd German soldiers also escorted French girls, prettily gotten up and glowing with kittenish vivacity.

Perhaps because Natalie was in an aroused state, with the adrenalin pumping at the alarming proximity of Dr. Beck, this plunge into the opera lobby dazzled her not only with light, but with a searing mental flash. Who then, she thought, were the "collaborationists," derided and excoriated by the Allied press and the de Gaulle broadcasts? Here they were. Wasn't it so? They were the French. They were the people. They had lost. They had spilled rivers of blood to win the first war, paid their taxes for twenty years, done what their politicians had demanded, built the Maginot Line, gone to war under prestigious generals; and the Germans had taken Paris. *Eh bien, je m'en fiche!* If the Americans would come to the rescue, well and good. Meantime, they would pursue their French ways under the Boches. And since the hardships were many and the pleasures few, these few were all the more to be savored. In this moment Natalie felt she half-understood the Comtesse de Chambrun. There was one difference from 1937, she realized, as she and Beck moved through the crowd to their seats. Then there had been many Jewish faces in every opera audience. Here there was not one.

The first notes of the overture swept across her nerves like a wind through harp strings, setting up shuddery vibrations; the more so because of her terrific tension. She tried to give herself to the music, but within a few measures her mind was racing back over Beck's disclosures. Who could have made that futile and damaging approach when they were in Lourdes? As she puzzled and wondered and worried, the curtain rose on a setting as opulent as any in peacetime. Figaro and Susanna, both excellent singers, launched into their immortal high-spirited antics. Natalie did not get much out of this *Marriage of Figaro,* though it was a polished performance. Her mind kept darting here and there over her predicament.

For the entr'acte Beck had reserved a little table in one of the smaller lounges. The waiter greeted them with an amiable smile and bow. *"Bonsoir, Madame, bonsoir, Monsieur le Ministre."* He whisked away the *reservé* sign, and brought champagne and sugar cakes.

"By the bye," Beck said, after some judicious comments on the singers as he ate cakes and sipped wine, "I've been rereading your uncle's broadcast scripts. He was truly prescient, do you realize that? The things he wrote a year ago are being said now all over the Allied world. Vice President Henry Wallace recently gave a speech that might have been lifted from your uncle's pages. Bernard Shaw, Bertrand Russell, many such first-class minds, have been saying these things. Astonishing."

"I haven't had much contact with the Allied world."

"Yes. Well, I have the press cuttings. When Dr. Jastrow is stronger, he ought to see them. I've been sorely tempted to publish his scripts.

Really, all that talk about further polishing was silly. They are gems. Memorable essays, with a beautiful intellectual progression to them." Beck paused as the waiter refilled his glass. Natalie wetted her lips with wine. "Don't you think he might want to broadcast them now? Perhaps over Radio Paris? Really, he owes me that much."

"He's too weak to discuss anything like that."

"But his doctor told me today that he should have his strength back in a couple of weeks. Is he comfortable at the Victoria Home?"

"He has had the best of everything."

"Good. I insisted on that. The Frankfurt hospital is very good, but I knew that he'd be happier here—ah, the first bell already, and you've hardly touched your wine. Isn't it all right?"

Natalie drank off her glass. "It's very good."

The torrent of brilliant music thereafter passed by Natalie like distant train noises. Fearful possibilities crowded on her, as the singers on the stage capered through their farcical disguises and misunderstandings. Once again, the worst possibility was proving the reality. The move to a hospital in Paris had not been innocuous. Dr. Beck had wanted to get them here, had bided his time, and had used the mischance of Aaron's illness to do it, since more brutal tactics might have embarrassed him with the Swiss. And what now? Aaron would still balk at broadcasting; and even if he agreed, wouldn't that only seal his fate and probably hers? Obviously he could repudiate the broadcasts as soon as he returned to the United States, and Dr. Beck was smart enough to know that. Therefore once the Germans had those recordings, they would hold on to Aaron in one way or another, and very likely to herself as well. Could the Swiss "protection" hold in such a case, considering their dubious status?

Yet what would happen if Aaron confronted Werner Beck with an outright refusal? In Follonica he had played out the procrastination game.

The trap, in fact, had sprung, or so it seemed to her. It was the most horrible imaginable sensation to be sitting there in the Paris Opera in a borrowed Worth original, with a thickly painted face, with a nervous stomach rebelling at the glass of wine she had gulped, beside a polite and intelligent man, a former Yale graduate student, in every nuance of word and manner a cultivated and civilized European, who nevertheless when it came right down to it was threatening her and her baby with a veiled hideous future. And this was not a preposterous dream from which she would wake up; it was reality.

"Perfectly charming," said Dr. Beck, as the curtain descended to great applause, and the singers came out to bow. "And now for a bite of supper, eh?"

"I must get home to my baby, Dr. Beck."

"You'll be home very early, I promise you."

He took her to a crowded dim restaurant nearby. Natalie had heard about it in the old days: far too expensive for student purses, requiring reservations a day in advance. Here the uniformed German customers were bald or grizzle-haired generals, and the Frenchmen tended to potbellies and naked pates. She recognized two politicians and a famous actor. Some of the women were gray and plump, but for the most part they were, once again, exquisite young Parisiennes, dressed to kill and bubbling with charm.

The very smell of food nauseated Natalie. Beck advised her to try the Loire salmon; this was the only place in Paris where one could get Loire salmon just now. She begged off, asking for an omelette, and when it came she ate only a fragment, while Beck devoured his salmon with serene appetite. Around them the Germans, the prosperous French insiders, and their women were eating duck, whole fresh fish, and roast meats, quaffing good wines, arguing, laughing, on top of the world. It was an incredible sight. Rationing was very severe in Paris. The papers were full of feature articles and sourly humorous pieces on the food shortage. At the convalescent home Aaron's daily ration of custard, requiring an egg, was regarded as royal fare. But for enough influence or money, at least in this obscure oasis, Paris was still Paris.

Natalie drank a little white wine to quiet Beck's urging. There was something so gross, she thought, about what he was doing; the swanky entertainment to soften her up, and the simultaneous harsh pressure of his demands, which he kept up over supper in wheedling tones. Even before the food came, he was at it again. When they had first turned up in Lourdes, he said, Gestapo headquarters in Paris had wanted to take them into custody at once, as Jewish fugitives from Italy with faked papers. Luckily, Ambassador Otto Abetz was a cultured and spiritual man. Thanks only to Dr. Abetz they had gone on to Baden-Baden. Dr. Abetz had read Dr. Jastrow's broadcast scripts with tremendous enthusiasm. In Dr. Abetz's view, the only way to achieve a positive outcome of the war now was for the Anglo-American allies to realize that Germany was fighting their fight, the fight of Western civilization, against brutish Slav imperialism. Anything that could promote understanding with the West was of huge importance to Ambassador Abetz.

That was the sugar. The pill came as they were eating. Beck let her have it casually, while smacking his lips over the salmon. The Gestapo pressure to arrest them had never ceased, he informed her. The Gestapo was exceedingly anxious to question them about their trip from Siena to Marseilles. Policemen, after all, had their job to do. Dr. Abetz had been shielding Dr. Jastrow thus far, said Beck, and if he withdrew his protection, the Gestapo would at once sweep them in. Beck could not be responsible for what happened after that, though he would be most enormously distressed. Swiss diplomatic protection, in such a case, would be like a straw fence against a fire. The Swiss had the whole record of their illegal escape from Italy. In view of Natalie's and Dr. Jastrow's clear criminal record the Swiss would be powerless. Dr. Otto Abetz was their shield and their hope.

"Well," Dr. Beck said, turning off the motor as he parked outside her house, "I trust the evening proved not so bad, after all."

"Thank you very much for the opera and the supper."

"My pleasure. Despite all your vicissitudes, Mrs. Henry, I must say you look more lovely than ever."

Good God, was he going to make a pass at her, too? She said hastily and coldly, "Every stitch I'm wearing is borrowed."

"The comtesse?"

"Yes, the comtesse."

"So I assumed. Dr. Abetz will be awaiting a report from me on our evening. What can I tell him?"

"Tell him I enjoyed *The Marriage of Figaro.*"

"That will charm him," Beck said with his eye-shutting smile, "but he will be strongly interested in your position on the matter of the broadcasts."

"It will be up to my uncle."

"You yourself are not rejecting the idea out of hand?"

Natalie bitterly thought how much simpler it would be—however skin-crawling—if all he really wanted was to sleep with her.

"I don't have much choice, do I?"

He nodded, a pleased look on his shadowy face. "Mrs. Henry, our evening has been well spent if you understand that. I would love to have a glimpse of your delightful boy, but I suppose he is asleep now."

"Oh, for hours."

After a long moment, during which Beck silently smiled at her, he got out and opened the door.

The flat was dark.

"*Maman?*" A wide-awake voice.

Natalie turned on a light. In a chair in the sitting room beside Louis's cot, the old lady dozed under a blanket. Louis was sitting up, blinking and joyously smiling, though his face was tear-streaked. The light woke the old woman. She apologized for going to sleep and waddled out, yawning. Quickly Natalie rubbed off all the paint with a ragged towel, and scrubbed her face with soap. She came to Louis and hugged and kissed him. He clung to her.

"Louis, you must go to sleep now."

"*Oui, maman.*" Since Corsica, she had been *maman*.

As he snuggled down under his blanket, she began to sing in Yiddish the lullaby that had become his bedtime ritual in Marseilles, and ever since:

> *Under Louis's cradle*
> *Lies a little white goat.*
> *The little goat went into business,*
> *That will be your career.*
> *Raisins and almonds,*
> *Sleep, little boy, sleep, dear.*

Louis drowsily sang along, mangling the Yiddish in his babyish way.

> *Rozhinkes mit mandlen,*
> *Shlof, mein ingele, shlof.*

One glance at Natalie's face next day told the comtesse that the opera evening had not been an unalloyed delight. She asked, as Natalie set down the two bags of clothing by the desk, how it had gone.

"All right. It was terribly generous of your cousin."

With that, Natalie went silently to work on catalogue cards in her own tiny office. After a while the Comtesse de Chambrun came in and shut the door. "What's up?" she twanged, sounding very little like a French noblewoman.

Turning haunted eyes on her, Natalie did not reply. In her fog of fear she hesitated to take any step, not knowing what pits surrounded her. Could she trust this collaborationist woman? That question, with others as hard, had kept her awake all night. The comtesse sat down on a small library stool. "Come on, we're both Americans. Let's hear."

Natalie told the Comtesse de Chambrun the whole story. It took a long time. She was under such strain that twice she lost her voice, and had to drink water from a carafe. The comtesse listened wordlessly, eyes bright as a bird's, and said when she finished, "You had better go back to Baden-Baden at once."

"Back to Germany? How will that help?"

"Your best protection is the chargé d'affaires. Tuck's a flaming New Dealer but he's competent and tough. You have no advocate here. The

Swiss can only go through the motions. Tuck will fight. He's got t|
threat of the German internees in the U.S.A. You're in a situatic
where once things happen, it's too late to protest. Can your unc
travel?"

"If he must, he will."

"Tell the Swiss you want to rejoin your group. Your uncle misses h
fellow journalists. The Germans have no right to hold you here. Mo|
quickly. Ask them to get in touch with Tuck right away, and to arran|
your return to Baden-Baden. Or I will."

"It's risky to involve yourself, Comtesse."

With a grim writhing smile of ribbon lips, the comtesse stood u|
"Let us go and talk to the comte."

Natalie went along. It was a plan; otherwise she was at the end of t|
road. The comtesse stopped at the hospital, and Natalie went on to t|
convalescent home. Aaron's vitality was too low for a violent reaction
the news about Beck. He shook his head wearily and murmure|
"Nemesis." To the proposal that they return to Baden-Baden, he sa|
he left it in Natalie's hands; they must do whatever was best for herse
and Louis. He felt strong enough for the journey, if that was the dec
sion.

When Natalie rejoined the comtesse at the hospital, her husband ha
already talked to the Swiss minister, who had promised to get in tou|
with Tuck and arrange for the return to Baden-Baden, anticipating r
difficulty.

Nor did there seem to be any. The Swiss legation telephoned Natal|
next day at the library to say that everything was in order. The Ge|
mans had approved the return, the railroad tickets were in hand. Tel|
phone communication with Tuck in Baden-Baden was limited, and ha|
to be routed through the Berlin switchboard, but they expected to |
able to notify him before Jastrow left Paris. That same afternoon t|
Swiss telephoned again: a snag. Ambassador Abetz was personally i|
terested in the famous author, and was sending his own physician to e
amine Jastrow and certify his fitness for travel.

When she heard that, Natalie knew the game was lost. So it was. Tl
Swiss legation reported the following day that the German doctor ha
declared Jastrow was in very poor condition and should not be move
for a month. Ambassador Abetz therefore felt he could not take the r|
sponsibility of permitting him to leave Paris.

*   *   *

66

Fortress Europe Crumbles

(from "Hitler as Military Leader," the epilogue to *Land, Sea, and Air Operations of World War II,* by General Armin von Roon)

TRANSLATOR'S NOTE: *Armin von Roon's epilogue gives a vivid picture of the Führer in action, especially as he was falling apart. In this reminiscence Roon is much harder on Hitler than in the operational analysis. His German editor notes that Roon drafted this memoir on his last sickbed, and did not revise it.*

The memoir opens with these words:

For more than four years I observed Adolf Hitler at close hand in Supreme Headquarters. Keitel and Jodl, who had the same opportunity, were hanged by the Allies. Most of the generals who knew the Führer well were executed by him, or sickened and died from the strain, or fell on the battlefield. I have seen no military memoir which truly portrays him as a man. The books of Guderian and Manstein pass over his personal aspects in understandable silence.

In my military history I have acknowledged his adroitness and his inspiring force as a politician, and have cited his flare for strategic and tactical decision-making in war, especially involving surprise. I have indicated that at his peak he seemed to us the soul of Germany reborn. I have also suggested his serious failings as a supreme commander that led to catastrophe.

Personally, he more and more revealed himself in adversity as a low and ugly individual. In his behavior after the July 20, 1944, assassination attempt he showed his true colors. Nobody who sat beside him as I did, and saw him gloat and giggle and applaud at motion pictures of great German generals, my revered superiors and friends, strangling naked in nooses of piano wire, their eyes popping from their discolored faces, their purple tongues thrust out, blood, urine, and feces streaking down their jerking bodies, could thereafter feel anything for Adolf Hitler but distaste.

If Germany is ever to rise again, we must uproot the political and cultural weaknesses that led us to follow a man like this to defeat, disgrace, and partitioning. Hence I have written this unsparing personal description of the Führer as I saw him in his headquarters.

This is a far cry from Roon's encomiums in the first volume of Land, Sea, and Air Operations; *such as, "A romantic idealist, an inspiring leader dreaming grand dreams of new heights and depths of human possibilities, and at the same time an icy calculator with iron willpower, he was the soul of Germany."*

Roon seems to have decided to level about the Führer before he died. Or possibly he felt more kindly toward him in writing about the victorious years; then, as he worked through the second volume, the bitterness of collapse came back to mind. At any rate, the epilogue is a warty picture of Hitler and a brisk recapitulation of the war. My translation of World Holocaust *concludes with excerpts which sketch the war to the end.—V.H.*

Tunis and Kursk

Hitler's phantom "Fortress Europe," a pure propaganda bluff, began to crumble visibly in July 1943, when the Red Army smashed our big summer offensive at Kursk, the Anglo-Americans landed in Sicily, and Mussolini fell.

These disasters stemmed straight from Hitler's two most colossal and pigheaded blunders: Stalingrad and Tunis. When I returned from my inspection trip to Tunis I told Hitler that Rommel was right, that our successes against the green American soldiers at Kasserine Pass were ephemeral, that in the long run we couldn't supply three hundred thousand Italian and German troops across a sea dominated by enemy navies. But Göring airily assured Hitler that Tunis was "just a hop" from Italy, and that the Luftwaffe would keep the armies supplied. Despite Göring's abject failure to make good the identical boast at Stalingrad, Hitler accepted this and kept pouring troops into North Africa, when he should have been evacuating the ones who were there. Had he taken out all those troops to Italy as an operating reserve, they might well have pushed the Allies off Sicily, and kept Italy in the war. We never recovered in the south from the Tunis bloodletting.

The Kursk offensive was just as ill-advised. My son Helmut fell there on July 7 at the head of a tank battalion under Manstein. He was a studious gentle lad who perhaps would not have been a professional soldier if not for his father's example. He died for Germany in the gigantic and futile operation called *Citadel,* the last gasp of German strategic initiative.

Like Guderian and Kleist, I was against Citadel. The Anglo-Americans were bound to attack the continent somewhere soon, and we had to stay uncommitted and mobile till we knew where the blow would fall. The sensible course was to straighten our lines in the east, gather strong reserves, let the Russians commit themselves, and then smash them with a counterattack as we did at Kharkov. Manstein was the master of this backhand stroke;* another such bloody setback and the Soviets might have proved more flexible in the secret peace talks. The Russians were showing interest, but their demands were still too cocky and unrealistic. No doubt what Hitler wanted at Kursk was a big victory that would improve his bargaining position with Stalin.

But Manstein and Kluge fell in love with the Citadel plan. As an actor offered a star part in a bad play will take it and hope to pull off a success, so generals become intoxicated by plans for large-scale operations which they will command. In the hinge of our front between Manstein's Army Group South and Kluge's Army Group Center, the Russians in their winter counterattacks had punched a deep westward bulge around the city of Kursk. Manstein and Kluge were to drive armored pincers in from north and south, cut off this bulge of territory, bag a reverse Stalingrad of Russian prisoners, and then drive on to God knows what great victories through this gaping hole torn in the Soviet lines.

A charming vision, but we lacked the means.

Hitler loved to reel off figures of divisions available for combat. We had hordes of such "divisions," but the figures were poppycock. Nearly all these divisions were understrength, and the men they had lost were the best troops, the fighting head, leaving the flabby administrative tail. Other divisions had been wiped out and were mere names on charts. But Hitler had ordered these "reconstituted"; and behold, by the breath of his mouth, they were again—in his mind—the full-strength trained fighting forces he had squandered forever on the Volga, in the Caucasus, and in Tunis. He was retreating into a dream world where he was still the triumphant master of the continent, commanding the strongest army on earth. This retreat went on until it ended in outright paranoia. But out of that private dreamland, until April 1945, there issued a stream of insensate orders which the German fighting man had to carry out on the harsh and bloody field of battle.

Moreover, while the Wehrmacht had been going downhill, the Red Army had been reviving and growing. The Soviet generals had been studying our tactics for two years. American Lend-Lease trucks, canned food, tanks, and planes, together with new Russian tanks from factories behind the Urals, had stiffened the real, not phantom, fresh divisions from Russia's limitless

---

* German—*aus der Rückhand schlagen,* a military term borrowed from tennis.—V.H.

manpower. Of all these adverse factors our intelligence warned us, but Hitler paid no attention.

Still, the Kursk attack might have had a chance in May, as first planned, when the Russians were worn out by their counterattacks and had not yet dug into the salient. But he put it off for six weeks so as to use our newest tanks. I warned Jodl that this would put Citadel squarely into the time-frame of the probable Anglo-American landing in Europe, but as usual I was ignored. The Russians used the time well to harden up the haunches of the Kursk bulge with mine fields, trenches, and antitank emplacements, while bringing in more and more forces.

Our intelligence spoke of *half a million railroad cars* entering the salient with troops and matériel! Hitler's response was to commit more and more divisions and air wings to Citadel. As in an American poker game, the stakes of this gamble kept building up on both sides, until Hitler had thrown in as many tanks as we had used in the entire 1940 campaign in the west. At last, on July 5, despite serious second thoughts of even Manstein and Kluge because of the two-month delay, Hitler unleashed the attack. What ensued was the world's biggest tank and air battle, and a total fiasco. Our pincers made very heavy weather against the Russian static defenses and swarms of tanks, achieving penetration of only a few miles. The attack was five days old and going very badly, north and south, when the Allies landed in Sicily.

What was Hitler's reaction? At a hurriedly summoned conference, he announced with great assumed glee that since the Anglo-Americans had now presented him with an opportunity to smash them in the Mediterranean, "the true theatre of decision," Citadel would be called off! That was his way of wriggling out of his failure. Not a word of apology, regret, or acknowledgment of error. Eighteen of our best remaining armored and motorized divisions, a striking force which we could never replace, and which should have been hoarded as a precious operational reserve, had been thrown away in the Kursk battle on a dreamy echo of the grand summer campaigns of the past. With Citadel all German offensives were over. Any attacks we made for the rest of the war were tactical counterthrusts to stave off defeat.

Hitler soon learned that we could not just "call off" a major offensive. There was the little matter of the enemy. On both sides of the Kursk salient the Russians struck back, and within a month freed the two central anchors of our eastern line, the cities of Orel and Belgorod. After Citadel our whole front slowly and inexorably crumbled before a Russian advance that stopped only at the Brandenburg Gate. If Stalingrad was the psychological turning point in the east, Kursk was the military pivot.

My feelings about my son have no place here. He died advancing at Kursk. Thereafter millions of Germany's sons were to die retreating, so as to keep the heads of men like Hitler and Göring on their shoulders.

The Fall of Mussolini

Meantime, my inspection trip to Sicily and Rome convinced me that Italy was about to drop out of the war or change sides. I saw that we must cut our losses and form a strong defense line in the Apennines at the northern end of the Italian boot. There was nothing to be gained by trying to hold on to Italy. From the start of the war this nation had been one gigantic *bouche inutile,* gulping enormous quantities of Germany's war resources to no result. The southern front was a chronic abscess. The Anglo-Saxons were welcome to occupy and feed Italy, I wrote in my summary report, and our forces thus released would help stabilize the eastern front and defend the west.

When I told this to Keitel at Berchtesgaden, he drew a face like an undertaker's and warned me to change my tune. But I was past caring. My only son was dead. I was suffering seriously from high blood pressure. To be transferred from Supreme Headquarters to the field seemed to me a welcome prospect.

So at the briefing conference I presented the picture as I had seen it. The Allies had total air superiority over Sicily, and Palermo had been flattened. The Sicilian divisions assigned to defend their island were fading into the countryside. In the German-held sector of Sicily the civilians were cursing and spitting at our soldiers. Rome looked like a city already out of the war, for soldiers were scarcely to be seen on the streets. Our German troops were staying out of sight, and the Italian soldiers were shedding their uniforms wholesale. I had encountered only evasiveness from Badoglio on the whole question of bringing more German divisions into Italy, and the Italians were *strengthening their Alpine fortifications,* an action which could only be directed against Germany. Such was the situation report I presented to Hitler.

He listened with his head down between his shoulders, glaring at me from under his graying eyebrows, now and then curling one side of his mouth in the half-smile, half-snarl that distorted his mustache, showed his teeth, and signalled extreme displeasure. His only comment was that "there still must be some worthwhile people in Italy. They can't have all turned rotten." As for Sicily, his inspiration was to assume command himself. Of course this made not the slightest difference.

Still, my report must have sunk in, because he arranged a meeting with Mussolini. It took place in a country house in northern Italy a few days before Il Duce fell, and it was a dismal affair. Hitler had nothing new to offer the sick-looking disheartened Mussolini and his staff. He spewed out optimistic statistics by the hour on manpower, raw materials, arms production, details of improved or new weaponry while the Italians looked at each other with their expressive miserable dark eyes. The end was written on their faces. During the meeting Mussolini received a dispatch saying that the Allies were making their first air raid on Rome. He handed the message to Hitler, who barely glanced at it, then resumed his boasting about our rising arms production and marvelous new weapons.

The scenes in Supreme Headquarters when Mussolini fell were horrendous. Hitler was beside himself with rage, howling and storming at the treachery of the Italian court, and the Vatican, and the Fascist leaders who had deposed Mussolini. His crude language and his threats were frightful. He would take Rome by force, he said, and get hold of "that rabble, that scum"—by which he meant King Victor Emmanuel, the royal Family, and the whole court—and make them creep and crawl. He would seize the Vatican, "clean out all that pus of priests," shoot the diplomatic corps hiding in there, lay hands on all the secret documents, then say it was a mistake of war.

He kept trying to get Göring on the phone. "There's an ice-cold fellow," he said. "Ice-cold. At times like these you need a man who's ice-cold. Get me Göring, I say! Hard as steel. I've been through any number of tough ones with him. Ice-cold, that fellow. Ice-cold." Göring hurriedly came, but all he did was agree with everything Hitler said, using vulgar language and bad jokes. That constituted being ice-cold.

The hundred urgent decisions and moves for keeping Italy in the war, at least while we peaceably introduced enough German troops to take over the country, were hammered out in our OKW headquarters. Hitler spent that time feverishly plotting a coup d'etat in Rome to restore Mussolini, which was impossible to execute and which he dropped; also the parachute rescue of the imprisoned Duce, which did come off and may have made them both feel better, but accomplished nothing. In fact, the photograph flashed around the world of a jolly uniformed Hitler, greeting the shrunken cringing ex-Duce in an ill-fitting black overcoat and black slouch hat, with a sickly smile on his white face, proclaimed louder than any headlines that the famous Axis was dead, and that Fortress Europe was doomed.

My Rise

All this had the surprising and unwelcome effect of restoring me to Hitler's favor. He asserted that I had seen through the Italian treachery before anybody else, that "the good Armin has a head on his shoulders," and so on. Also, he had heard of Helmut's death, and he put on a tragic face to commiserate with me. He praised me at briefings, and—a rare thing for a General Staff officer in those days—invited me to dinner. Speer, Himmler, and an industrialist were his other guests that night.

It was a miserable experience. Hitler must have talked for five consecutive hours. Nobody else said anything except a perfunctory word of agreement. It was all a high-flown jumble of history and philosophy, with a great deal about the Jews. The real trouble with the Italians, he said, was that the marrow of the nation had been eaten out by the cancer of the Church. Christianity was just a wily Jewish scheme to get control of the world by exalting weakness over strength. Jesus was not a Jew, but the bastard son of a Roman soldier. Paul was the greatest Jewish swindler of all time. And so on, ad nauseam. Late in the evening he made some interesting observations about Charlemagne, but I was too numbed to pay close attention. Everybody was stifling yawns. All in all the verbal flatulence was as unbearable as the physical flatulence. No doubt that was a weakness he could not control, due to his bad diet and irregular habits, but sitting near the Führer at table was no privilege. How a man like Bormann endured it for years I cannot imagine.

I was not asked again, but my hope of escaping from Headquarters and serving in the field went by the board. Jodl and Keitel now were all smiles to me. I did get a month's medical leave, and so was able to see my wife and console her. By the time I returned to Wolfsschanze, Italy had surrendered and our long-planned Operation Alaric to seize the peninsula was in full swing.

And so the drain to the south was to go on to the last. Adolf Hitler could not face the political setback of giving up Italy. While our armies humiliated the far stronger Anglo-Saxons there, forcing them to inch up the boot with heavy loses, it was all a terrible military mistake. This obtuse political egoism of Hitler, wasting our strength southward when we could have held the Alps barrier with a fraction of Kesselring's forces, set the stage for total national collapse under the squeeze from east and west.

* * *

67

THOUGH plunged in passion often, Pamela Tudsbury had experienced romantic love just once; and she flew from Washington to Moscow in August for a last glimpse of Captain Henry, the man for whom she felt that love, before she married somebody else.

Long after she had given up on the Soviet Union, in fact after she had given up on journalism and had decided to join Burne-Wilke in New Delhi, the visa suddenly came through. At once she changed her travel route so as to include Moscow, and to justify that, she put off quitting her job with the *Observer*. If Pamela's nature was excessively passionate, her head was on fairly straight, and she now knew beyond a doubt that her writing was but a thin echo of a dead man's. Cobbling up her father's dispatches when he was ill or weary had been one thing; but producing fresh copy with his insights and his verve was beyond her. She was not a journalist, but a ghost. Nor did she deceive herself about her reasons for marrying Burne-Wilke. Like the attempt at journalism, that decision had whirled into the vacuum left by Tudsbury's death. He had proposed at a vulnerable moment, when her life had loomed sad and empty. He was a gracious man, an extraordinary catch, and she had consented. She did not regret it. They could be happy enough together, she thought, and she was lucky to have attracted him.

Why then was she detouring to Moscow? Mainly because of what she had seen of Rhoda Henry in casual encounters at dances and parties, usually in the company of a tall gray-haired Army colonel. Rhoda had acted sprightly and cordial toward her, and—so it had struck Pamela—rather proprietary toward the imposing Army man. Before leaving Washington Pam had telephoned her, figuring she had little to lose. Rhoda had told her gaily that Byron was exec of his submarine now; Pamela must be sure to give Pug this news, and "tell him to watch his weight!" Not a trace of jealous concern or artificial sweetness; very puzzling. What had happened to the marriage? Had the reconciliation been so complete that Rhoda could act as she pleased? Or was she betraying Pug again, or working up to it? Pamela had absolutely no idea.

Since Midway she had had no word from him, not so much as a note of condolence on the much-publicized death of her father. Wartime mails were uncertain. In her letter from Egypt about Burne-Wilke, she had invited him to object to the engagement; no answer. But had it reached him before the sinking of the *Northampton?* Again, she had absolutely no idea. Pamela wanted to know how things stood with Victor Henry, and the only way to find out was to face the man. The thousands of extra miles of wartime travel in midsummer were nothing.

Nothing, yet prostrating. She all but collapsed into the embassy car that met her at the Moscow airport. Flying stop-and-go across North Africa, and then waiting three days in the dusty fly-ridden inferno of Tehran, had done her in. The driver, a little Cockney dressed in proper black, not visibly suffering from the Moscow heat, kept glancing at her in his rearview mirror. Weary though she was, Lord Burne-Wilke's slim fiancée, so un-Russian and so elegant in a white linen suit and white straw hat, looked to the homesick man every inch a future viscountess, and he was thrilled to be driving her. He was sure she must be doing newspaper work as a lark.

Moscow itself appeared much the same to the exhausted Pamela: flat stretches of drab old buildings, many unfinished structures abandoned to wind and weather because of the war, and fat barrage balloons still floating in the sky. But the people were changed. When she and her father had hastily left in 1941, with the Germans nearing the city and all the big shots skedaddling to Kuibyshev, the bundled-up Muscovites had looked a pinched harassed lot, trudging through the snowdrifts or digging tank traps. Now they strolled the sidewalks in the sunshine, the women in light print dresses, the men in sport shirts and slacks if they were not in uniform; and the pretty children were running and playing with carefree noise in the streets and the parks. The war was far away.

The British embassy, on a fine river-front site facing the Kremlin, had once been a czarist merchant's mansion like Spaso House. When Pamela stepped through the french windows in the rear, she came on the ambassador lounging stripped to the waist in the sunshine amid a loudly clucking flock of white chickens. The formal gardens had been turned into an enormous vegetable patch. Philip Rule, slouched on a campstool beside the ambassador, got up with a mock bow. "Ahhh! Lady Burne-Wilke, I presume?"

She returned drily, "Not quite yet, Philip."

The ambassador gestured around at the garden as he rose to shake hands. "Welcome, Pam. You see some alterations here. One's most likely to eat regularly in Moscow when food grows in the back yard."

"I can imagine."

"We tried to book you into the National, but they're jammed. Next Friday you'll get in, and we'll put you up here meantime."

"Very kind of you."

"Why do that?" Rule said. "I didn't know there was a problem. The U.P. just gave up a suite at the Metropole, Pam. The living room's an acre in size, and there's not a fancier bathroom in Moscow."

"Can I get it?"

"Come along, and let's see. It's five minutes from here. The manager's a distant cousin of my wife."

"The bathroom decides me," Pamela said, passing a hand over her wet brow. "I'd like to soak for a week."

The ambassador said, "I sympathize, but be sure to come to our party tonight, Pam. Best spot for watching the victory fireworks."

In the car Pam asked Rule, "What victory?"

"Why, the Kursk salient. You know about it, surely."

"Kursk didn't get much play in the States. Sicily's been the big story."

"No doubt, typical Yank editing. Sicily! It toppled Mussolini, but militarily it was a sideshow. Kursk was the biggest tank battle of all time, Pamela, the true turn of the war."

"Wasn't it weeks ago, Phil?"

"The breakthrough, yes. The counterattack swept into Orel and Belgorod yesterday. Those were the key German strong points of the salient, and the backbone of Jerry's line is broken at last. Stalin's ordered the first victory salute of the war, a hundred and twenty artillery salvos. It'll really be something."

"Well, I'd better come to the party."

"Why, you've got to."

"I'm perishing for sleep, and I feel rotten."

"Too bad. The Narkomindel's taking out the foreign press on a tour of the battlefields tomorrow. We'll be on the hop for a week. You can't miss that, either."

Pamela groaned.

"Incidentally, the whole Yank mission's coming to the embassy to watch the fireworks, but Captain Henry won't be there."

"Oh, won't he? You know him, then?"

"Of course. Short, athletic-looking, fifty or so. A bit dour, what? Doesn't say much."

"That's the man. Is he the naval attaché?"

"No, that's Captain Joyce. Henry does special military liaison. The inside word is that he's Hopkins's man in Moscow. Right now he's off in Siberia."

"Just as well."

"Why?"

"Because I look like death."

"Now, Pam, you look smashing." He touched her arm.

She pulled it away. "How's your wife?"

"Valentina? Fine, I guess. She's out touring the front with her ballet group. She dances on flatcars, on the backs of trucks, on air strips, wherever she can do a leap without breaking an ankle."

The suite at the Metropole was as Philip Rule had described it. The drawing room contained a grand piano, a vast Persian rug, and a cluttered array of very poor statues. Pamela said, peering into the bathroom, "Look at that tub! I shall be doing laps."

"Do you want the suite?"

"Yes, whatever it costs."

"I'll arrange it. And if you'll give me your papers, I'll check you in at the Nark for the battlefield tour. Suppose I call for you at half past ten? The guns and fireworks go off at midnight."

She was taking off her hat at a spotty mirror, and behind her he was frankly admiring her. Rule was going to fat, his blond hair was much thinner, his nose seemed bigger and broader. Except as a disagreeable memory, he meant nothing to her. Since the episode in the rainstorm on Christmas Eve in Singapore, she felt squeamish at being touched by him, that was all. She knew she still attracted him, but that was his problem, not hers. Kept at a distance, Philip Rule was quite tame, even helpful. She thought of his flowery eulogy for her father at the Alexandria cemetery: *An Englishman's Englishman, a reporter's reporter, a bard with a press card, singing the dirge of Empire to the thrilling beat of a triumphal march.*

She turned and with an effort gave him her hand. "You are kind, Phil. See you at ten-thirty."

Pamela was used to being undressed by men's glances, but a stripping by female eyes was a novelty. The Russian girls at the British embassy party stared her up and down, hair to shoes. She might have been a model, paid to go on display under hard scrutiny. There was no bitchiness in the looks, no deliberate rudeness, only intense wistful curiosity; and no wonder, considering their evening dresses; some long, some short, some flouncy, some tight, all atrociously cut and hideously colored.

Men soon surrounded Pam: Western correspondents, officers and diplomats relishing the sight of a chic woman from their world, and Russian officers in uniforms as smart as their women's dresses were dowdy, silently gazing at Pamela as at an objet d'art worth millions. The long wood-panelled room was not at all crowded by the forty or fifty guests, many clustered at a silver punch bowl, others dancing to an American jazz record on a bared patch of parquet floor, the rest talking and laughing, glasses in hand.

A big handsome young Russian officer, strung with medals and very fresh-faced, broke through the circle around Pamela and asked her in stumbling English to dance. Liking his nerve and his smile, she nodded. He was a very bad dancer, like herself, but the delight on his healthy red face at holding the beautiful Englishwoman by the waist, at an extremely respectful distance, charmed her.

"What are you doing in the war?" she asked, straining her rusty Russian to compose the sentence.

"Ubivayu nemtsev!" he returned, then hesitantly translated, "I— killing Chormans."

"I see. Lovely."

He nodded with a savage grin, eyes and teeth gleaming.

Philip Rule waited at the edge of the dance floor with two glasses of punch. When the record ended the Russian gave up Pamela with a bow. "That's one of their great tank commanders," said Rule. "He fought at Kursk."

"Really? He's hardly more than a boy."

"Boys fight the wars. We'd have the brotherhood of man tomorrow if the politicians had to get out and fight."

Rule was slipping, thought Pamela. Five years ago he would not have uttered the bromide with an air of saying something clever. Another record began: "Lili Marlene." They looked in each other's eyes. For Pamela, this song meant North Africa, and the death of her father. Rule said, "Strange, isn't it? The only decent war song of this whole bloody holocaust. A cheap weepy Hun ballad." He took the glass from her hand. "What the hell, Pamela, let's dance."

"Oh, all right."

To Pug Henry, who was just coming in with Ambassador Standley and an Air Corps general, "Lili Marlene" meant Pamela Tudsbury. The plaintive all-too-German melody had by some freak captured the bitter-sweet essence of fugitive wartime romance, the poignant sense of a fighting man's lovemaking in the dark before going off to battle, the sort of lovemaking he and Pamela would never know. He heard the tinny phonograph bleating as he walked in.

> *Bugler, tonight don't play the call to arms,*
> *I want another evening with her charms.*
> *Then we must say good-bye and part.*
> *I'll always keep you in my heart*
> *With me, Lili Marlene, with me, Lili Marlene.*

He was dumbfounded to come upon Pamela, of course. So the visa had gone through! Seeing her in Rule's arms intensified the surprise. Pug quietly loathed the man because of the Singapore episode; his reaction was not exactly a jealous one, for he had given up his dreams of Pamela, but the sight disgusted as well as amazed him.

Noticing the squat figure in blue and gold go by, Pamela guessed he had seen her, and was passing on because she was dancing with Rule. God in heaven, she thought, why did he have to turn up like this? Why does it never go right with us? And since when has he become so gray? She broke away and hurried after Pug, but he and the tall Air Corps general went into the crowd at the punch bowl, which closed around them. She hesitated to elbow through, but was about to try when the lights blinked several times. "Five minutes to midnight," the ambassador announced as the talk subsided. "We shall darken the room now, and open the curtains."

Pamela was swept by the excited guests to a railed open window. The night was starry, and a blessedly cool breeze was blowing. She stood there boxed in by noisy chatterers, unable to move, looking across the river toward the black mass of the Kremlin.

"Hello, Pamela." His voice, Victor Henry's voice, spoke in the dark beside her.

Rockets shot up into the sky at that moment and burst in a great crimson glare. Guns thundered. The floor shook beneath them. The party crowd cheered. A volcanic barrage rose from all over the city, not of fireworks but of ammunition: star shells, signal rockets, crimson tracers, shells that burst dazzling yellow, a canopy of colored battlefield fire, making a din that all but drowned out the gargantuan booming of a hundred and twenty big guns.

"Hello, there. Remind you of anything?" she gasped to the shadowy figure at her side. So they had stood watching the firebombing of London in 1940, when for the first time he had put his arm around her.

"Yes. That wasn't a victory display, though."

BOOM . . . BOOM . . . BOOM . . .

The barrage was exploding and blazing all over the sky, eerily lighting up the river, the cathedral, and the Kremlin. He spoke again between the roars of the big guns. "I'm sorry about your father, Pam, terribly sorry. Did you get my letter?"

"No. Did you ever get any of mine?"

BOOM . . .

"Just one that you wrote to me in Washington, saying you'd become engaged. Are you married?"

"No. I wrote another letter, a long one, to the *Northampton—*"

BOOM . . .

"That one I never got."

The salvos thundered on and on, and at last ceased. The eruption of fire died down, leaving puffs of black smoke spread across the stars. In the sudden quiet, a rattling and clattering started up on the embankment outside. "Great God, it's shrapnel falling!" the ambassador's voice rang out. "Away from the windows, everybody!"

When the lights came on, the Air Corps general, a tall lean man with wavy blond hair like Burne-Wilke's, and an unpleasantly cold expression, stood at Pug's elbow. "Lavish display of flak," he said. "Pity they're not that free with useful information."

Pug introduced him to Pamela. The general all at once looked pleasanter. "Well! I was with Duncan Burne-Wilke three weeks ago in New Delhi. He'd just gotten word you were coming, and he was a very happy man. I now see why."

She smiled. "Is he well?"

"Getting along. But that's a thankless war theatre, the CBI. Pug, we'd better get back at those charts. I'll make my farewells."

"Yes, sir."

The general went off. Pug said to her, "Sorry, I've got him on my hands, Pam. I'm pretty tied up. Business of getting new air routes for flying in Lend-Lease aircraft. Can we meet day after tomorrow, sometime?"

She told him about the Kursk tour. His face fell, and that slightly encouraged her. "A whole week, eh?" he said. "Too bad."

"I saw your wife in Washington. You've heard from her?"

"Oh, yes, now and then. She seems to be fine. How'd she look?"

"Very well. She told me to tell you that Byron's become the executive officer of his ship."

"Exec!" He raised heavy brows. Like his hair they were grayer now, and his face was heavier. "That's odd. He's very junior, and he's a reserve."

"Your general looks ready to go."

"So I see."

His handshake was friendly. She wanted to grip hard, to say in an act what would not come in words. But in this botched meeting, even that much might seem offensive disloyalty to Burne-Wilke. Oh, fiasco, she thought; fiasco, fiasco, fiasco!

"Well, see you in a week," he said. "If I'm not out of town again. So far I've nothing scheduled."

"Yes, yes. We have worlds to talk about."

"We do. Call me when you get back, Pam."

She rang the American embassy a week later, minutes after she returned to the Metropole suite, which she had wastefully retained and paid for. She was sure he would be away again, that they would go on missing each other, that this Moscow side trip would end as a doomed waste of time and spirit. But he was there, and he sounded glad to hear from her.

"Hello, Pam. How did it go?"

"Horribly. It's no good without Talky, Pug. What's more, I'm sick to my soul of devastated cities, smashed-up tanks, and stinking German corpses lying about. I'm sick of photographs of Russian women and children strung up on gallows. I'm sick of this whole insane and vile war. When do we see each other?"

"How about tomorrow?"

"Hasn't Philip Rule called you about tonight?"

"Rule?" His voice flattened. "No, he hasn't."

Hastily she said, "He will. His wife's back. It's her birthday, and he's having a party for her here in my suite. It's gigantic, and he got it for me, so I could hardly refuse. There'll be correspondents, a few embassy people, her ballet friends, that sort of thing. I'll gladly duck it if you'd rather not, and meet you somewhere else."

"N.G., Pamela. The Red Army's throwing a farewell banquet for my general. At the Metropole, in fact. We've got the agreement he came here to work out."

"How marvelous."

"That remains to be seen. Russian draftsmanship of an agreement can be surrealistic. Meantime there's this eating and drinking brawl to celebrate, and I can't possibly get out of it. I'll call you tomorrow."

"Damn," said Pamela. "Oh, bloody hell."

He chuckled. "Pam, you do sound like a correspondent."

"You don't know how I can sound. All right, tomorrow, then."

Rule's wife was almost too beautiful to be real: a perfect oval face, enormous clear blue eyes, heavy yellow hair, exquisitely molded hands and arms. She sat in a corner, hardly speaking or moving, never smiling. The suite was crowded, the music was blasting away, the guests were drinking and eating and dancing, but there was no real merriment in any of it, perhaps because the birthday girl was so conspicuously glum.

Far from showing any ballet grace in their Western dancing, the Russians were elephantine. Pamela danced with a man she had once seen as the prince in *Swan Lake*. He had a faun's face, a handsome shock of black hair and, even in his ill-fitting clothes, a superb physique; but he didn't know the steps, and he kept apologizing in incomprehensible Russian. The whole party was going like that. Phil was throwing down vodka, dancing awkwardly with one girl after another, and forcing foolish laughter. Valentina was beginning to look as though she wished she were dead. Pamela could not fathom what was wrong. Some of the trouble might be Russian awkwardness at socializing with foreigners, but there must be a strain between Rule and his fairy-tale beauty that she didn't know about.

Captain Joyce, the American naval attaché, a jolly Irishman with a knowing eye, asked Pamela to dance. Placing herself in his arms, she said, "Too bad Captain Henry is stuck downstairs."

"Oh, you know Pug?" Joyce said.

"Quite well." The knowing eye sparked at her. She added, "He and my father were good friends."

"I see. Well, the man is terrific. He's just pulled off a great feat."

"Can you tell me about it?"

"If you won't put it in your paper."

"I won't."

Speaking in Pamela's ear over the music as they shuffled here and there, Joyce said that Ambassador Standley had been trying in vain for months to get action on the Siberian route for the Lend-Lease aircraft. In a previous visit to the Soviet Union to push the thing, General Fitzgerald too had accomplished nothing. This time Standley had turned the problem over to Pug, and an agreement was now in hand. It meant that instead of flying a tough route via South America and Africa with a lot of crack-ups, or coming crated on convoy vessels which the U-boats could sink, the aircraft would now funnel in directly over a safe straight route. Fewer delays, more deliveries, and a cooling of much ill feeling on both sides would result.

"Will the Russians keep their word?" asked Pamela, as the music paused and they walked to the refreshment table.

"Remains to be seen. Meantime, that's a real love feast down below. Pug Henry is damn good at handling these tough ones." Pamela refused vodka. Tossing down a sizable glassful, Joyce coughed and glanced at his watch. "Say, they should be starting to carry them out of that fracas downstairs round about now. Why don't I try to fetch Pug?"

"Oh, please. *Please.*"

About ten minutes passed. Then into the room burst four Red Army officers in full regalia, followed by Joyce, Pug Henry, and General Fitzgerald. One of the Russians was an enormous bald general with a blaze of decorations, and an artificial hand in a leather glove. The others were much younger, and they did not seem nearly as jolly as the general, who entered with a roar in Russian of *"Happy Birthday!"* He marched up to Rule's wife, bowed over her hand, kissed her, and asked her to dance. Valentina smiled—for the first time, it seemed to Pamela, and it was like dawn over icy peaks—jumped up, and put herself in his arms.

"Recognize him?" Pug said to Pamela, as the pair went pounding out on the floor to "The Boogie-Woogie Washerwoman."

"Isn't he the one who gave us dinner in his field HQ, and then danced like mad?"

"Right. Yuri Yevlenko."

"By God, he's a live wire," said Captain Joyce. "That squinty little officer with the scar must be his political aide. Or an NKVD man. He tried to stop him from coming up. Muttered about fraternizing with foreigners. You know what the general said? He said, 'So? What can they do to me? Cut off my other hand?' "

. . . And the boogie-woogie washerwoman washes away . . .

"Seems to me," Pug said to Pamela, "that we've heard that imbecile noise before. Dance?"

"Must we?"

"You'd rather not? Thank God." He twined fingers in hers and led her to a small sofa. "They caught me at my white wine trick during the toasts. I had to switch back to vodka, and I'm reeling."

As Yevlenko clomped eccentrically about with the beaming Valentina, some Russians were abandoning their wooden fox-trots for the Lindy Hop. It better suited their springy dancing muscles. Though nobody could mistake them for Americans, several were flailing expertly away.

Pamela said, "You look sober enough." He sat erect in dress whites with bright gold buttons and shoulder-board stripes, and a rainbow bank of starred ribbons. The vodka had livened his eyes and heightened his color. Nothing had changed in fourteen months except for the grayed hair and added poundage. "By the way, your wife told me to admonish you about your weight."

"Ah, yes. She knows me. Go ahead, give me hell. When I've got duty like this, I eat and drink. On the *Northampton* I was a rail."

Nearly everybody was dancing now, except the three young Red Army officers ranged frozen-faced against the wall, and General Fitzgerald, who was flirting with a beautiful ballet girl in a ghastly red satin dress. Such was the noise that Rule had to turn up the music. Pamela all but shouted, "Tell me about the *Northampton*, Victor."

"Okay." As he talked about what had happened at sea after Midway, even about the Tassafaronga disaster, he glowed, or so it seemed to her. He told her of the post under Spruance that he might have had, and how he had taken this job instead at Roosevelt's request. He talked without bitterness or regret, laying out for her his life as it was. The party bubbled about them, and she sat listening, supremely content to be by his side, warmed by his physical presence, and sweetly disturbed by it, too. This was all she wanted, she kept thinking, just this closeness to this man until she died. She felt wholly alive again because she was sitting with him on a sofa. He was not happy. That was clear. She felt that she could make him happy, and that doing it would justify her own life.

Meantime, in a lull in the phonograph music, Yevlenko and the ballet people were talking excitedly around the piano. A girl sat down and rippled out-of-tune sour chords that brought general laughter. Yevlenko shouted, *"Nichevo! Igraitye!"* ("It doesn't matter! Play!") She drummed out a Russian melody, Yevlenko bawled an order, and all the Russians, even the three junior officers, formed up and performed a whirling group dance: everyone shouting, stamping, crisscrossing, spinning, while the Westerners in a circle clapped time and cheered them on. After that there was no ice left to be broken. Yevlenko stripped off his bemedalled coat, and in his sweat-stained blouse did the dance he had performed in the house at the Moscow front, squatting and bounding to applause; only, he held his lopped limb awkwardly and lifelessly. Next Valentina caused howls by putting on his coat, and improvising a wicked little dance burlesquing a pompous general.

More excited consultation at the piano, and Valentina gestured for silence, and friskily announced that she and her friends would do the ballet created for their tour of the fronts. She would dance Hitler, another girl Goebbels, a third Göring, and a fourth Mussolini, though they didn't have their masks. Four men would be dancing the Red Army.

Pug and Pamela broke off their talk to watch this satiric pantomime. The four villains strutted in to martial music, miming an invasion; gloated over their victory; argued about a division of the spoils; came to slapstick blows. Enter the Red Army, prancing to the "Internationale." Extravagant pantomime of cowardice and fear by the villains. Comic circular chase, round and round. Death of the four villains; and as they fell one by one, their four crooked bodies formed a swastika on the floor. Sensation!

Amid the applause the *Swan Lake* prince stripped off his coat and tie, kicked off his shoes, and signalled to the pianist. In open white shirt, trousers, and stocking feet, he launched into a stunningly brilliant dance with leaps and twirls that brought cheer after cheer. It was a climax impossible to top, or so it seemed. As he stood panting, surrounded by congratulations while refills of vodka were poured all around, the piano struck a harsh chord. Out on the floor stalked the ramrod-straight much-ribboned General Fitzgerald. He did not take off his coat. At his brusque signal the pianist began a fast *kozotzki;* whereupon the lean Air Corps general squatted and danced, arms folded, blond hair flying, long legs athletically kicking out and in, with appropriate sideward leaps. The surprise was magnificent. The *Swan Lake* prince dropped beside Fitzgerald and they finished the dance as a duo to a tumult of encouraging shouts, stamping, and clapping.

"I like your general," said Pamela.

"I like these people," said Pug. "They're impossible, but I like them."

General Yevlenko presented a glass of vodka to Fitzgerald and clinked with him. They drained their glasses to great applause. Fitzgerald walked to a refreshment table beside Pug's sofa and picked off two open vodka bottles—not very large, but full—saying, "Here goes for Old Glory, Pug." He strode back and handed Yevlenko a bottle with a challenging flourish.

"Eh? *Horoshi tshelovyek!*" ("Good fellow!") bellowed Yevlenko, whose big face and naked pate were now bright salmon color.

With all the guests urging them on—except, Pug noted, the Red Army officer with the scar, who looked as vexed as a disobeyed governess—the two generals tilted the bottles to their mouths, eyeing each other. Finishing first, Fitzgerald crashed his bottle into the brick fireplace. Yevlenko's bottle came flying after it. They embraced amid cheers, while the girl at the piano thumped out a barely recognizable "Stars and Stripes Forever."

"Christ, I'd better get him back to the embassy," Pug said. "He's been dodging booze ever since he got here."

But somebody had put "Tiger Rag" on the phonograph, and Fitzgerald was already dancing with the girl in red satin, who had cruelly mimicked the club-footed Goebbels in the ballet. Yevlenko took Pamela on the floor. It was past two in the morning, so this last burst of dancing did not last long. The guests began to leave, the party to dwindle down. Dancing again with the *Swan Lake* prince, Pamela noticed Pug, Yevlenko, and Fitzgerald huddled in talk, with Rule listening. Her dimming journalist instinct woke, and she went over to sit down beside Pug.

"Okay. Are we talking straight?" Fitzgerald said to Pug. The two generals were on facing settees, glaring at each other.

"Straight!" barked Yevlenko, with an unmistakable gesture.

"Then tell him I'm fed to the teeth, Pug, with this second front stuff. I've been getting it here for weeks. What about North Africa and Sicily, the two greatest amphibious attacks in history? What about the thousand-plane air raids on Germany? What about the whole Pacific war, where we're keeping the Japs from jumping on their backs?"

"Here goes for Old Glory," Pug muttered, bringing a chill grin to Fitzgerald's face. He translated, and kept translating as fast as he could during the ensuing exchange.

Yevlenko nodded and nodded at Pug's words, his face hardening. He thrust a finger at Fitzgerald's face. *"Concentrate forces and strike at the decisive point! Schwerpunktbildung!* Do they teach that principle at West Point? The decisive place is Hitlerite Germany. Yes or no? The way for you to strike at Hitlerite Germany is through France. Yes or no?"

"Ask him why Russia didn't open a second front for a whole year when England stood alone against Hitlerite Germany."

Yevlenko grated at Fitzgerald, "That war was an imperialist quarrel over world markets. It was of no concern to our peasants and workers."

Philip Rule, who kept refilling his own glass with vodka as he listened, now said to Fitzgerald rather thickly, "Should you go on with this?"

"He can call it quits. He started it," Fitzgerald snapped. "Pug, ask him why we should break our necks to help a nation that's committed to the destruction of our way of life."

"Oh, gawd," murmured Rule.

Yevlenko's glare grew more bellicose. "We believe your way of life will destroy itself through its inner contradictions. We won't destroy it, but Hitler can. So why don't you cooperate to beat Hitler? In 1919 Churchill tried to destroy our way of life. Now he is entertained in the Kremlin. History goes in steps, Lenin said. Sometimes forward, sometimes backward. Now is a time to go forward."

"You don't trust us for sour apples, so how can we cooperate?"

Pug had trouble with "sour apples," but Yevlenko got the idea. He sneered, "Yes, yes. An old complaint. Well, sir, your country has never been invaded, but we have been invaded over and over, invaded and occupied. Most of our allies have historically proved treacherous, and sooner or later have turned and attacked Russia. We have learned a little caution."

"America won't attack Russia. You have nothing we want."

"Well, we want nothing from you, once we beat Hitler, but to be left alone."

"On that note, can we all have a last drink?" said Rule.

"Our host is getting tired," said Yevlenko, dropping the harsh debating tone for a sudden amiable aside at Fitzgerald.

Rule began pontificating in Russian, with drunken gestures, and Pug muttered a running translation to Fitzgerald. "Oh, this is all talk in a vacuum. The white race is having another big civil war. Race, General Yevlenko, not economics, rules human affairs. The white race is mechanically brilliant but morally primitive. The German is the purest white man, the superman, Hitler's dead right about that. The white man like the red man is destined to fade from history, after laying waste half the planet in his civil wars. The white man's drivel about democracy is finished, too, after democracy elected creatures like Chamberlain, Daladier, and Hitler. Next will come China's turn. China is the Middle Kingdom, the center of gravity of the human race. The only genuine Marxist of world consequence is now living in a cave in Yenan. His name is Mao Tse-tung."

Rule delivered himself of this pronouncement with insufferable alcoholic positiveness, glancing often at Pamela as Pug translated.

Fitzgerald yawned and sat up, straightening his blouse and tie. "General, will I be able to fly my planes through Vladivostok, or won't I?"

"Keep your end of the bargain. We'll keep ours."

"Another thing. Are you going to make another deal with the Nazis, as you did in 1939?"

Pug was nervous about translating that, but Yevlenko retorted in a level tone, "If we get wind that you're negotiating another Munich, we'll turn the tables again and it'll serve you right. But if you fight, we'll fight. If you don't, we'll crush the Hitlerites ourselves."

"Okay, Pug. Now tell him I argued myself black in the face, as a war planner, against the North African campaign. Tell him I fought six long months for a second front in France this year. Go ahead. Tell him that."

Pug obeyed. Yevlenko listened, narrowed his eyes at Fitzgerald, and tightened his mouth.

"Tell him he'd better believe America is different from all other countries in history."

An enigmatic smile was Yevlenko's only reaction.

"And I hope his tyrannical regime will let his people realize that. Because it's the one chance for peace in the long run."

The smile faded, leaving a face of stone.

"And you, General," said Fitzgerald, standing and offering his hand, "are one hell of a guy. I am dead drunk. Any words of offense I spoke don't count. Pug, lead me back to Spaso House. I've got to pack up fast."

Yevlenko got to his feet, stretched out his left hand, and said, *"I will take you back to Spaso House."*

"Really? Most handsome of you. In the name of Allied amity, I accept. Now I'll say good-bye to the birthday beauty."

By now only the Red Army officers and Valentina had not yet left the suite. Yevlenko growled some words at the junior officers, whereupon they stiffened. One of them spoke to Fitzgerald—in fair English, Pug noted, using the language for the first time that evening—and the Air Corps general went out with him. Valentina pulled Rule from a slump in an armchair, and led him stumbling out. Pug, Pamela, and General Yevlenko remained alone amid the desolation of the ended party.

Yevlenko took Pamela's hand in his left, saying, "So you will marry Air Vice Marshal Duncan Burne-Wilke, who stole forty Aircobras from us."

Getting the grammar wrong, Pam replied, "General, we are fighting the same enemy with those Aircobras."

"I yevo?" ("And him?") Yevlenko directed his lifeless hand at Pug Henry.

She opened wide eyes and mimicked his gesture. *"Sprasitye yevo!"* ("Ask him!")

Pug spoke rapidly to Yevlenko. Pamela interrupted, "Now, now, what's all that?"

"I'm saying he misunderstands. That we're dear old friends."

Yevlenko spoke in slow clear Russian to Pamela, thrusting an index finger into Pug's shoulder. "You are in Moscow, dear lady, because *he* got you your visa. *Genry,"* he went on, buttoning the top of his tunic, *"ne bood durakom!"*

Abruptly he walked out, closing the door.

"Ne bood durakom—don't be—what?" asked Pamela. "What's *durakom?"*

"Goddamned fool. Instrumental case."

"I see." Pamela burst out with a throaty peal of female joy. She put her arms around his neck and kissed his mouth. "So you brought me to Moscow because we're dear old friends." He crushed her to him, kissed her hard, and let her go. Walking to the windows, he pulled back the curtains. It was day, the early Russian day of midsummer. The cool light made the after-party scene sadder and drearier. Pamela came beside him, looking out at clouds faintly flushed with sunrise. "You love me."

"I don't change much."

"I don't love Duncan. That's what I wrote you in the letter to the

Northampton. He knows I don't. He knows about you. In that letter I asked you to speak, or forever hold your peace. But you never got it."

"Why are you marrying a man you don't love?"

"I wrote you that, too. I was sick of floating, I wanted to land. That's doubly true now. I had Talky then, now I have nobody."

It was a while before he spoke. "Pamela, when I got home, Rhoda acted like a Turkish harem girl. She was my slave. She's guilty, and sorry, and sad, and bereft. I'm sure she has nothing to do with that other fellow any more. I'm not God. I'm her husband. I can't chuck her out."

Guilty and sorry! Sad and bereft! How little that resembled the woman Pamela had seen in Washington! Pug was the sad and bereft one, it was written in every line of his face. *And if she's unfaithful to you again?* The question was on the tip of Pamela's tongue. Looking into Pug Henry's seamed decent face and somber eyes, she couldn't utter it. "Well, here I am. You got me here. What do you want of me?"

"Look, Slote wrote that you were having trouble with your visa." She was facing him, staring into his eyes. "All right, do I have to say it? I wanted you here because to see you is happiness."

"Even when I'm dancing with Phil Rule?"

"Well, that just happened."

"Phil means nothing to me."

"I know."

"Pug, we have the rottenest luck, don't we?" Her eyes filled with tears that did not fall. "I can't hang around Moscow just to be near you. You don't want lovemaking, do you?"

With an ardent and bitter look he said, "I'm not free for lovemaking. Neither are you."

"Then I'll go on to New Delhi. I'll marry Duncan."

"You're so young. Why do that? There'll be a man you'll love."

"God almighty, there's no *room.* Don't you understand me? How explicit do I have to be? Duncan's sexual taste runs to pretty young poppies, and they swarm and swoon around him, so that more or less solves a difficulty for me. He wants a lady in his life, and he's very affectionate and romantic about me. He thinks I'm a dashing creature, decorative as well." She put both hands on Pug's shoulders. "You are my love. I'd help it if I could. I can't."

He took her in his arms. The sun came through low clouds and made a yellow patch on the wall.

"Ye gods, sunup," he said.

"Victor, just keep your arms around me."

After a long, long silence he said, "This may not come out right in words. You said we've had rotten luck. Well, I'm grateful as things are,

Pam. It's a miraculous gift from God, what I feel for you. Stay here awhile."

"A week," Pamela said, choking. "I'll try to stay a week."

"You will? A week? That's a lifetime. Now I've got to go and pour General Fitzgerald on an airplane."

She caressed his hair and eyebrows and kissed him. He strode out without looking back. At her window she watched until the erect small figure in white came in view, and vigorously walked out of sight on the quiet sunlit boulevard. The melody of "Lili Marlene" was running over and over in her head, and she was wondering when he would find out what was happening to his wife.

68

I N a wild ravine high in the Carpathian Mountains, wan light diffused through yellowing leaves shows a meandering forest path which might be a hunters' trail or an animal track, or no path at all but a trick of the light falling among the trees. As the sun sets and clouds redden overhead a bulkily clad figure comes striding down this trail carrying a heavy pack, with a rifle slung on a shoulder. It is a woman of slight build, her face close-wrapped by a thick gray shawl, her breath smoking. Passing a lightning-blasted oak trunk, she vanishes like a forest spirit sinking into the earth.

She is no forest spirit, but a so-called forest wife, a partisan commander's woman; and she has jumped down into a dugout, through a hole so masked by brush that if not for the ruined oak she herself might have missed it in the gloom. Partisan discipline forbids such creature comforts to lesser men, but a woman sharing his bed is a prestige symbol of the leader, like a new Nagant pistol, a separate dugout, and a leather windbreaker. Major Sidor Nikonov has grown quite fond of Bronka Ginsberg, whom at first he more or less raped; besides using her body he talks a lot to her, and listens to her opinions. He has been waiting for her, in fact, to help him decide whether or not to shoot the suspected infiltrator lying tied up in the cook dugout.

This fellow swears he is no infiltrator, but a Red Army soldier who escaped from a prison camp outside Ternopol, and joined a partisan band which the Germans wiped out. He got away, so he says, and has been wandering westward in the mountains, living on roots and berries or handouts from peasants. His story is plausible, and he is certainly emaciated and ragged enough; but his Russian accent is odd, he looks over sixty, and he has no identification at all.

Bronka Ginsberg goes to size up the man. Hunched in the dirt in a corner of the cook dugout, more tortured by the food smells than by the ropes cutting his ankles and wrists, Berel Jastrow takes one look at her face and decides to gamble.

"*Yir zeit a yiddishe tochter, nane?*" ("You're a Jewish daughter, no?")

"Richtig. Und ver zeit ir?" ("Right. And who are you?")

The Galician Yiddish, toughly rapped out, falls on his ears like som He gives straight answers to Bronka's probing questions.

The two bearded cooks stirring the soup vats exchange winks at tl Yiddish gabble. Bronka Ginsberg is an old story to them. Long ago tl major dragged this thin-lipped, hard-faced creature out of the fami camp of Jews up in the mountains, to nurse men wounded in a rai Now the damned Jew-bitch bosses the whole show. But she is a skille nurse, and nobody makes trouble about her. For one thing Sidor N konov would shoot any man who looked cross-eyed at the woman.

As she jaws away in Yiddish with the infiltrator, the cooks lose inte est. Since the fellow is a Yid, he can't really be an infiltrator; so th won't get to take him out in the woods and shoot him. She'll see to tha Too bad. It can be fun when they beg for mercy. These two are Ukrai ian peasants drafted into the band; in the cook dugout they stay warr fill their bellies, and avoid the food raids and railroad dynamiting They loathe Bronka Ginsberg but aren't about to cross her.

Why, she is asking Jastrow, didn't he tell his captors the truth? Tl partisans know about the mass graves; why did he make up that yan about Ternopol? Glancing at the cooks, he says she ought to know ho treacherous the Ukrainian backwoods are, worse even than in Litl uania. The Benderovce gangs are just as apt to kill a Jew as to feed hin or to let him go on his way. In Auschwitz some of the worst guare were Ukrainians. So he invented that story. Other partisan bands hav believed him and given him food. Why is he tied up here like a dog?

Bronka Ginsberg explains that a unit of turncoat Russian soldiers le by Germans infiltrated the ravine a week ago to destroy Nikonov band. One fellow doublecrossed the Fritzes, and alerted the partisan They ambushed the outfit, killed most of them, and have been huntin the stragglers ever since. Jastrow is lucky, she says, that he wasn't she at sight.

Berel is untied and fed. Later in the command dugout he repeats b story in Russian to Major Nikonov and the political officer, Comrae Polchenko, a wizened man with black teeth. Bronka Ginsberg sits b sewing. The officers make Berel cut the slender aluminum cylinde containing the film rolls out of his coat lining. They are peering at tl cylinders by the oil lamp when the evening Central Partisan Sta broadcast from Moscow starts up. They put aside the film containers t listen. Through a square wooden box that whistles and squeals, di patch orders come gargling out in plain language to various code-name detachments; also cheery bulletins about a victory west of recapture Kharkov, big bombing raids on Germany, and the surrender of Italy.

Their discussion about Berel resumes. The political officer is for sending the films to Moscow in the next ammunition delivery plane, and turning the Jew loose. Major Nikonov is against that; the films will get lost or nobody will know what they mean. If the films go to Moscow, the Jew should be sent along.

The major is curt with Polchenko. Political officers in partisan detachments are an irritation. Most of these bands consist of Red Army soldiers trapped behind German lines who have taken to the woods to survive. They attack enemy units or the local gendarmerie to seize food, arms, and ammunition, or to take revenge for peasants who are punished for helping them. But the heroic partisan stories are propaganda romance, by and large; these men have mostly turned forest animals, thinking first of their safety. This does not suit Moscow, naturally; hence men like Polchenko have been airlifted to the partisan forests, to stir up activity and see that Central Staff orders are obeyed.

As it happens, Nikonov's band is a brave and venturesome one, with a good record of sabotaging German communications. Nikonov himself is a regular Red Army officer, thinking of his own future once the tide of war has turned. But the Carpathians are far from Moscow, and the Red Army is far from the Carpathians. The Soviet bureaucracy, represented by the black-toothed man, doesn't swing much weight; Nikonov is boss here. So Berel Jastrow observes, listening anxiously to the talk. Polchenko is civil, almost ingratiating, as he argues with the leader.

Bronka Ginsberg looks up from her sewing. "You're both talking nonsense. Why bother with this fellow? What's he to us? Did Moscow ask for him or his films? Send him up to Levine's camp. They'll feed him, and then he can go on to Prague, or to the devil. If his Prague contact can really reach the Americans, then maybe the *New York Times* will have a story about the heroic Sidor Nikonov band. Eh?" She turns on Berel. "Wouldn't you give Major Nikonov credit? And his partisan detachment, that's blowing up Fritz's trains and bridges all over the western Ukraine?"

"I will get to Prague," says Berel, "and the Americans will hear about the Nikonov partisan brigade."

Major Nikonov's band is far from a brigade—a mere four hundred men, loosely held together by Nikonov. The word pleases him.

"All right, take him to Levine tomorrow," he says to Bronka. "You can use mules. The fellow's half-dead."

"Oh, he'll drag his own carcass up the mountain, don't worry."

The political officer makes a disgusted face, shakes his head, and spits in the dirt.

Dr. Levine's Jews, refugees from the last massacre in Zhitomir, are squatting in a tumbledown hunters' camp by a small lake, not far from the Slovakian border. The carpenters have long since repaired the leaky roofs of the abandoned cabins and main lodge, sealed the walls, put in shutters, knocked together rough furniture, and made a habitable retreat for the survivors of some eighty families, much reduced by frost, malnutrition, and disease in their long westward trek. Sidor Nikonov raided these Jews when they first came here, took most of their food and weapons, and dragged off Bronka. Bronka pointed out to him, after her rape, that Levine's men are craftsmen spared by the Germans in Zhitomir; electricians, carpenters, blacksmiths, mechanics, a gunsmith, a baker, a watchmaker, and the like. Ever since, the partisans have supplied food, clothing, bullets, and weapons to the Jews—very little, but sufficient to keep them alive and able to fight off intruders—and in return the Jews have serviced their machines, fashioned new weapons, made crude bombs, and repaired their generators and signal equipment. They are like a maintenance battalion, very useful.

The partnership has paid off both ways. Once when an SS patrol, tipped off by an anti-Semite down in the flats, climbed the mountain to scoop in the Jews, Nikonov warned them. They melted into the woods with their children, their aged, and their sick. The Germans found an empty camp. While they were still engaged in stealing everything they could lift, Nikonov's men fell on them and murdered them all. Germans have not come again looking for Jews. On the other hand, while Nikonov was off attacking a troop train, a gang of renegade Ukrainians happened upon his dugouts, and in a brief fierce fight with the guards set fire to the weapons cache. It burned for hours, leaving a smoking pile of twisted red-hot gun barrels. The Jews straightened the barrels, repaired the firing mechanisms, made new stocks, and restored the weapons to Nikonov's arsenal, usable again in a fashion until he could steal more guns.

Such are the stories that Bronka Ginsberg tells Jastrow while toiling up the mountain trail. "Sidor Nikonov is really not a bad man, for a *goy*," she sums up, sighing. "Not a wild beast like some. But my grandfather was a rabbi in Bryansk. My father was the president of the Zhitomir Zionists. And look at me, will you? A forest wife. Ivan Ivanovitch's whore."

Jastrow says, "You are an *aishess khayil*."

Bronka, ahead of him on the trail, looks back at him, her weatherbeaten face coloring, her eyes moist. *Aishess khayil*, from the Book of Proverbs, means "woman of valor," the ultimate religious praise for Jewess.

Late that night, the only woman in the council circle at the lodge is Bronka Ginsberg. The other firelit faces, except for the clean-shaven doctor's, are bearded, rough, and grim. "Tell them about the chains," she says. Her face is as hard as any man's there. "And about the dogs. Give them the picture."

Jastrow is talking to the executive committee of Dr. Levine's band, seated around a big stone fireplace where massive logs blaze. The prompting is helpful. What with the long climb and the bellyful of bread and soup, he is dropping off with fatigue.

Blobel's Jews had to work in chains, he relates, after his pal broke free, seized a gun, and shot some SS guards. Every fourth man in the gang, counted off at random, was hanged; the rest were chained in sections by the neck, with ankle chains on each man. The number of guard dogs was doubled.

Still, the escape of his section was planned for months. They waited for two minimum simultaneous conditions: a river nearby, and a heavy rainstorm. They worked during those months on their chains with screwdrivers, keys, picks, and other tools filched from the clothes of the dead. Though they were a sick, beaten, frightened lot, they knew that they were overdue to be shot and burned up, so the feeblest of them was game to try the break.

A thunderstorm just before sunset, in the woods outside Ternopol, at a mass grave on a bluff near the Seret River, gave them their chance. A thousand bodies, piled up on two frames with timber and waste oil, had just been put to the torch. The cloudburst caused dense dark clouds of stinking smoke to roll over the SS men, who backed off with their dogs. Jastrow's gang shed its chains amid the smoke and downpour, scattered into the woods, and made for the river. As Jastrow scrambled and slid down the bluff he heard the dogs, and shouts, and shots, and screams; but he reached the water and plunged in. He allowed the current to sweep him far downstream, and crawled ashore on the other side in darkness. Next morning, groping through dense dripping woods, he came on two other escapees, Polish Jews who were heading for their home towns, hoping for food and concealment there. As to the others, he feels that perhaps half got away, but he never saw them again.

"You still have the films?" asks Dr. Levine, a round-faced, black-haired man in his thirties, dressed in a patched Wehrmacht uniform. With his rimless glasses and kindly smile he looks like a city intellectual rather than the leader of the roughnecks around the fire. According to Bronka, he is a gynecologist, and also a dental surgeon. In the mountain hamlets, and in the villages down in the flats, the inhabitants like Levine: he will come great distances to treat their sick.

"Yes, I have them."

"You'll let Ephraim develop them?" Levine jerks a thumb at a long-nosed man with red whiskers bristling all over his face. "Ephraim is our photography specialist. Also a professor of physics. Then we can have a look at them."

"Yes."

"Good. When you're stronger, we'll send you on to people who'll get you over the border."

The red-whiskered man says, "Do the pictures show the crematoriums?"

"I don't know."

"Who took them? And with what?"

"Auschwitz has thousands of cameras. Mountains of film." Berel's reply is weak and weary. "Auschwitz is the biggest treasure house in the world, all the stuff robbed from our dead people. Jewish girls sit in thirty big warehouses, sorting out the loot. It's all supposed to go back to Germany, but the SS steals a lot. We steal, too. There is a very good Czech underground. They are good Jews, those Czechs. They are tough, and they stick together. They stole the cameras and the films. They took the pictures." Berel Jastrow is so tired that as he talks his eyes droop, and he half-dreams, and seems to see Auschwitz's long rows of horse stalls in floodlit snow, the trudging bent Jews in their striped suits, and the big "Canada" warehouses with the loot piled up outside them under snow-covered tarpaulins, and in the distance dark chimneys vomiting flames and black smoke.

"Let him rest," he hears Dr. Levine say. "Put him in with Ephraim."

Berel has not lain in a bed for weeks. The straw mattress and the ragged blanket in a rude three-tier bunk are blissful luxury. He sleeps and sleeps. When he wakes an old woman brings him hot soup with bread. He eats and dozes again. Two days of this and he is up and about, bathing in the lake at high noon when the sun warms the icy water, then walking around the camp dressed in the German winter uniform Ephraim gives him. It is a curiously peaceful scene, this lakeside cluster of mountain cabins surrounded by peaks russet with autumn. Ragged clothes dry in the sun, women scrub, sew, cook, and gossip, men in small workshops saw and hammer and clank, a blacksmith makes his forge blaze as little children watch. Older children drone in open-air classes: Bible, mathematics, Zionist history, even Talmud. There are few books, no pencils, no paper; the instruction is rote oral repetition in Yiddish. The pinch-faced shabby children look as bored and harassed here as in any schoolroom, and here as everywhere some are at surreptitious mischief. The Talmud boys sit in a circle around one large tome, some reading aloud from the upside-down text.

Young men and women armed with rifles patrol the camp. Ephraim tells Berel that radio-equipped sentinels are posted far down the trails and passes. The camp is not likely to be surprised. The armed guards can take care of infiltrators or small bands, but for protection from serious threats they must signal Nikonov. Their best young people are gone. They wanted vengeance for the killings at Zhitomir; some have joined Kovpak's famous partisan regiment, others the one led by the legendary Jew, Uncle Moisha. Dr. Levine approved their going.

In the week that Berel stays he hears a flood of stories, most of them horrible, a few heroic, some funny, drawn from the Jewish forest grapevine. He too has his adventures to relate. In this way, as he is reminiscing at supper one evening about his days with the early Jewish partisans outside Minsk, he learns that his own son is alive! There is no mistake about it. A skinny, pimply young fellow with an eyepatch, who served with Kovpak until a German grenade half-blinded him, marched with a Mendel Jastrow, through the Ukraine for months. So it comes out that not only is Mendel alive, but a partisan—quiet Mendel, the superreligious yeshiva boy—and that the daughter-in-law and her child, from what this young fellow last heard, are in hiding on a peasant's farm outside Volozhin.

This is the first word Berel has had of his family in two years of wanderings and imprisonment. Through all the abuse, pain, and hunger that have ground him down, he has never totally lost hope that things would yet turn around. He takes the news quietly, but it seems a signal that the darkest part of the dark night may be starting to pass. He feels stronger, and he is ready to forge on to Prague.

In the big room of the main lodge, the night before he leaves, Ephraim puts on a lantern-slide show for selected adults: Berel's developed films, copied to larger slides, and flashed on a sheet gray with age and washings, through a crude projector using the arc light of two battery carbons. The sputtering and flickering of this improvised light lends a bloodcurdling animation to the slides. The naked women appear to shiver, marching into the gas chamber with their children; the prisoners wrenching gold from the corpses' teeth under SS guard seem to heave and strain; over the long open pit, where huge rows of human bodies burn, and Sonderkommandos with meat hooks are dragging up more bodies, the smoke wavers and billows. Some pictures are too blurred to show much, but the rest tell the story of the Oswiecim camp in crushing truth.

The bad light makes the photographed documents hard to read. A long ledger page shows several hundred deaths of "heart attacks" in the same day; there are inventories of jewels, gold, furs, currency, watches, candlesticks, cameras, fountain pens, itemized and priced in neat German; six pages of a report of a medical experiment on twenty identical twins, with measurements of their response to extremes of heat, cold, and electric shock, length of time for expiring after phenol injection, and elaborate comparative anatomy statistics after autopsy. Berel Jastrow has never seen the documents nor witnessed the scenes pictured. Horrified and sorrowful, he is yet reassured to know that the material is so utterly and unanswerably damning.

Silently, those who have watched the slides trudge out of the main house, leaving only the council. Dr. Levine stares at the fire for a long time. "Berel, they know me in the villages. I'll take you over the border myself. The Jewish partisans in Slovakia are well organized, and they'll get you to Prague."

The train from Pardubice to Prague is crowded, the aisles of the second-class carriages jammed with standees. Czech policemen patiently work their way down the compartments, examining papers. In this docile Protectorate, betrayed at Munich, gobbled up before the war by the Germans, crushed by the reprisals for the Heydrich assassination, nothing ever turns up in the train inspections. Still, the Gestapo headquarters in Prague continues to require them.

An old man reading a German paper has to be nudged for his papers by a policeman entering the compartment. Absentmindedly he pulls out a worn wallet containing his cards and permits, and hands it over while continuing to read. Reinhold Henkle, German construction worker from Pardubice, mother's maiden name Hungarian, which goes with the broad smooth-shaven Slavic face; the policeman glances at the threadbare suit and toilworn hands of the passenger, returns the papers, and takes the next batch. So Berel Jastrow surfaces.

The train bowls along the valley of the Elbe by the glittery river through fruit-laden vineyards and orchards full of harvesters, and grain fields spiky with stubble. The other people in the compartment are a fat old lady with an irritated look, three young women giggling together, and a uniformed young man with crutches. This confrontation with the policeman, for which Berel rehearsed for a week, has come and gone like a quick bad joke. He has been through grotesque times, but this passage from the wild world of mass graves and mountain partisans to what he once took for everyday reality—a seat on a moving train, girls in pretty dresses diffusing cheap scent and laughing, his own tie, creased hat, white shirt that cuts his neck—what a jolt! Coming back from the dead would have to be something like this; normal life seems a mockery, a busy little make-believe game that shuts out a terrible truth beyond.

Prague astounds him. He knows it well from business trips. The lovely old city looks as though the war has never happened, as though the past four years recorded in his mind have been a long bad dream. The swastika flags flapping noisily in a high wind were all too visible in Prague in peacetime, when the Nazis were agitating for the return of the Sudetenland. Just as always the people crowd the streets in the afternoon sunshine, for it is just about quitting time. Well-dressed, looking stolidly content with things as they are, they fill the sidewalk cafés. If anything, Prague is more serene now than in the turbulent days when Hitler was breathing fire against Beneš. In the sidewalk crowds Berel sees not one Jewish face. That is new. That is the one clear sign in Prague that the war is no dream.

His memorized instructions give him an alternate address if the bookshop should be gone; but there it is, in a crooked alley of the Mala Strana, the Little Town.

N. MASTNY

BOOKS

NEW AND SECOND-HAND

The opening door jangles a bell. The place is packed with old books on shelves, in piles on the floor, and the smell is very musty. A white-haired woman in a gray smock sits at a desk heaped with books, marking catalogue cards. She looks up benignly, with a smile that is more like a twitch, and says something in Czech.

"*Sprechen Sie Deutsch?*"

"*Ja.*"

"Do you have, in your second-hand section, any books on philosophy?"

"Yes, quite a number."

"Do you have Immanuel Kant's *Critique of Pure Reason?*"

"I'm not sure." She blinks at him. "Forgive me, but you do not look like a man whom such a book would interest."

"It is for my son Eric. He is writing his doctoral thesis."

After a long appraising stare, she gets up. "Let me ask my husband."

She goes out through a curtain in the back. Soon a short, stooped, bald man in a torn sweater, wearing a green eyeshade, emerges sipping from a cup. "Excuse me, I just made my tea and it is still hot."

Unlike the other dialogue, this is not a signal. Berel makes no reply.

The man potters about among the shelves, noisily drinking. He takes down a worn volume, blowing off dust, and hands it to Berel, open to the flyleaf, on which a name and address are inked. "People should never write in books." The volume is about travels in Persia, and the author's name is meaningless. "It is such a desecration."

"Thank you, but that is not what I had in mind."

The man shrugs, murmurs a blank-faced apology, and vanishes behind the curtain with the book.

The address is on the other side of town. Berel takes a trolleybus there, and walks several blocks through a shabby section of four-story houses. On the ground-floor entrance of the house he seeks, there is a dentist's sign. A buzzer admits him. Two doleful elderly men sit waiting on a bench in the foyer. A housewifely woman in a dirty uniform comes out of the dentist's office, from which groans and the noise of a drill can be heard.

"I'm sorry, the doctor can see no more patients today."

"It's an emergency, madam, a very bad abscess."

"You'll have to wait your turn, then."

He waits almost an hour. The doctor, his white coat spattered with blood, is washing his hands at a sink when Berel comes into the office. "Sit down, I'll be right with you," he says over his shoulder.

"I come from Mastny, the bookseller."

The doctor straightens and turns: bushy sandy hair, a heavy square face, a hard big jaw. He scans Berel with narrowed eyes, and says words in Czech. Berel gives the memorized reply.

"Who are you?" asks the dentist.

"I come from Oswiecim."

"Oswiecim? *With films?*"

"Yes."

"My God. We've long since given you fellows up for dead." The doctor is tremendously excited. He laughs. He seizes Berel by the shoulders. "We expected two of you."

"The other man is dead. Here are the films."

With a sense of solemn exaltation, Berel hands the aluminum cylinders to the dentist.

That night, in the kitchen on the second floor of the house, he sits with the dentist and his wife at a supper of boiled potatoes, prunes, bread, and tea. His voice is giving out, for he has been talking so much, recounting his long journey and his adventures along the way. He is dwelling on his week in Levine's camp, and the great moment when he learned that his son was alive.

The wife, bringing glasses and a bottle of slivovitz to the table, casually says to her husband, "It's an odd name, at that. Didn't someone at the last committee meeting tell about a Jastrow they've got in Theresienstadt now? One of the *Prominente?*"

"That's an American." The dentist makes a gesture of dismissal. "Some rich Jewish writer who got himself caught in France, the damn fool." He says to Berel, "What route did you take to get over the border? Did you go through Turka?"

Berel does not reply.

The two men look at each other.

"What's the matter?" asks the dentist.

"Aaron Jastrow? In Theresienstadt?"

"I think his name is Aaron," says the dentist. "Why?"

PART SIX

The Paradise Ghetto

69

U NLIKE Auschwitz there is really nothing secret about Theresienstadt. The German government has even been at some pains to publicize, with news stories and photographs, the "Paradise Ghetto" in the Czech fortress town of Terezin near Prague, where Berel now hears his cousin is immured.

This anomalous Nazi-sponsored haven for Jews, also called *Theresienbad* ("Terezin Spa"), is almost a byword in Europe. Jews of influence or means desperately try to get sent there. The Gestapo collects enormous fees for selling them commodious Terezin apartments with guaranteed lifetime medical care, hotel service, and food allotments. Jewish leaders of some large cities are shipped there, once disease, hunger, and transportation "to the east" have erased their communities. Half-Jews, deserving old people, distinguished artists and scholars, decorated Jewish war veterans, dwell in this town with their families. Privileged Jews of the Netherlands and Denmark also end up there.

News pictures in European journals show these fortunate Jews, some recognizable by name or face, all wearing yellow stars, sitting at their ease in small cafés, attending lectures and concerts, happily at work in factories or shops, strolling in a flowery park, rehearsing an opera or a play, watching a local soccer game, wrapped in their prayer shawls and worshipping in a well-appointed synagogue, and even dancing in crowded little nightclubs. Outside Nazi Europe information about the place is distorted and sparse, but its existence is known through favorable Red Cross reports. European Jews who have not yet gone "east" would joyously trade places with Aaron Jastrow, and throw into the bargain all they possessed.

Such a comfortable resort for Jews in the midst of a Europe swamped in anti-Semitic propaganda and wartime hardships has naturally caused resentment. Dr. Goebbels has given voice to this in a speech:

> . . . While the Jews in Terezin are sitting in the café, drinking coffee, eating cake, and dancing, our soldiers have to bear all the miseries and deprivations, to defend their homeland . . .

Hints are not lacking in neutral and Allied countries, to be sure, that Theresienstadt is just a Potemkin village, a cynical show staged by the Nazis; so German Red Cross representatives have been invited to come and see for themselves, and have publicly confirmed the existence of this curious sanctuary. The Germans claim that Jewish camps in "the east" are all like Theresienstadt, just not quite so luxurious. For this the Red Cross and the world has to take their word.

There are few American Jews in Theresienstadt, or indeed anywhere in Nazi Europe. Most of them fled before the war. As for the scattering that remain, some are surviving by dint of influence, reputation, wealth, or luck, like Berenson and Gertrude Stein; some have gone into hiding and are making it through the war that way; some have already been gassed in Auschwitz, their American citizenship a useless mockery. Natalie, her uncle, and her baby have landed in the Paradise Ghetto.

$$\bullet \quad \bullet \quad \bullet$$

National Socialist Germany seems to have been something new in human affairs. Its roots were old, and the soil was old, but it was a mutant. In the ancient world, Sparta and Plato's imaginary Republic were but the dimmest foreshadowings. Despite Hitler's copious borrowings from Lenin and Mussolini, no modern political comparisons hold. No philosopher from Aristotle to Marx and Nietzsche ever foresaw such a thing, and none gave an account of human nature that could accommodate it. The Third Reich erupted into history as a surprise. It lasted a mere dozen years. It is gone. Historians, social scientists, political analysts, still stammer and grope in the mountainous ruins of unprecedented facts about human nature and society that it left behind.

Ordinary people prefer to forget it: a nasty twelve-year episode in Europe's decline, best swept under the rug. Scholars force it into one or another academic pigeonhole: populism plus terror, capitalist counterrevolution, recrudescence of Bonapartism, dictatorship of the right, triumph of a demagogue; bookish labels without end, developed into long, heavy tomes. None really accounts for the Third Reich. The still-spreading, still-baffling, sinister red stain on all mankind of National Socialist Germany—more than the population explosion, nuclear bombs, and the exhaustion of the environment—is the radical though shunned question in present human affairs.

Theresienstadt sheds light on it, because unlike Auschwitz, the Paradise Ghetto is not unfathomable. It was a National Socialist deed; but by an effort of the imagination, because it had a trace of recognizable sense, we can grasp it. It was just a hoax. The resources of a great government went into it, and so it worked. Natalie Henry's best hope for survival with her child lay, strangely enough, in this enormous fake painstakingly staged by the Germans.

The intention to kill every Jew in Europe—and every Jew in the world, as German domination expanded—was, for Hitler and his trusted few, probably never in doubt. It crystallized in deeds and documents early in the war. The paper trail remains exiguous, and Hitler apparently never signed anything; but that the order came down from him to execute his threats in *Mein Kampf* appears self-evident.

However, old-fashioned notions in the world outside Germany presented difficulties: mercy, justice, the right of all human beings to life and safety, horror of killing women and children, and so forth. But for the National Socialists, killing was the nature of war; German women and children were dying under bombs; the definition of *enemy* was a matter of government decision. That the Jews were Germany's greatest enemy was an article at the core of National Socialist policy. This was why, even as Germany in 1944 began to crumple, crucial war resources continued to go to murdering Jews. To the critical military mind this made no sense. To the leaders whom the German nation passionately followed to the last it made total sense. In the last will and testament that Adolf Hitler wrote, before blowing his brains out in his Berlin bunker, he boasted of his "humane" massacre of the Jews—he used that word—and exhorted the defeated German people to go on killing them.

In dealing with the softhearted prejudices of the benighted outside world during the great slaughter, the essential National Socialist policy was *hoax*. Wartime secrecy made possible the job of covering up the actual killings. No reporters travelled with the *Einsatzgruppen,* or got into Auschwitz. It was a question first of counteracting the ever-growing flood of leaks and rumors about the slayings, and second of getting rid of the evidence. The corpse-burning squads of Paul Blobel, and the Paradise Ghetto of Terezin, were complementary aspects of the great hoax. Theresienstadt would show that the slaughter was not happening. The corpse-burning squads would erase any evidence that it had ever happened.

Today the notion of forever concealing the murder of many millions of people may seem utterly crazy. But the energy and ingenuity of the entire German nation were at Hitler's disposal. The Germans were performing many other prodigious mad feats for him.

The most triumphant part of the hoax was directed at the Jews themselves. All through the four years of the giant slaughter, most of them never knew, few suspected, and fewer truly believed that the trains were taking them to their deaths. The Germans soothed them with the most diverse and elaborate lies about where they were going, and what they would do when they arrived. This faking lasted to the final seconds of their lives, when they were led naked into the "disinfection shower baths" which were asphyxiation dungeons.

Today, again, the millions of doomed Jews may seem crazily simple-minded to have swallowed the hoax and walked like oxen to the knife. But as the patient refuses to believe he has leukemia but grasps at any straws of reassurance, so the European Jews willed not to believe the ever-mounting rumors and reports that the Germans meant simply to kill them all.

To believe that, after all, they had to believe that the legal government of Germany was systematically and officially perpetrating a homicidal fraud gigantic beyond imagining. They had to believe that the function of the state itself, created by human society for its self-protection, had mutated in an advanced Western nation to the function of secretly executing multitudes of men, women, and children who had done nothing wrong, with no warning, no accusation, and no trial. This happened to be the truth, but to the last most of the Jews who died could not grasp it. Nor can we, even in hindsight, altogether blame them, since we ourselves still find this one stark fact absolutely incomprehensible.

The Theresienstadt part of the hoax was complex, and in the tangle of its cross-purposes lay Natalie's chance of living.

The Paradise Ghetto was nothing but a transit camp, a way station to "the east." The Jews there called it a *"schleuse,"* a sluice or floodgate. But it was a transit camp with a difference. The privileged Jews on arrival were cordially received, served a meal, and encouraged to fill out forms detailing what sort of hotel accommodations or apartments they preferred; also what possessions, jewelry, and currency they had brought with them. Then they were robbed down to their bare skins, and their bodily orifices searched for valuables. The cordial prelude of course facilitated the plundering. Thereafter they were treated exactly like the ordinary Jews who overflowed the houses and streets of the ghetto.

When large transports of Jews arrived the welcoming farce was sometimes omitted. The newcomers were simply herded into a hall, robbed en masse of whatever they had brought, issued cast-off clothing, and marched out into the crowded, verminous, disease-ridden town, to find shelter in four-tier bunks, in drafty attics already swarming with sick starving people, or in a room for four now housing a writhing mass of forty, or in a hallway or on a staircase just as jammed with wretched living bodies. Still, the arrivals were not asphyxiated straight off. To that extent it was a Paradise Ghetto.

Things unplanned by the Germans added to the paradisal façade. At the outset, the well-organized Jews of Prague had persuaded the SS to let them set up a Jewish municipality in the fortress town, a government half-joke and half-real; a joke, because it simply had to do whatever the Germans ordered, including drawing up lists for shipment "to the east"; yet real, since the departments did manage health, labor, food distribution, housing, and culture. The Germans cared only about tight security, their own comfort and pleasure, the production quotas of the factories, and the delivery of live bodies to fill up the trains. In other matters the Jews could look after themselves.

There was even a bank that printed special decorative Theresienstadt currency, with an astonishing engraving on all the bills, made by some anonymous artist, of a suffering Moses holding the tablets. The money was a ghetto jest, of course. One could buy nothing with it. But the Germans required the bankers and the Jewish workers to keep elaborate records of salaries, savings accounts, and disbursements, which also looked good to the casual eye of a casual Red Cross observer. The German effort in Terezin was a total hoax first to last; it never extended to raising the food ration above the starvation level, or providing medicines, or keeping down the incoming torrents of Jews.

Terezin was a pretty town; not, like Auschwitz, an expanse of horse stalls in a sandy marsh. The stone houses and long nineteenth-century barracks set along rectilinear streets pleased the eye, if one did not look inside at the crowds of sick and hungry inhabitants driven out of sight whenever visitors came. Including the soldiers quartered in the barracks, Terezin in normal times could house four or five thousand people. The ghetto averaged fifty or sixty thousand souls. It was like a town on the edge of a flood or earthquake area, overrun with disaster survivors; except that the disaster kept mounting and the survivors piling in, their numbers relieved only by the enormous mortality rate and by the sluice gate "to the east."

The lectures, the concerts, the plays, the operas, did actually go on. The talented inmates were permitted by the Germans to forget the hunger, the sickness, the crowding, the fear, in these paradisal activities. The cafés and the nightclub existed. There was nothing to eat or drink, but musicians abounded, and the Jews could go through the ghostly motions of peacetime pleasure till their turn came to be shipped off. The library in which Aaron Jastrow worked was a fine one, for the books were all looted from the arriving Jews. There were even shop façades, with windows full of goods stolen from the half-dead throngs drifting by. Naturally, nothing was for sale.

For a while only German Red Cross commissioners were allowed into Theresienstadt. No great effort was needed by the SS to elicit favorable reports from them. However, the very success of the hoax put the Germans in an unanticipated fix. A very pressing demand developed for a visit to the Paradise Ghetto *by neutral Red Cross observers.* This led to the most bizarre episode in Theresienstadt's bizarre history, the *Verschönerungsaktion,* or Great Beautification. On this Natalie's fate turned.

70

NATALIE is unrecognizable at work because a handkerchief masks her face below the eyes. The mica dust drifts from trimming and grinding machines over rows of long tables where women sit all day splitting the laminated mineral into sheets. Natalie is one more bent back in this large shabby array. The work takes dexterity and it is very boring, but not hard.

What the Germans use the stuff for she is not sure. Something to do with electrical equipment. It is evidently a rare material, for scraps and table sweepings go to the grinder, and the powder is crated and shipped to Germany like the trimmed sheets. Her job is to take a block or "book" and split the laminations into thinner, more transparent sheets until the tool will not wedge off another layer; and in the process to avoid tearing a sheet and getting clubbed by the armbanded French-Jewish harridan who patrols her section. Simple enough.

In this long low crowded shed of rough wood she spends eleven hours a day. Dimly lit by low-wattage bulbs hanging on long black wires, unheated and almost as cold as the snowy outdoors, damper because of the muck underfoot and the breath of the close-packed women, stinking from one loathsomely overflowing latrine, which is cleaned out only once a week by the pitiful squad of yellow-starred college professors, writers, composers, and scientists whom the Germans delight to put at hauling ordure; malodorous too from the body smells of the crowded ragged unwashed females who can scarcely get water to drink, let alone to bathe in or to launder their clothes—to a visitor from the outside this shed would seem a very hell. Natalie is used to it.

Most of the women are of refined background like hers. They are Czech, Austrian, German, Dutch, Polish, French, Danish. Terezin is a true melting pot. Many were once wealthy, many are as highly educated as Natalie. The mica factory is for favored women in the ghetto. The grisly ill-defined menace of "transport to the east" hangs over Terezin, much as death haunts normal life. The transport toll is spasmodic, cutting deep wide sudden swaths like a plague; but mica workers and their families do not go. As yet, anyway, they have not.

Most of the women doing this easy handwork are elderly, and Natalie's assignment to the mica factory suggests some veiled *"protectsia."* So does Aaron's library job. Their chute into Theresienstadt, though baffling and terrible, is not a random mischance. Something is behind it. They do not know what. Meantime, from day to day they endure.

The six o'clock bell.

The machines stop. The bent women get up, store their tools, and shuffle outside in a mob, clutching shawls, sweaters, rags around them. They move stiffly but fast, to get to the food queues while the slops are still warm. Outside, Natalie pulls the handkerchief off an almost unchanged face: sharper, paler, still beautiful, the mouth thinner, the jaw set harder. A brisk wind has swept from these straight snowy streets the prevailing Theresienstadt stench of clogged sewers, random excretions, rotting garbage, and sick filthy people; a slum smell with added gruesome whiffs of the dead from hand-pulled hearses that roll night and day, and of the crematorium beyond the wall that disposes of them; Jews dead of "natural" causes, not murder, at a mortality rate that extermination camps do not greatly surpass.

Between the straight lines of the barrack roofs, as she strikes out across the town to the toddlers' home, stars glitter overhead. A crescent moon hangs low over the fortress wall, beside a brilliant evening star. Rare clean sweet air rushes into her grateful lungs, and she thinks of Aaron's wry remark that morning, "Do you know, my dear, that today is Thanksgiving? Take it all in all, we have things to be thankful for."

She detours around the high wooden walls that shut Jews out of the main square, where she can hear the musicians playing at the SS café. At mealtime the streets are quiet and less crowded, though some of the feeble old people who poke in the rubbish heaps are still creeping around. The long food lines curl from some courtyards into the street. People stand scooping messes from tin dishes into their mouths, eyes popping with eagerness. It is one of the sadder sights of the ghetto, these cultured Europeans gulping slops like dogs.

A lean figure in a long ragged coat and cloth cap comes up beside her. *"Nu, wie gehts?"* ("So, how goes it?") says the man called Udam.

In Yiddish intonations no longer self-conscious she replies, "How should it go?"

She is beginning to talk the language as readily as her grandmother did. Now and then a Dutch or French inmate will even take her for a Polish Jewess. When she uses English she switches back easily to her old American tones, but they sound odd here. She and Aaron often fall into Yiddish, for he too uses it a lot in the library and in his Talmud course, though he lectures in German and French.

"Jesselson's string quartet is playing again tonight," Udam says. "They want us afterward. I have some new material."

"When can we rehearse?"

"Why not after we see the kids?"

"I teach an English class at seven."

"It's simple stuff. Won't take long."

"All right."

Louis is waiting in the doorway of his dormitory room. With a yell of joy, he leaps into her embrace. Feeling his sturdy body in her arms, Natalie forgets mica, boredom, misery, fear. His high spirits flood her and cheer her. Whatever hell winds blow, this is not a flame destined to be snuffed out.

Since his birth, Louis has been the light of her life, but never so much as here. Separated from her in the toddlers' home amid several hundred children, seeing her for only a few minutes most evenings, regimented by strange women in this damp dark old stone house, sleeping in a wooden box like a coffin, fed coarse scrappy food—though the children's rations are the best in the ghetto—Louis is thriving like a weed. Other little children pine, sicken, fall into listlessness and stupor, weaken in uncontrollable fits of crying, starve, die. The mortality in this home is terrible. But whether his travels—with the ever-changing water, air, food, bedding, and company—have hardened him, or whether, as she often thinks, the crossbreeding of the tough Jastrows and the tough Henrys has produced a Darwinian super-survivor, Louis is blazing with vitality. He leads in his classes. Finger painting, dancing, singing, are all one to him. He excels without seeming to try. He leads in mischief, too. The house women love him, but he is their despair. More and more he looks like Byron, with his mother's enormous eyes. His smile, at once enchanting and melancholy, is just his father's.

This is where she eats, since she takes turns on the night-duty staff. Udam eats here, too. He usually manages to fix things his way, and this is how he spends extra time with his three-year-old daughter. His wife is gone, transported. Tonight the soup is thick with potatoes, spoiled by frost and rotten-tasting, but substantial. As they eat he runs through his new dialogue, while his daughter plays with Louis. The portable puppet theatre is folded away in the basement playroom, and afterward the two children come down to watch them rehearse. Natalie's puppet show, a Punch and Judy which she got up to amuse the children, has become, with Udam's corrosive dialogue, a sub-rosa ghetto hit. It has given her more distinction than her American identity, which was briefly a wonder and soon taken for granted. Unlucky or stupid, here she is, and that is that to the ghetto people.

Natalie can become happily and totally absorbed in this revival of a teenage pastime neglected for years: making the dolls, dressing them, manipulating them, working up comic gestures to match Udam's words. Once she even put on a show in the SS café where he sings. She had to sit trembling through Udam's salacious German songs at which the boisterous SS men roared, and some sentimental ballads like "Lili Marlene" that had them all misty-eyed; and then her hands shook so that she could scarcely work the puppets. Happily the show wasn't a success. Udam left out all his good material, and they weren't asked again. There are other, far more masterly puppet shows in the ghetto that the SS can commandeer. Natalie's little display is feeble without Udam's bite.

Udam is a Polish cantor's son, a cadaverous crane of a man with burning eyes and a red mop of curly hair. A composer and singer of racy, even obscene songs, he nevertheless conducted the Yom Kippur service in the synagogue. He came to Theresienstadt with the early shipments from Prague, in the Zionist crowd that organized and ran the shadowy Jewish municipality. Berlin and Vienna types are now edging them out, for the SS favors the German Jews. Udam works in the farcical Theresienstadt bank, though it is a fief of these latecoming Jews, who still cling to their sense of superiority and tend to exclude others. Udam knows more about ghetto politics and angles than Natalie can absorb. His name is Josef Smulovitz, but everyone calls him "Udam." She has even heard the SS address him so.

Tonight he is adding new jokes to their most popular sketch, *The King of Frost-Cuckoo Land.*

Natalie puts a crown on Punch, and a very long red nose edged with icicles, and that is the king. Frost-Cuckoo Land is losing a war. The king keeps blaming the reported disasters on the Eskimos in the country. "Kill the Eskimos! Kill them all," he rages and rages. The comedy lies in the rushing in and out of a minister puppet in a vague uniform, also with an icicle-draped red nose, alternately announcing shortages, rebellions, and defeats, which make the king weep and bellow, and reports of more Eskimos killed at which he jumps with glee. At the end the minister bounces in to declare that all Eskimos have at last been liquidated. The king starts to rejoice, then abruptly roars, "Wait, wait! Now who can I blame? How will I run my war? This is terrible! Rush a plane to Alaska for more Eskimos! Eskimos! I need lots and lots of Eskimos!" Curtain.

Strange to say, the Jews find this crude macabre parallel extremely funny. The disasters resemble the latest news about Germany. The minister reports them in the orotund double-talk of Nazi propaganda.

This sort of risky underground humor is a great relief to ghetto life; there is a lot of it, and nobody seems to inform, because it goes on and on.

Natalie works the puppets with bitter zest. She is no more an American Jewess terrified of falling into German talons, and hugging the talisman of her passport for safety. The talisman has failed. The worst has happened. In a strange way she feels freer at heart, and clearer in her mind. Her whole being has a single focus now: to make it through with Louis, and live.

Udam's new dialogue refers to recent ghetto rumors: Hitler has cancer, the Germans are running out of oil to fight the war, the Americans will make a surprise landing in France on Christmas Day; the sort of wishful thinking that abounds in Theresienstadt. Natalie works up puppet business to match Udam's jokes, while his daughter and Louis, to whom the words mean nothing, chortle at the red-nosed dolls. Rehearsal done, she hugs Louis, feeling an invigorating electricity in the embrace, and goes on to her English class.

At the teenage boys' house lessons proceed day and night. Education of Jewish children is officially forbidden, but there is nothing else for them to do. The Germans do not really check, knowing what the ultimate destiny of the children is, and not caring what noises they make in the slaughter pen. These big-eyed scrawny boys put out a small newspaper, learn languages and instruments, work up theatricals, debate Zionism, sing Hebrew songs. On the other hand, they are for the most part cynical, accomplished scroungers and liars, believe in nothing, know their way around the ghetto like rats, and are sexually very precocious. Their greeting glances sometimes make Natalie uneasy, though in her baggy brown yellow-starred wool suit she considers herself a sexless, not to say a revolting, female object.

But once the boys get down to the lesson they are all sharp attention. They are bright volunteers, beginners, a mere nine of them, who want to know English "to go to America after the war." Two are missing tonight, off at a rehearsal of *Abduction from the Seraglio.* This ambitious Mozart opera is being undertaken to follow up on the big hit of the ghetto, *The Bartered Bride,* which even the SS enjoyed. Natalie saw a weak performance of this favorite because the cast had just been decimated by a transport. She has even heard that Verdi's *Requiem* is being rehearsed somewhere in a barracks cellar, though that seems fantastic. The class over, she hurries through the windy starry night to the loft where she will perform.

The quartet is already playing at the far end of the long low slope-roofed room, which was once usable for big gatherings, but is now filling up with bunks as more and more Jews sluice into the ghetto; far faster, as yet, than they are sluicing out "to the east." The whole hope of the ghetto Jews is that the Americans and the Russians will smash Frost-Cuckoo Land in time to save those piling up in the Theresienstadt floodgate. The object of life meantime is to avoid being transported, and to make the days and nights bearable with culture.

Jesselson's quartet makes excellent music: three gray-headed men and a very ugly middle-aged woman, playing on instruments smuggled into the ghetto, their shabbily dressed bodies swaying to the brilliant Haydn melodies, their faces intent and bright with inner light. The loft is packed. People hunch or lie on the bunks, squat on the floor, line the walls on their feet, beside the hundreds sitting jammed together on long wooden benches. Natalie waits for the piece to end, so as not to cause a commotion, then pushes through the crush. People recognize her and make way.

The puppet stage stands ready behind the musicians' chairs. She sits by Udam on the floor in front, and lets the balm of the music—Dvorak now—flow over her soul: the sweet violins and viola, the sobbing and thundering cello, weaving a pretty arabesque of folksong. After that the musicians play a late Beethoven quartet. The Theresienstadt programs are long, the audiences rapt and grateful, though here and there the sick or the elderly nod off.

Before the puppet show begins Udam sings a new Yiddish composition, *Mi Kumt* ("They're Coming"). This is another of his ingenious double-meaning political numbers. A lonely old man is singing on his birthday that everybody has forgotten him, and he is sitting sadly alone in his room in Prague. Suddenly his relatives begin to arrive. He turns joyful in the refrain, capering about the stage and snapping his fingers:

> *Oy they're coming, they're coming after all!*
> *Coming from the east, coming from the west,*
> *English cousins, Russian cousins,*
> *American cousins,*
> *All kinds of cousins!*
> *Coming in planes, coming in ships—*
> *Oy what joy, oy what a day,*
> *Oy thank God, from the east, from the west,*
> *Oy thank God, they're coming!*

Instant hit! In the encore, the audience takes up the refrain, clapping in rhythm: *Coming from the east, coming from the west!* On this high note the puppet show commences.

Before *The King of Frost-Cuckoo Land,* they do another favorite sketch. Punch is a ghetto official, in the mood to have sex with his wife. Judy puts him off. There is no privacy, she's hungry, he hasn't bathed, the bunk is too narrow, and so forth, familiar ghetto excuses which bring roars of laughter. He takes her to his office. Here they are alone; she coyly submits, but as their lovemaking commences, his underlings keep interrupting with ghetto problems. Udam's amorous coos and grunts of man and wife, alternated with Punch's irascible official tones and Judy's frustrated squawking, with some ribald lines and action, add up to a very funny business. Even Natalie, crouched beside Udam manipulating the dolls, keeps bursting into giggles.

The revised *Frost-Cuckoo Land* draws great laughter, too; and Udam and Natalie emerge flushed from behind the curtains to take bow after bow.

Calls arise here and there in the loft: "Udam!"

He shakes his head and waves protesting hands.

More calls: "Udam, Udam, Udam!"

Gesturing for quiet, he asks to be excused, he is tired, he is not in the mood, he has a cold; another time.

"No, no. Now! *Udam! Udam!*"

This happens at every puppet performance. Sometimes the audience prevails, sometimes Udam does beg off. Natalie sits. He strikes a somber singer's attitude, hands clasped before him, and in a deep cantorial baritone begins a mournful chant.

Udam . . . udam . . . udam . . .

Chills creep along Natalie's spine each time he starts it. This is a passage of the Yom Kippur liturgy. "*Udam yesoidoi may-ufar vay soifoi lay-ufar . . .*"

> *Man is created of the dust, and his end is in the dust. He is like a broken potsherd, a fading flower, like a floating mote, a passing shadow, and like a dream that flies away.*

After every pair of images comes the refrain of the opening melody, which the audience softly chants:

Udam . . . udam . . . udam.

It means

Man . . . man . . . man. The word in Hebrew for *man* is *adam.* *Udam* is a Polish-Yiddish variant of *adam.*

This brokenhearted low chant from the throats of the Theresienstadt Jews—*Adam, adam, adam*—all in the shadow of death, all recently howling with mirth, now murmuring what may be their own dirge, stirs deeps in Natalie Henry that she never knew were there before her imprisonment. As he works into the florid cantorial passage, Udam's voice sobs and swells like a cello. His eyes close. His body weaves before the little puppet stage. His hands stretch out and up. The agony, the reverence, the love of God and of humanity in his voice, are beyond belief in this man, who minutes before was performing the rawest ribaldry.

"Like a floating mote, a passing shadow . . ."

Udam . . . udam . . . udam . . .

He rises on tiptoe, his arms stiffen straight upward, his eyes open and glare at the audience like open furnace doors:

"And like a DREAM . . ."

The fiery eyes close. The hands fall, the body droops and all but crumples. The last words die to a crushed whisper

". . . that flies away."

He never does an encore. He acknowledges the applause with stiff bows and a strained white face.

This wrenching liturgical aria, words and melody alike, once seemed to Natalie a strange, almost gruesome way to close an evening of entertainment. Now she understands. It is pure Theresienstadt. She herself feels the catharsis she sees on the faces around her. The audience is spent, satisfied, ready to sleep, ready to face another day in the valley of the shadow. So is she.

"What the devil is *that?*"

A gray yellow-starred woolen suit lies across her cot. Beside it are lisle stockings and new shoes. A man's suit and shoes are on Aaron's cot opposite. He sits at the little table between the cots, poring over a large brown Talmud volume. He holds up a hand. "Just let me finish this."

The *protectsia* hovering over them is most apparent here; a separate room for the two of them, though it is only a tiny space with one window, partitioned off with wallboard from a larger chamber, formerly the dining room of a prosperous Czech family's private house. Beyond the partition hundreds of Jews are crowded in four-tier bunks. Here are two cots, a dim little lamp, a table, and a cardboard wardrobe like a telephone booth, the acme of ghetto luxury. Council officials do not live better. There has never been an explanation for this kind of treatment, other than that they are *Prominente.* Aaron gets his food here, but not by standing in line. The house elder has assigned a girl to bring it to him. However, he scarcely eats. He seems to be living on air. Usually when Natalie returns there are scraps and slops left, if she cares to choke them down. Otherwise the people beyond the partition will devour the stuff.

Now what is this gray suit? She holds it up against her; excellent material, well cut; a fair fit, a bit loose. The suit exudes a faint charming rose scent. A woman of quality owned this garment. Alive? Dead? Transported?

Closing the volume with a sigh, Aaron Jastrow turns to her. His hair and beard are white. His skin is like soft mica; bones and veins show through. Ever since his recovery he has been placidly frail, yet capable of surprising endurance. From day to day he teaches, lectures, attends concerts and plays, and puts in a full day's work on the Hebrew cataloguing.

He says, "Those things arrived at dinnertime. Quite a surprise. Eppstein came by later to explain."

Eppstein is Theresienstadt's present head of the municipality, a mayor of sorts with the title of *Ältester*. Formerly a lecturer in sociology, and the head of the "Association of Jews in Germany," he is a meek, beaten-down man, a survivor of Gestapo imprisonment. Trapped in subservience to the SS, he tries in his unnerved way to do some good, but the other Jews see him as hardly more than a puppet of the Germans. He has little choice, and little strength left to exercise what choice he has.

"What did Eppstein say?"

"We're to go to SS Headquarters tomorrow. But we're *not* in danger. It will be pleasant. We're due for more special privileges. So he swears, Natalie."

Feeling cold in her stomach, in her very bones, she asks, "Why are we going?"

"For an audience with Lieutenant Colonel Eichmann."

"*Eichmann!*"

The familiar SS names around Theresienstadt are those of the local officers: Roehn, Haindl, Moese, and so forth. Lieutenant Colonel Eichmann is a remote evil name only whispered; despite the modest rank, a figure standing not far below Himmler and Hitler in the ghetto mind.

Aaron's expression is kindly and sympathetic. He shows little fear. "Yes. Quite an honor," he says with calm irony. "But these clothes do bode well, don't they? Somebody at least wants us to look good. So let's do that, my dear."

71

"Mark! Haleakala, zero eight seven. Mark! Mauna Loa, one three two."

Crouched at the alidade, Byron was calling out bearings to a quartermaster writing by a red flashlight, as the *Moray* scored a phosphorescent wake on the calm sea. The warm offshore breeze smelled to Byron—a pleasant hallucination, no doubt—like the light perfume Janice often wore. The quartermaster went below to plot the bearings, and called up the position through the voice tube. Byron telephoned Aster's cabin.

"Captain, the moon's bright enough so I got a fix of sorts. We're well inside the submarine restricted area."

"Well, good. Maybe the airedales won't bomb us at dawn. Set course and speed to enter the channel at 0700."

"Aye aye, sir."

"Say, Mister Executive Officer, I've just been going over your patrol report. It's outstanding."

"Well, I tried."

"You're no dud at paperwork, Briny. Not anymore. Unfortunately, the clearer you put the story the lousier it comes out."

"Captain, there'll be other patrols." Aster's irritable depression had been troubling Byron all during the return voyage. The captain had holed up in his cabin, smoking cheap cigars by the boxful, reading tattered mysteries from the ship's library, leaving the running of the sub to the exec.

"Zero is zero, Byron."

"They can't fault you for aggressiveness. You volunteered for the Sea of Japan."

"I did, and I'm going back there, but next time with electric torpedoes. Otherwise the admiral can beach me. I'm all through with the Mark Fourteen." Byron could hear the slam of the telephone into the bracket.

Driving in a pool jeep to Janice's cottage next day, Byron was afire to crush his sister-in-law in his arms and forget the patrol. Loneliness,

he passage of time, the disappearance of Natalie, the warmth of Jan-
:e's home, the quiet shows of affection by his brother's pretty widow—
ll these elements were fusing into something like an undeclared ro-
1ance, mounting in sweetness each time he came back from the sea.
'he flame was feeding on an explosive mixture of intimacy and un-
ulfillment. Guilt tormented Byron over his flashes of thought about a
ife with Janice and Victor, if it should happen that Natalie never came
)ack. He suspected Janice of harboring similar notions. Normal rela-
ionships can be wrenched out of shape or destroyed by the tensions and
eparations of war, and what Byron was experiencing was very common-
)lace just now, all over the world. Only his conscience pangs were
lightly unusual.

Something was wrong this time. He knew when she opened the door
ind he saw her serious unpainted face. She was expecting him, for he
ad telephoned, but she had not changed out of a drab blue housedress,
or in any way smartened herself up; nor did she hand him the usual
)lanter's punch in welcome. He might have interrupted her at her cook-
ng or cleaning. She said straight off, "There's a letter from Natalie, for-
varded by the Red Cross."

"What! My God, finally?" Through the International Red Cross he
ad written several letters to Baden-Baden, with this return address.
Everything about the envelope she handed him was disturbing: the
limsy gray paper; the purple block lettering of the address and of "N.
IENRY" in a corner; the overlapping rubber stamps in different colors
ind languages, almost obliterating the Red Cross symbol; above all, the
)ostmark. "Terezin? Where's that?"

"Czechoslovakia, near Prague. I've telephoned my father about this,
3yron. He's talked to the State Department. Read your letter first."

He sank on a chair and slit the envelope with a penknife. The single
:ray sheet was block-lettered in purple.

KURZESTRASSE, P–I
THERESIENSTADT
SEPT. 7, 1943

DEAREST BYRON SPECIAL PRIVILEGE FOR "PROMINENTS"
MONTHLY HUNDRED-WORD LETTER. LOUIS WONDERFUL.
AARON ALL RIGHT. MY SPIRITS GOOD. YOUR LETTERS
DELAYED BUT LOVELY TO HAVE. WRITE HERE. RED CROSS
FOOD PACKAGES EXTREMELY DESIRABLE. DON'T WORRY.
THERESIENSTADT SPECIAL HAVEN FOR PRIVILEGED WAR
HEROES ARTISTS SCHOLARS ETC. WE HAVE GROUND-
FLOOR SUNNY APARTMENT BEST HERE. AARON LIBRAR-

IAN HEBRAIC COLLECTION. LOUIS KINDERGARTEN STAR ALSO CHIEF TROUBLEMAKER. MY WAR FACTORY WORK TAKES SKILL NOT BRAWN. LOVE YOU HEART SOUL. LIVE FOR DAY HOLD YOU IN ARMS. TELEPHONE MY MOTHER. LOVE LOVE NATALIE.

Byron glanced at his watch. "Would your father still be at the War Department?"

"He gave me a message for you. You're to call a Mr. Sylvester Aherne at the State Department. The number's by the telephone."

Byron rang the operator and put in the call. Lunch on his return from a patrol had developed into a merry ritual: strong rum concoctions, a Chinese meal, a bowl of scarlet hibiscus on the table, a laughing exchange of anecdotes. But this time neither the drinks nor Janice's tasty egg foo yong and pepper steak could lift the pall of the letter. Nor could Byron talk about the failed patrol. They ate glumly, and he leaped at the telephone when it rang.

Sylvester Aherne's way of talking made Byron picture a little man in a pince-nez, pursing his mouth and dancing his fingers together. As Byron read the letter to him, Aherne said, "Hm! . . . Hmmmm! Hmm! . . . *Hmmm!* Well! Quite a ray of light, that—isn't it? Reassuring, all in all. Very reassuring. Gives us something solid to work on. You must airmail a copy to us at once."

"What do you know about my family, Mr. Aherne, and about Theresienstadt?"

Speaking with slow prim care, Aherne disclosed that some months ago Natalie and Jastrow had failed to check in with the Swiss in Paris, simply dropped from sight. Insistent inquiries by the Swiss, and by the American chargé in Baden-Baden, had brought no response as yet from the Germans. Now that State knew where they actually were, efforts on their behalf could be redoubled. Since hearing from Senator Lacouture, Aherne had been looking into the Theresienstadt situation. The Red Cross had no record of any releases from the model ghetto; but the Jastrow case was unique, he said, and—so he concluded with a high little giggle—he always preferred to be an optimist.

"Mr. Aherne, are my wife and baby safe in that place?"

"Considering that your wife is Jewish, Lieutenant, and that she was caught travelling illegally in German-occupied territory—for as you know, her journalist credentials were trumped up in Marseilles—she's lucky to have landed there. And as she herself writes, at the moment all is well."

"Can you switch me to another officer in your division, Mr. Leslie Slote?"

"Ah—Leslie Slote? Leslie resigned from the State Department, quite awhile ago."

"Where can I reach him?"

"Sorry, I can't say."

Byron asked Janice to try to call his mother, who might know where Slote was; and he went back to the *Moray* in as low a frame of mind as he had ever been.

As soon as he left Janice began the beautifying routine that she had skipped for Byron's visit. Whether the feeling between them would ever warm up again she could not tell, but she knew that right now she had to keep her distance. Janice was very sorry for Natalie. She had never intended to steal Byron from her. But what indeed if she did not come back? The Theresienstadt letter struck Janice as ominous. She honestly wished Natalie would extricate herself and come home safely with the baby, but the chances seemed to be fading. Meantime, she enjoyed the cornucopia sense of pouring herself out to two men, each time the *Moray* made port. She preferred Byron on the whole; but Aster had his points, and he certainly deserved a good time when he returned from combat. Janice was, in fact, doing a very fair job of eating her cake and having it. She had given Byron his ritual lunch, and the next thing was the ritual rendezvous with Aster.

Byron found Aster waiting in the *Moray*'s wardroom, dressed for the beach and hollowly cheerful. "Well, Briny, the admiral was okay. All is forgiven. We get our Mark Eighteens, and a target ship for training runs. Two weeks for turnaround, and back to the Sea of Japan." He made a bravura flourish with his cigar. "Tomorrow, captain's inspection. Friday Admiral Nimitz comes aboard to give us a unit citation for the first patrol. Saturday, under way at 0600 for electric torpedo exercises. Questions?"

"Hell, yes, what about rest and recreation for the crew?"

"Coming to that. One week in drydock for the new sonar head, and repairs to the stern outer doors. Liberty for all hands. Three more days of training, and we're off to Midway and La Pérouse Strait."

"One week for the men isn't enough."

"Yes, it is," Aster snapped. "This crew has been hurt in its pride. It needs victories a lot more than R and R. Why are you so down in the mouth, anyway? How's Janice?"

"She's all right. Look, Captain, I thought we'd be getting a telephone line over from the dock today, but Hansen just told me no soap. Would you give her a ring while you're ashore? Tell her to call me at the officers' club about ten o'clock."

"Will do," Aster said with a strange grimace, and he left.

Byron assumed that Aster had a woman in Honolulu, but it had never once crossed his mind that the woman might be Janice. So far Aster had been playing along with Janice's pretense, but not liking it much. He thought she was making a fool of her brother-in-law. Byron's naïve obtuseness troubled him; couldn't he sense what was going on? Aster saw nothing wrong in what he and Janice were doing. They were both free, and neither wanted marriage. He didn't think that Byron would mind, but Janice claimed that he would be shocked and alienated, and she insisted on discretion. That was that. It was a subject they no longer talked about.

But he was in an evil mood and a lot of drinking did little to improve it. It grated on him when she telephoned the officers' club at ten o'clock, sitting up on the bed naked, her skin still glistening with amorous perspiration.

"Hi, Briny. Leslie Slote will be waiting for your call in his office tomorrow afternoon at one," she said with sweet calm, as though she sat at home with knitting in her lap. "That's seven in the morning our time, you know. Here's the number." She read it off a slip of paper.

"Did you talk to Slote?"

"No. Actually it was a Lieutenant Commander Anderson who tracked him down, and called me back. Do you know him? Simon Anderson. He seems to be living temporarily at your mother's place. Something about a fire in his apartment house, and she's putting him up for a couple of weeks."

"Simon Anderson's an old beau of Madeline's."

"Oh, well, maybe that explains it. Your mother wasn't there. Madeline came on the line first, sounding all bubbly. She was about to go out for a job interview, so she put Anderson on."

"Madeline's back in Washington to stay, then?"

"She seems to be."

"Why, that's marvelous."

"Will you come to lunch tomorrow, Briny?"

"No can do. Captain's inspection."

"Call me and tell me what Slote says."

"I will."

Aster had been around women; he had been in such a situation with the sweethearts of other men, and with a wife, too. He usually felt sympathy, tinged with contempt, for the poor fish on the other end of the line; but this was Byron Henry being taken in by Janice's coy charade.

"Jesus Christ, Janice," Aster said when she hung up, "are you still playing games with Byron, when Natalie's in a goddamn concentration camp?"

"Oh, just shut up!" Aster had been peevish and difficult all evening. He had said nothing whatever about the patrol, and he had gotten quite drunk; the sex in consequence had been a sputtering business, and Janice was feeling testy herself. "I didn't say she was in a concentration camp."

"Sure you did. In Czechoslovakia, you said."

"Look, you're too smashed to know what I said. I'm sorry you had a disappointing patrol. The next one will be better. Suppose I just go home now?"

"Do as you please, baby." Aster rolled on his side and went to sleep. After thinking it over, Janice did the same.

By the next morning a telephone had been rigged aboard the *Moray*. Byron got his call through to Leslie Slote, though it took several hours. The connection was a scratchy one, and when he finished reading Natalie's letter there was such a long noisy pause that he asked, "Leslie, are you still there?"

"I'm here." Slote uttered a sigh close to a groan. "What can I do for you, Byron? Or for her? What can anybody do? If you want my advice, just put all this from your mind."

"How can I?"

"That's up to you. Nobody knows much about that model ghetto. It does exist, and it may in fact prove a haven for her. I just can't tell you. Send her the letters and Red Cross packages, and keep sinking Japs, that's all. It doesn't help to go out of your head."

"I'm not going out of my head."

"Good. Neither am I. I'm a new man. I've made five training parachute jumps. Five! Remember the incident on the Praha road?"

"What incident?" Byron asked, though he never talked to Slote without thinking of his cowardly collapse under fire outside Warsaw.

"You don't recall? I'll bet you do. Anyway, do you see me making parachute jumps?"

"I'm in submarines, Leslie, and I always hated the Navy."

"Bah, you're from a warrior family. I'm a diplomat, a linguist, altogether a bespectacled cream puff. I die forty deaths in every jump. Yet I enjoy myself in an eerie fashion."

"Parachute jumps for what?"

"OSS. Intelligence. Fighting a war is the best way to forget what it's all about, Byron. That's a novel perception for me, and enormously illuminating."

"Leslie, what are Natalie's chances?"

Another very long scratchy pause.

"Leslie?"

"Byron, she's in a damnable situation. She has been, ever since Aaron wouldn't leave Italy in 1939. As you recall, I begged him to. You were sitting right there. They've done stupid and rash things, and now the fat's in the fire. But she's tough and strong and clever. Fight the war, Byron. Fight the war, and put your wife from your mind. Her, and all the other Jews. That's what I've done. Fight the war, and forget what you can't help. If you're a praying man, pray. I wouldn't talk like this if I were still employed at State, naturally. Good-bye."

When the *Moray* sailed, there were more defections from the crew than there had been in all previous patrols put together: requests for transfers, sudden illnesses, even some AWOLs.

The sky over Midway was low and gray, the wind dankly cold. Fueling was almost complete. Hands jammed in his windbreaker pockets, Byron paced the deck in a strong stench of diesel oil, making a last topside inspection before the long pull to Japan. Each departure from Midway made him think long dark thoughts. Somewhere around here, on the ocean floor in a shattered airplane, his brother's bones lay. Leaving Midway meant sallying forth from the last outpost, on the long lonely hunt. It meant calculation of distances, chances, fuel capacity, food stores; also of the state of nerves of the captain and the crew. Aster emerged on the bridge in fresh khakis and overseas cap, with eyes cleared and color restored by a few sober days under way; very much the killer-captain, Byron thought, even laying it on a bit to cheer up his depressed and edgy sailors.

"Say, Briny, Mullen's going with us, after all," he called down to the forecastle.

"He is? What changed his mind?"

"I talked to him."

Mullen was the *Moray*'s first-class yeoman. His orders to chiefs' school had arrived, and he was due to fly back to the States from Midway. But like all submarine sailors, the *Moray* crew were a superstitious lot, and many of them believed that this yeoman was the ship's good luck charm, simply because his nickname was Horseshoes. The name had nothing to do with his luck; Mullen tended to lose at cards and dice, also to fall off ladders, get himself arrested by the shore patrol, and so on. Nevertheless, Horseshoes he was, so dubbed at boot camp years ago because he had won a horseshoe-pitching contest. Byron had overheard many foreboding comments by crewmen on the transfer of Mullen, but it jarred him that Aster had gone and worked the ma-

over. He found Mullen thumping a typewriter in the tiny ship's office, a cigar thrust in his round red face; if Byron was not mistaken, one of the captain's Havanas. The tubby little sailor had been dressed in whites to go ashore, but he was wearing his washed-out dungarees again.

"What's all this, Mullen?"

"Just thought I'd grab one more patrol on this hell ship, sir. The food is so lousy I'll lose weight. The Stateside gals will like that."

"If you want to get off, say so, and you'll go."

The yeoman took a long puff at the expensive cigar, and his genial face toughened. "Mr. Henry, I'd follow Captain Aster to hell. He's the greatest skipper in SubPac, and now that we've got those Mark Eighteens, this is going to be the *Moray Maru*'s greatest patrol. I'm not about to miss it. Sir, where is Tarawa?"

"Tarawa? Down in the Gilberts. Why?"

"Marines are catching hell there. Look at this." He was making carbon copies of the latest news broadcast from Pearl Harbor. The tone of the bulletin was grave: *fierce opposition . . . very heavy casualties . . . outcome in doubt. . . .*

"Well, the first day of a landing is the worst."

"People think we've got rough duty." Horseshoes shook his head. "Those Marines sure bought the shit end of this war."

The *Moray* left Midway in a melancholy drizzle. For days the weather kept worsening. The submarine never rode well on the surface, and in these frigid stormy latitudes, shipboard life was a bruising routine of treacherous footing, seasickness, cold meals half-spilled, and chancy sleep through interminable dull days and nights. In the northwest Pacific, an inactive waste of tempestuous black water, the Japanese were unlikely to be doing much patrolling, and visibility was poor. Still, Aster maintained a combat alert all day. Frostbitten lookouts and OODs were coming off watch cracking ice from their clothes.

Making a transit of the rocky Kuriles within air range of Japan, Aster sailed on at fifteen knots, merely doubling the lookouts. The *Moray* was not a submarine, but a "submersible," he liked to say—that is, a surface ship that could dive—and skulking under the sea was no way to get places. Byron agreed, but he thought Aster sometimes crowded the line between courage and rashness. By now several submarines had patrolled the Sea of Japan; the *Wahoo* had disappeared there; the enemy might well have an air patrol out. Fortunately the *Moray* was travelling most of the time in fog and sleet. Byron's dead reckoning was getting a hard workout.

Seven days out of Midway, a shift in the wind thinned the fog, and the hills of Hokkaido ridged the gray horizon ahead. To starboard a higher black lump showed: the headlands of Sakhalin.

"*Soya Kaikyo!*" Aster jocularly hailed La Pérouse Strait by the Japanese name, and clapped Byron's shoulder. "Well done, Mister Navigator." The *Moray* was wallowing on heavy quartering swells, and a bitter stern wind whipped the captain's thick blond hair as he squinted landward. "Now then, how close do we go before we pull the plug? Do the Japs have radar yet on those hills, or not?"

"Let's not find out," said Byron. "Not now."

With a slow reluctant nod, Aster said, "Concur. Clear the bridge."

Riding at periscope depth was a restful change after a week of plunging and rolling. Seasick sailors climbed out of their bunks and ate sandwiches and hot soup at level tables. At the periscope, Byron was struck by the romance of the view in the glass. As the *Moray* neared the eastern entrance, the setting sun shot red rays under the low clouds, haloing in rosy mist the Hokkaido hill called Maru Yama. Across Byron's mind there flashed an old lovely vision. Japanese art had charmed him in his undergraduate days; the paintings, novels, and poetry had conjured up fairyland landscapes, delicately exotic architecture, and quaintly costumed little people with perfect manners and subtle esthetic tastes. This picture did not mesh at all with "the Japs," the barbarians who had smashed Pearl Harbor, raped Nanking, taken the Philippines and Singapore, killed his brother, and stolen an empire. He took grim pleasure in torpedoing "Japs." But this glimpse of misty Maru Yama in the sunset brought back that early vision. Did "the Japs"—it occurred to him to wonder—consider Americans barbarians? He did not feel like a barbarian, nor did the dungareed sailors on watch look barbarous. Yet the *Moray* was approaching the quaint fairyland to murder by stealth as many "Japs" as it could.

In short, war.

Byron summoned the captain to show him through the scope two vessels steaming eastward with running lights on: sparks of red, green, and white vivid in the twilight.

"Russkis, no doubt," said Aster. "Are they in the designated Russian route?"

"Dead on," said Byron.

"Good. That's where the mines aren't."

Last time, Aster had commented wryly on this freak aspect of the war: Soviet ships plying the Lend-Lease run through Jap waters with impunity, though Germany's defeat was bound to drag down Japan. Now, peering through the periscope, he remarked in businesslike tones, "Say, why don't we go through showing lights? If the Nips have installed radar up here, that's better deception than running darkened."

"Suppose we're challenged?"

"Then we're stupid Russians who didn't get the word."

"I'm for it, Captain."

In full view of the Japanese coast, about an hour after dark, the dripping *Moray* turned on its lights. For Byron, standing on the bridge in the strong freezing wind, it was the strangest moment of the war. He had never yet sailed on an illuminated submarine. The white masthead lights fore and aft dazzled like suns; the red and green glows seemed to shoot out to port and starboard half a mile. The ship was so visibly, so horribly a *submarine!* But only from the bridge; surely nothing could be seen from the Japanese headland ten miles away but the lights, if that much.

The lights were seen. As the *Moray* plunged along through the coal-dark strait, a signal searchlight on Hokkaido blinked. Aster and Byron were flailing their arms and stamping on the bridge. The signaller blinked again. And yet again. "No spikka da Joponese," said Aster.

The signalling ceased. The *Moray* bore on into the Sea of Japan, doused its lights before dawn, and submerged.

Toward noon as they were crawling southward they spotted a small freighter, perhaps eight hundred tons. Aster and Byron debated whether to shoot. It was worth torpedoing, but the attack might trigger SOS signals and a full air-and-sea submarine search in the Sea of Japan. If the Japs were not alerted now, the pickings further south tomorrow would be easier and fatter. Aster was calculating on three days of depredations, and one day to escape. "The Mark Eighteen can use a firing test," he said at last, lighting up a Havana. "Let's have an approach course, Mister Navigator. We'll shoot one fish." He returned a frigid defiant grin to Byron's quizzical look. "The Mark Eighteen leaves no wake. If it misses, our Nip friend up there will know from nothing, right? If it hits, he may get too busy to send messages."

Aster ran off the attack in a curt businesslike way, and Byron was heartened by the crew's spirited responses. The electric torpedo was longer-legged than the Mark Fourteen, but slower. Byron was not used to the additional lag before impact; watching in the glass, he was about to report a miss, when a column of smoke and white water burst over the freighter; and a second or so later a destructive rumble sounded through the *Moray*'s hull. He had never seen a vessel go down so fast. Less than five minutes after the hit, while he was still taking periscope photographs, it sank out of sight in a cloud of smoke, flame, and steam.

Aster seized the loudspeaker microphone. "Now hear this. Scratch one Jap freighter. And score one victory for the Mark Eighteen electric torpedo, the first of many for the *Moray Maru!*"

The yells sent prickling thrills through Byron. It had been a long time since he had heard this triumphant male baying, the war cry of a submarine.

That night Aster ran south to get athwart the ship lane to Korea, where the targets had been so numerous and the results so dismal on the last patrol. Toward dawn the OOD reported running lights ahead; so as yet, despite the attack on the freighter, there was no submarine alert in the Sea of Japan. Aster ordered a dive. In the periscope, brightening day showed what he called a mouth-watering sight, ships moving peaceably and unescorted wherever the glass turned. Byron found himself with a problem in relative movement worthy of an Annapolis navigation course: how to attack one target after another, with maximum scoring and minimum warning to the victims.

From the captain downward the *Moray* came alive. The killing machine was back in swing. Aster chose first to attack a large tanker; he bore in to nine hundred yards, fired a single torpedo, and struck. Leaving the cripple ablaze, settling, and pouring volcanic black smoke from the flammable cargo, he swung around in a long approach to what looked like a big troop carrier, by far the fattest target in sight. Maneuvering to close this prize took hours. Aster paced the conning tower, went below to his cabin, came up and paced again, gobbled a large steak from the galley at the chart desk, and ripped the pages of a girlie magazine with his impatient flipping. In attack position at last, with Byron at the periscope, he fired a spread of three torpedoes as soon as he could, at extreme range. After a prolonged wait Byron cried, *"Hit! By God, he's disappeared!"* When the obscuring curtain of smoke and spray cleared, the vessel was still there, sharply down by the bow and listing, clearly a dead loss. Aster's announcement brought more lusty cheers.

He had selected this target with a view to two others, a pair of large freighters steaming on the same course not far off. These vessels now turned away from the stricken troopship and put on speed.

"I can't catch them submerged. We'll pursue on the surface after nightfall," Aster said. "They're running back east for home and air cover. Things will be tougher tomorrow. *However*"—he slapped Byron on the back—"not a bad day's haul!"

This buoyant spirit was everywhere in the submarine: in the conning tower, the control room, the wardroom, even down in the engine rooms, when Byron laid below for a routine check. The perspiring half-naked grease-streaked sailors greeted him with the happy grins of football players after a big win. While he was below the submarine surfaced, and the diesels churned into deafening action. He hurried topside. On the bridge, in a parka and mittens, Carter Aster was eating a thick sandwich. The night was starry, with one dim red streak of sunset, and dead ahead on the horizon were the two tiny black blobs of the freighters.

"We'll nail both those monkeys at dawn," said the captain. "How are we on fuel?"

"Fifty-five thousand gallons."

"Not bad. This roast beef is great. Get Haynes to make you a sandwich."

"I think I'll grab some sleep."

"Staying in character, eh?"

Aster had not laughed much in recent weeks, nor poked fun at Byron. Actually, Byron had been getting by on very little rest, but the sleepyhead joke was permanent, and he was glad that Aster was in a joshing mood again.

"Well, Lady, it's a stern chase. Not much doing till about 0300." Looking up at the sky, Byron leaned on the bulwark. He felt relaxed and in no hurry to go below. "Nice night."

"Beautiful. One more day's hunting like today, Briny, and they can rotate me to the States any time."

"Feeling better, eh?"

"Christ, yes. How about you?"

"Well, on a day like today, I'm just fine. Otherwise, not so hot."

Long silence, except for the splash of the sea and the sighing of the wind.

"Natalie's on your mind."

"Oh, she always is. And the kid. And for that matter, Janice."

"Janice?" Aster hesitated, then asked, "Why Janice?"

They could barely see each other's faces in the starlight. The OOD stood close by, his binoculars trained on the horizon.

Byron's reply was scarcely audible. "I've treated her abominably."

Aster called down for another sandwich and coffee, then said, "In what way, for Pete's sake? I think you've been a downright Sir Galahad around Janice." Byron did not answer. "Well, you don't have to talk about it."

But in the release of long tension, Byron did want to talk about it, though the words came hard. "We're in love, Lady. Haven't you seen that? It's all my doing, and it's a stupid dream. That letter from Natalie woke me up. I've got to cut it off, and it'll be rotten for both of us. I don't know what the hell's possessed me, all these months."

"Look, Byron, you're lonesome," Aster commented after a pause, in a low gentle tone not like him. "She's a beautiful woman, and you're quite a guy. You've been sleeping under the same roof, for crying out loud! You ask me, you rate a Bronze Star for staying faithful to Natalie."

Byron gave his captain a light punch on the shoulder. "Well, that's how you'd figure it, Lady. Superlative fitness report. But from my viewpoint, she's fallen for me because I've encouraged her. I've been damned obvious about that. Yet while Natalie's alive, it's hopeless, isn't it? And do I want Natalie dead? I've been a shit."

"Jesus Christ and General Jackson," exclaimed Aster, "that tears it. Briny, in some ways I admire you, but on the whole you're to be pitied. You live off on some other planet, or you've never grown up, I don't know which, but—"

"What's all this, now?"

Byron and Aster were side by side, leaning elbows on the bulwark and looking out to sea. Aster glanced over his shoulder at the shadowy OOD.

"Listen, you fool, I've been laying Janice for a year. How could you be so goddamned blind, not to realize that?"

Byron straightened up. *"Wha-a-at!"* The word was an animal growl.

"It's true. Maybe I shouldn't tell you, but when you—"

At this moment the wardroom steward came up the ladder with a sandwich on a plate and a steaming mug. Aster picked off the sandwich, and took a gulp of coffee. "Thanks, Haynes."

Byron stood staring at Aster, rigid as an electrocuted man.

Aster resumed as the steward left, "Christ, man, with all your troubles, the idea of you eating out your heart because you've misled Janice! It would be hilarious, if it weren't so pathetic."

"For a year?" Byron repeated, dazedly shaking his head. "A year? You?"

Biting into the sandwich, Aster spoke with a half-full mouth. "Jesus, I'm hungry. Yes, I guess about a year. Since she got over the dengue fever. Between that, and your brother's death, and you off in the Med, she was a mighty sad cookie at that time. Now, don't get me wrong, she *likes* you, Byron. She missed you a lot when you were in the Med. Maybe she does love you, but Christ, she's *human*. I mean what harm have we done? She's a great kid. We've had a lot of laughs. She's been afraid of you and your father. Thought you'd disapprove." He drank coffee, and took another bite, peering at the silent and unmoving Byron. "Well, maybe you do, at that. Do you? I still don't know how your mind works. Just don't waste any more energy feeling guilty about Janice. Okay?"

Byron abruptly left the bridge.

At three o'clock in the morning he came into the control room and found Aster at the plotting board with the plot party, smoking a stogie and looking white and tense. "Hi, Briny. The SJ radar has picked one hell of a time to fail. We're socked in again. Visibility down to a thousand yards. We're trying to track them by sonar, but listening conditions stink. Our last position on them is two hours old, and if they change course we can lose them." Aster peered through smoke at Byron. "I don't know why they would change course. Do you?"

"Not if they're returning to port."

"Okay. We agree. I'm holding course and speed."

He followed Byron into the wardroom. Over coffee, after a lengthy silence, he asked, "Sleep?"

"Sure."

"Sore at me?"

Byron gave him a straight hard look that reminded Aster of Captain Victor Henry. "Why? You took a load off my mind."

"That was the idea."

At dawn they were topside, straining their eyes through binoculars. The radar still was not functioning. The visibility had improved, though heavy clouds still hung low over the sea. The freighters were not in sight. It was Horseshoes Mullen, their best lookout, who sang out from the cigarette deck, *"Target! Broad on the starboard bow, range ten thousand!"*

"Ten thousand?" said Aster, swinging his binoculars to starboard. "Son of a bitch. They did change course. And one of them's gone."

Byron discerned in his glass the faint small gray shadow. "Yes, that's one of those freighters. Same samson posts."

Aster yelled down the hatch, *"All ahead flank! Right full rudder!"*

"Five miles," Byron said. "Unless he zigzags, he's made it."

"Why? We can overtake him."

Byron turned to peer at him. "You mean on the *surface?"*

Aster jerked his thumb up at the low thick cloud cover. "What kind of air searches can they be running in this?"

"Lady, those freighters took evasive action. There's probably a full submarine alert on. You've got to assume that that freighter's been reporting his course, speed, and position all night, and that planes are in the area."

"Steady on one seven five!" Aster called.

Byron persisted, "They can swarm down like bees through any break in the clouds. What's more, we don't even know that they haven't got airborne radar."

The submarine was heeling and speeding up. Green water came crashing over the low forecastle, dousing everyone on the bridge with spray. Aster grinned at Byron, patted his arm, and snuffed the air. "Great morning, hey? Sound the happy hunting horn."

"Listen, we're still in the shipping lane, Lady. Plenty of other targets will be coming along. Let's submerge."

"That freighter's our pigeon, Briny. We've been tracking him all night, and we're going to get him."

The surface chase lasted almost an hour. The lighter the day grew, the more nervous Byron felt, though the clouds stayed low and solid overhead. They came close to overtaking the freighter, close enough to confirm that it was certainly the same ship. Byron never saw the planes. He heard Mullen yell, *"Aircraft dead astern, coming in low,"* and another, *"Aircraft on the port—"* The rest was drowned out in the stutter, whine, and *zing!* of many bullets. He threw himself on the deck, and as he did so a monstrous explosion almost broke his eardrums. Water showered over him; the heavy splash from a close miss, a bomb or a depth charge.

"Take her down! Dive, dive, dive!" Aster bawled.

Bullets went pinging all over the wallowing ship. The sailors and officers, staggering and leaping for the hatch, one by one dropped through in a rapid automatic routine. Within seconds the conning tower was crowded with the dripping deck watch.

BAMMMM!

Another close miss. Very close.

RAT-TAT-TAT! PING! PING! A hail of bullets topside. Solid water flooded down through the open hatch, sloshing all over the deck, wetting Byron to his knees.

"The captain! Where's the captain?" he bellowed.

As though in answer, an anguished voice shouted out on the deck, "BYRON, I'M HIT! I CAN'T MAKE IT! *TAKE HER DOWN!*"

Stunned for an instant, then wildly glancing around, Byron shouted at the crew, "Anybody else missing?"

"Horseshoes is dead, Mr. Henry," the quartermaster yelled at him. "He's out on the cigarette deck. He got it in the face. I tried to bring him down, but he's dead."

Byron roared, "Captain, I'm coming up for you!" He darted into the water showering down the ladder and began to climb.

"Byron, I'm *paralyzed.* I can't move!" Aster's voice was a cracking scream. "You can't help me. There's five planes diving at this ship. TAKE HER DOWN!"

BAMM!

The *Moray* rolled far over to starboard.

A torrent of salt water cascaded through the hatch, flooding up against control instruments. Sparks flew in smoke and sudden stink. The crewmen were slipping and stumbling about in swirling water, white-rimmed eyes on Byron as he desperately calculated the time he would need to fight his way topside and drag the paralyzed captain to safety. In this attack, probably in seconds, the *Moray* would almost surely be lost with all hands.

"Take her down, Byron! I'm done for. I'm dying." Aster's voice was fading.

Byron thrust himself up the ladder against the foaming waterfall in a last effort to climb out. He could not do it. With terrific exertion he barely succeeded in slamming the hatch shut. Drenched, coughing salt water, his voice breaking with grief, he gave his first order in command of a submarine.

"Take her to three hundred feet!"

The only knell for Captain Aster was the sound he perhaps loved best, though nobody could know whether he heard it.

A-OOOGHA . . . A-OOOGHA . . . A-OOOGHA . . .

72

October 1, 1943

Dear Pug:

Bill Standley has come home singing your praises. I am ever so grateful for all you've gotten done over there.

Now I have asked Harry to write the attached letter to you. At least it will get you out of Moscow! You have a feeling for facts, so please take on this job and do what you can. A cable about Tehran very soon would be much appreciated.

By the way, we are launching several splendid new battleships nowadays. One will be for you, as soon as we can shake you loose.

FDR

THIS was scrawled on one sheet of the familiar pale green notepaper. Hopkins's typewritten letter was much longer.

Dear Pug:

You've certainly been doing some grand work with the Russians. Thanks to your survey of shuttle-bombing sites the Joint Chiefs' planners are already working on the Poltava idea. General Fitzgerald wrote me a fine letter about you, and I sent the Bureau of Personnel a copy. Also, getting our servicemen's hospital and rest center finished up at Murmansk was a triumph over the ways of their bureaucracy. I'm told it has improved convoy morale.

Now about the forthcoming heads of state conference: Stalin won't travel farther than Tehran, just south of his Caucasus frontier. He claims he has to stay in close touch with his military situation. Whether that's true, or he's being coy, or worrying about his prestige we can't tell, but he absolutely will not budge on this.

The President will travel almost anywhere to get this damnable war won, but Tehran poses a constitutional snag. If Congress passes a bill he wants to veto, he has to do this with his own hand in ten days, or it automatically becomes law. A cabled or telephoned veto won't work. Tehran is reachable from Washington in less than ten days, with all equipment pushing in fair weather. But we're told Tehran weather is unpredictable and horrendous. We're also told it's not all that bad.

Nobody around here seems to know much about Persia. To Washington types it's like the moon.

I suggested that you fly down there, look around, ask some questions, and shoot us a word on the weather prospects at the end of November, and on the security angle too, since we hear the place crawls with Axis spies. Also, the President is fortifying himself with facts and figures for talking with Stalin, and Lend-Lease is bound to come up. We have sheaves of reports, but we could use a good eyewitness account of how things are really going in the Persian supply corridor. Unlike most report-writers you have no axe to grind!

General Connolly is the man in charge at our Amirabad base outside Tehran. He's a good man, an old Army engineer. I knew him well years ago when I headed the WPA and he handled some big construction projects. I have cabled him about you. Connolly will give you a rapid tour of our Lend-Lease port facilities, rail and truck routes, factories, and depots. You can ask any questions, go anywhere, talk to anybody. The President will want to see you before he meets Stalin; and if you can sum up your observations on one sheet of paper that will be a real help.

Incidentally, the landing craft problem has now reached a critical stage, as I foresaw. It's the strangling bottleneck of all our strategic plans. Production is increasing, but it could be a lot better. However, you'll soon be returning to your first love, the sea. The President is aware that you feel like a stranded whale.

> Yours,
> Harry Hopkins

The letters came as a cheering reprieve. Admiral Standley had not lasted long after his outburst; Harriman had succeeded him, bringing a large military mission headed by a three-star general, which spelled the end of Victor Henry's job. But as yet he had received no orders, and he was beginning to think BuPers had lost track of him. Moscow was again snowbound. He had not heard from Rhoda or his children in months. At last he could escape from the boredom of Spaso House talk, the bitching of the frustrated vodka-soaked American newspapermen, and the unfriendly deviousness and obduracy of the Russian bureaucrats. The same afternoon that he got the letters he was on a Russian military plane to Kuibyshev, thanks to a last assist from General Yevlenko. Next day General Connolly met Pug at the airport, put him up in his own quarters on the huge newly built base in the desert, served him venison for dinner, and over coffee and brandy handed him an itinerary that made him blink.

"It'll take you a week or so," said Connolly, a bluff West Pointer in his sixties who bit out rapid words, "but then you'll have something to tell old Harry Hopkins. What we're doing here is sheer lunacy. One country, the U.S.A., is trying to deliver stuff to another country, the USSR, under the control, or rather interference, of a third country, England, through the territory of a fourth country, Persia, where none of us have any goddamned business being. And—"

"You lose me. Why should England interfere?"

"You're new to the Middle East." Connolly blew out an exasperated breath. "Let me try to explain. The British are here by right of invasion and occupation, see? So are the Russians. They partitioned this country by armed force back in 1941, so as to suppress German activity here. That was the reason given, anyhow. Now, follow me carefully. *We* have no right to be here, because we *haven't* invaded Persia. See? Clear as mud, what? Theoretically we're merely helping the British help Russia. The striped-pants boys are still dingdonging about all that. Meantime we're just shoving the goods through any old way, insofar as the Limeys will let us, and the Persians don't steal it, and the Russkis will come and get it. It keeps piling sky-high in the Soviet depots."

"It does? But in Moscow they keep screaming for more."

"Naturally. That has nothing to do with their own transport foul-up. It's monumental. I had to call an eight-day rail embargo back in August, till they came and took away a mountain of stuff at the northern railhead. Once their pilots, drivers, and railroad men get out of the workers' paradise they tend to linger outside. Being fresh from Moscow, you probably can't understand that."

"Beats me." They grinned tart American grins at each other. Pug said, "I also have to look into the weather here."

"What about the weather?"

As Pug described the President's legal difficulty, General Connolly's face wrinkled in a pained frown. "Are you kidding? Why didn't somebody ask me? The weather's changeable, and the dust storms are a nuisance, sure. But we've had maybe two scheduled military flights held up all year. He and Stalin must be playing games. Stalin wants to make him come all the way to his back fence, and the Great White Father is standing on his dignity. I hope he sticks to that. Old Joe should move his tail himself. Russians don't admire people they can shove around."

"General, there's a lot of ignorance about Persia in Washington."

"Christ, you said a mouthful. Well, look, even assuming big winter storms at both ends"—Connolly scratched his head with a hand holding a thick smoking cigar—"that bill he might want to veto could be delivered to Tunis in five days, and we could fly him there in a B-24. He'd go there and back and miss maybe one day here. It's not a real problem."

"Well, I'll cable all that to Hopkins. I have to check into security here, too."

"No sweat, I'll give you the whole drill. How's your backgammon game?" Connolly asked, pouring more brandy for both of them.

Pug had played a lot of acey-deucey over the years. He beat the general two games running, and was winning the third when Connolly said, looking up at him from the board and half-closing one eye, "Say, Henry, we have a mutual acquaintance, don't we?"

"Who?"

"Hack Peters." At Pug's blank look he elaborated, "Colonel Harrison Peters, Engineers. Class of 1913. Big tall guy, bachelor."

"Oh, right. I met him at the Army-Navy Club."

Connolly heavily nodded. "He wrote me about this Navy captain who was Harry Hopkins's boy in Moscow. Now here we meet in this godforsaken neck of the woods. Small world."

Pug played on without further comment, and lost. The general happily folded away the elegantly inlaid board and the ivory counters. "Hack's working on something that can end this war overnight. He's cagey about it, but it's the biggest job the Army engineers have ever tackled."

"I don't know anything about that."

Bedding down in the chilly desert night on an austere Army-issue bed under three coarse blankets, Pug wondered what Colonel Peters could have written about him, after meeting him for a casual raucous hour of drinking champagne and wearing paper hats at a club table. Rhoda had mentioned Peters now and then as a church acquaintance. A possible connection with Palmer Kirby through the uranium bomb crossed Pug's mind, giving him a sick ugly qualm. After all, why had Rhoda's letters ceased? Communication with Moscow was difficult, but possible. Three silent months . . . His fatigue and the brandy helped him blot out these thoughts in sleep.

General Connolly's itinerary called for Pug to traverse Iran, south to north, by railroad and truck vonvoy; a man from the British legation, Granville Seaton, would go along partway on the train trip. The truck convoys were an all-American show to back up the railroad, which suffered—so Connolly said—from sabotage, washouts, pilfering, breakdowns, collisions, hijacking raids, and the general inefficiency built in by the Germans, and compounded by Persian and British mismanagement.

"Granville Seaton really knows the whole Persian setup," said Connolly. "He's a history scholar, a strange duck, but worth listening to. He loves bourbon. I'll give you some Old Crow to pack along."

On the flight down to Abadan the small plane was too noisy for talk. In the long sweaty tour of an astonishingly large American airplane assembly plant on the desolate seaside flats, where the temperature must have been well over a hundred degrees, Granville Seaton trudged alongside Pug and the factory manager, smoking and saying nothing. Then they drove up to Bandar Shahpur, the rail terminal on the Persian Gulf. Seaton chatted over their dinner at a British officers' mess, but the flutey sing-song words came out so blurry and strangled that he might as well have been talking Persian. Pug had never seen a man smoke so much. Seaton himself looked rather smoked; dried-out, brownish, weedy, with a wide gap between large yellow upper front teeth. Pug had the fancy that if injured the man would bleed brown as a tobacco stain.

Next day at breakfast Pug produced the bottle of Old Crow. At this Seaton smiled like a boy. "Most decadent," he said, and held out his water glass.

The single-track railway crossed dead salt flats and twisted up toward dead mountains. Seen from an airplane the barrenness of this country was bad enough, but from a train window it was worse. No brush grew, miles without end; sand, sand, sand. The train halted to take on another diesel locomotive, and they got off to stretch their legs. Not so much as a jackrabbit or a lizard moved on the sand. Only flies swarmed.

"This may have been the actual garden of Eden," Seaton suddenly spoke up. "It could be again, given water, energy, and a people to work the ground. But Iran lies on this landscape inert as a jellyfish on a rock. You Americans could help. And you had better."

They got back aboard. Clanking and groaning, the train ascended a rocky gorge on a hairpin-turning roadbed. Seaton unwrapped Spam sandwiches, and Pug brought out the Old Crow.

"What should we do about Iran?" Pug asked, pouring bourbon into paper cups.

"Save her from the Russians," replied Seaton. "Either because you're as altruistic and anti-imperialist as you say, or because you'd rather not see the Soviet Union come out of this war dominating the earth."

"Dominating the earth?" Pug asked skeptically. "Why? How?"

"The geography." Seaton drank bourbon, giving Pug a severe stare. "That's the key. The Iranian plateau bars Russia from warm-water ports. So she's landlocked half the year. Also bars her from India. Lenin hungrily called India the depot of the world. Said it was the main prize of his policy in Asia. But Persia, jammed by a thoughtful Providence against the Caucasus like a huge plug, holds back the Bear. It's as big as all western Europe, and mostly it's harsh mountains and salt deserts, such as you're looking at. The people are wild mountain tribes, nomads, feudal villagers, wily lowlanders, all very independent and un-manageable." His paper cup was empty. Pug quickly poured more bourbon. "Ah, thank you. The prime truth of modern Persian history, Captain, is simply this and remember it: *Russia's enemy is Iran's friend.* That's been the British role since 1800. Though on the whole we've bungled it, and come off as perfidious Albion."

The train howled into a long inky tunnel. When it clattered back into the sunglare, Seaton was toying with his empty paper cup. Pug refilled it. "Ah, lovely."

"Perfidious Albion, you were saying."

"Just so. You see, from time to time we've needed Russia's help in Europe—against Napoleon, against the Kaiser, and now against Hitler—and each time we've had to turn a blind eye to Persia, and the Bear each time has seized the chance to claw off a chunk. While we were al-lied against Napoleon, the Czar snatched the whole Caucasus. The Per-sians fought to regain their land, but we couldn't support them just then, so they had to quit. That's how Russia happens to possess the Baku and Maikop oil fields."

"All this," said Pug, "is complete news to me."

"Well, the tale gets sorrier. In 1907, when Kaiser Bill was getting nasty, we needed Russia in Europe again. The Kaiser was probing the Middle East with his Berlin-Baghdad railway, so we and the Russians partitioned Persia: sphere of influence in the north for them, in the south for us, with a neutral desert belt in between. Quite without con-sulting the Persians. And now again we've divided the country by armed invasion. Not pretty, but the Shah was decidedly pro-German, and we had to do it to secure our Middle East position. Still, one can't blame the Shah, can one? From his viewpoint, Hitler was striking at the two powers who've gnawed at Persia north and south for a century and a half."

"You're being very frank."

"Ah, well, among friends. Now look at it from Stalin's viewpoint for a moment, if you can. He partitioned Poland with Hitler. That we con-sider sinful. He partitioned Persia with us. That we consider quite all right. Appeals to his better nature may therefore confuse him a bit. You Americans have just got to take this thing firmly in hand."

"Why should we get into this mess at all?" asked Pug.

"Captain, the Red Army now occupies northern Iran. We're in the south. The Atlantic Charter commits us to get out after the war. You'll want us to comply. But what about the Russians? Who gets them out? Czarist or communist, Russia acts exactly the same, I assure you."

He gave Pug a long solemn stare. Pug stared back, not replying.

"Do you see the picture? We vacate. The Red Army stays. How long will it be before they control Iranian politics, and advance by invitation to the Persian Gulf and the Khyber Pass? Changing the world balance beyond recall, without firing a shot?"

After a gravelled silence, Pug asked, "What do we do about it?"

"Here endeth the first lesson," said Seaton. He tilted his yellow straw hat over his eyes and fell asleep. Pug dozed, too.

When the train jolted them awake, they were in a huge railway yard crowded with locomotives, freight cars, flatcars, tank cars, cranes, and trucks, where a great noisy activity went on: loading, unloading, shunting about of train sections on sidings, with much shouting by unshaven American soldiers in fatigues, and a wild gabble from crowds of native workers. The sheds and carbarns were newly erected, and most of the rails looked freshly laid. Seaton took Pug on a jeep tour of the yard. Breezy and cool despite a strong afternoon sun, the yard filled hundreds of acres of sandy desert, between a little town of mud-brick houses and a range of steep brown dead crags.

"Yankee energy endlessly amazes me. You've conjured up all this in months. Does archeology bore you?" Seaton pointed at a flinty slope. "There are Sassanid rock tombs up there. The bas-reliefs are worth a look."

They got out of the jeep and climbed in gusty wind. Seaton smoked as he went, picking his way upward like a goat. His stamina violated all physical rules; he was less out of breath than Pug when they reached the dark holes in the hillside, where the wind-eroded carvings, to Pug's unpracticed eye, looked Assyrian: bulls, lions, stiff curly-bearded warriors. Here all was quiet. Far below, the railroad yard clanged and squealed, a small busy blotch on the ancient silent desert.

"We can't stay in Iran once the war's won," Pug remarked, pitching his voice above the wind. "Our people don't think that way. All that stuff down there will just rust and rot."

"No, but there are things to do before you leave."

A loud hollow groan sounded behind them in the tomb. Seaton said owlishly, "The wind across the mouth of the sepulchre. Odd effect, what? Rather like blowing over an open bottle."

"I damned near jumped off this hill," said Pug.

"The natives say it's the souls of the ancients, sighing over Persia's fate. Not inappropriate. Now look here. In 1941, after the invasion and partition, the three governments—Iran, the USSR, and my country—signed a treaty. Iran promised to expel the German agents and make no more trouble, and we and Russia agreed to get out after the war. Well, Stalin will just ignore that scrap of paper. But if *you* join in the treaty—that is, if Stalin promises *Roosevelt* he'll get out—that's something else. He may actually go. With grunts, shoves, and growls, but it's the only chance."

"Is it in the works?"

"Not at all."

"Why not?"

Seaton threw up skinny brown hands.

Toward evening the train passed a string of smashed freight cars lying twisted and overturned by the roadbed. "This was a bad one," said Seaton. "German agents planted the dynamite. Tribesmen looted the cars. They had good intelligence. The cargo was food. Worth its weight in gold, in this country. The big shots are hoarding all the grain, and most other edibles. The corruption here boggles the Western mind, but it's how things are done in the Middle East. Byzantium and the Ottomans have left their mark."

He talked far into the night about the ingenious pilfering and raiding devices of the Persians, which were a real drain on Lend-Lease. To them, he said, this river of goods suddenly rushing through their land, south to north, was just another aspect of imperialist madness. They were fishing in it for dear life, knowing it couldn't last. Copper telephone wire, for instance, was stolen as fast as it was strung up. Hundreds of miles of it had vanished. The Persians loved copper trinkets, plates, and bowls, and the bazaars were now flooded with them. These people had been robbed for centuries, said Seaton, by conquerors and by their own grandees. *Loot or be looted* was the truth they knew.

"Should you succeed in getting Stalin out," he said, yawning, "for God's sake don't try to install your free enterprise system here, with party elections and the rest. By free enterprise, Persians mean what they're doing with your copper wire. A democracy in a backward or unstable country simply gets smashed by the best-organized power gang. Here it'll be a communist gang that will open the gates of Asia to Stalin. So forget your antiroyalist principles, and strengthen the monarchy."

"I'll do my best," said Pug, smiling at the cynical candor of the man.

Seaton smiled sleepily back. "One is told you have the ear of the great."

The Tehran Conference was an off-again, on-again thing until the last minute. Suddenly it was on. A presidential party of seventy fell out of the sky on General Connolly: Secret Service men, generals, admirals, diplomats, ambassadors, White House stewards, and assorted staff people, swirling through the Amirabad base in unholy confusion. Connolly told his secretary that he was too busy to see anybody, but on hearing that Captain Henry had reappeared he jumped up and went out to the anteroom.

"Good God. Look at you." Pug was unshaven, haggard, and covered with grime.

"The truck convoy got caught in a dust storm. Then in a mountain blizzard. I haven't been out of my clothes since Friday. When did the President get here?"

"Yesterday. General Marshall's in your room, Henry. We've moved you over to the officers' quarters."

"Okay. I got your message in Tabriz, but the Russians sort of garbled it."

"Well, Hopkins asked where you were, that's all. I thought you'd better get the hell back here. So the Russians did let you through to Tabriz?"

"It took some talking. Where's Hopkins now?"

"Downtown in the Soviet embassy. He and the President are staying there."

"In the *Soviet* embassy? Not here? Not in our legation?"

"Nope. There are reasons. We've got nearly everybody else."

"Where's the Soviet embassy?"

"My driver will take you there. And I think you should hurry." Pug rubbed a hand over his grimy stubby face. Connolly gestured at a bathroom door. "Use my razor."

Despite a few new boulevards which the deposed Shah had bulldozed through Tehran, most of the city was a maze of narrow crooked streets lined by blank mud-wattle walls. Seaton had told Pug that this Persian way of building a town was meant to slow and baffle an invading horde. It slowed the Army driver until he struck a boulevard and roared downtown. The walls around the Soviet embassy gave it a look of a high-security prison. At the entrance, and spaced all along the street and around the corners, frowning soldiers stood with fixed bayonets. One of these halted the car at the iron gates. Victor Henry rolled down the window and snapped in clear sharp Russian, "I am a naval aide to President Roosevelt." The soldier fell back in a stiff salute, then leaped on the running board to guide the driver through the compound, a spacious walled park with villas set here and there amid autumnal old trees, splashing fountains, and wide lawns dotted with ponds.

Russian sentries and American Secret Service men blocked the veranda of the largest villa. Pug talked his way into the foyer, where civilians and uniformed men, British, Russian, American, bustled about in a polyglot tumult. Pug spied Harry Hopkins slouching along in a gray suit by himself, hands in his pockets, looking sicker and skinnier than ever. Hopkins saw him, brightened, and shook hands. "Stalin just walked over to meet the Chief." He gestured at a closed wooden door. "They're in there. Quite a historic moment, hey? Come along, I haven't unpacked yet. How's the Persian Gulf Command doing?"

Behind the door, Franklin Roosevelt and Joseph Stalin sat face to face. There was nobody else in the room but two interpreters.

Across the narrow street that separated the Russian and the British compounds, Winston Churchill sulked in a bedchamber of his legation residence, nursing a sore throat and a sorer spirit. Since arriving in separate planes from Cairo, he and Roosevelt had not spoken. He had sent an invitation to Roosevelt to stay at his legation. The President had declined. He had asked urgently for a meeting before any talks with Stalin. The President had refused. Now those two were meeting without him. Alas for the old intimacy of Argentia and Casablanca!

To Ambassador Harriman, who went across the street to calm him, Churchill grumbled that he was glad to "obey orders," that all he wanted was to give a dinner party two nights later on his sixty-ninth birthday, get thoroughly drunk, and leave the next morning.

Why was Franklin Roosevelt staying in the Russian compound?

Historians casually note that on arrival he had declined invitations from both Stalin and Churchill, so as to offend neither. At midnight Molotov had urgently summoned the British and American ambassadors to warn them of an assassination plot afoot in Tehran. Stalin and Churchill were scheduled to come to the American legation in the morning for the first conference session. It was over a mile from the British and Russian compounds, which adjoined each other. Molotov urged that Roosevelt move to one of these, hinting that otherwise business could not safely proceed.

So when Roosevelt woke in the morning, a choice was thrust on him: either move in with Churchill, his old trusted ally, offering comfortable English-speaking hospitality and reliable privacy; or with Stalin, the ferocious Bolshevik, Hitler's former partner in crime, offering a goldfish bowl of alien attendants and perhaps of concealed microphones. An American Secret Service man had already checked the Russian villa Roosevelt was being offered; but could such a cursory inspection detect the sophisticated Soviet bugging?

Roosevelt chose the Russians. Churchill writes in his history that the choice pleased him because the Russians had more room. Chagrin is not something a great man often acknowledges.

Was there an assassination plot?

Nobody really knows. A book by an aged Nazi ex-agent asserts that he was part of one. Of making such books there is no end. At the least, Tehran's streets were risky; German agents were there; public men do get killed riding through streets; the First World War had started that way. The weary disabled Roosevelt no doubt was better off staying downtown.

Yet—*why with the Russians,* when the British were across the street? Franklin Roosevelt had come all the way to Stalin's back fence. So he had bowed to the brute fact that Russia was doing the main suffering and bleeding against Hitler. To take this last step, to accept Stalin's hospitality, to show openness and trust to a tyrant who knew only secrecy and distrust, was perhaps the subtle gamble of an old lion, the ultimate signal of goodwill across the political gulf between east and west.

Did it signal to Stalin that Franklin Roosevelt was a naïve and gullible optimist, a soft touch, a man to push around?

Stalin seldom disclosed his inner thoughts. But once, during the war, he told the communist author Djilas, "Churchill merely tries to pick your pocket. Roosevelt steals the big things."

The grim ultra-realist was not unaware, it would seem from this, that Russians were dying by the millions and Americans by the thousands, in a war that would give world preeminence to the United States.

We have a record of the first words they exchanged.

ROOSEVELT: *I have been trying for a long time to arrange this.*
STALIN: *I'm sorry, it is all my fault. I have been preoccupied with military matters.*

Or, translated into plain terms, Roosevelt was saying, as for the first time he shook hands with the second most powerful man on earth, *"Well, why have you been so difficult and mistrustful for so long? Here I am, you see, under your very roof."*

And Stalin, whom even Lenin called rude, was drawing instant first blood in his retort: *"We've been doing most of the fighting and dying, that's why."*

So these two men in their sixties met at Stalin's back fence in Persia and chatted: the huge crippled American in a blue-gray sack suit, the very short potbellied Georgian wearing an army uniform with a broad red stripe down the full trousers; the one a peaceful social reformer three times elected, guiltless of any trace of political violence, the other a revolutionary despot with the blood of unthinkable millions of his own countrymen on his hands. A strange encounter.

Tocqueville had predicted that America and Russia would between them rule the earth, the one as a free land, the other as a tyranny. Here was his vision made flesh. What drew these opposites together was only the mutual need to crush a mortal menace to the entire human race, Adolf Hitler's Frost-Cuckoo Land, coming from the east, and coming from the west.

A Secret Service man looked into Hopkins's room. "Mr. Stalin just left, sir. The President's asking for you."

Hopkins was changing his shirt. Hurriedly he tucked the shirttail inside baggy trousers, and pulled over his head a red sweater with a hole in one elbow. "Come along, Pug. The President was inquiring about you this morning."

Everything about this villa was oversize. Hopkins's bedroom was huge. So was the crowded foyer. The room in which Roosevelt sat might have accommodated a masquerade ball. Tall windows admitted a flood of golden sunshine through the sere leaves of high trees. The furniture was heavy, banal, randomly scattered, and none too clean. In an armchair in the sun Roosevelt smoked a cigarette with the holder in his teeth, exactly as in the caricatures.

"Why, hello there, Pug. Grand to see you." His arm swept out for a hearty handclasp. The President looked drawn, lean, much older, but a massive man still, radiating strength and—at the moment—triumphant good humor. The color of the big-jawed face was high. "Harry, it went beautifully. He's an impressive fellow. But bless me, the translation does eat up the time! Terribly tedious. We're meeting at four for the plenary session. Does Winnie know that?"

"Averell went over to tell him." Hopkins glanced at his wristwatch. "That's in twenty minutes, Mr. President."

"I know. Well, Pug!" He gestured at a sofa on which seven men might have sat. "We get gorgeous statistics about all the Lend-Lease aid going to Russia through this Persian corridor. Did you see any sign of it out there? Or is it all just talk, as I strongly suspect?"

The facetiousness went with a broad smile. Roosevelt clearly was still winding down from the excitement of meeting Stalin.

"It's all out there, Mr. President. It's an unbelievable, a magnificent effort. I'll have a report for you later today on one sheet of paper. I'm just back from the road."

"One sheet, eh?" The President laughed, glancing at Hopkins. "Grand. The top sheet is all I ever read, anyway."

"He toured Iran from the gulf to the north," said Hopkins. "By rail and by truck."

"What can I tell Uncle Joe, Pug, if Lend-Lease comes up?" Roosevelt said a shade more seriously. In an aside he remarked to Hopkins, "I don't think it will today, Harry. That wasn't his mood."

"He's changeable," Hopkins said.

Pug Henry swiftly described the pile-ups he had seen at the northern depots, especially at the truck terminal. The Russians had refused to permit the truck convoys to drive any distance into their zone of Iran, he said, allotting only one unloading terminal far from the Russian frontier. That was the big bottleneck. If the trucks could go straight on to Caspian ports and Caucasus border points, the Russians would get more matériel, much faster. Roosevelt listened with sharp attention.

"That's interesting. Put it on your one sheet of paper."

"Don't worry," said Pug without thinking, making Roosevelt laugh again.

"Pug's been boning up on Iran, Mr. President," Hopkins said. "He's on to Pat Hurley's idea, that we should become a party to the treaty guaranteeing withdrawal of foreign armies after the war."

"Yes, Pat keeps harping on that." On Roosevelt's expressive face impatience fleetingly came and went. "Didn't the Russians reject the notion at the Moscow Conference?"

"They stalled." Hopkins, sitting beside Pug, held out a bony hand in an argumentative gesture. "I agree, sir, that we can hardly initiate it. That would be pushing ourselves into the old imperialist game. Still—"

"Exactly. And I won't have that."

"But what about the Iranians, Mr. President? Suppose *they* ask for a guarantee that we'll get out? Then a new declaration would be in order, which would include us."

"We can't ask the Iranians to ask us," Roosevelt replied with casual candor, as though he were in the Oval Office, and not in a Soviet building where all his words were almost certainly being overheard. "That won't fool anybody. We've got three days here. Let's stick to essentials."

He dismissed Victor Henry with a smile and a handshake. Pug was making his way out through the noisy crowded foyer when he heard a very British voice: "I say, there's Captain Henry." It sounded like Seaton. He glanced about, and first noticed Admiral King, standing straight as a telephone pole, looking around with visible lack of love at the swarming uniformed Russians. Beside him a tanned man in a beribboned RAF blue uniform was smiling and beckoning. Pug had not seen Burne-Wilke in several years, and remembered him as taller and more formidable-looking. Beside King the air vice marshal appeared quite short, and he had a mild harassed look. "Hello, there," he said as Pug approached. "You're not on your delegation's roster, are you? Pamela said she'd looked, and you weren't."

"Henry, I thought you were in Moscow," Admiral King said in cold harsh tones. In their rare encounters King always made Pug uneasy. It was a long time since he had thought of the *Northampton,* but now in a mental flash he saw his burning cruiser going down, and sensed a hallucinatory stench of petroleum in his nostrils. `

"I came to Iran on special assignment, Admiral."

"You're in the delegation, then?"

"No, sir."

King stared, not liking the vague responses.

Burne-Wilke said, "Pug, if we can manage it, let's get together while we're here."

As coolly as he could, Pug replied, "Pamela's with you, you say?"

"Yes indeed. I was summoned from New Delhi on very short notice. Problems with the Burma campaign plans. She's still sorting out the maps and reports that we hustled together. She's my aide-de-camp now, and jolly good at it. One realizes what she must have done for poor old Talky."

Despite King's look of distaste for this chitchat, Pug persisted, "Where is she?"

"I left her at our legation, hard at work." Burne-Wilke gestured toward the open doorway. "Why don't you pop over and say hello?"

73

A Jew's Journey
(*from Aaron Jastrow's manuscript*)

I T will not be easy to record my meeting with Obersturmbannführer
Adolf Eichmann. In a sense I am starting this narrative over; and
not only this narrative! Whatever I have written, all my life long, now
seems to have been composed in a child's dream.

What I must put down is so dangerous that the former hiding place
of my papers will not do. As for the encipherment in Yiddish translit-
eration, the SS here would penetrate the poor mask instantly. Any one
of a thousand wretches in Theresienstadt would read it all off for a
bowl of soup or to avoid a beating. I have discovered a more secure
place. Not even Natalie will know about it. If I go in one of the transports (at the moment this still seems unlikely) the papers will molder
until wreckers or renovators, probably long after this war is over, let
sunlight into the walls and crevices of Theresienstadt's mournful old
buildings. If I survive the war, I will find these papers where I hid
them.

Eppstein himself came by this morning, to accompany us to the SS
headquarters. He tried to be agreeable, complimenting Natalie on her
looks and on the healthy appearance of Louis, whom she was clutching
in her arms. Eppstein is in a pitiful position: a Jewish tool, the figurehead "mayor" (*Ältester*) who carries out the SS orders; a shabby Jew
like the rest of us with his yellow star, making a point of wearing a
clean if frayed shirt and a threadbare tie to show his high position. His
wan, puffy, worried face is a truer badge of office.

We had never been in or near SS headquarters before; a high wooden
fence separates it and the entire town plaza from the Jews. The sentry
passed us through the fence and we went along a street bordering the
park, past a church and into a government building with offices and
bulletin boards and stale-smelling corridors echoing with typewriter
noise. It was very strange to come out of the grotesque and squalid
ghetto into a place that, except for the large picture of Hitler in the

lobby, belonged to the old familiar order of things. In its ordinariness, it was almost reassuring: the last thing I expected of SS headquarters. Of course I was very, very nervous.

Despite a balding broad forehead, Lieutenant Colonel Eichmann looks surprisingly young. The remaining hair is dark, and he has the alert, live-wire air of a middle-level official who is ambitious and on the climb. When we came into the office he sat behind a wide desk, and beside him in a wooden chair sat Burger, the SS boss of Theresienstadt, a cruel rough man one avoids if at all possible. Without getting up, yet not disagreeably, Eichmann motioned Natalie and me to chairs in front of the desk, and with a tilt of his head directed Eppstein to a grimy settee. So far, except for the cold nasty look of Burger, and the black uniforms on both men, we might have been calling on a bank manager for a loan, or on a police supervisor to report a theft.

I remember every word of the German conversation that followed, but I mean to put down only essentials. First Eichmann made businesslike inquiries about our health and accommodations. Natalie did not utter a word; she let me reply that we felt well-treated. When he glanced to her she jerkily nodded. The child, completely at his ease, sat in her lap looking wide-eyed at Eichmann, who then said that conditions in Theresienstadt did not satisfy him at all. He had made a thorough inspection. In the next weeks we would see remarkable improvements (*"gewaldige Verschönerungen"*). Burger had instructions to treat us as very special *Prominente*. As things improved in Theresienstadt we would be among the first to benefit.

Next he cleared up—as much as it ever will be, I fear—the mystery of how we come to be here. We were brought to his attention, he says, when I was in the hospital in Paris. The OVRA demanded that the Gestapo hand us over as fugitives from Italian justice. As he tells it, Werner Beck wanted first to extract recordings of my broadcasts from me, and then let the Italian secret police take us away. He paints a very black picture of Werner, which may well be distorted.

At any rate, our case fell in his lap for disposition. To hand us over to the Italians might well have meant our deaths, and could have complicated the negotiations for exchanging the Baden-Baden group. Yet to allow us to return to Baden-Baden, once we were discovered, would have offended Germany's one European ally; for Italy was then still in the war. Sending us to Theresienstadt, while taking the Italian request "under advisement," seemed the most considerate solution. He had brushed aside Werner Beck's pleas to extort the broadcasts from me. That was no way to treat a prominent personage, even a Jew. He always tried, Eichmann said, to be as fair and humane as possible in carrying out the strict Jewish policies of the Führer; with which, he was frank to say, he totally agreed. Moreover, he did not believe the broadcasts would have served any purpose. So in short, here we were.

Now, he said, he would let Herr Eppstein talk.

The *Ältester,* sitting hunched on the sofa, proceeded to reel off words in a monotone, occasionally looking at me and Eichmann, but throwing many worried glances at Burger, who was glaring at him. The Council of Elders had recently voted, he said, to split off the Culture Section from the Education Department. Cultural activities had greatly increased; they were the pride of Theresienstadt; but they were not properly supervised or coordinated. The council wanted to designate me as an Elder to head the new Department of Culture. My lectures on Byzantium, Martin Luther, and Saint Paul were the talk of the town. My status as an American author and scholar commanded respect. No doubt in my university career I had learned administration. Abruptly Eppstein stopped talking, looking straight at me with a mechanical smile, a mere lifting of the upper lip from stained teeth.

My only possible motive for accepting the offer would have been pity for the man. Clearly he was doing as he had been ordered. It was Eichmann who for some reason wanted me to head this new "Department of Culture."

I do not know how I summoned the courage to reply as I did. Here is almost exactly what I said. *"Herr Obersturmbannführer,* I am your prisoner here, bound to obey orders. Still, I permit myself to point out that my German is only fair. My health is frail. I have little appreciation for music, which is the backbone of Theresienstadt's cultural activities. My library work, which I enjoy, absorbs all my time. I am not refusing this honor, but I am ill-suited for it. Do I have a choice in this matter?"

"If you did not have a choice, Dr. Jastrow," Eichmann answered briskly, without annoyance, "this conversation would be pointless. I am a rather busy man. Sturmbannführer Burger could have given you an order. However, I think this job would be a fine one for you."

But I was appalled at the prospect of becoming one of the wretched Elders, who for a few miserable privileges—most of which I already enjoy—bear the awful burden of the ghetto on their consciences, transmit to the Jews all the harsh SS decrees, and see that these are carried out. It meant giving up my obscure but at least endurable existence for the limelight of the council, for daily dealing with the SS, for unending wrangling over terrible problems which have no decent solution. I screwed up my nerve for one more try.

"Then, if I may, sir, and only if I may, I should like to decline."

"Of course you may. We'll say no more about it. We do have one other matter to discuss." He turned to Natalie, who was sitting through all this with a face of white stone, gripping the boy. Louis was behaving like an angel. That he sensed his mother's terror and was doing his best to help seems to me beyond doubt. "But we are keeping you from your work. The mica factory, I believe?" Natalie nodded. "How do you like it?"

She had to speak. The voice came out hoarse and hollow. "I am very glad to be working there."

"And your son looks well, so it seems the children of Theresienstadt are properly treated."

"He is very well."

Lieutenant Colonel Eichmann stood up, gesturing to Natalie, and walked with her to the door. There he spoke a few offhand words to an SS man in the corridor, with whom she passed from sight. Eichmann closed the door and walked to his seat behind the desk. He has a thin mouth, a long thin nose, narrow eyes, and a sharp chin. Not a good-looking man; but now, all at once, he looked very ugly. His mouth was crazily twitched to one side. He burst out in a terrible roar, "WHO DO YOU THINK YOU ARE? WHERE THE DEVIL DO YOU THINK YOU ARE?"

Burger jumped up at this, charged at me, and slapped me. It made my ear ring, and as he raised his hand I winced, so that the blow knocked me off the chair. I fell hard on my knees. My glasses dropped off, so what happened next I saw very blurrily. Burger kicked me, or rather shoved me, with a boot so that I rolled over on my side. Then he kicked me in the stomach; not with all his might, though it hurt and nauseated me, but in utter contempt, as though kicking a dog.

"*I'll* tell you what you are," Burger shouted down at me. "You're nothing but AN OLD BAG OF FILTHY JEWISH SHIT! You hear? Why, you stinking old pile of shit, did you think you were still in America?" As he walked around me I could barely see the moving black boots. Next he kicked me hard in the backside. "You're in THERESIENSTADT! Understand? Your life isn't worth a pig's fart if you don't get that through that old shithead of yours!" With this, he delivered a really ferocious kick with the point of his boot. It struck my spine. Red-hot pain shot all through me. I lay there, stunned, blinded, agonized, shocked. I heard him walking away, saying, "Get up on your knees."

I obeyed, shaking all over.

"Now tell me what you are."

My throat was clamped shut by fear.

"Do you want more? Say what you are!"

God forgive me for not letting him kill me. The thought pierced my fog of shock that if I were to die now, Natalie and Louis would be in still greater danger.

I choked out, "I'm an old bag of fifthy Jewish shit."

"Louder. I didn't hear you."

I repeated it.

"Scream it, shit pile! Scream it at the top of your lungs! Or I'll kick you, you stinking Jew pig, until you do scream it!"

"I'M AN OLD BAG OF FILTHY JEWISH SHIT."

"Give him his glasses," Eichmann said in a matter-of-fact tone. "All right, get up."

As I staggered to my feet, a hand caught my elbow to steady me. I felt the glasses placed on my eyes. Into my vision there sprang the face of Eppstein. On that pale face, in those haunted brown eyes, were scarred two thousand years of Jewish history.

"Sit down, Dr. Jastrow," said Eichmann. He was sitting at the desk, smoking a cigarette, looking quite composed and bank-managerial. "Now let's talk sensibly."

Burger sat down beside him, grinning with enjoyment.

What happened after that is less clear in my recollection, for I was dazed and in great pain. Eichmann's tone was all business still, but with a new sarcastic edge. What he said was almost as upsetting as the physical abuse. The SS knows that I have been teaching the Talmud; and since education in Jewish subjects is forbidden, I could be sent to the dread prison in the Little Fortress, from which few return alive. Even more staggering, he disclosed that Natalie takes part in scurrilous underground shows mocking the Führer, for which she could be arrested and forthwith executed. Natalie has never talked to me about this. I only knew that she did puppet shows for children.

Obviously Eichmann told me these things to drive home the lesson of Burger's brutal assault: that no vestige remains of our rights as Americans, or as human beings in Western civilization. We have crossed the line. Any claim to our former Baden-Baden status has been erased by our offenses, and the sword hangs over our heads. With peculiar acid frankness he commented, "Not that we really give a damn how you Jews amuse yourselves!" He told me to teach away, and added that if Natalie ceases her satires it will only go harder with both of us, for I am not to tell her what happened after she left SS headquarters. I must never breathe a word of it to anybody. If I do, he will be sure to find out, and that will be too bad. He said that Eppstein would show me the ropes of my new Elder status; and so, with an offhand wave, he dismissed me. I could hardly rise from the chair. Eppstein had to help me hobble out. Behind us we could hear the two Germans joking and laughing.

As we left SS headquarters together, Eppstein said not a word. Passing the sentry at the fence, I forced myself to walk more normally. The pain was less, I found, if I stood straight and took firm strides. Eppstein brought me to the barber shop to have my hair and beard trimmed. We went on to the council chamber, where a photographer was setting up for news pictures of the gathered Elders. A reporter, a rather pretty young German woman in a fur coat, was asking questions and scrawling notes. I posed with the Elders. I had my own picture taken. The reporter chatted with me and with the others. I'm sure that these two newspaper people were genuine, and that they left with a highly plausible story—which they may even have believed—about the Jewish council which governs the Paradise Ghetto, a serene well-dressed group of distinguished gentlemen, including the eminent Dr. Aaron Jastrow, author of *A Jew's Jesus*.

That Natalie and I are beyond diplomatic rescue is self-evident in this public use of my name and face. Even if the story is meant for European consumption, word is bound to seep back to the United States. The slight gloss I lend to Theresienstadt seems to outweigh any trouble the State Department can now give the Germans about us. Exchanges of official correspondence can go on for years. Our fate will be decided before anything comes of that footling process.

Some notes on all this, before I proceed to write about the counterweight to all this shock, pain, and degradation: my cousin Berel's return from the dead.

In all my sixty-five years I have encountered strangely little physical violence. The last instance that I can recall, in fact, was the slap Reb Laizar gave me in the Oswiecim yeshiva. Reb Laizar slapped me out of my Jewish identity, as it were, and an SS officer kicked me back into it. What I did when I returned to my room will perhaps make no sense to anybody but me. Since leaving Siena I have carried a well-concealed pouch of last resort, containing the diamonds and the photocopied documents of my juvenile conversion to Catholicism. As *Prominente* we have never yet, thank God, been bodysearched. I got out those worn folded conversion papers dated 1900, and tore them to bits. This morning for the first time in about fifty years I put on phylacteries. I borrowed them from a pious old man next door. I mean to do this in all the days remaining to me on this sick and stricken earth.

Is this a return to the old Jewish God? Never mind. My Talmud teaching has certainly not been that. I drifted into it. Young people in the library began to ask me questions. A circle of questioners gradually formed, I found I enjoyed the elegant old logical game, and so it became a regular thing. The phylacteries, the old black-stained leather boxes containing Mosaic passages, gave me no intellectual or spiritual uplift as I tied them on head and arm. In fact, though I was alone, I felt self-consciously showy and silly. But I will persist. Thus I answer Eichmann. As for the old Jewish God, He and I both have accounts to settle, for if I have to explain my apostasy, He has to explain Theresienstadt. Jeremiah, Job, and Lamentations all teach that we Jews tend to rise to catastrophe. Hence phylacteries. Let it go at that.

It says much about human nature—or at least about my own personal foolishness—that for many years I have refused to believe the stories of Nazi atrocities against the Jews, and even the evidence of my eyes; yet now I am certain that the most alarming reports are the true ones. Why this turnabout? What was so very convincing about the encounter with Eichmann and Burger?

After all, I have already seen much atrocious German conduct here. I have seen an SS man clubbing an old woman to her knees in the snow because he caught her peddling cigarette butts. I have heard of children being hanged in the Little Fortress for stealing food. Then there was the census. Three weeks ago, the SS marched the entire ghetto population out into the fields, in blowing freezing weather, counted us over and over for about twelve hours, and left upwards of forty thousand persons standing around in the rainy night. Rumors swept the huge famished crowd that we were all about to be machine-gunned in the dark. A stampede to the town gates ensued. Natalie and I ducked the mob and got back without incident, but we heard that the field in the morning was littered with sleet-covered bodies of trampled old people and children.

Yet none of this signalled to me the truth. My meeting with Eichmann did. Why? It is the oldest psychological fact, I suppose, that one cannot really feel another's misery. And worse; let me face for once in my life this raw reality; the misery of others can make one glad and relieved that one has been spared.

Eichmann is not a low police brute. Nor is he a banal bureaucrat, though that is the role he brilliantly puts on when it suits him. Much more than the flamboyant fanatic Hitler, this businesslike Berlin official is the dread figure that has haunted the twentieth century and precipitated two wars. He is a reasonable, intelligent, brisk, even affable fellow. He is one of us, a civilized man of the West. Yet in a twinkling he can order horrible savagery perpetrated on an old feeble man, and look on calmly; and in another twinkling can return to polite European manners, without the slightest sense of any inconsistency, even with a sardonic smirk at the discomfiture of the victim who cannot conceive of this version of human nature. Like Hitler, he is an Austrian. Like him, in this dread century, he is *the German.*

I have grasped this difficult truth. Nevertheless, I will go to my death refusing to condemn an entire people. We Jews have had enough of that. I will remember Karl Frisch, the historian, who came to Yale from Heidelberg, a German to the bone, a sweet, liberal, profound man with a superb sense of humor. I will remember the wonderful yeasting of art and thought in Berlin in the twenties. I will remember the Hergesheimers, with whom I stayed for six months in Munich, people of the first quality with—I will swear—no taint of anti-Semitism, at a time when it was becoming a volcanic political rumble. Such Germans exist. They exist in large numbers. They must, to have created the beauty of Germany, and the art, and the philosophy, and the science; what was known as *Kultur* long before it became a name of execration and horror.

I do not understand the Germans. Attila, Alaric, Genghis Khan, Tamerlane, in the fury of conquest exterminated all who resisted them. The Moslem Turks slaughtered the Christian Armenians during the World War, but the Armenians were taking the part of the enemy, czarist Russia, and it happened in Asia Minor.

The Germans are part of Christian Europe. The Jews have passionately embraced and enriched the German culture, the arts, the sciences. In the World War the German Jews had a record of insensate loyalty to the Kaiser. No, there has been nothing like this before. We are caught in a mysterious and stupendous historical process, the grinding birth pangs of a new age; and as at the dawn of monotheism and of Christianity, we are fated to be at the heart of the convulsion, and to bear the brunt of its agony.

My lifelong posture of learned agnostic humanism was all very fine. My books about Christianity were not without merit. But taking it all in all, I have spent my life on the run. Now I turn and stand. I am a Jew. A fine earthy vulgarism goes, "What that man needs is a swift kick in the arse." It would seem to be my biography.

————

Berel Jastrow is in Prague.

That is almost all I know: that he is there, working in the underground, having escaped from a concentration camp. He sent me word through a communist grapevine that links Prague and Theresienstadt. To identify and authenticate himself, he used a Hebrew phrase that on Gentile tongues (for the Czech gendarmerie is the main transmitter) became almost undecipherable. Still, I puzzled it out: *hazak ve'emats,* "Be strong and of good courage."

It is amazing that this iron-willed resourceful cousin of mine is alive, close by, and aware of my incarceration here; but nothing is too amazing in the chaotic maelstrom that the Germans have made of Europe. I have not seen Berel in fifty years, yet Natalie's description has made him a commanding presence in my mind. That he can do anything for us is unlikely. My health would not endure an escape effort, even if such a thing were possible. Nor could Natalie risk it, with the child on her hands. What, then? My hope is only that of every other Jew in this trap: that the Americans and British will land in France very soon, and that National Socialist Germany will be smashed between assaults coming from the east and the west, in time to set us free.

Still, it is wonderful that Berel is in Prague. What an odyssey he must have lived, since Natalie last saw him in falling Warsaw, four eternal years ago! His survival must be called a miracle; the fact that he is so near, another miracle. Such things give me hope; make me, in fact, *"strong and of good courage."*

74

Pug Henry had been feverish for days, victim of some endemic Persian bug. Riding trains and trucks day and night through towns, farmlands, dust storms, blistering deserts, and snowy mountain passes, he had fallen into a lethargy in which—especially at night—fever dreams and reality had run together. He had arrived at Connolly's headquarters light-headed, and had been hard put to it to stay alert even talking to Hopkins and Roosevelt. Through those long whirling hours on the convoy route, Pamela and Burne-Wilke had come and gone in his hectic visions much as his dead son and his living family had. Pug could consciously seal off Pamela, like Warren, in a forbidden section of memory, but he could not help his dreams.

So the sight of Burne-Wilke in the Russian embassy villa was startling: a fever-dream figure, standing there beside the cold real Ernest King. *Pamela in Tehran!* He could not, under King's hard eye, ask straight out, "Are you married?" He left Roosevelt's villa not knowing whether he should inquire at the British legation for Lady Burne-Wilke or Pamela Tudsbury.

Stalin and Molotov were approaching on a gravel path as Pug came out, Molotov talking earnestly, Stalin smoking a cigarette and glancing about. Seeing Pug he nodded and half-smiled, his wrinkled eyes flashing clear recognition. Pug was used to politicians' memories, but this surprised him. It was over two years since he had delivered Hopkins's letter to Stalin. The man had borne the weight of a gigantic war all that time; yet he really seemed to remember. Tubby, gray, shorter than Victor Henry, he strode bouncily up the steps into the villa. Pug had had almost a year of the Moscow iconography—statues, paintings, gigantic photographs—presenting Stalin as a remote legendary all-wise Savior, one of a cloud-riding trinity with the dead Marx and Lenin; and there went the flesh and blood reality, a small paunchy old fellow in a beige uniform with a broad red stripe down the pants. Yet the icons in a way were more true than that reality; so Pug thought, recalling scenes on the vast Russian front that Stalin's will controlled, and remembering too his history of murdering millions. A stone-hearted colossus had gone by in that little old man.

Winston Churchill, whom he had met more often, did not recognize Pug. Accompanied by two stiff-striding generals and a pudgy admiral, chewing on a long cigar, he left the British compound as Pug was identifying himself at the gate. The filmy shrewd eyes looked straight at Pug and through him, and the stooped rotund figure in a white suit ambled on. The Prime Minister appeared dull and unwell.

Inside the British legation a few armed soldiers walked about the gardens, and civilians in little knots chatted in the sunshine. This was a much smaller and quieter establishment. Pug paused to take thought under a tree shedding golden leaves. Where to find her? How to ask for her? He was able to grin wryly at his own pettiness. An earth-shaking event was happening here, yet on this peak of high history, what excited him was not the sight of three world giants, but the prospect of laying eyes on a woman he saw once or twice a year by the chances of war.

Their week in Moscow, cut to four days by a whim of Standley's, remained in his memory as a burst of beauty like his honeymoon: serene, sweet, nothing but companionship at meals, in long walks, in Spaso House, at the Bolshoi, at a circus, in her hotel suite. They had talked endlessly, like lifelong friends, like husband and wife, meeting after a separation. In the last evening at her hotel he had even talked about Warren. The thoughts and feelings had broken from him. In Pamela's face, and in her brief gentle comments, he had found comfort. They had managed to part next day with smiles and casual words. Neither had said that it was an ending, but to Pug, at least, it had been nothing else. Now here she was again. He could no more resist looking for her than he could will to stop breathing.

"Hullo! There's Captain Henry." This time it really was Granville Seaton, standing with some men and women in uniform. Seaton came and took his arm, with far more warmth than he had displayed in their journeying together. "What cheer, Captain? Wearing business, that truck route, what? You look fairly done up."

"I'm all right." Pug gestured in the direction of the Soviet embassy. "I just told Harry Hopkins your ideas about a new treaty."

"You did? You actually did? Smashing!" Seaton hugged his arm close, exhaling a strong tobacco breath. "What was his reaction?"

"I can tell you the President's reaction." In his light-headedness Pug blurted this. His temples throbbed and his knees felt weak.

Seaton spoke intensely, his eyes searching Pug's face. "Tell me then."

"The thing was discussed at the Moscow Conference of foreign min isters last month. The Russians stalled. That's that. The President won't thrust the United States into your old rivalries. He's got a war to win and he needs Stalin."

Seaton's face fell into lines of sadness. "Then the Red Army will never leave Persia. If what you say is accurate, Roosevelt's pronouncing a long-range doom on all free men."

Victor Henry shrugged. "I guess he figures on fighting one war at a time."

"Victory is meaningless," Seaton exclaimed, "except in its effect on the politics of the future. You people have yet to grasp that."

"Well, if an initiative came from the Iranians that might be different. So Hopkins said."

"The Iranians?" Seaton grimaced. "Forgive me, but Americans are tragically naïve about Asia and Asian affairs. The Iranians won't take the initiative, for any number of reasons."

"Seaton, do you know Lord Burne-Wilke?"

"The air vice marshal? Yes, they've brought him here on the Burma business. He's over at the plenary session now."

"I'm looking for his aide, a WAAF."

"I say, Kate!" Seaton called and beckoned. A pretty woman in a WAAF uniform left the group he had been chatting with. "Captain Henry here is looking for the future Lady Burne-Wilke."

Green eyes snapped in a snub-nosed face, giving Pug a quick pert inspection. "Ah, yes. Well, everything's in such a muddle. She brought masses of maps and charts and whatnot. I think they installed her in the anteroom outside the office that Lord Gore is using."

"I'll take you there," Seaton said.

Two desks jammed the little room on the second floor of the main building. At one of them a pink-faced officer with a bushy mustache was hammering at a typewriter. Yes, he said peevishly, the other desk had been shoved into the room for Burne-Wilke's aide. She had worked at it for hours, but had left not long ago to shop at the Tehran bazaar. Seizing a scrap of paper on Pamela's desk, Victor Henry scrawled, *Hi! I'm here, at the U.S. Army base officers' quarters. Pug,* and jammed it on a spike. He asked Seaton as they walked outside, "Where's this bazaar?"

"I don't recommend that you go looking for her there."

"Where is it?"

Seaton told him.

General Connolly's driver took Pug into the old part of Tehran, and left him at the bazaar entrance. The exotic mob, the heavy smells, the foreign babble, the garish multitudinous signs in a strange alphabet, dizzied him. Peering past the stone arcades at the entrance, he saw crowded gloomy passageways of shops receding out of sight. Seaton was right. How could one find anybody here? Yet the conference was due to last only three days. This day was already melting away. Communication in this Asian city, especially amid the helter-skelter doings of an improvised conference, was chancy. They might even miss each other entirely if he did not make an effort to find her. "The *future* Lady Burne-Wilke," Seaton had called her. That was what mattered. Pug went plunging in to look for her.

He saw her almost at once, or thought he did. He was passing by shop after shop of tapestries and linens, when a narrow passageway opened off to the right, and glancing down it past the crowd of black-veiled women and burly men, through hanging leather coats and sheep-skin rugs, he spotted a trim little figure in blue, wearing what looked like a WAAF cap. Shouting at her was hopeless, above the din of merchant cries and bargaining. Pug shouldered through the mob and came to a broader cross-gallery, the section of carpet dealers. She was not in sight. He set off in the direction she had been moving. In an hour of sweaty striding through the pungent, crowded, tumultuous labyrinth, he did not see her again.

Had he not been in a fever it would still have seemed dreamlike, this frustrated quest for her through a thronged maze. All too often he had had just such nightmares about Warren. Whether he was looking for him at a football game, or in a graduation crowd, or aboard an aircraft carrier, the dream was always the same: he would glimpse his son just once, or he would be told that Warren was close by, and he would pursue and pursue and never find him. As he tramped sweatily round and round the galleries, feeling ever lighter in the head and queerer about the knees, he came to realize that he was not behaving normally. He groped back to the entrance, bargained in sign language with a cab driver in a rusty red Packard touring car, and paid a crazy price for a ride to the Amirabad base.

The next clear thing that happened to Pug Henry was that somebody shook him and said, "Admiral King wants to see you." He was lying clothed on a cot in the officers' quarters, bathed in sweat.

"I'll be with him in ten minutes," Pug said through chattering teeth. He took a double dose of pills that were supposed to control the ailment, and a heavy slug of Old Crow; showered and rapidly dressed, and hurried through the starlit darkness in his heavy bridge coat to General Connolly's residence. When he came into King's suite, the admiral's glowering glance changed to a look of concern. "Henry, get yourself to sick bay. You're damned green around the gills."

"I'm okay, Admiral."

"Sure? Want a steak sandwich and a beer?" King gestured at a tray on the desk between piles of mimeographed documents.

"No, thank you, sir."

"Well, I saw history made today." King talked as he ate, in an unusually benign vein. "That's more than Marshall and Arnold did. They missed the opening session, Henry. Fact! Our Army Chief of Staff and the boss of the Air Corps flew halfway around the world for this meeting with Stalin, then, by God, they didn't get the word, and tooled off sightseeing. Couldn't be located. Ha ha ha! Isn't *that* a snafu for the books?"

King emptied his glass of beer and complacently touched a napkin to his mouth. "Well, *I* was there. That Joe Stalin is one tough gent. Completely on top of things. Doesn't miss a trick. He put a hell of a spoke in Churchill's wheel today. *I* think all the talk about pooping around in the Mediterranean is finished, over, done with. It's a new ball game." King looked hard at him. "Now you're supposed to know something about landing craft."

"Yes, sir."

"Good." Searching through piles of documents, King pulled several out as he talked. "Churchill turns purple, just talking to me about landing craft. I spoil his fun. We've got thirty percent of new construction allotted to the Pacific, and I have to be a son of a bitch about them, or they'd melt away in his wild invasion schemes." He brandished a sheaf of documents. "Here's a British op-plan for a landing on Rhodes, for instance, which I consider absolutely asinine. Churchill asserts that it'll pull Turkey into the war, set the Balkans aflame, and blah blah blah. Now what I want you to do—"

General Connolly knocked, and entered in a heavy checkered bathrobe. "Admiral, Henry here has been invited to dinner by the Minister of the Imperial Court. This just arrived by hand. A car's waiting."

Connolly gave Pug a large cream-colored unsealed envelope.

"Who's the Minister of the Imperial Court?" King asked Pug. "And how do *you* know him?"

"I don't, Admiral." A scrawled note clipped to the crested card explained the invitation; but he did not mention it to King.

Hi—I'm a houseguest here. Talky and the minister were old good friends. It was this or the YWCA for me. Do come. P.

"Hussein Ala is the second or third man in the government, Admiral," said General Connolly. "Sort of a grand vizier. Better send Pug along. The Persians have peculiar ways of doing things."

"Like the heathen Chinee," said King. He threw the documents on the desk. "Okay, Henry, see me when you return. No matter what time."

"Aye aye, sir."

The black Daimler driven by a silent man in black went twisting through the walls of old Tehran, and halted in a narrow moonlit street. The driver opened a small door in a wall; Victor Henry had to stoop to go through. He walked down into a lantern-lit garden spacious as the Soviet embassy, with fountains spouting sparkling waters, rivulets murmuring in canals among the towering trees and sculptured shrubbery, and at the other side of this opulent private park, many lighted windows showing. A man in a long crimson garment, with enormous drooping black mustaches, bowed to Pug as he came in, and led him around the fountains and through the trees. In the foyer of the mansion Pug got a peripheral impression of inlaid wood walls, a high tiled ceiling, and rich tapestries and furniture. There stood Pamela in uniform. "Hi. Come and meet the minister. Duncan's late for dinner. He's staying at the officers' club."

The mustachioed man was helping Pug take off the bridge coat. Unable to find words for the joy he felt, Pug said, "This is somewhat unexpected."

"Well, I got your note, and I wasn't sure I'd see you otherwise. We're flying back to New Delhi day after tomorrow. The minister was very sweet about inviting you. I told him a thing or two about you, of course." She put her hand to his face, looking worried, and he saw the glitter of a large diamond. "Pug, are you all right?"

"I'm fine."

Despite a well-tailored dark British suit and pleasant clear English, it was a grand vizier who welcomed Pug in a magnificent sitting room: a commanding nose, wise brilliant brown eyes, thick silvering hair, a lordly bearing, an antique smooth manner. They settled in a cushioned alcove and the minister fell to talking business almost at once, while Pug and Pamela drank highballs. Lend-Lease, he said, had its very bad aspect for Iran. The American wages were causing a wild inflation: prices spiking, shortages mounting, goods vanishing into the warehouses of hoarders. The Russians were making matters worse. They occupied much of the best farming lands, and they were taking the produce. Tehran was not far from food riots. The Shah's one hope lay in the generosity of the United States.

"Ah, but the United States is already feeding nearly the whole world," Pamela remarked. "China, India, Russia. Even poor old England." The sound of her voice speaking these simple words enthralled Pug. Her presence transformed time; every moment was a celebration, a drunkenness; this was his reaction to seeing her again, perhaps fevered but true.

"Even poor old England." The minister nodded. His faint smile, the tilting of his head, conveyed ironic awareness of the dwindling of the British empire. "Yes, the United States is now the hope of mankind. There has never in history been a nation like America. But with your generous nature, Captain Henry, you must learn not to be too trusting. There truly are wolves in the woods."

"And bears," said Pug.

"Ah, just so." Ala smiled the formal bright smile of a grand vizier. "Bears."

Lord Burne-Wilke arrived, and they went in to dinner. Pug feared that he faced a heavy meal, but the fare was plain, though everything else was grand—the vaulted dining room, the long dark table polished to a mirror shine, the hand-painted china, and what looked like platinum or white-gold plate. They had a clear soup, a chicken dish, and sherbet, and with the help of wine Pug managed to eat.

Burne-Wilke did most of the talking at first, in an autumnal vein. The conference had started very badly. Nobody was to blame. The world had come to a "discontinuity of history." Those who knew what should be done lacked the power to do it. Those who had the power lacked the knowledge. Pug discerned in Burne-Wilke's gloom the spoke that Stalin had put in Churchill's wheel, to the glee of Ernest King.

The minister took up the theme and discoursed mellifluously on the ebb and flow of empires; the inevitable process by which conquerors became softened by their conquests, and dependent on their subjects to keep them in luxury, and so sooner or later fell to a new nation of hard rude fighters. The cycle had rolled on from Persepolis to the Tehran Conference. It would never end.

During all this Pug and Pamela sat silent opposite each other. Each time their eyes met it was a thrill for him. He thought she was tightly controlling her eyes and her face, as he was; and this necessity to mask his feelings only intensified them. He wondered what there could ever be again in life to match what he felt for Pamela Tudsbury. She wore Burne-Wilke's large diamond on her finger, as she had once worn the smaller diamond of Ted Gallard. She had not married the aviator, and she had not yet married Burne-Wilke, four months after the wrenching farewell in Moscow. Was she still caught as he was? This love kept triumphing over time, over geography, over shattering deaths, over year-long separations. A random meeting on an ocean liner had led step by step to this unlikely meeting in Persia, to these profoundly stirring glances. Now what? Would this be the end?

Pug scarcely knew Duncan Burne-Wilke, and the excited warmth with which the man began to expatiate on Hinduism astonished him. The air vice marshal grew flushed, his eyes softened and moistened, and he spoke for a long time, while his sherbet melted, about the *Bhagavad-Gita*. Serving in India, he said, had opened his eyes. India was old and full of wisdom. The Hindu view of the world was a total break from Christian and Western ideas, and wiser. The *Bhagavad-Gita* offered the only acceptable philosophy he had ever come upon.

The warrior hero of the *Gita,* he said, disgusted with the senseless killing of war, wanted to throw down his arms before a great battle. The god Krishna persuaded him that as a warrior his task was to fight, however stupid the cause and however revolting the murders, leaving the sorting out of the whole to Heaven and to destiny. Their long dialogue, said Burne-Wilke, was greater poetry than the Bible; it taught that the material world was not real, that the human mind could not grasp the workings of God, that death and life were twin delusions. A man could only face up to his lot, and act according to his nature and his place in life.

With a slight face twitch, Pamela conveyed to Pug that all this meant little to her, that Burne-Wilke was off riding a hobbyhorse.

"I know the *Bhagavad-Gita,*" said the minister placidly. "Some of our Persian poets write much in that vein. It is too fatalistic. One cannot control all the consequences of one's actions, true. But one must still think about them, and make choices. As to the world's not being real, I always humbly ask, '*Compared to what?*'"

"Compared to God, possibly," said Duncan Burne-Wilke.

"Ah, but by definition, He is beyond compare. So that is no answer. But we are caught in a very old revolving door. Tell me, what will come out of the conference to benefit Iran? We are your hosts, after all."

"Nothing. Stalin is dominating the proceedings. The President is just drifting with him, I suppose to show his good intentions. Churchill alone, great as he is, can't pull against two such weights. An ominous state of things, but there you have it."

"Perhaps President Roosevelt is cleverer than we know," said the minister, turning shrewd old brown eyes at Victor Henry.

Now Pug felt as he had in his Berlin post, just before sending in his report on the combat readiness of Germany. It had been a presumptuous thing to do. It had led to his meeting with Roosevelt. It had probably destroyed his naval career. Yet there sat Pamela opposite him, and that was how he had met her. Perhaps there was something to the *Bhagavad-Gita,* to the working of destiny, to the need for a man to act according to his nature. He was a plunger at crucial moments. He always had been. He plunged.

"Wouldn't it be a good thing to come out of the conference," he said, "if the United States joined in your treaty with England and Russia? If all three countries agreed to pull out their troops after the war?"

The minister's somewhat hooded eyes glinted. "A wonderful thing. But this idea has been rejected at the Moscow meeting of foreign ministers. We were not present, but we know."

"Why doesn't your government ask the President to take it up with Stalin?"

Glancing at Burne-Wilke, who was regarding Pug quizzically, the minister said, "Let me ask you an indiscreet question. On your tour of the Lend-Lease installations here, were you not a personal emissary of President Roosevelt?"

"Yes."

The minister nodded, contemplating him through eyes lidded almost shut. "Do you actually know your President's views on this matter of a new treaty?"

"Yes. The President won't initiate such a move, because it might look to the Russians like an imperialist intrusion. But he might respond to Iran's request for reassurance."

The minister's next words came rapid-fire. "But that idea has already been explored. A hint to your legation not long ago met no encouragement. It was not pressed. It is an extremely serious thing to push a powerful nation in such a delicate matter."

"No doubt, but the conference will break up in a couple of days. When will such a chance come again for Iran? If the President's doing everything Stalin's way, as Lord Burne-Wilke says, then Stalin might be in a mood to oblige him."

"Shall we have coffee?" The minister stood, smiling, and led them into a glassed-in veranda facing the garden. Here he left them, and was gone for about a quarter of an hour. They lolled on cushioned divans, and servants brought them coffee, brandy, and confections.

"Your point is well-taken," Burne-Wilke commented to Pug as they settled down. "The conference is such an utterly disorganized muddle that by sheer luck the Iranians might just pull it off. It's worth a try. There's no other way the Soviet Union will ever get out of Persia."

He talked about the China-Burma-India theatre. It was always feast or famine there, he complained; the forces were either starved, or suddenly glutted with supplies and asked to perform miracles. President Roosevelt was obsessed with keeping China in the war. It was bloody nonsense. Chiang Kai-shek wasn't fighting the Japanese. Half the Lend-Lease aid was lining his pockets, the other half was going to suppress the Chinese communists. General Stilwell had told Roosevelt the brute facts at Cairo. Yet the President had promised Chiang a campaign to reopen the Burma Road, though the only troops on hand to fight such a campaign were British and Indian, and Churchill opposed the whole idea. Mountbatten had wisely avoided coming to Tehran, unloading the whole wretched Burma tangle on Burne-Wilke. The discussions with the American staff were going round and round in circles. He was heartily sick of it, and looked forward to escaping in a day or two.

"Pug, you don't look well," Pamela said quite suddenly, sitting up.

There was no use denying it. The relief of bourbon, Scotch, and wine, and the pulse of adrenalin from seeing Pamela, were all ebbing away. The room was swimming, and he felt like death. "It comes and goes, Pam. The Persian crud. Maybe I'd better get back to base."

The minister just then returned, and he at once ordered the car and driver brought around to the garden door.

"I'll walk with you to the car," Pamela said.

Wearily, with a gracious intelligent smile, Burne-Wilke rose to shake hands. The minister accompanied them through the ornate foyer.

"Thanks for dinner," Pug said.

"I am pleased you could come," said Hussein Ala, with a penetrating look into Pug's face. "Very pleased."

In the garden Pamela paused in a darkened space between lanterns, seized Pug's sweaty hand, and turned him toward her.

"Better not, Pam," he muttered, "I'm probably infectious as hell."

"Really?" She took his head in her hands and pulled his mouth down on hers. She kissed him three times, light sweet kisses. "There. Now we've both got the crud."

"Why haven't you married Burne-Wilke?"

"I'm going to. You've seen my ring. You couldn't take your eyes off it."

"But you're not married."

Her tone turned exasperated. They were both talking breathlessly and low. "Oh, look, when I got to New Delhi, Duncan had this blinding imbecile of an aide who was driving him bonkers. He asked me to step in. I've done a fair job. He seems pleased. It would be sort of sticky, Lady Burne-Wilke manning the outer office, but this way it's okay. We're together constantly. Everything's fine. When it seems suitable we'll get married, but possibly not till we go back to England. There's no hurry."

"He's a grand fellow," Pug said.

"He's terribly depressed tonight. That brought on the *Bhagavad-Gita*. He's a brilliant administrator, a fearless flier, and altogether a lamb. I love him."

"You saw Rhoda several times in Washington, didn't you?"

"Yes, three or four times."

"Was she ever with an Army colonel named Peters? Harrison Peters?"

"Why, no. Not that I know." She turned and started to walk.

"You're sure?" He put his hand on her arm.

She shook it off and strolled on, speaking nervously. "Don't do this. What a pointless question! It's wretched of you to fish like that."

"I'm not fishing. I want to know."

"About *what?*" She halted and turned to him. "Look, didn't we explore this haunting—*thing*—of ours to weariness, darling, in Moscow? There's a bond between you and Rhoda that nothing can break. Nothing. Not since Warren died. I understand. It's taken me a while, but I've got the idea. It's a terrible mistake to open it all up. Don't do it."

They stood by a large fountain in the middle of the garden. The tall man in the crimson robe was waiting, a dim figure, at the steps to the garden door.

"Why did you get the minister to ask me to dinner?"

"You damned well know why. I won't change till I'm dead. Maybe not then. But I'm not raving with fever, and you are, so *go*. Get yourself doctored. I'll look for you tomorrow."

"Pamela, I've lived four days this year, those four days in Moscow. Now what about this Colonel Peters? You're not very good at pretending."

"But what brings this on? Have you had more poison-pen letters?" He did not answer. She took both his hands, looking him straight in the eyes. "All right, listen. Once at a big dance—I don't remember what it was—I ran into Rhoda, and a tall gray-haired man in Army uniform was escorting her. Very casual, very correct. All right? She introduced him, and I think the name was Peters. That's it. That's *all* of it. A woman can't go to a dance without an escort, Pug. You startled me with your abrupt question, or I'd have told you that straight off."

He hesitated, and said, "I don't think that's all of it."

Pamela burst out at him, "Pug Henry, these fleeting encounters of ours are all very romantic, and I freely confess I'm as dotty as you are. I can't help it. I can't hide it. I don't. Duncan knows all about it. Since it's utterly hopeless, and since we've had the best of it, why not just *forget it?* Call it a chimera feeding on loneliness, separation, and these tantalizing glimpses. Now for God's sake, *go!*" Her cold hand touched his cheek. "You're terribly sick. I'll look for you tomorrow."

"Well, I'd better go, at that. They'll think you've fallen in a fountain." They walked through the garden. She was clutching his hand like a child.

"What about Byron?"

"So far as I know, he's all right."

"Natalie?"

"No news."

The crimson-robed man went up the steps and opened the garden door. Moonlight glinted on the Daimler. They halted at the steps.

"Don't marry him," Pug said.

Her eyes opened wide, gleaming in the moonlight. "Why, I most certainly will."

"Not until I get back to Washington, and find out where Rhoda stands."

"You're delirious. Just go back to her and make her as happy as you can. When this ghastly war ends, maybe we'll meet again. I'll try to see you tomorrow before I go."

She kissed him on the mouth and strode off into the garden.

The car roared through the quiet chilly town and out into the desert silvered by the moon. At the gate to the Amirabad base, a soldier on guard came to the window and saluted. "Cap'n Henry?"

"Yes."

"General Connolly lak to see you, suh." The Virginia accent gave Pug a homesick twinge.

In the checkered bathrobe, wearing horn-rimmed glasses, Connolly was writing at a desk in his sitting room on the ground floor of the residence, his feet in heavy stockings stretched toward a small oil stove. "Hello, Pug. How are you feeling?"

"I could use a slug of booze."

"Christ, you're shivering! Sit by this stove. It gets damned cold toward midnight, doesn't it? Don't disturb Admiral King, he's turned in. What was on Hussein Ala's mind?"

"A British friend of mine is staying with him. We all dined together."

"That's all?"

"That's all." Pug downed the whiskey. "Incidentally, General, what did Hack Peters write you about my wife?"

Connolly was settling back in his desk chair. He took off his glasses and stared at Pug. "Beg your pardon?"

"You mentioned last week that Peters wrote you about us."

"I said nothing about your wife."

"No, but he's her friend, actually, not mine. They met at church, or something. What did he say? Is she all right? It's been a long time since I've heard from her." The general was flushing, and looking very uncomfortable. "Why, what's the matter? Is she ill?"

"Not in the least." Connolly shook his head and rubbed a hand on his brow. "But this is blasted awkward. Hack Peters is my oldest friend, Pug. We write each other with our hair down. Your wife seems to be some kind of paragon. He's taken her dancing and whatnot, Hack's a great dancer, but—oh, hell, why pussyfoot around? Here's what he wrote about her. I'll read you every word, though I probably shouldn't have mentioned the letter."

Rummaging in his desk, Connolly pulled out a small dark V-mail sheet, and read from it with a magnifying glass. Pug listened, sitting hunched in his bridge coat by the smelly stove, the whiskey flaming in his stomach and chills racking his frame. It was a sentimental, flowery picture of a perfect woman—beautiful, poised, sweet, clever, modest, rigidly faithful to her husband, unapproachable as a vestal virgin, and yet a marvelous companion at dances, the theatre, and concerts. Peters praised her gallantry about Warren's death at Midway, the long silences of her submariner son, and the prolonged absence of her husband in Russia. The gist of all this was a moan that, after a long frivolous bachelor existence, he had found the one impossible right woman; and she was totally out of reach. He had to be grateful that she would even let him take her out now and then.

Connolly tossed down the letter and the magnifying glass. "I call that a superb tribute. I wouldn't mind a man writing it about my wife, Pug! Your gal must be quite something."

"She is. Well, I'm glad he's giving her some diversion. She's entitled to it, she's got a rotten deal. I thought the admiral was expecting me."

"No, he seems to be coming down with what you've got. The President got taken queer at dinner tonight, too. Had to leave Churchill and Stalin chewing the fat without him. The Secret Service had a poison scare, but I hear he's sleeping it off all right. Just the crud. Persia's kind of hard on newcomers."

"It is that."

"If you're not better in the morning, go to the hospital, Pug, and get some blood tests."

"I have a report to finish before I turn in. The President expects it in the morning."

Connolly looked impressed, but his reply was offhand. "No sweat. Call the base duty officer and it'll be picked up, any hour of the night."

Coming into the officers' quarters, Pug said to a sergeant sleepily reading a comic book at the entrance desk, "Is there a typewriter in this place?"

"This desk has a fold-away typewriter, sir."

"I'd like to use it."

The sergeant squinted at him. "Now, sir? It makes a racket."

"I won't be long."

He went to his room, took a dram of strong bourbon, and returned to the silent lobby with his notes on the Lend-Lease tour. His ailment tended to retreat before alcohol, leaving him briefly euphoric; and the one-page report that he thunderously clattered off seemed brilliant to him. That it might look like drunken drivel in the morning was a risk he had to accept. He sealed it up and called the duty officer. In his unheated small room he tumbled into the cot, piling on every blanket and also his bridge coat.

He woke in sweat-soaked sheets. By the blurry look of his wristwatch, the spinning of the sunlit room, and his weakness when he tried to stand, he knew he had no choice but the hospital.

75

THE "spoke in Churchill's wheel" was nothing less than the expulsion of the British Empire from its leading position in world affairs, all in a few hours of polite talk around a table in the Soviet embassy.

Churchill had met Stalin before. Roosevelt had not. With the first face-to-face encounter of Stalin and Roosevelt, the center of gravity of the war and of the world's future shifted. The one person who felt this shift in its full crushing force was Winston Churchill. Hints had not been lacking from the start at Tehran that his intimacy with Roosevelt in war leadership was fading: the President's private first meeting with Stalin, for one thing, and his acceptance of Russian hospitality for another. But only in the plenary sessions did the change bite into Churchill's role in history.

A great man, an astute historian, Churchill at Tehran could play only the cards he held. They were relatively weak. Roosevelt might feel affection for him, and total distrust toward Stalin. But in this new deal, shuffled up by world war, of the ancient great game, the Soviet Union now held the cards of manpower and willpower. At Tehran the British were dealt out; some three hundred years of Western European leadership in history ended; and the present day gloomily dawned.

The very hardest thing to imagine, in looking back on this old war, is that it could have gone other than it did. Yet the overwhelming reality during the war—which one must try to grasp, to get a sense of the time—is that nobody knew how it would go. Franklin Roosevelt had done well to journey to the Bolshevik's back fence. Fighting men were dying in masses all over the world, tanks were burning, ships sinking, planes falling, cities toppling, resources wasting; yet the outcome was still very much in doubt, and no plan for winning existed among Hitler's foes. After two years of talk, the American and British staffs remained at loggerheads: the Americans adamant for an all-out smash into France in 1944, the British holding out for less risky operations in the Balkans and the eastern Mediterranean. Roosevelt had no assurance that the Soviet Union would not make a separate peace, or like the Chinese quit fighting beyond a point; and that Stalin would ever declare war on Japan, or join a union of nations after the war, were mere hopes.

Tehran changed all that. In the space of three days, in three round-table strategy meetings lasting but a few hours, the President with bland art—and what looks in the record like simulated clumsiness—led Josef Stalin to veto once for all Winston Churchill's proposed nibblings at Europe's periphery, and to swing the decision at last for *Overlord,* the grandiose cross-Channel landing in France. Stalin promised a synchronized all-out smash from the east; also, once Germany was beaten, an attack on Japan. He pledged, too, that Russia would join a postwar United Nations. The long suspicious fencing among the Big Three ended at Tehran in a tough solid alliance, with a firm plan for wiping out National Socialism. The alliance would not last in the riptides of postwar change, but it would win the war. Franklin Roosevelt went to Tehran to win the war.

The plan rode roughshod over Churchill's cherished ideas. In the opening session, Roosevelt almost chattily asked Stalin whether he preferred the great assault on France, or one or another Mediterranean plan; and when the formidable Russian approved the Overlord attack, Churchill found himself outvoted two to one, with his vote the least powerful of the three. It was the "spoke in the wheel," the quietus on his long dogged struggle to conduct the war so as to preserve his old Empire.

Next day in the second formal meeting he fought back, arguing long and frantically for his Mediterranean proposals, until Stalin stopped him cold by asking, "Do the British really believe in Overlord, or are they only saying so to reassure the Russians?" It was such a raw moment that Roosevelt said they had all better get ready for dinner. Stalin rode Churchill hard, all during the meal that evening, about his tenderness for the Germans. The Prime Minister at last stalked in fury from the room; whereupon the Russian followed and good-humoredly brought him back.

Early on the third morning Hopkins visited Churchill. Perhaps he brought the crusty old battler word from Roosevelt that it was time to quit; we do not know. Anyway, at the combined Chiefs of Staff meeting shortly after that, the British all at once conceded that the staff had better set the date for Overlord or go home. Thus the two-year wrangle ended. The Americans showed no elation or triumph. A one-page agreement on Overlord was rushed to Churchill and Roosevelt. At lunch, Churchill gamely suggested that Roosevelt read it to Stalin, and he did. With grim delight, Stalin responded that the Red Army would show the gratitude of Russia by a full-scale matching attack from the east.

That night Churchill's birthday dinner took place in the British legation. Churchill presided, with Roosevelt at his right, Josef Stalin at his left, and military leaders and foreign ministers ranged up and down the glittering table. All was conviviality and wassail, optimism and friendship. The sense of a great turn in history was strong. The toasts went round and round. It was Churchill's prerogative to give the last one, but Stalin surprised the gathering by requesting the privilege. These were his words:

"I want to tell you, from the Russian point of view, what the President and the United States have done to win the war. The most important things in this war are machines. The United States has proven that it can turn out from eight thousand to ten thousand airplanes per month. Russia can only turn out, at most, three thousand airplanes per month. England turns out three thousand to thirty-five hundred, which are principally heavy bombers.

"The United States, therefore, is a country of machines. Without these machines, through Lend-Lease, we would lose the war."

It was more than Stalin ever said publicly to his own people about the American contribution to the war until he died. He might have been expected, given the occasion, to compliment Churchill and the British; instead the old monster chose to praise America and Lend-Lease. He had never allowed Churchill to forget his enmity to Bolshevism; perhaps this was his oblique last thrust at the aging Tory.

There would be another day of political chaffering, leaving the sore issue of Poland uppermost and unresolved, but the Tehran Conference was over. All three leaders could go home in triumph. Stalin had his full-scale invasion of France, which was what he had been demanding since the day Germany had invaded his country. Put down though Churchill was, he could bring to the British people assurance of victory in the war they had all but lost; and if his Mediterranean plans had been subordinated to Overlord, he would fight on for them, and push some through.

The chief gain was Roosevelt's. He had a firm alliance against Germany at last, the exact Allied strategy he wanted, elimination of a separate peace, Stalin's pledge to attack Japan, and his commitment to join the United Nations: a clean sweep of objectives. Franklin Roosevelt bore himself at Tehran, the memoirs suggest, as though it were his finest hour. Perhaps it was.

Yet no human mind can peer very far into the coming time; less so, in the smoke of war. In the end, the United States would not need

Russia's help in the Pacific, indeed would be embarrassed by it. But now the atomic bomb project was a limping question mark, and capturing one small atoll, Tarawa, had been a very bloody business. The war against Japan was expected to go on after Germany's fall for a year or more, ending in an invasion of the Tokyo plain that might cost a million casualties. Stalin's pledge seemed a godsend. As for the eventual dismal decline of the United Nations, who could foresee that? What was there to do but try?

For the Jews still alive in Europe's dreadful night, Tehran was also a dawn; but for them, too, a gloomy dawn. The Overlord assault could not traverse the stormy English Channel before the mild weather of May or June. Roosevelt jocosely observed to Stalin, in breaking this bad news, that the Channel was "a disagreeable body of water." Churchill interjected that the British people had reason to be glad it was so disagreeable. On this waggish byplay turned countless Jewish lives. By the time of Tehran the "territorial solution" was going full blast. Most of Europe's Jews were dead or en route to their deaths. Yet multitudes might yet be saved by the quick smashing of Nazi Germany.

Nobody talked at Tehran about the Jews, but among the high stakes of the conference was this race for the rescue of a remnant. Franklin Roosevelt had made sure that Hitlerism would not much longer darken the earth; but meantime the German murder machinery was working very fast.

What remains of the Tehran Conference, besides old words and old photographs, is the shape of the modern world. If you would see the monument of Tehran, look around. The quaint Persian city in which it took place has been engulfed by a roaring metropolis. The war leaders, having strutted and fretted their hour, are gone. Their work still turns history's wheels. The rest is for the tellers of tales.

. . .

A fat pale Army doctor, moving along the double row of beds, came upon Pug Henry sitting up in a khaki hospital gown. "How are you?" the doctor wearily said. He was himself a newcomer, and had a touch of some Persian ailment.

"Hungry. Can I order breakfast?"

"What have you in mind?"

"Ham and eggs and hashed brown potatoes. Maybe I should go over to the officers' mess."

The doctor sadly grinned, felt his pulse, and handed him a letter. "Will you settle for powdered eggs, dehydrated potatoes, and Spam?"

"Sounds great." Pug was eagerly tearing open the envelope, addressed in Pamela's mannish vertical hand. It was dated the previous day.

My love,

I am beside myself. They won't let me see you!

They tell me you're still too sick to come out to the visitors' room, and a female can't enter the ward. Blast, hell, damn! They say you don't have amoebas, malaria, or any of the other local horrors, so that's a relief, but I'll worry about you all the way back to New Delhi. *Please* go to the British legation before you leave, look for Lieutenant Shingle-wood (a nice green-eyed girl) and tell her you're all right. She'll get word to me.

Duncan is abysmally disgusted with the way the conference has gone. He says it's the end of the Empire. I am hearing a lot of the *Bhagavad-Gita.*

Now *listen,* very quickly and no doubt very clumsily, here it is. I put on an idiotic show that other night in the garden. Possibly there was no "right" way to behave when you threw those questions about Rhoda at me. I reacted on pure instinct, squirting an ink cloud like an alarmed octopus. Why? Not sure. Solidarity of the sex, reluctance to stick a knife into a rival, whatever. Now I've thought it over. Matters are too serious for any of that. The happiness of several people may be at stake. Anyway, you obviously know something, possibly more than I do.

I *don't* know that Rhoda's done anything wrong. I *did* meet her with a Colonel Harrison Peters, and not once but several times. Their relationship may be innocent. In fact I would venture from her demeanor that it is. However, I don't think it's trivial. You had better get back to Washington by hook or by crook, and have it out with her.

Meantime, my love, I *cannot* sit on the sidelines holding my breath for news. I am in very deep with Duncan. We'll probably be married before you and I see each other or even communicate again. I confess this tenuous but iron tie between us is beyond me. It's like a fairy-tale thread that giants cannot break. But there's nothing we can do about it, except to be glad that we've known such painful and exquisite magic.

Write me when you settle something, anyway. With all my heart I urge you to give Rhoda the benefit of every doubt. She's a remarkable woman, she gave you stunning sons, and she's had a terrible time. I'll always love you, always want to hear from you, always wish you well. We've lived five days now this year, haven't we? So many people never live a day from the cradle to the grave.

I love you.
Pamela

Pug was downing the breakfast, thinking that Spam was a grossly maligned delicacy—especially with powdered eggs, another underrated treat—when the doctor looked into the ward and said that he had a visitor. Pug walked out as fast as he could on shaky legs, the hospital bathrobe flapping. On a cheap settee in the deserted outer room, Harry Hopkins sat. He raised a tired hand. "Hi. We're flying off to Cairo in half an hour. The President asked me to see how you are."

"That's incredibly thoughtful of him. I'm better."

"Pug, your Lend-Lease memo was a dandy. He wants you to know that. He didn't use it, but I did. Molotov started to gripe to me about Lend-Lease at a foreign ministers' meeting. I socked him with your facts, and not only did I shut him up, but he apologized and said the bottlenecks would be eliminated fast. When I told the President he laughed like anything. Said it made his day. Now, you haven't talked to Pat Hurley, have you?"

"No, sir. I've been pretty much out of things."

"Well, that idea for a new agreement on troop withdrawals has worked out. The Iranians asked for a statement of intent from the three occupying powers, and that was all the President needed. He got an okay from Stalin, and Hurley rushed hither and yon getting the thing drafted and signed. It's called 'The Declaration of Iran.' The Shah signed at midnight."

"Mr. Hopkins, what about the landing craft situation?"

"That's shot up in importance and urgency at this conference." Hopkins gave him an acute questioning glance. "It'll be top priority next year. Why?"

"That's what I'd like to do next."

"That, rather than command a battleship?" The long lean sickly face expressed lively skepticism. "You, Pug? You're up for a command, I know that."

"Well, for narrow personal reasons, Mr. Hopkins, yes. I'd like to spend some time with my wife."

Hopkins stuck out a bony hand. "Come back by fastest transportation."

The first situation ever brought before the United Nations, in April 1946, was a complaint by Iran that the Soviet Union, unlike America and Great Britain, had failed to withdraw its troops in accordance with the Tehran agreement, and was trying to set up a puppet communist republic in the north. President Harry Truman forcibly backed up Iran

The Russians, with considerable snarling, finally got out. The puppet republic collapsed. Iran recovered its territory. During that crisis, Victor Henry wondered whether a few words at a Persian dinner table might have been his chief contribution to the war. He could never know.

76

SOME twenty seedy men wearing yellow stars sit around a long table in the Magdeburg barracks, Aaron Jastrow among them, awaiting their first meeting with the new commander of Theresienstadt. After several days of driving around in gray February gloom and slush, making a thorough inspection of the ghetto, the new man has summoned the Council of Elders. The Board of Three heading the table—Eppstein and his two deputies—are not saying much, but their faces are long.

The newcomer, SS Sturmbannführer Karl Rahm, is not unknown here. For years he ran the Registry for Jewish Property, in the Central Office for Jewish Affairs of nearby Prague. The registry is the official German government office for despoiling Jews. Most European capitals have such agencies, patterned after Eichmann's pioneer bureau in Vienna, and men like Rahm manage them. By reputation he is a run-of-the-mill Nazi, an Austrian, with a dangerous way of exploding on small provocation; but his manners are reputed a bit less coarse and cold than Burger's.

These Elders, the sham government of Theresienstadt, are worried about the change of commanders. Burger was a devil they were used to. The ghetto was functioning under him on a wretched but stabilized basis. There have been no transports for many weeks. What will the unknown devil bring? That is the question written on the faces around the table.

Major Rahm enters the room with the camp inspector, Haindl. The Elders rise.

Only the black dress uniform with silver flashes and buttons, Jastrow thinks, gives this very common-looking fellow Rahm any presence. One saw such types by the thousands in the old days, jowly thirtyish blonds with bulging stomachs and haunches, strolling on the boulevards of Munich or Vienna. But Scharführer Haindl looks as evil as he is: a real plug-ugly. This Austrian inspector with the cigarette obsession is a feared and loathed man. He will jump through barracks windows to catch Jews smoking; spy on field gangs with binoculars; pop into hospitals, cabarets, even latrines. For possessing a single cigarette he will beat a victim half to death, or send him or her off to the Little Fortress to be tortured. Nevertheless people smoke voraciously in Theresienstadt; cigarettes rate just below gold and jewelry as currency; but a very sharp watch is kept for Haindl. Today he has a mild look, and his gray-green uniform is less sloppy than usual.

Major Rahm tells the Elders to sit down. From the head of the table he addresses them, feet apart, black swagger stick clutched behind him. His opening words are an amazement. He means to make Theresienstadt the Paradise Ghetto in fact as well as in name. The Elders know the town. They know their departments. It is up to them to give him ideas. Present conditions are disgraceful. Theresienstadt is run-down. He is not going to tolerate it. He is initiating a great beautification (*eine grosse Verschönerungsaktion*).

Jastrow is struck by this Eichmann phrase. Rahm's entire speech echoes what Eichmann said two months ago. Under Burger too there was talk about "beautification," but the idea was so preposterous, and Burger himself seemed so uninterested, that the Elders took it as just one more mendacious German façade of words; and the Board of Three gave only desultory orders for cleaning up the streets and painting some huts and barracks.

Rahm is talking a different language. "The Great Beautification" is going to be his prime concern. He has issued important orders. The old Sokol hall will be rebuilt at once as a community center, with studios, lecture halls, and an opera house and theatre with fully equipped stages. All Theresienstadt's other auditoriums and meeting halls will be smartened up. The cabarets will be enlarged and newly decorated. More orchestras will be created. Operas, ballets, concerts, and plays will be scheduled, also various amusements and art exhibits. Materials for costumes, settings, paintings, and so forth will be provided. The hospitals are going to be spic-and-span. A children's playground will be built. A beautiful park will be laid out for the old folks' leisure.

As Jastrow listens to this astonishing harangue, wondering whether it can be serious, the catch in the whole business becomes clear. Rahm is not mentioning any of the things that really make Theresienstadt a hell instead of a paradise: the starvation diet, the hideous overcrowding, the lack of warm clothes, of heat, of latrines, of care centers for mental cases and for the old and crippled, all generating the terrible death rate. Of these things, not a word. He is proposing to paint a corpse.

Jastrow has long suspected that Eichmann made him a figurehead Elder, and possibly even sent him to Theresienstadt, in anticipation of a visit from the Vatican or the neutral Red Cross. Something like that must be in the wind now. Even so, Rahm's approach seems simpleminded. No matter how laboriously he renovates the buildings and grounds, how can he conceal the overwhelming squalor, the crowding, the sickly faces, the malnutrition, the death rate? A little more food, some attention to health, would quickly and easily create a sunburst of happiness in the ghetto that would fool anybody. But the concept of treating the Jews themselves any better, even to create a brief useful illusion, seems beyond the Germans.

Rahm finishes up and asks for suggestions. Around the table eyes shift in gray faces. Nobody speaks. The so-called Elders—in actuality department heads of varying ages—are a mixed lot: some decent, some corrupt, some narrowly self-seeking, some humane. But all hug their posts. Private living quarters, exemption from transport, the chance to give and receive favors, outweigh the tension and guilt of being SS tools. None will risk opening his mouth first, and the silence grows nasty. Outside, a gray sky; inside a gray silence, and the ever-prevailing Theresienstadt smell of dirty bodies. Faintly from afar one can hear "The Beautiful Blue Danube"; the town orchestra is starting the morning concert, off behind the fence in the main square.

Jastrow's department does not deal in the vital things Rahm has ignored. He will do nothing that might hurt Natalie and her child, but for himself, since the encounter with Eichmann, he is strangely unafraid. The American in him still finds this European nightmare in which he is caught disgusting and ludicrous; and the miasma of fear all around him, pathetic. For the barking fat-faced mediocrity in the stagy black uniform he feels chiefly contempt, modified by caution.

He raises his hand. Rahm nods. He stands up and salutes. *"Herr Kommandant,* I am the stinking Jew, Jastrow—"

Rahm interrupts, pointing a thick finger at him. "Now then! That kind of shit will cease at once." He turns to Haindl, who is smoking a cigar in an armchair. "New regulations! No more idiotic saluting and removing of caps. No more 'stinking Jew' talk. Theresienstadt is not a concentration camp. It is a comfortable and happy residential town."

Haindl's malevolent face twists in surprise. *"Jawohl, Herr Kommandant."*

Surprise, too, on all the Elders' countenances. Hitherto, failure to pull off one's head-covering and to salute in a German's presence has been a major ghetto offense, punishable by instant clubbing. Sounding off as a "stinking Jew" has been mandatory. The reflexes will take much unlearning.

"I beg leave to mention," Jastrow goes on, "that in my department the music section badly needs paper."

"Paper?" Rahm's face wrinkles up. "What kind of paper?"

"Any kind, *mein Kommandant."* Jastrow is speaking the truth.

Scraps of wallpaper, even of linen, are being used to note down music. It is a small harmless item, worth a try. "The musicians will rule it themselves. Though of course, ruled musical score paper would be best."

"Ruled musical score paper." Rahm repeats this as though it were a foreign language. "How much?"

Jastrow's deputy, a cadaverous orchestra leader from Vienna, whispers from the seat beside him.

"Mein Kommandant," says Jastrow, "for the kind of great cultural expansion you are planning, five hundred sheets to start with."

"See to it!" Rahm says to Haindl. "And I thank you, sir. Gentlemen, that is the kind of idea I want. What else?"

One by one the other Elders now timidly rise with innocuous requests, which Rahm receives warmly. The atmosphere improves. On cue, the day brightens outside and the sun shines into the room. Jastrow rises again. May the music section also request more musical instruments, of better quality? Rahm laughs. By all means! The Central Registry in Prague has two big warehouses stuffed with musical instruments: violins, cellos, flutes, clarinets, guitars, pianos, the lot! No problem at all; just put in a list.

Not one Elder mentions food, medicine, or living space. Jastrow feels capable of bringing up these things, but what good could come of it? He would quench the sunny moment, bring trouble on himself, and accomplish nothing. Not his department.

When Rahm and Haindl leave, Eppstein rises. On his face the fixed obsequious smile fades. There is one more thing, he announces. The new commander has found the overcrowding of the town most unhealthy and unsightly, so five thousand Jews must at once be transported.

In an ordinary town of fifty thousand, struck by a tornado that wiped out five thousand inhabitants, the people might feel somewhat as the Jews do at a transport.

There is no getting used to this intermittent scourge. Each time the fabric of the ghetto is torn apart. Optimism and faith dim. The sense of doom rises again. Though nobody is sure what "the east" really means, it is a name of terror. The unlucky ones move around in shock, making their farewells, giving away what meager belongings they cannot pack into one suitcase. The Central Secretariat is besieged by frantic petitioners pulling every string and trying every loophole to get exemptions. But an iron proscenium of number frames the tragedy: *five thousand.* Five thousand Jews must get on the train. If one is exempted, another must take his place. If fifty are excused, fifty who thought themselves safe must be struck as by lightning with gray summons cards.

The Jews who run the Transport Section are a sad harried lot. They are their brothers' keepers, saviors, and executioners. It is a ghetto joke that in the end Theresienstadt will shrink to the commander and the Transport Section. Everybody smiles on them; but they know they are cursed and despised. They have life-and-death power they never wanted. They are Sonderkommando clerks, disposing of Jews' living bodies with pens and rubber stamps.

Are they to blame? Many desperate Jews stand ready to seize their places. Some of these transport bureaucrats belong to the communist or Zionist undergrounds, spending their nights in vain plots for uprisings. Some never think of anything but their own skins. A few brave ones try to correct the worst hardships. Some wretched ones show favoritism, take bribes, satisfy grudges.

In this spectrum of human nature blasted by German cruelty, what man can say where he would have fit? What man who was not there can judge the *Judenräte,* the Central Secretariats, and the Transport Sections? *"God pardons the coerced,"* says an ancient Jewish proverb, distilled from bitter millennia.

A parody of German thoroughness, the Central Secretariat reaches everywhere with its gray summons cards. In half a dozen different catalogue systems, Jews are indexed and cross-indexed by other Jews. Wherever a body can lie down for the night, that space is catalogued, with the name of the body occupying it. Each day a roll call of the town is taken. The dead and the transported are neatly crossed off the cards. Newcomers upon arrival are indexed as they are robbed. One can get out of the card catalogues only by dying or "going east."

The real power in Theresienstadt under the SS is not Eppstein, or the Board of Three, or the Council of Elders; it is the Central Secretariat. Yet the Secretariat is nobody you can talk to. It is friends, neighbors, relatives, or just other Jews. It is a Bureau, bureaucratically carrying out the orders of the Germans. The Complaint Section of the Secretariat, a row of sour Jewish faces behind desks, is an impotent mockery; but it provides a lot of jobs. The Secretariat is monstrously overstaffed because it has been a refuge. Yet this time the gray cards strike even inside the Secretariat. The monster is starting to eat its own bowels.

The strangest thing is that a few people actually apply to go in each transport. In a previous shipment their spouses, parents, or children have gone. They are lonesome. Theresienstadt is not such a bed of roses that they should want to stay on at all costs. So they will brave the unknown, hoping to find their loved ones in the east. Some have received letters and postcards, so they know that those they seek are at least still alive. Even from the mica factory, the most reliable refuge in Theresienstadt, several women have volunteered and gone east. That is one request about which the Germans are invariably gracious.

When Natalie meets Udam outside the children's home after work he stuns her by showing her his gray card. He has already been to the Secretariat. He knows Eppstein's two deputies. The head of the transport section is an old Zionist pal from Prague. The bank manager has intervened. Nothing helps. Perhaps the SS got irked by his performances. Anyway, it is all finished. Tonight they give their last show. At six in the morning he must collect his daughter and go to the depot.

Her first reaction is cold fright. She too has been performing; has a gray card come to her apartment during the day? Seeing the look on her face, Udam tells her he has inquired, and there is no summons for her. She and Jastrow have the highest exempt classification. If nobody else is here when "the cousins arrive from the east and the west," they will be. He has some new topical jokes for Frost-Cuckoo Land, and they may as well rehearse, and make this last show a good one.

She lays a hand on his arm as he starts inside, and suggests that they call it off. Jastrow's audience will be small and in no mood to laugh. Maybe nobody will come. Aaron's lecture subject, "Heroes of the *Iliad*," is heavily academic, and hardly inspiring or cheering. Aaron requested the puppet show because he has never seen it, but Natalie suspects that professorial vanity dies hard, and that he really wants to draw an audience. It is his first lecture since he became an Elder, and he must know that he is unpopular.

Udam won't hear of cancelling. Why waste good jokes? They go in to the children. Louis greets her with the usual wild joy, in the great moment of his day. During their meal, Udam talks optimistically about "the east." How much worse can it be, after all, than Theresienstadt? His wife's postcards, coming about once a month, have been short but reassuring. He shows Natalie the last card, dated only two weeks ago.

Birkenau, Camp II-B

My dearest

 Everything is all right. I hope Martha is well. I miss you both. Much snow here.

    Love,
    Hilda

"Birkenau?" Natalie asks. "Where is that?"

"Poland, outside Oswiecim. It's just a village. The Jews work in big German factories around there, and get plenty of food."

Udam's tone does not match his words. Natalie passed through Oswiecim with Byron years ago, on the way to the wedding of Berel's son in Medzice. She barely remembers it as a flat dull railroad town. There is remarkably little talk in the ghetto about "the east," the camps there, and what happens there; like death, like cancer, like the executions in the Little Fortress, these are shunned topics. Nevertheless, the word *"Oswiecim"* vibrates with horror. Natalie does not press Udam. She does not want to hear any more.

They rehearse in the basement, while Louis romps with the playmate he will not see after tonight. Udam's new jokes are pallid, except for the touch about the Persian slave girl. The Frost-Cuckoo minister has brought her for the king's pleasure. She comes in, a veiled waggling female puppet. Natalie puts on a husky sexy voice for the billing and cooing she does with the amorous king. He asks her name. She is coy and reluctant. He teases it out of her. "Well, I'm named after my home town." "And that is?" She giggles. "Tee-hee. Tehran." The king shrieks, the icicles fall off his nose—a standard trick Natalie has worked up—and he chases her off the stage with a club. That will go well. Reports of the Tehran Conference have much cheered the ghetto.

Afterward Natalie hurries back to the new apartment, still fearing a gray card may be there. Who was safer than Udam? Who had more inside contacts? Who could have felt more protected? But she sees at once on Aaron's face that there is no gray card; though he says nothing, merely looking up and nodding, at the quite decent desk where he is marking his lecture notes.

The luxury of these two rooms and a bath still makes Natalie uneasy. Ever since Jastrow reversed himself and accepted the post and privileges of an Elder, there has been a coldness between them. She saw Eichmann accept his refusal. He has never explained why he changed his mind. Did his old selfish love of comfort overcome him? Being an SS tool does not seem to trouble him at all. The religiosity is the only change. He puts on phylacteries, spends a lot of time over the Talmud, and has withdrawn into a quiet frail placidity; perhaps, she thinks, to shut out her disapproval, or his own self-contempt.

Jastrow knows what she thinks. He can do nothing about it. The explanation would be too terrifying. Natalie already lives on the brink of panic; she is young, and she has the baby. Since his illness he is reconciled to dying when he must. Let her go about her business, he had decided, not knowing the worst. If the SS chooses to pounce, her scurrilous performances have already condemned her. It is now a race against time. His aim is to last, until rescue comes from the east and the west.

She tells him about Udam, and without much hope asks him to intercede. He replies drily that he has very little influence; that it is a bad business to venture prestige and position on a request likely to be refused. They hardly talk again until they set out together for the barracks where Aaron is to lecture in the loft.

A large silent audience has gathered, after all. Usually there is lively chatter before the evening's diversion. Not tonight. They have turned out in surprising numbers, but the mood is funereal. Behind the crude lectern, off to a side, stands the curtained puppet theatre. As Natalie takes the vacant seat beside Udam, he gives her a little smile that cuts her heart.

Aaron places his notes on the lectern and looks about, stroking his beard. Softly, in a dry classroom manner, speaking slow formal German, he begins.

"It is interesting that Shakespeare seems to find the whole story of the *Iliad* contemptible. He retells it in his play, *Troilus and Cressida,* and he puts his opinion in the mouth of Thersites, the cynical coward— *'The matter is only a cuckold and a whore.'*"

This quotation Aaron Jastrow cites in English, then with a prudish little smile translates it into German.

"Now Falstaff, that other and more celebrated Shakespearean coward, thinks like Emerson that war in general is nothing but a periodic madness. *'Who hath honor? He that died o' Wednesday.'* We suspect that Shakespeare agreed with his immortal fat man. *Troilus,* his play of the Trojan war, is not in his best tragic vein, for madness is not tragic. Madness is either funny or ghastly, and so is much war literature: either *The Good Soldier Schweik,* or *All Quiet on the Western Front.*

"But the *Iliad* is epic tragedy. It is the same war story as *Troilus,* but with one crucial difference. Shakespeare has taken out the gods, whereas it is the gods who make the *Iliad* grand and terrible.

"For Homer's Hector and Achilles are caught in a squabble of the Greek deities. The gods take sides. They come down into the dust of the battlefield to intervene. They turn aside weapons hurled straight to kill. They appear in disguises to make trouble or to pull their favorites out of jams. An honorable contest of arms becomes a mockery, a game of wits among supernatural, invisible magicians. The fighting men are mere helpless pieces of the game."

Natalie glances over her shoulder at the listeners. No audiences like these! Famished for diversion, for light, for a shred of consolation, they hang on a literary talk in Theresienstadt, as elsewhere people do on a great concert artist's recital, or on a gripping film.

In the same level pedantic way, Jastrow reviews the background of the *Iliad:* Paris's awarding of the golden apple for beauty to Aphrodite; the hostilities on Olympus that ensue; the kidnapping by Paris of Helen, the world's prettiest woman, Aphrodite's promised reward; and the inevitable war, since she is a married Greek queen and he a Trojan prince. Splendid men on both sides, who care nothing for the cuckold, the whore, or the kidnapper, become embroiled. For them, once it is war, honor is at stake.

"But in this squalid quarrel, what gives the heroes of the *Iliad* their grandeur? Is it not their indomitable will to fight, despite the shifting and capricious meddling of the gods? To venture their lives for honor, in an unfair and unfathomable situation where bad and stupid men triumph, good and skilled men fall, and strange accidents divert and decide battles? In a purposeless, unfair, absurd battle, to fight on, fight to the death, fight like men? It is the oldest of human problems, the problem of senseless evil, dramatized on the field of battle. That is the tragedy Homer perceived and Shakespeare passed over."

Jastrow pauses, turns a page, and looks straight at the audience, his emaciated face dead pale, his eyes large in the sunken sockets. If the audience has been silent before, it is now as quiet as so many corpses.

"The universe of the *Iliad,* in short, is a childish and despicable trap. The glory of Hector is that in such a trap he behaves so nobly that an Almighty God, if He did exist, would weep with pride and pity. Pride, that He has created out of a handful of dirt a being so grand. Pity, that in His botched universe a Hector must unjustly die, and his poor corpse be dragged in the dust. But Homer knows no Almighty God. There is Zeus, the father of the gods, but who can say what he is up to? Perhaps he is off mounting some bemused mortal girl in the disguise of her husband, or a bull, or a swan. Small wonder that Greek mythology is extinct."

The disgusted gesture with which Jastrow turns his page surprises an uncertain laugh from the rapt audience. Thrusting his notes into his pocket, Jastrow leaves the lectern, comes forward, and stares at his listeners. His usually placid face is working. He bursts out in another voice, startling Natalie by shifting to Yiddish, in which he has never lectured before.

"All right. Now let us talk about this in our mother-language. And let us talk about an epic of our own. Satan says to God, you remember, 'Naturally, Job is upright. Seven sons, three daughters, the wealthiest man in the land of Uz. Why not be upright? Look how it pays. A sensible universe! A fine arrangement! Job is not upright, he is just a smart

Jew. The sinners are damned fools. But just take away his rewards, and see how upright he will remain!'

" 'All right, take them away,' God says. And in one day marauders carry off Job's wealth, and a hurricane kills all his ten children. What does Job do? He goes into mourning. 'Naked I came from the womb, naked I will return,' he says, 'God has given, God has taken away. Blessed be God's name.'

"So God challenges Satan. 'See? He remained upright. A good man.'

" 'Skin for skin,' Satan answers. 'All a man really cares about is his life. Reduce him to a skeleton—a sick, plundered, bereaved skeleton, nothing left to this proud Jew but his own rotting skin and bones—' "

Jastrow loses his voice. He shakes his head, clears his throat, passes a hand over his eyes. He goes on hoarsely. "God says, 'All right, do anything to him except kill him.' A horrible sickness strikes Job. Too loathsome an object to stay under his own roof, he crawls out and sits on an ash heap, scraping his sores with a shard. He says nothing. Stripped of his wealth, his children senselessly killed, his body a horrible stinking skeleton covered with boils, he is silent. Three of his pious friends come to comfort him. A debate follows.

"Oh, my friends, what a debate! What rugged poetry, what insight into the human condition! I say to you that Homer pales before Job; that Aeschylus meets his match in power, and his master in understanding; that Dante and Milton sit at this author's feet without ever grasping him. Who was he? Nobody knows. Some old Jew. He knew what life is, that's all. He knew it as we in Theresienstadt know it."

He pauses, looking straight at his niece with sad eyes. Shaken, perplexed, on the verge of tears, Natalie is hungry for his next words. When he speaks, though he looks away, she feels he is talking to her.

"In Job, as in most great works of art, the main design is very simple. His comforters maintain that since one Almighty God rules the universe, it must make sense. Therefore Job must have sinned. Let him search his deeds, confess and repent. The missing piece is only what his offense was.

"And in round after round of soaring argument, Job fights back. The missing piece must be with God, not with him. He is as religious as they are. He knows that the Almighty exists, that the universe must make sense. But he, poor bereft boil-covered skeleton, knows now that it does not in fact always make sense; that there is no guarantee of good fortune for good behavior; that crazy injustice is part of the visible world, and of this life. His religion demands that he assert his innocence, *otherwise he will be profaning God's name!* He will be conceding that the Almighty can botch one man's life; and if God can do that, the whole universe is a botch, and He is not an Almighty God. That Job will never concede. He wants an answer.

"He gets an answer! Oh, what an answer! An answer that answers nothing. God Himself speaks at last out of a roaring storm. *'Who are you to call me to account? Can you hope to understand why or how I do anything? Were you there at the Creation? Can you comprehend the marvels of the stars, the animals, the infinite wonders of existence? You, a worm that lives a few moments, and dies?'*

"My friends, Job has won! Do you understand? God with all His roaring has *conceded Job's main point, that the missing piece is with Him!* God claims only that His reason is beyond Job. That, Job is perfectly willing to admit. With the main point settled, Job humbles himself, is more than satisfied, falls on his face.

"So the drama ends. God rebukes the comforters for speaking falsely of Him, and praises Job for holding to the truth. He restores Job's wealth. Job has seven more sons and three more daughters. He lives a hundred and forty more years, sees grandchildren and great-grandchildren, and dies old, prosperous, revered."

The rich flow of literary Yiddish halts. Jastrow goes back to the lectern, pulls the notes from his pocket, and turns over several sheets. He peers out at the audience.

"Satisfied? A happy ending, yes? Much more Jewish than the absurd and tragic *Iliad?*

"Are you so sure? My dear Jewish friends, what about the ten children who died? Where was God's justice to them? And what about the father, the mother? Can those scars on Job's heart heal, even in a hundred and forty years?

"That is not the worst of it. Think! What was the missing piece that was too much for Job to understand? *We* understand it, and are we so very clever? Satan simply sneered God into ordering the senseless ordeal. No wonder God roars out of a storm to silence Job! Isn't He ashamed of Himself before His own creature? Hasn't Job behaved better than God?"

Jastrow shrugs, spreads his hands, and his face relaxes in a wistful little smile that makes Natalie think of Charlie Chaplin.

"But I am expounding the *Iliad*. In the *Iliad*, unseen powers are at odds with each other, and that brings about a visible world of senseless evil. Not so in Job. Satan has no power at all. He is not the Christian Satan, not Dante's colossal monster, not Milton's proud rebel, not in the least. He needs God's permission to make every move.

"Then who is Satan, and why does God leave him out of the answer from the storm? The word *satan* in Hebrew means *adversary*. What is the book telling us? Was God arguing with Himself? Was He asking Himself whether there was any purpose in the vast creation? And in reply pointing, not to the dead glittering galaxies that sprawl over thousands of light-years, but to man, the handful of dirt that can sense His presence, do His will, and measure those galaxies? Above all to the upright man, the speck of dirt who can measure himself against the Creator Himself, for dignity and goodness? What else did the ordeal establish?

"The heroes in the *Iliad* rise superior to the squabbling injustice of weak and contemptible gods.

"The hero in Job holds to the truth of One Almighty God through the most senseless and horrible injustice; forcing God at last to measure up to Himself, to acknowledge that injustice is on His side, to repair the damage as best He can.

"In the *Iliad* there is no injustice to repair. In the end there is only blind fate.

"In Job God must answer for everything, good and bad, that happens. Job is the Bible's only hero. There are fighting men, patriarchs, lawgivers, prophets, in the other books. This is the one man who rises to the measure of the universe, to the stature of the God of Israel, while sitting on an ash heap; Job, a poor skeletal broken beggar.

"Who is Job?

"Nobody. *'Job was never born and never existed,'* says the Talmud. *'He was a parable.'*

"Parable of what truth?

"All right, we have come to it now. Who is it in history who will never admit that there is no God, never admit that the universe makes no sense? Who is it who suffers ordeal after ordeal, plundering after plundering, massacre after massacre, century after century, yet looks up at the sky, sometimes with dying eyes, and cries, 'The Lord our God, the Lord is One'?

"Who is it who in the end of days will force from God the answer from the storm? Who will see the false comforters rebuked, the old glory restored, and generations of happy children and grandchildren to the fourth generation? Who until then will leave the missing piece to God, and praise His Name, crying, 'The Lord has given, the Lord has taken away, blessed be the Name of the Lord'? Not the noble Greek of the *Iliad*, he is extinct. No! Nobody but the sick, plundered skeleton on the ash heap. Nobody but the beloved of God, the worm that lives a few moments and dies, the handful of dirt that has justified Creation. Nobody but Job. He is the only answer, if there is one, to the adversary challenge to an Almighty God, if there is One. Job, the stinking Jew."

Jastrow stares in a stunned way at the still audience, then stumbles toward the first row. Udam jumps up and gently helps him to his seat. The audience does not applaud, does not talk, does not move.

Udam begins to sing.

Udam . . . udam . . . udam . . .

So there will be no puppet show. Natalie joins in the chorusing of the tragic refrain. Udam sings his song for the last time in Theresienstadt, driving it to a heartrending crescendo.

When it ends, there is no reaction. No applause, no talk, nothing. This silent audience is waiting for something.

Udam does something he has never before done; an encore; an encore to no applause. He starts another song, one Natalie has heard in Zionist meetings. It is an old simple syncopated refrain, in a minor key, built on a line from the liturgy: *"Let the temple be rebuilt, soon in our time, and grant us a portion in Your law."* As he sings it, Udam slowly begins to dance.

> *Sheh-yi-boneh bet-hamikdash*
> *Bim-hera b'yomenu—*

He dances as an old rabbi might on a holy day, deliberately, awkwardly, his arms raised, his face turned upward, his eyes closed, his fingers snapping the rhythm. The people softly accompany him, singing and clapping their hands. One by one they rise to their feet. Udam's voice grows more powerful, his steps more vigorous. He is losing himself in the dance and the song, drifting into an ecstasy terrible and beautiful to see. Barely opening his eyes, twisting and swaying, he moves toward Aaron Jastrow, and holds out a hand. Jastrow gets to his feet, links his hand with Udam's, and the two men dance and sing.

It is a death dance. Natalie knows it. Everybody knows it. The sight both freezes and exalts her. It is the most stirring moment of her life, here in this dark malodorous loft in a prison ghetto. She is overwhelmed with the agony of her predicament, and the exaltation of being Jewish.

> *Oy let the temple be rebuilt*
> *Oy speedily in our time*
> *Oy and grant us a portion in Your law!*

When the dance ends, the audience starts to leave. Everybody slowly goes from the loft, as if from a burial. There is almost no talking. Udam folds up the puppet theatre, and gives Natalie one kiss in farewell.

"I did not think they wanted my jokes," he says. "I'll put this back in the children's home. Keep up your shows for the children. Good-bye."

"Tehran was a good joke," she says, through a choked throat.

Aaron leans heavily on her as they go down the stairs and into the shadowy street. Amid the dispersing crowd, a burly man sidles up to them, and says in Yiddish, *"Gut gezugt, Arele, und gut getantzed."* ("Well said, little Aaron, and well danced.") "Natalie, *sholem aleichem.*"

In the gloom she sees a square tough elderly smooth-shaven face, a total stranger.

"Who are you?" she asks.

Aaron Jastrow, who has not seen him in fifty years, says, "Berel?"

77

Jeffersonville Plaza Motor Hotel
Jeffersonville, Indiana
2 March 1944

Pamela, my love—

Here I am in a place you never heard of, doing what I've been doing ever since I returned to the States—namely, persuading various obtuse or confused sons of bitches to do things they ought to be doing anyway, if this country's to get the landing craft it urgently needs.

This is my first chance to write you, because Rhoda and I didn't get down to cases until recently. I've been on the run since I got back. Besides, Rhoda has a sort of genius for keeping her mouth shut when in doubt or in trouble; and as you know, I'm not a ready talker about such things.

Brigadier General Old came to Washington from New Delhi last week, to blast loose more transport planes for Burma. He has great regard for Burne-Wilke, and rather likes you, too. To my immense relief he called you Pamela Tudsbury, not Lady Burne-Wilke. Hence, all that follows. Rhoda's supposed to telephone me tonight or tomorrow about her situation with Peters. Then I can spell it all out for you. Meantime, my other news—quite a lot since Tehran:

To begin with, I'm now the Deputy Chief, Production Branch, Office of Procurement and Materials; and collaterally, Material and Products Control Officer; that is, another anonymous man in uniform running around Washington's corridors. My task boils down to industrial liaison and troubleshooting.

I came into this business late, with the landing craft program well along. So I'm the outsider, the roving player, with no bureaucratic position to build up or protect; SecNav's professional alter ego, you might say, watching for problems, cutting across agency lines, forestalling major delays. When I do my job right, there's no sign of it; disasters just fail to occur.

Our industrial mobilization has become an absolute marvel, Pam. We've sprung to life, turning out weapons of war, ships, planes, internal combustion engines in quantities that add up to the eighth wonder of the world. But it's all been improvised; new people in new factories doing new jobs. Tempers are short, pressure is terrific, and everybody's competitive and tight-nerved as hell. When priorities clash, whole agencies harden into battle posture. Big shots get their dander up and memos start flying.

Well, I know a good deal about landing craft, as an engineer and as a war planner, and about available factories and materials. Serving on the main war boards I can usually spot developing trouble. The tough part is persuading hard-charging bosses to do as I say. As the secretary's man I have a lot of leverage. I seldom have to go to Hopkins, though I've done it on occasion. The Navy is going to come up with an amazing number of landing craft for Eisenhower, Pamela. Our civilian sector is unruly and spoiled, but ye gods, it turns out the stuff.

No doubt I'll stay in production until the war ends. I've fallen behind in the career race. My classmates will fight the remaining battles at sea. There's a lot of life left in the Japs, but I've passed up my last chance at the blue water. It doesn't matter. For every star performer in this war you need a dozen good backup men in industrial logistics, or you don't get your victories.

One A.M. and old Rhoda hasn't called. My plane to Houston leaves at the crack of dawn, so I'll break off. More tomorrow.

3 March
Houston

Hi.

Wild rainstorm here. Wind whipping the palm trees outside my room, rain lashing the windows. Texas weather, like the inhabitants, tends to extremes. However, Texans are okay once they understand (a) that you're right, (b) that you mean business, and (c) that you have some negotiating strength. Haven't heard from Rhoda yet, but expect to tonight, for sure.

More news: Byron's passed through Washington, en route to his new duty post, exec of a submarine undergoing overhaul in Connecticut. He's come through some bad personal ordeals.

[*The letter narrates the death of Carter Aster, and the news about Natalie in Theresienstadt.*]

I've obtained the record of the court of inquiry about Aster's death. It was touch-and-go for Byron. He made a very poor witness for himself. He would not say that he *couldn't* have saved the captain by a delay in submerging. But the old chief of the boat wrapped the thing up in his testimony when he said: "Maybe Captain Aster was wrong and he could have survived, but he was right that the *Moray* couldn't have. He was the greatest submarine skipper of this war. He gave the right orders. Mr. Henry only obeyed them." That's what the court concluded. Forrestal is proposing a posthumous Congressional Medal of Honor for Aster. Byron may get a Bronze Star, but it won't help his spirits much.

Warren's widow came back around Christmastime, and Rhoda took her in. She's planning to go back to law school in the fall. She's a beautiful woman with a fine son and her whole life ahead of her. Usually she's very cheerful, but when Byron was with us she went into a deep depression. Byron looks more and more like Warren as he fills out. No doubt that got Janice down. A couple of times Rhoda came on her crying. Since he left she's been okay.

And what a kid that Vic is! Handsome, affectionate, and deep. He's very active and naughty, but in a stealthy way. His mischief is not impulsive but *planned*, like tactics, for maximum destruction and minimum detection. He'll go far.

Madeline finally dropped that grinning, pot-bellied, oleaginous radio mountebank I told you about, relieving me of the need to horsewhip him, which I was working up to. She's living at home, working in a Washington radio station, and she's taken up again with an old admirer, Simon Anderson, a first-rate naval officer who's on duty here in new weaponry. Last week she had a long tearful talk with Rhoda on whether, and what, she should tell Simon about the radio man. I asked Rhoda what her advice was. She gave me a funny look and said, "I told her, wait till he asks you." I would have advised Madeline to have it out with Sime, and start on an honest basis. No doubt that's why she consulted Rhoda.

There goes the telephone. It has to be my wife.

It was.

Okay. Now I can backtrack and tell you what happened last week. We were sitting around after dinner, the same day General Old let me know you were still unmarried. I said, "Rho, why don't we talk about Hack Peters?" She didn't turn a hair. "Yes, why not, dear? Better mix us a couple of stiff drinks." Rhoda-like, she waited until I asked her. But she was quite ready for this showdown.

She acknowledged the relationship, declared it's the real thing, not guilty but deep. I believe her. Colonel Peters has been an "irreproachable gentleman," thinks she's twenty times as good as she is, and in short looks on her as the perfection of womankind. Rhoda says that it's embarrassing to be so idolized, but also very sweet and rejuvenating. I asked her point-blank whether she'd be happier divorcing me and marrying Peters.

Rhoda took a very long time to answer that one. Finally she looked me in the eye and said, yes, she would. The main reason, she said, is that she's lost my good opinion and can't get it back, though I've been kind and forgiving. After being loved by me for years, it's wretched just to be tolerated. I asked her what she wanted me to do. She brought up that talk you had with her in California. I said that I had great affection for you, but since you were engaged, that was that. I told her to decide on her own best prospects for happiness, and that I would do whatever she wanted.

She apparently had been waiting for this sort of green light from me. Rhoda's always been a bit afraid of me. I don't know why, since it seems to me I've been rather henpecked. Anyway, she said that she'd need some time. Well, she didn't need much. That was what the phone call was about. Harrison Peters is dying to marry her. No question. She's landed him. She expects to talk to our lawyer, and then to Peters's lawyer, in the next couple of days. Peters also wants to talk to me "man to man" when I get back to Washington. I may forgo that delight.

Well, Pamela darling, so I'll be free, if by some miracle you'll still have me. Will you marry me?

I'm not a rich man—serving one's country one doesn't get rich—but we wouldn't be badly off. I've saved fifteen percent of my salary for thirty-one years. Working in BuShips and BuOrd I could observe industrial trends, so I've invested and done well. Rhoda's in fine shape, she's got a substantial family trust. Anyway, I'm sure Peters will take excellent care of her. Am I being too mundane? I'm not expert at proposing. This is only my second try.

If we do marry, I'll take an early retirement so that we can be together all the time. There are many jobs for me in industry; I could even work in England.

If we did have a kid or two, I'd want to give them a church upbringing. Is that all right? I know you're a freethinker. I can't make much sense out of life, myself, but none whatever without religion. Maybe in my fifties I'd make a hard-shelled mossy crab of a father; still, I get along pretty well with little Vic. I might in fact spoil kids now. I'd like the chance to try!

So there it is! If you're Lady Burne-Wilke by now, take my letter as a wistful farewell compliment to an unlikely and wonderful love. If I hadn't casually booked passage on the *Bremen* in 1939, mainly to brush up on my German, I'd never have known you. I was happy with Rhoda, in love with her, and not inclined to look further. Yet despite the differences in age, nationality, and background, despite the fact that over four years we've spent perhaps three weeks together in all, the simple truth is that you seem to be my other half, found when it was all but too late. The bare possibility of marrying you is a glimpse of beauty that stops my breath. Very likely Rhoda's been groping for that beauty outside our marriage, because it wasn't quite there; she's been a good wife (till she fell away) but a discontented one.

In the Persian garden you suggested that this whole thing might be a romantic illusion. I've given that a lot of thought. If we'd been snatching at our rare meetings to go to bed together, I might agree. But what have we ever done but talk, and yet feel this closeness? Marriage will not be, I grant you, like these tantalizing encounters in far-off places; there'll be shopping, laundry, housekeeping, the mortgage, mowing the lawn, arguments, packing and unpacking, headaches, sore throats, and all the rest. Well, with you, all that strikes me as a lovely prospect. I don't want anything else. If God gives me that much, I'll say—with everything that's gone wrong with my life, and all my scars—that I'm a happy man, and I'll try to make you happy.

I hope this letter doesn't come too late.

All my love,
Pug

The battle for Imphal was already on when Pug wrote. Since Burne-Wilke's headquarters was no longer in New Delhi but at the forward base at Comilla, the letter did not reach her until mid-April, after Burne-Wilke had disappeared in a flight over the jungle, and while a search was still on for him.

• • •

Luck figures not only in war, but in the writing of war journalism and history. Imphal was a British victory which lifted the cloud of Singapore; a classic showdown like El Alamein, fought out on worse terrain over a larger front. It was unique among modern battles, in that the RAF did at Imphal what the Luftwaffe failed to do at Stalingrad: it supplied a surrounded army by air for months until breakout and victory. But the Normandy invasion and the fall of Rome, with hordes of reporters and cameramen in attendance at both events, spanned the same block of time. So at Imphal, in a remote valley near the Himalayas, two hundred thousand men fought a long series of sanguinary engagements unnoticed by the newspapers. History continues to overlook Imphal. The dead of course do not care. The survivors with their faded recollections are passing from the scene unnoticed.

Imphal itself is a real-life Shangri-La, a cluster of native villages around golden-domed temples, on a fertile and beautiful plain in the northeast corner of vast India bordering Burma, ringed by formidable mountains. The freakish tides of world war brought the British and the Japanese to death-grips there. Ignominiously kicked out of Malaya and Burma by the Japanese in 1942, the British had one war aim in Southeast Asia, to retrieve their Empire. The conquering Japanese armies had halted at the great mountain ranges that separate Burma from India. The Americans, from Franklin Roosevelt down, had no interest in the British war aim, regarding it as backward-looking, unjust, and futile. Roosevelt had even told Stalin at Tehran that he wanted to see India free. But the Americans did want to clear a corridor through northern Burma to keep China supplied and fighting, and to set up bases on the China coast for bombing Japan.

The beautiful plain of Imphal was the key to such a supply corridor, a gateway among the mountain passes. The British had been building up here for counterattack, and perforce they accepted the American strategy. Their commanding general, a brilliant warrior named Slim, piled in a large army of mingled English and Asian divisions, with the mission of fighting through northern Burma to join hands with Chinese divisions driving south under the American General Stilwell, thus opening the supply corridor. At this, the Japanese too moved up north in force to confront Slim. His appetizing buildup offered a chance to destroy India's defenders with a counterstroke; and then perhaps to march in and set up a new puppet government of India under Subhas Chandra Bose, a red-hot Indian nationalist who had defected to Japan.

The Japanese attacked first, employing their old jungle-fighting tactics against the British: rapid thrusts far beyond supply lines with quick flanking encirclements, feeding and fueling their army from captured supply dumps as they advanced. But this time Slim and his field commander, Scoones, accepting battle on the Imphal plain, bloodily fought the Japanese to a standstill there, denying them their usual replenishment until they starved, wilted, and ran. This took over three months. The battle evolved into two epic sieges—of a small British force surrounded at a village called Kohima, and of Slim's main body at Imphal itself, invested by a seasoned and fierce Japanese jungle army.

Airlift tipped the balance of the sieges. The British consumed supplies more rapidly than the Japanese, whose soldiers could survive for a while on a bag of rice a day; but American transport planes daily flew in hundreds of tons of supplies, landing some at overburdened airfields, the crews kicking the rest out of open plane doors to parachute down. Burne-Wilke's tactical command protected the airlift, and harried the Japanese army with bombing and strafing.

• • •

Upon investing Imphal, however, the Japanese overran several radar warning outposts, and for a while the air picture was not good. Burne-Wilke decided in a conference at Comilla to fly into Imphal to see things for himself. His Spitfire squadrons stationed on the plain were reporting that without adequate radar warning, maintaining control of the air was becoming a problem. He took a reconnaissance aircraft and flew off solo, ignoring Pamela's mutterings.

Burne-Wilke was a seasoned pilot, a World War I flyer and a career RAF man. The premature death of his older brother had made him a viscount, but he had stayed in the service. Too senior now to fly in combat, he seized chances to fly alone when he could. Mountbatten had already reprimanded him once for this. But he loved flying over the jungle without the distracting chatter of a co-pilot. It afforded him something like the calming peace of flight over water, this solid green earth cover passing underneath for hours, unbroken except by the rare brown crooked crawl of a river speckled with green islands. The bouncing curving ride through mountain passes amid thick-timbered peaks towering high above his wings, ending in a sudden view of the gardened valley and the gleaming gold domes of Imphal, with here and there on the broad plain a smoky plume of battle, gave him a dour delight that helped shake off his persisting fatalistic depression.

For to Duncan Burne-Wilke, Imphal was a battle straight out of the *Bhagavad-Gita*. He was not an old Asia hand, but as an educated British military man he knew the Far East. He thought American strategic ideas about China were pitifully ignorant; and the gigantic effort to open the north Burma corridor, into which they had pushed the British, a futile waste of lives and resources. In the long run, it would not matter much who won at Imphal. The Japanese, slowly weakening under the American Pacific assault, now lacked the punch to drive far into India. The Chinese under Chiang Kai-shek would not fight worth a damn; Chiang's concern was holding off the Chinese communists in the north. In any case, Gandhi's unruly nationalist movement would shove the British out of India, once the war was over. The handwriting was on the wall; so Burne-Wilke thought. Still, events had swirled into this vortex, and a man had to fight.

As usual, talking to the combatants on the spot proved worth it. Burne-Wilke gathered his pilots in the large bamboo canteen at Imphal, and asked for complaints, observations, and ideas. Out of the crowd of hundreds of young men came plenty of response, especially complaints.

"Air Marshal, we'll take the red ants and the black spiders, the heat rashes and the dysentery," spoke up one Cockney voice from the rear, "the short rations, the itches and the sweat, the cobras, and the rest of this jolly show. All we ask in return, sir, is enough petrol to fly a combat air patrol from dawn to dusk. Sir, is that askin' so bleedin' much?" This brought growls and applause, but Burne-Wilke had to say that Air Transport could not bring in that much fuel.

An idea surfaced, as the meeting went on, which the fliers had been discussing among themselves. The Japanese raiders came and went over the Imphal plain through two passes in the mountains. The notion was to scramble not after the raiders, but directly into patrol positions in the passes. Returning Jap pilots would either face the superior Spitfires in these narrow traps, or they would crash from engine failure or lack of fuel, trying to evade over the mountains. Burne-Wilke seized on the idea, and ordered it put into effect. He promised alleviation of other shortages, if not of fuel, and he flew off to cheers. On this return flight, he disappeared in a thunderstorm.

Pamela endured a bad week before word came from Imphal that some villagers had brought him in alive. It was during this week that Pug's letter arrived from New Delhi, in a batch of delayed personal mail. She was busier than usual, working for the deputy tactical commander. The disappearance of Burne-Wilke was preying on her mind. As his fiancée, she was the focus of all the concern and sympathy on the base. These pages typed on stationery of the Jeffersonville Plaza Motor Hotel seemed to come from another world. For Pamela, everyday reality was now Comilla, this hot mildewy Bengali town two hundred miles east of Calcutta, its walls stained and rotting from monsoons, its foliage almost as green and rank as the jungle, its main distinction a thick sprinkling of monuments to British officials murdered by Bengali terrorists, its army headquarters aswarm with Asian faces.

Jeffersonville, Indiana! What did it look like? What sort of people were there? The name was so like Victor Henry himself—square, American, obscure, unprepossessing, yet with the noble hint of "Jefferson" in it. Pug's marriage proposal, with its sober financial statement and brief clumsy words of love, both amused and dizzied Pamela. It was endearing, but she could not cope with it at this bad time, so she did not write an answer. When she thought about the letter, in the ensuing turbulence of Burne-Wilke's return, it seemed less and less real to her. At bottom, she could not believe that Rhoda Henry would bring off this latest maneuver. And it was all happening so far, far away!

After a few days in the Imphal hospital, Burne-Wilke was flown to Comilla. His collarbone was broken, both ankles were fractured, and he was running a high fever. Worst of all, at least to look at, were his suppurating sores from leeches. He ruefully told Pamela that he had done this to himself, tearing the leeches off his body and leaving the heads under his skin. He knew better, but he had regained consciousness in a swamp with his uniform almost torn off, and black fat leeches clustering on him. In dazed horror he had begun plucking at them, before remembering the rule to let them drink their fill and drop off. The plane had spun in, he said, but he had managed to level off at the tree tops for a stalling crash. Coming to, he had hacked through the jungle to a riverbed, and stumbled along it for two days until the villagers came on him.

"I was rather lucky, actually," he said to Pamela. He lay in a hospital bed, swathed in bandages, his wanly smiling face puffed and hideously discolored by the leech sores. "One's told the Nagas are headhunters. They could have helped themselves to my head, and nobody would have been the wiser. They were dashed kind. Frankly, my dear, I don't care if I never see another tree."

She was at his bedside for hours every day. He was very low, and movingly dependent on her for affection and encouragement. They had been close before in a quiet way but they now seemed really married. Pamela finally and rather despairingly wrote to Pug on her plane trip from New Delhi to London. After two weeks in hospital, Burne-Wilke was being sent back, very much against his will, for further treatment. She recounted what had happened to explain her delay in replying, and went on,

> Now, Pug, about your proposal. I put my arms around your neck and bless you. I find it very hard to go on, but the fact is that it mustn't be. Duncan's sick as a dog. I can't jilt him. I don't want to. I'm terribly fond of him, I admire him, and I love him. He's a superb man. I've never pretended to him—or to you—that I feel for him the strange love that has bound us. But I'm about ready to give up passion as a bad job. I've not had much luck with it!
>
> He's never pretended, either. At the outset, when he proposed, I asked, "But why do you want me, Duncan?" With that shy subtle smile he answered, "Because you'll do."
>
> My dear, I really don't quite believe your letter. Don't be angry with me. I just know that Rhoda hasn't landed her new fellow yet. Until he's marched her into a church, she won't have done. There's many a slip! The unattainable other man's wife, and the prospective spouse, may look very different to a confirmed bachelor threatened with the altar.
>
> You will always take Rhoda back, and actually I feel you should. It's impossible to blame you. I can't give you a Warren (I *wouldn't* mind the church upbringing, you dear thing, but—oh well) and whatever ties us, it's nothing like that thick rope of memories between you and Rhoda.
>
> I look back at these hastily scrawled paragraphs and find it hard to believe my blurring eyes.
>
> I love you, you know that, and I always will. I've never known anyone like you. Don't stop loving me. The whole thing was just fated not to be; bad timing, bad luck, interfering commitments. But it was beautiful. Let's be great friends when this damned war ends. If Rhoda does get her man, find some American beauty who will make you happy. They abound in your country, oh my sweet, like daisies in a June meadow. You have just never looked around. Now you can. But don't ever forget
>
> Your poor loving
Pamela

78

A Jew's Journey
(*from Aaron Jastrow's manuscript*)

APRIL 22, 1944.

I am waiting for Natalie to return from a clandestine Zionist meeting; waiting and worrying on a cool spring night, with pleasant scents drifting into the apartment from window boxes of geraniums, placed on our sills only yesterday by Beautification workers. I think she is stumbling into acute danger. Though it may cause a scene for which I haven't the strength, I intend to have it out with her when she returns.

How long is it since I wrote a diary entry? I'm not sure. The last sheets are hidden away, long since. The Beautification has more or less overwhelmed me, both at the library and in the council. Also, Berel's stunning appearance after my *Iliad* lecture was a very difficult thing to write about, so I put it off, put it off, and let the whole diary slide. Now I will try to fill it in. I've prepared tomorrow's Talmud section, and this is the best way left to kill time. I won't sleep till she shows up.

Berel gave me the start of my life that night, coming out of the gloom. What an eerie encounter! I had not seen him for close to fifty years. Alas, the transformations of time; the red-cheeked plump boy has become a hard-looking elderly man with bushy gray hair, a big outthrust jaw, heavy frowning eyebrows, and deep lines scored on a clean-shaven face. There's a ghostly familiarity in the smile, and that is all. Shabbily dressed, with a yellow star for camouflage on his torn sheepskin jacket, he looked more Polish then Jewish, if there is anything to these notions of racial physiognomies; a formidable suspicious old Silesian peasant. He was nervous and wary in the extreme. While he walked with us he kept looking around and behind. He had a mission to perform in the ghetto, he said, and would leave before dawn; no explanation of when and how he had come, or how he would go.

He walked to our apartment with us, and there without ado he offered to get Louis out of Theresienstadt! Natalie paled at the very thought. But a new transport had just been ordered, she was in a shaken mood, and she was willing to listen. Berel's idea was to place the child with a Czech farm family, as some Prague Jews managed to do with their tots before being hauled off to Theresienstadt. It has worked well; the parents hear news of the children from time to time, and even receive smuggled letters from the older ones. To get Louis out, he would be hospitalized on some fraudulent diagnosis, for which Berel says he has the necessary connections in the Health Department. A death certificate would be provided to satisfy the Central Secretariat index, and there might be a faked burial or cremation. The child would be removed from the hospital in secret and spirited to Prague. There Berel would receive him and take him to the farm, visit him regularly, and send news about him to Natalie. The war might go on another year or more; but whatever happened, Berel would watch over him.

Natalie's face grew longer and grimmer as Berel talked. Why, she asked, was this necessary? Louis was adaptable and thriving. Seeing his mother every day was the best thing for him. Berel did not argue about any of that, but he urged that, all in all, the best thing was to let Louis go. Sickness, malnutrition, transport, and German cruelty were ever-present dangers here, worse than the temporary risk of getting him out. Natalie gave no ground. I am abstracting here a low-toned Yiddish conversation that took more than an hour, before Berel dropped it and said he had business with me. She went off to bed. We talked Polish, which she doesn't understand.

Now my pencil halts. How to write down what he told me?

I will not try to recapitulate his journeyings and ordeals. Imagination numbs, belief fails. Berel has passed through all seven circles of the inferno that Germany has made of eastern Europe. The very worst rumors about the Jewish fate are not only true, but very pale and gentle intimations of the truth. With his own hands my cousin has disinterred from mass graves and burned thousands of murdered men, women, and children. Such graves dot all of eastern Europe near cities where Jews once lived. A million and a half buried corpses, is his conservative guess.

In certain camps, including the one outside our old yeshiva town of Oswiecim, huge poison gas cellars exist for killing thousands of people at a time. A crowd to fill a great opera house, crammed into an enormous basement and asphyxiated all at once! Arriving fresh off sealed trains from all over Europe, they are murdered then and there. Great crematoriums burn up the bodies. Tall chimneys dominate the camp landscape, vomiting flames, greasy smoke, and human scraps and ash twenty-four hours a day, when an "action" is on. Berel was not recounting rumors. He worked in a construction gang that built such a crematorium.

The Jews who are not killed at once are worked to death as slave labor in gigantic armaments factories, on rations calculated to murder them by rapid attrition.

We Theresienstadt Jews, he says, are oxen in the pen, waiting our turn. The Beautification is a lucky reprieve, but the day after the neutral Red Cross visit the transports will again roll. Our hope is an Allied victory. The war is certainly going against the Germans, but the end is a way off, and the destruction of the Jews is accelerating. His organization, which he did not identify (I would guess the communists), is planning an uprising in case of a mass transport order, or a killing action launched by the SS here in Theresienstadt. But that will be a desperate business in which Natalie and Louis are unlikely to survive. The Jewish people must look to the future, he said. Louis is the future. He is the one to save.

He did not want to tell Natalie about the murder camps because he could see that her spirits are good, and that is the secret of survival under the Germans. I must try to persuade her to let Louis go, without frightening her too much.

I asked him how widespread in Theresienstadt was knowledge of the murder camps. He said that high-placed people had been told of it; he had spoken to two himself. The usual reaction was incredulity, or anger at the tellers of such "scare stories," and a quick change of subject.

I asked if the outside world yet had any inkling. Newspaper stories were just starting to appear abroad, he replied, and radio broadcasts. The microfilmed documents and pictures he brought from Oswiecim did reach Switzerland and these may be figuring in the accounts. But the people in England and America seem no more inclined as yet to believe the thing than are the Jews right here in Theresienstadt, who know the SS so well. In the Oswiecim camp itself, Berel said, where one saw the chimneys flame out at night, and smelled the burning hair, meat, and fat, many inmates shunned the topic of the gassings, or even denied that they were happening.

(My hand has been shaking as I write these things, that is why the words straggle on the page.)

To wind up quickly the visit of Berel, we had a sad interlude of family gossip. Except for himself and one son's family, our Jastrow clan in Europe has been extirpated, root and branch. His eldest son fights with Jewish partisans behind the German lines in White Russia. The daughter-in-law and grandson are safe on a Latvian farm. Berel has lost everyone else, and so have I; a network of clever and lovable relatives I never saw after I went to America but pleasantly remembered. Through all his wanderings he has preserved a tattered picture of the grandchild, so scuffed and water-stained that one sees only a vague blurred infant face. "The future," Berel said as he showed it to me. *"Der osed."*

He explained how I could notify him if Natalie changed her mind about Louis. We embraced. I had last hugged Berel half a century ago in Medzice, when we left for America; nothing is stranger than what actually happens. As he released me, he shot me the kind of keen look, with head aslant, that in the old days preceded an acute question about the Talmud; and one shoulder humped up, a mannerism unchanged by years and sufferings. "Arele, I heard you wrote books about that man." (*Oso ho-ish,* Jesus.)

"Yes."

"Why did you *dafka* have to write about that man?"

Dafka is an untranslatable Talmud word. It means many things: *necessarily, for that very reason, perversely, defiantly, in spite of everything.* The Jews have a tendency to do things *dafka.* That is the essence of the stiff-necked people. They had to worship the golden calf *dafka,* for instance, at the foot of Mount Sinai.

It was a moment of truth. I answered, "I wrote to make money, Berel, and a name for myself among the Gentiles."

"See how it helped you," he said.

I took from a drawer the phylacteries for which I recently gave a diamond, and showed them to him.

"So?" He sadly smiled. "In Theresienstadt?"

"In Theresienstadt, *dafka,* Berel."

We embraced again, and he slipped out. In two months I have heard nothing more from him or about him. I assume he got safely away. In the First World War Berel escaped twice from prisoner-of-war camps. He is made of wiry stuff, and he is very ingenious.

Past midnight. No sign of her. It is unwise to be walking the streets at this hour, though I suppose her nurse's aide card covers her.

Now let me hurriedly sketch the Beautification. This is a story which in years to come must be told. Future generations may find it harder to believe even than the Oswiecim gassing cellars. After all, however gruesome, those are but the natural end product of National Socialism.

One has simply to grasp that Hitler meant it, and that the obedient Germans went and did it.

The Beautification is stranger. It is a painstaking pretense that the Germans are Europeans just like the others, conforming to the tenets of Western civilization; that the rumors and reports about the Jews are too silly for words, or else cruel Allied atrocity propaganda. The Germans are playacting here an elaborate denial of their central effort in this war, the eradication of a people and of two world religions. Yes, two. I believe with whole faith that Jews and Judaism will in the end live on; but Christianity cannot survive this deed by a Christian nation. Nietzsche's Antichrist has come, in boots and swastika armband. In the flames and smoke of the Oswiecim chimneys, all the crucifixes of Europe are going up.

Our new commander, Rahm, is a coarse but thorough brute. His planning of this Beautification carries hypocrisy into new realms. Because I am the Elder in charge of culture, I am much involved. I have spent hours in his office over a table map of the town, where the route of the visitors is marked in red, with every stopping place numbered. A wall chart shows the progress of renovation and new construction at each numbered halt. My department is staging the musical and dramatic events along the route, but my deputies are doing the real work. My role on "the day" will be to show the visitors around a marvelously renovated library; I already have twenty people working on the catalogue, and beautiful books keep pouring in. We are amassing the finest Judaica collection left on European soil, all for one day's fakery.

The visit is being planned like a Passion play; it will be a spectacle involving an entire town. The action, however, will be limited to the route traced in red on the map. A hundred yards on either side of that route, the old filth, illness, overcrowding, and starvation will prevail. A narrow simulacrum of an idyllic spa is being created with immense labor, and no expense spared, wherever the visitors' eyes may look. Do the Germans really expect to get away with this grotesque fake? It seems so. Previous inspections by German Red Cross officials proved no problem, of course. The visitors came and went and spread glowing reports about the Paradise Ghetto. But this time the visitors will be neutral outsiders. How can the Germans be sure of controlling them? A determined Swede or Swiss Red Cross man has only to say, "Let us go down that street," or "Let us have a look in yonder barracks," and the bubble will pop. Beyond the iridescent film of fakery will lie horror to make a neutral's hair stand on end; though we of course are used to it, and though it is nothing compared to an Oswiecim.

Does Rahm have some wily plan to deflect such embarrassing requests? Does he count on suave bullying to keep the visitors in line? Or, as I strongly suspect, is this whole Beautification just a master instance, a paradigm, of the idiot thoroughness which has characterized what the Germans have done since Hitler took power?

In their ability to get things done, their energy, their attention to detail, their sheer scientific and industrial prowess, they equal and perhaps surpass the Americans. Moreover, they are capable of the greatest charm, intelligence, and taste. It is their peculiarity as a people that with no reservations, with whole hearts, with singular élan, they can throw themselves into the executing of plans and orders crazy or monstrous beyond previous human conceptions. Why this should be, the world may be a thousand years puzzling out; meantime it is happening. It has loosed a holocaust of war which must almost certainly end in the destruction of Germany. At the heart of that vast hecatomb is what they are doing to my people. And at the heart of the heart is this Beautification, the German face turned innocently to the outside world, with the plaintive statement, "See how unjust you are, to accuse us of doing bad things?"

The idiot thoroughness of this Beautification is awesome. There is nothing Rahm and his advisers haven't thought of, assuming that he can hold his visitors to the red line. Very little is finished yet, but the scenario is all laid down. The bustling disorder in Theresienstadt these days is that of a stage halfway ready for a dress rehearsal. Two or three thousand ablebodied Jews are toiling from dawn to dusk for the Technical Department—and, here and there, all night under floodlights—to build this fantastic narrow path of illusion.

The itinerary of the visitors has been fixed for months. Rahm carries around a thick document bound in black and red striped cloth, which we of the council call (among ourselves) the "Beautification Bible." All our department heads have contributed to it, but the final minuteness of detail could only be German. It includes the selections the municipal orchestra will play in the town square, though the Technical Department is only now laying the foundation for the pavilion. Our musicians are busy copying out the parts—two Rossini overtures, some military marches, several Strauss waltzes, and potpourris from Donizetti and Bizet. Copying paper is now available in profusion. Excellent new instruments have flooded in. Theresienstadt, like Prospero's magic island, is becoming a place where melody fills the air.

Looking into the opera house in the Sports Hall, the visitors will observe a full orchestra and large chorus rehearsing Verdi's *Requiem:* more than a hundred fifty talented Jews in neat clean clothing, yellow stars and all, producing music worthy of performance in Paris or

Vienna. Downstairs in a smaller theatre they will happen upon a costumed run-through of the delightful original children's opera, *Brundibar,* the hit of the ghetto. Walking in the flower-lined streets, they will hear a string quartet in one private house doing Beethoven, a superb contralto singing Schubert lieder in another, a great clarinetist practicing Weber in a third. In the cafés they will come on costumed musicians and singers performing, as patrons sip coffee and eat cream pastries. The visitors will refresh themselves at one café, where customers will pay, depart, and arrive in a thoroughly drilled natural fashion.

The visitors will see shops well-stocked with all manner of fine goods, including luxury foods, and shoppers casually coming and going, buying what they please, paying in the Theresienstadt paper currency engraved with a picture of Moses. This worthless currency is the sourest joke of the ghetto, of course, and Rahm's Bible contains a stern warning that as soon as the visitors depart these "customers" must return all the "purchases." Any shortage will be punished. For a missing food item, the offender will go to the Little Fortress.

The plan ramifies through every phrase of ghetto life. A mock superclean hospital, a mock children's playground, a mock printing plant for men, a mock clothing factory for women, a mock sports field, are all in the works. The bank is being redecorated. A mock boys' school is already finished, a new building complete to the last detail of blackboards, chalk, and textbooks, which has never been and will never be used, except for musicians' rehearsals. A "main mess hall," a commodious hut, is being erected for the serving of exactly one meal, the visitors' lunch, where Jews all around them will also heartily dine. The SS have yet to figure out a way to avoid feeding some Jews just this once. It is the only lapse in Rahm's Bible. The café customers, of course, are to indulge in coffee and cakes only while the visitors are in sight, otherwise they will go through motions over brown slop, and plates of cakes they may not touch.

It is after one o'clock. Why do I go on with this bitter drivelling? Well, even the gallows jest of the Beautification is some relief from thoughts of Berel's disclosures, and my worry over Natalie's tardiness. She must get up at six. Before she goes to work at the mica factory, she has to rehearse for the visit, at the children's playground and the kindergarten. She has just received that assignment, with several other attractive women. They will have their work cut out for them, training the kids to speak their little pieces and simulate happiness. At lunch, she tells me, the kids are supposed to cry out, "What, sardines again?"

A whole twenty-minute charade like that has been written out. Here the Beautification is doing some real good, for the SS have increased the rations of the children. They want the visitors to see roly-poly tots at play; so they are stuffing them as the witch did Hansel and Gretel.

I cannot believe that so blatant a comedy can hoodwink anybody. Yet say it does succeed: what are the Germans hoping to gain by it? The Jews are disappearing, millions are gone, and can this vast horror be long concealed? I cannot understand it. There is no sense to it. No, it is the backward child, on a monumental and terrible scale; the backward child caught at the empty jam jar, his face, hands, clothes smeared red, smiling and denying that he ate the jam.

For that matter, what sense is there to the Oswiecim gas cellars? I have thought and thought about that for weeks, with dizzied brain. Calling the Germans sadists, butchers, beasts, savages explains nothing, for they are men and women like us. I have an idea, and I will scribble it down, with much more certainty than I feel. The root of the matter cannot be Hitler. I start with that premise. Such a thing must have been brewing for centuries, to have encountered so little resistance among the Germans when it happened.

Napoleon forced liberty and equality on the Germans. From the outset they gagged on it. With cannon and tramping boots, he invaded a patchwork of absolutist states hardly out of feudalism. He ground the faces of the Germans in the brotherhood of man. Freeing the Jews was part of this new liberal humanism. It was not natural to the Germans, but they conformed.

Alas, we Jews believed in the change, but the Germans in their hearts never did. It was the conqueror's creed. It swept Europe, but not Germany. Their Romantic philosophers inveighed against the un-German Enlightenment, their anti-Semitic political parties sprouted, while Germany grew and grew to an industrial giant, never convinced of the "Western" ideas.

Their defeat under the Kaiser, and the great inflation and crash, generated in them a terrible frustrated anger. The communists threatened chaos and overthrow. Weimar was falling apart. When Hitler rose from this witches' brew, like an oracular spook in Macbeth, and pointed at the Jews in the department stores and the opera promenades; when he thundered that not only were they the visible beneficiaries of Germany's wrongs, but the actual cause of them; when that frenzied historical formula rolled forth, as mendaciously simple as the Marxist slogans, but more candidly bloodthirsty; then the German rage was released in an explosion of national energy and joy, and the plausible maniac who had released it had his murder weapon in hand. Bottomless lack of compunction in the Germans peculiarly fitted the weapon to the man. Awareness of this baffling trait had to be kicked into me. I am still puzzling over it.

Does my work on Luther shed light on it? Only Luther, before Hitler, ever so wholly spoke with the national voice to release plugged-up national rage; in his case, against a corrupt Latin-droning popery. The resemblances in the forceful, coarse, sarcastic rhetoric of the two men gave me anxious pause even when I was Luther's admiring biographer. Luther's Protestantism is a grand theology, a sonorous earnest hardheaded Christianity, well worthy of the Christ whom Luther claimed to be rescuing from the Whore of Babylon. But even this homegrown product sat hard on the German stomach, did it not?

The German has never been quite at home in Christian Europe, has never quite made up his mind whether he is Vandal or Roman, the destroyer from the north or the *comme il faut* Western man. He oscillates, vacillates, plays the one or the other role, as historic circumstances change. To the Vandal in him, Christian compunction and British and French liberalism are nonsense; the reason and logic of the Enlightenment are a veneer over real human nature; destruction and dominance are the thing; slaughter is an ancient joy. After centuries of Lutheran restraint, the rude rough German voice bellowed forth once again, in Nietzsche, radical revulsion from Christianity's meek tenets. Quite accurately Nietzsche blamed all this kindness and compunction on Judaism. Quite accurately he foretold the coming death of the Christian God. What he failed to foresee was that the freed Vandal, in lunatic industrialized vengeance, would set out to nail eleven million Christs to the cross.

Oh, scribble, scribble, scribble! I look back over these hastily pencilled pages and my heart sinks. No wonder I have neglected the diary; my small mind cannot cope with what I now know. How can one move on this theme without a general theory of nationalism? Without tracing socialism to its sources, and demonstrating how the two movements converge in Hitler? Without giving the menace of the Russian Revolution its due weight?

Have I made any contact whatever with the German in all this glib scrawling? Am I, the stinking Jew Jastrow, putting on phylacteries in Theresienstadt, and he, striking out all over Europe with clanking armies and roaring air fleets, really following the same human impulse, to preserve a threatened identity? Is that why he wants to kill me, because the Jew and Judaism are the everlasting challenge, reproach, and hobble to primitive Germanism? Or is all this an empty conceit, the vaporings of the tired and overwrought brain of a lifelong liberal, trying to find one shred of sense in Oswiecim and in the Beautification, trying to bridge the gulf between myself and Karl Rahm, because the truth is that though he slay me we are brothers, in Darwinian taxonomy if not under God?

————————

Here is Natalie!

NEXT MORNING.

It is even graver than I thought. She is in very deep. She came back weary, but in a glow. These Zionist meetings have been debating ways and means to defeat the Beautification, to signal the truth about Theresienstadt to the Red Cross visitors, without alerting the SS. She thinks they have hit on something. At each of the stops, a Jew in charge will be primed to say one and the same sentence, in response to any Red Cross comment: *"Oh yes, it is all very, very new. And there is much more to see."*

They worked this out, I gather, with great wrangling and revisions. They voted on words. These exact repetitions, they believe, will strike the visitors as a signal. The Jews will speak the sentence casually, with meaningful looks, if possible beyond SS earshot. The hope, or rather the fantasy, is that the visitors will catch on that they are seeing brand-new faked installations, and will push beyond the planned route, because of the "much more to see."

I listened patiently. Then I told her that she was slipping into the endemic ghetto dreaminess, and endangering her life and Louis's. The Germans are trained wary prison guards. The visitors will be soft polite welfare executives. The Beautification is a major German effort, and the most obvious thing to guard against is just such Jewish schemes to tip off the visitors. So I argued, but she retorted that one way or another the Jews must fight back. Since we have no weapons but our brains, we must use them.

Then I took the drastic step of disclosing Berel's revelations about Oswiecim. My intent was to shock her into greater awareness of her danger of being transported. She was, of course, badly shocked; not quite flabbergasted, since such stories do float around. But she took it the wrong way. All the more reason, she said, to waken the suspicions of the Red Cross; anyway, Berel's story must be exaggerated, because Udam had received postcards from his wife in Oswiecim, and her friends were getting cards now from relatives in the February transport.

I repeated what Berel told me: that the Oswiecim SS keeps up a "Theresienstadt family camp," in case the Red Cross ever manages to negotiate a visit to that terrible place; that on arrival in Oswiecim everyone must write postcards dated months ahead; and that the Theresienstadt camp is periodically cleared of the sick, the weak, the elderly, and the children, all gassed in a body, to make room for further Theresienstadt transports. Udam was undoubtedly getting mail from a cremated woman.

Next she asserted that her group has heard, via their grapevine to Prague, that according to German military intelligence, the Americans will definitely land in France on May 15. This may well touch off uprisings all over Europe, and lead to the rapid collapse of the Nazi empire. In any case, the SS officers will begin worrying about their own necks, and so further transports are unlikely.

Against such wishful thinking hardened into delusion there is no arguing. I urged her, if she meant to go on with this business, at least to send word to Berel to get Louis out. She wouldn't hear of it; denied that she was putting Louis in any greater danger than he already faced; turned decidedly snappish, and went off to bed.

That was only a few hours ago. She was in a better mood when she awoke, and apologized before she left for her display of short temper. She said nothing more about Louis. Nor did I.

Far from objecting to her newfound Zionism, I am glad of it. It seems to be for her the assertion of threatened identity that I have found in my old religion. One needs some such spiritual stiffening to survive in the ghetto, if one is not a conniver or a black marketeer. But suppose her circle is penetrated by an informer? With scurrilous puppetry already on record in her SS dossier, that will be the end of her.

I myself was never a Zionist. I remain enormously skeptical of the notion of returning the Jews to that desolate patch of the Middle East inhabited by unfriendly Arabs. True, the Zionists did foresee this European catastrophe, when it was a cloud no bigger than a man's hand. But does it follow that their visionary solution was a possible or correct one? Hardly. Only a handful of dreamers ever went to Palestine before Hitler. Even they were driven there by pogroms, rather than drawn by the desiccated Holy Land.

I am no longer sure about this, I confess, or about any of my former notions. Certainly Jewish nationalism is a powerful means of identity, but I regard nationalism as the curse of modern times. I simply cannot believe that we poor Jews are ever meant to have an army and a navy, a parliament and ministers, boundaries, harbors, airports, universities, on Mediterranean sands. What a sweet and hollow dream! Let Natalie dream it, if it helps her get through Theresienstadt. She says that if a Jewish state the size of Liechtenstein had existed, all these horrors wouldn't be happening; and that such a state must arise to prevent their happening again. Messianic rhetoric; my fear is only that this new febrile enthusiasm, overcoming her usual tough good sense, may lead her into rashness that will destroy her and Louis.

79

THROUGH the closed bedroom door it sounded like crying, but Rhoda cried so seldom that Victor Henry shrugged and passed on to the guest room where he now slept. It was very late. He had sat up for hours in the library after dinner, working on landing craft documents for his meeting with Colonel Peters; something he was not looking forward to, but a priorities conflict was forcing it. He undressed, showered, drank off his nightcap of bourbon and water, and before turning in stopped to listen at Rhoda's door. The sounds had become unmistakable: keening moans, broken by sobs.

"Rhoda?"

No answer. The sounds ceased as though switched off.

"Rho! Come on, what is it?"

Muffled sad voice: "Oh, I'm all right. Go to sleep."

"Let me in."

"The door's not locked, Pug."

The room was dark. When he turned on the light Rhoda sat up in an oyster-white satiny nightdress, blinking and dabbing a tissue at swollen red eyes. "Was I making a racket? I tried to keep it low."

"What's up?"

"Oh, Pug, I'm done for. Everything's in ruins. You're well rid of me."

"I think you can use a drink."

"I must look GRUESOME. Don't I?" She put her hands to her tumbled hair.

"Want to come down to the library and talk?"

"You're an angel. Scotch and soda. Be right there." She thrust shapely white legs and thighs out of bed. Pug went to the library and mixed drinks at the movable bar. She soon appeared in a peignoir over her nightgown, brushing her hair in familiar charming gestures he had not seen since moving to the guest room. She was lightly made-up and she had done something to her eyes, for they were bright and clear.

"I washed my face and FLUNG myself into bed hours and hours ago, then I couldn't sleep."

"But why? Because I have to see Colonel Peters? It's just a business meeting, Rhoda. I told you that." He handed her the drink. "Maybe I shouldn't have mentioned it, but I won't make any trouble for you."

"Pug, I'm in such distress!" She took a deep gulp of her drink. "Somebody's been writing Hack anonymous letters. He's received, oh, five or six. He tore up the first ones, but he showed me two. With abject apologies, but he showed them. They've gotten under his skin."

Rhoda gave her husband one of her most melting, appealing looks. He thought of mentioning the anonymous letters he too had received, but saw no purpose in that. Pamela might have told Rhoda about them; in any case, no use stirring up that mud. He did not comment.

She burst out, "It's so unfair! I didn't even KNOW Hack, then, did I? Talk about your double standard! Why, he's slept with all KINDS of women, to hear him talk. Single, married, divorced, he makes no bones about it, even reminisces, and the point always is how different I am. And I am too, I *am!* There was only Palmer Kirby. I still don't know how or why THAT happened. I'm not one of those cheap flirts he's run around with all his life. But these letters are wrecking everything. He seems so unhappy, SO CRUSHED. Of course I denied everything. I had to, for HIS sake. For such an experienced man, he's strangely NAÏVE."

What surprised Pug most was that this casual outright admission of her adultery—"There was only Palmer Kirby"—could give him pain; not the agony of the first shock, her letter asking for a divorce, but still, real pain. Rhoda had skirted a specific admission until this very moment. Her habit of silence had served her well, but the words had slipped out because Peters was now the man who mattered. This was the real end, thought Pug. He, like Kirby, was part of her past. She could be careless with him.

"The man loves you, Rhoda. He'll believe you, and forget about the letters."

"Oh, will he? And suppose he asks *you* about them tomorrow?"

"That's unthinkable."

"Not so unthinkable. You're meeting for the first time since all this happened."

"Rhoda, we've got a very urgent priorities problem to thrash out. He won't bring up personal matters. Certainly not those anonymous letters. Not to me. His skin would crawl at the idea."

She looked both amused and miserable. "Male pride, you mean."

"Call it that. Forget it. Go to sleep, and pleasant dreams."

"May I have another drink?"

"Sure."

"Will you tell me afterward what happened? I mean, what you talked about?"

"Not the business part."

"I'm not interested in the business part."

"If anything personal comes up, I'll tell you, yes." He handed her the drink. "Any idea who's writing the letters?"

"No. It's a woman. Some vicious bitch or other. Oh, they abound, Pug, they abound. She uses green ink, writes in a funny up-and-down hand on little tan sheets. Her facts are all cockeyed, but she does mention Palmer Kirby. Very nastily. Dates, places, all that. Disgusting."

"Where's Kirby now?"

"I don't know. I last saw him in Chicago when I was coming back from California, right after—after Midway. I stopped there for a few hours to break it off once for all. Funnily enough, that's how I met Hack."

As she drank, Rhoda described the encounter in the Pump Room, and finding Colonel Peters afterward on the train to New York.

"I'll never know why he took a fancy to me, Pug. I was *very* distant in the club car that night. Actually, I FROZE him. I was feeling wretched about Palmer, and you, and the whole mess, and I was by no means over Warren. I wouldn't accept a drink. Wouldn't get into conversation. I mean, he was so OBVIOUSLY fresh from a roll in the hay with that creature in green! He still had that glint in his eye, and I wasn't about to give him IDEAS. Then next morning in the dining car the steward seated him at my table. It was crowded for breakfast, so I couldn't object, although I don't know, maybe he SLIPPED that steward something. Anyway, that was it. He said Palmer had told him about me, and he admired my brave spirit so much, and all that. I still kept my distance. I always have. He really PURSUED me, in a gentlemanly way, showing up at church, and Navy affairs, and Bundles for Britain, and so on. It was a very gradual business. It was MONTHS before I even agreed to go to the theatre with him. Maybe that's what intrigued Hack, the sheer novelty of it all. It couldn't have been my girlish charm. But when he thinks back to when we met, there I WAS, after all, visiting Palmer Kirby. It makes those horrid letters so PLAUSIBLE."

This was more than Rhoda had said about her romance in all the months that Pug had been back. She was being positively chatty. Pug said, "Feeling better now, aren't you?"

"Heaps. You're sweet to be so reassuring. I'm not a crybaby, Pug, you know that, but I am in a STATE about those letters. When you told me you were meeting him tomorrow, I panicked. I mean, Hack can't possibly ever ask Palmer. That's not done. Palmer wouldn't tell, anyway. You're the only other one who knows. You're the aggrieved husband, and, well, I just got to thinking of all kinds of awful possibilities." She had finished her drink and was slipping pink mules back on her bare feet.

"I really didn't know anything, anyway, Rhoda. Not until tonight."

She went rigid, staring at him, one mule in her hand, her mind obviously racing back over the conversation. "Oh, nuts." She slammed the slipper down on the floor. "Of course you knew. Don't be like that, Pug. How could you NOT know? What was it ever all about?"

Pug was sitting at the desk where the big leather-bound Warren album still lay, beside a pile of his file folders. "I'm sort of waked up now," he said, picking up a folder. "I'll do a little more work."

MANHATTAN ENGINEERING DISTRICT
Brig. Gen. Leslie R. Groves, U.S.A., Chief
Colonel Harrison Peters, Deputy Chief

The signs on the two adjoining doors, on an upper floor in the State Department building, were so inconspicuous that Pug walked by them and had to backtrack. Colonel Peters strode from behind his desk to shake hands. "Well! High time we met again."

Pug had forgotten how tall the man was, perhaps six feet three, and how handsome: brilliant blue eyes, healthily colored long bony face, straight body in a sharply tailored uniform, no trace of a bulge at the middle. Despite the gray hair the general effect was youthful, manly, and altogether impressive, except for an uncertain quality in his broad smile. No doubt he was embarrassed. Yet Pug felt very little resentment toward the Army man. It helped a lot that the fellow had not cuckolded him. Pug did believe he hadn't, mainly because that had been the only way for Rhoda to play this particular fish.

The small desk was bare. The only other furniture was an armchair. There were no pictures on the wall, no files, no window, no bookcase, no secretary; a low-level operation, one would think, assigned to a run-of-the-mill colonel. Pug declined coffee, and sat in the armchair.

"Before we get down to business," said Peters, flushing a little, "let me say one thing. I have the greatest respect for you. Rhoda is what she is, a woman in a million, because of her years with you. I regret we haven't yet talked about all that. We're both busy as hell, I know, but one of these days we'll have to."

"By all means."

"Do you smoke cigars?" Peters took a box of long Havanas from a desk drawer.

"Thanks." Pug did not want a cigar, but accepting it might improve the atmosphere.

Peters took his time about lighting up. "Sorry I was slow getting back to you."

"I guess the phone call from Harry Hopkins helped."

"That would have made no difference, if your security clearance hadn't checked out."

"Just to shortcut this a bit," Pug said, "when I was naval attaché in Berlin I supplied the S-1 committee, at their request, with dope on German industrial activity in graphite, heavy water, uranium, and thorium. I know the Army's working on a uranium bomb, with a blank-check triple-A priority power. That's why I'm here. The landing craft program needs those couplings I mentioned over the telephone."

"How do you know we've got them?" Peters leaned back, clasping his long arms behind his head. A harder professional tone came into his voice.

"You haven't got them. They're still warehoused in Pennsylvania. The Dresser firm wouldn't say anything except that they're on Army order. The prime contractor, Kellogg, wouldn't talk at all. I ran into a blank wall at the War Production Board, too. The fellows there just clammed up. The landing craft program hasn't conflicted with the uranium bomb before. I figured it couldn't be anything else. So I called you."

"What makes you think I'm in the uranium bomb business?"

"General Connolly told me in Tehran that you were working on something very big. I took a shot in the dark."

"You mean," Peters asked, tough and incredulous, "that you telephoned me on a guess?"

"Right. Do we get the couplings, Colonel?"

After a long pause, and a mutual staring contest, Peters replied, "Sorry, no."

"Why not? What are you using them for?"

"Jesus Christ, Henry! For a manufacturing process of the highest national urgency."

"I know that. But is this component irreplaceable? All it does is connect pipes. There are many ways to connect pipes."

"Then use another way on your landing craft."

"I'll tell you my problem, if you'll listen."

"Sure you won't have coffee?"

"Thanks. Black, no sugar. This is a fine cigar."

"Best in the world." Peters ordered coffee over the intercom. Pug was liking the man better as he toughened up. This rapid exchange over the desk was a little like a long point in tennis. Peters's returns so far were hard but not sneaky or tricky.

"I'm listening." Peters leaned back in his swivel chair, nursing a knee.

"Okay. Our shipyards have gotten so jammed that we've subcontracted some construction to Britain. We're sending sections which can be put together by semiskilled help and launched in a few days. That is, *if* the right components are on hand. Now, these Dresser couplings go in faster than welded or bolted joints. They require little experience or strength to install. Also, uncoupling them to check faulty lines is simple. The *Queen Mary* sails Friday, Colonel, with fifteen thousand troops aboard, and I've reserved cargo space for shipping that stuff. I've got trucks standing by in Pennsylvania, ready to take the lot to New York. I'm talking about components for forty vessels. If they're launched on schedule, Eisenhower will hit the French beaches with more force than he'll have otherwise."

"We hear this kind of thing all the time," Peters said. "The British will connect up those lines, one way or another."

"Look, the decision to put these vessels together in England turned on hard specifications for speed of assembly. When we shipped the sections those couplings were available. Now you've overridden our priority. Why?"

Peters puffed at his cigar, squinted through the smoke at Pug, and replied, "Okay. For a very large network of underground water lines. Our requirements for speed and simplicity are the same as yours, and our urgency is greater."

"I have an idea for solving this," Pug said, "less messy than going to the President, which I'm also prepared to do."

"Let's hear your idea."

"I checked all the stuff Dresser has on hand. They could modify a larger coupling to meet your specs. Delivery would be delayed ten days. Now, I have samples of that substitute coupling. Suppose I take them to your plant, and talk to the engineers in charge?"

"Christ, not a chance."

"Why not? Peters, the fellows on the spot can clear this thing up, yes or no, in a few hours. President Roosevelt has other things on his mind, and anyway, General Groves wouldn't appreciate being overruled by him. Why not try to avoid that?"

"How do you know what the President will do?"

"I was at Tehran. The landing craft program is a commitment not only to Churchill but to Stalin."

"Clearing you for such a visit—if it could be done at all—would take a week."

"N.G., Colonel. Those trucks have to load up and leave Bradford, Pennsylvania, Thursday morning."

"Then you'll have to go to the President. I can't help you."

"Okay, I will," Pug said, grinding out his cigar.

Colonel Peters stood up, shook hands, and walked out with Pug into the long hallway. "Let me look into one possibility, and ring you before noon."

"I'll wait for your call."

Peters telephoned Pug about an hour later. "Can you come with me for a little trip? You'd be away from Washington two nights."

"Sure."

"Meet me at Union Station at five to seven, track eighteen. I'll have the Pullman berths."

"Where are we going?"

"Knoxville, Tennessee. Fetch along that substitute coupling."

Match point, thought Pug.

Oak Ridge was a huge backwoods area on a little-known Tennessee river, cordoned off from the world, where a secret industrial complex had sprung up to effect mass murder in a new way, on an unprecedented scale. Some would therefore argue today that it was comparable to Auschwitz.

Nobody was being murdered at Oak Ridge, to be sure. Nor was there any slave labor. Cheerful Americans were working at very high pay, constructing enormous buildings and installing gigantic masses of machinery, with no idea of what it was all for. The secret of Oak Ridge was better kept than that of Auschwitz. Inside, only very high-level personnel knew. Outside, few rumors leaked.

As in Germany it was bad form to talk about the state of the Jews, so in Oak Ridge it was antisocial to discuss the purpose of the place. In Germany, people did know that something ghastly must be happening to the Jews, and the Germans in Auschwitz knew exactly what was happening; whereas the Oak Ridge workers were in the dark until the day the bomb fell on Hiroshima. In beautiful wooded country they drudged by day in ankle-deep mud, and amused themselves as they could by night in rude huts and trailers, asking no questions; or they passed jocular rumors, such as that they were creating a plant for mass-producing front ends of horses, to be shipped to Washington for assembly.

Still, the postwar argument goes that when one contemplates the results of Auschwitz and Oak Ridge, there is little to choose between the Americans and the Nazis; both were equally guilty of the new barbarism. It is a challenging point. After every war there is a great and sensible revulsion at the whole horrible bloodletting. Distinctions tend to blur. All was atrocity. All were equally criminal. That is how the cry runs. It was in truth a nasty war; so nasty that mankind does not want another; which is a start, anyway, toward abolishing this old human craziness. But it really should not be seen in remembrance as a mere blur of universal guilt. There were differences.

The Oak Ridge effort, to begin with, broke new ground in physics, chemistry, and industrial invention by producing uranium-235. As a feat of applied engineering and of human scientific genius, it was remarkable, possibly unique in scale and brilliance. The German gas chambers and crematoriums were not brilliant innovative works of genius.

Again, once one is attacked in war one can either give up and submit to looting, or one can fight. To fight means to try to frighten the other side, by a lot of murder, into stopping the war. Political conflicts between states must occur; and certainly, in an age of reason and science, they should be resolved by some more sane means than wholesale murder. But that was the means the German and Japanese politicians chose, thinking it would work, and they could only be dissuaded by the same means. When the Americans began their race to make uranium bombs, they had no way of knowing that their attackers would not make and use them first. It was a scary and highly motivating thought.

So on the whole, the analogy between Auschwitz and Oak Ridge seems forced. Resemblances exist. Both were stupendous secret wartime improvisations for slaughter; both opened terrible new problems in human experience that remain unsolved; and if not for National Socialist Germany, neither would have existed. But the purpose of Auschwitz was insane useless killing. The purpose of Oak Ridge was to stop the global war unleashed by Germany, and it worked.

However, when Pug Henry came to Oak Ridge in the late spring of 1944, the Manhattan Project loomed as a vast wartime bust, the boondoggle of the ages. The whole thing was uneconomical to the point of lunacy. Only the rush for a decisive new weapon could justify it. Fear was fading in 1944 that the Germans or Japanese might beat America to the bomb; the new goal was to shorten the war. So on three different theories, the Army had built three different giant industrial complexes for making bomb stuff. The Hanford plant on the Columbia River was striving to produce plutonium. A dubious enough venture, it was a bright hope compared with the two colossal installations at Oak Ridge intended to separate uranium-235 by two different methods, both still sputtering and failing.

Few people even at the highest levels knew the extent of the threatening failure. Colonel Peters knew. The scientific mastermind of the bomb project, Dr. Robert Oppenheimer, knew. And the resolute, thick-hided Army man bossing the show, Brigadier General Leslie Groves, knew. But nobody knew what to do about it. Dr. Oppenheimer had an idea, and Colonel Peters was going to Oak Ridge to meet with Oppenheimer and a small senior committee.

As against this crisis, Captain Henry's request for the Dresser couplings was small potatoes. Rather than risk trouble with the White House, Peters was taking him along, since Pug's security clearance was flawless. Oppenheimer's idea involved bringing in the Navy, and Army–Navy relations were touchy. A cooperative gesture made some sense at this point.

Peters knew nothing about the Navy's thermal diffusion system. "Compartmentalization" was General Groves's first rule: noncommunication walls between sections of the bomb effort, so that people in one track would not know what was happening elsewhere. Groves had investigated thermal diffusion in 1942 and concluded that the Navy was wasting its time. Now Oppenheimer had written to Groves suggesting a second very urgent look at the Navy's results.

Pug Henry had been passing through military checkpoints all his life, but the Oak Ridge roadblock was something new. The gate guards were processing a crowd of new workmen in a considerable uproar, letting them through one by one like counted gold coins, to buses waiting beyond the gate. The substitute coupling Pug had brought along was scrutinized by hardfaced MPs and passed before a fluoroscope. He himself went through a body search and some stiff questioning, then got back into Peters's Army car, wearing various badges and a radiation gauge.

"Let's go," Peters said to the sergeant driver. "Stop at the overlook."

They went bowling along a narrow tarred road through dense green woods, flowering here and there with redbud and dogwood.

"Bob McDermott will be at the castle. I phoned," said Peters. "I'll turn you over to him."

"Who's he? What's the castle?"

"He'll have to pass on your request. He's the boss engineer. The castle is the administration building."

The ride through wild woods went on for miles. The colonel worked on papers as he had on the train, and during the drive from Knoxville. The two men had scarcely spoken since leaving Washington. Pug had his own paper sheaf, and silence always suited him. It was a warm morning, and the forest scent through the open windows was delightful. The car climbed a twisting stretch of road through solid dogwood. Rounding a bend, the driver pulled off the road and stopped.

"God Almighty," Pug gasped.

"K-25," said Peters.

A long wide valley stretched below, a chaotic muddy panorama of construction centered around an unfinished building that looked like all the airplane hangars in America put together in a U-shape; the most gigantic edifice Pug had ever seen. Around it sprawled miles of flat-roofed huts, acres of trailers, rows of military barracks, and scores of buildings, clear out of sight. The general look, from this distance, was a strange mélange of Army base, science-fiction vision, and gold-rush town, all in a sea of red mud. A sense of an awesome future rose from this view like the shock wave of a bomb.

"The water lines are for that big plant," said Peters. "Something, hey? The technicians get around in there on bicycles. It's operating, but we keep adding units. Over the ridge there's another valley, and another installation. Not quite as big, different principle."

They drove down through the booming valley past rough huts interlined with wooden boardwalks built over the mud, past long queues of workingmen and women at bus stops and stores, past a hundred noisy construction jobs, past the gigantic K-25 structure, to the "castle." Pug was not expecting to encounter a familiar face, but there in the corridor was Sime Anderson in uniform, talking to shirt-sleeved civilians. Sime returned a salute to Pug's startled informal wave.

"Know that young fellow?" asked Peters.

"Beau of my daughter's. Lieutenant Commander Anderson."

"Oh, yes. Rhoda's mentioned him."

It was the first reference to Rhoda on the trip.

The walls of the chief engineer's small office were covered with maps, his desk with blueprints. McDermott was a heavyset mustached man with a grimly amused look in bulging brown eyes, as though he were hanging on to his sanity by regarding Oak Ridge as a great mad joke. His neatly pressed suit trousers were tucked into rubber knee boots crusted with fresh red muck. "Hope you don't mind walking in mud," he said to Pug as he shook hands.

"If it'll get me those couplings, not at all."

McDermott looked over the substitute coupling Pug showed him. "Why don't you use this on your landing craft?"

"We can't accept the delay needed for modification."

"Can we?" McDermott asked Colonel Peters.

"That's the second question," Peters replied. "The first question is whether you can use that thing."

McDermott turned to Pug, and pointed a thumb at a pile of muddy boots. "Help yourself and let's go."

"How long will you be?" Peters asked.

"I'll bring him back by four."

"Good enough. Did the new barriers come in from Detroit?"

McDermott nodded. Grim amusement came on his face like a mask. "Unsatisfactory."

"Jesus God," said Peters. "The general will go up in smoke."

"Well, they're still testing them."

"Ready," Pug said. The boots were too large. He hoped they would not come off in the mud.

"On our way," said McDermott.

In the corridor, a short bespectacled colonel, almost bald, with a genial very sharp expression, had joined Anderson and the civilians. Peters introduced Pug to the Army boss of Oak Ridge, Colonel Nichols.

"Is the Navy going to get those landing craft made in time?" Nichols asked Pug, his bluntness modified by a pleasant manner.

"Not if you keep preempting our components."

Nichols asked McDermott, "What's the problem?"

"The Dresser couplings for the underground water lines."

"Oh, yes. Well, do what you can."

"Gonna try."

"Hi, there," Pug said to Anderson. The junior officer diffidently grinned. Pug went off with McDermott.

A frail-looking, young-looking man smoking a pipe entered the building as Pug left. The prospect of addressing a meeting that included Dr. Oppenheimer had Sime Anderson shaking at the knees. Oppenheimer was, in Anderson's view, probably the brightest human being alive; his mind probed nature as though God were his private tutor, and he was cruel to fools. Sime's boss, Abelson, had casually sent Sime off to Oak Ridge to describe the thermal diffusion plant for a few key Oak Ridge personnel and corporation executives. Only on arriving had Sime learned that Oppenheimer would be there.

There was no help for it now. Feeling appallingly ill-prepared, he followed Dr. Oppenheimer into the small conference room, where a blackboard gave the place of a classroom look. Some twenty men, mostly in shirt-sleeves, made it crowded, smoky, and hot. Anderson was sweating in his heavy blue uniform when Nichols introduced him and he got to his feet. But chalk in hand, talking about his work, he soon felt all right. He avoided looking at Oppenheimer, who slouched smoking in the second row. By the time Anderson paused for questions, forty minutes had sped by, and the blackboard was covered with diagrams and equations. His small audience appeared alert, interested, and puzzled.

Nichols broke the short silence. "That separation factor of two—that's the theoretical performance you're hoping for?"

"That's what our system is putting out, sir."

"You're getting that concentration of U-235? *Now?*"

"Yes, sir. One point four. One part in seventy."

Nichols looked straight at Oppenheimer.

Oppenheimer stood, walked forward, and shook hands with Sime, smiling in remote recognition. "Well done, Anderson." Sime sat down, his heart swelling with relief.

Oppenheimer looked around with large sombre eyes. "The figure of one point four is the reason for this meeting. We have made a very fundamental, very serious, very embarrassing mistake," he said in a slow weary voice, "all of us have, who share responsibility for this effort. It seems we were bemused by the greater elegance and originality of gaseous diffusion and electromagnetic separation. We were obsessed, too, with going to ninety percent enrichment along a single path. It didn't occur to us that combined processes might be a speedier way. Now here we are. From the last word on barriers, K-25 will not work in time for this war. Hanford too is a question. Out in New Mexico we're testing bomb configurations for an explosive that doesn't yet exist. Not in usable quantities."

Picking up chalk, Oppenheimer went on, "Now thermal diffusion itself won't provide the enrichment we need, but a combination of thermal diffusion and the Y-12 process will give us a bomb by July 1945. That is clear." He rapidly scrawled on the board figures that showed a fourfold increase in the electromagnetic separation of the Y-12 plant, given feed enriched to one part in seventy. "The question is, can a thermal plant on a very large scale be erected within a few months to feed Y-12? I've recommended this urgently to General Groves. We're here to discuss ways and means."

Stooped, skinny, melancholy, Oppenheimer returned to his seat. Now that the meeting had a direction, ideas and questions sparked around in quick insiders' shorthand. Sime Anderson was called on to answer many questions. The meeting pressed him hard on the core of the Navy system, the forty-eight-foot vertical steam pipes of concentric iron, copper, and nickel cylinders.

"But the Navy's using only a hundred of them, hand-fashioned at hat," exclaimed a big red-faced civilian in the front row. "That's lab equipment. We're talking here about several thousand of the damn things, aren't we? A whole forest of them, factory-made! It's a plumber's nightmare, Colonel Nichols. You won't get a corporation in his country to take on such a contract. Three *thousand* pipes of that ength, with those tolerances, in a few *months?* Forget it."

The meeting split into two groups for lunch: one to talk about design with Oppenheimer and Anderson, one to confer with Nichols and Peters on construction and manufacturing. "The general wants this hing done," Colonel Nichols summed up in adjourning. "So it will be. We'll all meet back here at two o'clock, and start making some decisions."

With a wave of his pipe, Oppenheimer stopped Sime from leaving the room. When they were alone he said, walking to the blackboard, "A-minus, Anderson." He picked up chalk, corrected an equation with a nervous rub of a fist and a scrawl of symbols; then asked a series of quick questions, dazzling the naval officer with his total grasp of thermal diffusion in every aspect. "Well, let's get on to the cafeteria," he said, dropping the chalk, "and join the others."

"Yes, sir."

Leaning against the desk, arms folded, Oppenheimer made no move to go. "What next for you?"

"I'm returning to Washington tonight, sir."

"I know that. Now that the Army will get into thermal diffusion, what about a new challenge? Come and join us out in New Mexico."

"You're sure the Army will do it?"

"They have to. There's no alternative. The weapon itself still poses some nice problems in ideas. Not lion hunting, so to say, but a lively rabbit shoot. Are you married, Anderson?"

"Ah—no, I'm not."

"Better so. The mesa is a strange place, quite isolated. Some of the wives take to it, but others—well, that won't concern you. You'll soon be hearing from Captain Parsons."

"Captain Parsons? Is he in New Mexico now?"

"He's a division head. You'll come, won't you? There's a lot of excellence out there."

"I go where I'm ordered, Dr. Oppenheimer."

"Orders won't be a problem."

All the trudging in ropy mud wore Victor Henry down. McDermott drove a jeep, but the narrow rutted roads ended abruptly in brush or muck, sometimes far from where they wanted to go. Pug didn't mind the slogging here and there, because they were getting the answers he wanted. One after another, the technicians concurred that with a modified sleeve and a thicker gasket, the substitute coupling would answer. It was the old story—administrative rigidity in Washington, good-humored horse sense among the men with hard hats, dirty hands, and muddy shoes. Pug had broken many a supply impasse this way.

"I'm convinced," McDermott shouted over the grinding and bumping of the jeep, as they headed back under lowering storm clouds. They had been at this for hours, pausing only for sandwiches and coffee at a field canteen. "Now convince the Army, Captain."

80

SHARING a drawing room on the train back to Washington, Pug and Peters hung up wet clothes as the train started, and Pug declined the whiskey the Army man offered him. He did not feel much like drinking with his wife's current love. Sime Anderson came in, summoned by the colonel. "Stay here," Peters said to Pug, when their discussion began and he offered to leave. "I want you in on this."

Pug quickly gathered that the Army was taking a sudden urgent interest in a Navy system for processing uranium. He kept his mouth shut while the colonel, whose frame bulked large in the tiny room, puffed at a cigar, sipped whiskey, and asked Anderson questions. The train picked up speed, the wheels clattered, rain beat on the black windows, and Pug began to feel hungry.

"Sir, I'm on special detached duty, assigned directly to the lab," Anderson replied to a query about the Navy chain of command on the project. "You'll have to talk to Dr. Abelson."

"I will. I see only one way through this mess," Peters said, putting his notebook into a breast pocket. "We'll have to build twenty Chinese copies of your plant. Just duplicate it and string 'em in series. Designing a new two-thousand-column plant can take many months."

"You could design for greater efficiency, sir."

"Yes, for the next war. The idea is to make a weapon for this one. All right, Commander. Many thanks."

When Anderson left, Peters asked Pug, "Do you know Admiral Purnell? I'm wondering how I go about getting the Navy's blueprints for thermal diffusion real fast."

"Your man is Ernest King."

"But King may not even be clued in on uranium. Purnell's the Navy man on the Military Policy Committee."

"I know, but that doesn't matter. Go to King."

"Will you do that?"

"What? Approach Admiral King for the Army? *Me?*"

At the incredulous tone, Colonel Peters's fleshy mouth widened in the grin which no doubt charmed the women; the naïve, cheery grin of a mature man who had not known much grief, a gray-haired boyish man. "Look, Henry, I can't proceed through channels in the uranium business, and I can't write letters. Ordinarily I'd go with this thing to the next meeting of the Military Policy Committee, but I want to get moving. The trouble is—and it hasn't been my doing—we've cold-shouldered the Navy for years. We've shut Abelson out. We even got snotty about giving him a supply of uranium hexafluoride, when it was Abelson, for Christ's sake, who first produced the stuff for us. I just found that out today. Stupid policy, and now we need the Navy. You know King, don't you?"

"Quite well."

"I have a feeling you could broker this thing."

"Look, Colonel, just getting in to see Ernest King can take days. Tell you what, though. You release those couplings—I mean telephone that firm in Pennsylvania from Union Station tomorrow—and I'll get right in a cab and try to break in on the CNO."

"Pug, only the general can waive this priority." Peters's wide grin was wary and uncertain. "I could get my head cut off."

"So you said. Well, I can get my head cut off for barging in on Ernest King without an appointment. Especially with an Army request."

Staring at Pug, Colonel Peters rubbed his mouth hard, then burst out laughing. "Hell, those Oak Ridge fellows approved your coupling, didn't they? You're on. Let's have a drink on it."

"I'd rather have dinner. I'm hungry as a bear. Coming?"

"Go ahead." Peters clearly did not like this second refusal. "I'll be along."

Sime Anderson stood in the queue outside the dining car, pondering a common quandary of wartime—whether to propose marriage before going off to serve in a distant place. He could take Madeline out to that mesa in New Mexico, but would she agree to go, and even if she did, would she be happy in such a place? Oppenheimer had hinted at difficulties with wives. When Madeline's father showed up on the queue, Sime seized the chance to sit with him in the jammed dining car at a table for two. While they ate tepid tomato soup and very greasy fried pork chops, and the car swayed and rattled, and rippling rain slanted in streaks on the window, he told Pug his problem. Pug did not speak until he finished, and not for a while after that.

"You love each other?" he asked at last.

"Yes, sir."

"Well, then? Navy juniors are used to living in strange places."

"She went to New York to break the mold of a Navy junior." Sime had said nothing as yet about Hugh Cleveland. His sad tone, his miserable glance at the father, revealed to Pug that Madeline had told all, and that it had gone down hard.

"Sime, she came home."

"Yes. To another big city, and another radio job."

"Are you asking for my advice?"

"Yes, sir."

"Ever hear about faint hearts and fair ladies? Take your chances. I think she'll go with you, and stay with you." The father offered his hand. "Good luck."

"Thank you, sir." They gripped each other's hands.

In the club car, Pug drank a large brandy in a contented glow. Madeline for years had seemed an irretrievable disaster; and now this! He mulled over images of Madeline through the years: the enchanting girl baby, the fairy princess in the school play, the disconcerting flirt with budding breasts, shining eyes, and inexpert makeup going to her first dance, the brassy horror in New York. Now it seemed that poor Madeline would make it; at least there was a damned good chance for her, after a rotten start.

Pug did not want to spoil his good mood by spending the night bedded down in a room with Colonel Harrison Peters. He was used to sleeping sitting up in trains and planes, and he decided to snooze in the club car. Peters had not appeared for dinner; probably he had quaffed several whiskeys and turned in. Pug dozed off with the lights on and drinkers' noise all around him, having slipped the barman ten dollars to buy his peace.

The car was dimmed, and quiet except for the rapid clacking of the wheels, when he was poked awake. A tall figure in a bathrobe swayed over him. Peters said, "There's a nice berth all made up for you."

Yawning, stiff, Pug could think of no gracious way out. He stumbled after Peters to the drawing room, which for odors of whiskey and stale cigars was no better than the club car; but the crisply sheeted upper berth looked good. He quickly undressed.

"Nightcap?" Peters was pouring from an almost empty bottle.

"No, thanks."

"Pug, don't you want to drink with me?"

Without comment Pug accepted the glass. They drank, got into their berths, and turned out the lights. Pug was glad to be under covers after all. He relaxed with a sigh, and was sinking into sleep.

"Say, Pug." Peters's voice from below, warm and whiskeyish. "That Anderson's a comer. Rhoda thinks he and Madeline are serious. You'd approve, wouldn't you?"

"Yep."

Silence. Train sounds.

"Pug, can I ask you a very personal question?"

No reply.

"Sorry as hell to disturb you. This is damned important to me."

"Go ahead."

"Why did you and Rhoda ever break up?"

Victor Henry had tried to avoid a night with the Army man, to duck the risk of just such a probe. He did not answer.

"It wasn't my doing, was it? It's unbelievably shitty to move in on a guy's wife when he's overseas. I understood you were already estranged."

"That's true."

"Otherwise, believe me, attractive as she is, I'd have steered clear."

"I believe you."

"You and Rhoda are two of the finest people I know. What happened?"

"I fell in love with an Englishwoman."

Pause.

"That's what Rhoda says."

"That's it."

"It doesn't seem like you."

Pug was silent.

"Are you going to marry her?"

"I thought I was, but she refused me." So Peters wrung from Victor Henry his first reference to Pamela's astounding letter, which he had tried to bury from mind.

"Jesus! You never know with a woman, Pug, do you? Sorry to hear that."

"Good-night, Colonel." It was a sharp cut-off tone.

"Pug, just one more question. Did Dr. Fred Kirby have anything to do with all this?"

There it was. The thing Rhoda had feared was coming to pass because of this forced intimacy. What Victor Henry said next could make or break the rest of Rhoda's life; and he had to answer fast, for every second of hesitation was a slur on her, on him, and on their marriage.

"What the hell does that mean?" Pug hoped he put the right puzzlement, tinged with anger, in his tone.

"I've been getting letters, Pug, damnable anonymous letters, about Rhoda and Dr. Kirby. I'm ashamed of myself for paying them any attention, but—"

"You should be. Fred Kirby's an old friend of mine. We met when I was stationed in Berlin. Rhoda had to come home when the war broke out. Fred was in Washington then, and he played tennis with her, and took her to shows and such, sort of the way you've been doing, but with no complications. I knew about it, and I appreciated it. I don't like this conversation much, and I'd like to turn in."

"Sorry, Pug."

"Okay."

Silence. Then Peters's voice, low, troubled, and drunk. "It's because I idolize Rhoda that I'm so upset. I'm more than upset, I'm tortured. Pug, I've known a hell of a lot of women, prettier than Rhoda, and sexier. But she's virtuous. That's where her preciousness lies. That sounds strange coming from me, but that's how I feel. Rhoda's the first lady in every sense of the word that I've ever known, except for my own mother. She's perfect. She's elegant, modest, decent, and truthful. She never lies. Christ, most women lie the way they breathe. You know that. You can't blame them. We keep trying to screw them, they play a desperate game, and all's fair. Don't you agree?"

Peters had drunk up the bottle, Pug thought, to nerve himself for this. The maundering could go on all night. He made no reply.

"I mean I'm not talking about these stodgy wives, Pug. I'm talking about stylish women. My mother was a knockout till she was eighty-two. Christ, she looked like a chorus girl in her coffin. Yet I want to tell you, she was a saint. Like Rhoda, she went to church every Sunday, rain or shine. Rhoda's as stylish as a movie queen, yet there's something saintly about her, too. That's why this thing's hit me like an earthquake, Pug, and if I've offended you I'm sorry, because I think the world of you."

"We've got a busy day tomorrow, Colonel."

"Right, Pug."

In a few minutes Peters was snoring.

There were two admirals in King's outer office, when Pug came there straight from Union Station. He prevailed on the flag lieutenant to send in a short note, and King at once summoned him inside. The CNO sat behind his large desk in the bleak room, smoking a cigarette in a holder. "You look better than you did in Tehran," he said, not offering Pug a chair. "What's this about uranium now? I've shredded your note into the burn basket."

Pug sketched the situation at Oak Ridge in spare sentences. King's bald long head and seamed face turned very pink. His severe mouth puckered strangely, and Pug surmised that he was trying not to smile. "Are you saying," King broke in harshly, "that the Army, after commandeering all the nation's scientists and factories, and spending billions, hasn't got a bomb, while we've cooked one up in that tinpot Anacostia lab of ours?"

"Not quite, Admiral. There's a technical gap in the Army's method. The Navy process closes that gap. They want to take our system and blow it up on a huge industrial scale."

"And that way they'll get this weapon made? Not otherwise?"

"So I understand. Not in time for use in this war."

"Hell, I'll give 'em anything they need, then. Why not? This should make us look pretty good in the history books, hey? Except the Army will write the history, so we'll probably get left out. How did you become involved in it?"

King listened to the tale of the couplings, nodding and smoking, his face rigid again. "Colonel Peters has telephoned the Dresser company," Pug concluded. "It's all set. I'm flying to Pennsylvania to make sure that the stuff gets on the trucks and rolls out."

"Good idea. Flying how?"

"Navy plane out of Andrews."

"Got transportation?"

"Not yet."

King picked up the telephone and ordered a car and driver for Captain Henry. "Now then. What do you want me to do, Henry?"

"Assure Colonel Peters of Navy cooperation, Admiral. Before pushing this idea of duplicating our plant, he wants to be sure of his ground."

"Give his phone number to my flag lieutenant. I'll call the man."

"Yes, sir."

"I've heard about your expediting of the landing craft program. The Secretary is pleased." King got up and held out a long lean arm crusted with gold to the elbow. "On your way."

As Pug was paying off the taxicab on his return from Pennsylvania, Madeline opened the front door. She looked almost as she had, going to her first dance: flushed, shiny-eyed, too painted-up. She said nothing, but gave him a hug and led him into the living room. There sat Rhoda, looking very dressy for a weekday at home, behind a coffee table on which champagne was cooling in a silver bucket. Sime Anderson stood beside her with a bewildered, foolishly pleased look on his face.

"Good evening, sir."

"Well! Return of the warrior!" said Rhoda. "You remembered you had a FAMILY! How nice! Are you busy next Saturday?"

"Not that I can think of, no."

"Oh, no! Well, fine. How about coming to Saint John's Church, then, and giving Madeline away to this sailor boy?"

Mother, daughter, and suitor burst into joyous laughter. Pug seized Madeline in his arms. She clung to him, hugging him hard, her wet cheek to his. He shook hands with Sime Anderson and embraced him. The young man wore the shaving lotion Warren had used; the smell gave Pug a small shock. Rhoda jumped up, kissed Pug, and exclaimed, "OKAY! Surprise is over, now for the champagne." Practical talk followed: wedding arrangements, trousseau, caterer, guest list, accommodations for Sime's family, and so forth; Rhoda kept making neat notes in a stenographic pad. Then Pug took Anderson off into the library.

"Sime, how are your finances?"

The young man confessed to two expensive hobbies: hunting, which he had learned from his father, and classical music. He had put more than a thousand dollars into records and a Capehart, and almost as much into a collection of rifles and shotguns. No doubt it hadn't been sensible to clutter up his life that way; he could hardly turn around in his apartment; but then, he hadn't bothered much with girls. Now he would store the stuff, and one day sell it off. Meantime he had saved only twelve hundred dollars.

"Well, that's something. You can live on your salary. Madeline has savings, too. Also some stock in that damned radio show."

Anderson looked very uncomfortable. "Yes. She's better off than I am."

"Don't live higher on the hog than your own salary warrants. Let her do what she likes with her money, but not that."

"That's my intention."

"Now, look, Sime, I've got fifteen thousand dollars put aside for her. It's yours."

"Ye gods, that's marvelous!" An innocently greedy pleasure lit the young man's face. "I didn't expect that."

"I'd suggest you buy a house around Washington with it, if you plan to stay in the Navy."

"Sure, I'm staying in the Navy. We've talked that all out. R and D will be very big after the war."

Pug put his hands on Anderson's shoulders. "She's said a thousand times, down the years, that she'd never marry a naval officer. Well done."

The young couple went off in a happy flurry to celebrate. Pug and Rhoda sat in the living room, finishing the wine.

"So," said Rhoda, "the last fledgling takes wing. At least she's made it before the mother flew off." Rhoda blinked archly over the rim of her wineglass at Pug.

"Shall I take you out to dinner?"

"Oh, no. I've got shad roe for the two of us. And there's another bottle of champagne. How was your trip? Was Hack helpful?"

"Decidedly."

"I'm so glad. He has got a big job, hasn't he, Pug?"

"Couldn't be bigger."

Fresh-cut flowers from the garden on the candle-lit table; a tossed salad with Roquefort dressing; perfectly done large shad roe with dry crisp bacon; potatoes in their jackets, with sour cream and chives; a fresh-baked blueberry pie; obviously Rhoda had planned all this for his return. She cooked and served it herself, then sat and ate in a gray silk dress, with beautifully coiffed hair, looking like a chic guest at her own table. She was in a wonderful mood, telling Pug her ideas for the wedding, or else she was giving a superb performance. The champagne sparkled in her eyes.

This was the Rhoda who, for all her familiar failings—crabbiness, flightiness, moodiness, shallowness—had made him a happy man, Pug was thinking, for twenty-five years; who had captivated Kirby and Peters, and could ensnare any man her age; beautiful, competent, energetic, attentive to a man's comforts, intensely feminine, capable of exciting passion. What had happened? Why had he frozen her out? What had been so irreparable? Long, long ago he had faced the fact that the war had caused her affair with Kirby, that it was a personal mischance in a world upheaval; even Sime Anderson had shrugged off Madeline's past, and made a happy start on a new life.

The answer never changed. He did not love Rhoda any more. He had no use for her. He could not help it. It had nothing to do with forgiveness. He had forgiven her. But a live nerve now bound Sime Anderson and Madeline, and Rhoda had severed the nerve of their marriage. It was withered and dead. Some marriages survived an infidelity, but this one had not. He had been ready to go on with it because of the memory of their lost son, but it was better for Rhoda to live with someone who loved her. That she was in trouble with Peters only made him pity her.

"Great pie," said Pug.

"Thank you, kind sir, and you know what I propose next? I propose coffee and Armagnac in the garden, that's what. All the iris have popped open, and the smell is sheer HEAVEN."

"You're on."

It had taken Rhoda a couple of years to weed out and replant the neglected quarter-acre. Now it was a charming brick-walled nook of varied colors and delicious fragrances, around a musically splashing little fountain she had installed at some cost. She carried the coffee service out to a wrought-iron table between cushioned lounge chairs, and Pug brought the Armagnac and glasses.

"By the bye," she said as they settled down, "there's a letter from Byron. In all the excitement, I clean forgot. He's fine. It's just a page."

"Any real news?" Pug tried to keep relief out of his voice.

"Well, the first patrol was a success, and he's been qualified for command. You know Byron. He never says much."

"Did his Bronze Star come through?"

"Nothing on that. He worries and worries about Natalie. Begs us to cable any word we get."

Pug sat staring at the flower beds. The colors were dimming in the fading light, and a breeze stirred a rich scent from the nodding purple iris. "We should call the State Department again."

"I did, today. The Danish Red Cross is supposed to visit Theresienstadt, so maybe some word will come through."

Pug was experiencing the sensation of a slipped cog in time, of reliving an old scene. Rhoda's *"By the bye, there's a letter from Byron"* had triggered it, he realized. So they had sat drinking Armagnac in twilight before the war, the day Admiral Preble had offered him the attaché post in Berlin. *"By the bye, there's a letter from Byron,"* Rhoda had said, and he had felt the same sort of relief, because they had not heard from him in months. It had been the first letter about Natalie. That day, Warren had announced he was putting in for flight training. That day, Madeline had tried to go to New York during the school week, and he had stopped her with difficulty. In hindsight, quite a turning point, that day.

"Rhoda, I said I'd report any personal talk I had with Peters."

"Yes?" Rhoda sat up.

"There was some."

She gulped brandy. "Go ahead."

Pug narrated the conversation in the dark train compartment. Rhoda kept taking nervous sips of her brandy. She sighed when he described Peters's subsiding into snores. "Well! You were very, very gallant," she said. "It's no more than I expected of you, Pug. Thank you, and God bless you."

"That wasn't the end of it, Rho."

She stared at her husband, her face white and strained in the gloom. "He went to sleep, you said."

"He did. I woke early, and slid out of there for some breakfast. The waiter was bringing me orange juice when your colonel showed up, all shaved and spruce, and sat down with me. We were the only two people in the diner. He asked for coffee, and right off he said—in a very sober and calm way—'I take it you preferred not to give me a straight answer last night about Dr. Kirby.'"

"Oh, God. What did you say?"

"Well, he caught me off guard, you realize. I said, 'How could I have been any straighter?' Something like that. Then here's what he answered—and I'm trying for his exact words—'I'm not about to cross-examine you, Pug. And I'm not about to throw over Rhoda. But I think I should know the truth. A marriage shouldn't start with a lie. If you get a chance to tell Rhoda that, please do. It may help clear the air.'"

"And what did you say to that?" Her voice shook, and her hand shook as she poured her glass full.

"I said, 'There's no air to clear, except in your mind. If poison-pen letters can get to you, you don't deserve any woman's love, let alone Rhoda's.'"

"Beautiful, darling. Beautiful."

"I'm not sure. He looked me in the eye and just said, 'Okay, Pug.' He changed the subject and talked business. He never referred to you again."

Rhoda drank deeply. "I'm lost. You're not a good liar, Pug, though God knows you tried."

"Rhoda, I can lie, and on occasion I do it damned well."

"In the line of duty!" She flipped her hand in scorn. "That's not what I'm talking about." She drank, and poured more, saying, "I'm sunk, that's all. That accursed woman! Whoever she is, I really could kill her —oops!" The glass was overflowing.

"You'll be blotto."

"Why not?"

"Rhoda, he said he's not throwing you over."

"Oh, no. He'll go through with it. Soul of honor, and all that. I'll probably have to let him. What's my alternative? Still, it's all ruined."

"Why don't you just tell him, Rhoda?"

Rhoda sat and peered at him without replying.

"I mean that. Look at Madeline and Sime. She told him. They couldn't be happier."

With some of her old feminine sarcasm she said, "Pug, my dear dumb love, what kind of comparison is THAT? For God's sake, I'm a HAG. Sime's not thirty years old, and Madeline's a luscious girl. Hack's fastened on to me, and it's all been terribly charming, but at our age it's mostly mental. Now I'm CORNERED. I'm damned if I do and damned if I don't. I'm a good wife, *you* know I am, and I know I could make him happy. But he had to have this perfect picture of me. It's GONE."

"It was an illusion, Rho."

"What's WRONG with illusions?" Rhoda's voice strained and broke. "Sorry. I'm going to bed. Thank you, darling. Thank you for trying. You're a grand man, and I love you for it."

They stood up. Rhoda took a lithe step or two, put her arms around him and gave him a sensuous brandy-soaked kiss, pressing her body to his. They had not kissed like this in a year. So far as it went, it still worked. Pug could not help pulling her close and responding.

With a husky laugh, she broke half-free. "Save it for Pamela, honey."

"Pamela turned me down."

Rhoda went rigid in his arms, opening eyes like saucers. "Is THAT what was in that letter last week? She DIDN'T!"

"Yes."

"My God, you're close-mouthed. Why? How *could* she? Is she marrying Burne-Wilke?"

"She hadn't yet. Burne-Wilke was wounded in India. They're back in England. She's been nursing him and—well, Rhoda, she said no. That's it."

Rhoda uttered a coarse chuckle. "You accepted that?"

"How do I not accept it?"

"Honeybunch, I'm potted enough to TELL you how. Woo her! That's all she wants."

"I don't think she's like that. The letter was pretty final."

"We're ALL like that. I declare, I am STONE drunk. You may have to help me up the stairs."

"Okay, let's go."

"Just fooling." She patted his arm. "Finish your brandy, dear, and enjoy that gorgeous moon. I can navigate."

"You're sure?"

"Sure. Night, love."

A cool gentle kiss on the mouth, and Rhoda walked unsteadily inside.

When Pug came upstairs almost an hour later, Rhoda's door was wide open. The bedroom was dark. The door had not been open since his return from Tehran.

"Pug, is that you?"

"Yes."

"Well, good-night again, darling."

It was all in the tone. Rhoda was a signaller, not a talker, and Pug read the signal, loud and clear. Clearly she had weighed her chances again, in the light of Peters's suspicions, Pam's refusal, and the family glow of Madeline's happiness. Here was his old marriage, asking him back in. It was Rhoda's last try. *"They play a desperate game,"* Peters had said. True enough. It was a powerful game, too. He had only to step through the doorway, into the remembered sweet odors of that dark room.

He walked by the door, his eyes moistening. "Good-night, Rhoda."

81

P AST midnight. Overhead the full moon rides, silvering the deserted streets; silvering too the long, long freight train that comes clanking and squealing into the Bahnhofstrasse and jars to a halt outside the Hamburg barracks. Reverberating through the straight streets, the noises awaken the restless sleepers. *"Did you hear that?"* In many languages these words are whispered through the crowded rows of three-tier bunks.

There has not been a transport in a long time. The train could be bringing more materials for the crazy Beautification. Or perhaps it has come to take away the products of the factories. So the worried whispers go, though trucks and horse-drawn wagons, not trains, usually haul in and out everything but human beings. Of course it could be an arriving transport, but those usually come by day.

Aaron Jastrow, poring over the Talmud in his preposterously well-furnished ground floor apartment on the Seestrasse (it is to be a stop for the Red Cross visitors) hears the train. Natalie does not wake. Just as well! The Council of Elders has been wrestling for days with the transport order. The controlling figures are burned in Jastrow's brain:

All Jews now in Theresienstadt	35,000
Protected by Germans (*Prominente, half-Jews, Danes, medal bearers, wounded war veterans and their families*)	9,500
Protected by the Central Secretariat (*officials bureaucrats, staff artists, war factory workers*)	6,500
Total protected	16,000
Available for transport	19,000

Seven thousand, five hundred persons must go—almost half of the "available," one-fifth of the whole ghetto. The grating irony of the dates! The expectation of an Allied landing on May 15 has swept

Theresienstadt. People have been waiting and praying for that day. Now the Transport Section is frantically shuffling and reshuffling index cards for the first shipment on May 15 of twenty-five hundred; the transport will go in three trains on three successive days.

This transport will badly disrupt the Beautification. The Technical Department will lose much of the work force that is repainting the town, laying out flower beds, putting down turf, building and renovating. The orchestras, the choruses, the drama and opera casts, will be cut to pieces. But the SS is unconcerned. Rahm has warned that the work will be done and the performances will shape up, or those in charge will be sorry. The Beautification is the cause of the transport. As the Red Cross visit draws nearer, the commander is getting nervous about his ability to steer it along a restricted route. The whole ghetto is being cleaned up, and to relieve the overcrowding, the sluice to the east has once more been opened.

Jastrow is heartsick over the general tragedy, and over a private bereavement. Headquarters has ordered all orphans in the town shipped off. Red Cross visitors asking a child about its parents must not hear that they are dead or—forbidden word—"transported." Half of his Talmud class are orphans. His star student, Shmuel Horovitz, is one: a shy gaunt lad of sixteen with long hair, a silky beard, huge infinitely sad eyes, and a lightning mind. How can he bear to lose Shmuel? If only the Allies will indeed land! If only the shock will delay or cancel this transport! Saving seven thousand, five hundred Jews out of the massacre would be a miracle. Saving Shmuel alone would be a miracle. In Jastrow's fond view, the blaze of this boy's brain could light up the future of the whole Jewish people. He could be a Maimonides, a Rashi. To lose such a mind in a brief horrible flare over Oswiecim!

Natalie departs for the mica factory in the morning, unaware of the waiting train. Jastrow goes to the newly located, superbly equipped library, which would not disgrace a small college: whole rooms full of new steel book stacks, bright lighting, polished reading tables, good chairs, even carpeting; and a richly varied collection of books in the major European languages, as well as the stunning Judaica collection, all smartly indexed and catalogued. Of course nobody is using this luxurious facility. Readers and borrowers will be suitably rehearsed in due time, to make it all look natural for the Danish visitors.

Nobody on Jastrow's staff mentions the train. The day fades into late afternoon. Nothing has happened, and he begins to hope that all will be well. But they come, after all: two shabby Jews from the Transport Commission, a big fellow with wavy red hair carrying the bundle of

ummons cards, and a yellow-faced gnome with the roster to be signed.
Their expressions are bitter. They know they move in an aura of hatred.
They plod about the rooms, hunting down each transport recruit, serving him with his card, and getting his signature. The library is badly hit;
out of seven staff workers Jastrow loses five, including Shmuel Horovitz. With the gray card on the desk before him, Shmuel strokes his
youthful beard and looks to Jastrow. Slowly he turns his palms up and
outward, his dark eyes wide, black-rimmed, and grieving as the eyes of
Jesus in a Byzantine mosaic.

When Jastrow returns to the apartment, Natalie is there. Regarding
him with eyes like Shmuel Horovitz's, she holds out two gray cards to
him. She and Louis are assigned to the third train, departing on the
seventeenth *"for resettlement in the direction of Dresden."* Their transport numbers are on the cards. She must report with Louis to the Hamburg barracks on the sixteenth, bringing light luggage, one change of
linen, and food for twenty-four hours.

"This is a mistake," says Jastrow. "I'll go to Eppstein."

Natalie's face is as gray as the card. "You think so?"

"No doubt of it. You're a *Prominent,* a mica worker, and the
headmistress of the children's pavilion. The Transport Commission is a
madhouse. Somebody pulled the wrong card. I shall be back within the
hour. Be cheerful."

Outside the Magdeburg barracks, there is a riotous crush. Cursing
ghetto guards are trying to shove the people into a queue, using fists,
shoulders, and here and there rubber clubs. Jastrow passes through a
privileged entrance. From the far end of the main hallway comes the
angry anxious tumult of petitioners jamming the transport office. Outside Eppstein's suite there is also a line. Jastrow recognizes high officials
of the Economic and Technical Departments. This transport is biting
deep! Jastrow does not get in line. The rank of Elder is a wretched
burden, but at least it gives one access to the big shots, and even—if one
has real business with them—to the SS. Eppstein's pretty Berlin secretary, looking cross and worn, manages a smile at Jastrow, and passes
him in.

Eppstein sits with hands clasped on his handsome new mahogany
desk. The office would suit a Prague banker now, for furnishings and
decoration; a long briefing for the Red Cross is scheduled here. He
looks surprised to see Jastrow, and is cordial and sympathetic about
Natalie. Yes, a mistake is not at all unlikely. Those poor devils in transport have been running around without heads. He will look into it. Has
Jastrow's niece been up to any mischief, by chance? Jastrow says,

"Nothing of the kind, certainly not," and he tries to give Eppstein the gray cards.

The High Elder shrinks from them. "No, no, no, let her keep them, don't confuse things. When the error is corrected she'll be notified to turn the cards in."

For three days no further word comes from Eppstein. Jastrow tries over and over to see him, but the Berlin secretary turns cold, formal, and mean. Pestering her is useless, she says. The High Elder will send word when he has news. Meantime Natalie learns, and reports to Jastrow, that every member of her Zionist circle has received a transport card. Sullenly she acknowledges that Jastrow was prescient; an informer must have betrayed them, and they are being gotten rid of. They include the hospital's head of surgery, the deputy manager of the food administration, and the former president of the Jewish War Veterans of Germany. No protection avails this group, obviously.

The first two trains leave. Natalie's little cabal, except for herself, are all shipped off. A third long string of cattle cars squeals into the Bahnhofstrasse. All over Theresienstadt, transportees trudge toward the Hamburg barracks in bright afternoon sunshine, carrying luggage, food, and small children.

Jastrow returns to the apartment from a last try to see Eppstein. He has failed, but there is a ray of hope. One of his students, who works in the Central Secretariat, has whispered news to him. Gross errors were made by the Transport Commission. Over eight thousand summonses went out, but the SS has contracted with the Reichsbahn, the German railroad company, for exactly seven thousand five hundred transportees. The Reichsbahn calls the transports *Sonderzüge,* "special trains," charging the SS reduced third-class group fares. There are cars for only seventy-five hundred in all. So at least five hundred summonses may be cancelled; five hundred transportees reprieved!

Natalie sits on the couch sewing, with Louis beside her, as Jastrow pours out this news. She does not react with joy. She hardly reacts at all. Natalie has withdrawn into the old shell of narrow-focused numbness that protects her in bad times.

Right now she is wondering, she tells Jastrow, what to wear. She has dressed Louis up like Little Lord Fauntleroy, buying or borrowing clothes from families who are not going. With calm, dreamy, almost schizoid logic, she explains that her appearance will be important, since she will no longer be shielded by a famous uncle. She will be on her own. She must look her best. If only she can find instant favor in the eyes of the SS men where she is going, identify herself as an American and a *Prominent,* then her sex appeal and Louis's charm, and sympathy for a young mother, can all work for her. Shall she wear her rather seductive purple dress for the journey? She is sewing a yellow star on the dress as they talk. In this warm weather, she says, it might just do for the trip. What does Aaron think?

He gently falls in with her frame of mind. No, the purple dress might provoke liberties from the Germans, or even from low Jews. The tailored gray suit is elegant, Germanic, and it sets off her figure. She and Louis will stand out when they arrive. Solemnly nodding as he talks, she agrees, and folds away the starred dress in her suitcase, saying it may come in handy yet. She continues fussing at her packing, talking half to herself about the choices she must make. Aaron unlocks a desk drawer, takes out a knife, and severs a couple of stiches in the stout walking shoe on his right foot. Numb as she is, this strikes her as strange. "What are you doing?" The shoe is too tight, he says, going off into his own room. When he comes out, he is wearing his best suit and his old fedora. He looks rather like a transportee. His face is very grave, or upset, or scared, she cannot tell which.

"Natalie, I'll follow up on this matter of the cancelled summonses."

"But I must go to the Hamburg barracks soon."

"I shan't be long, and anyway, I can visit you there tonight."

She peers at him. "Honestly, do you think there is any hope?" Her tone is skeptical and detached.

"We'll see." Aaron drops on a knee beside Louis, who is playing with Natalie's Punch puppet on the floor. "Well, Louis," he says in Yiddish, "good-bye, and God watch over you." He kisses the boy. The tickling beard makes Louis laugh.

Natalie finishes her packing, closes the suitcases, and ties the bundles. Now she has nothing to do. This is what she finds hard to bear. Keeping busy is her best surcease from dread. She knows well that she and Louis are on a brink. She has not forgotten Berel's account, reported by Aaron, of what happens "in the east." She has not forgotten it, but she has suppressed it. She and Aaron have not referred to Oswiecim again. The transport summons says nothing about Oswiecim. She has shut her mind and heart to the thought that she is probably going there. She does not even yet repent of her involvement with the underground Zionists. It has kept her spirits high, given her a handle on her fate, made some sense of it.

The great German oppression is due to the homelessness and defenselessness of the Jews. Bad luck has caught her up in the catastrophe. But Western liberalism was always a mirage. Assimilation is impossible. She herself has lived an empty Jewish life until now, but she has found herself. If she survives, her life will go to restoring the Jewish nation to its ancient soil in Palestine.

She believes this. It is her new creed. At least, she believes she believes it. A small resistant mocking American voice has never quite died in her, whispering that what she really wants is to survive, go back to Byron, and live in San Francisco or Colorado; and that her sudden conversion to Zionism is mental morphine for the agony of entrapment. But morphine or creed, she has risked her life for it, is about to pay the price, and still does not regret it. She regrets only that she did not jump at Berel's offer to deliver Louis. If only she might still do it!

She can wait no longer for Aaron. With Louis toddling beside her, she sets out for the Hamburg barracks, a bundle of food and toilet things on her back, a suitcase in either hand. She falls into a stooped shabby procession of Jews with their packs, all headed that way. It is a beautiful balmy afternoon. Flowers bloom everywhere, bordering fresh green lawns that have been laid down in the last couple of weeks. Theresienstadt's streets are clean. The town smells like springtime. The buildings gleam with new yellow paint. Though the Beautification has a long way to go, the Red Cross visitors could almost be fooled right now, Natalie dully thinks, as she squints into the sinking sun dead ahead in the street; fooled, that is, if they would not enter the barracks, or if they would not inquire about the railroad spur into the town, or about the mortality rates.

She gets into the long line outside the Hamburg barracks, holding tight to Louis, pushing her suitcases forward with a foot. Across the street under the terminal shed stands the black locomotive. At the courtyard entrance, under the eyes of SS men, Transport Commission Jews at raw lumber tables are officiously checking in the transportees—asking questions, calling out names and numbers, slamming papers with rubber stamps, all with the worn-down irritability of emigration inspectors at any border.

Natalie's turn comes. The official who takes her papers is a small man wearing a red cloth cap. He shouts at her in German, stamps the papers, and scrawls notes. He collects her cards, and bawls the numbers over his shoulder. A man with a three-day stubble brings him two cardboard signs looped with string. The numbers of Natalie's gray cards are painted on the signs in huge black digits. Natalie hangs a number around her neck, and the other on Louis.

At the SS headquarters, Aaron Jastrow stands hat in hand outside the commander's office, the adjutant having ordered him to wait in the hall. Uniformed Germans pass him without a glance. A Jew Elder sum-

moned to Sturmbannführer Rahm's office is no uncommon sight, especially during the Beautification push. Fear weakens the old man's knees,
yet he does not dare lean against the wall. A Jew in a lounging attitude
in the presence of Germans invites a fist or a club, Beautification or no.
The wariness is soaked into his bones. With great effort, he holds himself stiffly straight.

The fear was worst when he made the decision back at the apartment. His hand trembled so, when he cut into the shoe, that at first try
the knife slipped and gashed his left thumb, which still oozes blood
through the rag he has tied over it. That, happily, Natalie did not notice
in her stunned state, though she did see him sever the stitches. But the
decision once taken, he has mastered the fear enough to go ahead. The
rest is in God's hands. The time for the ultimate gamble is upon him.
The Allies will land; if not in May, then in June or July. On all fronts
the Germans are losing. The war may end quite suddenly. Natalie and
Louis must not go in this transport.

"*Doron, t'fila, milkhama!*"

Over and over Aaron Jastrow keeps muttering these three Hebrew
words. They give him courage. "*Doron, t'fila, milkhama!*" He remembers them from a childhood Bible lesson about Jacob and Esau.
After a twenty-year separation, the brothers are about to meet, and
Jacob hears that Esau is coming with four hundred armed men. Jacob
sends ahead huge gifts, whole herds of cattle, donkeys, and camels; he
arrays his caravan for combat; and he implores God for help. Rashi
comments, "The three ways to prepare for the foe: tribute, prayer, and
battle—*doron, t'fila, milkhama.*"

Jastrow has prayed. He has brought costly tribute with him. And if
he must, he is ready to fight.

The adjutant, a big pink-faced Austrian who cannot be twenty-five,
yet whose Sam Browne belt strains his green-clad paunch into two rolls,
opens the office door. "All right, you. Get in here."

Jastrow walks through the anteroom, and through the open door to
Rahm's office, where the scowling commander sits writing at his desk.
Behind Jastrow, the adjutant shuts the door. Rahm does not look up.
His pen scratches and scratches. Jastrow has a bad urge to urinate. He
has never been in this office before. The big pictures of Hitler and
Himmler, the swastika flag, the double lightning-flash insignia of the
SS, blown up on the wall in a large silver and black wall medallion, all
unnerve him. In almost any other circumstances he would beg the use
of a bathroom, but he dare not open his mouth.

"What the devil do you want?" Rahm all at once shouts, glaring up
at him and going red in the face.

"*Herr Kommandant,* may I respectfully—"

"Respectfully what? You think I don't know why you're here? Say one word on behalf of that Jew-whore niece of yours, and you'll be thrown out of here covered with blood! You understand? You think because you're a shitty Elder you can barge into these headquarters, to beg for a Jewish sow who plotted treason against the German government?"

This is Rahm's way. He has a fulminating temper and at such moments he can be very dangerous. Jastrow is near collapse. Pounding the desk, rising to his feet, Rahm screams at him, "WELL, JEW? You asked to see the commander, *ja?* I give you two minutes, and if you mention that cunt of a niece even once, I'll knock your teeth down your swinish throat! TALK."

In low tones, Jastrow gasps out, "I have committed a serious crime, which I want to confess to you."

"What? What? A crime?" The choleric face distorts in a look of puzzlement.

Jastrow pulls from his pocket a small velvety yellow pouch. With a violently shaking hand, he lays it on the desk before the commander. Glaring from him to the pouch, Rahm picks it up, and empties out on the desk six sparkling stones.

"I bought them in Rome, *Herr Kommandant,* in 1940, for twenty-five thousand dollars. I lived in Italy then. In Siena." Jastrow's voice slightly firms as he talks. "When Mussolini entered the war, I took the precaution of putting money into diamonds. As a *Prominent,* I was not searched on arrival in Theresienstadt. Regulations required the turning in of my jewelry. I know that. I regret this very serious offense, and I have come to make a clean breast of it."

Rahm sits down in his chair, contemplating the diamonds with a sour grin.

"I thought I had better turn them in directly to the *Herr Kommandant,*" Jastrow adds, "because of their value."

After a long, cynical stare at Jastrow, Rahm abruptly laughs. "Value! Probably you bought them from a Jew swindler, and they're glass."

"I bought them at Bulgari, *Herr Kommandant.* No doubt you have heard of the finest jeweler in Italy. The trademark is on the pouch."

Rahm does not look at the pouch. He brushes the stones aside with the back of his hand, and they scatter on his blotter.

"Where did you keep them hidden?"

"In my shoe."

"Ha! An old Jew trick. How much more have you got hidden away?"

Rahm's tone is conversationally sarcastic. This is his way, too. Once his rage blows over, one can talk to him. Eppstein says, *"Rahm barks more than he bites."* However, he does bite. There lies the bribe on the desk. Rahm is not taking it. Jastrow's fate is in the balance now.

"I have nothing more."

"If your balls got twisted in the Little Fortress, you might remember something you overlooked."

"There is nothing else, *Herr Kommandant.*" Jastrow is convulsed with shivers; but his reply is persuasive in its steady tone.

One by one Rahm picks up the diamonds and holds them to the light. "Twenty-five thousand dollars? You were swindled blind, wherever you got them. I know cut stones. These are shit."

"I had them appraised in Milan, a year later, for forty thousand, *Herr Kommandant.*" Jastrow is here putting in a beautification touch of his own. Rahm's eyebrows lift.

"And your whore of a niece knows all about the stones, naturally."

"I never told her. It was wiser so. Nobody in the world knows of them, *Herr Kommandant,* but you and me."

Sturmbannführer Rahm's bloodshot eyes bore at Jastrow for long seconds. He drops the stones into the pouch, the pouch into a pocket. "Well, the whore and her bastard go in the transport."

"Herr Kommandant, there was an excess of summonses, I understand, and many will be cancelled."

Obstinately Rahm shakes his head. "She goes. She's lucky not to get sent to the Little Fortress and shot. Now clear out of here." He takes a pen and resumes writing.

Yet the *doron* has had some slight effect. The dismissal is curt but not fierce. Aaron Jastrow now has to make a quick judgment at highest hazard. Of course Rahm cannot acknowledge that the bribe has worked. But will he in fact see to it that Natalie does not go?

"I said, get your shitty ass out of here," snaps Rahm.

Jastrow decides to wield his pitiful weapon.

"Herr Kommandant, if my niece is transported, I must tell you I will resign as Elder. I will resign from the library. I will take no part in the Beautification. I will not talk to the Red Cross visitors in my apartment. Nothing will force me to change my mind." In nervous rapid-fire, he blurts out these rehearsed sentences.

The audacity catches Rahm by surprise. The pen drops. A horrible ferocity rumbles in his voice. "You are interested in committing suicide, Jew? Right away?"

More rehearsed sentences tumble out. *"Herr Kommandant,* Obersturmbannführer Eichmann went to great trouble to bring me from

Paris to Theresienstadt. I make good window dressing! My picture has been taken by German journalists. My books are published in Denmark. The Red Cross visitors will be very interested to meet me, and—"

"Shut your dribbling asshole," Rahm says in an oddly unemotional way, "and get out of here this instant, if you want to live."

"*Herr Kommandant,* I don't value my life much. I'm old and not well. Kill me, and you'll have to explain to Herr Eichmann what became of his window dressing. Torture me, and if I survive, what impression can I make on the Red Cross? If you cancel my niece's summons, I guarantee our cooperation when the Red Cross comes. I guarantee she will do no more foolish things."

Rahm presses a buzzer and picks up his pen. The adjutant opens the door. At Rahm's murderous glare and dismissive gesture with his pen, Jastrow rushes out.

The square in front of the HQ is a mass of blossoming trees. As Jastrow emerges on the street, the sweet smell fills his nostrils. The band is playing the evening concert; at the moment, a waltz from *Die Fledermaus.* The moon hangs red and low over the trees. Jastrow staggers to the outdoor café, where Jews may sit and drink black water. As an Elder he can walk past the queue of waiting customers. He falls in a chair, and buries his face in his hands in exhausted relief. He is alive and unhurt. What he has accomplished he does not know, but he has done his all.

Searchlights blaze down on the lawn from the roof of the Hamburg barracks. Blinded, frightened, Natalie snatches up her sleeping son. He whimpers.

"*On your feet! Form a queue by threes!*" Ghetto guards are stalking the lawn and yelling. "*Everybody out of the barracks! Into the courtyard! Queue up! Hurry up! On your feet! Line up by threes!*"

Transportees swarm into the courtyard, hastily pulling on clothes. These are the foresighted ones who have reported in early to grab bunks, knowing the SS has cleared the barracks for use as an assembly center. The two thousand or more Jews who lived there are gone, staying wherever they can.

Word sweeps among the transportees, "*Exemptions!*" What else can be happening but that? Everybody knows by now about the excessive summonses. The Elders, led by Eppstein himself, are trooping into the courtyard, as guards set up two tables on the cleared grass. Transport officials sit down with their stacks of cards and papers, their wire baskets, their rubber stamps. Commander Rahm arrives, swinging a swagger stick.

The line of three thousand Jews commences a shuffling march around the yard before Rahm. He points his stick to exempt this one and that. The freed ones go to a corner of the yard. Sometimes Rahm consults the Elders, otherwise he simply picks handsome men and pretty women. The entire line passes in review, and starts around again. It takes a long time. Louis's legs give out, and Natalie has to sling him on her back, for she is dragging the suitcases, too. As she comes around again, she sees Aaron Jastrow address Rahm. The commander menaces him with the stick and turns his back on him. The march goes on and on under the floodlights.

Suddenly, tumult and confusion!

The guards shout, "Halt!" Sturmbannführer Rahm is bellowing obscenities and swinging his stick at squirming, dodging transport officials. There has been some kind of miscount. A long delay ensues. Whether Rahm is drunk, or the Jews at the tables are incompetent or terrorized, this botch with people's lives has now gone on past midnight. At last the line starts moving again. Natalie trudges in a hopeless daze, following the back of a limping old lady in a ragged coat with a black feathery collar, the same back that she has been trailing for hours. A rough tug at her elbow all at once spins her stumbling out of line. "What's the matter with you, you stupid bitch?" mutters a whiskered guard. Commander Rahm is pointing his stick at her, with a sneering expression.

The floodlights go out. The commander, the Elders, the transport officials leave. The exempted Jews are trooped off into a separate bunk room. A transport official, the same redheaded man who distributed summonses, tells them that they are now "the reserve." The commander is very angry about the bungled count. There will be another tally tomorrow when the train loads up. Till then they are confined to this room. Natalie spends a hideous sleepless night with Louis slumbering in her arms.

Next day the official returns with a typewritten list, and calls out fifty names to proceed to the train. The list is not alphabetical, so until the last name is read off, the tension on the listening faces deepens. Natalie is not called. The fifty unfortunates pick up their suitcases and go out. Another long wait; then Natalie hears the wail of the train whistle, the chuffing of the locomotive, and the clank of moving cars.

The redheaded man looks into the room and shouts, "Pile your numbers on the table and get out of here. Go back to your barracks."

Sick at heart as she is about the people on the train, especially those with whom she spent the night, taking Louis's number off his neck gives Natalie the greatest joy of her life.

Aaron Jastrow waits outside the barracks entrance amid a crowd of relatives and friends. The reunions all about them are subdued. He only nods to her. "I'll take the suitcases."

"No, just pick up Louis, he's exhausted." She lowers her voice. "And for God's sake, let us get in touch with Berel."

At the mica factory about noon, a few days later, a ghetto guard comes to Natalie and tells her to report to SS headquarters at eight in the morning with her child. When the workday ends, she runs all the way to the Seestrasse apartment. Aaron is there, murmuring over the Talmud. The news does not seem to upset him. Probably she is due for a warning, he says. The SS knows, after all, about the scheme to alert the Red Cross, and she is the only one of the group left in the ghetto. She must be humble and contrite, and she must promise to cooperate from now on. That is undoubtedly all the Germans want of her.

"But why Louis? Why must I bring him?"

"You brought him there last time. The adjutant probably remembers that. Try not to worry. Keep your spirits up. That's crucial."

"Have you heard from Berel yet?"

Jastrow shakes his head. "They say it may take a week or more."

Natalie does not close her eyes that night, either. When the windows turn gray she gets up, feeling very ill, puts on the gray suit, and does her best with her hair, and with touches of color from her dry old rouge pot, to look presentable.

"All will be well," Jastrow says, as she is about to go. He looks ill himself, for all his reassuring smiles. They do something unusual for them; they kiss.

She hurries to the children's house, and dresses and feeds Louis. As the clock on the church strikes eight, she enters SS headquarters. The bored-looking SS man at the desk by the door nods when she gives her name. "Follow me." They go down the hall, descend a long staircase, and walk through another gloomier hall. Louis, in his mother's arms, is looking around with bright-eyed curiosity, holding a tin soldier. The SS man halts at a wooden door. "In here. Wait." He shuts the door on Natalie. It is a windowless whitewashed room, with a cellar smell, lit by a bulb in a wire mesh. The walls are stone, the floor cement. There are three wooden chairs against a wall, and in a corner a mop and a pail full of water.

Natalie sits on a chair, holding Louis on her lap. A long time goes by. She cannot tell how long. Louis prattles to the tin soldier.

The door opens. Natalie gets to her feet. Commander Rahm comes in, followed by Inspector Haindl, who closes the door. Rahm is in black dress uniform; Haindl wears the usual gray-green. Rahm walks up to her and roars in her face, "SO, YOU'RE THE JEWISH WHORE WHO PLOTTED AGAINST THE GERMAN GOVERNMENT! YES?"

Natalie's throat clamps shut. She opens her mouth, tries to talk, but no sounds come.

"ARE YOU OR AREN'T YOU?" Rahm bellows.

"I—I—" Low hoarse gasps.

Rahm says to Haindl, "Take the shitty little bastard from her."

The inspector pulls Louis from Natalie's arms. She is losing any belief that this is really happening, but Louis's wail forces hoarse words out of her throat. "I was insane, I was misled, I will cooperate, don't hurt my baby—"

"Don't hurt him? He's GONE, you dirty cunt, don't you realize that?" Rahm gestures at the mop and the pail of water. "That's for cleaning up the bloody garbage he'll be in ONE MINUTE. You'll do that yourself. You thought you got away with it, did you?"

Haindl, a squat burly man, turns Louis upside down, holding one leg in each hairy hand. The boy's jacket hangs around his face. The tin soldier clinks to the floor. He utters muffled cries.

"He is DEAD," shouts Rahm at her. "Go ahead, Haindl, get it over with. Rip him in half."

Natalie shrieks, and rushes toward Haindl, but she trips and falls to the cement. She raises up on her hands and knees. "Don't kill him! I'll do anything. *Just don't kill him!*"

Rahm, with a laugh, points his stick at Haindl, who is holding the wailing child upside down still. "You'll do anything? Fine, let's see you suck the inspector's cock."

It does not shock her. Natalie is nothing but a crazed animal now, trying to protect a baby animal. "Yes, yes, all right, I will."

Haindl takes both of Louis's ankles in one hand, holding the whimpering boy head down like a fowl. Unbuttoning, he pulls out a small penis in a bush of hair. On her hands and knees, Natalie crawls to him. The exposed penis is limp and shrunken. Odious and unspeakable as all this would be if she were sane and conscious, Natalie only knows that if she takes that object in her mouth her child may not be hurt. Haindl backs away from her as she crawls. Both men are laughing. "Look, she really wants it, *Herr Kommandant*," he says.

Rahm guffaws. "Oh, all these Jewesses are cocksuckers at heart. Go ahead, let her have her fun. German cocks is what they want most."

Haindl halts. Natalie crawls to his feet and raises her mouth to do the horrible thing.

Haindl lifts a boot, puts it in her face, and pushes her tumbling backward on the floor. Her head hits the cement hard. She sees zigzag lights. "GET away from me. Think I'd let your Jewish shit-mouth dirty my cock?" He stands over Natalie, spits down at her face, and drops Louis on her stomach. "Go suck off your uncle, the Talmud rabbi."

She sits up, clutching at the child, pulling the jacket away from his purpled face. He is gasping, his eyes are red and staring, and he has vomited.

"Get to your feet," says Rahm.

Natalie obeys.

"Now LISTEN, Jew-sow. When the Red Cross comes, YOU will be the guide for the children's department. You will make the finest impression on them. They will write you up in their report, you will be such a happy American Jewess. The children's pavilion will be your pride and joy. *Ja?*"

"Of course. Of course. Yes."

"After the Red Cross goes, if you've misbehaved in any way, you'll come straight here with your brat. Haindl will tear him in half like a wet rag before your eyes. You'll clean up the bloody crap with your own hands and take it to the crematorium. Then you'll go to the hut of the POW road gang. Two hundred stinking Ukrainians will fuck you by turn for a week. If your whore's carcass survives, you'll go to the Little Fortress to be shot. Understand, cunt?"

"I will do everything you say. I'll make a wonderful impression."

"All right. And one word about any of this, to your uncle or anybody else, and you're *kaputt!*" He shoves his face directly into her spittle-wet face, and howls with a corpse-smelling breath, so loud that her ears ring, "DO YOU BELIEVE ME?"

"I do! I do!"

"Get her out of here."

The inspector pulls her by the arm out of the room, up the stairs, along the hall, and shoves her, with the inert child in her arms, out into the square glorious with spring blossoms. The band is playing the morning concert, selections from *Faust*.

Jastrow is waiting when she returns. The child, his face still smeared with vomit, looks stunned. Natalie's face sickens Jastrow; the eyes are round and white-rimmed, the skin dirty green, the expression one of deathbed fright.

"Well?" he says.

"It was a warning. I'm all right. I must change my clothes and go to work."

He is still there a half hour later, when she comes out in her threadbare brown dress with the child, who is washed and seems better. Her face is dead gray but the hellish look has faded. "Why aren't you at the library?"

"I wanted to tell you that word has come from Berel."

"Yes?" She grasps at his shoulder, her eyes wild.

"They'll try."

*   *   *

82

$\mathfrak{Finis\ Germaniae}$

(from *World Holocaust* by Armin von Roon)

TRANSLATOR'S NOTE: Roon treats the Normandy landings and the Soviet attack in June as a combined operation. This is valid only in a very general sense. At Tehran the Grand Alliance did agree to strike at Germany simultaneously from east and west. But the Russians did not know our operational plans, nor we theirs. Once we landed it was touch and go for two weeks whether Stalin would actually keep his word and attack.

This chapter combines passages from Roon's strategic essay and his concluding memoir about Hitler.—V.H.

In June 1944, the iron jaws of the vise forged at Tehran began to close. The German nation, the last bastion of Christian culture and decency in middle Europe, was assailed from west and east by the long-plotted double onslaught of plutocratic imperialism and Slav communism.

In Western writings, the Normandy landings and the Russian assault still pass as a triumph for "humanity." But serious historians are beginning to penetrate the smokescreen of wartime propaganda. At Tehran, Franklin D. Roosevelt delivered eastern Europe into Red claws. His motive? To destroy Germany, the strongest rival on earth to American monopoly capital. England was already skinned like a rabbit, in Hitler's colorful phrase, by her overstrained war-making, and by Roosevelt's wily anticolonialism. Brave Japan was sinking to her knees in the unequal contest with von Nimitz's ever-swelling fleets. Only Germany still blocked the way to the world hegemony of the dollar.

It is a shallow commonplace that Roosevelt was "outsmarted" at the later conference in Yalta and gave away too much to Stalin. In fact, he had already given everything away at Tehran. Once he pledged the assault on

France, he made the Red Asian sweep into the heart of Europe inevitable. To assure this, he flooded Lend-Lease to the Soviet Union. The figures still beggar the imagination: some four hundred thousand motor vehicles, two thousand locomotives, eleven thousand railway cars, seven thousand tanks, and more than six thousand self-propelled guns and half-tracks, with the two million seven hundred thousand tons of petroleum and other products required to put the primitive Slav horde on wheels; to say nothing of fifteen thousand aircraft, and millions of tons of food, together with raw materials, factories, munitions, and technical equipment beyond calculation.

The picture of Roosevelt as a naïve outwitted humanitarian in his dealings with Stalin was his greatest propaganda swindle. These two icy butchers thoroughly understood each other; they just struck dissimilar poses for domestic consumption and for history. Of the two, Roosevelt always had the upper hand, because Soviet Russia was half-devastated and in desperate straits, while America was rich, strong, and untouched. Stalin had no choice but to sacrifice millions of Russian lives to clear the way for world rule by American monopolists. He did explore the possibility of making peace with us on reasonable terms, in very secret parleys that we at Headquarters knew nothing about at the time; but here Roosevelt's Lend-Lease "generosity" frustrated us. Naturally Hitler was not prepared to yield all our gains. Given all that matériel, Stalin decided he would do better by fighting on, at the cost of rivers of German and Russian blood.

The quarrelsome and impoverished lands of eastern Europe were Roosevelt's sop to Stalin for his country's terrible sacrifices. Roosevelt's policy was simply to let them fall to the Russians. Of course, the treacherous Balkans were a dubious prey. The Soviets already belch with indigestion from those swallowed but intransigent nationalities. The strategic importance of that turbulent peninsula is not what it was in past centuries, or even to us in 1944 as a conduit for Turkish chrome. But even so, to invite Slav communism to march to the Elbe and the Danube was monstrous. Churchill's itch to funnel the main Allied thrust into the Balkans at least showed some political sensitivity, and some sense of responsibility for middle Europe and for Christian civilization. His blood was not as cold as Roosevelt's. Roosevelt cared nothing for the Balkans or for Poland; though in a strange moment of candor he told Stalin at Tehran that he had to make some sort of fuss about Poland's future, because of the large Polish vote in the election he faced.

Clash of the Warlords

Franklin Roosevelt took a great risk with the Normandy landings. This is not well-known. When one weighs the opposing forces, the elements of space and time, and the sea–land transfer problem, one sees that Churchill's foot-dragging made sense. The landings were very chancy and might have ended disastrously. A pyramiding of mistakes and bad luck on our side gave Roosevelt success in his one audacious military move.

Eisenhower himself knew the riskiness of Overlord. Even as his five thousand vessels were steaming toward the Normandy coast in the stormy night, he drafted an announcement of the operation's failure, which by chance has been preserved: *"Our landings in the Cherbourg–Havre area have failed to gain a satisfactory foothold and I have withdrawn the troops. My decision to attack at this time and place was based upon the best information available. The troops, the air, and the Navy did all that bravery and devotion to duty could do. If any blame or fault attaches to the attempt it is mine alone."*

That this document did not become the official Allied communiqué was due to several factors, chiefly:

a. Our abominable intelligence;
b. Our confused and sluggish response to the attack in the first decisive hours;
c. Unbelievable botching by Adolf Hitler;
d. Failure of the Luftwaffe to cope with Allied air superiority.

The mounting of the invasion armada was certainly a fine technological achievement; as was the production of the huge air fleets, with crews to man them. General Marshall's raising, equipping, and training of the land armies that poured into Normandy showed him to be an American Scharnhorst. The U.S. infantryman, while requiring far too luxurious logistical support, put up a nice fight in France; he was fresh, well fed, and unscarred by battle. The British Tommy under Montgomery, though slow-moving as usual, showed bulldog courage. But essentially what happened in Normandy was that Franklin Roosevelt beat Adolf Hitler, as surely as Wellington beat Napoleon at Waterloo. In Normandy the two men at last clashed in head-on armed shock. Hitler's mistakes gave Roosevelt the victory; just as at Waterloo it was less Wellington who won than Napoleon who lost.

The core of Franklin Roosevelt's malignant military genius lay in these simple rules: to pick generals and admirals with care; to leave strategy and tactics to them, and attend only to the politics of the war; never to interfere in operations; never to relieve leaders who encountered honorable reverses; and to allow all the glory to those who won victories. When Roosevelt died, his supreme command in the field was virtually the original team. This steadiness paid dividends. Shake-ups in military command can cost much momentum, élan, and fighting effectiveness. The shuffling of generals by Hitler was our plague.

For the Führer had arrogated supreme operational command to himself, and we were suffering bad reverses. He could never admit that he was responsible for any setback. Hence, heads had to keep rolling. Ambitious rising commanders abounded, eager to plunge in where their elders had been sacked for Hitler's failures. I watched these temporary Führer favorites come and go, taking over with zest, only to be worn down by Hitler's meddling and at last fired for his bad moves; likely as not to kill themselves or die of heart failure. It was a sad business, and absurd war-making.

The Normandy Landings

Three questions governed the invasion problem, on which the fate of our nation hung:

1. Where will they land?
2. When will they land?
3. Where do we fight them?

By all military logic, the place for the Anglo-Americans to land was the Pas de Calais, opposite Dover. It offered the shortest route to the Ruhr, our nation's industrial heart. The Channel is there at its narrowest. Waterborne troops are all but helpless, and common sense demands getting them ashore the quickest way. The turnaround time for ships and for air support would have been shortest on the Dover-Calais axis. The Normandy coast, where the enemy struck, was a much longer pull by sea and air.

By preparing so well for invasion at the Pas de Calais, we set our minds in one groove, and gave the foe the chance to spring a surprise. Hitler somehow guessed that Normandy might be the place. At one staff meeting he literally put his finger on the map and said, "They will be landing here," with what we used to call his undeniable *coup d'oeil*. But he made many such guesses during the war, as often as not extremely wild. Of course he remembered only the ones that turned out right, and made a great noise about them. Rommel, charged with repelling the invasion, also became concerned about Normandy. So, very late, we hardened up those beaches, and augmented the armed forces poised there; and we could have crushed the landings despite the surprise, except for the unspeakable manner in which the first day was bungled.

The chief British planner of the landings, General Morgan, has written: "One hopes and plans for battle as far inland from the beach as may be, *for if the invasion battle takes place on the beach, one is already defeated.*" I confess that we of the OKW staff erred on this. We agreed with Rundstedt that the mobile reserve should lie in wait far enough inland to avoid the naval and close air bombardment; and that once Eisenhower was ashore and moving inland in force, we should attack and wipe out the whole enterprise, as we had repeatedly bagged Russian armies. It was an "eastern front" mentality. Rommel knew better. In North Africa he had tried to fight a war of maneuver against an enemy controlling the air. We were between the devil and the deep, and the only time to stop the Normandy invasion was when the enemy was floundering ashore under our guns. Rommel fortified the so-called Atlantic Wall and made all his plans on that principle. Had we fought D-day as he planned it, we might have won and turned the war around.

TRANSLATOR'S NOTE: *Roon gives no credit to the superb deception tactics, mainly British, that encouraged the Germans in their wishful "logic" about where we would land. An enormous effort was laid on: air attacks and naval bombardment of the Pas de Calais exceeding those in Normandy, aerial bombing of the railroads and highways leading to it, vast arrays of dummy landing craft and fake army hutments near Dover, and a variety of still-secret intelligence tricks. The Germans were not very imaginative. They swallowed all hints confirming their clever judgment that we were coming to the Pas de Calais.—V.H.*

What Went Wrong—Preparations

We German generals are sometimes accused of blaming Hitler, the dead politician, for losing the war it was our job to win. Still, the defeat in France was Hitler's work. He fumbled the one slender chance we had. This fact cannot be blinked in a professional analysis.

His *fundamental* estimate was not bad. As far back as November he issued his famous Directive Number 51 for shifting strength to the west. Quite properly he pointed out that we could trade space for time in the east, whereas an enemy lodgment in France would have immediate "staggering" implications; the Ruhr, our war-making arsenal, would come within enemy reach. The directive was sober, its program realistic. If only he had followed through on it! But from January to June he dithered and waffled, actually draining western forces into three other theatres: the occupation of Hungary, the eastern front, and the Allied front south of Rome. Also, he froze large forces in Norway, the Balkans, Denmark, and the south of France to ward off possible landings, instead of massing all these near the Channel coast.

Certainly he was under pressure. Europe's three thousand miles of coastline lay exposed to assault. In the east the Russians were fighting on, in Hitler's phrase, like "swamp animals"; freeing Leningrad, recapturing the Crimea, and threatening our whole southern flank. Partisan activity was making all Europe restive. The satellite politicians were wavering. In Italy the enemy kept crawling up the boot. The barbarous Allied air bombings were intensifying in size and accuracy, and for all Göring's loud mouth, his battered Luftwaffe was tied down in the east and over our factory cities. Like England in 1940, we were stretched too thin with diminishing troops, arms, and resources. The tables had turned, and there was no untouched ally beyond the seas to pull our chestnuts out of the fire.

At such times a great leader should supply the steadying hand. If Directive Number 51 was correct, Hitler's course was clear:

1. Firm up political faltering with victory, not with wasteful armed occupation as in Hungary and Italy;
2. Withdraw in Italy to the easily defended line of the Alps and Apennines, and send the released divisions into France;
3. Slow the enemy in the east with elastic harrying tactics, instead of rigid costly stands for prestige;
4. Leave skeleton forces in unlikely invasion areas, and gamble all strength at the Channel.

That is how von Nimitz and Spruance won the Battle of Midway against odds; by accepting great risks to concentrate at the decisive point. This principle of warfare is eternal. But Hitler's nervousness precluded adhering to principle. Obstinate he was, but not firm.

His much-vaunted "Atlantic Wall" along the Channel was ill-conceived. In his solitary wisdom he decided that the invasion forces would head for a major port. A million and a half tons of concrete and countless man-hours went into pillboxes and heavy gun emplacements, designed by the supreme genius himself, that bristled around the main French harbors. Rommel presciently ordered the open beaches fortified too: belts of mines on land, in the sea, underwater obstacles to tear up and blast approaching vessels, sharpened stakes in areas behind the beaches to destroy gliders, myriads of more pillboxes and gun emplacements along the shore.

But lack of manpower hampered this new effort, because of the excavating of grandiose bomb-proof caverns for aircraft factories, and the repair of bomb damage in our cities. Compared to INVASION, how important were such things? Yet Hitler did not back up Rommel's supplementary Atlantic Wall orders, and the "Wall" remained largely a propaganda phantom. One instance suffices. Rommel ordered fifty million mines planted in the glider areas behind the beaches. Had he been obeyed the airborne landings would have failed, but not even ten percent of the mining was done, and they succeeded.

On paper we had a force of about sixty divisions to defend France; but the static divisions strung along the coast consisted mainly of substandard troops scraped from the bottom of the barrel. Some attack infantry divisions were scattered here and there, but with the ten motorized and armored divisions lay our hope. Five of these, stationed not far from the Channel coast, could strike at either the Pas de Calais or Normandy. Rommel intended to annihilate on the beaches the first wave arriving in landing craft; actually, as it turned out, only five divisions in all. He therefore pleaded for operational control of the panzers.

In vain. Rundstedt, the overall *Ob West*, advocated hitting the invaders after they were well-lodged. Dithering between the two tactical concepts, Hitler came down on neither side. He issued orders dividing the panzers among three different commands; and *he reserved to himself, six hundred miles away in Berchtesgaden, operational control of the four panzer divisions nearest the Normandy beaches.* This decision was a grievous one. It tied Rommel's hands, when all depended on a quick free-swinging punch. But the invasion found the German command in such a state of chaos that it is hard to say which omission, which mistake, which folly, brought *finis Germaniae.* Invasion day was a cataract of omissions, mistakes, and follies.

What Went Wrong—D-day

The overwhelming failure was the Pas de Calais mistake. That we lacked agents in England to ferret out a "secret" involving two million men; that deception measures took us in, and that our reconnaissance could not pinpoint the direction of an attack organized a few score miles away in plain sight; there is a bitter mystery!

We failed to discern that they would land at low tide. Our guns bore on the high-tide line; the thought was, why should they elect to slog across eight hundred additional yards of mushy sand under fire? They did. Eisenhower's shock troops came in when our formidable underwater obstacles were exposed for swift clearing by sappers, and his troops made it across the sand.

We abjectly failed on the question, *When?* As the enemy armada was crossing the Channel, Erwin Rommel was visiting his wife in Germany! A near-gale was blowing on the fifth of June, predicted to last three days. This bad weather lulled Rommel and everyone else. Eisenhower had meteorological intelligence showing a marginal break in the weather. He risked a go-ahead. The scattered airborne descents in the wee hours of the morning somehow did not alarm us. Not till our soldiers in the Normandy pillboxes saw with their naked eyes the monstrous apparition of Overlord—thousands and thousands of vessels, approaching in the misty gray dawn—did we go on battle alert.

Actually we had one intelligence break which was pooh-poohed. Our informers in the French Resistance had obtained the BBC signals that would call for D-day sabotage. Our monitoring posts heard these signals. All operational commands received the warning. In our Supreme Headquarters the report went to Jodl, who thought nothing of it. Later I heard that Rundstedt, laughing off the alarm, remarked, "As though Eisenhower would announce the invasion on the BBC!" This was the general attitude.

* * *

My Trip to the Front

(from "Hitler as Military Leader")

. . . It seemed that Hitler would never wake up that morning. Repeatedly I telephoned Jodl to rouse him, for Rundstedt was demanding the release of the panzers. Obviously the Normandy attack was serious! Jodl put off Rundstedt, a decision for which historians now excoriate him. Yet when Hitler did see Jodl at about ten o'clock, after a leisurely private breakfast, he quite approved denying Rundstedt's frantic requests.

The Berchtesgaden command situation was absurd. Hitler was up at his mountain eyrie, Jodl in the "Little Chancellery," and operational headquarters were in a barracks at the other end of town. We were never off the telephone. Rommel was out of touch, returning to the front; Rundstedt in Paris, and Rommel's chief of staff, Speidel, at the coast, and the panzer general, Geyr, were all scorching the telephone lines and teleprinters to Berchtesgaden. The midday briefing conference was scheduled for Klessheim Castle, a charming spot about an hour out of town, in honor of some Hungarian visitors of state. It never occurred to Hitler to call this off. No, the staff had to motor out there to meet him in a small map room, where he rehearsed the "show" briefing for the visitors; then we had to hang around for the briefing, while our troops were dying under Allied bombs and naval shelling, and enemy lodgments were expanding by the hour.

I can still see the Führer bouncing into that map room about noon, his bloated pasty face wreathed in smiles, his mustache aquiver, greeting the staff with some such remark as, "Well, here we go, eh? Now we've got them where we can hit them! Over in England they were safe." He showed no concern whatever over the grave reports. This landing was all a fake that we had anticipated long ago. We weren't fooled! We were all ready for them at the Pas de Calais. This feint would turn into another bloody Dieppe fiasco for them. Splendid!

So he also declaimed in the large briefing chamber, with its soft arm-chairs and impressive war maps. He bombarded the Hungarians with disgusting boasts about the strength of our forces in France, the superiority of our armaments, our miraculous "new weapons" soon to be launched, the greenness of the U.S. army, etc. etc. etc. He pooh-poohed the fall of Rome two days earlier, even making a coarse joke about his relief at turning over a million and a half Italians, syphilitic whores and all, for the Americans to feed. What the obsequious Hungarians thought of all this, nobody could tell. To me, Hitler was convincing only himself, talking his daydreams aloud. As soon as this charade was over, I requested permission to go to Normandy. Not only did the unpredictable Führer agree, he waived the rule against airplane travel by senior officers. I could fly as far as Paris, and find out what was going on.

When my plane circled down several hours later over the swastika fluttering on the Eiffel Tower, I couldn't help thinking, *How long will it fly there?* In Rundstedt's situation room everything was at sixes and sevens. Hitler had meantime released one panzer division, and a staff argument was raging about where to use it. Junior officers rushed about in a din of teleprinters and shouting. The battle map bristled with little emblems of ships and parachute-drops. Red infantry markers delineated a fifty-mile front in surprising depth, except in one spot where we had the Americans pinned down at the waterline.

Rundstedt appeared calm enough, and as usual bandbox-neat, but weary, thin, and pessimistic. He did not act at all like the *Ob West;* rather, like an old man with worries but no power. He tried to argue that I should not risk capture by paratroopers, but he was half-hearted about that, too. He still believed this was a diversion in force. But throwing the invaders back into the sea would buck up the Fatherland and give the enemy pause, so it had to be done.

Next morning the beautiful French landscape, with its fat cows and drudging peasants, was strangely quiet. The young aide of Rundstedt's who was riding with me had to order the chauffeur to detour time and again around knocked-out bridges. The damage from the weeks of methodical Allied air bombings was manifest: devastated railroad yards, smashed trestles, burned-out trains and terminals, overturned locomotives, Churchill's "railway desert" with a vengeance. Tactically the ground was a blotch of islands, rather than a terrain suited to overland supply. No wonder; *fifteen thousand enemy air sorties on D-day alone,* with virtually no opposition! So the postwar records show.

Passing through Saint-Lô, I fell in with trucks carrying our paratroopers toward Carentan. I took the major into my car. French saboteurs had cut his telephone lines, he said, and he had been out of touch on invasion day, but late at night had gotten through to his general. His mission now was to counterattack the thin American beachhead east of Varreville.

The strange bucolic quiet persisted as we neared the coast. The major and I climbed the steeple of a village church to have a look around. A stunning panorama greeted us: the Channel dotted with enemy ships from horizon to horizon, and boats like a million water-insects swarming between the shore and the vessels. Through field glasses a colossal and quite peaceful operation was visible on the beach. Landing craft were lined up hull to hull as far as one could see, disgorging men, supplies, and equipment. The shore was black for miles with crates, boxes, bags, machines, and soldiers doing stevedore labor, and a crawling parade of trucks heading inland.

The "Battle of France" indeed! These troops were preparing to destroy Germany, and they looked like picnickers. I heard no gunfire but a scattering of rifle shots. What a contrast to the Führer's gory boasts at Klessheim Castle about "squashing the invaders into the sand," and "meeting them with a curtain of steel and fire"!

As we drove eastward small gun duels sputtered and villages burned in the persisting quiet. Interrogating officers wherever I could, I learned the reason for the strange calm. A vast combined naval and air bombardment at dawn had poured a deluge of shot and shell on our defenses. The wounded I spoke to had horror-stricken faces. One older noncom with a smashed arm told me that he had lived through Verdun and experienced nothing like it. Everywhere I encountered fatalism, apathy, lost communications, broken-up regiments, and confusion over orders. The gigantic sea armada, the air fleets roaring overhead, and the fearful bombardments had already spread a sense of a lost war.

That a possibly fatal crisis was at hand I could no longer doubt. Speeding back to Paris I told Jodl over the telephone that this was the main assault, and that we must concentrate against it, moving at night to evade the air interdiction, and effecting transport repair on a crash basis. Jodl's response was, "Well, get back here, but I advise you to be very careful about what you say." It was unnecessary advice. I never got a hearing. At the next few briefing conferences I was not called on. Hitler pointedly avoided my eye. The Normandy situation deteriorated rapidly, and my information was soon out of date.

Two impressions remain with me of this lovely June, when our German world was crumbling while Hitler socialized over tea and cakes in Berchtesgaden. On June 19 a great storm blew up on the Normandy coast and raged for four days. It set back the invaders far more than our forces had. It broke up the artificial harbors, and threw almost a thousand vessels up on the beach. Reconnaissance photographs showed such a gigantic disaster that I felt my last flicker of hope. Hitler was in seventh heaven, reeling off giddy disquisitions on the fate of the Spanish Armada. When the weather cleared, the enemy resumed his attacks by land, sea, and air, as though a summer shower had passed by. His resources, pouring out of the unreachable U.S. cornucopia, were frightening. We heard no more about the Spanish Armada.

Stamped on my memory too is a briefing conference about the time Cherbourg was falling. Hitler was standing at the map, wearing his thick glasses, and with a compass and ruler he was gleefully showing us what a small part of France the invaders held, compared to the area we still occupied. This he was telling to senior generals who knew, and who had been warning him for weeks, that with the defensive crust at the coast smashed, and a major port gone, the rest of France was open country for enemy operations, with no tenable German position short of the West Wall at the border and the Rhine. What a sorry moment; scales fell from my eyes, and I knew once for all that the triumphant Führer had degenerated to a pathological monster, trembling for his life behind a mask of bravado.

• • •

Normandy: Summary

(from *World Holocaust*)

. . . Had Hitler accepted the suggestions of Rommel and Rundstedt late in June to end the war, we would have had to kneel down to a draconic peace. We might have ended up partitioned as we are now, we might not have; but certainly our people would have been spared a year of savage air bombings, including the gruesome horror of Dresden, and Eisenhower's ruinous march to the Elbe; and from the east, the horror of universal Bolshevik pillage and rape, which the world smiled at and overlooked, while millions of our civilians had to flee westward from their homes, never to return.

In 1918, while we stood on foreign soil, Ludendorff and Hindenburg had similarly counseled surrender, before others could inflict on German territory the ruin of war. But in 1918 there had been a political state and a military arm; and by the abdication of the Kaiser, the politicians could effect this timely surrender. Now there was no political state, no military arm; all was merged in Hitler. Politically, how could he surrender, and stretch out his neck to the hangman? He could only fight on.

Very well, what of his strategy in fighting on: was it good, or bad? It was rigid, complacent, and dull-witted. He lost Normandy. Only five divisions in the landing force! Had the panzers been freed and concentrated, then in spite of all—intelligence failure, enemy air superiority, naval bombardment—Rommel's able chief of staff, Speidel, could have unleashed them against the floundering G.I.'s and Tommies. The result would have been a historic bloodbath. At Omaha Beach, the Americans were almost thrown back into the sea by one attack infantry division, the 352nd, which happened to be operating there. What would a planned concentrated counterattack in those first hours not have achieved?

Had we smashed those five divisions, that might well have been the turning point. The Anglo-Americans were not Russians; politically and militarily they could not take such bloodletting. If all those fantastic preparations, all that outpouring of technology and treasure, could not prevent the slaughter of their landing force on that crucial first day, I believe Eisenhower, Roosevelt, and Churchill would have quailed and announced a face-saving "withdrawal." The political results would have been spectacular: the fall of Churchill, Roosevelt's defeat in the election, charges of bad faith by Stalin; even some kind of endurable separate peace in the east, who can say? But Adolf Hitler wanted to control the panzers from Berchtesgaden.

As doom closed in, Hitler clung to, and interminably mouthed, three self-comforting fantasies:

1. The breakup of the Alliance against us;
2. The turning of the tide by miraculous new weapons;
3. A sudden outpouring from the factory caverns of new jet fighters that would sweep the enemy from the skies.

For seven fatal weeks he insisted on immobilizing the Fifteenth Army at the Pas de Calais awaiting the "main invasion," because the launching platforms for his precious V-1 and V-2 rockets were there. But the rockets, when they finally flew, were minor terror weapons, causing random death and damage in London without military effect. The fighter planes came trickling out of the caverns only in 1945, much too late. As for the only new weapon that mattered, the atom bomb, Hitler had frittered away our scientific lead in atom-splitting by failing to support the project, and he had driven out the Jewish scientists who produced it for our enemies.

The breakup of the enemy coalition had indeed been our one escape hatch; but Franklin Roosevelt's supreme political stroke at Tehran had slammed it shut and sealed it. And so there burst on us from the east on June 22, three years to the day after we invaded the Soviet Union, the worst catastrophe yet, the Battle of White Russia, Stalin's assigned role in the Tehran plan.

To this grim tale I now turn.

———————

TRANSLATOR'S NOTE: *In this much-abridged compilation of Roon's views, I have tried to highlight how the Germans saw the Normandy landing, omitting much operational detail familiar from popular history and movies.*

Stalin's telegram to Churchill remains as good a summary as any of the grandeur of Overlord: "The history of war knows no other like undertaking, from the point of view of its scale, its vast conception, and its masterly execution."

The blaming of Hitler can be overdone. Even if the panzers had been released to Rommel, our forces would probably have known it. Our intelligence—from air reconnaissance, the French Resistance, and code penetration—was superb. We might have battered up the panzers from the air before they ever went into action. This is not to say that the landing was not a close thing. It was an extreme risk calculated to a cat's whisker, and it succeeded.

As for Hitler "degenerating" into a pathological monster, he never was anything else, though he had a good run in his first flush of brigandage. Why his demagogic bunkum ever spurred the Germans to their wars and their crimes remains a vastly puzzling question.

The scales did not fall from Roon's eyes. They had to be shot off.—V.H.

*   *   *

83

JEDBURGH TEAM "MAURICE"

U.S.A.:   *Leslie Slote, OSS*
French: *Dr. Jean R. Latour, FFI*
British: *Leading Aircraftsman Ira N. Thompson, RAF*

WHEN Pamela saw Slote's name in the top-secret schedule of the Jedburgh air drops, she at once decided to go and see him. She was getting desperate for some word of Victor Henry. Since sending her letter of refusal, the thought of which was making her more and more miserable as time passed, she had heard nothing. Utter silence. She found an official reason to go to Milton Hall, the stately home some sixty miles north of London where the Jedburghs trained, and she went whizzing out there next day in a jeep. At Milton Hall she quickly attended to her official business. Leslie Slote, she was told, was off on a field exercise. She left a note for him with her telephone number, and was walking disconsolately back to her jeep, when she heard from behind her, "Pamela?"

Not a hail; an uncertain call. She turned. Heavy drooping blond mustache, close-cropped hair, no insignia on the untidy brown uniform; a very different Leslie Slote, if the same man. "Hello! It is Leslie, isn't it?"

The mustache spread in Slote's old frigid grin. He came and shook her hand. "I guess I'm a bit changed. What the devil are you doing at Milton Hall, Pam? Got time for a drink?"

"I'd rather not, thanks. I have to drive forty miles. My jeep's just down in the lot."

"Is it Lady Burne-Wilke yet?"

"Well, no, he's still recuperating from an air crash in India. I'm going to Stoneford now, that's his house in Coombe Hill." She glanced curiously up at him. "So you're a Jedburgh?"

His face stiffened. "What do you know about that?"

"Sweetie, I'm in the Air Ministry section that's arranging to drop you in."

He laughed, a coarse hearty guffaw. "How much time have you got? Let's sit down and talk somewhere. Christ, it's wonderful to see an old face. Yes, I'm a Jed."

Here was an opening of sorts for Pamela.

"Victor Henry mentioned that you were in some branch of the OSS."

"Ah, yes. Seeing much of the admiral these days?"

"I've had an occasional letter. Nothing lately."

"But Pamela, he's here."

"Here? In England?"

"Of course. Didn't you know that? He's been here quite a while."

"Really! Would we be out of the wind down at that lily pond? I see a stone bench. We can chat for a few minutes."

Slote well remembered Pamela's great urge to go to Moscow when Henry was there. Her nonchalance seemed overdone; he guessed that the news was a hell of a jolt. They strolled to the bench and sat down by the pond, where frogs croaked as the sun sank behind the trees.

Pamela was indeed silenced by pure shock, and Slote did all the talking. He foamed words. For months he had had nobody to talk to. He told Pam, who sat listening with grave brilliant eyes, that he had joined the OSS because his knowledge of the German massacre of the Jews—which more and more each month was coming to public light, proving he hadn't been a monomaniac after all—and the callous inertness of the State Department had been driving him crazy. The drastic move had transformed his life. He had discovered to his surprise that most men were as full of fear as himself. He had done no worse in parachuting than anybody else, and better than some. As a boy he had loathed violence; bullies had discerned this, he said, picked on him, and fixed him in a timorousness which had fed on itself and became an obsession. Other men concealed their fears even from themselves, for a hearty swagger was the American male way; but he had always been too self-analytical to pretend that he was anything but a coward.

"I've come a long way, Pam!"

On the first airplane jump, back in the States, the man ahead of him in line, a beefy Army captain who had done very well in training, had refused; had looked out at the landscape far below and had frozen, resisting the dispatcher's shove with hysterical obscene snarling. Once he was pushed aside, Slote had jumped out into the roaring slipstream with, in his words, "imbecile joy"; the static line had opened his chute, and the shock had jerked him upright; he had yanked on his webs, floated down in proud ecstasy, and landed like a circus acrobat. Afterward he had shivered and sweated and gloried for days. He had never made another jump half as good. To him, jumping was a hideous business. He hated it. Quite a few OSS men and Jeds felt as he did, and were ready to admit it, though others liked to jump.

"Passing the psychological tests really stunned me, Pamela. I was having very shaky second thoughts about volunteering. I told the Jedburgh board straight out that I was a high-strung coward. They looked skeptical and asked why I had put in for the duty. I gave them my song and dance about the Jews. They rated me 'questionable.' After weeks of being observed by psychiatrists, I passed. They must have been damned hard up for Jeds. Physically I'm very fit, of course, and my French is dazzling, at least to Americans."

It was obvious to Pamela that he would go on and on in this vein and say no more about Victor Henry. "I've got to go, Leslie. Walk me to my jeep." Over the whirring of the motor, as she turned the key, Pamela asked, "Where is Captain Henry, exactly? Do you know?"

"It's Admiral Henry, Pam," said Slote, suppressing a smile. "I told you that."

"I thought you were being facetious."

"No, no. Rear Admiral Henry, ablaze with gold braid, battle ribbons, and stars. I ran into him at our embassy. Try the U.S. Amphibious Base in Exeter. He said he was going there."

She reached out and clasped his hand. He gave her a quick kiss on the cheek. "Till we meet again, Pam. Lord, isn't it a million years since Paris? I did some drinking with Phil Rule last month in London. He's gotten utterly gross."

"It's the liquor. I saw him in Moscow last year. He was all stout and tallowy then, and he got falling-down drunk. Victor wrote me that Natalie's waiting out the war in a Czech ghetto."

"Yes, so he told me." Slote nodded, his face falling. "Well, Pamela, we were young and gay in Paris, anyway."

"Were we? I think we labored awfully sweatily at being Ernest Hemingway characters. Too too raffish and mad. I remember how Phil would hold that black comb under his nose and do Hitler reciting Mother Goose, and we would roar." She ground the jeep into gear, and raised her voice. "Very funny. Those were the days. Good luck on your mission, Leslie. I admire you."

"I had a time tracking you down." Pamela's voice over the telephone was affectionate and cheerful. Hearing those husky tones was very painful to Victor Henry. "Will you by some chance be in London on Thursday?"

"Yes, Pamela, I will be."

"Wonderful. Then come to dinner with us—with Duncan and me—at Stoneford. It's only half an hour from town."

Pug was sitting in the admiral's office in the Devonport dockyard. Seen from the window, landing craft stretched out of sight in the gray drizzle, tied up in the estuary by the hundreds; an array of floating machinery so thick that no water was visible from shore to shore. Back home Pug had dealt in abstractions: production schedules, progress reports, inventories, projections. Here was the reality: multitudes on multitudes of ungainly metal vessels—LCIs, LCMs, LSTs, LCVPs— strange shapes, varying sizes, seemingly numberless as the wheat grains of an American harvest. But Pug knew the exact number of each type here, and at every other assembly point along the coast. He had been hard at work, travelling from base to base, exerting willpower not to telephone Pamela Tudsbury; but she had found him.

"How do I get there?"

"Take one of the SHAEF buses to Bushey Park. I'll pick you up at four or so, and we can talk a bit. Duncan sleeps from four to six. Doctor's orders."

"How is he?"

"Oh—not too well. There will be a few others for dinner, including General Eisenhower."

"Well! Exalted company for me, Pamela."

"I don't think so, Admiral Henry."

"That's two stars, and only temporary."

"Leigh-Mallory will be coming, too, Eisenhower's commander for air." A silence. Then Pam said jocularly, "Well, let's both get on with the war, shall we? See you Thursday at four, out at SHAEF."

Pug could not guess what this invitation was really about. Nor was Pamela free to tell him. She was dying to see him, of course, but bringing him into the high-brass dinner had a special purpose.

During these anxious last days before D-day, the planned airborne attack at "Utah Beach," the westernmost American landing area, was in hot controversy. A swampy lagoon behind the beach was passable only over narrow causeways. These had to be seized by airborne troops before the Germans could block them or blow them up. Otherwise, the landing force could be stranded on the sands, unable to advance and vulnerable to quick destruction. Utah Beach was the closest landing area to Cherbourg. In Eisenhower's view it had to be captured for Overlord to succeed.

Sir Trafford Leigh-Mallory, who had the responsibility for flying in the gliders and parachute troops, opposed the air operation. It would run into devastating flak over the Cotentin peninsula, he argued; the losses would exceed fifty percent; the remnant who got through would be overwhelmed on the ground; it would be a criminal waste of two crack divisions. Even if it meant cancelling the Utah Beach landing, he wanted the air assault dropped. The American generals would not hear of abandoning the Utah landing or its air operation. But Leigh-Mallory had been fighting the Germans in the air for five years. His knowledge and his fortitude were beyond dispute. It was a deadlock.

In the history of coalition warfare such impasses have been common, and sometimes disastrous. Adolf Hitler could well hope to the last that his foes would fall out in some such way. The Anglo-American invasion was riven by disagreements from start to finish, but Dwight Eisenhower held the grand assault together until his troops met the Russians at the Elbe. So he won his place in military history. To wind this matter up— for the Utah Beach attack is no part of our narrative—Eisenhower in the end took the responsibility and ordered Leigh-Mallory to do it. With the air reinforcement, Utah was a swift smooth landing. The causeways were secured. The airborne casualties were lighter than the estimates. Leigh-Mallory apologized to Eisenhower next day by phone "for adding to his burdens." Years later, Eisenhower said that his happiest moment in the whole war was the news that the two airborne divisions had gone into action at Utah Beach.

When Pamela called Pug, Leigh-Mallory was still resisting the Utah operation. Burne-Wilke had contrived the dinner with Eisenhower so that his old friend might urge his case. Telegraph Cottage, Eisenhower's country place, was near Stoneford. The ailing Burne-Wilke kept a good stable, and Eisenhower liked to ride; Burne-Wilke was a passable bridge player, and that was Eisenhower's game. They had hit it off as neighbors, having already worked together in North Africa.

Burne-Wilke too thought that the Utah Beach air drop was a calamitous idea. In general, Burne-Wilke was seeing the world and the war through a veil of invalid gloom. To him the torrent of American manpower and weaponry flooding England had an end-of-the-world feeling; he saw the pride of Empire crumbling before candy bars, chewing gum, Virginia cigarettes, and canned beer. Still, when Pamela suggested inviting Pug Henry he warmly approved. The bone of jealousy was either missing in Lord Burne-Wilke's makeup, or concealed beyond detection. He thought Rear Admiral Henry's presence might dilute the tension of the dinner.

Pug had briefly met Eisenhower once; on arriving in England, he had brought him an oral message from President Roosevelt about bombing the French railway yards, terminals, locomotives, and bridges. The political consequences of slaughtering Frenchmen, their former comrades-in-arms, was troubling the British, and they were pressing Eisenhower to let up on the French. Roosevelt sent word by Victor Henry that he wanted the bombing to go on. (Later, since Churchill kept making trouble, the President had to put this hard-boiled view in writing.) At their meeting Eisenhower received the grim message with a cold satisfied nod, and made no other comment. He said some genial words about Pug's football prowess against Army in the old days; then he queried him sharply on the close-support bombardments in the Pacific, and asked incisive questions about the Overlord naval fire-support plans. Pug left after half an hour feeling that this man had a trace of Roosevelt's leadership aura; that under a mild warm manner and a charming smile he was at least as tough a customer as Ernest King; and that the invasion was going to succeed.

The prospect of dining with him gave Pug no thrill. He had had enough of the war's heavyweights. He was not sure how he would react to seeing Pamela again. Of one thing he was sure: that she would not inflict on him twice the pain of rejection; that by no word or gesture would he try to change her mind.

As she drove Burne-Wilke's Bentley to Bushey Park Pamela was dreading, and at the same time yearning, to look on Pug Henry once more. A woman can handle almost anything but indifference, and the revelation that he was in England had all but shattered her.

Since returning to England, Pamela had been finding out the gritty aspects of her commitment to Duncan Burne-Wilke. His family, she now knew, included an abrasively vigorous mother of eighty-seven who talked to Pam, when she visited, as to a hired nurse; and a numerous train of brothers and sisters, nephews and nieces, all of whom seemed unanimous in snobbish disapproval of her. By and large she and Burne-Wilke still enjoyed the old easy RAF intimacy, though illness and inactivity were making him querulous. In the stress of war she had become extremely fond of him; and bereft of any other future, she had accepted him. Pug's abrupt proposal had come much too late. Still, Stoneford struck her as a big burden, however imposing; Duncan's family was another burden; both bearable had she been deeply in love, but as things stood, gloomily disconcerting. The real trouble was that her letter of rejection to Pug had really settled nothing in her own mind. Not a word in reply for weeks! And then to learn from somebody else that he was here! Could he have turned stone-cold after that one letter, her only offending move, as he had with his wife? What a scary man! In this state of turmoil she drove into Bushey Park and saw Victor Henry standing at the bus stop.

"You look smashing." The schoolgirl words and tones gushed from her.

His smile was wry and reserved. "The big gold stripe helps."

"Oh, it isn't that, Admiral." Her eyes searched his face. "Actually, you're a bit war-worn, Victor. But so *American*. So totally American. They should carve you on Mount Rushmore."

"Kind words, Pam. Isn't that the suit you wore on the *Bremen?*"

"So! You remember." Her face burned with a blush. "I'm out of uniform. I *felt* like being out of uniform. There it was in the closet. I wondered whether I could still get into it. How long will you be here?"

"I'm flying back tomorrow night."

"Tomorrow! So soon?"

"Overnight in Washington, and on to the Pacific. Tell me about Duncan."

Thoroughly rattled (*tomorrow!*) she described Burne-Wilke's puzzling symptoms as calmly as she could while they drove: the abdominal pains, the recurring low fevers, the spells of extreme fatigue alternating with days of seemingly restored health. At the moment he was low again, scarcely able to walk around the gardens. The doctors guessed that injury and shock had allowed some tropical infection to get going in his bloodstream. Months or a year could go by before he shook it off; then again, it might suddenly clear up. Meantime, an invalid regime was mandatory: curtailed activity, much sleep, long bed rest every day, and many pills.

"He must be going mad."

"He was. Now he reads and reads, sitting in the sun. He's taken to writing, too, rather mystical stuff à la Saint-Exupéry. Flying plus the *Bhagavad-Gita*. Aviation and Vishnu really don't mix, not to my taste. I want him to write about the China-Burma-India theatre, it's the great untold story of this war. But he says there are too many maggots under the rocks. Well, here's Stoneford."

"Pam, it's magnificent."

"Yes, isn't the front lovely?" She was driving the car between brick pillars and open wrought-iron gates. Ahead, bisecting a broad green lawn, stretched a long straight gravel road lined with immense oaks, leading to a wide brick mansion glowing rose-red in the sun. "The first viscount bought the place and added the wings. Actually it's a wreck inside, Pug. Lady Caroline took in masses of slum children during the blitz, and they quite laid waste to the place. Duncan's had no chance to fix it up. We live in the guest wing. The little savages never got in there. I have a nice little suite. We'll have tea there, then walk in the garden until Duncan wakes up."

When they mounted to the second floor, Pamela casually pointed out that she and Burne-Wilke lived at opposite sides of the house; he looked out on the oaks, she on the gardens. "No need to tiptoe," she said as they walked past his door. "He sleeps like a dormouse."

An elderly woman in a maid's costume served the tea very clumsily. Pug and Pamela sat by tall windows overlooking weed-choked flower beds. "It's all going to jungle," she said. "One can't hire the men. They're fighting all over the world. Mrs. Robinson and her husband look after the place. She's the one who bungled the tea, she used to be the laundress. He's a senile drunk. Duncan's old cook has stayed on, so that's good. I have a job in the ministry, and I manage to come out most nights. That's my story, Pug. What's yours?"

"Madeline married that young naval officer."

"Wonderful!"

"They're in New Mexico. Pleasantest turnabout in my life. Byron's got his Bronze Star, and by all accounts he's a good submariner. Janice is in law school. My grandson at three is a formidable genius. There's some hope about Natalie. A neutral Red Cross delegation will visit her camp, or ghetto, or whatever it is, very soon, so maybe we'll get some word. If the Germans are letting the Red Cross in, the place can't be too bad. That's my story."

Pamela could not help it, though Pug's tone was so final. "And Rhoda?"

"In Reno, getting her divorce. You said something about a walk in the gardens."

Getting her divorce! But his manner was so estranged, cold, and discouraging, she could say no more about that.

They were outside before he spoke again. "This isn't jungle." The terraced rose garden was massed with well-tended bushes coming into bud.

"Roses are Duncan's hobby. When he's well he spends hours here. Tell me about your promotion."

Pug Henry brightened. "Actually, that's quite a yarn, Pam."

The President, he said, had invited him to Hyde Park. He had not seen Roosevelt since Tehran, and had found him shockingly withered. They had dined at a long table with only one other person, his daughter. Afterward in a small study Roosevelt had talked about the landing craft program. A curious anxiety was haunting the haggard President. He feared enemy action in the first few days might damage or sink a large number of the craft. Weeks might pass before Cherbourg was captured and big supply ships could take over the logistics; meantime speedy salvage and relaunching of sunk or damaged landing craft would be imperative. He had asked for reports on such arrangements and had gotten nothing satisfactory. He would "sleep better" if Pug would go to England and inspect the facilities. In the morning as Pug took his leave, the President had said something jocose and puzzling about "fair sailing weather ahead." Immediately on Pug's return to Washington from Hyde Park, Admiral King had summoned him to tell him face to face that he was getting his two stars and a Pacific battleship division.

"A battleship *division*, Pug!" They were walking through a densely blossoming apple orchard. Pamela seized his arm. "But that's absolutely marvelous! A *division!*"

"King said it was my reward for work well done, and he knew I could fight a BatDiv if I had to. It's two ships, Pam. Two of our best, the *Iowa* and the *New Jersey*, and—what the devil is the matter?"

"Nothing, nothing at all." Pamela was putting a handkerchief to her eyes. "Oh, Pug!"

"Well, it's the best I could hope for in my career. A monumental surprise." Pug wearily shrugged. "Of course it's a carrier war out there, Pam. The battlewagons mainly bombard beaches. I may just ride around in fancy flag quarters till the war ends, initialing papers and acting pompous. An admiral afloat can be a futile fellow."

"It's terrific," Pamela said. "It's absolutely, utterly, bloody flaming terrific."

Pug gave her the bleak smile she had loved on the *Bremen* and loved now. "I agree. Won't Duncan be waking up?"

"Good Lord, six o'clock. Where did the time go? Let's run like deer."

They had drinks before dinner on the terrace. Eisenhower arrived late, looking pale and acting edgy. He declined a highball, and when his driver, Mrs. Summersby, cheerfully accepted one, he gave her a grumpy glance. This was Pug's first glimpse of the woman that all the gossip was about. Even in uniform Kay Summersby looked like the fashion model she had been before the war: tall, lissome, with a seductive high-cheekboned face and big eyes that glinted self-assurance; a professional beauty to her fingertips, with a faintly mischievous military veneer. Since the general wasn't drinking, the others gulped their highballs and conversation lagged.

The small dining room opened out on the gardens, and through the french doors pleasant flower scents drifted in. For a while this was the only pleasant thing going on. Sunburned, scarred, spectral, Burne-Wilke talked with Mrs. Summersby while the laundress waddled about clumsily serving lamb, boiled potatoes, and Brussels sprouts. Pamela, with Eisenhower on her right and Leigh-Mallory on her left, could not get a rise out of either. They just sat there eating glumly. The dinner seemed to Pug Henry a disaster. Leigh-Mallory, a stiff correct RAF sort, stocky and mustached, kept furtively shifting his eyes at Kay Summersby beside him, as though the woman were sitting there stark naked.

But Burne-Wilke's good claret and Pug's presence in time helped matters. Leigh-Mallory mentioned that the drive to relieve Imphal was picking up steam, and Burne-Wilke observed that perhaps only Leningrad had been besieged longer in this war. Pamela piped up, "Pug was in Leningrad during the siege."

At that Eisenhower shook his head and rubbed his eyes like a man wakened from a doze. "You were, Henry? In Leningrad? Let's hear about it."

Pug talked. The imminent invasion was apparently weighing down the two high commanders, so a yarn was in order. His account of silent snowy Leningrad, the apartment of Yevlenko's daughter-in-law, the horror tales of the siege, rolled out easily. Leigh-Mallory's rigid face relaxed to lively attention. Eisenhower stared straight at Pug, chain-lighting cigarettes. He commented when Pug finished, "Most interesting. I was unaware that any of our fellows had gotten in there. I saw no intelligence on this."

"Technically I was a Lend-Lease observer, General. I did send a supplement on combat aspects to ONI."

"Kay, tell Lee tomorrow to get that stuff from the Office of Naval Intelligence."

"Yes, General."

"This chap, Yevlenko—he took you to Stalingrad too, you say?" asked Leigh-Mallory.

"Yes, but the fighting had already ended there."

"Tell us about that," said Eisenhower.

Burne-Wilke signalled the laundress to bring more claret. The atmosphere was clearing by the minute. When Eisenhower laughed at Pug's description of the rough drinking party in the Stalingrad cellar, Leigh-Mallory too uttered a reluctant chortle.

Eisenhower said, his face hardening, "Henry, you know these people. Once we go, will they attack in the east? Harriman's assured me that the attack is on, but there's a lot of skepticism around here."

Pug took a moment to think. "They'll go, sir. That's my guess. Politically, they're unpredictable, and may strike us as treacherous. They truly don't see the world, or use language, as we do. That may not change, ever. Still, I think they'll keep this military commitment."

The Supreme Commander emphatically nodded.

"Why?" asked Leigh-Mallory.

"Self-interest, of course," Eisenhower almost snapped. "I agree, Henry. The time to hit the other fellow is when he has his hands full. They're bound to go."

"Also," said Pug, "out of a sense of honor. That they've got."

"If they've got that much in common with us," Eisenhower said soberly, "we'll eventually get along with them. We can build on that."

"I wonder," said Leigh-Mallory in a heavily jesting tone. "Look at the trouble we have getting along, General, and we have the English language in common."

Kay Summersby remarked sweetly, in Mayfair accents, "It only seems we do."

Turning on her, Sir Trafford Leigh-Mallory genuinely laughed, and raised his glass to her.

Eisenhower gave Mrs. Summersby a wide warm grin. "Well, Kay, now I have to talk for a while with these two RAF fellows—in sign language, of course." A joke from the Supreme Commander naturally brought loud laughter. Everybody stood up. Eisenhower said to Burne-Wilke, "Maybe we can get in a rubber afterward."

Pamela invited Pug and Mrs. Summersby to the terrace for brandy and coffee, but once outside Kay Summersby did not sit down. "See here, Pam," she said with an ironic little glance from Henry to Pamela, "they'll be talking for quite a while. I have simply masses of things to do at the cottage. You and the admiral will forgive me, won't you, if I just pop over there and come back for the bridge?"

And she was gone. The general's car rattled down the gravel road.

Pamela was perfectly aware that Mrs. Summersby, with sharp intuition, was giving her what might be her last chance at Victor Henry in this life. She went right on the attack. She had to provoke a scene to accomplish anything. "No doubt you deeply disapprove of Kay. Or do you bend your rules for great men?"

"I know no more about her than meets the eye."

"I see. As a matter of fact, and I know them rather well, I'm sure that's all there is to it." Pug made no comment. "Pity you couldn't be more broadminded about your wife."

"I was ready to stick it out. You know that. Rhoda chose differently."

"You froze her."

Pug said nothing.

"Will she be happy with the fellow?"

"I don't know. I'm worried, Pam." He told her about the anonymous letters, and his talk with Peters on the train. "I've met him once since then, the day Rhoda left for Reno. He came to take her to the station, and while she primped we talked. He didn't act happy. I think at this point he's doing the honorable thing."

"Poor Rhoda!" This was all Pamela could say, in the rush of emotion at what Pug Henry was now telling her. Here was the last bit of the jigsaw puzzle. Colonel Peters had looked to Pamela like a hard and clever man; and her instinct had been that he would see through Rhoda Henry before she got him to the altar, and would drop her. He *had* seen through her; yet the marriage was on. Victor Henry was really free.

The night was dark now. They sat in starlight. A bird nearby was pouring out rich song. "Isn't that a nightingale?" Pug asked.

"Yes."

"Last time I heard one was on the airfield, before I took off on the flight over Berlin."

"Oh, yes. And didn't you put me through the hell of an ordeal *that* time, too. Only it lasted twenty hours, not six weeks."

He peered at her. "Six weeks? What are you talking about?"

"Six weeks and three days, exactly, since I wrote you. Why didn't you ever answer my letter? Just a word, any word? And why did I have to find out by chance that you've been in England? Do you hate me that much?"

"I don't hate you, Pam. Don't be ridiculous."

"Yet all I deserved was to be cast into the outer darkness."

"What could I have written you?"

"Oh, I don't know. Let's say, a gallant good-bye. Conceivably, even, a dashing refusal to take 'no' for an answer. Any little sign that you didn't loathe and despise me for an agonized decision. I told you I was blinded with tears when I wrote. Didn't you believe me?"

"I wrote the gallant good-bye," he said dully. "Can't you image that much? I wrote the refusal to take 'no' for an answer. I tore up many letters. There was no graceful way to answer. I don't see begging a woman to change her mind, and I don't imagine begging helps. Anyway, I'm no good at it."

"Yes, you do find it awkward to write your feelings, don't you?" Gladness surged through Pamela to hear of the torn-up letters, and she drove on in forcible tones. "That marriage proposal of yours! The way you went on and on about money—"

"Money's important. A man should let a woman know what she may be getting into. Anyhow, what is all this about, Pamela?"

"Goddamn it, Victor, I'll have my say! Your letter couldn't have been more horribly mistimed. I've been wretched ever since I answered you. I've never been more shocked in my life than when Slote said you were here. I thought I'd expire of the pain. Seeing you is incredibly sweet, and it's sheer torture." Pamela stood up. Stepping to Pug, who remained in his chair, she held out her arms to him, dim white in the light of the rising moon. "I told you in Moscow, I told you in Tehran, I tell you for the last time that I love you and not Duncan. Now there it is, and now *you* talk. Speak up, Victor Henry, at long last! Will you have me, or won't you?"

After a pause, he said blandly, "Well, I'll tell you, Pamela. I'll think about it."

It was such an unexpected deflating response that it took Pam a second or two to suspect teasing. She pounced on him, seized his shoulders, and shook him.

"You're shaking Mount Rushmore," he said.

"I'll shake it down! The damned stuffy banal Yankee monument!"

He gripped her hands, rose, and embraced her for a long hard kiss. Then he held her a little away from him, keenly scanning her face. "Okay, Pamela. Six weeks ago you refused me. What's changed?"

"Rhoda's gone. I couldn't believe that. Now I know she is. And you and I are here together, not separated by the whole damned planet. I've been sad since I wrote you, and now I'm happy. I've got to do Duncan dirt, that's all. It's my life."

"This is astounding. Old Rhoda said all you needed was some wooing."

"She said that? Wise woman, but I've never gotten it, and I never would have done. It's a good thing I'm such a forward slut, isn't it."

He sat on the parapet and pulled her beside him. "Now listen, Pamela. That Pacific war can last a long time. The Japs are still raising plenty of hell out there. If it comes to a fleet action, I'll probably be in it, and I could come out on the short end, too."

"So? What are you saying? That I'd be prudent to keep Duncan on the string? Something like that?"

"I'm saying you needn't make up your mind. I love you, and God knows I want you, but just remember what you said in Tehran."

"What did I say in Tehran?"

"That these very rare meetings of ours generate an illusion of romance, a wartime thing of no substance, and so on—"

"I'll gamble the rest of my life that it's a lie. I'll have to tell Duncan straight off, darling. There's no other possibility now. He won't be surprised. Hurt, yes, damn it, and I dread that, but—oh, Christ, I hear them." The voices of the other men sounded faintly in the house. "They weren't at it long, were they? And we've arranged nothing, nothing! Pug, I'm dizzy with happiness. Call me at the Air Ministry at eight o'clock, my dear sweet love, and now for God's sake kiss me once more."

They kissed. "Is it possible?" Pug murmured the words, looking searchingly into her face. "Is it possible that I'm going to be happy?"

He rode back to London with Leigh-Mallory. All the while the car raced down the moonlit highway to the city, and twisted through blacked-out streets to Pug's quarters, the air marshal said not a word. The meeting with Eisenhower clearly had not gone well. But the lack of talk was a blessing for Pug, who could dwell on the amazed supreme joy suffusing him.

When the car stopped, Leigh-Mallory spoke hoarsely and abruptly. "What you said about the Russian sense of honor interested me, Admiral. D'you think we British have a sense of honor, too?"

The emotion in his voice, his strained expression, forced Pug to collect himself fast.

"Marshal, whatever we Americans have, we learned from you."

Leigh-Mallory shook his hand, looked him in the eye, and said, "Glad we met."

The night before D-day. Ten o'clock.

In a lone Halifax bomber flying low over the Channel, the Jedburgh team "Maurice" was on its way. The Jeds were a small cog in the giant invasion machine. Liaison with the French Resistance was their mission; to arm and supply the maquisards and link them to the Allied attack plan. These three-man teams parachuted into France from D-day onward, had colorful adventures, did some good, had some losses. Without them the war would doubtless have been won, but the thorough Overlord plan had provided for this small detail, too.

And so it was that Leslie Slote—a Rhodes Scholar, a resigned Foreign Service officer, a man who had despised his own timidity all his life—found himself crouching in the noisy Halifax with a baby-faced aircraftsman from Yorkshire, his radio operator, and a French dentist, his contact with the Resistance; calculating, as the plane roared over moonlit water toward Brittany, his chances for living very long. A Rhodes Scholar had had to excel in sports, and he had always kept up his physical fitness. His mind was nimble. He had mastered the guerrilla crafts in a fashion: jumping, knife and rope work, silent movement, silent killing, and the rest. But to the last, to this moment when he found himself going in, it had all seemed strenuous make-believe, a simulation of Hollywood combat. Now here was the real thing. His uppermost feeling was relief, whatever the dread that was muttering underneath; the waiting at least was over. The hundred twenty-five thousand embarking troops probably felt much the same way. There were few hurrahs on D-day. Honor consisted in keeping one's head in the convulsive maelstrom of machinery, explosives, and fire, and doing one's assigned job unless shot or blown up.

Leslie Slote did his assigned job. The moment came, and he jumped. The opening shock of the chute was violent; and seconds later, so it seemed, the ground hit him another hard shock. Dropped too damned low by the damned RAF again; made it, anyway!

Powerful arms embraced him, even as he was unhooking the parachute. Whiskers scratched him. There was a gabble of idiomatic French, a smell of wine and garlic on heavy breaths. The dentist appeared out of the night, and the young Yorkshireman, in a mill of happy armed Frenchmen with wild faces.

I've done it, thought Leslie Slote. *I want to live, and by God I'm going to.* The surge of self-confidence was like nothing he had known before. The dentist was in command. Slote carried out his first joyous order, which was to drink down a stone mug of wine. Then they set about gathering up the dropped supply containers in the peaceful fragrant meadow under a glittery moon.

84

A Jew's Journey
(from Aaron Jastrow's manuscript)

JUNE 22, 1944.

I am utterly spent from the day's "dress rehearsal." Tomorrow the Red Cross comes. Cleanup and painting squads are still at work under floodlights, though already the town looks far better than Baden-Baden did. The spanking new paint everywhere, the clipped lawns, the lush flower beds, the fine sports fields and children's playgrounds, together with the artistic performances and the well-dressed Jews playacting vacationers at a happy peacetime spa, all add up to a musical comedy in the open air, utterly unreal. Not knowing what humaneness is, the Germans have worked up an elephantine parody of humaneness. It shouldn't deceive anybody who is not determined to be deceived.

Rabbi Baeck, the wise and gentle old Berlin scholar, a sort of spiritual father of the ghetto, hopes for much from this visit. The Red Cross people will not be taken in, he is sure; they will ask searching questions and probe behind the façade; and their report will force genuine changes in Theresienstadt, and perhaps in all the German camps. He reflects the prevailing optimism. We are an unstable lot in Theresienstadt. The prison mentality, the overcrowding, the haunting fear of the Germans, the subhuman nutrition and medical care, and the nerve-wracking jumbling together of Jews from many countries with little more than the yellow star in common, all make for unrealistic gusts of mood. What with the Allied landings in France and this imminent visit from the "outside," the mood is for the moment manic.

But I try to keep a grip on reality. The Allied invasion of Normandy has in fact bogged down. The Russians have in fact failed to attack in the east. What treachery is beyond Stalin? Has the monster decided to let a death struggle waste both sides in France, after which he can roll over all Europe at his leisure? I greatly fear so.

Today, June 22, three years ago, the Germans sprang at the Soviet Union. Today, if ever, the Russians, with their love of dramatic anniversary gestures, should have launched their Tolstoyan counterblow.

No sign of it. The BBC evening bulletin was glum and vague. (BBC is always covertly monitored here and the word quickly spreads, although the penalty for listening is death.) Radio Berlin was cock-a-hoop again, crowing that Eisenhower's armies are trapped in the bocage and marsh country of Normandy; that Rommel will soon drive them into the sea; and that Hitler's new "wonder weapons" will then deliver a frightful knockout to the Anglo-Americans. As for the Russians, the Germans say that they paid "with oceans of blood" for their drive in the Crimea and the Ukraine, and have now come to the end of their strength, hence their long halt. Is there any truth to that? Even the German home front cannot tolerate total nonsense in war bulletins. Unless the Russians do attack very soon, and in great force, we will yet again know the foul taste of hope soured to despair.

Oh, what a revolting farce this long day was! Some small-fry German officials from Prague stood in for the visitors. Only Rahm was in uniform. It was absolutely dreamlike to watch Haindl and the other SS thugs in ill-fitting suits, ties, and felt hats bowing and scraping to us Elders, helping us in and out of our chauffeured cars, stepping aside smilingly for Jewish women in the cafés, in the streets, or in corridors. The whole thing went off like clockwork. Concealed messenger boys, as the party progressed, ran ahead and triggered off a singing chorus, a café performance, a string quartet in a private house, a ballet workout, a children's dance, a soccer game. Wherever we passed we saw happy, well-dressed, good-looking holiday strollers smoking cigars and cigarettes. "Clockwork" is just the word. The Jews played their little happy parts with the stiffness of living dolls; and the "visitors" once past, their motions stopped, and they froze into poor scared Theresienstadt prisoners waiting for the next signal.

Three battered Red Cross parcels from Byron are piled on the floor beside me. Trucks trundled through the ghetto tonight heaped high with the packages, withheld by the Germans for months. Thus the visitors will see a ghetto swamped with Red Cross provisions. The Germans have thought of everything. From the Prague storehouses of Jewish loot they have brought a great load of finery for those inmates who will be on show. Right now I am wearing a superb suit of English serge and two gold rings. A beauty parlor has been set up for the women. Cosmetics have been distributed. Pretty Jewesses with neat yellow stars on their elegant clothes strolled today like queens on the arms of well-dressed escorts in the flower-bordered squares. Almost, I could believe I was back in peacetime Vienna or Berlin. Poor females! Despite themselves, they glowed in the brief delight of being bathed, perfumed, coiffed, decked out, and gemmed. They were as pathetic in their way as the wagonloads of dead bodies that used to pass by day and night, before all the sick were transported.

At the children's pavilion Natalie wears a beautiful blue silk dress, and Louis, in a dark velvet suit with a lace collar, is a joy to watch at his games. The SS have fattened up the tots like Strasbourg geese. They are rotund, red-cheeked, and full of vim, none more so than Louis. If anything can fool the visitors it will be this lovely pavilion, completed only a few days ago, charming and quaint as a dollhouse, and its enchanting little children playing on the swings and roundabout or splashing in the pool.

———

Natalie has just come in with the news that the Russians have attacked, after all! Two separate radio reports were picked up at midnight; an exultant BBC bulletin, and a long Czech-language broadcast from Moscow. The Soviets called the attack "our drive to crush the Hitlerite bandits in cooperation with our Allies in France." When she told me this, I murmured the Hebrew blessing on good news. Then I asked her if she would go ahead with the plans for Louis. Who knows, I said—suddenly manic myself—but what Germany may now quickly collapse? Is the risk still worth it?

"He goes," she said. "Nothing will change that."

I drop my pen with poor Udam's song running in my brain: *"Oy they're coming, they're coming after all! Coming from the east, coming from the west . . ."*

God speed them!

• • •

From 𝔚𝔬𝔯𝔩𝔡 𝔥𝔬𝔩𝔬𝔠𝔞𝔲𝔰𝔱

by Armin von Roon

Bagration

On the night of June 22, 1944, the third anniversary of Barbarossa, the Russians struck at us with full fury in the east. Partisan uprisings all over White Russia derailed our troop trains and blew up bridges. Reconnaissance probes stabbed at Army Groups Center and North from the Baltic Sea to the Pripet Marshes. Next day rolling artillery barrages from perhaps a hundred thousand big guns, massed in some places wheel to wheel, turned the four-hundred-fifty-mile front into an inferno. Then rifle divisions, tank divisions, and motorized divisions advanced in hordes, under a sky dark with Soviet aircraft. No Luftwaffe fighters rose to oppose them. The Russians were attacking us with a million two hundred thousand men, five thousand tanks, and six thousand airplanes. Here with a vengeance was the other jaw of Roosevelt's vise, grinding westward to meet the eastward thrust of Overlord.

BAGRATION! Revenge of Barbarossa!

Like us, the Soviets invoked the name of a great war leader, their hero of the Battle of Borodino, for their June 22 assault. Like us, they aimed at the speedy capture of all of White Russia, and the envelopment of the armies stationed on that vast wooded plain. Indeed, Bagration as it unfolded on our OKW maps was a spine-chilling mirror image of Barbarossa, reflecting back in our amazed faces the military lessons we had taught the Soviets only too well.

In their gory winter campaign to relieve Leningrad, and in their slogging rout of Manstein's forces from the Ukraine and the Crimea in the spring, we had seen their frightening resilience, and Stalin's brute resolve to go on squandering lives. But here in White Russia was something new: our own best tactical concepts, skillfully turned against us. To make the mirror image complete, Adolf Hitler would repeat the wooden-headed orders of Stalin in 1941—"Stand where you are, no retreat, no maneuvers, hold or die" —with the identical catastrophic results, in the opposite direction.

The Soviets even achieved the same kind of surprise.

In 1941, expecting Hitler to strike for the Ukrainian breadbasket and the Caucasus oil fields, they had weighted their forces to the south. Thus our main thrust through White Russia had quickly shattered their central front. This time, despite the big Red buildup in the center, the infallible Hitler "knew" that the Russians would exploit their salient in the south to drive at the Rumanian oil fields and the Balkans. The central buildup he dismissed, in his usual airy-fairy way, as a feint, and he concentrated our forces to face the Soviet front in the Ukraine.

The anxious intelligence warnings by Busch, the commanding general of Army Group Center, and his pleas for reinforcements, went unheeded. When the Russian blow fell and the front caved in, Hitler of course fired Busch for his own pigheaded miscalculation; but the new commander, General Model, was just as hamstrung by Hitler's meddling, especially by his insistence that our divisions hole up in "strong points," towns left behind by the swift Russian onslaught—Vitebsk, Bobruisk, Orsha, Mogilev—instead of fighting their way out. This folly wrecked the front. The "strong points" fell in days, and all the divisions were lost. Gaping holes opened in our line, through which the Soviets came roaring like Tatars, on their limitless Lend-Lease wheels.

My operational analysis of Bagration, called "The Battle of White Russia," is very detailed, for I consider this little-studied event the pivot of Germany's final collapse in World War II, even more than the much-touted Normandy landings. If there was a true "second Stalingrad" in the war, it was Bagration. In less than two weeks the Russians advanced some two hundred miles. Sweeping pincer thrusts closing on Minsk trapped a hundred thousand German soldiers, and in the fighting we lost perhaps a hundred fifty thousand more. The remnants of Army Group Center reeled westward beyond Minsk, its formations sliced and skewered by Soviet armored spear points. By the middle of July Army Group Center had virtually ceased to exist. Melancholy ragged columns of German prisoners were again parading in Red Square. The Red Army had recaptured White Russia and marched into Poland and Lithuania. It was threatening the east Prussia frontier, and Army Group North faced being cut off by a Red thrust to the sea. All this time, the Anglo-Americans were still struggling to break out of Normandy.

And all this time Adolf Hitler kept his eyes obsessively on the west! The swelling eastern crisis he brushed off, at our briefing conferences, with short-tempered snap judgments. Our controlled press and radio drew a veil over the catastrophe. As for the Americans and the British, they were preoccupied then, and their historians still are, with operations in France. The Soviets put out little more than the bald facts of their advances; and after the war, during Stalin's decline into bloodthirsty lunacy, their military historians were gagged by fear. Not much useful writing about the war emerged from that wretched land for a long time.

So it happens that Bagration has slipped into obscurity. But it was this battle that irretrievably broke our front in the east, toppled Finland out of the war, and set the Balkan politicians plotting the treachery that led to our even larger disaster the following month in Rumania. And Bagration was the real fuse that, on July 20, set off the bomb in Supreme Headquarters.

———

TRANSLATOR'S NOTE: *In recent years the Soviets have been putting out more and better books on the war. Marshal Zhukov's memoirs treat Bagration at length. These books, while informative, are not necessarily truthful by our standards. The communist government owns all the printing presses in Russia, and nothing sees the light that does not extol the Party; which, like Hitler, never makes mistakes.—V.H.*

• • •

At the first gray light on June 23, Natalie gets up and dresses for the Red Cross visit, in a bedchamber befitting a good European hotel:

blond wood furniture, a small Oriental carpet, gay flowered wallpaper, armchair, lampshades; even vases of fresh flowers, delivered last night by the gardening crew. The Jastrow flat will be a stop in the tour. The noted author will show the visitors through the rooms, offer them cognac, and take them to the synagogue and the Judaica library. So Natalie tidies the place as for military inspection before hurrying off. There is much yet to do at the children's pavilion. Rahm has ordered a last-minute rearrangement of the furniture and many more animal cutouts for the walls.

It is just sunrise. Squads of women are out on the streets already, scrubbing the pavements on their hands and knees in the slant yellow light. The stench of these tattered scarecrows from the overcrowded lofts fouls the morning breeze. Their work done, they will vanish, and the perfumed pretty ones in fancy clothes will come out. Natalie's senses are too blunted to register such Beautification ironies. A recurring nightmare has been destroying her sleep for a month—Haindl, swinging Louis by the legs and smashing his skull on the cement floor. By now the picture of the child's head splitting apart, the blood spurting, the white brains spattering, is as real to her as her memory of the SS cellar; in a way even more familiar, because that short horror came and went in a blur of shock, whereas she has seen this ghastly vision a score of times. Natalie is a reduced creature, scarcely normal in the head. One thing keeps her going, and that is the hope of getting Louis out of the ghetto.

The Czech gendarme who conveys Berel's messages says the attempt is set for the week after the visit. Louis will sicken and disappear into the hospital. She will not see him again. She will be told only that he has died of typhus. Then she has to hope that she will one day hear he is safe. It is like sending him off to emergency surgery; no help for it, whatever the risk.

From a handcart parked outside the Danish barracks, gardeners are unloading rose bushes full of blooms, carrying them into the courtyard, and tamping them down into holes in the lawn. Heavy rose perfume deliciously sweetens the air as Natalie walks by. Clearly something special is going on with the Danish Jews. But that is not her concern. Her concern is to get through this day without a mistake, without angering Rahm and endangering Louis. The children's pavilion is the last stop on the scheduled tour, the star attraction.

As it happens, the Danish Jews are the important ones today: a handful, four hundred fifty Jews amid thirty-five thousand, but a special handful.

The whole story of Danish Jewry is astonishing. All but these few are free and safe in neutral Sweden. The Danish government, getting wind of an impending roundup of Jews by the German occupying force, secretly alerted the population; and in an improvised fleet of small craft, in one night, Danish volunteers ferried some six thousand Jews across a narrow sound to neutral and hospitable Sweden. So only this tiny group was caught by the Germans and sent to Theresienstadt.

Ever since, the Danish Red Cross has been demanding to visit its Jewish citizens in the Paradise Ghetto. The Danish Foreign Ministry has been forcefully pressing this demand. The Germans, curiously enough, instead of shooting a few Danes and squelching the nuisance, have acted irresolute in the face of such unprecedented moral courage on behalf of Jews, displayed by this one small nation and by no other. Though postponing the visit time and again, they have, in fact, at last knuckled under.

Four men, dim in history, but their names still on record, make up the visiting party.

Frants Hvass, the Danish diplomat who has been pressing Berlin about Theresienstadt.

Dr. Juel Henningsen, of the Danish Red Cross.

Dr. M. Rossel, of the German office of the International Red Cross in Berlin.

Eberhard von Thadden, a German career diplomat. Thadden handles Jewish affairs in the Foreign Ministry. Eichmann transports Jews to their deaths; Thadden pries them out of the countries where they hold citizenship, and delivers them to Eichmann.

The tour begins at noon. It lasts eight hours. It is to impress these two Danes and these two Germans, in these eight hours, that the whole stupendous six-month Beautification has been carried out. It proves well worth it. The written reports of Hvass and the Red Cross man have survived. They glow with approbation of the splendid conditions in Theresienstadt. "More like an ideal suburban community," one sums up, "than a concentration camp."

And why not?

The four visitors, with a train of high Nazi officials from Berlin and Prague, traverse Rahm's route by the timetable without a hitch. Their approach sets off one charming sight after another—pretty farm girls singing as they march with shouldered rakes to the truck gardens, masses of fragrant fresh vegetables unloading at the grocery store and Jews happily queueing up to buy, a robed chorus of eighty voices bursting forth with a breathtaking "Sanctus," a soccer goal shot to the cheers of a joyous crowd, just as the visitors reach the sports field.

The hospital looks and smells Paradise-clean, the linen is snow-white, the patients are cheerful and comfortable, replying to all questions by praising the superb treatment and meals. Wherever the visitors go—the slaughterhouse, the laundry, the bank, the Jewish administration offices, the post office, the ground-floor apartments of the *Prominente,* the Danish barracks—they see order, brightness, cleanliness, charm, and contentment. The Danish Jews outdo each other in assuring Hvass and Henningsen that they are well off and handsomely treated.

And the outdoor scenes are so pleasant! The quaintly decorated street signs are a treat to the eye. Well-dressed Jews stroll at leisure in the sunshine, as few Europeans can do in the harsh wartime conditions. The café entertainment is first-class. The cream pastries are delicious. Of the coffee Herr von Thadden remarks, "Better than you can get in Berlin!"

And what a fine last impression the children's pavilion makes! The lovely svelte Jewess in charge, the niece of the famous author, appears so happy in her work, and is so quick with positive responses to questions! Clearly she is on the friendliest terms with Commander Rahm and Inspector Haindl. It is a beguiling close to the visit: healthy pretty children swinging, sliding, dancing in a circle, splashing in the pond, riding a roundabout, casting comic long shadows in the sunset light on the fresh grass of the playground, their laughter chiming like light music. Pretty young matrons watch them, but none half as handsome or cheerful as the one in the blue silk dress. With the commander's permission, the Berlin Red Cross man takes photographs, including one of her holding her son in her arms, a lively imp with a heart-melting smile. In a burst of good feeling, Herr Rossel tells her that a print will be forwarded to her family in America.

. . .

After the war, challenged in the Danish Parliament to explain how he was duped by the Germans, Frants Hvass replies that he was not in the least fooled. He could see the visit was staged. He turned in a favorable report to assure continued good treatment for the Danish Jews and the flow of food parcels to them. That was his mission, not the exposure of German duplicity. Hvass confesses to Parliament, nevertheless, that he was relieved by the visit. In view of the terrible reports of the German camps already in the hands of the Red Cross, he had half-feared seeing corpses lying all over the streets, Musselmen stumbling about in a miasma of filth and death. Despite all the fakery, there was none of that.

The world keeps wondering why the International Red Cross—and for that matter, the Vatican—kept silent all through the war when they certainly knew about the great secret massacre. The nearest thing to an explanation is always Frants Hvass's: that accusing the Germans of crimes that could not be proven in wartime would only have made matters worse for the Jews still alive in their hands. The Red Cross and the Vatican knew the Germans well. Possibly they had a point, though the next question is, "How could matters have been made worse?"

• • •

The success of the Great Beautification gives the higher-ups in Berlin an idea. Why not shoot a film in Theresienstadt showing how well off the Jews are under the Nazis, giving the lie to all the mounting Allied atrocity propaganda about murder camps and gas cellars? Orders go out to prepare and shoot such a film at once. Title: *Der Führer schenkt den Juden eine Stadt,* "The Führer Grants the Jews a Town." Assigned to the script committee is Dr. Aaron Jastrow; and the children's pavilion will be prominently featured.

From "Hitler as Military Leader"

July 20—The Attempt to Kill Hitler

. . . The briefing conference was taking place in a wooden hut, because the heavy concrete command bunker was being reinforced against air attack as the Russian front drew nearer Rastenburg. This saved Hitler's life. In the bunker we would all have been wiped out by the confined explosion.

It was a familiar boring scene until the bomb went off. Heusinger was droning on glumly about the eastern front. Hitler leaned over the table map, peering through his thick spectacles, and I stood beside him among the usual staff officers. There came a shattering noise, and the room was swathed in yellow smoke. I found myself lying on the wooden floor in terrible pain, involuntary groans issuing from my throat. I thought we had been bombed from the air. My first idea was to save myself from being burned alive, for there was a crackling of flame and a smell of burning. Despite my broken leg I dragged myself outside, stumbling over fallen bodies in the smoke and gloom. The groans and screams all around me were frightful. On the ground outside I collapsed in a sitting position. I saw Hitler come out of the smoke leaning on somebody's arm. There was blood on his face, his hair stood on end caked with plaster dust, and I could see his naked legs through his ripped black trousers. Those white spindle legs, those pudgy knees, for the moment made him seem an ordinary and pathetic man, not the ferocious warlord.

A favorable literature has sprung up about the conspirators. I myself cannot sentimentalize over them. That I was almost killed is beside the point. Count von Stauffenberg certainly was brave and ingenious to get by the formidable gate systems and security checks of Wolfsschanze and to place the briefcase full of explosives under the table; but to what avail? He was already a mutilated wreck, as is well known, minus an eye, a right hand, and two fingers on the left, lost in North Africa. Why did he not give his all? True, he was the head of the conspiracy, but the whole purpose was to kill Hitler; and the only sure way to do that was to walk up to him, camouflaged bomb in hand, and detonate it. The count's vague Christian idealism, it seems, did not extend to martyrdom. Ironically, he only lived a few more hours, anyway. He was caught and executed that same night in Berlin.

I knew nearly all the Wehrmacht conspirators. That some of them turned out to be involved astounded me. The identity of others I would have guessed, for I too was sounded out, early on. I silenced the inquirer and was not approached again. The concept of ending the war by murdering the Head of State—whatever his defects, so evident to us insiders—I considered treasonous, contrary to our oath as officers, and unsound. I still do.

On July 20, 1944, the Wehrmacht stood everywhere deep in foreign territory, nine million strong, fighting magnificently despite erratic leadership. The Fatherland, though battered from the air, was intact. The political spine of Germany was, for better or worse, the bond between the German people and Hitler. Murdering him would have let loose chaos. Himmler, Göring, and Goebbels, who still controlled all the state machinery, would have launched a vengeful blood bath beyond imagining. Every German's hand would have been against his brother. Our leaderless armies would have collapsed. The military situation, bad as it was, did not call for such a solution, really no solution at all: to plunge ourselves into anarchy, and invite the Bolshevik barbarians to spread rapine and pillage to the Rhine!

In fact, the July twentieth bombing bomeranged into a second Reichstag Fire. It gave Hitler the one excuse he needed to slaughter all surviving opposition. At least five thousand people died, most of them innocent. The General Staff and the independent intellectual elite—politicians, labor leaders, priests, professors, and the remnants of the old German aristocracy —were all but exterminated. My judgment is that July twentieth may have prolonged the war. We were at the very brink of the August disasters, which might have forced the Nazis themselves to ease out Hitler for an orderly capitulation. Instead, July twentieth shocked all Germany into rallying around the Führer. This lasted until he shot himself nine fearful months later. Among the German people, there was no support for the bungled attempt. The conspirators were execrated, and Hitler was riding high again.

In the infirmary at Wolfsschanze, as I can well recall, Hitler sat not ten feet from me talking to Göring, while doctors worked on his burst eardrums. *"Now I have got those fellows where I want them,"* he said, or words to that effect. *"Now I can act."* He knew that the fiasco had reprieved his regime.

Hitler's apologists claim he did not see the films he ordered taken of the generals' executions, but I myself sat beside him during the screening. His giggles and remarks were more appropriate to a Charlie Chaplin comedy than to the ghastly distortions of my old comrades-in-arms, going through death agonies naked, in nooses of piano wire. I could never respect him after that. I cannot respect his memory when I recall it.

For me, the July twentieth affair was in every way a calamity. I have walked with a bad limp ever since. I lost the hearing in my right ear, and I am subject to dizzy spells and falling episodes. Also, it ended my chances of getting out of Supreme Headquarters. Coming from a conservative landowning family like most of the July twentieth men, I might well have fallen victim to Hitler's irrational suspicions and been executed myself. But possibly my injuries made my innocence seem self-evident. Or perhaps the Gestapo knew that I was in the clear. At any rate, I became again "the good Armin," different from those "others," treated more decently by Hitler than almost any general except Model and Guderian; and I was forced to witness his progressive degeneration down to the bitter end in the Berlin bunker, swallowing every day the foulest abuse of my profession and my class.

TRANSLATOR'S NOTE: *The tiny band of conspirators had a sort of Keystone Cops quality. They kept setting bombs that failed to go off, planning actions in which someone goofed, and generally falling all over themselves. But they were very brave men, and their story is complex and fascinating. Roon's disapproval of them is not widely shared in Germany. I get the impression that Roon feels guilty about staying out of it, and protests too much.—V.H.*

* * *

From A Jew's Journey

JULY 23.

Rahm toured the ghetto today with the Dutch Jew who will direct the film. The script calls for a big scene at the children's pavilion. Natalie knew they were coming, and by the time the two cars arrived, she tells me, she was close to nervous prostration. But Rahn took very airily the news that Louis was dead. "Well, too bad. Use one of the other brats,

hen," was all he said. "Pick a lively one, and teach him that French
song your kid sang." It seemed quite a matter of course to him that the
child had died of typhus; no condolences, and apparently no suspicions.
Of course we must wait and see. He may still investigate. Meantime, the
relief is enormous.

Possibly none of Natalie's macabre precautions have been necessary:
the urn of Louis's ashes in her bedroom, the memorial candles, the consultations with the rabbi on mourning procedures, the synagogue attendance to say *kaddish,* and the rest. But they have eased her mind.
Nor has she had to playact! The continuing uncertainty has been crushing her. In three weeks there has been no further word; just the official
death notice, and the grisly offer from the crematorium of his ashes, at
a price. For all we know as yet, those really are Louis's ashes in Natalie's room. Of course we don't believe that; still, it has been all too convincing a business, first to last.

(Alas! Whose are they?)

The war news is becoming glorious. One wakes each day hungry for
the latest word. German newspapers, smuggled in or pilfered from SS
quarters, are now passed eagerly from hand to hand, for they have become fountains of good cheer. Whatever the Goebbels press admits
must be true; and recent stories cause one to blink with amazed happiness. It is an absolute fact that a cadre of German generals have tried to
kill Hitler! I read a full account in the scrawny *Völkischer Beobachter,*
boiling with moral indignation at the "tiny clique of crazy traitors."
German army morale is clearly cracking. In the far-off Pacific—the
BBC, again—our Navy has won another victory while capturing the
Mariana islands, which brings Japan within the range of American
B-29s; and the Japanese government has fallen.

Meantime, the whole mad Beautification extravaganza is on again;
rehearsals, refurbishing, and construction of even more fake Theresienstadt delights: a public "beach" on the river, an open-air theatre, and
Heaven knows what else. The film is a God-given reprieve. Preparing
for it will take a month; shooting, another month. The Germans are as
fully bent on it as they were on the Beautification. If somebody in the
collapsing Berlin regime doesn't think of countermanding the film, the
cameras may be inanely grinding away when Russian or American
tanks come crashing through the Bohusovice Gate.

For the Anglo-Americans have at last begun to break out of their
Normandy bridgehead. The German papers tell of heavy fighting
around Saint-Lô, a new place-name. On the eastern front, old place-
names of my youth fill the German communiqués, as the Soviets have
driven deep into eastern Poland. Pinsk, Baranovitch, Ternopol, Lvov—

great Jewish cities, homes of famous yeshivas and eminent Hassidi
dynasties—have been recaptured by the Red Army.

From Lvov, as the crow flies, Theresienstadt is some four hundre
miles.

In the past three weeks, the Russians have advanced two hundre
miles. *In three weeks.*

It is a race. Because of the film, we have a chance. Thank God—thi
once—for the Nazi passion for crude fraud!

AUGUST 6.

I have been drafted to work on the film script, hence the gap in thi
record. I suggested a simple visual running theme—the flow of water, i
and out of the ghetto—thinking that some clever viewers might catch th
symbolism of the "sluice." The director grasped it without words; I sav
it in his eyes. The blockhead Rahm approves. He is taking childis
pleasure in the film project; especially in selecting the bathing girls fo
the beach scene.

And still no word about Louis. Nothing. He disappeared into th
hospital a month ago yesterday. Natalie puts in her day's work at th
mica factory, then plods to the children's pavilion for film rehearsal
She does not eat, she never mentions Louis, and she looks gaunt an
haunted. A few days ago in desperation she went to the hospital an
demanded to talk to the doctor who wrote Louis's death certificate. Sh
was very roughly turned away.

AUGUST 18.

Filming began. I have been rewriting the half-witted script night an
day with four collaborators, under the interminable meddling of th
dullard Rahm. No time to breathe, but thank God still for the film. Ei
senhower's armies have swarmed out over France and surrounded th
German armies at a place called Falaise. The BBC talks of a "wester
Stalingrad." The Allies have now landed in southern France, too, an
the Germans there are retreating in panic. "The south of France i
going up in flames," says the Free French radio, and the Russians hav
reached the Vistula. They are in Praga, across the river from Warsav
in great force. The Poles are rising against the Germans. In Warsav
there is bloody street fighting. One's hopes brighten and brighten.

AUGUST 30.

Louis is all right! Paris is liberated!
This is the brightest day in all my years.
During a filming session in the library today, a Czech cameraman—

honestly don't know which one, it happened so fast, in the glare of the klieg lights—shoved into my pocket an off-focus photograph of Berel and the boy. They stand by a haystack in strong sunlight. Louis looks plump and well. As I write these words, Natalie sits opposite me, still weeping with joy over the picture.

The good news from the battlefields is becoming a cataract. The American armies moved so fast across France that they captured Paris undamaged. The Germans simply pulled out and fled. Rumania has suddenly changed sides, and declared war on Germany. This caught the Nazi regime by surprise, it seems. Between the invading Red Army and the Rumanian turncoat forces, so says the Moscow radio, the Germans are snared in a colossal Balkan entrapment. They are being shattered on all fronts, no doubt of that. The Allied air bombing, complains the *Völkischer Beobachter,* is the most horrible and remorseless in history. How pleasant! The Goebbels editorials take on a strident tone of *Götterdämmerung.* This war can end at any moment.

SEPTEMBER 10.

How far off can the end be now? Bulgaria has declared war on Germany. Eisenhower's armies are driving for the Rhine, scarcely opposed by the fleeing Wehrmacht. The uprising in Warsaw goes on. Somehow the Russians have not managed to cross the Vistula to help the Poles. Of course those lightning advances strained their supply lines. No doubt that is the reason for the lull.

Now Rahm, after much meddling and dawdling, has abruptly ordered the film finished. No explanation. I can think of only one. When the Soviets captured Lublin, they overran a vast concentration camp for Jews there called Maidanek. They found gas chambers, crematoriums, mass graves, thousands and thousands of living skeletons, and countless corpses lying about, all exactly as Berel described Oswiecim. The Russians brought in thirty Western correspondents to see the horror for themselves. The details are being told and retold on Radio Moscow. The worst reports and rumors turn out to have been plain fact.

So the gruesome German game is up. "The Führer Grants the Jews a Town," an idyllic documentary of the Paradise Ghetto almost two hours long, will probably never be shown. After the Lublin exposure the film is a self-evident, clumsy, hopeless fabrication. Our reprieve expires in five days. Then what? Nobody knows yet.

It is very strange. All these crashing war developments are for us distant thunder. We read words on paper, or we hear whispers of what was said on some foreign radio. Theresienstadt itself remains a stagnant little prison town where every sticky summer day is the same; a noisome ghetto jammed with undernourished, sick, scared people; faintly animated by the filming nonsense, but otherwise quiet as a morgue.

• • •

From 𝔚𝔬𝔯𝔩𝔡 𝔥𝔬𝔩𝔬𝔠𝔞𝔲𝔰𝔱

The September Miracle

During August our doom appeared to some giddy Western journalists "a question of days." The jaws of the east-west vise had closed to the Vistula and the Meuse. On the southern fronts the Anglo-Americans were driving up the Rhone valley almost unchecked, and ascending the Italian boot far north of Rome; and the Russians, wheeling in a great mass through our wide-open southern flank in the treacherous Balkans, had arrived at the Danube. On nearly every active front large numbers of our forces were either retreating or encircled.

Later Hitler himself called August 15 "the worst day of my life." That was the day the Allies landed in the south of France, and in the north General von Kluge disappeared into the Falaise pocket. Pathologically suspicious after July 20, the Führer feared that Kluge might have vanished to negotiate; the situation actually looked that bad at Headquarters. But the gallant Kluge soon managed to restore communications with us. Shortly afterward he killed himself; whether in despair over Hitler's stupid commands which were destroying his army, or because he was really involved in the bomb plot, I do not know. In August, I confess, the thought of suicide more than once crossed my own mind.

But September passed and no enemy soldier had yet set foot on German soil!

After Rundstedt's forces brilliantly repulsed Montgomery's foolhardy narrow thrust with airborne troops at Arnhem, trying to flank the Westwall through Holland, Eisenhower's rush toward the Rhine faded away. Gas tanks were empty, generals at loggerheads, strength dispersed from the Low Countries to the Alps. The Russians were halted along the Vistula, coping with our counterattacks, while across the river the Waffen SS levelled Warsaw with fire and explosives to wipe out the uprising. The southern drives against us were all halted. Under the worst pounding and against the worst odds of modern history, Germany stood bloodied and defiant, holding its ring of foes at bay.

If the lone British stand in 1940 merits praise, why not this heroic rebound of the Wehrmacht in September 1944?

The analytical elements of the "September miracle" are clear. West and east, our enemies outran their supplies in their spectacular and speedy advances; while German discipline hardened and total mobilization took place, under the threat to our sacred soil. Nor can one overlook the letdown in the invaders' fighting morale, especially in the west: the euphoric feeling of "well, we've won the war, we'll be home by Christmas," induced by long advances, the fall of Paris, and the attempt on Hitler's life. Also, Hitler's one-sided insistence on hardening up the French ports was at last paying some dividends. Eisenhower had two million men ashore, but through the distant bottlenecks of Cherbourg and an artificial harbor he could not supply an all-out assault on the Westwall. He needed Antwerp, and we still dominated the Scheldt estuary.

In postwar military writings there is much armchair scoffing at Eisenhower. These authors dwell on map distances and troop counts, overlooking the sweaty, gritty, complex logistics that decide modern war. Eisenhower was the typical American military man, a plodder in the field but something of a genius in organization and supply. His caution and broadfront strategy were not unsound, if scarcely Napoleonic. We were still a very dangerous foe, and he deserves credit for resisting specious gambles in September.

Advocates of both Montgomery and Patton argue that given enough gasoline, each of their heroes could have thrust on to Berlin and quickly ended the war. General Blumentritt told British interrogators that Montgomery could certainly have done it. I shall demonstrate in my operational analysis the decisive adverse factors. Briefly, the flanks of such a narrow thrust on extended supply lines would have invited a disastrous repulse, a much greater Arnhem. I knew Blumentritt well, and I doubt that those were his professional views. He was telling his conquerors what they wanted to hear. Given the port facilities and communications available to Eisenhower, the thing could not be done. The consumption rate of his troops was quite shocking: seven hundred tons per division per day! A German division did its fighting on less than two hundred tons a day.

Eisenhower could not afford a massive risk and setback; not with hundreds of American correspondents breathing down his neck, and a presidential election two months away. The enemy coalition was unstable enough. All through the summer campaign the Anglo-Americans pulled and tugged at bad cross-purposes. And the Russian failure to aid the Warsaw uprising —and what was worse, their refusal to allow the Anglo-Americans even to send airborne assistance—already planted the poison of the Polish question, which would in time destroy the strange alliance of capitalists and Bolsheviks.

Unfortunately we lacked the punch to exploit these strains among our foes. Hitler's mulish "stand or die" policy on the battlefield had bled us too much. In the three colossal summer defeats—Bagration, the Balkans, and western France—and a score of smaller entrapments, one million five hundred thousand German front-line troops had been killed, captured, cut off, or routed in disorder without arms. Had these battle-hardened forces fought an elastic defense instead, harrying our foes' advance while withdrawing in good order to the Fatherland, we might well have salvaged something from the war.

As it was, the "September miracle" could not avert *Finis Germaniae,* it could only postpone the doom. Yet even as he went down, Hitler retained the hypnotic power to draw suicidal reserves of nervous energy and fighting heart from Germany. Already at the end of August he had issued his startling directive for the Ardennes counterattack. With heavy hearts we were making plans and issuing preliminary orders at Headquarters. However badly the man was failing, his feral willpower was not to be opposed.

———————

TRANSLATOR'S NOTE: *This Ardennes operation became the "Battle of the Bulge." It is interesting that Roon commends Eisenhower's cautious broadfront strategy, which many authorities condemn. The true judgment would lie in unravelling very complicated logistical statistics of Overlord. Fortune favors the bold, but not when they are out of gas and bullets. The strange Red Army inaction while Warsaw was destroyed by the Germans in plain sight across the river remains controversial. Some say that from Stalin's viewpoint the wrong Poles were leading the uprising. The Russians maintain that they had reached the limit of their supplies, and that the Poles did not bother to coordinate their uprising with Red Army plans.—V.H.*

• • •

From A Jew's Journey

OCTOBER 4.

The fourth transport since the filming ended is now loading. I have just come from the Hamburg barracks, where I said my last good-bye to Yuri, Joshua, and Jan. That is the end of my Theresienstadt Talmud class.

We stayed up all night in the library, studying by candlelight until dawn broke. The boys had packed their few belongings, and they wanted to learn to the last. A strange and abstruse topic we had reached, too: the *met-mitzva,* the unidentified body found in the fields, whose burial is a strict duty to all. The Talmud drives to a dramatic extreme to make the point. A high priest, enjoined by special laws of ritual purity against contact with a corpse, is forbidden to bury even his own father or mother. So is a man under Nazirite vows. Yet a high priest who has taken a Nazirite vow—thus being doubly restricted—is commanded to bury a *met-mitzva* with his own hands! Such is the Jewish regard for human dignity, even in death. The voice of the Talmud speaks across two thousand years to teach my boys, as its last word to them, the gulf between ourselves and the Germans.

Joshua, the brightest of the three remaining lads, asked abruptly as I closed the old volume, "Rebbe, are we all going to be gassed?"

That yanked me back to the present! The rumors are rife in the ghetto now, though few people are tough-minded enough to face up to them. Thank God I was able to answer, "No. You're going to join your father, Joshua—and you, Yuri and Jan, your older brothers—at a construction project near Dresden. That's what we in the council have been informed, and that's what I believe."

Their faces shone as though I had set them free from prison. They were high-spirited still at the barracks, with the transport numbers around their necks, and I could see that they were cheering up other people.

Was I deceiving them, as well as myself? The Zossen construction project outside Berlin—temporary government huts—is a fact. The workers from Theresienstadt and their families are being very well treated there. This labor project in the Dresden area, Rahm has firmly assured the council, is the same sort of thing. Zucker heads the draft; an able man, an old Prague Zionist and council member, very supple at handling the Germans.

The pessimists in the council, who tend to be Zionists and long-term ghetto inmates, don't believe Rahm at all. The draft of five thousand able-bodied men, they say, denudes us of the hands needed for an uprising, should the SS decide to liquidate the ghetto. There have been uprisings in other ghettos; we hear the reports. When Eppstein was arrested after the filming stopped, and the order came down for this huge labor draft, the false security of the Beautification and the movie foolishness dissolved, and the council was plunged in dismay. We had had no transport order in almost five months. I heard mutinous mutterings around the table that astonished me, and there were Zionist meetings about an uprising to which I was not invited. But the draft went off on schedule in three transports, with no disturbance.

This fourth transport is extremely worrisome. True, they are the relatives of the construction workers who have gone. But last week the SS permitted relatives to volunteer to go along, and about a thousand did. These are being railroaded out willy-nilly. The one shred of reassurance is that the four shipments do make up one group, the big labor draft and its families. Rahm explains that it is the policy to keep families together. This may be a soothing lie; conceivably it could still be true.

The endless talk in the council about our probable fate comes down to two opposed views: (1) Despite the lull in the war, the Germans have lost, and they know it; and we can expect a gradual softening of our SS bosses as they start thinking of self-preservation. (2) The lust of the Germans to murder all the Jews of Europe will only be aggravated by looming defeat; they will rush to complete this "triumph" if they can gain no other.

I hesitate between the two probabilities. One is sensible, the other insane. The Germans have both faces.

Natalie is a total pessimist. She is recovering much of her old toughness, now that Louis is gone and safe; eating the worst slops voraciously, and gaining weight and strength every day. She means to survive, she says, and find Louis; and if transported, she intends to be strong enough to survive as a laborer.

OCTOBER 5.

A fifth transport was ordered *two hours* after the fourth left; a random selection of eleven hundred people. No explanation this time, nothing to do with the Dresden construction project. Many families will have to be broken up. Large numbers of the sick, and women with small children, will go. Natalie probably would have gone, if Louis were still here. The Germans simply lied again.

I will not yield to despair. Despite the strange lull on the battlefronts, Hitler's Reich is falling. The civilized world can yet smash into this lunatic enclave of Nazi Europe in time to save our remnant. Like Natalie, I want to live. I want to tell this story.

If I do not, these scrawls will speak for me in a distant time.

85

THE wind was high, the swells huge, as Battleship Division Seven stood in to Ulithi atoll with the *Iowa* in the van, and the *New Jersey* in column astern flying Halsey's flag. When the battleships pitched, gray water broke clear over their massive forecastles, and the dipping long guns vanished in spray. The screening destroyers were bobbing in and out of sight on the wind-streaked black swells of the typhoon's aftermath. Blue patches were just starting to show in the overcast after the storm.

Ye gods, Victor Henry was thinking—as the warm sticky wind, sweeping salt spray all the way up to the *Iowa*'s flag bridge, wetted his face—how I love this sight! Since the newsreels of his boyhood days showing dreadnoughts plowing the seas, battleships under way had always stirred him like martial music. Now these were *his* ships, more grand and strong than any he had ever served in. The accuracy of the radar-controlled main batteries, in the first gunnery exercises he had ordered, astounded him. The barrage thrown up by the bristling AA made a show like the victory blaze over Moscow. Halsey's staff in its happy-go-lucky fashion had not yet put out the Leyte operation order, but Pug Henry was convinced that this landing in the Philippines meant a fleet battle. Avenging the *Northampton* with the guns of the *Iowa* and the *New Jersey* was a grimly pleasing prospect.

Signal flags ran snapping and fluttering up the halyards, ordered by Pug's chief of staff: *Take formation to enter channel.* Responding flags showed on the *New Jersey* and the carriers and destroyers. The task group smoothly reshuffled its stations. Pug had one reservation about his new life; as he had told Pamela, there wasn't enough to do. Paperwork could keep him as busy as he pleased, but in fact his staff—nearly all reserves, but good men—and his chief of staff had things under control. His function was close to ceremonial, and would continue so until BatDiv Seven got into a fight.

He could not even explore the *Iowa* much. At sea he had an ingrained busybody instinct, and he yearned to nose around the engine spaces, the turrets, the magazines, the machine shops, even the crew's quarters of this gargantuan vessel; but it would look like snooping on the work of the *Iowa*'s captain and exec. He had missed out on commanding one of these engineering marvels, and his two stars had lifted him forever beyond the satisfying dirty work of seagoing, into airy spotless flag quarters.

As the *Iowa* steamed up Mugai channel, Pug had his eye out for submarines; he had not seen Byron or heard from him in months. Fleet carriers, new fast battleships, cruisers, destroyers, minesweepers, support vessels, were awesomely arrayed in this lagoon ten thousand miles from home; one could scarcely see the palms and coral beaches of the atoll for the warships. But no subs. Not unusual; Saipan was their forward base now. The dispatch that his flag lieutenant brought him as the anchor rattled down was therefore a disquieting surprise.

FROM: CO BARRACUDA
TO: COMBATDIV SEVEN
RESPECTFULLY REQUEST PERMISSION CALL ON YOU

It had come in on the harbor circuit. The submarine was berthed in the southern anchorage, the flag lieutenant said, blocked from view by nests of LSTs.

But why the commanding officer, Pug wondered? Byron was the exec. Was he ill? In trouble? Off the *Barracuda?* Pug uneasily scrawled a reply.

FROM: COMBATDIV SEVEN
TO: CO BARRACUDA
MY BARGE WILL FETCH YOU 1700 DINNER MY QUARTERS

For Halsey's command conference, deferred by the typhoon sortie, long black barges fluttering white-starred blue flags came bouncing through the choppy waters to the *New Jersey*. Soon admirals in starched open-collared khakis ranged the long green table of Halsey's quarters. Pug had never seen so many starred collar pins and flag officers' faces in one room. There was still no operation order. Halsey's chief of staff, standing with a pointer at a big Pacific chart, described the forthcoming strikes at Luzon, Okinawa, and Formosa, intended to squelch land-based air interference with MacArthur's landing. Then Halsey, though looking very worn and aged, talked zestfully about the operation. The Nips could hardly stand by idly while MacArthur recaptured the Philippines. They might well hit back with everything they had. That would be the chance to make a killing, to annihilate the Imperial Fleet once for all; the chance Ray Spruance had passed up at Saipan.

His pouchy eyes glinting, Halsey read aloud from Nimitz's directive. He was ordered to cover and support the forces under MacArthur *"in order to assist in the seizure and occupation of all objectives in the Central Philippines."* That much he intoned in a level voice. Then giving the assembled admirals an amused yet menacing glare, he grated slow words: *"In case opportunity for destruction of major portion of the enemy fleet is offered or can be created, SUCH DESTRUCTION BECOMES THE PRIMARY TASK."*

That was the sentence, he said, that had been missing from Ray Spruance's directive for Saipan. Getting it into his own orders for Leyte had been a job, but there it was. So everybody at the conference now knew what the Third Fleet was going to Leyte for; to destroy the Japanese navy, once the invasion forced it out of hiding.

At the eager exclamations of approval around the table, the old warrior grinned with tired happiness. The talk moved to routine details of the air strikes. The chief of staff mentioned that some newspapermen flown out by Cincpac to observe the Third Fleet in action would be berthed in the *Iowa* as guests of ComBatDiv Seven.

Amused glances all turned on Pug Henry, who blurted, "Oh, Christ, no! I'd rather have a bunch of women aboard."

Halsey wagged gray thick eyebrows. "Ha! Who wouldn't?"

Barks of laughter.

"Admiral, I mean old, bent, toothless women, with skin ailments."

"Of course, Pug. We can't be all that fussy out here."

The conference broke up in ribald merriment.

When Pug returned to the *Iowa* his chief of staff told him that the newspapermen were already aboard, berthed in wardroom country. "Just keep them away from me," Pug growled.

"The fact is," said the chief of staff, a pleasant and able captain of the class of '24, with thick prematurely white hair, "they've already asked for a press conference with you."

Pug used obscenity sparely, but he let fly at the chief of staff, who departed fast.

Mail lay on the desk in two baskets: official, stacked high as usual, and a small personal pile. He always looked first for Pamela's letters. There was one, promisingly thick. Pulling it out, he saw a small pink envelope, with the address on the back that still jarred him:

MRS. HARRISON PETERS

1417 FOXHALL ROAD

WASHINGTON, D.C.

The letter was brisk. The longer Hack lived in the Foxhall Road house, Rhoda wrote, the better he liked it. In fact, he wanted to buy it. She knew Pug had never really been fond of the place. It was a messy thing, since the divorce settlement had given her rent-free occupancy, but left the house in his name until she felt like disposing of it. If Pug would just write to his lawyer and suggest a sale price, the "legal beagles" could get started. Rhoda reported that Janice was seeing a lot of a law school instructor, and that Vic was doing admirably in nursery school.

> Madeline has been a great comfort, too. She actually writes every month or so, cheering me up. She seems to love New Mexico. I got one lovely letter from Byron at last. I wondered and wondered how he would take it. Frankly I sort of *cringed*. He doesn't understand, any more than I do, exactly, but he wished me and Hack happiness. He said that to him I would always be just Mom, no matter what. Couldn't be sweeter. Sooner or later you'll see him out there. When you explain, don't be too hard on me. The whole thing's been hard enough. However, I am perfectly happy.
>
> Love,
> Rho

Pug rang for coffee, and told his Filipino steward that he would be dining in his quarters with one guest. He wrote a terse reply to Rhoda, sealed it up, and tossed it in his out-basket. The thickness of Pam's envelope, perhaps because of the pall of Rhoda's letter, now seemed ominous. He settled down with coffee in an armchair to read.

It was indeed a grave letter. It began, "Sorry, love, but I'm going to write about nothing but death." Three shocks had struck her in two weeks, the first by far the worst, the others hitting her hard because of her low state. Burne-Wilke had died, swept away by a fulminating pneumonia. She had left Stoneford months ago, and the family had not notified her, so she had first learned about it at the Air Ministry, and had missed the funeral. Guilt was gnawing at her. Would he have sickened if she had stayed on with him, cared for him, and said nothing about the future until the end of the war? Had the hurt and the loneliness weakened him? She could never know, but she was having an unhappy time over it.

> There's something awful altogether about this September. It's a brown wet ugly fall. The buzz bombs were bad enough, but these new horrors, huge rockets that arrive and fall without a sound, have thrown us into a funk. After all the wretched years of war, after the great Normandy landing and the sweep through France, with victory apparently days away, we're back in the blitz! It's just too damned much—the sirens, the all-night fires, the frightful explosions, the roped-off streets,

the acres of smoking rubble, the civilian death lists, all over again—ghastly, ghastly, ghastly!

And Montgomery has had an atrocious fiasco in Holland, with an enormous commitment of airborne troops. It's probably killed any chance of ending the war before mid-1945. The worst of it is that Monty keeps telling the papers it was a "partial victory." Ugh!

It was a rocket that killed Phil Rule, poor wretch. It blew to smithereens the newsmen's pub he haunted, leaving nothing but a crater for two blocks in all directions. Days went by before there even was a reliable death list. Phil has simply vanished. Of course he was killed. I had no feelings left about Philip Rule, as you well know, but too much of my youth was thrown away on him, and his death hurts.

As for Leslie, it's conceivable that he's still alive, but not likely. The French dentist who was in the team made his way to Bradley's army, and I've read his report. The team was betrayed by an informer in Saint-Nazaire. They got into the town hidden inside big wine casks, in a huge vanload of wine delivered to the German garrison. They managed to obtain and send out excellent intelligence about the defenses. In trying to organize an uprising, they got careless about the Frenchmen they took into their confidence, and the Germans trapped them. The dentist, before he escaped from the house where they were ambushed, saw Leslie fall, shot. Another pointless death! As you know the Brittany ports are no longer significant. Eisenhower is just letting the German garrisons wither there. Leslie's death, if he died, was sheer waste.

Leslie Slote, Phil Rule, and Natalie Jastrow! Pug, you dear good upright man of arms, you can't picture what it was like to be young in Paris with those three in the mid-thirties. What in God's name has become of poor Natalie? Is *she* dead, too?

What has this gruesome war all been for? Can you tell me? Poor Duncan believed—and I'm sure he was right—that as soon as the war ends and we pull out of India, the Hindus and Moslems will butcher each other in the millions. He predicted, too, that a Chinese civil war "will turn the Yellow River red." Certainly the Empire is finished. You saw Russia, a gutted slaughterhouse to the Volga. And what have we achieved? We have almost succeeded in murdering enough Germans and Japanese to convince them to quit trying to plunder the world. That's all. We haven't finished with that dirty business yet, after five long years.

Duncan said—it was on our last night together at Stoneford, actually, and he was of course melancholy, but unfailingly gentle and decent as always—that the worst part of this century would not be the war, but the aftermath. He said the young would be left with such utter contempt for their elders, after this stupid bath of world carnage, that there would be a general collapse of religion, morals, values, and politics. "Hitler will have his *Götterdämmerung*," Duncan said. "He's pulled it off. The West is done for. The Americans will seem all right for a while, but they'll go too, at last, in a spectacular and probably sudden racial blowup."

I wonder what you'd say to that! Duncan was rather down on Americans, for complicated reasons, not wholly excluding you and me. He saw the world going Buddhist in the end, after perhaps another half century of horror and impoverishment. I could never follow him into the *Bhagavad-Gita,* but he was morbidly persuasive that night, poor darling.

———————

Well, now it's a rainy morning.

Can you guess that I was pretty tipsy last night when I clattered out all those pages? I'm wondering whether to send such a depressing wail to you, out there in the Pacific, still with the job of fighting the war, and therefore still having to believe in it. Well, I'll send it. It's how I feel, and it's the news. In a day or two I'll write you another and more cheery one, I promise. I don't expect to be knocked on the head by a V-2, and if I should be, it's a quick painless exit from this crazed world. I only want to live to love you. Everything else is gone, but that's enough to build on, for me. I swear I'll be jolly in my next one, especially if my resignation from the WAAFs is accepted, and I can start planning to join you. It's in the works; very irregular, horribly unpatriotic, but I may just pull it off. I know people.

All my love,
Pamela

Pug took from a drawer and set on his desk the picture of Pamela, in the old silver frame from which Rhoda had smiled for almost thirty years, stowed away for the typhoon sortie. Pamela was in uniform, full-length, frowning. The picture was cropped from a news shot and blurrily blown up; far from flattering, but quite real, unlike Rhoda's old softly lit studio portrait, so many years out of date. He got at his official mail.

The gangway messenger of the *Barracuda* knocked at Byron's cabin door. "Captain, the admiral's barge is coming alongside."

"Thanks, Carson." In jockey shorts, his body shining with sweat, Byron was taking down from a bulkhead the Red Cross photograph of Natalie and Louis. "Ask Mr. Philby to meet me topside."

He came out on deck buttoning a faded gray shirt. The new exec was at the gangway; a foxy-faced Academy lieutenant who (Byron already surmised) did not much relish serving under a reserve skipper. The *Barracuda* was tied up port side to an ammunition ship. A working party aft was making a great profane noise around a torpedo swinging down on a crane.

"Tom, when all the fish are aboard, cast off, and take her alongside the *Bridge* for provisioning. I'll be back by 1900."

"Aye aye, sir."

ComBatDiv Seven's long barge, all gleaming white cordwork and white leather cushioning inside, purred away from the submarine. The luxury charmed Byron for what it said of his father's new status, but his mind was mainly on the divorce. Madeline had written that she had "seen it coming for a long time." Byron could not understand her. To him, until the arrival of the long sad surgary letter from Rhoda, his parents' marriage had been a monolithic fact, literally the Bible's "one flesh." No doubt his flighty mother was at fault, yet one passage in a letter his father had written from London still puzzled him: "I hope your mother will be happy. Things have been happening in my life, too, better discussed face to face, when the occasion offers, than written about."

Now they would come face to face. It would be awkward, possibly painful for his father, but at least the identity of the *Barracuda*'s captain should give him a nice surprise.

The watch book of the *Iowa*'s OOD noted, *At 1730 admiral's guest will arrive. JOOD escort to flag quarters.* But at 1720 the admiral himself appeared, squinting toward the south anchorage. In the glittering weather after the typhoon, the low sun blazed and the lagoon blindingly sparkled. The officer of the deck had seldom seen Rear Admiral Henry up close, this bloodless force called ComBatDiv Seven, a spruce squat grizzled man, a tongue-tying icy presence. The barge came alongside and a tall officer in dingy wrinkled grays leaped up the steps, jingling the guy chains.

"Request permission to come aboard."

"Permission granted."

"Good evening, Admiral." A sharp unsmiling salute by the officer in gray.

"Hello there." A casual return salute. ComBatDiv Seven said to the OOD, "Log my visitor aboard, please. Commanding officer of the *Barracuda,* SS 204. Lieutenant Commander Byron Henry, USNR."

The OOD, glancing from father to son, ventured a grin. A brief cool smile was the admiral's response.

"When did all this happen?" Pug asked as they left the quarterdeck.

"As a matter of fact, only three days ago."

The father's right hand momentarily gripped Byron's shoulder. They mounted the ladders inside the citadel at a run. "You're in pretty good condition," the son panted.

"I may drop dead doing that," said Pug, breathing hard. "But I'll be the healthiest man ever buried at sea. Come out on my bridge for a minute."

"Wow!" Byron shaded his eyes to look around.

"You don't get this view from a submarine."

"God, no. Doesn't it beat anything in history?"

"Eisenhower had a bigger fleet for the crossing to Normandy. But for striking power, you're right, the earth's never seen its like before."

"And the *size* of the *Iowa!*" Byron was looking aft. "What a beauty!"

"Ah, Briny, she's put together like a Swiss watch. Maybe later we'll mosey around."

Pug was still digesting the surprise. *Commander of a submarine!* Byron was growing into an eerie resemblance to the lost Warren; too pale, though, too tense in his movements.

"I'm pretty tight for time, Dad."

"Then let's go in to dinner."

"Snazzy setup," Byron said, as they entered the flag quarters. Sunlight streamed through the portholes, brightening the impressive outer cabin.

"Comes with the job. Beats a desk in Washington."

"I'll say—" Byron halted, his eyes widening at the silver-framed photograph on the desk. "Who's *that?*" Before Pug could answer he turned on his father. "Christ, isn't that Pamela Tudsbury?"

"Yes. It's a long story." Pug had not intended to break it this way, but the thing was done now. "I'll explain at dinner."

Byron's right hand shot up, palm and fingers stiff and flat. "It's your life." He yanked the snapshot of Natalie and Louis from a breast pocket. "I think I wrote you about this."

"Ah! The Red Cross picture." Pug scanned it avidly. "Why, Byron, they both look very well. How big the boy is!"

"It was taken in June. God knows what's happened since."

"They're in a playground, aren't they? Those children in the background look fine, too."

"Yes, it's encouraging, as far as it goes. But the Red Cross has ignored my letters ever since. The State Department remains a total zilch."

Pug handed back the picture. "Thanks. Seeing it does my heart good. Sit you down."

"Dad, maybe I'll just have a cup of coffee and run on back. We sortie at 0500. I've got a new exec, and—"

"Byron, dinner takes fifteen minutes." Pug gestured at his conference table, already set with two places at one end: white napery, silver and china, a vase of pink frangipani sprigs. "You've got to eat."

"Well, if it'll only take fifteen minutes."

"I'll see to that."

Pug strode out. Sinking into the chair at his desk, Byron peered incredulously at the photograph in the old silver frame that, as far back as he could remember, had held his mother's picture.

Sons find it uncomfortable to confront the reality of their fathers' sexual lives. Psychologists can analyze the reasons till the cows come home, and they tend to, but it is a clear fact of human nature. Had the picture of a woman his mother's age filled the frame, Byron could have absorbed the jolt. But *Pamela Tudsbury,* a girl who had helled around with Natalie in Paris! Byron had liked her well enough for the way she looked after her father. Even so, he had wondered, especially at Gibraltar, how such a hot dish—Pamela had been lightly clad on that Mediterranean midsummer day in a gauzy white sleeveless frock—could devote herself to following an old man about. She must have a lover, he had thought, if not several.

Her picture on his father's desk, in that frame, conjured up ugly visions of crude sex, mismatched sex, shacked-up sex, wartime London sex. There it stared, the proclamation of Pug Henry's weakness, the explanation of the divorce. To think that his idolized father—while he himself and Natalie were separated by the war—had groaned and thumped around on a bed in London with a girl Natalie's age! Byron resolved to keep utter silence, and at the first possible moment to get the hell off this battleship.

"Chow down," said his father.

They sat at the table, and the beaming Filipino steward served bowls of fragrant fish soup. Because this was such a rare moment for Pug—himself a flag officer, Byron a submarine captain, meeting for the first time in their new dignities—he put his head down and said a long heartfelt grace. Byron said, *"Amen,"* and not another word while he gulped soup.

There was nothing unusual about that. Pug had always had trouble conversing with Byron. His mere presence was satisfying enough. Pug did not realize that Pamela's picture had caused an earthquake in his son. He knew it was a surprise, a disconcerting one, and he intended to explain. To get talk going again he remarked, "Say, incidentally, aren't you the first reserve skipper in the whole submarine fleet?"

"No, three of the guys have S-boats by now, and Moose Holloway just got *Flounder*. He's the first one to get a fleet boat. Of course he's Yale NROTC from way back, and from an old Navy family. I guess being your son did me no harm."

"You had to have the record."

"Well, Carter Aster qualified me long ago, but I've not yet had a PCO cruise, and—what happened was, my skipper took sick out on station off Sibutu." Byron was glad to fill the time with talk that stayed off his father's personal life. "Woke up one morning in a fever and couldn't walk, not without terrible pain. Dragged himself around for a week, taking aspirin, but then he tried an attack on a freighter and botched it. By then he obviously was so damned sick we headed straight in here instead of returning to Saipan. They're still giving him blood tests on the *Solace*. He's half-paralyzed. I thought SubPac would fly out a CO, but they sent an exec instead, and I got the orders. Floored me."

"Talking of surprises," said Pug, by way of leading up to Pamela, "that fellow Leslie Slote is probably a goner. You remember him?"

"Slote? Of course. He's dead?"

"Well, that's Pam's information." Pug recounted his sketchy knowledge of the parachute mission on which Slote had been lost. "How about that? Would you have figured him as a volunteer for extra-hazardous duty?"

"Do you still have Mom's picture?" Byron said, looking at his wristwatch and pushing away his half-eaten food. "If you have, I'll take it."

"I have it, but not here. Let me tell you about Pamela."

"Not if it's a long story, Dad. I've got to go. What happened to you and Mom?"

"Well, son, the war."

"Did Mom ask for the divorce so as to marry Peters? Or did you want it because of *her?*" Byron jerked a thumb toward the picture.

"Byron, don't look for someone to blame."

Pug could not tell his son the truth. On the bald facts Byron would probably absolve him and despise his mother; this hard-faced young submariner was a black-or-white moralist such as he had himself been before the war. But Pug no longer condemned Rhoda for the Kirby business, he only felt sorry for her. These nuances went with being older, sadder, and more self-knowing than Byron could yet be. His son's silence and the rigid face made Pug very uneasy, and he added, "I know Pamela's young. That troubles me, and the whole thing may not come off."

"Dad, I don't know if I'm fit for command."

The sudden words hit Pug a hammer blow.

"ComSubPac thinks you are."

"ComSubPac can't look into my mind."

"What's your problem?"

"Possible instability under combat stress."

"You're cool by nature under the severest stress. That, I know."

"By nature, maybe. I'm in an unnatural state. Natalie and Louis haunt me. Warren's dead and I'm the one you've got left. Also, I'm a reserve skipper, one of the first, and that's a hot spot. I've been emulating you, Dad, or trying to. I came here today hoping for a shot in the arm. Instead—" again, the thumb pointing to Pamela's picture.

"I'm sorry that you're taking it that way, because—"

"There's always a shortage of aggressive COs," Byron rode over his father, something he never did. "I rate high for aggressiveness, I know that. The trouble is, my stomach for the whole thing is dropping out. This picture"—he touched his breast pocket—"is driving me crazy. If Natalie had listened to me and risked a few hours on a French train, she'd be back home now. It doesn't help to remember that. Nor does your divorce. I'm not in the best of shape, Dad. I can take the *Barracuda* back to Saipan and ask for a relief. Or I can go out on lifeguard station off Formosa as ordered, for the air strikes. What would you recommend?"

"Only you can make that decision."

"Why? You were willing to decide my whole life for me, weren't you? If you hadn't pushed me into submarine school—if you hadn't flown down to Miami the very day I proposed to Natalie, and forced the issue, with her sitting there and listening—she wouldn't have gone back to Europe. She and my kid wouldn't be over there now, if in fact they're even alive."

"I regret what I did. At the time it seemed right."

This answer caused Byron's eyes to redden. "Okay, okay. I'll tell you something, it's a bad symptom of my instability that I throw that up to you."

"Byron, when I was in bad shape myself, I requested the *Northampton*. I found that command at sea made life more bearable, because it was so all-absorbing."

"But I'm not a professional like you, and a submarine is a mortal responsibility."

"If you return to Saipan, some aviators may drown off Formosa that you might save."

After a silence Byron said, "Well, I'd better get back to my boat."

They did not speak again until they were out on the warm breezy quarterdeck in a magnificent sunset, leaning side by side on the rail.

Byron said as though talking to himself, "There's something else. My exec's an Academy man. Taking orders from me grates on him."

"Judge him on performance at sea. Never mind how he feels."

Below from astern came the clanging of the barge. Byron straightened up and saluted. It hurt Pug to look into his son's remote eyes. "Good luck and good hunting, Byron." He returned the salute, they shook hands, and Byron went down the accommodation ladder.

The barge thrummed away. Pug returned to his quarters, and found the operation order for the Formosa strike on his desk, just delivered. Concentrating on the thick pile of inky-smelling mimeographed sheets was almost impossible. Pug kept thinking that he could not survive as a functioning man the loss of Byron.

And with this strained parting, father and son headed out into the biggest fleet battle in the history of the world.

PART SEVEN

Leyte Gulf

86

THE great sea fight turned on four elements: two strategic, one geographical, one human. The fate of Victor Henry and his son now rode on these four elements, so they should be borne in mind.

The geographical element was simply the conformation of the Philippines. Seven thousand islands straggle roughly north and south over a thousand miles of ocean between Japan and the East Indies. Capture of the Philippines meant cutting off Japan from oil, metal, and food. Luzon, the northernmost and largest island, was the key to the archipelago; and Lingayen Gulf, the classic landing area on Luzon for a drive to Manila, opens northwestward into the South China Sea.

Choosing as his stepping-stone to Luzon the smaller island of Leyte far to the southeast, MacArthur planned a landing in force on the shores of Leyte Gulf; a body of water hemmed in by island masses and small islets, opening eastward into the Philippine Sea. From the east, the American attackers could steam straight into the gulf, but from the west, the land masses and islets of the archipelago barred the way. Nearly all the water passages that threaded through the island maze were too shallow for fleet use.

Getting to Leyte from Japan itself, counterattacking Japanese units could steam down the eastern side of the archipelago and head straight in. Coming from the west or southwest, however—say from Singapore, or Borneo—there were but two usable ways through the archipelago to Leyte Gulf for warships: San Bernardino Strait, which would bring a task force past the big island of Samar for a turn down into the gulf from the north, or Surigao Strait, which enters the gulf from the south.

To be near fuel sources, the Main Striking Force of the Imperial Fleet was based off Singapore. It was scheduled to refuel in Borneo, if it had to do battle for the Philippines.

The human element was Admiral Halsey's frame of mind. This was dominated by an event five months in the past.

Back in June, the Pacific Fleet under Spruance had taken Saipan, an island in the Marianas chain, as a long hop toward Japan. The landing had provoked a major carrier duel, at once dubbed by American naval aviators as the "Marianas Turkey Shoot"; an aerial disaster for Japan, in which most of her surviving first-line pilots were shot down with small loss to Spruance. The Japanese carriers fled. The Americans in a short brutal land fight for Saipan gained an air base within bomber range of Tokyo. Spruance's opponent of Midway, Admiral Nagumo, the man who had bombed Pearl Harbor, committed suicide on Saipan; for with this breach of the Empire's inner defenses he deemed the war lost. So did many of Japan's leaders. The fall of Tojo, the militarist prime minister, was a world sensation, but the cause was not. The battle for Saipan was fought while Eisenhower's troops were grinding toward Cherbourg; so, like Imphal and Bagration, it was eclipsed in the newspapers.

Despite this historic if obscure victory, Spruance came in for savage insiders' criticism. His carrier commanders had yearned to steam out from Saipan to meet the oncoming Japanese for a head-on battle; they felt they could have annihilated the Imperial Fleet once for all. Spruance had reluctantly vetoed the idea. He would not be pulled away from the landing force he was there to shield, not knowing what other enemy forces might cut in behind him and wipe out the beachhead. So the Japanese aircraft had attacked in a cloud the Spruance forces hugging Saipan, and had fallen in the "Turkey Shoot," but their flattops and support forces had for the most part gotten away. King and Nimitz afterward praised Spruance's decision, but it remains in controversy. There were no other enemy forces at sea, critics still argue, and Spruance in his caution had passed up a chance for a big killing that might have shortened the war.

That was certainly Admiral Halsey's view. His character was eagerly aggressive, and at Leyte, he did not intend to repeat what he regarded as Spruance's great mistake.

As to strategy: on the American side two conflicting concepts for the Pacific war at last collided head-on—MacArthur's push northwest from Australia in land campaigns, the "South Pacific strategy"; and the Navy's island-to-island thrust across the broad watery wastes between Pearl Harbor and Tokyo, the "Central Pacific strategy."

The Navy planners wanted to bypass the Philippines altogether, land on Formosa or the China coast, and so "cork the bottle" of East Indies supplies. The bombing of shipping lanes, ports, and cities, they contended, with the submarine stranglehold, would in time force a surrender. MacArthur held the classic Army view that the enemy armed forces had to be defeated on land. New Guinea, the Philippines, then the home islands: that was his path to victory. King and Spruance, the chief Navy strategists, thought this would waste blood and time. Spruance even argued for a waterborne thrust straight to Iwo Jima and Okinawa. From these two small manageable objectives, he believed, air and submarine warfare could finish off Japan.

After Saipan, the Joint Chiefs of Staff got interested in the Navy strategy. MacArthur was outraged. In 1942 he had fled the Philippines by air on Roosevelt's orders. On arriving in Australia, he had publicly vowed, *I shall return.* He did not mean to return in a civilian airliner, after the Japanese had been beaten the Navy way. He demanded a personal meeting with the President, and he got it at Pearl Harbor in July.

Roosevelt had just been nominated for a fourth term. With the war going brilliantly in Europe, he undoubtedly wanted no trouble with MacArthur, whom the political opposition was portraying as a neglected and mistreated military genius. Arriving at Pearl Harbor an ailing man, Roosevelt heard out MacArthur's impassioned appeal for recapturing the Philippines as a "requirement of the national honor"; also Nimitz's quiet professional argument for the Navy plan.

MacArthur won. The invasion of the Philippines was on. Yet the radical Army–Navy split persisted. Nimitz assigned to MacArthur for his amphibious operation the entire Seventh Fleet under Vice Admiral Thomas Kinkaid; a grand armada of old battleships, with cruisers, escort carriers, and a train of destroyers, minesweepers, and oilers. But Nimitz kept tight control of the new fleet carriers and fast battleships, his striking arm; called Fifth Fleet when Spruance was leading it, and Third Fleet during Halsey operations.

Thus Kinkaid was heading a large sea force under MacArthur; Halsey was heading another large sea force under Nimitz; *and there was no supreme commander of the Leyte invasion.*

As to the Japanese strategy: Halsey's Formosa strikes before the battle had lead to a vast Japanese victory celebration. Imperial General Headquarters jubilantly announced that the rash Yankees had at last come to grief; Japanese army and navy planes had swarmed out over the Third Fleet and crushed it!

Eleven aircraft carriers sunk, eight damaged; two battleships sunk, two damaged; three cruisers sunk, four damaged; destroyers, light cruisers, and dozens of other unidentified ships destroyed or set afire.

So ran the official communiqué. With this stunning reversal of fortunes, Saipan was avenged! The threat of invasion to the Philippines was over! Mass demonstrations of joy broke out all over Japan. Hitler and Mussolini sent telegrams of congratulation. "Victory is within our grasp," the new premier announced, and the Emperor himself issued a rescript commemorating the triumph.

In rude fact, Halsey's Third Fleet had retired after the strikes without losing a single ship. The Japanese army air squadrons had been slaughtered, and their bases razed. The toll was about six hundred aircraft shot down, with two hundred more smashed and burned on the ground. The Japanese high command, taken in by overoptimism, had stripped the navy's carriers too, and flung their squadrons into the fight. Army and navy pilots alike were nearly all green recruits. Halsey's veteran aviators had made sport of them, but the few returning stragglers had brought back ridiculous victory reports. Splashing bombs, or their own comrades' aircraft exploding in the sea, had seemed to their excited innocent eyes flaming sinking battleships and carriers. The Japanese command had discounted the reports by fifty percent, but they were pure moonshine.

Then MacArthur's advance units landed on islands in Leyte Gulf, and reconnaissance reported a giant invasion expedition—Kinkaid's Seventh Fleet under MacArthur, seven hundred vessels or more—headed for the Philippines. Search planes from Luzon also found Halsey's Third Fleet afloat, intact, and on the prowl. The war-weary Japanese woke from the victory dream to the real nightmare. Word flashed out to the Imperial Fleet: *Execute Plan SHO-ONE.* The Japanese code name *Sho* meant "conquer." There were four versions of *Sho* to oppose a stab at four probable points of the Empire's shrinking perimeter. *Sho-One* was the Philippines plan.

Sho was a strategy of desperation. The whole Imperial Fleet would sail, covered by army air forces in the Philippines and Formosa, to blast through the American support forces, sink the troop transports, and wipe out the landing parties with gunfire. The plan assumed that the Japanese would be outnumbered about three to one; and that Halsey alone, with his carriers and fast battleships, would wield striking power the Imperial Fleet could not match.

The whole theme of *Sho* was therefore *deception*. To neutralize the lopsided advantage of the foe, Japan's remaining aircraft carriers would decoy Halsey's Third Fleet far away from the beachhead, in quest of a carrier duel. The Main Body would then shoot its way past the support ships of Kinkaid's Seventh Fleet, wreak its havoc on MacArthur's landing force, and depart.

But the Formosa "victory" had already crippled *Sho*. Land-based support from the decimated army air force would be scant; and the decoy carriers, stripped of their squadrons, could no longer fight. They could at best tantalize the Third Fleet into roaring far away from the beachhead to butcher them. This would suffice, the Japanese command bitterly decided. If only Halsey would take the bait and get out of the way, the Main Striking Force of battleships and cruisers might still penetrate Leyte Gulf and wipe out MacArthur's beachhead. The goal of all this sacrifice was only a tolerable peace settlement after a success. The operation was in essence a giant kamikaze attack. In itself the fleet advancing to the sacrifice was formidable, but it faced almost hopeless odds.

Was it wrong to sacrifice the remnant of a great navy at a blow? Hardly, in Japanese thinking. What was there to lose? With the Philippines gone, the oil supply would be cut off anyway. The warships would be like toys with broken springs. Surrender now? A logical course, but logic in war is for the strong. For the weak there is proud defiance, deemed laudable in most cultures, and noble in Japan.

The problem of oil further complicated *Sho*. So low had the nation's supply sunk from the submarine attrition that the fleet could not even fuel at home. That was why the Main Striking Force under Vice Admiral Kurita—two new monster battleships, the biggest and most powerful in the world, with three other battleships and many cruisers and destroyers—laid off Singapore, so as to have access to the oil of Java and Borneo. The decoy carriers were in the home waters of the Inland Sea.

So the gigantic *Sho* deception, which hinged on many precise interlocking moves, had to start with its forces far apart, in touch only by radio. Yet communication personnel, like pilots, were in low supply. The best technicians had mostly drowned in the Coral Sea, at Midway, around Guadalcanal, and at Saipan. The Imperial Fleet sallied forth to execute *Sho,* in short, scattered over thousands of miles by the oil shortage, and stuttering with communication failures; still powerful, however, and bent on victory or self-immolation.

On October 20, MacArthur's forces landed on Leyte. The general waded up on the beach to broadcast, *"People of the Philippines, I have returned! Rally to me! . . . For your homes and hearths, strike! For future generations of your sons and daughters, strike! . . . Let no heart be faint. Let every arm be steeled. . . . Follow in His name to the Holy Grail of righteous victory!"* etc. These glorious thoughts provoked much unseemly snickering and snorting in the Navy crews gathered at radios.

The Japanese hardly seemed to oppose the invasion at first. Their fleet did not visibly move. Admiral Halsey, panting for his great fleet killing, talked of cutting through the archipelago into the South China Sea to smoke out the enemy, leaving the beachhead for Kinkaid to defend. A severe dispatch from Nimitz cooled that notion. It did not however, cool Halsey's itch to trounce the Japanese navy.

Here was the human element coming into play. Halsey's war record and his public reputation were curiously at odds. He was the only admiral the home front knew about. He radiated the he-man aura of a Western movie star. He had led many carrier strikes. In the South Pacific his pugnacious spirit had revived sagging American morale and rescued the Guadalcanal campaign. The newspapers and the nation loved this rough tough Pacific gunfighter with his quotable taunts like "The Japs are losing their grip, even with their tails." But with the war winding down, he had yet to get into an actual gunfight. He had missed them all, while Spruance, his junior and his old friend, had fought and won big sea victories.

Halsey's staff was not sure that the enemy would fight for Leyte by risking a transit from the west of either of the two narrow straits, San Bernardino or Surigao. The Japs might well wait until MacArthur landed on Luzon, it was thought, for there they had a powerful army and big air bases. There, moreover, the Imperial Fleet would have a clear run in to Lingayen Gulf, and MacArthur could be heavily blasted by land, sea, and air. On some such reasoning, once Nimitz vetoed the South China Sea dash, Halsey released the strongest of his four task groups, a group of five carriers—he had nineteen in all—for rest and replenishment at Ulithi, some eight hundred miles away. Another task group was ordered to sail for Ulithi October 23, removing four more carriers from the scene.

These releases deeply troubled Pug Henry. Remembering Halsey from destroyer days, he could well picture the old man chafing and fuming aboard the *New Jersey,* as his great Third Fleet slowly patrolled empty tropic seas a hundred miles off the Philippines, burning up oil. The idea of charging westward through the islands into the China Sea was Halsey all over. So were the impulsive last-minute shifts of plans and orders. So to Pug's mind was the airy release of half his carrier strength only three days after the landing. Halsey worked in two modes, casual or ferocious. True, the task force had been at sea for ten months, refueled and replenished by ComServPac's remarkable ship-to-ship system. Men were weary. Ships needed time in port. But wasn't the chance for battle paramount? Halsey was behaving as though the sea threat to Leyte had faded away, but in fact the whereabouts of the foe was still a mystery.

Pug also wished Halsey would leave management of the carriers to their commander, Marc Mitscher, the most skilled air admiral in the Navy. Halsey was directly ordering the flattops about, and their real boss had become a silent passenger on the *Enterprise.* It was as though Pug had taken to running the *Iowa* himself. A very bad business! Spruance had let Mitscher fight his ships at Saipan, overriding him only on the idea of abandoning the beachhead.

Still, the fleet loved Halsey. The sailors liked to say they would follow the "Bull" to hell, and they had hardly been aware of Spruance. Pug himself was excited to be sailing under Halsey again. The electricity of Halsey had the whole Third Fleet hot for the fight. That was something. But cool good sense in the fog of battle was just as important. That was Spruance's demonstrated strong point, and whether Halsey possessed it, the Navy was now for the first time going to find out.

87

TO: COM THIRD FLEET
FROM: DARTER
MANY SHIPS SIGHTED INCLUDING THREE PROBABLE BB'S X AM CHAS-
ING X

"KICKOFF!" Pug thought. The dispatch came from a picket submarine far out to the west, in the Palawan Passage, about halfway
from Borneo to Leyte; sent during the night, it gave the position, course,
and speed of the heavy enemy force. At once Pug marked the information in orange ink on the chart in his office. It was just sunrise of the
twenty-third of October.

So there would be a fight, after all. Those battleships were heading
for the Sibuyan Sea and San Bernardino Strait. Halsey's prompt orders
quickened Pug's pulse. He was cancelling the release to Ulithi of a carrier group. Good! The three flattop groups on hand were to space themselves along two hundred fifty miles of the eastern Philippine coast for
air searches and strikes next morning, when the Jap battleships would
be steaming within range. Halsey's own group, including Victor Henry's
BatDiv Seven, would stand off San Bernardino Strait to meet the foe as
he came.

The ships the submarine had sighted were in fact Vice Admiral
Kurita's Main Striking Force, on its way from Borneo to storm into
Leyte Gulf and wipe out MacArthur's beachhead. The two chief opponents in the vast melee, Halsey and Kurita, were thus touching gloves at
a range of about six hundred miles. Admirals would be plentiful as black-
berries around Leyte Gulf, but the battle would turn on what these two
would do as they drew together.

Takeo Kurita was a hard-willed dried-up salt of fifty-five. His force—
five battleships, ten heavy cruisers, with light cruisers and destroyers—
made a mighty parade as it plowed the blue swells of the Palawan Passage. Two of his battleships were the seventy-thousand-ton monsters
Musashi and *Yamato,* with secret eighteen-inch guns built in violation

of arms limitation treaties, and never yet fired at a foe. Pug Henry's *Iowa* and *New Jersey* carried sixteen-inch guns. No United States ship packed bigger armament. The two-inch difference in bore meant that Kurita could stand off beyond Henry's range and smash at him with shells perhaps twice as destructive as any he could fire back. Conceived in 1934, built over fifteen years at a nation-straining cost of manpower and treasure, these were the strongest gunships on the globe. Reckoning only with BatDiv Seven types they might have been invincible, but warfare had moved past them. Submarines and carrier aircraft were menaces the great guns could not fight.

From Admiral Kurita's viewpoint, therefore, all depended on the decoy carriers. If they would but suck Halsey out of the way, he could perhaps bull through San Bernardino Strait and annihilate the MacArthur beachhead with his giant guns. Under the able Vice Admiral Ozawa, those decoy carriers were already at sea, heading down from Japan toward Luzon. That was about all Kurita knew, for thirty parallels of latitude separated the two forces when they sailed.

Kurita had one more major factor to bear in mind. The Tokyo strategists, with their obsessive taste for razzle-dazzle, had improvised a third force—battleships and cruisers with their destroyer screens—to run far south and come up into Leyte Gulf through the other access route, Surigao Strait. On the war game boards *Sho* must have looked very pretty indeed: Kurita with the powerhouse armada driving through the central Philippines to steam at Leyte Gulf from the north; the other force closing a pincer from the south; and Ozawa, in waters far north of Luzon, teasing the bellicose Halsey clear of the troops he was supposed to protect.

But in such a slow-moving ballet of great ships over thousands of miles, precise timing was critical. Kurita had to get to Leyte on the morning of the twenty-fifth, when the Surigao force would arrive. Well before that morning, the decoy flattops had to lure Halsey northward. None of this could come off, on the face of it, except at high cost. The question was whether early losses would stop *Sho* cold, or whether it would bloodily go through.

A hint of the answer came at sunrise of the twenty-third. Without warning, four torpedoes one after the other struck Kurita's flagship. The whole force had just begun its daylight zigzagging. As the flag bridge of the heavy cruiser *Atago* shuddered under Kurita's feet, he saw the next cruiser astern get hit too in smoke, flame, and great climbing showers of white water. Within minutes the *Atago* was wrapped in fire, shaking with explosions, and going down. Kurita's attention narrowed to saving himself. Destroyers approached the burning wreck to take him off, but there was no time. The admiral and his staff had to swim for their lives in heaving warm salt water.

A destroyer fished Kurita aboard. There another sad sight met his brine-stung eyes: a third heavy cruiser nearby, blowing apart like a firecracker in pale flame and dense black smoke, its pieces going down while he stood there dripping. This day was not half an hour old, and he had lost two heavy cruisers out of ten to submarine assault; a third was dead in the water and afire; and he was two full days' steaming from Leyte Gulf.

The picket submarines *Darter* and *Dace* had detected Kurita's force in the night, chased it on the surface, and submerged for this dawn attack. They escaped the cascade of destroyer depth charges that raised great geysers all over the sea, but tracking the crippled cruiser, the *Darter* ran up on a reef. The *Dace* rescued its crew. The *Darter* had sounded the alarm and drawn first blood, but its day was done.

Panicky false periscope sightings disarrayed Kurita's force most of that day until he managed to transfer with his staff to the *Yamato*. There, in the world's mightiest gunship, in spacious elegant flag quarters, he regained his grip on the situation. His grand armada was, after all, mainly intact. He had not expected to advance without losses. Night would soon fall and cover his movements. Tokyo radioed him that the decoy force had as yet made no contact with Halsey; so aircraft attacks, as well as the submarine menace, lay ahead for the morrow. The day after that, it now seemed, he would run straight into Halsey at the mouth of San Bernardino Strait. But Takeo Kurita had this command because he was a man who would push on through fire walls. As the sun set he went to full speed.

Night gave him twelve hours of a peaceful fast run. With the sunrise on October twenty-fourth the carrier attacks came, and never stopped coming. Five major strikes, hundreds of sorties, repeated and repeated assaults with bombs and torpedoes, kept the air buzzing over the Main Striking Force all day. Kurita had been promised air cover from Luzon and Formosa. There was none.

Still he steamed doughtily on, winding a course past beautiful mountainous islands, throwing up AA fire from hundreds of guns, in desperation shooting his main batteries at oncoming clusters of airplanes. In this greatest of all fights between aircraft and surface ships, on October twenty-fourth, called now the Battle of the Sibuyan Sea, Kurita did very well. Only the supergiant *Musashi*, hit early by a torpedo, attracted the full fury of the waspish Yank planes. Supposedly unsinkable, it absorbed in the five strikes nineteen torpedoes and uncounted bombs; sank lower and listed farther as it fell astern, the hours passed, and the punishment went on; and toward sundown it rolled over and sank with half its crew, never having fought except with tiny flying machines.

That was the worst. A tragic loss, but the Main Striking Force had weathered the storm with plenty of power to carry out its mission. However, no word had ever come from Ozawa's decoy force. Was there to be no relief, all the way to Leyte? Halsey obviously had not yet been tricked; this day's harsh pounding had come from carrier aircraft. Kurita's radioed pleas for air cover were going unheeded. The day's attrition so far—the *Musashi* in tragic death throes, the disabling of yet another cruiser, and much bomb damage to other ships—could be accepted; but how long could a force defenseless from the air survive against fifteen or twenty carriers?

About four o'clock Kurita turned his ships around and retreated westward, to increase the range from Halsey's flattops and stay in open water, where his captains could at least continue their successful squirming and dodging; for once in the straits, they would lose maneuverability and become easy targets. Again he beseeched Tokyo and Manila for air cover, citing the damage he was sustaining. Manila made no answer. The air commander there had decided to use his planes against enemy carriers, not in covering Kurita.

It seemed to Takeo Kurita at this juncture, as his ships milled about on a calm sea bounded by the ridges of green islands, and the blasted *Musashi* dropped out of sight trying to beach itself and "become a land battery," that the *Sho* plan was already collapsing. The air and submarine attacks had thrown off the timing. The air cover element was missing. The deception was not working. Still, having put off entering narrow waters until darkness was near, he reversed course once again, and made for San Bernardino Strait. As he went he notified the southern force to slow down and postpone the pincer attack on the gulf by several hours. Tokyo headquarters in a helpful mood now sent this message: *"All forces will dash to the attack, counting on Divine assistance."*

Night once more veiled the Main Striking Force. Yet even so, Kurita faced mounting perils. Ahead lay narrow heavily mined waters. In traversing San Bernardino Strait, he would have to take his force through in column. Halsey's battleships and cruisers would undoubtedly be patrolling the entrance, waiting to cross the *T* and pick off his ships one by one as they came out. In precisely such a maneuver, during the great Battle of Tsushima Strait in 1905, the Japanese navy had crushed the czarist fleet and won a war. Now Kurita was cast in the Russian role of that battle he had studied all his life, with no way to escape; no alternative but to steam on to his fate, "counting on Divine assistance."

Astern, a yellow quarter-moon was setting over the dark Sibuyan Sea. Ahead, the Japanese command in Manila had turned on the navigation lights of San Bernardino Strait. The night was clear. Posting himself on the flag bridge of the giant *Yamato,* Takeo Kurita sent a blunt final dispatch to his crews: *Chancing annihilation, we are determined to break through to the anchorage and destroy the enemy.* The force passed into the narrows, forming into column, and all ships went to battle stations. Despite the hellish day the haggard crews stood to their guns. They were good men, well trained in night action. Kurita could count on them to give the Americans up ahead a real fight, and die for the Emperor if they must.

At midnight the moon went down. Half an hour later, in starlit darkness, the Main Striking Force began to emerge, ship by ship, between the headlands of Luzon and Samar into the quiet open waters of the Philippine Sea. Admiral Kurita could see nothing ahead. Nor could the lookouts on any of his vessels. Radar sweeping the sea for fifty miles in all directions found nothing.

Nothing! Not so much as a single picket destroyer guarding the entrance to San Bernardino Strait!

Astounded, his hopes rebounding, Kurita formed up for battle and made full speed south along the coast of Samar for Leyte Gulf. He had to accept the evidence of his senses. By some fantastic chance of war Halsey was gone, and MacArthur lay at the mercy of the Emperor's biggest guns.

88

THE strange events on the American side which led to this incredible circumstance will remain in controversy as long as anybody cares about naval battles. The events are clear enough. The controversy lies in how and why they happened. Victor Henry lived through them in the *Iowa*'s flag quarters.

. . .

He was up well before dawn of that October twenty-fourth, in flag plot, checking his staff's setup for following the situation, for joining battle, and even for taking command of the task group if necessary. Pug knew very well how junior he was in Halsey's force, yet misfortune might thrust extraordinary responsibility on him. He intended to stay as fully informed as though he were Halsey's chief of staff.

Flag plot was a large dimly lit room over his quarters, reached by a private ladder. Here radar scopes showed in phosphorescent green tracery movements of ships and aircraft, storm patterns, configuration of nearby land, and—especially in night action—a better picture of the foe than eyes could discern on the sea. Here large Plexiglas displays manned by telephone talkers gave at a glance in vivid orange or red grease hand-printing abstract summaries of what was happening. Here dispatches poured in to the watch officer for quick digest and display. Coffee, tobacco smoke, and ozone from the electronic gear stewed together in an unchanging flag-plot smell. Loudspeakers hoarsely spouted bursts of signal jargon: *"Baker Jig How Seven, Baker Jig How Seven, this is Courthouse Four. Request Able Mike Report Peter Slant Zed. Over,"* and the like.

But sometimes—as now at five in the morning, when the admiral looked in—flag plot was quiet. Shadowy sailors sat at the scopes, their faces ghastly in the glow, drinking coffee, smoking, or munching candy bars. Telephone talkers murmured into their receivers or wrote on the Plexiglas; stationed behind the display, they were adept at printing backward. Officers bent over charts, calculating and talking low. The chief of staff was already at the central chart desk. In the Formosa strikes Captain Bradford had satisfied Pug that he could run flag plot and sort out pertinent facts from the torrent of noise. Pug went below and alone in his quarters heartily ate canned peaches, cornflakes, ham and eggs, and fresh biscuits with honey. It might be a long time before he sat down to a meal again. He was drinking coffee when Bradford buzzed him.

"Preparing to launch air searches, Admiral."

"Very well, Ned."

Pug ran up the ladder, went out on the flag bridge in a clear warm violet dawn, and watched the dive-bomber squadrons soaring off under the morning stars from the *Intrepid,* the *Hancock,* and the *Independence.* A quiet pain stirred in his heart. (*Absalom, Absalom!*) When the last planes left he returned below to a small office off his sea cabin. Pug meant to keep his own command chart here. Only in combat would he post himself in flag plot near the radars, the TBS, and the flag bridge. For many hours yet, bald plotted facts would matter most: sightings, distances, courses, speeds, damage reports, and what these implied.

It was Blue versus Orange again, after all, the old clash of the War College game boards and the peacetime fleet exercises. The real thing was flaringly different, yet one factor would not change. Even in make-believe combat the hardest thing to do was to keep one's head; how much more so now! Let Bradford enjoy the excitement and the hot news in flag plot. Pug meant to weigh essentials here until the fight was on, and talk to his staff only when he had to.

In the peace of this office, as he plotted on his chart in orange and blue ink reports of the morning sightings and strikes, what struck him most was the steady Jap advance. This fellow heading for San Bernardino Strait meant business. The reported submarine sinkings the day before had failed to shake him. Unless the air strikes could turn him back, it looked like night battle off the strait, perhaps only sixteen to twenty hours hence.

An early sighting of a second surface force far to the south heading for Surigao Strait didn't surprise Pug. Diversionary end run, standard Jap tactics. This was exactly why Spruance had refused to leave the Saipan beachhead. The Japs were really throwing everything in! Davison's task group, to the south, would probably go after that force. No, wrong guess, Halsey was ordering him to concentrate off San Bernardino, too. Well, Kinkaid's fleet down in the gulf had six old battleships, five of them resurrected from the Pearl Harbor graveyard, including the good old *California*—also plenty of cruisers and escort carriers, to hit that diversionary force making for Surigao. The jeep flattops were converted merchantmen, slow as molasses, small and flimsy; but in the aggregate they could launch a fair air strike.

First damage to the Halsey fleet! Sherman's flattops, the northernmost group, under air attack at nine-thirty A.M.; *Princeton* bombed and on fire. Planes could be from Luzon or Jap carriers, according to Sherman. His aviators massacring the enemy pilots. Now a welcome intercept: Halsey calling back the fourth carrier group, until now bound for Ulithi. At last, and none too soon! The chart indicated that they would have to fuel at sea, and were a full day's run away. If the blow to the *Princeton* had jolted this decision out of Halsey, it might prove worth the cost.

More air strikes against the oncoming Japs in the center; more jubilant damage reports; battleships and cruisers bombed, torpedoed, on fire, turned turtle. On Pug's chart these reports looked thrilling. The symbols for sunk or damaged ships crowded the Sibuyan Sea. If the reports were true the Jap would never make it, he was a goner already. But why in that case was he continuing to advance? Strikes by thirty to seventy planes were hitting him at will, yet on he came.

Why did he have no air cover? *Where were the Jap carriers?* The question had been nagging at Victor Henry all day, and not only at him; it was troubling William Halsey and his staff, and his group commanders, and Admiral Nimitz in Pearl Harbor, where night had already fallen, and Admiral King in Washington. Those missing flattops weren't covering the oncoming San Bernardino force. They weren't with the end runners to the south. What then was their role in this supreme gamble of the Imperial Fleet? It was unthinkable that they could be idling in the Inland Sea. Pug saw two possibilities. He wrote them, for his own future smiles or groans, on a separate sheet of paper.

24 October, 1430, off Leyte.
  Q: Where are the enemy carriers?
  A: (1) Hanging back outside search range in the South China Sea. They'll run in toward us at high speed once the sun gets low, to strike at dawn tomorrow the cripples of the coming night action off San Bernardino Strait.
  (2) They're heading down from the north to decoy us away from San Bernardino Strait. If so, they'll make certain they're seen before dark, probably well north of Luzon.

There was nothing prescient in Pug's second guess. Several of Halsey's group commanders were making the same surmise. A captured Japanese tactical manual recently sent out by ONI had discussed sacrificing carriers as a diversion gambit. Somehow the carrier force had gotten out of the Inland Sea undetected by submarine pickets. They might just now be moving into air search range. The answer—so Pug felt as the last Halsey strike was heading home—would come before sundown.

Vice Admiral Ozawa's gambit carriers were in fact already to the north of Luzon, and Ozawa was doing everything to attract Halsey's attention except—so to say—stand on his head and wiggle his ears. But Halsey had assigned the northward search to Sherman, and in the confusion of the air attack and the *Princeton* fire the launch had stalled. So Ozawa had dispatched the motley aircraft in his flattops—only seventy-six in all—to attack Sherman's group, hoping to alert Halsey if nothing else. This flight had less luck than the land-based strike that had fired the *Princeton*. Many of the pilots were shot down; most of the rest were too green to land on a moving carrier, so they flew on to Luzon or else dropped in the sea. Halsey was not alerted; this straggling strike was evaluated as probably coming from Luzon.

Ozawa also broadcast copious radio signals, hoping to be detected. Late in the day, desperate to be seen and pursued, he sent southward two hermaphrodite battleships—bizarre gunships with flight decks grafted on—to engage Sherman's group in surface combat. Ozawa notified Kurita by radio of all these actions. The two forces were about a thousand miles apart, well within radio range. But Kurita received no messages from him, either directly or via Tokyo or Manila.

Halsey's battle plan for the night came through about three o'clock. It named four battleships, including the *Iowa* and the *New Jersey,* two heavy cruisers, three light cruisers, and fourteen destroyers.

THESE SHIPS WILL BE FORMED AS TASK FORCE 34 UNDER VICE ADMI-RAL LEE COMMANDER BATTLE LINE X TASK FORCE 34 WILL EN-GAGE DECISIVELY AT LONG RANGES X

Form Battle Line!

Pug Henry had studied battle-line tactics all his life. He knew the manual by heart. He had gamed, times beyond counting, Jutland and Tsushima Strait, and Nelson's classic actions at Trafalgar and Saint Vincent. The showdown between ships of the line was the supreme historical test of navies. So far in this war, the graceless weak floating barns called carriers had eclipsed the battleship. Well, by God, here was Japan sending its battle line through San Bernardino Strait to smash the Leyte invasion, and all Halsey's carriers were not stopping it from coming on.

Form Battle Line! It was the sounding of the charge. His blood racing as though he were twenty, Victor Henry pulled the telephone from its bracket and buzzed Captain Bradford. "Staff meeting in my quarters at sixteen hundred. Leave one watch officer in flag plot. You come down."

It did not escape Pug's notice that Halsey, in the *New Jersey,* would be OTC of the Battle Line. Willis Lee would form the task force, and he would do a superb job, but Halsey would take over and fight the engagement. What wild excitement must be fizzing over in the flag quarters of the *New Jersey!* If Pug Henry had been waiting thirty years for this, Bill Halsey had been waiting forty years. Of all admirals in history, not one had been more hungry or ready for an all-out fleet battle. The man and the moment had come together for the forging of a famous victory.

Pug ran up to the flag bridge to air out his lungs. He had gone through three packs of cigarettes. The scene on the sea could not be more tranquil: carriers, battleships, and their screening vessels spreading as far as the eye could see in afternoon sunshine, extending below the horizon north and south, gray familiar shapes of war steaming slowly in AA formation on the mildly foaming blue ocean. No land was in sight, no foe, no smoke, no fire. All the excitement was in the chatter of the flag plot loudspeakers, in the facts tumbling out of the coding machines in Navy abracadabra. Wireless communications, airplanes, and black oil had made for a new kind of sea warfare reaching out hundreds, thousands of miles for contact, encompassing millions of square miles as the field of battle. Yet the signal of signals was unchanged from Trafalgar, and no doubt from Salamis.

Form Battle Line!

Battle was the ultimate risk. The giant *Iowa* could go down like any other warship. The sinking of the *Northampton* was much on Pug's mind, and he was running over what he would say to the staff about torpedo attack. Yet he felt, as he stood there alone in rumpled khakis, taking deep breaths of the streaming tropic sea air, that this night would do much to justify his life. He was filled with exaltation that was half-guilty because the business was only slaughter, and many Americans might die, and yet he was so damned happy about it.

The staff conference was not fifteen minutes along when flag plot called him with a new position report on the Japs in the Sibuyan Sea. Noting the latitude and longitude on a scratch pad, Pug snapped, "Check the decoding, that's a mistake," and hung up. Soon the watch officer apologetically called again. The decode checked out. There was another sighting, a much more recent one. Pug wrote down the numbers, abruptly went off into his office, and presently called in the chief of staff.

"What do you make of that?"

On his chart the orange track of the Jap force now hooked around to westward. Retreat!

"Admiral, I didn't see how he could keep coming as long as he did." Running his fingers through his white hair, Bradford shook his head. "He was like a snowball rolling along on a hot stove. He'd have arrived with nothing."

"You think he's quit?"

"Yes, sir."

"I don't. Meeting's suspended. Get on up there, Ned. Sift the dispatches. Pick up what you can on TBS. Double the coding watch on command channel intercepts. Let's get the word on these position reports."

Soon Bradford telephoned down that the whole fleet was buzzing with the Jap turnaround. Pug stared at the chart, calculating the possibilities, as in a chess game after a surprise move. He began to write:

24 October, 1645. Central Force turns west.
Why?

1. Beaten by air strike. Slinking home to Nippon.

2. Ahead of schedule. Carriers not yet in search range. Rendezvous off Leyte fouled up. Killing time. Also confusing us.

3. Avoiding a night action. Jap minor forces prefer night fighting, what with long-range torpedoes, etc. This fellow wants good visibility for his big guns.

4. Preserving maneuverability in daylight hours.

5. Made damage report to Tokyo and awaits further orders.

6. Remember Spruance "retreating" at Midway? This is a tough individual, a strong force, and a resourceful mind at work. May be tantalizing Halsey to charge through San Bernardino Strait after him, whereupon he'll come about and cross our T.

As Pug sat mulling over these possibilities an excited knock came at his door. "Admiral, I thought I'd better bring you this." Eyes gleaming, Bradford laid a decode on his desk, strips of tape pasted on a blank form. It was from Halsey.

TO: ALL GROUP COMS AND DIV COMS THIRD FLEET
SHERMAN REPORTS X 3 CARRIERS 2 LIGHT CRUISERS 3 DESTROYERS
18–32 N 125–28 E X

Pug darted his orange pen to the chart. Northeast of Luzon, two hundred miles off shore; there was the answer on the Jap carriers.

"Hm! Any late word on that force in the Sibuyan Sea?"

"None, Admiral."

They looked at the chart, and at each other, wryly grinning. Pug said, "Okay, you're Halsey. What do you do?"

"Take off like a bat out of hell after those carriers."

"What about San Bernardino Strait? What about that fellow in the Sibuyan Sea?"

"He's still retreating. If he turns around and comes back, the Battle Line will fix him."

"So you go north with the carriers only, leaving the battleships behind? Isn't that risky?"

"The carriers can pick up Sherman's two battleships as they steam north. That's enough power to handle any carrier force the Japs have got."

"What about concentration of force?"

Bradford scratched his head. "Well, the Japs haven't done that, have they? They're coming at me from two directions. They're too far apart for me to hit one outfit and then the other with a concentrated force. I'd say the tactical situation prevails over the principle. I've got to divide my force to make sure I hit both his teams. My two sections are much stronger than his two, anyway." Pug gave him a horrible frown. Bradford added uncertainly, "Admiral, I get paid for saying what I think, however stupid, when asked."

"You've made Mahan turn over in his grave. However, I agree with you. Get back up there, Ned."

The steward knocked and offered to bring the admiral dinner on a tray. Pug felt he could not force an olive down his throat. He asked for more coffee, and sat smoking cigarette after cigarette, trying to think himself into Halsey's brain.

Here was an embarrassment of riches for the old gunfighter—*two* great engagements within his grasp! He could be the Lord Nelson of either one, but not of both; too far apart, as Bradford said. The *New Jersey* would have to be detached from the Battle Line, if he decided to run north with the carriers. In that case Willis Lee would fight the Battle Line night action, with one of Sherman's battlewagons replacing the *New Jersey*. Or Halsey could stay off San Bernardino with the battleships, and turn Mitscher's flattops loose to run north and get the carriers. That was what Ray Spruance had declined to do at Saipan.

The San Bernardino fight, Pug thought, would be the more decisive one. That was the big immediate menace to the beachhead. But suppose the Jap didn't reverse course and come on? In that case Bill Halsey would patrol at dead slow all night with silent guns, while Marc Mitscher sailed off to the biggest carrier victory since Midway.

Not a chance, Pug Henry thought. Not a chance. Bradford was right. In Halsey's place he, Pug, might well go north himself.

But he hoped Halsey would take only the *New Jersey* and not drag the *Iowa* along. Those Jap flattops would be meat for Mitscher's aviators. The battleship function in the north would be merely sinking cripples. At San Bernardino Strait there would be battle. That Jap had not quit; so a sixth sense told Pug.

Down from flag plot came an intercepted visual signal from Willis Lee to Halsey, sent just before dark. It was a situation analysis close to Pug's, which made him feel good. Lee was a shrewd veteran strategist. The Jap carriers were weak decoys, Lee said, low on aircraft; the Sibuyan turnaround was temporary; that force would return and come through the strait at night.

Division of opinion in Halsey's staff quarters must be deep and debate furious, Pug surmised. Time was slipping by. No orders were forthcoming, not even the "Execute" for the Battle Line plan, and Willis Lee needed time to organize and form up his force. Shortly after eight o'clock the orders did at last come through. Bradford did not deliver or telephone this crucial dispatch. He sent it down by messenger, a very odd thing to do. When Pug read the long battle order, he understood why.

Halsey was going north after the carriers, all right; but he was taking with him the entire Third Fleet, *leaving not one vessel behind to guard San Bernardino Strait*.

Pug was still digesting this sickening surprise when another dispatch came down, again by messenger. It was a sighting report of the Sibuyan Sea force by a night search plane. The longitude numbers made his hair prickle before he put his pen to the chart. The Jap had turned around and was heading for San Bernardino Strait at twenty-two knots.

The date-time of the dispatch was 2210; ten minutes past ten at night, October 24, 1944.

89

A Jew's Journey
(from Aaron Jastrow's manuscript)

OCTOBER 24, 1944.

Natalie and I have received our deportation notices. We leave in the eleventh transport on October 28. Appeal is quite useless. Nobody gets excused from these October transports.

Theresienstadt is a desolate and terrible scene. Perhaps twelve thousand people are left. In less than a month since the filming ended, the trains have taken away almost twenty thousand, all under sixty-five. Above that age one is still safe, unless, as in my case, one has offended. The young, the strong, the able, the good-looking, are gone. The aged remnants of a jammed and bustling ghetto creep about the nearly empty streets, freezing, frightened, and starving. The town's institutions and services have broken down. There is no hot food, not even the wretched slops of former days. No cooks are left. Garbage piles up, for there is nobody to remove it. In empty barracks abandoned clothes, books, carpets, and pictures are strewn around. There is nobody to clean up, and nobody is interested in looting. The hospitals are empty, for all the sick were transported. Everywhere there is the smell of decay, abandonment, and rot.

The gimcrackery of the Beautification—the quaint signposts, the shop fronts, the bandstand, the cafés, the children's pavilion—is falling apart in the harsh weather, the colors fading, the paint peeling. Despite dire posted penalties, the old people pilfer the planks of these Potemkin constructions for firewood. There is no music. Hardly a child is left, except for those of mixed couples, war veterans, municipal officials, and *Prominente*. But this eleventh transport, a big one of more than two thousand souls, is cutting like a scythe into the ranks of privilege. There will be plenty of children in it.

My offense was refusal to cooperate. The new High Elder, who replaced the pathetic, mysteriously vanished Eppstein at the end of September, is a certain Dr. Murmelstein of Vienna, a former rabbi and university lecturer. I am sure that the SS put him up to designating me as his chief deputy. The motive must have been window dressing again, in case of a sudden end to the war. It would look good for them, these twisted minds must calculate, if an American Jew would be on hand as a high official to greet the conquerors. Not that the war looks to be ending. East and west it appears to have bogged down for the winter, and the crimes of the Germans will go on for many more months unchecked, perhaps multiplying because this is their last chance to commit them.

Murmelstein worked on me for hours with a wearisome flood of flattery and argument. To cut it off, I said I would think about it. Natalie's reaction that night was the same as mine. I pointed out to her that if I were transported for refusing, she would probably share my fate. "Do as you please," she said, "but don't accept it on my account."

When I gave Murmelstein my answer next day, I had to endure the whole rigmarole again, ending in threats, grovelling, beseeching, and real tears. No doubt he feared the displeasure of his masters upon conveying my refusal. A sketch of this man and how he thinks is worth preserving in these last sheets. He is a type. There have surely been Murmelsteins all over Europe. His theme in brief is that the Germans as direct overseers are far more brutal and murderous than the Jewish officials who are willing to interpose themselves as buffers, carry out their orders, absorb their anger at delays, exemptions, and evasions, endure the hatred and contempt of the Jews, and work unceasingly at reducing hardships and saving lives.

I retorted that even if this had once been so in Theresienstadt, the officials now were doing nothing but organizing and sending off the transports, and that I would not be part of it. I refrained from pointing out that such officials are saving their skins, or at least postponing their fates, by designating fellow Jews for death. Epicurus said that everything in this world can be taken by two handles. I don't condemn Murmelstein. There may be a color of truth in his argument that things would be worse if Jews like him did not administer the orders of the Germans, and try to soften the impact. Nevertheless, I will not do it. I knew when I refused that I risked torture, but I was not going to yield.

Among his blandishments was an appeal to me as between fellow scholars. Our fields overlap, for he taught ancient Jewish history at Vienna University. I have heard him lecture here in the ghetto, and don't think much of his scholarship. He cited Flavius Josephus, a figure he clings to in his desperate self-justification; a man hated by the Jews as a collaborationist and a tool of the Romans, whose whole aim was to benefit his people. History's verdict on Josephus is equivocal at best. The Murmelsteins will not come out that well.

After warning me with popping eyes and a skull-like expression of the SS anger that hung over me, he broke down and wept. He was not acting, or else he is very good at it, for the tears really gushed. His burdens were overpowering, he wailed. He respected me more than almost anybody in the ghetto. As an American, at this stage of the war, I had unusual power to intercede with the Germans and do good. He was ready to go down on his knees to change my mind, save me from going to the Little Fortress, and get me to share his frightful responsibilities. He could no longer carry on alone.

I told him he would have to carry on without me, and that as to my own fate, I would risk anything my frail body could still endure. So I left him, shaking his head and drying his eyes. That was almost three weeks ago. I trembled with fear for days. I have not become any braver, but there are really things worse than pain, worse than dying; not to mention that, in the grip of the Germans, a Jew probably has no way in the long run of escaping pain or death, unless the outside world rescues him. He may as well do what is right.

I heard nothing further until the blow fell today. I feel sure that Murmelstein is not to blame. Of course he countersigned the orders, as he does for all the transportees. But I was simply on the SS list. Not being able to use me, or not interested in forcing me, as they were for the Red Cross visit, they are getting rid of me. Unless they can have me on their side, as a tool of theirs and therefore an accomplice of sorts, I am not one they want to have around when the Americans arrive. Or the Russians, either.

The notices came in the morning, just before Natalie went off to the mica factory. The thing has become commonplace, and we both half-expected it. I offered to go to Murmelstein and say I had reconsidered. I meant it. I pointed out that she has her son to live for, and that though we have had no word in months (all communication with the outside has long since broken down) she has every reason to hope that he is all right, and that when this long nightmare ends, if she can manage to survive, she will find him.

She said sombrely, her face drawn and somewhat scared—and I want to record this little exchange before I seal away these pages—"I don't want you to protect me by sending Jews off in trains."

"Natalie, that is how I talked to Murmelstein. But you and I know that the transports will go anyway."

"Not by your hand, though."

I was moved. I said, "*Ye-horeg v'al ya-harog.*"

She has learned some Hebrew from me and from the Zionists, but not much. She looked puzzled. I explained, "It's from the Talmud. There are three things a Jew must die rather than do under compulsion, and that's one of them. *Let yourself be killed, but do not kill.*"

"I call that common decency."

"According to Hillel the whole Torah is only common decency."

"What are the other two things a Jew must die rather than do?"

"Worship of false gods, and forbidden sexual conduct."

She looked thoughtful, then smiled at me like the Mona Lisa, and went off to the mica factory.

———————

I, Aaron Jastrow the Jew, began this record of a journey aboard a vessel docked in Naples harbor, in December 1941. It was bound for Palestine. My niece and I left that vessel before it sailed and were interned in Siena. We escaped from Fascist Italy through the help of the underground, intending to return to America via Portugal. Mischances and misjudgments brought us to Theresienstadt.

Here I have seen German barbarism and duplicity with my own eyes, and have tried to record the truth in bald hurried language. I have not recorded one one-thousandth of the daily agony, brutality, and degradation I have witnessed. Yet Theresienstadt is a "model ghetto." The accounts I have heard of what the Germans are doing in camps like Oswiecim exceed all human experience. Words break down as a means of describing them. So, in writing what I have heard, I have put down the plainest possible words that come to mind. The Thucydides who will tell this story so that the world can picture, believe, and remember may not be born for centuries. Or if he lives now, I am not he.

I am going to my death. I have heard that strong young people are spared to work in Oswiecim, so my niece may survive. I am in my sixty-eighth year, and will not lack much of the Biblical threescore-and-ten. Millions of Jews, I now believe, have already perished at German hands with half or less than half of their lives lived. A million or more of these must have been little children.

The world will be a long time fathoming this fact about human nature, this new fact, the thing the Germans have done. These scribbled sheets are a miserable fragment of testimony to the truth. Such records will be found all over Europe when the National Socialist curse passes.

I was a man of nimble Talmudic wit, insight quick rather than profound, with a literary gift graceful rather than powerful. I was at my best in my youth, a prodigy. My parents took me from Poland to America. I expended my gifts there in pleasing the Gentiles. I became an apostate. I dropped my Jewishness outside and inside, and strove only to be like other people, and to be accepted by them. In this I was successful. This period of my life stretched from my sixteenth year, when I arrived in New York, to my sixty-sixth year, when I arrived in Theresienstadt. Here under the Germans I resumed my Jewishness because they forced me to.

I have been in Theresienstadt about a year. I value this year more than all my fifty-one years of *hefkerut,* of being like others. Degraded, hungry, oppressed, beaten, frightened, I have found myself, my God, and my self-respect here. I am terribly afraid of dying. I am bowed to the ground by the tragedy of my people. But I have experienced a strange bitter happiness in Theresienstadt that I missed as an American professor and as a fashionable author living in a Tuscan villa. I have been myself. I have taught bright-eyed, sharp-minded Jewish boys the Talmud. They are gone. I do not know whether one of them still lives. But the words of the Talmud lived on our lips and burned in our minds. I was born to carry that flame. The world has greatly changed, and the change was too much for me, until I came to Theresienstadt. Here I mastered the change, and returned to myself. Now I will return to Oswiecim, where I studied in the yeshiva and where I abandoned the Talmud, and there the Jew's Journey will end. I am ready.

There is such a world still to write about Theresienstadt! And ah, if a good angel would but give me a year to tell my story from my early days! But these scattered notes, much more than anything else I have written, must serve as the mark over the emptiness that will be my grave.

Earth, cover not their blood!

Aaron Jastrow
October 24, 1944
Theresienstadt

90

WHEN it is midnight in Leyte, the sun rides high over Washington. About halfway between them lies Pearl Harbor. From there, Chester Nimitz was transmitting to Ernest King in his Washington headquarters all the Leyte events as they broke. In Tokyo, of course, the naval HQ was following the battle step by step.

So far had the art of communication advanced, so powerful were the transmitters, so swift the coding, so deliberate the movements of fleets traversing long distances at twenty or twenty-five miles an hour, that the far-off high commands could watch this entire battle like Homeric gods hovering overhead, or like Napoleon on a hill at Austerlitz. The Battle of Leyte Gulf was not only the biggest sea fight of all time, it was unique in having all these distant spectators; unique, too, in the flood of on-the-spot facts pouring out of transmitters and cryptographic machines.

It is interesting, therefore, that nobody on the scene, or anywhere else in the world, really knew what the hell was going on. There never was a denser fog of war. All the sophisticated communication only spread and thickened it.

Halsey totally confused everybody. In a very terse dispatch he notified Kinkaid down in the gulf of his decision to leave San Bernardino Strait unguarded, making Nimitz and King information addressees:

CENTRAL FORCE HEAVILY DAMAGED ACCORDING TO STRIKE REPORTS X AM PROCEEDING NORTH WITH THREE GROUPS TO ATTACK CARRIER FORCE AT DAWN X

That was all. Kinkaid assumed this meant that Halsey was taking his three *carrier* groups north, leaving Task Force Thirty-four, the Battle Line, to guard the strait. That is what Nimitz assumed. That is what King assumed. That is what Mitscher assumed. To all of them the dispatch could mean nothing else, for leaving the strait open to the enemy was unthinkable. But to Halsey and his staff it was crystal clear that since he had not ordered the battle plan *executed,* there was no Battle Line. Therefore San Bernardino was unguarded. Therefore Kinkaid was duly warned. Therefore he would have to look out for himself and for the beachhead.

In Pearl Harbor Raymond Spruance, standing at Nimitz's side by the chart table when the dispatch came in, softly remarked, "If I were there, I would keep my forces right here," placing his hand off San Bernardino Strait. But he too was referring to the carriers; it did not even cross his mind that Halsey was pulling out the battleships.

Halsey confused the Japanese by waiting until after dark to sally northward. Kurita therefore thought his Main Striking Force was steaming head-on into the Third Fleet. Ozawa in the decoy carriers was doubly confused; he had received word of Kurita's turn west, but not of his reversal toward San Bernardino Strait, so he did not know whether *Sho* was off or on, and whether or not he had succeeded in luring Halsey. First he fled north, then getting the "Divine assistance" message, turned back south to resume his role of worm on a hook, then again went north. As for the Japanese commanders in Manila and Tokyo, they no longer had the dimmest idea of what to think.

However, the admirals Halsey was taking north with him did have ideas.

Pug Henry was haunting flag plot, hoping for new orders from Halsey. For long dragging hours, there was only dead silence in the transmitters, while the unguarded strait fell farther and farther astern. What was going on? Could Halsey *possibly* have failed to get the word that the Central Force was heading for Leyte again?

Suddenly the TBS began grating out tense harsh questions and answers between Admiral Bogan, the commander of Pug's task group, and the captain of the *Independence,* the carrier of the night search planes. Pug recognized the admiral's voice through the gargling wireless distortion. Were those position reports on the Sibuyan Sea force accurate? Had the captain closely questioned the pilots? Absolutely, the captain replied. Those Japs were coming on fast, no doubt of it. In fact, a snooper pilot out on search now had just reported the navigation lights in San Bernardino Strait brilliantly lit.

Pug heard the admiral exclaim in a most irregular and refreshing way, "Jesus Christ!" Within minutes Bogan was on the TBS again, calling "Blackjack personally," the inter-ship call sign for Admiral Halsey. This took some temerity, but it was fruitless. Not "Blackjack" but an unidentifiable voice responded. Bogan repeated the news of the illuminated strait, underlining its import with his urgent excited tones. The voice said in audible boredom, "Yes, yes, we have that information."

Again, long silence. Pug was working up his nerve to speak his own view over the TBS—for the little it was worth—that the San Bernardino situation was getting desperate, when Willis Lee beat him to it, calling Halsey to say he was sure the Central Force would be coming through San Bernardino Strait in the darkness. Pug heard the same bored voice say, "Roger," and no more. That decided Pug against inviting a similar squelching.

Long after the battle it turned out that both Bogan and Lee intended to urge Halsey to send the Battle Line back to the strait. The bland cold anonymous voice silenced both of them. It turned out, too, that talking to Halsey wouldn't have helped. The old man had made up his mind to get the Jap carriers. He had shut off all further debate in his staff, and gone to sleep. It also turned out that Marc Mitscher's chief of staff, a belligerent sort nicknamed "Thirty-one Knot" Burke, had awakened Mitscher at midnight, imploring him to tell Halsey to send back the Battle Line. Mitscher's answer is immortal: "If he wants my advice, he'll ask for it." With that he rolled over in his bunk.

So the mighty fleet went pottering north at varying moderate speeds—no faster, for Halsey did not want to run past the elusive Japs in the dark. Halsey's admirals, in varying states of disagreement, apprehension, and consternation, held their tongues. October twenty-fourth melted at midnight into October twenty-fifth, the day of reckoning at Leyte Gulf; also, as it happened, the ninetieth anniversary of the Charge of the Light Brigade.

On October twenty-fifth, three different battles broke out, touched off by the three-pronged *Sho* approach. The Sibuyan Sea battle of the twenty-fourth is merged with these three, when Leyte Gulf is called "a combat of four engagements."

Broad wastes of peaceful sea separated the three massive fights on the twenty-fifth. They had no tactical connection. No commander on either side coordinated them, or had any grasp of the whole picture. They started and ended at different times. Any one of the engagements might have gone down in history as the great Battle of Leyte Gulf, had the other two not occurred. In military records they have coalesced into one vast impenetrably tangled sea fight. Each of the three battles would need a long book to tell its violent smoky tale in full. A brief bare sorting out of the famous October twenty-fifth triple melee, which was spaced over six hundred sea miles, is this:

In the southern battle of Surigao Strait, the action took place in early morning darkness and lasted to the dawn, a smashing American victory.

In the northern battle off Luzon, Mitscher's air strikes went on all day against Ozawa's empty carriers and his supporting force; the carriers were sunk, but most of the supporting force escaped.

In the central battle off Samar, Seventh Fleet jeep carriers were surprised at sunrise by Kurita as he sped toward Leyte Gulf. In this chance encounter, the odds were totally reversed, in favor of the Japanese. The awesome Main Striking Force stumbled on a cheap victory to be had for the taking, in routine gunnery, on the way to the beachhead: six slow tubby little flattops and a few destroyers and DEs, not one armed with more than a five-inch gun.

Here took place the crucial battle for Leyte Gulf.

The most spectacular battle, however, was fought in the south, in the dark: a crossing of the *T,* the first on earth's waters since Jutland, no doubt the last the world will witness.

The Japanese diversionary force, ignoring Kurita's order to slow down, entered Surigao Strait—the southern entrance to Leyte Gulf— shortly after midnight. Every gunship of Kinkaid's Seventh Fleet lay in wait, in textbook Battle Line formation: in all, forty-two warships against eight, six battleships against two.

Advancing blindly and doughtily in column, the Japanese first ran a gauntlet of thirty-nine PT boats, which they drove off with searchlights and secondary battery fire. Next they butted into destroyer attacks; one column after another, steaming past neatly as in a fleet exercise, discharging volleys of torpedoes, which ran through four miles of black water and blew up one battleship, holed the other, which was the flagship, sank one destroyer and crippled two more. A pitiful little tail for the *T* limped up the strait to be crossed: one battleship, one cruiser, and one destroyer, all damaged. The Battle Line blasted them into oblivion. Pursuit of retreating cripples lasted well into daylight. Only one destroyer escaped to tell the grisly story of Surigao Strait back in Japan.

A second Japanese group of cruisers and destroyers, sailing down from Japan to join the southern attack, failed to arrive in time for this massacre. Coming on the scene before dawn, seeing the flaming hulks drifting on the sea, hearing the anguished radio exchanges among the doomed ships, the admiral turned and departed, after sustaining one PT boat torpedo hit on a cruiser. A cowardly or a prudent act? Judgments will vary on such discreetness in war.

By all accounts the Battle of Surigao Strait was ferocious fun for the Americans. They took many chances, absorbed some hits, and executed classic slaughter. Men wrote afterward of the beauty and the color of this last Battle Line fight: the long long wait for the enemy on the calm sea in the warm night under a setting moon, the tightening of nerves, the once-in-a-lifetime exaltation of destroyer run-ins against heavy ships in searchlight beams, under star shells, under the red blazing flying arches of tracers; the breathless wait for torpedoes to find their marks in the night; the ships blowing up and burning on the sea, the blue-white searchlights blindingly sweeping the black waters, the great guns erupting in salvo after salvo. The Japanese lost all their ships but one, and thousands of lives. The Americans lost thirty-nine lives and no ships.

So to the south Leyte Gulf was safe. But what of the north? At about four in the morning, with the battle going so well, Kinkaid decided to eliminate any farfetched concern by inquiring directly from Halsey whether Task Force Thirty-four was indeed guarding San Bernardino Strait. Off went the dispatch. By that time, the distance between Halsey and Kurita, who was well along toward the gulf, was widening to two hundred miles.

On the flag bridge of the *Iowa*, Victor Henry paced, sleepless. He knew he should be in his sea cabin, resting before the battle. But whenever he tried to lie down the miles kept clicking off in his mind as on a taxi meter, with the price in hours to get back to Leyte Gulf. Blocking San Bernardino Strait, crossing the *T* of the Central Force; blasted dreams! The Jap was certainly through the strait by now, going hell for leather for the beachhead. When would the first howl for help come? The sooner the better, Pug thought; a historic disgrace eclipsing Pearl Harbor was in the making, and the margin of time for averting it was melting away.

The fleet was moving with slow majesty on a smooth sea under thick-sown stars. Far below, the black swells sliding past the *Iowa*'s hull made a quiet slosh. Dead astern, high over the horizon, the Southern Cross blazed. Pug wanted to enjoy the sweet night air, the splendor of the stars, the religious awe of darkness on the ocean. He tried to force his thoughts away from the fleet's predicament. Why torture himself with this empty fretful masterminding? Who was he, anyway, to question his chief? Suppose Halsey had top-secret instructions to do exactly what he was doing? Suppose orders or information had come in on channels for which BatDiv Seven lacked the codes?

His watch officer spoke in the darkness. "Admiral? Urgent dispatch from Com Third Fleet."

Pug hurried into the smoky red-lit flag plot, where sailors slumped at the radars in tired mid-watch attitudes. On the chart desk lay the dispatch. His heart thumped painfully and joyously as his eye caught the words:

FORM BATTLE LINE.

Halsey was ordering Task Force Thirty-four into existence, after all!

But, alas, not to speed south; on the contrary. The six fast battleships, with cruisers and destroyers, were to rush ahead, still farther *northward,* to engage the Jap carriers if they showed up by daylight within gunfire range. Otherwise Mitscher's carriers would hit them, and the Battle Line would hound down and destroy the cripples. Pug's hopes died as quickly as they had flared.

Maneuvering the six giant black shapes out of a formation of sixty-odd vessels by starlight was a tedious tricky business. Pug Henry, almost dropping with weariness but unable to rest, prowled flag quarters and the bridge, tried to eat and failed, smoked and drank coffee until his hammering pulse warned him to take it easy. He had nothing to do; it was the captain's job to handle the ship. Daylight found the Battle Line on station, ten miles north of the carriers, foaming along on the sunlit sea. Squadrons of aircraft were roaring by overhead to strike the quarry, discovered by search planes a hundred fifty miles away.

Pug had ordered his communications officer to intercept every message between Kinkaid and Halsey that could be decoded, for he was starting a separate file of dispatches bearing on the Central Force crisis, noting the time he read each one. So far the file held three sheets:

0650. KINKAID TO HALSEY. AM NOW ENGAGING ENEMY SURFACE FORCES SURIGAO STRAIT. QUESTION. IS TASK FORCE 34 GUARDING SAN BERNARDINO STRAIT.

0730. HALSEY TO KINKAID. NEGATIVE. IT IS WITH OUR CARRIERS NOW ENGAGING ENEMY CARRIERS.

Pug thought bitterly that the face of Admiral Kinkaid, far down there in Leyte Gulf, would be a memorable study in shock when he read *that* one.

0825. KINKAID TO HALSEY. ENEMY VESSELS RETIRING SURIGAO STRAIT. OUR LIGHT FORCES IN PURSUIT.

That was the last calm message. Now came the howl for help Pug was partly dreading, partly hoping for:

0837. KINKAID TO HALSEY. ENEMY BATTLESHIPS AND CRUISERS REPORTED FIRING ON TASK UNIT 77.4.3 FROM 15 MILES ASTERN.

The coding officer had noted "Sent in the clear." Plain English! Kinkaid's dropping of secrecy for the sake of fast communication, allowing the Jap to copy, spoke more stridently than his words.

Quickly Pug thumbed through the thick operation order to identify Task Unit 77.4.3. Ye gods! The jeep carrier outfit of Ziggy Sprague had run afoul of the whole damned Jap battle line. Clifton Sprague was an old friend, class of '18, one of the smart ones who had gone into aviation early and had beaten many seniors like Pug to flag rank. God help Ziggy now, and God help those matchbox ships of his!

Pug was at the flag plot desk, with Bradford facing him. Here the messages began to pile up in his file, while the business of flag plot swirled around him, having to do with the fighting up ahead.

0840. KINKAID TO HALSEY. URGENTLY NEED FAST BATTLESHIPS LEYTE GULF AT ONCE.

Muttering "At once, hey?" Pug measured off the Battle Line's distance to Leyte Gulf: two hundred twenty-five miles. At flank speed, a nine-hour run would get them there by sundown. Too late to save Ziggy Sprague's unit and the landing force from a holocaust; but providing that Halsey acted at once and sent the battleships back they might yet cut off and sink the marauders.

But the only word from Halsey went to the fourth carrier group, still plodding back from Ulithi:

0855. HALSEY TO MCCAIN. STRIKE ENEMY VICINITY 11–20 N 127 E AT BEST POSSIBLE SPEED.

Pug's plotted track of McCain's force showed him over three hundred miles from Leyte. Even if he started maneuvers at once to launch his planes, they could not reach the battle scene for hours, and what would be left of Ziggy's ships?

Meanwhile, pilots' reports were coming in from the air strikes to the north. Cheers rang through flag plot as sailors posted the score in bold grease-pencil strokes on the Plexiglas. Halsey was chalking up his victory early: one carrier sunk, two carriers and a cruiser "badly hit," only one carrier left undamaged; all in the first strike! *"Little or no opposition,"* went up in big orange letters. Not much for the Battle Line to do here, obviously. Mitscher's four hundred planes would mince up this weak wounded force. It would be a sweep like Midway for ships sunk, though of no comparable significance.

The ship's captain buzzed Pug from the bridge to exult over the news. Flag plot was bubbling with the excitement of victory. Only Victor Henry sat glum and isolated. Even as the reports of triumph were spreading over the Plexiglas, a coding room ensign brought him several Kinkaid messages. Coming thick and fast now!

0910. KINKAID TO HALSEY. OUR ESCORT CARRIERS BEING ATTACKED BY 4 BATTLESHIPS, 8 CRUISERS, PLUS OTHERS. REQUEST LEE COVER LEYTE AT TOP SPEED. REQUEST FAST CARRIERS MAKE IMMEDIATE STRIKE.

0914. KINKAID TO HALSEY. HELP NEEDED FROM HEAVY SHIPS IMMEDI-
ATELY.

0925. KINKAID TO HALSEY. SITUATION CRITICAL, BATTLESHIPS AND FAST
CARRIERS WANTED TO PREVENT ENEMY PENETRATING LEYTE GULF.

God in Heaven, how long would Halsey hold out? The messages
were arriving in scrambled sequence. There seemed to be major foul-
ups in transmission. Still, the import was clear. Surely Nimitz must be
picking up these appalling messages from Com Seventh Fleet's powerful
transmitter, and sending them on to King. At this point it seemed to
Pug that Halsey's actual career was at stake; not only a defeat, but a
court-martial was building up in these dispatches.

0930. KINKAID TO HALSEY. TASK UNIT 77.4.3 UNDER ATTACK BY CRUISERS
AND BATTLESHIPS AT 0700. REQUEST IMMEDIATE AIR STRIKES. ALSO RE-
QUEST SUPPORT BY HEAVY SHIPS. MY OLD BATTLESHIPS LOW ON AMMU-
NITION.

This message did at last provoke a response.

0940. HALSEY TO KINKAID. I AM STILL ENGAGING ENEMY CARRIERS. MC-
CAIN WITH 5 CARRIERS 4 HEAVY CRUISERS HAS BEEN ORDERED TO ASSIST
YOU IMMEDIATELY.

Now for the first time Halsey gave his own latitude and longitude. So
Kinkaid had the bad news, flat out, that the Battle Line was about ten
hours from Leyte Gulf. What Kinkaid did not know was that it was still
going the other way at full speed.

1005. KINKAID TO HALSEY. WHERE IS LEE? SEND LEE.

The coding officer again noted "Broadcast in the clear."
A true bellow of agony in plain English for the Japs to pick up!
Pug's telephone buzzed. The coding officer said in a trembling voice,
"Admiral, we're breaking a message from Nimitz." Pug ran to the small
top-secret room, and looked over the decoder's shoulder through dense
cigarette smoke as he tapped the keys. The message came snaking out
of the machine on paper tape:

1000. NIMITZ TO HALSEY. TURKEY TROTS TO WATER GG. WHERE REPEAT
WHERE IS TASK FORCE 34 RR. THE WORLD WONDERS.

The nonsense padding set off by double letters was standard encod-
ing procedure. Yet "The world wonders" from "The Charge of the
Light Brigade" (though Pug had no idea that this day was an anniversary) was apt enough to the situation! Well, Pug thought, this does it;

this unprecedented rebuke from Nimitz in mid-battle would penetrate the hide of a dinosaur; here we go at last. He strode out on the bridge, absolutely certain that within minutes he would see the *New Jersey* streaming the colored signal flags ordering the Battle Line to reverse course: *Turn one-eight.*

Ten minutes passed, a quarter hour, a half hour.

One hour.

The Battle Line continued to steam away from Leyte Gulf at twenty-five knots.

91

WHAT Admiral Kinkaid did not know, and what Pug Henry could not possibly imagine, was the course the combat off Samar was taking. Of all the long books to be written about the three battles on October 25, the tale of this fray is the one any chronicler would most enjoy writing, for its theme is one that will stir human hearts long after all the swords are plowshares: gallantry against high odds.

Sprague's unit of six jeep carriers had the shortwave call sign Taffy Three. When it was surprised, Taffy Three was eighty miles north of the entrance to Leyte Gulf, doing the donkeywork of amphibious warfare; small air strikes at enemy fields, combat air patrol over the beachhead, antisubmarine patrol, bombing of truck convoys, parachuting of supplies to Army units.

These mass-produced runt flattops were not built to fight. Nor was the screen of three destroyers and four smaller destroyer escorts expected to do battle, except against submarines. Most of the sailors and officers of Taffy Three were reserves. A goodly number were draftees. The prima donnas Halsey had taken north, the fleet carriers and fast battleships, were manned by the professional Navy; not the likes of Taffy Three. But Taffy Three, not Halsey, was in Kurita's way as he bore down on Leyte Gulf, and so Taffy Three had to fight him.

Two other jeep carrier units, Taffy Two and Taffy One, were patrolling farther to the south. The gap between each unit was thirty to fifty miles. A glorious harvest for Kurita! Merely continuing to sweep southward, he could pick off most of these slow thin-skinned ships and their little screen vessels one by one. The carriers could not escape him, for his powerful gunships were much faster, and could shoot fifteen miles or more; a heaven-sent opportunity, in short, to lay waste an entire flotilla of flattops on his way to his main job of annihilating the invasion.

But Kurita had not planned to catch the Taffys unawares. He was as surprised by this encounter as they were. Relaxed by the luck of finding the strait unguarded, worn down by the swim for his life on the twenty-third, the air strikes of the twenty-fourth, the loss of the mighty *Musa-*

shi, and three sleepless nights culminating in the tense night passage through mine fields, Kurita was in no jolly mood for pursuing aircraft carriers. The first sight of the low flat shapes on the horizon in the sunrise confounded him. Who were they? Where had they come from? Was Halsey lying in wait here, instead of at the strait? Was the Main Striking Force in for another day of unopposed mayhem from the air?

The apparition met Kurita's eyes at a bad moment. His vessels were crisscrossing helter-skelter all around him, for he had ordered the force into AA formation for daylight steaming. To reshuffle his force into line of battle would take time. Yet the AA "ring formation" was no way to pursue a foe. As Kurita tried to think all this out, staring at the minute gray silhouettes to the south, frantic reports were pouring in from the *Yamato*'s lookouts and from other ships: *"Fleet carriers ahead! Cruisers! Battleships! Small carriers! Tankers! Destroyers!"*—a bedlam of agitated cries. Desperate for information, Kurita launched the *Yamato*'s two scout planes. They vanished and never reported in again. He had to make his decisions without knowing what force he had encountered, and he had to surmise the worst case: that this was Halsey.

Sprague, on the other hand, knew exactly what he faced. These vessels jutting up in a mass over the horizon were the Jap Central Force. Their foreign TBS gabble was coming in plainly. Sprague had assumed with everyone else that Halsey's Battle Line was guarding the strait, and that the Central Force would be none of his business. Now here it was. Most of his planes were already launched, flying CAP over the beachhead, or patrolling for submarines, or circling above his own outfit. The crews of his feeble ships were not even at General Quarters. It took them seconds to abandon their breakfasts and man battle stations, but this scarcely improved the ships' defense stance. Each had one five-inch gun; just one.

Kurita at last ordered "General Attack." The command let loose every ship in the Central Force to pick and chase its own target. They ran off in an uncoordinated pursuit, firing at will; some ships in column, some acting singly, all bearing down at flank speed on the Americans.

Sprague reacted like a War College student solving a battle problem. He went to full speed upwind, making smoke with his carriers. He ordered the escorts to lay a smoke screen. He launched all aircraft still on board his vessels. He notified Kinkaid of his danger, calling for battleship help. He put out an emergency combat call to all aircraft within range. Those things done, he headed for a rainsquall lying upwind, and his formation gradually disappeared into it, about a quarter of an hour after sighting the Japanese. Near-misses had jolted the force, but the ships were safe and whole. At the War College he would have received good marks for his solution, worked out while red, purple, green, and yellow splashes from the big guns sprang up all over the sea about him, and destruction seemed minutes away.

In the squall he was far from safe, of course. He was like a fugitive hiding from a cop behind a moving wagon. The rainsquall would not hold still. Nor could he. The enemy kept gaining on him, and could see him with radar. Sprague headed windward and southward through thick rain to keep sea room, and to close with whatever ships were coming to his aid. His tactic was to play for time and keep his carriers together and afloat until deliverance came from *some* quarter: Halsey, Kinkaid, the other Taffys, Army air, or a merciful God.

Through the drifting rain and smoke, he could see the battleships getting bigger astern, and cruisers drawing near on his quarters. He ordered his three destroyers to make a torpedo attack against the huge force. It was a hardhearted, cold-blooded delaying move. The three slim gray vessels pulled out of the rainsquall and steamed straight toward the battleships and cruisers, through a barrage of big shells. On opposing courses, the Main Striking Force and the little ships closed fast. Hit after hit smashed into the destroyers, but they shot off their torpedoes and limped away under fire. Two eventually sank. They got only a single hit on a cruiser.

Still, the pursuers had had to break off the chase to evade the torpedoes, giving Sprague a start on his escape dash. For Kurita the result was very bad. By his own orders the heavy *Yamato* wheeled north to evade while the fight ran southward. The super-battleship steamed seven miles northward before turning around again, for the destroyer attacks were not simultaneous and the torpedo tracks kept coming. Kurita lost contact with the engagement. His force was headless thereafter, committing itself piecemeal to no plan.

Meantime, aircraft were showing up: Sprague's planes, planes from Leyte, planes from Taffy One and Taffy Two; bombing, torpedoing, and strafing the Japanese. During the long fight the air attacks hit three cruisers; all three in the end went down. Yet the pursuers fought back hard, knocking down over a hundred aircraft while gaining on Sprague in a gun chase lasting two hours. As a last resort Sprague ordered his four destroyer escorts, equipped with torpedoes but untrained in their use, to make another delaying attack. These puny vessels too charged into the teeth of the big guns. They got no hits, took brutal damage, and one sank. They gained Sprague a little more time.

But after two hours his game was about played out. Heavy cruisers were pulling abeam to port and starboard, pumping shells into his carriers. Two battleships were rapidly coming up astern. He had no tricks left but violent zigzagging among the gruesomely beautiful shell splashes. American planes were smoking and burning all over the sea. None of his carriers was undamaged, and one was sinking. Impotently they kept firing their single five-inch guns.

At this point, Kurita on the distant *Yamato* ordered all his ships to cease fire and rejoin him.

The guns fell silent. The Japanese vessels turned away from their gasping prey and headed north. Taffy Three fled southward, its sailors—from the admiral down to the youngest seaman—incredulous at this mysterious deliverance. The Battle of Samar was over. It was about a quarter past nine.

Under sporadic air harassment, Takeo Kurita next gathered up his force for the thrust into Leyte Gulf. He steamed a slow circle off the entrance, reuniting the scattered units. It took three hours. Leyte Gulf now lay open before him. With Taffy Three distantly on the run, nothing any longer barred the way. Against unbelievable odds, despite mistakes, misfortunes, miscalculations, communication failures, and terrible punishment, the *Sho* plan had worked! Kinkaid's old battleships, trying to hurry back from their Surigao Strait pursuit, were far off and low on ammunition. The MacArthur invasion in the gulf, transports and troops alike, lay helpless before the Main Striking Force.

At half past twelve, Admiral Kurita, having regrouped his force, *decided on his own not to enter Leyte Gulf. Asking no permission from Tokyo, notifying nobody, he turned north to head home through San Bernardino Strait.*

The signal flags for reversing course ran up on the *New Jersey* halyards about a quarter past eleven.

TURN ONE-EIGHT

According to Pug's chart, the crippled carriers were only forty-five miles away, dodging and burning under the air strikes. Leyte Gulf was three hundred miles to the south. Now, less than an hour's steaming from the force he had run northward all night and half the day to destroy, Halsey was turning back.

The captain of the *Iowa* burst into flag plot. Could the admiral tell him what was happening? There was great hunting directly ahead. Why were they turning away?

"Looks like a bigger fight making up back at Leyte Gulf, Skipper."

"We can't get there until sunup tomorrow, Admiral. At best."

"I know," Pug said in a dry tone that guillotined the conversation, and the captain left.

Pug could not trust himself to talk to the captain. He was in the emotional turmoil of a mutinous ensign. Could Halsey really be throwing away one of the major battles of all time, covering the United States Navy with ignominy, endangering the Leyte landing force, fumbling the winning of the war? Or was he himself—deprived of the big chance of his life to fight a battle-line engagement—too upset to think straight?

Yet he could not stop his mind from working. Even on this turnaround, he judged Halsey was making serious mistakes. Why was he taking six battleships? Two could still press ahead to the Northern Force; surface fire was the right way to sink cripples. And why was he dragging along a mass of destroyers? They would all have to be fueled first.

Pug recalled how Churchill, coming to meet Roosevelt at Argentia aboard the *Prince of Wales,* had left the destroyer screen behind to speed through a gale faster than they could go. That was a man! Here was the redeeming moment, the very last chance to rush back and gun down the Central Force. Halsey had lost six hours by not turning back at Kinkaid's first bellow. Only desperate measures would answer now. The Central Force must be a weary battered outfit, perhaps with empty torpedo tubes, low fuel bunkers, possibly even low magazines. Surely it was a moment to pitch all on one throw; to forgo destroyer protection and destroyer torpedoes, and roar down there with the big guns.

But it was not to be. The "rescue run" became an exasperating leisurely saunter at ten knots in the hot humid afternoon. One by one, hour after hour, the destroyers pulled up alongside the battleships to fuel. The carriers went by the other way, at full speed in pursuit of the Northern Force. It was a bitter sight; bitter to be becalmed in this great Battle Line in the midst of vast engagements, not yet having fired a shot.

Bitterer yet was the stench of oil. Pug was observing the refueling from the flag bridge. It was a skillfully done business: each small ship nosing up alongside the giant *Iowa,* its young skipper on his bridge, far below Pug, matching speeds until relative movement was zero; then the touch-and-go passing of the swaying oil lines over the splashing blue swells between the ships, and the parallel steaming until the little nursing vessel dropped away sated. Pug was used to the sight, yet, like carrier flight operations, he usually enjoyed watching it.

But today, in his overwrought state, the smell of black oil brought back the night of the *Northampton*'s sinking. That remembrance twisted the knife of his present impotence. Division commander of two battleships, he was being robbed of vengeance for the men who had died in the *Northampton,* by the bellicose blundering of Bill Halsey.

A despairing vision came over Pug Henry as these dragging hours passed. It struck him that the whole war had been generated by this damned viscous black fluid. Hitler's tanks and planes, the Jap carriers that had hit Pearl Harbor, all the war machinery hurtling and clashing all over the earth, ran on this same stinking gunk. The Japs had gone to war to grab a supply of it. Not fifty years had passed since the first Texas oil field had come in, and the stuff had caused this world inferno. At Oak Ridge they were cooking up something even more potent than petroleum, racing to isolate it and use it for slaughter.

Pug felt on this October twenty-fifth, during this endless, nerve-wracking, refueling crawl toward Leyte Gulf at ten knots, that he belonged to a doomed species. God had weighed modern man in the balance with three gifts of buried treasure—coal, oil, uranium—and found him wanting. Coal had fueled Jutland and the German trains in the Great War, petroleum had turned loose air war and tank war, and the Oak Ridge stuff would probably end the whole horrible business. God had promised not to send another deluge; He had said nothing about preventing men from setting fire to their planet and themselves.

Pug's mood had reached this depth of dismalness when Captain Bradford came running out on the flying bridge. ComBatDiv Seven was being summoned on the TBS by "Blackjack."

"It's not a communicator, Admiral," said Bradford with some agitation, "it's Halsey."

Pug's apocalyptic vision vanished. He darted into flag plot and seized the TBS receiver.

"Blackjack, this is Buckeye Seven, over."

"Say, Pug," came Halsey's familiar voice, grainy and buoyant, using the informal style privileged to high flag officers, "we're about through refueling here, and time's a-wasting. Our division can sustain a long flank speed run. What say we mosey on ahead down there, and try to catch those monkeys? The others will follow. Bogan will back us up with his carriers."

The proposal knocked Pug's breath out. At that rate the *New Jersey* and the *Iowa* could reach San Bernardino Strait about one in the morning, Leyte Gulf at three or four. If they did encounter the enemy, it would mean a night action. The Japs were old hands at that, and Bat-Div Seven had no night fighting experience at all. Two battleships would be fighting at least four battleships, including one with eighteen-inch guns.

But, by God, here was *Form Battle Line,* at long last; wrong, rash, tardy, but the thing itself! And Halsey would be right there. Pug could not keep out of his voice a flash of reluctant regard for the crazy old fighting son of a bitch.

"I'm for it."

"I thought you would be. Form Task Group Thirty-four point five, Pug. Designate *Biloxi, Vincennes, Miami,* and eight DDs for the screen. You've got tactical command. Let's get the hell down to Leyte Gulf."

"Aye aye, sir."

* * *

92

Japan's Last Gasp

(from World Holocaust by Armin von Roon)

TRANSLATOR'S NOTE: *When* World Holocaust *first appeared in German, a translation of this controversial chapter was published in the U.S. Naval Institute* Proceedings. *As a BatDiv commander at Leyte, I was invited to write a rejoinder. It is appended here.—V.H.*

Our Ardennes offensive in late 1944, the so-called Battle of the Bulge, and the Battle for Leyte Gulf were parallel operations. In each case a nation close to defeat staked all on one last throw of the dice. Hitler wanted to panic the Western allies into a settlement that would give him a breather to hold off the Russians; he even harbored grandiose delusions of getting the Anglo-Americans to fight on his side. The Japanese wanted to make the Americans sick of the distant war, and willing to negotiate a peace.

Our Ardennes offensive, discussed in my next section, gave Roosevelt and Churchill anxious weeks. The two aging warmongers thought Germany was done for, but we split their front in France and made good progress for a while, though Hitler's overambitious battle plan and tactical meddling, plus Allied air power, probably doomed us from the start.

The Japanese, however, almost brought off a world-shaking success. The chance for this success was created by the imbecility of the American fleet commander, Halsey. It was thrown away by the greater imbecility of the Japanese fleet commander, Kurita. The Battle for Leyte Gulf is a study in military folly on the vastest scale. Its lessons should be pondered by the armed forces of all countries.

Politics and War

War is politics implemented by the use of force. A military undertaking seldom rises above its political genesis; if that is unsound the guns will speak and the blood flow in vain. These Clausewitzian commonplaces will shed light on the grotesque fiasco at Leyte Gulf.

The political situation in the Pacific in late 1944 was this. On the one hand, the Japanese nation, in its gallant try for hegemony in its own geographical area, had already been ruthlessly beaten by the American imperialists; but its leaders wanted to fight on. Unconditional surrender was unthinkable to these Samurai idealists. Yet Franklin Roosevelt had laid down those terms to suit the mentality of his countrymen, on whose soil not one bomb had yet fallen, and who were fighting a Hollywood war.

This being the political deadlock in the Pacific—for on military grounds the Japanese should have been suing for peace once Tojo fell—a military *shock* was needed to break the stalemate. In long wars, peace parties develop: in democratic systems openly, in dictatorships within the ruling cadre. A shock strengthens the peace party of the shocked side. The Japanese planned to lie back until the Americans struck the Empire's inner perimeter, and then smash them. At the end of extended supply lines, near Japanese air and naval bases, the Yanks would be at a transient disadvantage, and might be shocked by a bloody setback into a reasonable peace.

The American concept behind the invasion of the Philippines was a mere empty gratification of General MacArthur's vanity, which would also palliate some home-front grumbling. It brought major Japanese land forces in the Philippines unnecessarily into action. These were already stymied by the horrible unrestricted U-boat warfare of the Americans, and should have been left to wither on the vine. But Douglas MacArthur wanted to return to the Philippines, and Roosevelt wanted such a theatrical reconquest right before the election.

The ostensible reason for taking Leyte, a large central island of the archipelago, was to establish supply depots and a large air base for the attack on Luzon. But Leyte is mountainous, and its one important flat valley is a mass of soggy rice paddies. MacArthur's own engineers protested at choosing Leyte for such purposes. The generalissimo, in his hunger for his great Return, ignored them. Leyte after its capture never became a significant operational base. The world's most massive sea battle was fought for a trivial and useless prize.

Following the Nimitz strategy of a Central Pacific drive, Admirals King and Spruance had offered better plans for ending the war. Both proposed to bypass the Philippines. King wanted to take Formosa. Spruance—who has an undeserved reputation for caution—suggested the audacious project of landing on Okinawa. Such a landing, virtually in Japan's home waters, might well have been the shock to topple the war cabinet and bring peace. The atomic bomb was then still more than half a year from becoming a reality. The barbaric deed of Hiroshima might never have been necessary. But nine months later when the Americans did take Okinawa, the Japanese were hardened in last-ditch resistance, and only nuclear slaughter could jolt them out of the war.

In short, the overweening ego of Generalissimo MacArthur and the cold-blooded politicking of Franklin Roosevelt gave the Japanese their chance. They seized it, and they should have won. The Americans stumbled, fumbled, and flopped into a sorry "victory," thanks to one Japanese admiral's unbelievable folly.

My operational analysis gives the Japanese *Sho* plan in detail, with daily charts of the four main engagements. This sketch will be limited to the outstanding Leyte controversies.

A pincer attack on MacArthur's landing force through Surigao Strait and San Bernardino Strait was a sound idea. The use of Ozawa's impotent carriers as a decoy force was brilliant. Unless Halsey's Third Fleet could be lured from the scene, the pincer attack could not succeed. The chief controversies center around the battle decisions of Halsey and Kurita.

Halsey

The American commander who botched the battle, William F. Halsey, rushed into print after the war to cover his tracks with a book that ran serially in a popular magazine while the nations were still burying their dead. The book opens with these words, purportedly written by his collaborator, a staff officer: *Fleet Admiral Halsey was attending a reception in 1946 when a woman broke through the crowd around him, grasped his hand, and cried, "I feel as if I were touching the hand of God!"*

This first sentence in *Admiral Halsey's Story* characterizes the man. He was a seagoing George Patton, a blustering war lover with a gift for publicity; but one finds in his combat record nothing to match Patton's advance in Sicily, his flank march during "the Bulge" to relieve Bastogne, or his dashing drive across Germany.

The critique of Halsey's actions at Leyte goes to these questions:

a. Did he make the correct decision in pursuing Ozawa's carriers, even if the force was a decoy?

b. Why did he leave San Bernardino Strait unguarded?

c. Who was to blame for the surprise of Sprague's "jeep" carriers off Samar?

Admiral Halsey wrote a defensive dispatch to Nimitz on these very points the evening after the battle, when he and his staff were still gloomy at the fearful mess they had made, and had not yet worked up their alibi. By the time he wrote his book, Halsey's defense had hardened into an explicit position.

a. He was right to go after the carriers. They were the main threat of the Pacific war. Had he not attacked them, they might have "shuttle-bombed" his fleet, the planes hopping from the carrier decks to fields in the Philippines and back again. As to Ozawa's being a decoy, Halsey suggested he lied under interrogation. "*The Japs had continuously lied during the war. . . . Why believe them implicitly as soon as the war ends?*"

b. Staying at San Bernardino Strait was a bad idea, since the Japanese might also "shuttle-bomb" the Third Fleet there. Leaving the Battle Line to guard the strait was also a bad idea. "Shuttle-bombing" would be even more effective against divided forces. He took all his ships north to "preserve his fleet's integrity and keep the initiative."

c. Kinkaid was to blame for the surprise off Samar. He had been notified that Halsey was abandoning the strait. Protecting the MacArthur landing and his own jeep carriers was Kinkaid's job. He was derelict in not sending air searches north that would have spotted Kurita's approach.

This flimsy apologia may do for magazine readers, but not for military historians.

As for "shuttle-bombing," Halsey himself had successfully urged the Joint Chiefs to advance the date of the Leyte invasion, because of the weak air resistance he had encountered from Philippine bases. He had himself crushed most of Japan's residual air strength in the Formosa operation. He had himself observed the pitiful calibre of the raw Japanese pilots still flying. He had himself struck the Luzon airfields almost with impunity. His own admirals did not think Ozawa's carriers could be strongly manned. The strategist Lee warned him in so many words that they were a decoy force. The "shuttle-bombing" story is a weak attempt to make the facts fit Halsey's fatuous action in swallowing the Japanese bait.

His reason for taking all ships north and abandoning the strait—"to preserve his fleet's integrity"—is bombast. He did not need sixty-four warships to fight seventeen, or ten carriers to fight four. Common sense required leaving a force to guard the strait. All the high commanders thought he had done that. Only his sloppy communications failed to undeceive them in time.

In blaming Kinkaid for the surprise off Samar, Halsey sinks to his nadir. Guarding San Bernardino Strait was Halsey's responsibility, and he was the senior naval officer present. If he really was shifting such a heavy responsibility to Kinkaid's shoulders, he should have done so in clear terms by dispatch, preferably after consulting Nimitz, for which there was plenty of time.

At Leyte Halsey made the essential mistake of Napoleon at Waterloo. He faced two forces, and dealt one a hard but not a decisive blow; then, in his obsessive desire to strike the second force, he chose to believe that the first force was done for, and closed his ears and his mind to all evidence to the contrary. Kurita's advance after his retreat in the Sibuyan Sea parallels Blücher's advance after his retreat at Ligny. (The reader may wish to glance at my *Waterloo: A Modern Analysis,* published in Hamburg in 1937.)

Halsey was obsessed with the carrier force because he wanted to outdo Spruance. The sickness that had taken him out of the Battle of Midway had been the disappointment of his life. He was wild for a great carrier victory. He intended to be there in person, and in command, when it happened. Since he was riding a battleship, he disposed his forces so that the battleships could have a glorious time sinking cripples, and he went steaming north with the lot of them.

Roosevelt's straddling between the MacArthur and the Nimitz strategies for defeating Japan—between the naval drive across the central Pacific, and the long plod of armies up the South Pacific archipelagoes—came to catastrophe at Leyte. Halsey was Nimitz's man. Kinkaid by his orders was MacArthur's man. The Leyte invasion was the triumph of the MacArthur strategy. Halsey with his simple-minded dash after the carriers thought he was implementing the Nimitz strategy. In swallowing the Japanese bait, he forgot what he was at Leyte for; that is, if he had ever understood it.

Halsey never admitted making any mistake at Leyte Gulf except turning back to help Kinkaid. That, he asserted, was an error made in anger, and due to a misunderstanding. Nimitz's inquiry at ten in the morning, WHERE IS TASK FORCE 34, was astounding, so Halsey insisted, since he had notified everybody that the Battle Line was going north with him. But the next phrase, THE WORLD WONDERS, seemed a deliberate insult, and threw him into a rage. Only much later did he learn that it was padding added by a coding officer.

This is such foolishness that the worst would be if it were true, and if Halsey had acted in pique. Morison, the American navy's fine historian, charitably ignores this excuse in his volume on Leyte. So Halsey regrets the only sensible thing he did in the Battle of Leyte Gulf, and blames his putative mistake on some anonymous little "squirt," to use his own word, at a coding machine.

Halsey was a newspaper tiger the American navy did not dare disown. In the inner circles, after Leyte, there was talk of retiring him. But he stayed on to run the fleet into two typhoons, incurring as much damage and loss of life as in a major defeat. He was promoted to five-star admiral, and he stood on the deck of the *Missouri* by Nimitz's side when the Japanese signed the instrument of surrender. Spruance was then in Manila. Spruance never received a fifth star. Hitler's treatment of our General Staff was senselessly unfair, but the American Congress and the navy have something to answer for in this matter.

Kurita

Kurita's role at Leyte had elements of the noble and the pathetic, before his collapse into imbecility. He set out on a suicidal mission. He bore on bravely through submarine and air blows that staggered and shrank his force. His reward was finding the exit of San Bernardino Strait unguarded. He should have gone on to penetrate Leyte Gulf and crush MacArthur's landing. That he did not was high tragedy for Japan; also, as I shall show, for Germany.

Kurita's disintegration on the morning of October twenty-fifth was due to the human limits of strain and fatigue, and the failure of Japanese communications. American communications were poor, considering their wealth of sophisticated equipment, but the only word for the Japanese performance is *lamentable*. Kurita also suffered from the absence of air support and air reconnaissance, as we did in the Ardennes. To an extent hard to imagine, he fought blind.

He made three major blunders, and the third is the crux of Leyte Gulf. One man's mental blackout ruined the last hopes of two great nations.

The first mistake was to order "General Attack" on sighting Sprague's escort carriers. He should have formed for battle, then speeded up and wiped Sprague out. He could then have proceeded into the gulf after a shining victory, while scarcely breaking stride. "General Attack," a lapse into Asiatic excitability, released his ships like a pack of hounds each chasing its own rabbit. In the ensuing confusion Sprague escaped.

The second mistake was breaking off the action when his disorganized forces had managed to overhaul Sprague. Because of the abominable communications Kurita did not realize what had happened in the smoke and rainsqualls far to the south. He thought that he had done very well: surprised Halsey's big carriers, routed them from his path to Leyte Gulf, and sunk several, as his excited subordinates reported. So he decided to get on into the gulf.

The puzzle at which military writers stand confounded is Kurita's fatal third mistake: his turnabout and departure without entering Leyte Gulf, when he had fought his way to the entrance and could no longer be stopped.

Under American interrogation, Kurita later explained that by midday of October twenty-fifth he could accomplish little in the gulf. The landing was "confirmed," and the question was, what could he do instead? He got word of a large carrier force about a hundred miles to the north (a false report) and he decided to head that way to attack it, perhaps in conjunction with Ozawa. Northward was also the way to escape, but he always denied that intention.

One report Kurita certainly never received was that Ozawa was under attack by Halsey three hundred miles from Leyte Gulf. *Had Kurita received such a dispatch he would have entered the gulf and accomplished his mission. Kurita's ignorance of the fact that Halsey had been decoyed is the solution to the mystery of Leyte Gulf.*

This abysmal communication failure, so reminiscent—once again—of episodes at Waterloo, by no means absolves Kurita of imbecility. Like Halsey, he forgot what he was there for. Halsey was distracted by lust for a showy triumph. Kurita was distracted by bad information, fatigue, and the enemy's spate of plain-language messages. Kinkaid's cries for help, instead of reassuring Kurita, appear to have worried him with fears of enormous reinforcements on the way.

But none of these excuses will answer. It was not for Kurita to decide that MacArthur's landing was "confirmed." He was there to sail in, destroy that landing, and perish if he had to, like the wasp that stings and dies. This was the whole mission of *Sho.* Kurita had the prize in his grasp. He let it slip and fled the field. One short dispatch of less than ten words from Ozawa to Kurita—AM ENGAGING ENEMY FLEET NE OF LUZON—could have altered the outcome of the battle and the war.

For the American election was then less than two weeks away. There was growing disillusionment with the old hypocrite in the White House and his pseudo-royal family. There was also widespread suspicion that he was a dying man, as he was. His lead over his Republican opponent was fragile. Had Roosevelt fallen, and his relatively young and unknown Republican opponent, Dewey, taken office, the shape of the future might have been different. American antipathy for the Bolsheviks might have broken to the surface, in time to save Europe from the spectre of Soviet domination, which now rots our culture and our politics with the leprosy of communism.

Certainly a setback at Leyte would have called for a rethinking of American strategy, including "unconditional surrender." With a resurgent Japan at their backs, the Russians might have halted on the eastern front. Germany and Japan could no longer have won; but with less draconic peace terms, both nations would have recovered sooner from the war, and become more credible counterweights to Chinese and Russian communism.

As it was, thanks to his good luck at Leyte, the dying Roosevelt had his dear wish of crushing all competition to American capitalism in the short run. He may thereby have sold out Western Christian civilization to the Marxists in the long run. That seems not to have occurred to him or to have troubled him.

"Form Battle Line"

A Rejoinder
by Vice Admiral Victor Henry, USN (Ret.)

Not being equipped to discuss General von Roon's peculiar geopolitics, I will make one or two general comments and then get to the battle.

Roon's slurs on Roosevelt, our greatest President since Lincoln, are not worth discussing, coming as they do from a man imprisoned for faithfully abetting Adolf Hitler's crimes until the day that monster shot himself.

What he says about shock in the last stages of a war is interesting. The well-known Tet offensive in Viet Nam was such a shock; a last-gasp effort, and as an attack a costly failure. But President Johnson had assured the American people that the South Viet Nam communists were done for. The public was extremely shocked by Tet, the tepid support for the war evaporated, and the agitation for peace prevailed.

World War II was different. Annihilation of MacArthur's beachhead might have affected the peace terms, but Roon exaggerates its potential. The country was behind that war. The submarine throttling of Japan, the crushing of Germany between Eisenhower and the Russians, would have continued. Whether President Roosevelt would have lost the election is one of those "ifs" beyond determination.

Roon is a little shaky on some facts. Spruance's plan to take Okinawa depended on an unsolved logistical problem, the transfer of heavy ammunition at sea. Nimitz approved the advance on the Philippines, after study.

I find Roon's criticisms of Kurita and Halsey facile and trite. Insight into Leyte requires a detailed knowledge of what went on, and a sense of the geography, and what the sea and air distances meant in terms of hard-sweating time. I was there, and I can point out Roon's obvious sour notes.

Kurita's Mistakes

Taking Roon's criticisms of Kurita's actions on October twenty-fifth one by one:

a. The order, "General Attack"

Roon follows Morison in condemning this move.

Yet think about it. Kurita's surface force had surprised carriers. Carriers had given him a terrible pasting and had sunk the *Musashi*. Carriers needed time to maneuver into the wind for launching. If he could rush them and start gunning them down before they could get going, he stood his best chance with this target of opportunity. He hit out at once with **everything** he had. That was not "Asiatic excitability," it was desperate aggressiveness. Roon's racial phrasing is deplorable.

Kurita kept driving to windward to interfere with the carriers' launching and recovery operations during the running fight. He knew what he was about. In fact, his force did catch up at last with Sprague, and "the definite partiality of Almighty God," as Sprague put it in his action report, was all that saved Taffy Three.

b. Breaking off the fight with Sprague

Clearly a mistake, in 20/20 hindsight. But nothing was clear to Kurita at the time, far off to the north on the *Yamato*. He should have turned south into the torpedo tracks to comb them, rather than away. That would have kept him in the picture.

He got some very bum reports from his commanders. It was the Formosa business all over again. If he believed half of them, he had won the biggest victory since Midway. But the air attacks were stepping up, the day was wearing on, and three of his heavy cruisers were dead in the water and burning. His ships were scattered over forty square miles of ocean. He decided to rally them and proceed into the gulf. Considering his faulty information, it was a reasonable move.

c. Turning away from Leyte Gulf

Indefensible. Still, "imbecile" is hardly a professional term. Roon ignores the mitigating factors.

It took Kurita over three hours to round up his force. Air attacks slowed the process, and the buzzing planes and bursting bombs must have been driving him cuckoo. By the time he was ready to head into the gulf, it was getting on to one o'clock. His surprise was blown. He surmised—quite correctly—that wherever Halsey was, he was coming on fast. Ozawa was silent, and the Southern Force had evidently never made it into the gulf. To Kurita the gulf had become a death trap, a hornets' nest of land-based and carrier planes, where his whole force would be sunk in the remaining daylight hours without laying a glove on MacArthur.

Granted, he was in a funk. All of us like to think that in his place we would have plunged on into Leyte Gulf anyway. But if we are honest with ourselves we can understand, if not admire, what Kurita did.

The real "solution" of Leyte Gulf is that Ziggy Sprague, an able American few remember or honor, frustrated the *Sho* plan and saved Halsey's reputation and MacArthur's beachhead. He held up Kurita for six crucial hours: two and a half hours in the running fight, and three and a half hours in regrouping. After midday, proceeding into the gulf was a very iffy shot.

Kurita did not lose the Battle of Leyte Gulf because of one wrong decision or one missing dispatch. The U.S. Navy won it with some magnificent fighting. The long and the short of Leyte Gulf was that the Japanese navy was routed and broken, and never sailed again. For all our mistakes, Leyte was an honorable, not a "sorry" victory, and a very hard-fought one. We had superiority in Surigao Strait and in the north, but not off the gulf, where it mattered most.

The vision of Sprague's three destroyers—the *Johnston*, the *Hoel*, and the *Heermann*—charging out of the smoke and the rain straight toward the main batteries of Kurita's battleships and cruisers, can endure as a picture of the way Americans fight when they don't have superiority. Our schoolchildren should know about that incident, and our enemies should ponder it.

Halsey's Mistakes

I have never been madder at anybody in my life than I was at Halsey during Leyte Gulf. To this hour I can remember my rage and despair. I can get sick at heart all over again at the missed chance to fight the Battle Line action off San Bernardino Strait.

Nor am I about to defend either his swallowing the Ozawa lure, or his failure to leave a force to await Kurita. These were blunders. Roon's criticism of Halsey's published alibi is on target. His excessive eagerness for action, his lack of cool analytical powers—which I observed when I was an ensign on a destroyer he commanded—were his ruination. If he had stayed at San Bernardino Strait and sent Mitscher after Ozawa, or if he had simply left Lee and the Battle Line on guard, he would have creamed both Japanese forces, and William Halsey would stand in history with John Paul Jones. As it was, both partially escaped, and his name remains under a cloud.

And yet, I say Armin von Roon misses the truth about Admiral Halsey by a wide sea mile.

His concern about shuttle-bombing was not a mere weak excuse after the fact. October twenty-fifth was not two hours along when planes from Luzon knocked out the *Princeton*. Halsey was right to worry about more such attacks. If he gave that worry too much weight, that's another matter.

In Leo Tolstoy's *War and Peace*, which all military men have read (or should have), there are some pretty questionable historical and military theories; among them, the notion that strategic and tactical plans do not actually matter a damn in war. The variables are infinite, confusion reigns, and chance governs all. So says Tolstoy. Most of us have had that feeling in battle, one time or another. Still, it is not so. The battles of Grant and Spruance—to take American instances—show solid results from solid planning. However, the author makes one telling point: that victory turns on the individual brave spirit in the field, the man who snatches the flag, shouts

"Hurrah!" and rushes forward when the issue is in doubt. That is a truth we all know too.

In the Pacific war, William F. Halsey was that man.

After his botch at Leyte there was indeed thought of retiring him. The powers that be decided that he was a "national asset," and could not be spared. They were right. Nobody but the professional officers, and the high-ranking ones at that, knew who Spruance was. Scarcely any more knew of Nimitz and King. But every last draftee knew about "Bull" Halsey, and felt safe and proud sailing under him. In the dark days of Guadalcanal, he made our dispirited forces believe in themselves again with his "Hurrah!" and they came from behind to win that gory fight.

On the afternoon of October twenty-fifth, Halsey called me on the TBS. I commanded BatDiv Seven in the *Iowa*, and he was in the *New Jersey*. We were heading back with most of the fleet to help Kinkaid. With the gallant good humor of a star quarterback leading a team in trouble, he asked me —not ordered me, asked me—what I thought about making a high-speed run with BatDiv Seven, ahead of the fleet, to take on the Central Force. I agreed. He put me in tactical command, and off we roared at twenty-eight knots.

We missed Kurita. He had hightailed it through San Bernardino Strait a few hours earlier, thanks to his decision not to enter the gulf. We caught one lagging destroyer about two in the morning, and our screen vessels sank it. As Halsey writes in his book, that was the only gunfighting he ever saw, in his forty-three years at sea.

Furious as I was at Halsey, I forgave him that day as we talked on the TBS. Rushing two battleships into a night action against Kurita was fool-hardy, perhaps fully as bullheaded as his run after Ozawa. Yet I couldn't help shouting my "Hurrah!" to echo his. Spruance wouldn't have dashed ahead like that, perhaps; but then Spruance wouldn't have run six battle-ships three hundred miles north and then three hundred miles south during a great battle without firing a shot. That was Halsey, the good and the bad of him. I executed *Form Battle Line* with Halsey at Leyte Gulf, and went hunting the enemy through the tropical night with great trepidation against great odds. Nothing came of it, and I may be a fool, but that farewell "Hur-rah!" of my career remains a good memory.

"Form Battle Line"

This order will not be heard again on earth. The days of naval engage-ments are finished. Technology has overwhelmed this classic military con-cept. A very old sailor may perhaps be permitted to ramble a bit, in conclusion, on the real lessons of Leyte Gulf.

Leyte stands as a monument to the subhuman stupidity of warfare in our age of science and industry. War has always been violent blindman's buff, played with men's lives and nations' resources. But the time for it is over. As the race has outgrown human sacrifice, human slavery, and duelling, it has to outgrow war. The means now dwarf the results, and destructive machinery has become a senseless resort in politics. This was already the case at Leyte. It was truly "imbecile" to launch the colossal navies that clashed there, at a cost of manpower and treasure almost beyond imagining, and to pin the fate of nations on the decisions of a couple of agitated, ill-informed, fatigued old men, acting under impossible pressure. The silliness of it all would be slapstick if it were not so tragic.

Yet granting all that, *what alternative was there but to fight at Leyte Gulf?* That is the crack we were in, and still are.

Forty years ago, when I was a lieutenant commander and our pacifists were pointing out quite accurately the obsolete folly of industrialized war, Hitler and the Japanese militarists were arming to the teeth, with the most formidable weapons science and industry could give them, for a criminal attempt to loot the world. The English-speaking countries and the Russians fought a just war to stop the crime. At horrible cost, we succeeded. What would the world be like had we disarmed, and Nazi Germany prevailed and won world dominion?

Yet today, when every intelligent man is sick with unspoken fear of nuclear weapons, the benighted Marxist autocrats in the Kremlin, ruling the very great, very brave, very unlucky people who were our comrades-in-arms, are conducting foreign affairs as though Catherine the Great were still running the show there; only they call their grabby czarist policy the "struggle against colonialism."

I have no answer to this dilemma, and I will not live to see it resolved. I honor the young men in our armed forces who must man machinery of hideous potential, in a profession despised and feared by their fellow countrymen. I honor them to my very soul, and they have my sympathy. Their sacrifice is far greater than ours ever was. We could still believe in, and hope for, the great hour of *Form Battle Line*. We were looked up to for that by our country. We felt proud. That is no more. The world now loathes the very thought of industrialized war, after two big doses of it. Yet, while belligerent fools or villains anywhere on earth consider it an optional policy, what can free men do but confront them with what met the Japanese at Leyte Gulf, and Adolf Hitler in the skies over England in 1940—daunting force, and self-sacrificing brave spirits ready to wield it?

If the hope is not the coming of the Prince of Peace, it has to be that in their hearts most people, even the most fanatical and boneheaded Marxists, even the craziest nationalists and revolutionaries, love their children, and don't want to see them burn up. There is no politician imbecile enough, surely, to want a nuclear Leyte Gulf. The future now seems to depend on that grim assumption. Either war is finished or we are.

93

A<small>N</small> official Jew from the Transport Section stops Aaron Jastrow by bustling through the crowd and grabbing his arm, as he and Natalie are climbing the wooden ramp into the train.

"Dr. Jastrow, you'll ride up ahead in the passenger coach."

"I would rather stay with my niece."

"Don't argue or it will be the worse for you. Go where you're told, quick march."

All along the track SS men are bellowing obscenities and threats, and thrashing at the transportees with stout sticks. The Jews are panicking up the ramps into the cattle cars, dragging suitcases, bundles, sacks, and whimpering children. Natalie manages one hasty kiss on Aaron's bearded cheek. He says in Yiddish, which Natalie can barely hear over the German shouting, *"Zye mutig."* ("Keep up your spirit.") The shoving crowd thrusts them apart.

As the moving crush bears her inside the gloomy car, the cow-barn smell gives her an incongruous memory flash of childhood summers. Places to sit along the rough wooden walls are being fought over with exasperated yells and violent pushing and pulling. She makes her way as through a rush-hour subway mob to a corner under a barred window where two Viennese co-workers from the mica factory are sitting with husbands, children, and luggage crammed around them. They make a bit of room for her by moving their legs. Natalie sits down in a place which becomes hers for the next three days, as though she has bought a ticket for this one dung-caked spot on the slatted floor, where the wind whistles through a broad crack, the racket of the wheels sounds loud as the train rolls, and querulous people press against her from all sides.

They leave in rain, and they travel through rain. Though it is almost November the weather is not cold. When Natalie struggles to her feet and takes her turn at the high barred window to look out and breathe sweet air, she sees trees in autumn colors and peasants picking fruits. These moments at the window are delicious. They pass all too quickly and she must drop back into the fetor of the car. The barn odor and the smell of unwashed crowded people in old wet clothes is soon overwhelmed by a stink of broken toilets. The men, women, and children in the car, a hundred or more, must relieve themselves into two overflowing pails, one at each end, to which they must squirm and struggle through the crowd, and which are emptied only when the train stops and an SS man remembers to slide open the door a crack. Natalie has to face away from the pail not five feet from her; less to avoid the stench and the sounds, for that is futile, than to give the pitiful squatters some privacy.

This one breakdown of primitive human decency—more even than the hunger, the thirst, the crowding, the lack of sleep, the wailing of miserable children, the grating outbreaks of nerve-shattered squabbles, more even than the fear of what lies ahead—dominates the start of this journey; the stink and the humiliation of lacking a clean private way to dispose of one's droppings. Weak, old, sick people, helpless to get to the pails through the jam, even void where they sit, choking and disgusting those around them.

Yet there are brave spirits in the car. A strong gray-headed Czech Jewish nurse pushes around with one bucket of water, which the SS refills every few hours, doling out cupfuls to the sick and the children ahead of others. She recruits women to help tend the sick and clean up the unfortunates who foul themselves. A burly blond-bearded Polish Jew in a sort of military cap makes himself the car captain. He rigs blankets to screen the pails, puts a stop to the worst quarrels, and appoints distributors for the food scraps thrown into the car by the SS. Here and there in the lugubrious crush sour laughter can be heard, especially after a share-out of food; and when things have settled down, the car captain even leads some doleful singing.

Rumors keep rippling through the car about where they are going, and what will happen when they arrive. The announced destination is a "work camp outside Dresden," but the Czech Jews say that the line of stations they are going through points toward Poland. Each time the train passes a station the name is shouted around and fresh speculation starts up. Oswiecim is hardly mentioned. All eastern Europe lies ahead. Tracks branch off every few miles; if not toward Dresden, then to many other places. Why necessarily must they be travelling to Oswiecim? Most of these Theresienstadt Jews have heard of Oswiecim. Some have received cards from transportees who have landed there, though it is a long time since any postcards have come. The name evokes a shadowy terror laced with whispered details too gruesome to be believed. No, there is no reason to assume they are going to Oswiecim; or even if they are, that conditions there in any way resemble the frightful stories.

Such is the state of mind that Natalie discerns in the car. She knows better. She cannot rid herself of the information that Berel Jastrow imparted. Nor does she want to muffle her mind in fantasies. Her will to live, to see Louis again, demands that she think straight. She has plenty of time to think, sitting there over the drafty crack in the splintered floor hour after hour after hour, through long nights and long days, hungry, thirsty, sick from the stench, her teeth and bones jarring with the jolts of the train.

The abrupt separation from her uncle is clearing her mind and hardening her resolve. She is on her own, one more body in an anonymous rabble training eastward. The SS men who herded the Jews into the cattle cars took no roll calls, only head counts. Aaron Jastrow is still identified, still a name, still an Elder, still a *Prominent,* up front in the coach. She is a nameless nobody. He will probably survive in some clerkish job, wherever they are going, until the Allies smash through the failing German armies. Perhaps he will find her and protect her there, too; but instinct tells her that she has looked her last on Aaron.

Really believing that one is about to die is hard. Hospital patients rotted through with cancer, criminals walking to the electric chair or the gallows, sailors on a ship going down in a storm, cling to a secret hope that it is all a mistake, that some relieving word will come to lift the strangling nightmare; so why not Natalie Henry, young and healthy, riding a train through eastern Europe? She has her private hope, as no doubt each troubled Jew does all through the cattle cars.

She is an American. This sets her off from the others. By crazy circumstances and her own stupid mistakes she is trapped in this train, slowing and groaning up into the mountains on the second night, twisting through timbered valleys and rocky gorges, passing at dead slow through moonlit snowdrifts that spray glittering away from the wheels and whirl off on the wind. Looking out at this pretty scene, freezing and shivering, Natalie thinks of her Christmas vacation in Colorado when she was a college senior; so the moonlit snow sprayed from the train climbing up the Rockies to Denver. She is grasping for American memories. A moment lies ahead when she may live or die by her capacity to look a German official in the face and make him take pause with the words, "I am an American."

For, given the chance, she can prove it. Surprisingly, she still has her passport. Battered, creased, stamped *Ghetoisiert,* it lies in the breast pocket of her gray suit under the yellow star. With their peculiar respect for official paper, the Germans have not confiscated or destroyed it. In Baden-Baden they held it for weeks but returned it when she went to Paris. Arriving in Theresienstadt, she had to turn it in, but after many months she found it one day on her bed with Byron's picture still clipped inside. Perhaps German intelligence used it for forging spy documents; perhaps it merely moldered in an SS desk. Anyway, she has it. She knows it will not protect her. International law does not exist for her, or for any rider on this train. Still, in this crowd of unfortunates it is a unique identifying document; and to a German eye, the photograph of a husband in a United States naval uniform should also strike home.

Natalie pictures Oswiecim as a more dreadful Theresienstadt, larger, harsher, with gas chambers instead of a Little Fortress. Surely there will be work to do even there. The barracks may be as bad as this cattle car or worse, the weak, the old, the unskilled transportees may die, but the rest will be laborers. She intends to look her best, produce her passport, tell of her mica job, offer her language skills, flirt, prostitute herself if she is forced, but live till deliverance comes. That much, however short of the reality, is not entirely delusory. But her ultimate hope is a mirage: namely, that some farseeing SS officer will take her under his wing, so as to lean on her as a character witness after the German defeat. What she cannot conceive is that most Germans do not yet believe they will lose the war. Faith in Adolf Hitler keeps this maddened nation going strong.

Her surmise about the progress of the war is quite correct. German higher-ups know their game is almost played out. Little peace feelers like maggots are creeping out of the dying Nazi leviathan. Reichsführer SS Himmler is about to order the gassings halted. He is covering his tracks, preparing his alibi, stolidly setting about to refurbish his image. Natalie is riding the last train taking Jews to Oswiecim; bureaucratic delay in reversing policy has allowed it to roll. But to the SS staff waiting for it at the Birkenau ramp, with crematoriums fired up and Sonderkommandos on the alert, it is just one more routine job. Nobody is thinking of taking on a pet American Jewess as a shield in defeat. Natalie's passport may be a mental comfort, but it is just a scrap of paper.

Conditions in the car keep worsening. By the second day the sickest begin to die where they lie, stand, or sit. Shortly after dawn of the third day, a feverish small girl near Natalie goes into convulsions, writhes, beats her hands about, then becomes limp and still. There is no room to lay out bodies, so the moaning mother of the dead girl holds the corpse huddled to her as in life. The child's face is blue, the eyes shut and sunken, the jaw hanging loose. About an hour later an old woman whose feet touch Natalie dribbles blood, gasps, makes noisy rattling sounds, and topples from her wall space. The Czech nurse, who squirms tirelessly through the car trying to keep people alive, cannot revive her. Somebody else seizes the wall space.

The old woman lies under her own short coat in a heap. One skinny wool-stockinged leg with a green garter protrudes until Natalie pushes it under the coat, trying to suppress her horror with callous thinking of other days, other things. It is not easy. The smell of death comes through the excrement stink, more and more strongly as the train clacks, sways, and rolls on to the east. Farther down the car, where the SS crammed in the Theresienstadt sick, perhaps fifteen people are dead. The transportees, sunk in wretched apathy, doze or stare about in the asphyxiating miasma.

A halt.

Rough voices shout outside. Bells clang. The train moves jerkily backward and then forward again, changing locomotives. It stops. The car door opens to allow the emptying of the reeking slop pails. Sunshine and fresh air flood in like a burst of music. The Czech nurse gets her water bucket refilled. The car captain talks about the corpses to the SS guard bringing the water, who shouts, *"Na, die haben noch Glück!"* ("Well, they're lucky!") He slides the door shut, and turns a screeching bolt.

When the train moves again, the stations that glide by have Polish names. Now one hears "Oswiecim" spoken aloud in the car. A Polish couple near Natalie says they are heading straight for Oswiecim. It is as though Oswiecim is a giant magnet sucking in the train. Sometimes the route has seemed to turn in another direction and spirits have revived, but sooner or later it always bends back to Oswiecim—Auschwitz, the Viennese women call it.

Natalie has now been sitting up for seventy-two hours. The elbow she leans on is rubbed raw and staining her suit with blood. Her hunger is gone. Thirst is racking her, blotting out everything else. Since leaving Theresienstadt *she has had two cups of water*. Her mouth is as dry as if she has been eating dust. The Czech nurse gives water to people who need it more: the children, the sick, the old, the dying. Natalie keeps thinking of American drinks, of the times and the places where she drank them: ice-cream sodas in drugstores, Coca-Colas at high school dances, cold beer at college picnics, water from kitchen taps, water from office coolers, water from an icy brown mountain pool in the Adirondacks where she could see trout swimming, water in a cold shower after tennis that she caught in her hands and drank. But she has to shut off these visions. They are driving her crazy.

A halt.

Looking out, she sees farmlands, woods, a village, a wooden church. SS men in gray-green uniform pass outside, stretching their legs, smoking cigars she can smell, chatting amiably in German. From a farmhouse close to the railroad a whiskered man in boots and muddy clothes comes, carrying a large lumpy sack. He pulls off his cap to talk to an SS officer, who grins and makes a contemptuous gesture at the train. In a moment the door slides open, the sack is tossed through the aperture, and it closes.

"Apples! Apples!" The joyous unbelieving word sings through the car.

Who was this softhearted benefactor, this muddy bewhiskered man who knew there were Jews in the silent train and pitied them? Nobody can say. The transportees get to their feet, eyes gleaming, gaunt faces suffering and eager. Men move about putting fruit into snatching hands. The train starts. The jerk throws Natalie off her numb feet. She has to grab at the man bringing the apples. He glares at her, then laughs. He was the construction foreman at the children's pavilion. "Steady, Natalie!" he fishes in the sack and gives her a big greenish fruit.

The first squirt of apple juice in Natalie's mouth sets her stopped saliva flowing; it cools; it sweetens; it sends life stinging electrically through her. She eats the apple as slowly as she can. Around her everybody is crunching fruit. A fragrance of harvest time, the smell of apples, steals through the foul air. Natalie chews the apple down, bite by exquisite bite. She eats the core. She chews the bitter stem. She licks the streaks of sweet juice from her fingers and her palm. Then she gets as drowsy as though she has eaten a meal and drunk wine. Sitting cross-legged, her head leaned on her hand, her one raw elbow on the floor, she sleeps.

When she wakes moonlight makes a blue barred rectangle of the high window. It is warmer than before, when they were coming out of the mountains. Exhausted Jews slump or lean on each other in sleep all through the vile-smelling car. Almost too stiff to move, she pulls herself to the window for air. They are running through scrubby marshy wasteland. The moonlight glitters on patches of swampy water where cattails and leafy reeds grow thick. The train traverses a high barbed-wire fence, strung on concrete posts as far as the moon illumines, spaced with shadowy watchtowers. One tower is so close to the track that Natalie glimpses two guards silhouetted at their machine guns, under the cylinders of darkened searchlights.

Inside the fence, more wasteland. Up ahead, Natalie perceives a yellowish glow. The train is slowing down; the clacks of the wheels are lower in pitch and fewer. Straining her eyes she discerns in the distance rows of long huts. Now the train sharply turns. Some of the Jews rouse themselves at the screech of wheels and groan of the rickety car. Natalie sees up ahead, before the train straightens out, a wide heavy building with two arched entrances into which the moonlit railroad tracks disappear. Clearly this is the terminal, their destination, Oswiecim. Trembling and sickness seize her, though nothing frightening is in sight.

The train passes through a dark arch into a dazzling white glare. The train is gliding to a halt alongside a very long floodlit wooden platform. SS men line the track, some with large black dogs on leashes. Many strange-looking figures also await the train: bald-skulled men in ragged vertical-striped pajamas, dozens of them, all along the platform.

The train stops.

A terrifying din breaks out: clubs pounding at the wooden car walls, dogs barking, Germans roaring, *"Get out! Everybody out! Quick! Out! Out!"*

Though the Jews cannot know it, this reception is rather unusual. The SS prefers a quiet arrival that keeps up the hoax to the last: peaceable unloading, lectures about health examinations and work possibilities, reassurance of luggage delivery, and the rest of the standard game. But word has come that this transport may prove unruly, so the less common harsh procedure is on.

Doors slide open. Light glares in on the dazed crowded Jews. *"Down! Out! Jump! Leave your baggage! No baggage! You'll get it in your barracks! Out! Get down! Out!"* The Jews begin to vanish out into the white glare. Big uniformed men jump into the car, brandishing clubs and snarling, *"Out! What are you waiting for? Move your shitty asses! Out! Drop that baggage! Get out!"* As fast as they can crowd forward, Jews are stampeding out of the car. Natalie, far from the door, is caught in a crush thrusting her toward the light. Her feet scarcely touch the floor. Sweating with fear, she finds herself in the full blinding glare of a floodlight. God, it is a long jump to the platform! Children are sprawling all over down there, old ladies lie on their faces and backs where they have tumbled, showing their pitiful white or pink drawers. The striped spooks are moving among them, lifting up the fallen. So much registers on Natalie's nearly paralyzed consciousness. She hesitates, not wanting to jump on a child. There is no clear space to land. The thought flashes through her mind, "At least I spared Louis this!" A heavy blow cracks her shoulder, and she leaps with a scream.

Her uncle has a different experience.

He knows from Berel's revelations the precise fate that awaits him. In his final entry in *A Jew's Journey,* Aaron has recorded an almost Socratic acceptance of death, but this serenity is hard to sustain on a three-day train trip toward extermination by poison gas. Socrates, it will be recalled, drank the hemlock and faded off after a short noble discourse to sorrowing and admiring disciples. Jastrow has no disciples, but *A Jew's Journey*—though he has secreted it behind the planks of the library wall in Theresienstadt, with no hope of living until it is found—is addressed to an audience too, its eventual readers; and Jastrow, a writer to the core, has left the noblest last words he could muster. Thereafter, however, he remains very much alive, and the trip is long.

Seventeen *Prominente* are crammed with him into two rear compartments of the coach in which the SS rides. It is very close quarters. They must take turns standing and sitting, dozing when they can. They are fed watery soup and stale bread at night, one cup of brown slop in the morning. For a half hour each morning they have access to a toilet, which they must then scrub and disinfect, ceiling to floor, for German use. It is not first-class travel. Still, compared with their fellows in the cattle cars they are well off, and they know it.

That is, in fact, Jastrow's torment. The privileged coach ride gnaws at his fatalistic serenity. Can there be any hope? Certainly the seventeen others think so. They talk of little else, day and night, but the positive aspects of their favored treatment. Those who have wives and children in other cars are optimistic even about them. True, the train evidently is not heading for Dresden. But wherever it is going, on this transport *Prominente* remain *Prominente*. That's the main thing! Once at their destination, they will manage to look after their loved ones.

Common sense warns Aaron Jastrow that the coach ride can be more sadistic German foolery, or a bureaucratic mischance, or a calculated move to keep out of the cattle cars personages around whom a spark of resistance might flicker. But it is hard to hold out against the desperate ebullience of the others. He too yearns to live. These seventeen cultivated, highly superior men can argue persuasively: three Elders, two rabbis, a symphony conductor, a painter, a concert pianist, a newspaper publisher, three doctors, two army officers with war wounds, two half-Jewish industrialists, and the head of the Transport Section, a bitter-faced little Berlin lawyer, who alone does not talk to the others or even look at them. Nobody knows how he fell afoul of his bosses.

Except for one guard posted outside their compartments, the Germans pay no attention whatever to the Jews. Riding in the SS car, however great a privilege, is unnerving. Jews are usually quarantined from this elite like diseased animals. They can smell the hearty meals brought on board for the SS. At night jolly songs drunkenly roar out in the car, and loud arguments go on, sometimes sounding ugly. This Teutonic boisterousness close at hand makes the *Prominente* shudder, for at any time it can occur to the SS to work off their boredom by making sport with Jews.

Late on the second night, the SS men are beerily bellowing the *Horst Wessel* song, and Jastrow is remembering the first time he heard it, in Munich in the mid-thirties. Those early feelings flood over him. Ridiculous though he thought the Nazis were then, their song did embody a certain elemental German wistfulness; and now that he is probably about to die at their hands he can still hear that simple romantic *Heimweh* in this discordant chorus. The compartment door bursts open. The guard shouts, "The stinking Jew Jastrow! To compartment number four!" He is shocked into shivery alertness. With long faces the other Jews make way. He goes, the guard tramping behind him.

In compartment four, a gray-headed SS officer with a gross double chin, sitting with several other officers drinking schnapps, tells him to stand there and listen. This SS man is discoursing on a comparison of the Seven Years' War and World War II, pointing out the comforting analogies between Hitler and Frederick the Great. Both wars show, he argues, how a small disciplined nation under a great warlord can hold its own against a huge shaky coalition led by mediocrities. Frederick made brilliant use of diplomatic surprise just like the Führer; he always attacked first; time after time he reversed what looked like sure defeat by iron willpower; and in the end, the sudden death of Elizabeth of Russia gave him the break he needed for a favorable peace. Stalin, Roosevelt, and Churchill are all elderly ailing men of unhealthy habits. The death of any one of them could similarly explode the coalition overnight, says the grayhead. The other officers are most impressed, looking at each other and wisely nodding.

Abruptly he says to Jastrow, "They tell me you are a famous American historian. You must be familiar with all this."

The eighteenth century is not Jastrow's field, but he knows Carlyle's work on Frederick. "*Ach, ja! Carlyle!*" exclaims the gray-headed officer, encouraging him to proceed. Aaron says that the two wars are indeed amazingly similar; that Hitler seems an absolute reincarnation of Frederick the Great; and that the death of Elizabeth of Russia certainly was a providential break, such as could happen any day in this war. When he is dismissed, he returns to his compartment full of disgust with himself. But the guard brings him a roll and sausage which he gives to the others to share out, and that makes him feel better.

Next morning the gray-headed officer summons him again, this time for a private talk, just the two of them. He seems quite senior and quite sure of himself; he allows Jastrow to sit down, something unheard of for a Jew in an SS presence. He once taught history, he says, but a scheming Jew got a university professorship he was in line for, ruining his career. Puffing on heavy cigars, he treats Aaron to a three-hour pedantic harangue on the probable political structure of German Europe for the next three or four centuries, branching off into Germany's world leadership, quoting authors back to Plutarch and comparing Hitler to such great men as Lycurgus, Solon, Mohammed, Cromwell, and Darwin. Aaron has only to listen and nod. In a way this drivel is a diversion from the waves of fear and uncertainty about oncoming death which have been plaguing him like migraine. Dismissed, he receives another sausage and roll in the compartment, which he shares out again. He sees the grayhead no more. Once the train enters Poland, and the names of the towns they pass draw an arrow toward Auschwitz, Aaron finds himself wishing for some such distraction, even a rowdy SS songfest to kill the nerve-wracking hours. But this day the Germans have fallen silent.

Only when he descends on the Birkenau ramp does Aaron fully grasp what he has been spared so far. Standing huddled with the *Prominente* beyond the floodlights, he sees at a distance the detraining—the terrorized leaping, falling, and milling about of the Jews, the casual tossing out of bodies and luggage by bald-skulled prisoners in stripes, the long row the corpses make laid out along the platform; especially the far-stretching separate line of children's bodies, which the unloaders throw about like sawdust dolls. He looks for Natalie in the floodlight glare. Once or twice he thinks he sees her. But more than two thousand Jews have poured out of all those cattle cars. They crowd the long platform, lining up in fives under the shouts and club blows of the Germans, the men separately from the women and children. It is hard to be sure of anybody's identity in that confused mass of drooping heads.

After this first violent and noisy ejection of the Jews from the train, the scene on the ramp for a while looks tame and tedious, reminding Jastrow queerly of his own family's disembarkation at night from the steerage of a Polish ship at Ellis Island amid a throng of shabby Jewish immigrants. Uniformed officials strut about under floodlights now as then, shouting orders. The new arrivals, bewildered and helpless in a foreign place, stand and wait for something to happen. But at Ellis Island there were no dogs, no machine guns, and no rows of the dead.

In fact, something is happening. The living and the dead are being counted, to confirm that as many passengers arrived as departed. The SS pays a group fare to the Reichsbahn for every Jew transported to Oswiecim, and bookkeeping must be punctilious. Separated by sexes, the Jews stand quietly five abreast in two dark queues all the way down the track. The baldheads in stripes have time to empty the cars and stack all the belongings on the platform.

These make enormous mounds. The stuff looks like the rubbish of beggars, but Jastrow can guess what wealth may be hidden there. The Jews find desperate ways to carry a remnant of their lives' earnings with them, and it is all hidden in those shabby piles or concealed on their bodies. Knowing what lies in store for him, Aaron Jastrow has left his money belt behind the wall in Theresienstadt with the manuscript of *A Jew's Journey*. Let the finders have both, and may their hands not be German! Berel's description of the looting of the dead in Auschwitz gave Aaron Jastrow his first slippery grip on the crazy massacre. Murder for plunder is an ancient risk Jewry runs; the innovation of National Socialism is only to organize it as an industrial process. Well, the Germans may kill him but they will not plunder him.

The women's line at last begins to move. Now Jastrow sees before his eyes the process that Berel described. SS officers are separating the Jewesses into two lines. One tall thin officer seems to be making the final decision with a flick of a hand, left or right. It all goes in a quiet matter-of-fact official manner. The talk of the Germans, the rare yap of a dog, and hissing bursts of steam from the cooling locomotive are all one hears.

He stands in the shadows with the *Prominente,* watching. Evidently they are exempt from the selection process. Their baggage remains in the coach, so far. Can the optimists possibly have been right? One SS officer and one guard have been detailed to this special handful of Jews; average-looking young Germans who, except for their intimidating uniforms, are not menacing in aspect. The guard, rather short and in rimless glasses, looks as mild as he can with a submachine gun in his hands. Both seem bored with their routine chore. The officer has ordered the *Prominente* not to talk, that is all. Shading his eyes from the floodlights, Aaron Jastrow keeps peering down the platform for a sight of Natalie. He means to take his life in his hands if he can spot her; point her out to the officer as his niece, and tell him she has an American passport. The utterance will take thirty seconds. If he gets beaten or shot, let it be so. Conceivably the Germans may want to know about her. But he cannot pick her out, though he knows she is there somewhere. She was too strong to sicken and die on the train. Certainly she is not in the thin straggle of women going to the left. Those are easy to tell apart. She could be in the thick crowd of women sent to the right, many of them leading or carrying children, or in the long line of the unselected.

The women sent to the right come shuffling past the *Prominente,* with scared stunned faces. Half-blinded by the floodlight glare, Jastrow cannot discern Natalie as they go by, if she is among them. The children walk docilely, holding on to their mothers' hands or skirts. Some of the children are being carried, sound asleep, for it is after all the middle of the night; the full moon rides in the Zenith above the glare. The line passes by. Now two striped men board the SS coach and toss down the privileged Jews' luggage.

"Attention!" says the SS officer to the *Prominente.* "You will go along with those now, for disinfection." His tone is offhand, his gesture toward the departing women is forceful and unmistakable.

Dumbfounded, the seventeen look at each other, and at their tumbling luggage.

"Quick march!" The officer's voice hardens. "Follow them!"

The guard waves at the men with the submachine gun.

In a quavering, ingratiating voice, the Berlin lawyer exclaims, stepping forward, *"Herr Untersturmführer,* your honor, aren't you making a very serious mistake? We are all *Prominente,* and—"

The officer moves two stiff fingers. The guard drives the gun butt into the lawyer's face. He drops, bleeding and groaning.

"Pick him up," says the officer to the others, "and get along with you."

So Aaron has his answer. The uncertainty is finished, he is going to die. He will die very soon, probably within minutes. It is an exceedingly peculiar realization: awesome, agonizing, but at the same time sadly liberating. He is looking his last at the moon, at things like trains, at women, at children, at Germans in uniform. It is a surprise, but not such a great one. This was what he was ready for when he left Theresienstadt. He helps the others pick up the Transport Section head, whose mouth is a bloody mess, but whose frightened eyes are worse to see. In a last glance behind him, Jastrow observes the long lines still stretching down the floodlit platform, the selections still going on. Will he ever know what happened to Natalie?

A long trudge in cold air under the moon; a silent trudge, except for the crunch of footfalls on frozen muck, and the sleepy whimpering of children. The line arrives at a beautifully kept lawn, bright green under tremendous floodlights, in front of a long low windowless building of dark red brick, with tall square chimneys which fitfully flare. It might be a bakery or a laundry. The baldheads lead the line down broad cement steps, along a dim corridor and into a big bare room brightly lit with naked electric lights, rather like a bathhouse at a beach, with benches and hooks for undressing along the walls, and around pillars down the middle. On the pillar facing the entrance a sign in several languages, with Yiddish at the top, reads:

UNDRESS HERE FOR DISINFECTANT BATHS.
FOLD CLOTHES NEATLY.
REMEMBER WHERE YOU LEAVE THEM.

It is disconcerting that men and women must undress in the same place. The striped prisoners herd the few *Prominente* off in one corner, and to Aaron's surprise, they help the women and children undress, chattering apologies all the time. It is the rules of the camp, they say. None of this takes long. The main thing is to hurry, fold clothes neatly, and obey orders. Soon Aaron Jastrow sits naked on a rough wooden bench, murmuring psalms, his bare feet on chilly cement. One must not pray naked or utter God's name bareheaded, but this is *shat hadhak,* an hour of emergency, when the law is lenient. He sees that some women are young and enchanting to look upon, their rounded naked flesh rosy as Rubens nudes under the bright lights. Of course most of the figures are spoiled: scrawny or drooping, with pendulous breasts and stomachs. The children all look thin as plucked fowl.

A second group of women comes crowding into the disrobing room, with many more men behind them. He cannot tell if Natalie is there, it is such a mob. Strange brief reunions occur between naked women and their clothed husbands: joyous cries of recognition, embraces, fathers hugging their bare children. But the baldheads cut these scenes short. There will be plenty of time later! Now people must get on with the undressing.

German voices soon call flat harsh orders outside: *"Attention! Men only! Proceed by twos to the showers!"*

The striped prisoners shepherd the men out of the disrobing room. This lot of naked males jostling along with exposed dangling genitals in bushy hair is very like a bathhouse scene, except for the strange stripe-clothed baldheads among them, and the crowd of nude women and children watching them go and calling out to them affectionately. Some women are crying. Some, Aaron can see, must be stifling screams, with hands clutched to their mouths. They fear being beaten, perhaps, or they do not want to alarm the children.

It is cold in the corridor; not for the armed SS men who line the walls, but certainly for the naked Aaron and the men marching with him. His mind remains clear enough to note that the fraud grows thin. Why this cordon of armed booted men in uniforms for a few Jews going to the showers? The faces of the SS men are ordinary German faces, mostly young, such as one might see on the Kurfürstendamm strolling on a Sunday with their girls, but they frown in an unpleasant way, like police facing a disorderly crowd and watching for violence. But the naked Jewish men, young and old, are not at all disorderly. There is no violence on this short walk.

They are led into a long narrow room of raw cement floors and walls, almost large enough to be a theatre, though the ceiling filled with hundreds of shower heads is too low for that, and the rows of pillars would be in the way. On the walls and the pillars—some of solid concrete, some of perforated sheet iron—are soap racks with bars of yellow soap. This chamber too is lit to almost uncomfortable brightness by bare bulbs in the ceiling.

So much registers on Aaron Jastrow's consciousness, as in his detached and fatalistic frame of mind he murmurs Hebrew psalms, until physical discomfort erases his tightly controlled religious composure. The prisoners in stripes keep pushing the men farther and farther inside. *"Make room! Make room! All men to the back!"* He is being jammed against the clammy skin of other men taller than he is, a miserable sensation for a fastidious person; he can feel their soft genitals crushing against him. The women are coming in now, though Aaron can only hear them. He can see nothing but the naked bodies pressing in around him. Some children are bawling, some women weeping, and there are random forlorn shrieks amid distant German shouts of command. Also many women's voices are soothing their children or greeting their men.

The crowding, ever tighter, throws panic into Jastrow. He cannot help it. He has always had a fear of crowds, a fear that he would die trampled or smothered. He absolutely cannot move, cannot see, can hardly breathe, packed in on all sides by naked strangers in a gymnasium reek, jammed against a chilly perforated iron pillar, directly under a light that shines in his face as an elbow jams under his chin and roughly forces his head up.

The light suddenly is extinguished. The whole place goes black. From far down the chamber comes a slam of heavy doors, a screech of iron bolts, turning and tightening. In the huge chamber a mournful general wail rises. Amid the wail there is terrific shrieking and yelling: *"The gas! The gas! They are killing us! Oh, God have mercy! The gas!"*

Aaron smells it, strong, chokingly strong, the disinfectant smell, but far more powerful. It is coming from the iron pillar. The first whiff burns, stabbing into his lungs like a red-hot sword, shooting alarm through his frame, racking him with cramps. He tries in vain to shrink away from the pillar. All is howling chaos and terror in the dark. He gasps out a deathbed confession, or tries to, with congesting lungs, swelling mouth tissues, in breath-stopping pain: *"The Lord is God. Blessed be His name for ever and ever. Hear O Israel, the Lord our God is One God."* He falls to the cement. Writhing bodies pile on top of him, for he is one of the first adults to go down. He falls on his back, striking his head hard. Naked flesh presses on his face and all over him, stilling his contortions. He cannot move. He does not die of the gas. Very little enters his system. He goes almost at once, the life smothered out of him by the weight of dying Jews. Call it a blessing, for death by the gas can take a long time. The Germans allow a half hour for the process.

When the men in stripes pull apart the tangled dead mass, the sea of stiff human nakedness, and uncover him, his face is less contorted than others, though nobody notices one old thin dead body among thousands. Jastrow is dragged by a rubber-gloved Sonderkommando to a table in a mortuary where his gold-filled teeth are ripped out with pliers and dropped in a pail. This process goes on wholesale all over the mortuary, with the search of orifices and the cutting off of the women's hair. He is then loaded on a hoist which is lifting bodies in assembly-line fashion to a hot room where a crowd of Sonderkommandos is busily at work at a row of furnaces. His body on an iron cradle, with two children's bodies piled on top of him because he is so small, goes into an oven. The iron door with a glass peephole slams shut. The bodies rapidly swell and burst, and the flames burn the fragments like coal. Not until the next day are his ashes carted to the Vistula in a big truck loaded with human ash and bone fragments, and dumped into the river.

So the dissolved atoms of Aaron Jastrow float past the river banks of Medzice where he played as a boy, and float all the way through Poland, past Warsaw to the Baltic Sea. The diamonds he swallowed on the walk to the crematorium may have burned up, for diamonds burn. Or they may lie on the river bed of the Vistula. They were the finest stones, saved for an ultimate extremity, and he had meant to slip them to Natalie on the train. Their sudden parting prevented that, but the Germans never got them.

94

THE turning earth brings the same bright moon over a low black vessel cutting through rough waters off Kyushu. Spray glitters up over the bridge as the *Barracuda* speeds toward a dawn attack on a Leyte Gulf cripple; a big fleet tanker screened by four escorts, crawling at nine knots and down hard by the bow. An Ultra dispatch has vectored the *Barracuda* to this limping ship, and the new captain's test of fire is on. Tankers have become prime targets. The Japs cannot fight on without oil, and it all comes in by sea. Hence four escorts. A tough shot! Byron has rescued downed airmen, helped a grounded submarine free itself from a reef, and patrolled all during the battle with no results. He has yet to conduct an attack.

He and his exec are getting soaked by the cold spray. Lieutenant Philby wears foul-weather gear, but Byron has come topside for a look around at midnight in his khakis. He does not mind; the salt shower is cheering. On the sharp moonlit horizon the tanker is a smudge. The escorts are invisible.

"How are we doing?"

"Okay. We'll be on station at 0500, if he doesn't change course."

The exec's tone is reserved. He wanted to try a stern chase and a night attack up-moon. Had they done that they would now be in the approach phase. Byron doesn't regret his decision for an end-around run; not yet. The enemy is holding course. If the sky had clouded over the night attack would have been chancy. Carter Aster always favored an approach on the bow with good visibility.

"Well, I'll turn in, then. Call me at 0430."

The skeptical squint on the exec's wet face all but shouts, *Who are you kidding? Sleep before your first attack?*

"Aye aye, sir." A faint note of disapproval.

Byron is unoffended. Philby is a good exec, he has found. He hardly sleeps, he is getting ashen as a dead man, and he has the ship up to the mark in all departments. On torpedo maintenance and readiness he is red-hot. How he performs in an attack and holds up under depth charging is the real question. That will probably soon be clear.

Shucking off the wet uniform, Byron lies down in his cabin facing pictures of Natalie and Louis taped on the bulkhead. Often he no longer notices them; they have been there too long. Now he sees them afresh: the snapshots from Rome and Theresienstadt, and a studio photograph of Natalie. The old aches throb. Are his wife and son still in the Czech town? Are they even alive? How beautiful she was; how he loved her! The memory of Louis is almost unbearable. Frustration has turned the love he felt for that boy to a festering grudge: at his father for driving Natalie to Europe, at her for her funk in Marseilles. And Dad's involvement with Pamela Tudsbury . . .

Profitless thoughts! Out goes the light. In the dark Byron whispers a prayer for Natalie and Louis, something he used to do every night, but has been forgetting lately. His father was right about that, at least; command has proven a distraction and an anodyne. He falls asleep almost at once. What was a joke about him as a junior officer is an asset in command.

The steward brings him coffee at 0430. He wakes nervily confident. He is no Carter Aster, never will be, and twenty things can foul up in an attack, but he is ready to go. That is one hell of a target out there. Rough weather; his second cup sloshes over the wardroom table. Topside, the tossing dark ocean is flecked with whitecaps in stormy dawn light; a strong wind blows. Visibility way down, the tanker not in sight. Philby still mans the bridge, his rubber clothes streaming. Radar has the target at fourteen thousand yards, he says, heading 310 as before, target angle zero. The *Barracuda* now lies ahead of its prey.

Submerging for his approach, Byron sees the screen vessels appear through a misty dawn, coming straight on: four frigate types, gray small ships like American DEs. The station-keeping is ragged; inexperienced reserve skippers, no doubt. On the zigzag a gap opens to port, and Byron heads through it, undetected by the pinging, toward the huge listing tanker. Attack phase: range closing to fifteen hundred . . . twelve hundred . . . nine hundred yards . . . "I like short ranges," Aster used to say; greater peril, but a surer shot. Byron and Philby work smoothly together, and the sailors and officers in the conning tower are all old hands. In the tension of the hunt and the technical torpedo problem, Byron loses all sense that this is a debut. Many a time he has manned the scope during Aster's attacks. It is old stuff, scary and thrilling as ever. He has the last word on firing; only that is new.

When he calls "Up scope!" for a final bearing, the tanker hull looms ahead like the side of a stadium, a pathetic gigantic victim. How can he miss? He is so close he sees swarms of Japs repairing bomb damage on the steeply slanting deck.

He shoots. The submarine ejects four torpedoes, the slower and more reliable electrics. At this short range only a minute elapses. Then, *"Up scope! HIT, by God!"* Three white splashes leap high at the tanker's side. Earthquake rumblings shake the *Barracuda.* Cheers break out in the conning tower. Byron whips the scope around and sees the two escorts he evaded turning toward him.

"Take her deep! Level at three hundred feet!"

The first depth charges fall astern, thunderous jolts that do no harm. At three hundred feet the submarine creeps away, running silent, but a sonar picks up the trail. The pinging grows louder, and shifts to short scale. Screw noises approach, pass overhead. The seasoned sailors in the conning tower wince, crouch, hold their ears.

A pattern of depth charges drops all around the *Barracuda:* a perfect shot, a barrage of explosions. The vessel takes a sharp down angle and sinks like a rock, the lights going out, clocks, gauges, other loose objects flying around, anguished voices jabbering confused damage reports in the sound-powered telephones. Emergency lights show depth increasing alarmingly: three fifty, four hundred, four hundred fifty feet. Four hundred is maximum test depth. Never down this deep before, the submarine still descends.

Philby goes staggering down the ladder to check on damage, while Byron fights to arrest the plunge. The exec shouts up from the control room that the stern planes are jammed on hard dive. The steering planes are jammed too. At *five hundred and seventy feet,* Byron is dripping sweat amid ashen-faced sailors, in a conning tower half-lit by emergency lights and awash to his ankles. Philby has reported the hull dished in by sea pressure and leaking in several compartments, many hull fittings and valves spurting water, air and hydraulic systems out, electrical control panels shorting, and pumps not functioning. Byron blows the forward high-pressure group, his emergency reserve of compressed air, his very last resort, for an up-angle. That arrests the dive. Then he blows the after high-pressure group, and he has buoyancy.

Powering up to the surface, he orders all hands to battle stations as soon as they can crack the hatches. When the quartermaster opens the conning tower hatch, an astonishing waterspout rises through the hole, and for a long minute nobody can get up to the forward guns or the bridge. The diesels catch and roar, a welcome sound. When Byron does reach the bridge the enemy ship, about three miles off, is already firing, pale yellow flashes from guns that look like three-inch fifties, kicking up misses well astern of the partly disabled submarine. The other escorts are far off, rescuing survivors around the foundering tanker. The *Barracuda* fires back with its four-inch bow gun, and the escort stands off, peppering away. Its gunnery is poor. For fifteen minutes Byron avoids being hit, twisting here and there, while Philby roams the ship below, trying to restore diving condition. As things stand, one square hit on the thin old hull can probably finish the *Barracuda.*

The low-pressure blowers start up, and the submarine slowly rights a list to port. The jammed stern planes are freed. The steering planes are made to work by hand. The pumps begin to master the flooding. All this time, the gun duel goes on; and at last Philby comes up and tells Byron that the hull has been dangerously weakened. The submarine cannot dive again, probably not until major repairs are made in a Navy Yard. So the *Barracuda* is stripped of its chief defense, the safety of the deep.

All this time the frigate captain has not called for help; no doubt he wants sole credit for the kill. As Philby shouts his report between salvos of the bow gun, Byron keeps his eye on the Jap through the cloud of gunsmoke tumbling over the bridge, and sees him speed up and turn. Black smoke pours from the two stumpy stacks. He has surmised, it seems, the trouble the *Barracuda* is in, and has decided to ram. At about four thousand yards, closing at twenty knots or more, he will hit in a few minutes. A foaming bow-wave flies as his sharp antisubmarine prow cuts the sea. His outline swells.

The exec is at Byron's side. "What do we do, Captain?" he says, in a reasonably concerned tone, no note of hysteria.

A good question!

So far Byron has acted from experience. Aster too once had to blow his high-pressure group, on the third patrol, when depth charges jammed the controls and unseated a hatch, and the flooding *Moray* went down past five hundred feet. But that time they surfaced at night and Aster escaped into the darkness. Aster never faced a ramming.

Byron's best speed now is eighteen knots. Given time, the engineers can probably restore full power, but there is no time. Flight? A stern chase will gain time, but then the other frigates will pursue. The *Barracuda* will probably be outgunned and sunk.

Byron seizes the microphone. "Now engine rooms, this is the captain. Give me all the power you've got, we're about to be rammed . . . Helmsman, right standard rudder."

The helmsman turns startled eyes at him. *"Right,* Captain?"

The order will turn the submarine *toward* the charging gray frigate. "Right, right full rudder! I want to clear and pass him."

"Aye aye, sir. Right full rudder . . . Rudder is hard right, sir."

The submarine surges forward and turns. Both ships, smashing toward each other through high green waves, are throwing up curtains of foam. Byron shouts to Philby, "We've got him outgunned with small calibre, Tom. I'm going to rake him broadside. Let's have continuous fire from the AA while we pass him. Tell the four-inch to aim for the bridge!"

"Aye aye, sir."

The enemy captain's reaction is slow. By the time he starts his counterturn to port the submarine's stern is slipping past his prow. The *Barracuda* sails down the frigate's port side scarcely fifty feet away, the seas noisily splashing and spiring between them. The sailors over on the other deck are visibly Japanese. From the submarine there bursts a rattling din, a blaze of gun flashes, a cloud of smoke. Red tracer streams comb the frigate's deck. The four-inch blasts away, *Crumpp! Crumpp! Crumpp!* The frigate's guns stammer in reply, but by the time the *Barracuda* has sailed past the stern they have fallen silent.

"Byron, he's dead in the water," says Philby, as Byron orders a hard turn away. He is now heading straight toward the settling tanker and the other escorts. The tanker is on its side, its red bottom scarcely visible above the swells. "Maybe you killed the captain."

"Maybe. We've got three other captains to worry about. They're turning this way. Lay below to the maneuvering room, Tom, and bend on every possible turn, for God's sake. This is it."

Philby produces a speed of twenty knots. After a twenty-minute chase the *Barracuda* disappears from its pursuers into a broad black rainsquall. Soon the three escorts drop from the radar screen.

A tour of the damaged compartments convinces Byron that the *Barracuda* is no longer seaworthy. The dents in the pressure hull from the deep-sea squeeze are serious; the malfunctions beyond repair by the crew are many; the pumps are working full-time to keep the water out. But there has been no loss of life, and only a few injuries.

"Let me have a course for Saipan, Tom," he tells the exec, on returning to the rainy bridge. "Set the regular watch. Post a one-in-three standby watch for damage control. Tell the chief of boat to draw up the bill."

"Yes, sir." The word *sir* resonates with new respect.

In his cabin, taking off wet clothes, Byron says aloud to the photograph of Natalie, "Well, I guess I can command a submarine, if that proves anything." In the aftermath of the battle, to his own puzzlement, he is deeply depressed. He dries himself with a towel, and sticky with salt tumbles into his bunk.

Late that night, he and Philby are compiling the action report in the wardroom. Philby scrawls the narrative; Byron draws neat charts of the sinking and the gunfight, in blue and orange ink. At one point Philby looks up, dropping his pen. "Captain, can I say something?"

"Sure."

"You were magnificent today."

"Well, the crew was magnificent. I had a pretty competent exec."

The long white face of Philby turns bright pink. "Captain, you're a cinch for a Navy Cross." Byron says nothing, bent over his chart. "How do you feel about it?"

"About what?"

"I mean your first sinking, and then that great fight?"

"How do you feel?"

"Goddamn proud I was part of it."

"Well, as for me, I hope we get sent all the way back to Mare Island. And that the war ends before our overhaul does." He laughs wryly at the disappointment in Philby's face. "Tom, I saw hundreds of Japs walking around and working on that tanker. Killing Japs always gave Carter Aster a big charge. It leaves me cold."

"It's the way to win the war." Philby's tone is injured, almost piously so.

"This war is won. The agony may drag on, but it's won. If I had my choice, I'd sleep the war out on dry land. I'm not a professional naval officer. I never was. Let's finish the report."

Byron got part of his wish. The *Barracuda* went back to San Francisco, and the overhaul took a long time. For a Navy Yard captain swamped by destroyers, carriers, even battleships crowding in with kamikaze damage, an old crippled submarine was a low-priority customer. Nor was ComSubPac screaming for the *Barracuda*'s return. New submarines were out on patrol in a flock. Targets were actually becoming scarce.

At the end of the overhaul an experimental undersea sonar called the FM was put aboard, and Byron was ordered to test it in dummy mine fields off California. A mine picked up by this fancy short-range sonar set off a gong in the ship; in theory, therefore, a submarine so equipped could gong its way in the undersea dark through Japanese mine fields and into the Sea of Japan, where merchant traffic was still thick. ComSubPac was very high on the FM sonar; think of all those nice fat juicy targets still skulking in the Sea of Japan!

Byron had his doubts because the sonar was erratic; he bumped many a dummy mine on his runs. His crew, good submariners all, were appalled at the notion of nosing through rows of Jap mines with an electronic gadget. They knew Navy gadgets. Most of them had sweated through two years of dud torpedoes and BuOrd excuses. The chief of the boat warned Byron that he would lose a third of his crew by transfer requests or desertions if he sailed on an FM probe of the Sea of Japan.

But Byron was not sure he would ever leave the West Coast. In San Francisco the end-of-the-war feeling was marked. The blackout was over. Cars were crowding the streets and highways. The black market had made a farce of gasoline rationing. There were no food shortages. The headlines of Allied advances and Axis retreats were becoming boring. Only reverses made news: the kamikaze campaign, and the German last gasp dubbed the "Battle of the Bulge." Byron cared about Europe mainly because a German defeat might uncover news of Natalie. As for the Pacific, he hoped that the B-29 raids, the submarine blockade, and MacArthur's advance through the Philippines would bring a Jap surrender before he went gonging into their mine fields. How much longer could the agony really drag on?

His was a not uncommon American view of this peculiar phase of the war. Staggering events were being pureed by journalism into a pap of continuous victory. Surely the thing would end any day! But a war is easier to start than to stop. This one was now a worldwide way of life. Germany and Japan were resilient, desperate great nations under firm totalitarian control. They had no plans for quitting. The Allies had no way to make them quit but by more and more killing. Everything conspired to produce unprecedented military butcheries; while Byron (more or less oblivious to the horrors) pottered with the *Barracuda*'s machinery and the FM sonar.

Adolf Hitler, of course, had no way to quit. He could keep afloat only in blood. From the east, the west, the south, and from the air his end was closing in. His response at this time was the Ardennes offensive, the "Battle of the Bulge." Back in late August, with all his fronts crumbling, he had ordered a stand-fast on the Russian front and a giant surprise counterpunch in the west. The aim was vague: some kind of success, leading to a cease-fire that did not involve his extinction. The German army and people had rallied around him in fantastic preparations that took months, scraping together their remaining strength and concentrating it in the west.

But all this was essentially dreamy lunacy. In the east the Soviet Union was assembling five replenished army groups, more than two million men with mountains of supplies, for a drive to Berlin. Scarcely a German alive preferred a Russian to an Anglo-American occupation. Hitler was between a torrent and a trickle, so to say, of menace to Germany's future; and he was damming the trickle and neglecting the torrent, dreaming of a second 1940, another Ardennes breakthrough, a new march to the sea. When Guderian showed him accurate intelligence reports on the Soviet buildup he sneered, *"Why, it's the biggest fake since Genghis Khan! Who's responsible for this rubbish?"*

The Ardennes offensive lasted two weeks, from mid-December through Christmas. It lives on in American memory chiefly as the time a general said "Nuts!" to a German call for surrender. More prosaically, there were a hundred thousand German and seventy-five thousand Allied casualties, and on both sides, great loss of arms. The western Allies were briefly surprised but recovered. The end was German disaster. In his private circle Hitler was vocally very jolly about having "recovered the initiative in the west." He never spoke or showed himself publicly anymore.

As the Ardennes push collapsed, the Russians came roaring in from the Baltic to the Carpathians. In crossing Poland, the Red Army overran a vast industrial complex and prison camp at Oswiecim, abandoned except by a few dying scarecrows in striped rags, who pointed out some dynamited ruins as crematoriums where millions of people had been secretly murdered. Events on the Russian front got little play in California newspapers. If there was such a story Byron missed it.

Within four weeks the Russians stood everywhere deep in Germany on the Oder-Neisse River line, at some points only eighty miles from Berlin. Having run hundreds of miles, they paused for resupply. Now Hitler ordered the bulk of his forces pell-mell eastward, stripping the western front. At that time Eisenhower's armies, quite recovered from the Bulge, were preparing a Rhine crossing as big as the Russian attack. This frantic shuttling of dwindling armies across Germany from east to west and to the east again at a lunatic's whim may seem ludicrous today, but it unfolded early in 1945 as very serious military and railroading business inside the Reich. Certainly it prolonged the agony.

Of these tides of battle in Europe Byron had little grasp. He knew more about the Pacific. Even so, MacArthur's massive Philippines campaign came through to him mainly as a meteor shower of kamikazes on the naval forces. He knew that the British were driving the Japanese out of Burma, because of the dull daily stories about fighting along a river called the Irrawaddy; and that B-29 "Superfortresses" based in the Marianas were setting Japanese cities on fire. But to him the capture of Iwo Jima was the big event in the Pacific—some twenty-five thousand United States Marine casualties, a rock with airfields eight hundred miles from Yokohama! Surely the Japs would quit now.

It was in fact a time of peace feelers, German and Japanese; tenuous, unofficial, contrary to government public policy, and futile. Officially Germany and Japan bellowed defiance and the imminent collapse of their war-weary foes. But both nations were now helpless in the air, and plans took form to topple their intransigent governments with airborne massacres. Like Byron, the Allied leaders were getting impatient for the end.

In mid-February, British and American bombers killed more than a hundred thousand Germans with a single fire raid on Dresden.

In mid-March the Superfortresses killed more than a hundred thousand Japanese in a single fire raid on Tokyo.

These vast slaughters have since become notorious. They went by for Byron, and for nearly all Americans, as just undistinguished headlines of the day's far-off successes. More people died in these raids than at Hiroshima and Nagasaki, but there was no novelty in them. Albert Speer, Hitler's astute production chief, is reported to have chided an American Air Force general, after the war, for not laying on more raids like Dresden; it was the sovereign way to end the war, he said, but the Allies failed to follow through.

Nor did Byron make much of the Yalta Conference, which ended as the Dresden raid was taking off. It was hailed in the papers as a cordial triumph of Allied comradeship. Only gradually did a sour counterswell spread that Roosevelt had "sold out" to Stalin. Quite simply, he had traded Balkan, Polish, and Asian geography to Stalin for American lives. Stalin was glad of the trade, and pledged a lot more Russian deaths than he ever had to deliver. Given the facts, Byron Henry probably would have been for the trade. He just wanted to win the war, find his family, and go home.

At Yalta Roosevelt wanted and got from Stalin a renewed pledge to attack Japan once Germany fell. He did not know that the atom bomb would work. An invasion of Japan, he had been advised, might cost half a million casualties or more. As for the Balkans and Poland, the Red Army already practically held them. No doubt Roosevelt sensed the general American sentiment typified in Byron Henry for being done with the mess, and the indifference to foreign geography. Perhaps he foresaw that modern warfare must soon cease of its own impractical horror, and that geography would then become of little consequence. Dying men sometimes have visions denied to the active and the cunning.

Thus, at any rate, the agony went on and on, and in mid-March the *Barracuda* was ordered back to Pearl Harbor. There it was assigned to a submarine pack that would penetrate the Sea of Japan with FM sonar.

95

Eighth Air Force Command
Army Air Corps
U.S. Army Post Office
San Francisco

15 March 1945

Pamela, my love,

Remember the Air Corps general who slugged down a bottle of vodka and danced at your Moscow wingding for the ballet people? He's here in the Marianas on LeMay's staff. I'm batting out this letter in his office. He's flying to the States tomorrow and he'll mail it there. Otherwise I'd probably have to cable you. I want you to meet me in Washington instead of San Diego, and there's much for you to do meantime. Captain Williams, our naval attaché in London, is a whiz at air priorities. Tell him you're my bride-to-be and he'll get you to Washington.

The news is that Rhoda's husband offered his vacant apartment to me for the run of the lease. That broke the lawyers' deadlock. I didn't calculate the financial quid pro quo, I just wrote my lawyer, Charlie Lyons, to drop the arguing. So the house goes to Peters at his price, and we now have a flat on Connecticut Avenue to land in. Charlie will see to the lease and get you moved in; and Peters has quite decently offered to refurnish as you desire.

I'll be relieved soon, I'm sure. BuPers is speeding up the rotation of sea billets. It's like the fourth quarter of a won football game, when the substitutes come streaming out on the field for a few plays. I'll request duty in Washington, and we can start living our lives.

All my movable possessions are in Foxhall Road. If I know Rhoda she's already crated and boxed them out of sight. Have the stuff delivered to the apartment. There won't be room for my books, Peters doesn't strike me as a reader. Leave those crated and I'll buy bookcases.

Incidentally, Pam, once you're in Washington, start drawing on Charlie Lyons for expenses. Don't argue, you're not to blow in your funds at Washington prices. Please buy yourself all the clothes you need. "Trousseau" may not be an appropriate word, but call it what you will, your wardrobe's important. You've been living for years in uniforms and travel clothes.

Well, there I go again. You've chided me before about filling my letters with money matters. I'm a poor hand at "the love stuff," which is what Warren and Byron, when they were boys, called the romantic scenes in cowboy movies. I admit it. I've really cheated you out of the love stuff, haven't I? The fact is, Pam, I can read the love poems of Keats or Shelley or Heine with deeply stirred emotions, even gooseflesh, but I can no more express such emotions than I can saw a woman in half. I don't know the trick. You and I can talk at length about the inarticulateness of American men as we lie naked in bed together. (How's that?)

I'm waiting around here for dinner time. LeMay has invited me to dine. My flag's in the *New Jersey* while the *Iowa*'s getting a Stateside overhaul, and we just put in here for replenishment. This island, Tinian, is a rock off the southern coast of Saipan, designed by nature as a bomber airfield. It's a staggeringly vast airport, biggest on earth, they say. The B-29s take off from here to drop their fire bombs on the Japs.

I'm developing a grudging respect for the Japanese. I commanded the bombardment group at Iwo Jima. It was Admiral Spruance's show, so he gave me something to do. I had battlewagons, heavy cruisers, destroyers pounding away for days at that little island. I don't believe we left one square yard unblasted. Carrier aircraft bombed it, too. When the landing craft hit the beaches, that island was silent as a tomb. Then, by God, if Japs didn't swarm up out of the ground and inflict twenty-five thousand casualties on our marines. It was the bloodiest fighting of the whole Pacific. My ships kept socking them, the carrier planes too, but they wouldn't quit. When Iwo was secured I don't think there were fifty Japs left alive on it.

Simultaneously their suicide pilots were damn near panicking our task force. Fleet morale is way down. The sailors thought they had the war won, and along comes this menace. Our newspapers are abusing the kamikazes as fanatics, madmen, drug addicts, and whatnot. It's balderdash. Those same papers spread a legend right after Pearl Harbor about an Air Corps flier, Colin Kelly, diving his plane into a battleship smokestack off Luzon. The press to-do about Colin Kelly at the time was tumultuous. Yet the thing never even happened, Kelly was shot down in a bombing mission. The Japs have thousands of real Colin Kellys. The kamikaze pilots may be ignorant and misled, and they can't win the war, but there's a sad magnificence about such willingness to die in young men, and I ruefully admire the culture that has produced them, while I deplore the wasteful, useless tactic.

Spruance is now taking flak about the need for the capture of Iwo Jima, but LeMay wanted an emergency landing field halfway to Tokyo. The B-29s go in vast numbers, and Fitzpatrick tells me Iwo has already cut plane losses and picked up air crew morale. Whether it was worth it or not, the blood has been spilled.

I came ashore at Fitz's invitation to watch the biggest B-29 raid of the war take off and return. Pamela, it's an indescribable spectacle, these giant machines roaring off in succession for hours. My God, what the American factories have poured out, and what airmen the Army's trained! Fitzpatrick went along on the raid. It just about wiped out Tokyo, he says, set it on fire from end to end, all those square miles of matchbox houses burning away. He thinks maybe they left half a million dead.

Well, these airedales tend to overestimate their havoc, but I saw that armada take off. It must have created another "firestorm," like Hamburg and Dresden. An incendiary raid of that magnitude sucks all the oxygen out of the air, I'm told, and people suffocate even if they're not burned up. So far the Japs are saying nothing about it, but you'll see plenty of stories on this attack sooner or later.

Here in the officers' mess I've been reading in old papers and magazines about the Dresden raid. The Germans raised quite a howl. Evidently it was a honey. My tour of duty in the Soviet Union equips me to contemplate Dr. Goebbels's anguished tears over Dresden unmoved. If the Russians had our planes and pilots, they'd do a raid like that on a German city every week till this war ends. They'd do it with joy, and they still wouldn't half-repay the Germans for the devastation in the Soviet Union and the civilian deaths. I think the Germans hanged more Russian kids as partisans or in reprisals than have died in all the air raids on Germany put together. God knows I pity the Dresden women and children whose charred bodies are piled up in Goebbels's propaganda photographs, but nobody made the Germans follow Hitler. He wasn't a legitimate ruler. He was a man with a mouth, and they liked what he said. They got behind him, and they let loose a firestorm that's sucking all the decent instincts out of human society. My peerless son died fighting it. It's made savages of all of us. Hitler gloried in savagery, he proclaimed it as his battle cry, and the Germans shouted *Sieg Heil!* They still go on laying down their misguided lives for him, and the lives of their unfortunate families. I wish them joy of their Führer while he lasts.

The Japs seem to take their punishment differently. They richly deserve what's happening to them, too, but they bear themselves as though they know it.

God in Heaven, I wish all this brutalizing would end.

Pamela, did you hear Roosevelt's Yalta report to the Congress on the radio? It scared me. He kept wandering and slurring as though he were sick or drunk. He apologized for speaking seated, and talked about "all this iron on my legs." I have never before heard him refer to his paralysis. The one thing that can go wrong in the war now is his death or disability—well, here's General Fitzpatrick. Chow down. I didn't mean to get off on war and politics, and now there's no time for the love stuff, is there? You know that I adore you. I thought my life was finished after Midway. In a way it was, as you yourself saw. I was an ambulatory fighting corpse. I'm alive again, or I will be when we embrace as man and wife. See you in Washington!

Much love stuff,
Pug

H APPIER than she had ever believed she could be, but very edgy, Pamela kept looking out of the open window for the moving van. The blooming magnolia in front of the old apartment house perfumed the air clear up to the third floor. In a schoolyard across the windy sunny avenue, blossoming cherry trees were showering petals past the Stars and Stripes briskly flapping on a jonquil-bordered flagpole. Washington in springtime, again; but this time, what a difference!

She still felt half in a dream. To be back in this rich untouched beautiful city, among these well-dressed, well-fed bustling Americans; to be buying in shops crammed with fine clothes, feasting in restaurants on meats and fruits not seen in London for years; and not drifting in her poor father's wake, not fearing the collapse of England, not gnawed by guilt or grief or melancholy, but marriage to Victor Henry! Colonel Peters's apartment, with its broad rooms and masculine furnishings (except for the frilly pink and gold boudoir, a tart's delight), still chilled her a bit. It was so big and so much a stranger's, with nothing in it of Pug. But today that would change.

The van came. Two sweating men grunted in with trunks, filing cabinets, packing boxes, suitcases, and cartons—more, and more, and more. The living room filled up. When Rhoda arrived, Pamela was relieved. She had been dreading handling Pug's things with his ex-wife; a sticky business, she had thought. But it had been damned sensible, after all, to accept Rhoda's offer of help with this jumble. Mrs. Harrison Peters was cheery as a robin in an Eastery sort of outfit, pastel colors, big silk hat with veil, matching gloves and shoes. She was on her way to a tea, she said, a church benefit. She had brought a typed list of Pug's belongings several pages long. Every container was numbered, and the list described what each held. "Don't bother to open numbers seven, eight, and nine, dear. Books. No matter how you arrange them, he'll GROWL. Then, let's see, numbers three and four are winter civilian stuff—suits, sweaters, overcoats, and such. They're mothballed. Air them in September and have them cleaned, and they'll be fine. Better stash all that stuff in the spare room for now. Where is it?"

Surprised, Pamela blurted, "Don't you know?"

"I've never been here before. Young man, we'll have some of these things moved, please."

Rhoda took charge, ordering the men to shift containers about and open those that were nailed or roped up. Once they left she produced keys to the trunks and suitcases, and pitched in on the unpacking of Pug's clothes, chattering about how he liked his shirts done, the dry cleaner he used, and so on. Her affectionate proprietary manner and tone about Pug, a bit like a mother packing off a grown-up son on a long trip, deeply disconcerted Pamela. Passing her hand fondly over his suits as she hung them up one by one, Rhoda told where they had been made, which he favored, which he seldom put on. Twice she mentioned that his waist measurement was the same as it had been on their wedding day. She lined up his shoes in Peters's shoe cupboard with care. "You'll ALWAYS have to put the shoe trees in, honey. He wants his shoes to look just so, but will he take five seconds to put in the trees? Never. Not him. Away from the Navy, dear, he's a bit of an absent-minded PROFESSOR, you'll find. Last thing you'd expect of Pug Henry, hey?"

"Rhoda, I really think I can do the rest of this. I'm frightfully grateful—"

"Oh? Well then, there's still number fifteen. Let's get at that. It's hard, you know, to split the herring down the BACKBONE, as you might say. There are some things Pug and I really share. One of us will have to end up without them. It can't be helped. Pictures, mementos, that sort of thing. I've made a selection. Pug can have anything I've kept back. I'll take anything he doesn't want. Can't be fairer than that, can I?" Rhoda gave her a bright smile.

"Certainly not," said Pamela, and to turn the conversation she added, "Look, something is bothering me. Did you say you'd never been here before?"

"No."

"Why not?"

"Well, dear, before I married Hack I wouldn't have DREAMED of coming to his bachelor lair. Caesar's wife, and all that. And afterward, well—" Rhoda's mouth twisted to one side, and she suddenly looked coarser, older, and very cynical—"I decided I really wanted no part of his memories here. Do I have to draw you a PICTURE?"

At the brief uncomfortable meeting in a lawyer's office for signing documents about the house and the apartment—which Pamela had attended at Pug's lawyer's request, and at which Rhoda had offered to help with this move—Rhoda's face had flashed that look just once; when

Peters had overridden a remark of hers in an offhand contemptuous way.

"No, I guess not."

"All right. So let's just dig into number fifteen, shall we? Look here."

Rhoda pulled out and showed her photograph albums of the children, of houses the Henrys had lived in, of picnics, dances, banquets, of ships in which Pug had served, where Rhoda posed with him in sunlight at a gun mount, or on a bridge, or walking the deck, or with the commanding officer. There were framed pictures of the couple—young, not so young, middle-aged, but always close, familiar, happy; Pug's usual pose was a half-admiring, half-amused look at Rhoda, the look of a loving husband aware of his wife's foibles and crazy about her. Pamela felt as never before that she herself was a young interloper at the tail end of Victor Henry's life; that whomever he lived with and called his wife, his center of gravity was forever fixed in this woman.

"Now take this, for instance," Rhoda said, laying the leather-bound Warren album on top of a box and turning the pages. "I had a hard time deciding about THIS one, I can tell you. Naturally I never thought of making two of these. Maybe Pug finds it painful. I don't know. I love it. I made it for him, but he never uttered a single word about it." Rhoda glanced at Pamela with hard shiny eyes. "You'll find him tough to figure out sometimes. Or have you already?" She carefully closed the album. "Well, there it is, anyway. Pug can have it if he wants it."

"Rhoda," Pamela said with difficulty, "I don't think he'd want you to give up such things, and—"

"Oh, there's more, plenty more. I've got my share. You accumulate LOTS in thirty years. You don't have to tell me ANYTHING about what I've given up, honey. So let's have a look around at Hack's den of INIQUITY, shall we? And then I'll be on my merry way. Do you have a decent kitchen?"

"Immense," Pamela said hurriedly. "It's through here."

"I'll bet you found it FILTHY."

"Well, I did have to scrape and scrub some." Pamela nervously laughed. "Bachelors, you know."

"Men, dear. Still, there's a difference between Army and Navy. I've found that out." Showing Rhoda through the place, Pamela tried to slip past the closed door of the pink and gold room, but Rhoda opened it and walked in. "Oh, GAWD. Whorehouse modern."

"It is a bit giddy, isn't it?"

"It's ABOMINABLE. Why didn't you make Hack redecorate and refurnish it?"

"Oh, it's simpler just to close it off. I don't need it."

One entire wall consisted of sliding mirrors that covered a long closet. The two women stood side by side, looking into the mirror, and addressing each other's images: Rhoda smartly dressed for springtime, Pamela in a plain blouse and straight skirt. Pamela looked like her daughter.

I don't need it was a trivial remark, or Pamela meant it so. But Rhoda failed to answer. Their eyes met in the mirror. A silence lengthened. The words gained portentousness second by second, and tactlessness, too. In Pug's room there was only a double bed. The innocent statement swelled into something like this, and true enough: *I'll sleep with Pug, and live in that room with him. There are closets enough for both of us. I don't want a separate room. I love him too much. I want to stay near him.*

Rhoda's mouth twisted far to one side. The eyes of her image, cynical and sad, wandered from Pamela's face to the garish room. "I guess you don't. Hack and I are finding separate rooms pretty handy, but then I'm getting on, aren't I? Well, what else is on the tour?"

Back in the living room, she looked out of the window and said, "You face south. That's cheerful. What a fine magnolia tree! These older apartment houses are the best. Isn't that schoolyard noisy? Of course it's after hours now."

"I haven't noticed."

"Why is their flag at half-mast, do you suppose?"

"Is it? So it is. It wasn't half an hour ago."

"Are you sure of that?" Wrinkling her brows, Rhoda said, "Something about the war, maybe."

Pamela said, "I'll turn on the radio."

It warmed up gibbering a Lucky Strike commercial. Pamela turned the dial.

"*. . . and Chief Justice Stone is now on the way to the White House,*" said an announcer's smooth voice, in professional dramatic tones troubled with real emotion, "*to administer the oath of office to Vice President Harry Truman. Mrs. Eleanor Roosevelt is flying to Warm Springs, Georgia—*"

"God save us, it's the PRESIDENT," Rhoda exclaimed. She threw a hand to her forehead, knocking her hat askew.

The news was scanty. He had suddenly died of a stroke at his vacation home in Georgia. That was all. The announcer talked on and on about reactions in Washington. Rhoda gestured at Pamela to shut it off. She dropped in an armchair, staring. "Franklin Roosevelt DEAD! Why, it's like the end of the world." She spoke very hoarsely. "I knew him. I sat beside him at dinner at the White House. What an utter CHARMER he was! Do you know what he said to me? I'll never forget it as long as I live. He said, *'Not many men deserve a wife as beautiful as you, Rhoda, but Pug does.'* Those were his words. Just being NICE, you know. But he certainly looked at me as though he MEANT it. Dead! Roosevelt! What about the war? Truman's a NOBODY. Oh, what a nightmare!"

"It's ghastly," Pamela said, her mind racing across world strategy to discern whether this might delay Pug's return to Washington.

"Hack said he left some booze here," Rhoda said.

"There's lots."

"Well, you know what? The hell with that tea. Give me a good drink of straight Scotch, will you, dear? Then I'll just go home."

Pamela was pouring the drink in the kitchen when she heard sobs. She hurried back into the living room. Rhoda sat amid the empty boxes and crates and trunks, streaming tears, her hat crooked, with the Warren album open on her lap. "It's the end of the world," she moaned. "It's the end."

*   *   *

96

The Bitter End

(from "Hitler as Military Leader" by Armin von Roon)

Brief Joy

On 12 April when the news of Roosevelt's death came, I was out inspecting Berlin's defenses, mainly to ascertain for Speer how far along the demolition preparations were. Returning to the bunker, I could hear the sounds of rejoicing echo up the long stairs. I walked in on a celebration complete with champagne, cakes, dancing, music, and happy toasts. Amidst all the joy and wassail Hitler sat smiling around in a dazed benign way, holding his left hand with his right to still the trembling. Goebbels himself deigned to greet me, hobbling up and waving a newspaper. "Only cheerful faces here tonight, my good General! It's the big turnabout at last. The mad dog has croaked."

That was the tenor of the party. Here was the break Germany was waiting for, the "miracle of the House of Brandenburg" all over again, the deliverance of Frederick the Great by the Russian empress's death, 1945 version. This was quite a success for the astrologers. They had been predicting a grand deliverance in mid-April.

Of course the Russians under Zhukov were massing along the Oder, at one point only thirty-five miles from the bunker; and Eisenhower was marching to the Elbe; and southward the Anglo-Americans were breaking apart our lines in Italy; and another great Russian force under Konev was grinding through the Balkans to race Zhukov and the Americans to Berlin; and the skies over the city were raining bombs day and night. Our war production had virtually ceased. Our forces everywhere were running out of ammunition and gasoline. Millions of refugees from east and west were clogging the roads, bringing Wehrmacht movements to a standstill. Trains were being shunted here and there by the SS, blocking up the railroad system. But in the atmosphere of the cement molehole under the Chancellery, what did all that matter? It had become a place of dreams and fantasies. Any excuse for optimism was inflated into a "big turnabout," though nothing ever equalled the brief glee over Roosevelt's death.

Next day the Red Army secured Vienna, and that let some gas out of the balloon. Yet on that very day as Speer and I sat discussing the grave demolition problem in Berlin, the Nazi labor administrator Ley came bubbling up to announce that some German back yard genius had just invented "the Death Ray!" It was as simple and cheap to manufacture as a machine gun. Ley had seen the plans himself, and prominent scientists had analyzed the apparatus for him. This was the big turnabout, if Speer would only start mass-producing the thing at once. With a straight face Speer appointed Ley on the spot "Commissioner of Death Rays," with full authority to commandeer all German industry in Speer's name for production of the wonder weapon. Ley went off drivelling happily, and we got back to our painful discussion.

This whole swindle of "wonder weapons" and "secret weapons" was a trial for Speer, and for me once I became his liaison to OKW. Generals, manufacturers, bigwig politicians, and ordinary people would approach me with a nudge and a wink. "Isn't it about time the Führer unleashed the secret weapon? When will it happen?" My own wife, the daughter of a general and an army wife to the core, pathetically asked me this herself. So far had Goebbels spread this cruel delusion through "leaks" and whispering campaigns, just to keep the bloodshed going and the Nazi cancer flourishing.

The Party Takes Over

By 1945 that cancer had metastasized all through the Fatherland. Party fools and plug-uglies like Ley permeated the state and military structures. The Waffen SS had become a rival army, absorbing the best new troops and equipment. In January Hitler actually appointed Heinrich Himmler to command Army Group Vistula, facing the brunt of the Red Army breakthrough in the north. Of course the result was disaster. Himmler's idea of generalship was to execute officers who failed to hold hopeless positions he had ordered held. Later he threatened to execute their families, too. The bridges and villages in his area were festooned with the hanging bodies of German soldiers, labelled cowards or deserters.

Naturally, all this National Socialist "inspiration" only reduced further the waning capability of our forces. The Russians quickly broke through Himmler's front to the Baltic, cutting off much of our German power in East Prussia and Latvia. Only Dönitz's splendid evacuation by sea, a forgotten rescue much greater than Dunkirk, saved those forces and much of the civilian population. Himmler meanwhile, as has been subsequently revealed, was secretly making his own peace feelers through Sweden, and simultaneously conducting fantastic negotiations to release surviving Jews for a big ransom.

At last, much too late, Hitler sent General Heinrici to relieve this incompetent brute. Meanwhile, however, Hitler too was showing his true Nazi colors. When the Americans in a brilliant dash captured the Remagen bridge, he flew into a tantrum and ordered four fine officers shot for failing to blow up the bridge in time. One of them, as it happened, was my own brother-in-law. In such circumstances one's oath of loyalty was quite a burden.

Speer versus Hitler

As staff liaison to Speer, I found my loyalty tested to the limit, for I was caught squarely between him and Hitler in the matter of demolition. The Führer was decreeing a "scorched-earth policy" in the face of the advancing enemy, east and west. In Berlin, essential services were to be totally demolished by our own explosives. Everywhere the Wehrmacht in retreat was to blow up bridges, railroads, waterways, highways, and leave a "transportation desert"; we were to flood the coal mines of the Ruhr, dynamite the steel plants, the electric and gas works, the dams, and in effect render Germany uninhabitable for a hundred years. When Speer ventured to object, Hitler simply shouted that the Germans had shown themselves unfit to survive anyway, or some such obdurate and merciless nonsense.

Speer was as dedicated a Nazi as any of them. There was something doglike about his squirming deference to Hitler that always disgusted me; nevertheless he was a master of modern technology, and responsibility for the nation's war production had forced him to keep his sanity. He knew that the war was lost, and he risked his neck for months to foil Hitler's demolition orders. Sometimes he wheedled his way out of them by arguing that we would soon need all those bridges and other facilities, to support the Führer's brilliant plans for counterattacking and regaining the lost territory. At other times he fudged his orders, authorizing a bridge or two blown up and leaving the rest of an area intact.

Unfortunately, this double-dealing backed up to me, because I had to handle the generals who received Hitler's orders. My job was to induce delays in carrying them out. After the execution of the four Remagen officers, these generals became harder to convince. Then at the situation conferences I had to exaggerate the demolition that had been done, and prevaricate about the rest. I was risking my head, as Speer was. The Führer was so far gone, however, in his dream world, that with luck one could wriggle through each conference by answering a perfunctory question or two.

Besides, I was not alone now in lying to him. These conferences in April had become war games on paper, with no relation to the frightening realities outside the bunker. Hitler pored over the maps, ordered phantom divisions moved about, commanded big counterattacks, argued over minor withdrawals, just as in the old days, but none of it was actually happening. We were all in a tacit conspiracy to humor him with soothing pretenses. Yet his person continued to command our unswerving loyalty. Jodl and Keitel issued streams of methodical realistic orders to deal with the collapsing situation into which German honor had led us. Of course it could not go on. Reality had to come crashing into the dreamland.

The Blowup

On the twentieth of April, during the lugubrious little birthday party for Hitler, Jodl told me that I was to leave at once and set up a skeleton OKW North in conjunction with Dönitz's staff. Our land communications were about to be cut in two by the juncture at the Elbe of the Americans and the Russians. Our military orientation therefore had to shift at a right angle; instead of facing west and east, we would now have a northern and a southern "front"! Words cannot convey the gloomy eeriness of all this at the time. So I missed the historic blowup at the situation conference on the twenty-second, which led to Hitler's decision to die in Berlin, instead of flying to Obersalzberg to carry on the war from the southern redoubt.

In my operational analysis of the battle for Berlin, I describe in detail the events of the twenty-second, turning on the phantom "Steiner attack." For once Hitler could not be put off with soothing lies, because Russian shells were falling on the Chancellery and shaking the bunker. He had ordered a big counterattack from the southern suburbs under SS General Steiner. The staff had assured him, with the usual wealth of mendacious detail, that the attack was on. Well, then, he demanded, where was Steiner? Why weren't the Russians being driven back?

When he was at last brought face to face with the truth that there was no Steiner attack, Hitler threw a fit of rage so horrible that nobody present could write or talk coherently about it thereafter. It seems to have been the last eruption of a dying volcano; a frightening explosion that left the man a dull burned-out shell, as I myself later saw; a three-hour screaming fit about the betrayal, treachery, and incompetence all around him that had frustrated his genius, lost the war, and destroyed Germany. Then and there he made his decision for suicide. Nothing could alter it. The result was a big exodus next day from the bunker. Jodl and Keitel went northwest to meet up with Dönitz, and most of the Nazi entourage scuttled off westward into one hole or another. *Sauve qui peut!*

My Last Talk with Hitler

I saw Hitler once more, on the twenty-fourth. Things were becoming very confused in this period. I received a peremptory summons by telex from Bormann, the repulsive toad who was Hitler's shadow and appointments secretary, to report to the Chancellery. The Russians had the city surrounded, the air was thick with their fighters, their artillery made rings of bright fire, but with luck one could still fly over their lines at night and land near the Chancellery on the East-West Axis boulevard, which had been marked with red lanterns. Not caring much what happened to me, I found a young Luftwaffe pilot who regarded the thing as a sporting challenge. He got hold of a small Stork reconnaissance plane, and flew me in there and out again. I will never forget coming in over the Brandenburg Tor in the green glare of Russian star shells. That pilot is now, incidentally, a well-known newspaper publisher in Munich.

Hitler received me in his private chambers. He questioned me closely about Dönitz's headquarters at Plön, the efficiency of his staff, the communications with the south, and the state of Dönitz's spirits. Perhaps he was making up his mind about the succession. It was after one in the morning, and I was desperately weary, but he was wound up, and he talked on and on. His eyes were glazed, his face doughy white with purple streaks. He hunched down in an armchair, rolling a stubby pencil in his left hand.

Glowering at me from under his eyebrows, he disclosed that Speer, that very day, had confessed to him the sabotage of his demolition orders in the past months. "You are implicated, and you deserve to be treated accordingly," he said, in a nasty snarling tone full of the old menace. For an unpleasant moment I thought I had been summoned to be shot, as had happened to many of my comrades-in-arms, and I wondered whether Speer was still alive. Hitler went on, "However, I've forgiven Speer because of his service to the Reich. I forgive you because, contrary to the nature of your whole damned breed, and despite the lapses that have not once escaped me, you have on the whole been a loyal general."

This led into the threadbare tirade on how the German General Staff had lost the war. Hitler could not converse at all. He had certain monologues which at a cue he would play out again and again, like phonograph records or an actor's repertoire. That is why, though he had a sharp mind and a certain coarse wit, all the memoirs quite truly describe his company as stupefyingly boring.

Beginning with the assertion that he had been betrayed, let down, and doublecrossed by us ever since 1939, this soliloquy reviewed the entire war in astonishing detail, rehashing his favorite grievances against the military, from Brauchitsch and Halder to Manstein and Guderian, the whole tragic procession that had taken the blame for his blunders. His grand strategy for the war, as he described it, could not possibly have failed except for the incompetence and treachery of our General Staff. In every disagreement he had been proved right and the generals wrong; the invasion of Poland, the attack on France, the hold-or-die order in Russia in December 1941, and all the smaller tactical disputes and disappointments he treasured in his unusual memory, right down to the Steiner attack.

That is my final impression of "Hitler as Military Leader"—a maundering paranoiac in an underground shelter in Berlin which shuddered under the blast of Russian shells, explaining for the thousandth time how our nation's catastrophe had been everybody else's fault but his; how he, its absolute ruler who had run the war first to last, had never made a mistake.

In the document that turned up after the war as his last Will and Testament, he blamed the Jews. In this tirade he blamed our General Staff. But to the last, one thing remained perfectly clear to him: Adolf Hitler himself had never made a mistake.

* * *

My long labor draws to a close. I have, I believe, in the course of my operational analysis, given this strange historic figure due credit for his positive qualities. All writings about him tend to end in contradiction because the authors write of "Hitler" as though he were one person. But there was more than one Hitler.

The early Hitler, as I have written, was undeniably "the soul of Germany." He fully expressed our people's vigorous yearning for a place in the sun, and for a healthy German culture uncontaminated by the poisons of Asiatic communism, Western materialism, and the weak negative aspects of Judeo-Christian morality exposed by Friedrich Nietzsche. His domestic policies brought prosperity and tranquillity. His foreign policies brought diplomatic victories over the world's strongest nations, our recent conquerors. When he led us to war, against the forebodings of our General Staff because we were far from ready, our nation won magnificent military triumphs. I have acknowledged his flair for adventurist opportunities in military strategy. None of this can be denied.

But at Stalingrad the later Hitler was born. This was another person, an insane monster. He more and more revealed himself as such, as adversity stripped away the glamour of the early Hitler, the protean masks he devised fell off one by one, and he dwindled to the broken jabberer I last glimpsed in the bunker.

In passing my own final judgment on the man, I must suspend the military historian's critical detachment, and speak from a soldier's heart.

His manner of death laid bare his character. A general may fall on his sword when the battle ends, a captain may go down with his ship, but a head of state is different. Was this the act of a head of state in wartime—to desert his office in the hour of his nation's greatest agony; to leave his disasters and his crimes for others to liquidate; to shoot his dog, poison his mistress, and seek Lethe at the muzzle of a pistol? His apologists call it "a Roman death." It was the death of a hysterical coward.

Napoleon in defeat behaved like a proper head of state. For two decades he had made all Europe run red with blood. Yet he faced up to his conquerors, accepted his fate, and purged France of his personal guilt. He was a soldier. Hitler was not, though he talked endlessly about his service in the trenches.

The unconscionable Nuremberg trials proved nothing but our foes' frustrated rage at the escape of Hitler from their hands. This vengeful and unjust farce condemned a whole nation for the deeds of one vanished man, and hanged and imprisoned the generals who were honor bound to obey him. Had Hitler abdicated, let Dönitz surrender, and offered himself to the fury of the victors, such a show of dignified courage would have done much to redeem his failures. Had he done so, I would not now be writing from a prison cell; of that I am convinced. As a master demagogue Hitler tricked his way to absolute power in Germany; then, as our Supreme Warlord, he betrayed our trust.

Epitaph

We are too vigorous a nation not to recover in time. However badly we lost, the German spirit strides on. All modern military strategy, as well as the world's hopes for an adequate energy supply, now turn on nuclear fission, a discovery of German science. Americans have walked on the moon, propelled there by an improved German V-2 rocket, in a program administered by German brains. The Soviet Union dominates Europe with its German-organized Red Army, administered on the German model. Captive German science and engineering have equipped Russia to confront the U.S.A. with intercontinental missiles armed with atom bombs.

In world politics, Hitler's brew of nationalism plus socialism—with its revolutionary egalitarian propaganda, terror apparatus, and one-party dictatorship—is the worldwide political trend. It governs Russia, China, and most developing countries. Perhaps it is nothing to be proud of, but such is the fact. The ideas of the great German philosopher Hegel, popularized and twisted by the converted German Jew Karl Marx, are becoming a new Islam.

In the arts, the Western perverters of form and beauty only echo the avant-garde abstraction and corruption of the Weimar Republic in the 1930s. They are doing nothing now that our clever decadents did not do half a century ago, in the period of anarchy that brought on the Hitler regime.

We Germans have been the bellwether people of the twentieth century, with our triumphs and our tragedies. Though we lost our gallant bid for world empire, our great marches to the Atlantic, the Volga, and the Caucasus will shine forever in the chronicles of war.

But one historical fact we can never live down: that at the apogee of our national strength we gambled our destiny, and shot our bolt, for the sake of a common poltroon. Napoleon lies in the splendid tomb of the Invalides, a world shrine. Hitler ended as a mess of charred carrion in flaming gasoline. Only Shakespeare could write the appropriate epitaph for him:

Nothing in his life became him like the leaving it.

TRANSLATOR'S NOTE: *In Roon's view the early "Dr. Jekyll" Hitler made it to Stalingrad. There he turned into "Mr. Hyde." I am sure Roon meant this. Stalingrad occurred at the end of 1942. By then Hitler had led his people to commit virtually all the crimes for which the world execrates National Socialist Germany. However, he was still winning the war. He became "an insane monster," by Roon's lights, when he began to lose.—V.H.*

*   *   *

97

WHAT startled Pug Henry most was seeing the President stand up. To come on this small new man at Roosevelt's seat in the Oval Office was itself unsettling, but Truman's bouncy walk around a desk cleared of the familiar clutter gave Pug the queer sensation that the flow of history had left him stranded in the past; that reality was becoming dreamlike, and that this perky little "President" in a double-breasted suit and bright bow tie was some sort of imposter. Harry Truman shook hands briskly, told his secretary to buzz him the moment Mr. Byrnes arrived, and invited Pug to sit down.

"I need a naval aide, Admiral Henry." The voice was tart, high, businesslike, the tone flat, midwestern, abrasive; the other American pole from Roosevelt's creamy Harvard accent. "Now, Harry Hopkins and Admiral Leahy have both recommended you. Would you like the job?"

"Very much, Mr. President."

"You're hired. That does our business. Wish all the transactions in this office were that simple." President Truman uttered a short self-conscious laugh. "Now it's in the nature of things, Admiral, that the military and the President don't see eye to eye on lots of things. So let's get that straight right from the start. Who will you work for—me, or the Navy?"

"You're my Commander-in-Chief."

"Good enough."

"However, if I think you're wrong in a disagreement with the Navy, I'll tell you so."

"All right. That's what I want. Just remember that the military can be wrong, too. Very wrong!" Truman emphasized his words with short chops of both hands. "Why, the day after I was sworn in, the Joint Chiefs gave me a briefing on the war. Six more months to lick Germany, they said, and another year and a half to beat Japan. Well, here's old Hitler dead or disappeared, and surrender talks under way, and it's been all of three weeks. Hey? How about that? Will the Joint Chiefs be just as far off about the Pacific? You've just come from there."

"That sounds like an Army estimate."

"Now exactly what does that mean? And just remember I'm a field artillery man."

"General MacArthur projects long land campaigns, Mr. President. But the submarine blockade and the destruction from the air should make the Japs quit sooner than that."

"Why, they're fighting like devils on Okinawa."

"They do fight hard. But they'll run out of the wherewithal."

"Without our invading Honshu?"

"That's my judgment, Mr. President."

"Then we won't need the Russians' help to finish the war out there?"

"No. I don't think so."

Resting both hands on the desk before him, Truman stared through glittering glasses at the admiral. Pug's short assured answers were instinctive returns of the hard straight quizzing. He did not know how else to handle it. This man's style was not Roosevelt's at all. FDR would first have made or elicited some mild jokes, inquired about Pug's family, put him at ease, and made him feel that they might chat all day. Like a new ship's captain, Truman seemed not quite the real thing because of the change in look and manners. But no matter how long in office he would never acquire Roosevelt's lordly authority. That seemed plain.

"Well, I hope you're right," Truman said.

"I can be as wrong as the Joint Chiefs of Staff, Mr. President."

"What about that big Jap army on the Chinese mainland?"

"Well, sir, you cut off an octopus's head, and the arms go kind of limp."

A natural smile softened the President's stiff expression and relaxed the tight mouth. He sat back, clasping his hands behind his head. "Say, what's the matter with those Russians, anyway, Admiral? You've had duty there. Why don't they stick to their agreements?"

"Which agreements, sir?"

"Why, any agreements."

"In my experience they usually do."

"Is that so? Well, you're dead wrong, right there. Stalin agreed at Yalta to hold free elections in Poland, and that's a serious commitment. Now they're handpicking all the candidates, so as to force in that puppet Lublin government of theirs. Figure they can get away with it because their army's occupying Poland. Churchill's up in arms about that, and so am I. I told Molotov just how I felt about it last week. He said he'd never been talked to like that in his life. I said, 'Keep your agreements and you won't get talked to like that!' "

Truman looked and sounded comfortable now, and quite pleased with himself. As he talked, Pug Henry had flashing memories of the devastated landscape in the Soviet Union, the trips with General Yevlenko, the ruins of Stalingrad, the burned-out German and Russian tanks, the corpses; memories too of trying to deal with Russians, of drinking with them, of hearing their songs and watching them dance. Harry Truman was a straight-shooting fellow from Missouri. He expected everybody else to behave like prosperous, unbombed, uninvaded, straight-shooting fellows from Missouri. Quite a gap. Roosevelt had understood that gap, and had bridged it long enough to win the war. Maybe nothing more was possible with the Soviet Union.

"Mr. President, you've got Russian experts to advise you on that. I'm not one. I don't know the language of the Yalta agreements. With the Russians, if there's a single loophole in the language of an agreement, they'll drive a truck through it. That much you can count on."

A buzzer, and a voice: *"Mr. Byrnes is arriving, Mr. President."*

Truman stood up. Again it surprised Pug. This would take getting used to. "I'm told you've just been married."

"Yes, Mr. President."

"I suppose you'll want a few weeks for your honeymoon."

"Sir, I'm prepared to report for duty now."

Again the smile. Roosevelt's world-famous smile had been more spectacular, but Pug was beginning to like Truman's better. It was genuine, with no trace of condescension. Here was a simple smart man, and he was the President, after all; that showed in the confident natural smile. He was still somewhat ill at ease in the presidency, not an unlikable trait. "Well, very good. The sooner the better. Is your bride a Washington lady?"

"No, sir. An Englishwoman." Truman blinked. "Her father was the British war correspondent, Alistair Tudsbury."

"Oh, yes. The fat man. He interviewed me once. He stuck to the truth in that article. Didn't he get killed in North Africa?"

"Yes."

"I'll look forward to meeting her."

Playing with her gloves, Pamela was strolling along the sunny tulip beds near the old Dodge she had acquired. The uniformed White House guards were watching her swaying walk. When she waved the gloves at the admiral, they took their eyes off her. Her look was affectionate and subtly inquiring.

"Where to now?" he said. "That thing at your embassy?"

"If you're free, darling. And if you don't mind."

"Let's go."

She drove out of the gate and around toward the north in the old too-quick way, with jerky stops and fast starts at the lights of Connecticut Avenue. The traffic was heavy, the gasoline fumes choking through the open car windows. Again the feeling stole over Victor Henry of being stranded in the past. On Connecticut Avenue what was different from 1939? Franklin Roosevelt had kept the war from this untouched avenue, this untouched capital, this untouched land. Had he been too successful? Did these contented people swarming in automobiles up and down Connecticut Avenue have any idea of what war was? The Russians knew, and the future required the toughest realism about war.

"Penny for your thoughts," Pamela said to her silent husband, with a jackrabbit start away from a red light at Dupont Circle.

"I'd be overcharging you. Tell me again what this embassy shindig is about."

"Oh, just a little reception. Our press corps, the British purchase mission, and such."

"But what's the occasion?"

"Frankly, so that I can show you off." She gave him a sidewise glance. "Okay? Mostly my friends will be there. Lady Halifax is curious to meet you."

"Okay."

Pamela took his hand as she drove, and twined cool fingers in his. "It isn't every little British popsie, you see, who hooks herself an American admiral."

"And the naval aide to the President." Pug had held out long enough. By now Rhoda would have asked him.

The grip on his hand tightened. "That's what it was about then. Are you pleased?"

"Well, the alternative was BuOrd or BuShips again. You'll enjoy this more. So will I."

"How did he strike you?"

"He's no Roosevelt. But Roosevelt's dead, Pamela."

Victor Henry was clearly on display at the party. Pam walked around the embassy garden on his arm, introducing him. For all the British nonchalance with which he was greeted in the sparse little gathering, the studied avoidance of stares or questions, he felt himself measured by all eyes. Thirty years ago, Rhoda had dragged her Navy quarterback to a luncheon of her Sweetbriar classmates. Some things did not change much. Pamela in her flowered frock and cartwheel hat was enchanting to look at, and her proud glow was a little comical to Pug, and a little sad. He did not think himself much of a prize; though he cut a better figure than he perhaps realized, with his South Pacific tan and his banks of battle-starred campaign ribbons on dress whites.

Lord and Lady Halifax moved genially about among their guests. Pug kept watching this tall bald gloomy man who had spent so much time with Hitler during the Munich debacle, and right up to the outbreak of the war. There he stood, this man of history, holding a glass and making chitchat with ladies. Lord Halifax caught Pug's eye and walked straight up to him. "Admiral, I believe Sumner Welles told me about you, long ago. Didn't you see Hitler in 1939, with the banker your President sent over on a peace mission?"

"Yes. I was naval attaché in Berlin then. I translated."

"He wasn't easy to deal with, was he?" Halifax said morosely. "Anyway, we've done for him at last."

"Could he have been stopped before the war, Mr. Ambassador?"

Halifax looked thoughtful, and spoke straightforwardly. "No. Churchill's wrong about that. We made mistakes, but given the mood of our people and the French there was no stopping him. They thought war was a thing of the past."

"A misimpression," Pug said.

"Rather. Pamela is a lovely woman. Congratulations, and good luck." Halifax shook hands, smiled a shade wearily, and walked off.

Driving back to the apartment, Pamela remarked, "Lady Halifax says you're rather a lamb."

"Is that good?"

"The accolade."

Back at Peters's apartment Pug showered, and with the smell of a broiling steak drifting through the open bedroom door, he put on old gray slacks that fitted loosely, much to his satisfaction; an open white shirt, a maroon pullover, and moccasins. It was his customary off-duty dress of peacetime days. He heard the tinkle of ice in a jug. In the living room Pamela, wearing a plain dress and apron, handed him a martini. "My God, I can't get used to the sight of you like this," she said. "You look thirty."

Pug growled, "I don't function like thirty," and sat down with his drink. It was a glancing comment on the bedchamber: exquisite joy for him, and he hoped for her, but nothing record-breaking in the newly-wed line. Her reply was a throaty laugh and a caress on his neck.

Soon they sat facing each other in the breakfast nook; they ate all their meals there because the dining room was cavernous. They drank red wine, and ate with great gusto, and said many foolish and wise things, laughing almost all the time. Pug was quite reconciled in such moments to being out of the war, though at other times he had qualms about having hung up his arms too soon.

The telephone rang. Pamela went out to the living room to answer it, and came back looking very sober. "It's Rhoda."

The instant fear stabbed through Victor Henry's mind: *bad news about Byron.* He hurried out. Pamela heard him say, "Good God!" Then: "Wait a minute, let me get a pencil. Okay, go ahead. . . . Got it. No, no, Rhoda. I'll see to this myself. Of course, and I'll let you know."

Pamela stood in the doorway. He was picking up the telephone again and dialling. "Darling, what is it?"

Mutely he handed her the scrawl on the telephone pad. *Natalie Henry German internee hospitalized Army facility Erfurt condition critical malnutrition typhus American Red Cross Germany.*

Three days out from Guam, Byron received the message on the Fox schedule. Several submarines equipped with FM sonar were heading for some final training in Guam waters, and then for a wolf-pack penetration of the Sea of Japan. He could not break radio silence. Those were three long days for Byron. Coming into Guam, a mountainous gardenlike island breaking out in a rash of Navy construction and bulldozed roads, Byron paced the forecastle while Philby brought the vessel alongside. He leaped before the *Barracuda* tied up, and trotted across the decks and gangways of the submarine nest, and all the way to the communications office. No further messages for him; no quick way to get in touch with his father. "You can try a personal," said a sympathetic watch officer, "but we're loaded with urgent and operational priority traffic. The kamikazes are raising hell at Okinawa. A routine message won't hit the sked for maybe two weeks."

Still, Byron sent the dispatch:

FROM: CO BARRACUDA
TO: BUPERS
PERSONAL RADM VICTOR HENRY WHAT ABOUT LOUIS

The yeoman brought to his cabin the mail from the fleet post office. Amid all the official stuff lay a letter from Madeline. This was as rare an event as a total eclipse of the sun, and ordinarily Byron would have ripped it open on sight, but he went at the Navy correspondence instead, taking work like aspirin to dull his agitation.

What about Louis?

However worrisome the report on Natalie, she was alive, and in American hands. The silence about his son was doubly disturbing, since the boy was evidently not with her. German captivity had hospitalized her with "malnutrition and typhus." What had it done to a three-and-a-half-year-old child?

After dinner in the wardroom, at which he ate so little and looked so glum that his officers kept exchanging glances, he shut himself in his cabin with Madeline's letter.

> Los Alamos, New Mexico
> April 20, 1945

Dear Briny—

Sorry I threw you. I thought I'd get to San Francisco during your overhaul. Truly I did. I tried, but I lead a very strange and complicated life nowadays. Letters out of here are censored. I can't say much about it, but coming and going isn't all that simple. And Sime is working his fool head off day and night, and I guess I felt guilty about leaving him, and so I just let the whole thing slide. I'm fine, and all's well. No baby in sight, if you're curious; not while we're up on this weird hill cut off from the world, no thanks.

Now about Dad and Mom. The main reason I wanted to come to San Francisco was to have all that out with you. You're so misinformed and wrong-headed that it's pitiful. Dad's just come back to Washington and yes, he's going to marry Pam Tudsbury, just a quiet private ceremony. I thought of flying there to be with him, poor lonely man, but it isn't in the cards. I only hope she makes him happy. There's no reason she shouldn't, if she really loves him. The age difference doesn't matter. He's the best man alive.

Your resentment of that match is plain dumb. You don't know certain facts, and here they are. Remember Fred Kirby, the big tall engineer you all met in Berlin? Well, he got a job in Washington after that, *and he and Mom had a wild two-year affair.* Surprised? It's true. Mom wrote Dad and asked for a divorce. I don't know all the details, but after Warren died she took it back, and they patched things up. Then when he went to Russia she got into this big romance with Colonel Peters, and that was the end. Whether *they* had an affair, too, I don't know, and don't much care. Mom's all set now.

But Dad did not have an affair with Pamela Tudsbury, not that I'd condemn him if he had. Good God, what's the matter with you? It's *wartime.* I know he didn't, because Mama and I got very swozzled one night, when he was off in the Soviet Union and Colonel Peters was falling for her. Mom was all confused and upset, and just spilled everything. Said she'd hurt Dad so bad that the marriage was finished, even though he was sticking it out and had never reproached her, never even mentioned Kirby's name. Frankly I think Mom was choked by Dad's forbearance. Pamela told Mom in Hollywood that she and Dad had had an innocent romance, and that after Warren's death she was bowing out. She did, too.

You are an impossible fellow. Where did you get your fossilized morality from? Dad's from another generation, and it's understandable in him, but at that he's more tolerant than you. I confess you did me a favor in your quaint way, when you knocked out Hugh Cleveland's bridgework. God, was that ever hilarious. If you'd been any less stern I'd have dragged on and on with Hugh—he kept promising to get a divorce and marry me, you know, that was what *that* was all about—but a fat toothless man was just too much. And so, bless your neanderthal heart, I broke free in time to marry Sime Anderson, by the skin of my teeth.

Well, now *I'm* spilling more than I should, but when I do take up a pen once in seven years it just runs. I'll stop now because I have to cook dinner. Admiral ████████, no less, is coming, and that's quite an honor around here. Let's hope the roast doesn't burn. I do have the crappiest stove. Everything here is tacky and make-do. Most of the scientists' wives here are older and smarter than little Madeline, but thanks to my home training I cook better than most, and my showbiz background goes for something, too. Some of these big brains even like Hugh Cleveland.

Oh, Briny, I hope Natalie and your boy are all right! That war in Europe is folding up. You'll hear something very soon, I'm sure. I have painful memories of a mean thing or two I said about Natalie. She intimidated me, she was so beautiful and seemed so dignified and brilliant. And you were being pretty mean about Cleveland then. There's a church here and I do go on Sunday, which is more than Sime does, and I pray for your wife and kid.

I hope I've straightened you out about Dad. Don't you know that he worships the ground you walk on? He'd have done ANYTHING to keep your good opinion, except say a word against Mom. He'll go to the grave without doing that. You and I have an incredible father, as we once had an incredible brother. Mom is—well, she's Mom. She's all right.

Good hunting, darling, and good luck.

Love,
Mad

The name of the admiral had been neatly cut from the letter, leaving a rectangular hole.

Byron went ashore that night to the officers' club and got very drunk. Next morning he was on the bridge as the flotilla put out to sea for a training exercise, then he went to his cabin and slept for twenty-four hours, while Philby accumulated experience maneuvering underwater by the sound of gongs.

Two weeks later, the admiral who was so hot on the FM sonar held a farewell luncheon for the skippers of the wolf pack. Some Navy nurses came, too; to add glamour, as he put it. The Guam nurses were a tired beaten-down lot, what with the casualties pouring in from Okinawa, and the sexual demands of hordes of young servicemen, fended off or yielded to; but they smirked and giggled dutifully with the submarine captains. "You fellows are sailing to finish the job we started," shouted the admiral in his little speech, "to sink everything that floats and flies a Jap flag!"

Byron knew that the admiral meant well, and had even asked Nimitz in vain for permission to go with the wolf pack. But the whole FM caper was unnecessary, in his view. He had penetrated the Sea of Japan two years ago with Carter Aster in the *Moray,* via La Pérouse Strait. They could enter the same way now, probably at less hazard than through the Tsushima Strait mines. They were planning to leave that way, after all. But the FM sonar had been developed with much trouble, expense, and scientific ingenuity; and the admiral was damned well going to use it. Nobody was asking Byron's opinion. He had convinced his crew that he would get them through the mines; few sailors had transferred, and none had deserted.

The wolf pack sailed, and reached Japan without incident, seeing no shipping whatever on the way. Transiting the mine field was a long tense misery. The FM sonar, dubbed by the sailors, none too affectionately, "Hell's Bells," rang for fish, kelp beds, temperature gradients, and mine cables, with fine changes in tone. Byron bypassed the danger for the most part, by creeping along at maximum charted depth, below the antisubmarine mines that set off the bells at a hundred feet. The riskiest moment came when he surfaced, just once, to be sure where he was. He took quick bearings, satisfied himself that his submerged dead reckoning wasn't being thrown off by the current, and proceeded. On two occasions, mine cables grated slowly along the clearing wires, all the way down the hull. Nasty minutes, but that was the worst of it.

His patrol sector was in the southeast, so he had to wait while the rest of the wolf pack crawled north into station. The thick Jap traffic ran peaceably past his periscope, showing lights at night, moving unescorted by day, like shipping in New York harbor—small passenger vessels, coastal cargo carriers and tankers, assorted small craft, even pleasure sailboats. He saw no warships. When the slaughter began at a scheduled hour, Byron was holding a clumsy little freighter in his sights. He turned the periscope over to Philby, who neatly and exuberantly torpedoed the victim.

All in all, over the two weeks of the pack's assault, the *Barracuda* sank three ships. On the last two, in 1943, Aster would have scorned to expend torpedoes. All the torpedoes worked quite well now. The traffic dwindled after the first sinkings alarmed the Japs. Targets became scarce, and Byron crept here and there off the west coast of Honshu, admiring the pretty landscape.

At the rendezvous in La Pérouse Strait, eight of the nine submarines showed up. The wolf pack left in a welcome fog. Once clear of aircraft search range, they ran for Pearl Harbor on the surface, exchanging cheerful notes on their scores, and worried inquiries about the missing *Bonefish*. The *Barracuda* resumed copying Fox, but nothing came in for Byron. Entering port on July fourth, the flotilla encountered no jubilation, no ceremony. Byron went straight to the telephone office and put in a call to his mother, not knowing where his father was. It went through quickly, but there was no answer.

ComSubPac's operations officer jumped up to throw his arms around Byron when he came into the office. "Hey, Byron! Christ, what a sweep!"

"Bill, I request relief."

"*Relief!* Are you out of your mind? Why?"

The operations officer sat down and heard the story out, chewing his lips and looking hard at Byron. His comment was tentative and cool. "That's rough. But look here, your wife may be home by now. Maybe she's got your boy, too. Why don't you find out first? Don't go off half-cocked like this. You're on your way to a great record."

"I've made my record. I request relief, Bill."

"Sit down. Stop pounding my desk. That isn't necessary." Byron was in fact slamming his fist on the glass top.

"Sorry." Byron dropped in a chair.

The operations officer offered him a cigarette. Taking a confidential tone he began to reveal surprising secrets. Russia was coming into the war. SubPac had the word. MacArthur was going to land in Japan; first on Kyushu, then Honshu. The Sea of Japan was going to be zoned off between U.S. forces and the Russians. So it would be a whole new ball game. The only fat pickings left were in the Sea of Japan, and ComSubPac wanted to pour on the Hell's Bells forays, and really clean up while he could. "The submarines have won this war, Byron, you know that. But no job's done until it's over. You're doing superbly. Lady Aster would have been proud of you. Don't walk away from a fight."

"Okay," Byron said. "Thanks."

He was not angry at the operations officer. The man's purpose in life was fat pickings. He went to the office of the admiral, the enthusiast for FM sonar, and got right in. Byron calmly described to the admiral his talk with the operations officer.

"Admiral, here it is," Byron said. "You may want to court-martial me for desertion, or you may not. I'm going to see my wife, and find my son if he's alive. Please give me orders to enable me to do this. I've tried to serve. If I find my family, and the war's still on, I'll fly back here and take an FM submarine into Tokyo Bay. I'll take one into Vladivostok, if you want me to."

The admiral, with an annoyed squint and a jutting jaw, said, "You have one hell of a nerve." He began looking through papers on his desk. "Whatever your personal hardship, I don't appreciate being told off like that."

"Sorry, Admiral."

"I have a letter here from CNO, as it happens—now where the devil is it? Here we are. CNO wants a team of experienced skippers to inspect captured U-boats over in Germany. Preliminary reports are that those boats look better than ours. Embarrassingly so. The only way to get the real dope is to go out with the skippers and operate them. Do you know any German?"

"Sir, I speak it well."

"Interested?"

"God, I'll be so grateful, Admiral!"

"Well, you have the operational background. You'll have to qualify your relief on the FM sonar first. Give him a week of runs in the dummy field off Molokai."

"Aye aye, sir. Thank you and God bless you, Admiral."

"Say, Byron, how did your FM sonar perform?"

"Magnificently, sir."

"Greatest thing since canned beer," said the admiral.

98

THE usual pile of mail after a patrol lay on Byron's bunk, including a heavy manila envelope from his father. Byron pounced on it. A handwritten letter was clipped to the bulky sheaf of papers inside.

14 June 1945

Dear Byron:

I know you're out on operations, so I've opened your mail from Europe. Here it is, as of now. In case this envelope goes astray, I've made facsimiles. Natalie's story fills Pamela and me with horror. Horror is too weak a word. We still can't grasp that an American girl went through these things, but it seems she just got caught in the mill.

Here in the U.S.A. the true facts are only now starting to sink in. General Eisenhower brought the press into Buchenwald, Dachau, Bergen-Belsen, and all those places. The papers have been full of the pictures and the accounts. Natalie's survival shows her stamina, and perhaps the effect of our prayers, too. But prayer didn't help the millions who got massacred. The decisive thing was that this man Rabinovitz's outfit was working in Thuringia. That I call miraculous intervention. I believe that's why she's alive. His letter gives the details.

For a long time Pamela's been asking me, "What's this filthy war all about? Why did your son have to die? What have we achieved?" Now it's clear. The political system that could perpetrate such foul deeds had to be wiped off the planet. It was damned powerful, too. The combined strength of the Russians, the British, and ourselves barely contained the thing. It could have overrun the earth. Because the Japs made league with it, we had to crush Japan too. Warren died in a right and great cause. I know that now, and I will never think otherwise.

Your little boy was well many months after he was taken out of Theresienstadt, since Natalie saw that snapshot of him on the farm outside Prague. Don't give up hope. The search may take a long time. If you want to telephone me, I'm at the White House, office of the Naval Aide. That's my new job. Evenings, Republic 4698 is our apartment number. Pam joins me in sending love,

Dad

Below this, on a single sheet of paper with an Army Medical Corps heading, Byron read these few typed words:

20 May 1945

Dear Byron:

I am a little better. Berel came to Theresienstadt and got Louis last July. Then later I received a picture of him on a farm outside Prague. He looked well. Avram says they will find him. I love you.

Natalie

(Dictated to Nurse Emily Denny, Sergeant 1/c USANC)

The shaky signature was in green ink.

Avram Rabinovitz's long typed letter on flimsy onionskin paper was signed with the same pen.

17th May 1945

Dear Byron:

I speak better than I write English, and I am also very busy. So I will make this short and give you what happened. The important thing is that she is over the typhus. Now she has to build up, she is in very poor condition. The interviewer from the War Refugee Board was a stupid woman so Natalie sounds stupid in the affidavit. Her mind is now clear and she talks nicely, but she cries a lot, and she does not like to talk about what happened. She ran a fever for three days after the interview. That is not being allowed any more. She has asked me to write to you. As you will see, her handwriting is unsteady and she is weak. Also she does not want to remember and write things down.

To make it short, I am based in Paris with a rescue organization, I won't go into too many details. We are cleaning up the Nazi wreckage, putting the Jews who are wandering homeless and starving into camps, in order to get their health back and go to Palestine. It is terrible work. When Germany was falling apart the SS didn't know what to do with the Jews they had not yet killed. It all happened too fast to kill them all and cover up the camps, although they tried. They marched them around or moved them sealed in trains, no orders, no destination, no food or water, and when the Americans or the Russians came the Germans just ran and left the Jews where they were, I don't know how many thousands of them like that, all over Europe. Our people found Natalie in a train that came from Ravensbrück which was a women's concentration camp, and was stalled in a forest outside Weimar, just standing there. Probably it was heading for Buchenwald. Natalie was under the train, lying on the railroad bed. She crawled out because women were dying all around her in the car. I was with a different unit, we talked on the telephone at night and they told me they had found a woman under a train who said she was an American. A lot of Jews claim they are Americans to get better treatment. These fellows couldn't talk English, so I drove over from Erfurt, never expecting to find your wife, God knows, but even stranger things have happened to me in this work. She was not very recognizable, skin and bones, and she was delirious, but I knew her and besides she kept talking about Louis and Byron. So I went to the American Army HQ and told them we had an American woman. This was in the middle of the night, and they sent a field ambulance for her right away. The treatment the army gave her is marvelous since she is an American.

They are trying to move her to Paris and I think they will succeed. There is a fine American hospital there in which Natalie worked for a while. The administrator remembers her and although it's crowded he is willing to take her in. However, the red tape is tremendous, for instance the army officials are still trying to get her a new passport, but all that will be all right. Now about your son there is really no news. You will read in the affidavit how they got separated and Natalie did the right thing. That was very brave. However, it is not easy in Prague, because the Russians are occupying it, and they are not cooperative. Still, our people have been checking around Prague with no results yet. Just before the Russians arrived there was a lot of disorder in Prague, an uprising, Germans killing communists and so forth, and when the Germans retreated they looted a lot of the farms around there and set fire to them, so there is no telling what happened. Chances are your boy is certainly alive, but finding him is "looking for a needle in a haystack." The homeless Jewish children are a problem in themselves, hundreds of thousands of them are roaming Europe, and some of them have become savages, wolves, their parents were killed and they learned to live by stealing. What the Germans did will never be repaired enough. Big card indexes are being assembled in Paris and Geneva by Red Cross, UNRRA, the Joint, and other organizations, but so far it is only a drop in the bucket. I have given the information on your son to our people who visit the files but they are swamped. It will take time. So that is the story, and I am sorry it is not a pleasanter one, but Natalie is alive at least, and she is beginning to look better. She has no appetite or she would recuperate faster. Letters from you would be a big help, and you had better send them to me, I'll see that she gets them. Be as cheerful as possible when you write, tell her you believe your son is alive and we will find him.

> Yours truly,
> Avram Rabinovitz

The affidavit was a smudged faint single-spaced carbon copy, so poorly written that Byron could hardly follow some of it. It sounded nothing like Natalie. The interviewer obviously had taken notes, then typed them up in a hurry. The story began in peacetime in Siena, describing her entrapment by the Pearl Harbor attack and everything that had followed. Up to their meeting in Marseilles Byron knew most of it. The long Theresienstadt narrative, especially the scene in the SS cellar, made him cringe (though she or the interviewer had omitted the sexual details). The heading of the affidavit said there had been three interview sessions, but from Theresienstadt onward the narrative became sparse. The last words about Aaron Jastrow were oddly flat.

> When we were getting on the train, an official of the Transport Section separated us. I never saw my uncle again. I heard later that all the *Prominente* in the transport went to the gas. He was an old frail man. They only picked a few young strong ones to live, so I am sure he is dead.

That was all. Her Auschwitz narrative after that rambled: how it felt to have her head shaved and a number tattooed on her arm, the rags she was given to wear, the conditions in the women's brick blockhouse, the sanitary and feeding arrangements. A man called Udam, a friend from Theresienstadt, had obtained work for her in the warehouses of looted Jewish belongings. She had been assigned to the section of children's toys, taking apart dolls, teddy bears, and other stuffed toys in search of money and valuables, then restoring them for sale or distribution to children in Germany. The most vivid passage in the whole affidavit described a punishment at this job.

> I got very good at disassembling and reassembling the toys. There were mountains of them, and every one meant a little child murdered by Germans. But we stopped thinking about that, we were numb. Many toys were identical, from the same manufacturers. Occasionally we found something; jewelry, gold coins, or currency. There was pilfering, of course. We risked our lives when we kept things, because we were searched every afternoon when we left Canada. The warehouse section was called "Canada" because Polish people think Canada is a land of gold. We had to steal, because we could trade loot for food. Whose property was it, after all? Not the Germans'! I was never caught, but once I was beaten almost to death for nothing at all. I took apart a worn-out, ragged teddy bear with nothing in it. There was just no way to repair it. It fell to pieces in my hands. The supervisor was a loathsome Greek Jewess who strutted around dressed like an SS woman guard. She hated me because I was an American, and she jumped on the chance to make an example of me. She reported me to the SS. I was sentenced to twenty strokes of the cane on my bare skin, "for criminal destruction of Reich property." The sentence was carried out at a roll call of all the workers in Canada. I had to bend over a wooden frame naked, and an SS man flogged me. I have never known such agony. I fainted before he was finished. Udam and some of my women friends carried me to the blockhouse, and Udam got me into the hospital. Oth-

erwise I would have died from loss of blood. I couldn't walk for a week. I found out how strong my constitution is, however. I healed up and went back to the same job. The Greek woman acted as though nothing had happened.

The narrative passed into incoherent generalities about life in Auschwitz: the smell from the mass graves where the bodies were being dug up and burned, the black market, the exceptional steadfastness of Jehovah's Witnesses, a kindly SS man, having an affair with a woman in the blockhouse, who had brought them much good food. It described the rumors of the Russian approach, the distant sound of the guns, the three-day march of thousands of women in the snow to a railroad terminal, the train ride in open coal cars to Ravensbrück. She had gone to work in a clothing plant, living in terror of Ravensbrück medical experiments, of which she had heard rumors even in Auschwitz. Field whores for the Wehrmacht, also for SS brothels, were recruited from this camp; but about this her comment, even filtered through the interviewer's mind and style, was pitiful.

That was one threat that did not concern me. I had once been considered attractive, but a few months in Auschwitz had fixed that. Anyway, they only recruited the youngest, freshest Jewish girls. Some of the Hungarian Jewesses who came to Ravensbrück were really delicate beauties. Moreover, in Ravensbrück I had no way to get extra food, and I was shrinking to a skeleton, as I am now. Also, I would never have passed the physical examination because of the scars. The German men wouldn't have enjoyed the sight.

In April thousands of us were loaded onto trains. We had heard that the war was almost over, that the Russians and the Americans were about to join hands, and we were counting the days and praying to be liberated. But the Germans stuffed us into sealed cattle cars and sent us God knows where, with no provision whatever for food, water, or health. Typhus had already broken out in the camp. On the train it spread like wildfire. I remember very little after I left Ravensbrück. Just how horrible it was on that train, worse than anything yet. My car was a morgue, practically all the women were dead or dying. They tell me I was found under the train. I don't know how I got there, and I can't understand how it is that I'm still alive. If anything kept me going all these months it was the hope of one day seeing my son again. I think that was what gave me the strength to get out of that car. I can't tell you who opened the door or how I got out. I have told you all I know.

99

A STRONG child can hold fifteen pounds or so in his two hands, if the stuff is not bulky: say, two lumps of the man-made heavy element, plutonium. If the child holds the lumps far apart nothing will happen. If he can clap his hands together very fast, and if he is a big-city child, he can make a "critical mass" and kill a million people; that is, in theory. Actually no child can move his arms that fast; at worst he would make a fizzle that would kill him and cause a bad mess. One needs a device that zips the little lumps together, for an atomic blast and a city-destroying blaze of light.

This fact of nature, so earthshaking in 1945, is an old story now. Still, it remains strange and frightening. We prefer not to think about it, as we prefer not to think much about the attempted murder of all the Jews in Europe by a modern government. But these are ruling realities of the way we live now. Our little earth contains traces of the primordial ash of creation, powerful enough in handful sizes to wipe us all out: and human nature contains traces of savagery, persisting in advanced society, which can use the stuff to wipe us out. These were the two fundamental developments of the Second World War. Obscured in the dustclouds of conventional history kicked up by the great battles, they emerge plain as the dust settles. Whether in consequence the human story, like this tale, is entering its last chapter, nobody yet knows.

* * *

To go on with the story: the first time plutonium lumps blazed out in the new light, Sime Anderson was there.

"What on earth?" Madeline muttered, as the alarm went off at midnight.

"Sorry," he said with a yawn. "Duty calls."

"Again? Gawd," she said, turning over.

Sime dressed, went out in the chilly drizzle, and boarded one of the crowded buses carrying selected Los Alamos scientists and engineers to the test ground. Sime had been a small fish in the vast effort, but he was going with Captain Parsons, a large fish. The weather was bad for the test. For a while postponement was in the air, and the hour of the shot was delayed. The spectators waited in the dark many miles from the test tower, drinking coffee, smoking, and making airy or somber conversation. Nobody knew exactly what was going to happen when the shot went off. There was some talk, not quite persiflage, about the possibility that the explosion would set fire to the atmosphere, or start a process that would disintegrate the earth. There was nervous talk too about a fizzle.

That was the point of the test. Laboratory tickling of uranium 235 had satisfied the scientists that it would certainly go off with a proper bang in a critical mass; and so it did over Hiroshima without a previous test. The trouble was that the mountainous Manhattan Project had labored and brought forth only one small lethal mouse of U-235, just enough for a single bomb. Plutonium had turned out to be relatively simpler to produce, and there was more of it. But it was touchier stuff. Nobody could be sure whether it would not pre-detonate—that is, fizzle—as the lumps came together. There had to be a test of a device, worked out by the world's best brains, to whisk the lumps into an explosive mass in an eyeblink. The rain and wind abated, and the test went on. It worked. Flying from San Francisco to Washington on a night plane held up by weather, Byron saw the vague flash in the sky to the south, but he thought it was lightning. There were many electrical storms in the American West that morning. His sister, like most Los Alamos wives, slept straight through the test.

It did not look like lightning to Sime Anderson, of course. Standing twenty-five miles away, he saw through dark glasses a glare never before viewed by men on the earth's surface, though they had always seen it burning in the sun and twinkling in the stars. Sime fell on his face. It was instinct. When he got up, the cloud of fire—which reminded Dr. Oppenheimer of the apparition of Vishnu in the *Bhagavad-Gita*— already towered many miles high. A brigadier general and a scientist stood near Sime, paper coffee cups in hand, staring through goggles.

"There's the end of the war," he heard the scientist say.

"Yes," he heard the general say, "once we drop a couple of those on the Japs."

At the Andrews airfield, Pug and Pamela met Byron. After the warm letter Byron had written from Guam, Pug expected a bearhug, but it was his son's embrace of Pamela that gave him the feeling of a won war. Byron hugged and kissed his new stepmother, held her by the shoulders, looked her up and down, and shouted over the roar of a

MATS plane just taking off, "You know what? I'm damned if I'm going to call you mama."

She burst into a joyous laugh. "How about Pamela?"

"No change," said Byron. "Easy to remember. Dad, is there any news?"

"Since you called from San Francisco? None."

"When does she go into the convalescent home, did you say?"

"Day after tomorrow."

"I'd like to see Rabinovitz's letter."

"Here it is. There's another one from her."

Byron read his mail as Pamela drove wildly back to Washington. "She sounds better. Dad, I can't get on a plane to Europe. I was on the phone for hours in San Francisco, trying to wangle a priority."

"How much leave have you got?"

"Thirty days. Little enough."

"I'm flying there myself tomorrow."

"Where to?"

"Berlin. Potsdam."

"God, that would be perfect. I have to report to Swinemünde before my leave starts. Can I bum a ride?"

Pug's mouth wrinkled in a reluctant smile. "Let me find out."

Lunch with his mother at Foxhall Road was pleasanter than Byron had anticipated. Brigadier General Peters was not there. (He was, in fact, the general who had spoken at Los Alamos of dropping a couple on the Japs.) Janice showed up in a straight skirt, a plain brown blouse, and glasses, carrying a briefcase. She would not drink. She was working "on the hill" in a summer job, and did not want to get sleepy. She had put on weight, she wore little makeup, and her hair was pulled straight back. She was genially talkative about her plans after law school. When her eyes met Byron's he saw there only alert friendly intelligence. Her snapshots of little Victor, so much like Warren's kindergarten pictures, hurt Byron, but Rhoda made sweet grandmotherly noises over them.

"Mom's drinking too much," Byron said to his father that evening at the apartment.

"She has spells. What do you call too much?"

"Two Scotch-and-sodas before lunch, two bottles of white wine with the chicken salad. She polished off most of the wine herself."

"That's too much. I know she was tense about seeing you. She told me so."

"What about that plane ride?"

"Pack up in the morning and come with me. All they can do is bounce you."

"I haven't unpacked."

A courier in a special plane was rushing papers and pictures from Los Alamos to Secretary Stimson and President Truman in Potsdam, and Pug was going in that plane. This news was not being entrusted to the telephone or telegraph. It was still a secret of secrets. Only a short, enigmatic cable had been sent to the President, announcing the arrival of a healthy "baby," and he had informed Churchill. So these two knew. Most likely Stalin did too, since a leading scientist at Los Alamos was a faithful communist spy. Otherwise it was a secret of secrets. So Byron got rapid transportation to Europe on the courier plane, which turned out to make a great difference. As they say, it's an ill wind.

"There's no reason why he shouldn't be alive," Rabinovitz said. "She got him out of the Germans' hands. She took a hell of a chance, and I give her credit."

"How do I go about finding him?"

"That's another question. Very tough."

They sat drinking coffee at an outdoor café in Neuilly, waiting for Natalie to wake from her afternoon sleep. "Don't go into that with her," Rabinovitz said. "And don't stay too long, not this time. It'll be hard for her."

"We're bound to talk about Louis."

"Keep it vague. Just tell her that you're going to search for him. Twenty-five days isn't much time, but you can make an effort."

"Where's the best place to start?"

"Geneva. You'll find the big card files on kids there, the Red Cross, the Joint, the World Jewish Congress. They're starting a cross-index there, too. After Geneva, Paris. We have some files here. And I can give you a list of the D.P. camps that have a lot of children."

"Why don't I go straight to Prague? He ought to be around there somewhere."

"I went to Prague." Rabinovitz slumped over the coffee like an old man. He needed a shave, and his bloodshot eyes in sunken sockets were puffed almost shut. "I went to all four centers where they've got kids. I checked the card indexes and looked over the four-year-olds. I think I'd have recognized him, though they change a lot in a year and a half. Now as to the farmhouse, the name Natalie had, it's burned down and everything's overgrown and wild. Most of the neighbors are gone. Only one farmer would talk. He said he remembered a little boy, and he said the people weren't massacred, they got away. The Germans looted an empty house. Anyway, that was his story, and there you are. So it's tough. But kids can endure a lot, and Louis is a strong kid with plenty of spirit."

"I'll go to Geneva tomorrow."

Rabinovitz looked at the clock on the wall. "She's awake now. Do you want me to come with you?"

"I think so. Just to start with, you know."

"I can't stay long anyhow. Byron, she said more than once to me that if she ever finds Louis she'll take him to Palestine."

"Do you think she means that?"

Rabinovitz's shrug and look were skeptical. "She's not well yet. Don't get into an argument over it."

They gave their names at the reception desk, and waited in a flowery garden where patients sat about in the sunshine, some dressed, some in bathrobes. She came out and walked toward them with something of the old swing, in a dark dress, her hair cropped short. She was smiling uncertainly. Her legs were thin, her face gaunt.

"Well, Byron, so it's you," she said, holding out her arms. He embraced her and got a shock. Her body felt nothing like a woman's. The chest was almost flat. He was holding bones.

She leaned back in his arms, staring with strange eyes. "You look like a movie star," she said. Byron was wearing his dress whites and ribbons, because, as he had told Rabinovitz, the uniform helped him squelch fools behind desks. "And I look ghastly, don't I?"

"Not at all. Not to me, God knows."

"I should have gone with you in Marseilles." She recited the words dully, a rehearsed apology.

"None of that, Natalie."

She glanced at Rabinovitz, who stood stooped near them, smoking a cigarette. "Avram saved my life, you know."

Rabinovitz said, "You saved your own life. I'll go about my business, Byron."

Jumping at Rabinovitz, Natalie kissed him with much more feeling than she had shown Byron. She said something in Yiddish. Rabinovitz shrugged and walked out of the garden.

"Let's sit down," Natalie said to Byron with effortful politeness. "Your father has written me lovely letters. He's a fine man."

"Did you get any of mine?"

"No, Byron. Not that I remember. My memory is not too good, not yet." Natalie was speaking in a groping manner, almost as though trying to remember a foreign language. Her great dark eyes in shadowed hollows were scared and remote. They sat down on a stone bench by blooming rose bushes. "Not real letters. I dream, you know. I've dreamed a lot about you. I dreamed letters, too. But your father's letters, I know they were real. I'm sorry your parents broke up."

"My father's happy, and my mother's all right."

"Good. Of course, I knew Pamela in Paris. Strange, isn't it? And Slote, what about Slote? Do you know anything about Slote?"

For Byron, this conversation was starting very strangely. Her recent letters had been more affectionate and coherent. Now she seemed to be saying whatever came into her head, to cover fear or embarrassment; nothing that mattered, nothing about Louis, nothing about Aaron Jastrow, nothing intimate, mere forced chatter. He went along with it. He told her at length how Slote had ruined his career trying to get State Department action on the Jews, and about his end as a Jedburgh agent, what he knew of that from Pamela and his father. Natalie's eyes became more normal as she listened. Some of the alarm faded. "My heavens. Poor Slote, a parachutist! He couldn't have been very good at it, could he? But you see, I wasn't wrong to like him. His heart was in the right place, for a Gentile. I sensed that." She did not know how she brought Byron up short with those words. She was smiling at him. "You really do look so imposing. Were you in much danger?"

"*You* ask *me* that?"

"Well, there's danger and danger."

"I had narrow scrapes, sure. Ninety-nine percent of it was boring dead time. At least when I got in danger I could fight."

"I tried to fight. Maybe it was foolish, but that was my nature." Her mouth quivered. "Well, tell me about your narrow escapes. Tell me about Lady Aster. Is he a big hero now?"

Byron talked of Aster's exploits and his death. She seemed interested, though her eyes sometimes wandered. Then a silence fell between them. They sat in shade, in the fragrance of blooming roses, looking at each other. Natalie said brightly, "Oh, I finally got my new passport. It came yesterday. Lord, that little book looked good, Byron!"

"I'll bet."

"You know, I managed to keep my old one for a long, long time. Right into Auschwitz. Would you believe it? But there they took all my clothes away. One of the girls in Canada must have found it. She probably traded it for a nice big chunk of gold." Natalie's voice began to shake, her hands to tremble, her eyes to brim.

Byron decided to break through all this. He clasped her in his arms. "Natalie, I love you."

She clutched him with bony fingers, sobbing. "Sorry, sorry. I'm not in good condition yet. The nightmares, the nightmares! Every single night, Byron. Every night. And all the drugs, I get needles night and day—"

"I'm going to Geneva tomorrow to start looking for Louis."

"Oh, are you? Thank God." She wiped her eyes. "How much time have you got?"

"About a month. I'll come to see you, too."

"Yes, yes, but the main thing is to look for him." She seized his arm with both thin hands, her dark eyes widened, and her voice became an intense hissing whisper. *"He's alive. I know he is. Find him."*

"Darling, I'll give it the old college try."

She blinked, then laughed as she used to do. " 'The old college try.' How long since I've heard that!" She put her arms around his neck. "I love you, too. You're much, much older, Byron."

A nurse approached them, pointing at her wristwatch. Natalie looked surprised and rather relieved. "Oh, dear, already?" When she stood up, the nurse took her elbow. "But we haven't even talked about Aaron, have we? Byron, he was brave. The worse things got, the braver he was. I could tell you about him for hours. He wasn't the man we knew in Siena. He became very religious."

"I always thought he was, the way he wrote about Jesus."

Leaning on the nurse, Natalie frowned. At the entrance she again hugged him weakly. "I'm glad you're here. *Find him.* Forgive me, Byron, I'm in lousy shape. I'll do better next time." She kissed his mouth with dry rough lips, and went in.

"Lousy." The American slang word, ringing so naturally, slightly re-assured Byron. He hunted up the chief doctor, a prissy old Frenchman with a Pétain-like white mustache. "Ah, but she is doing very well, Monsieur. You have no idea. After the liberation, I worked for a month in the camps. Wreckage! Wreckage! Dante's Inferno! She will get well."

"She wrote me about scars on her legs and back."

The doctor's face twitched. "Not pretty, but ah, Monsieur, she is a lovely woman, and she is alive. The scars, *eh bien,* plastic surgery, and so forth. It is more a question now of mental scars, of restoring her flesh, and her spiritual balance."

After two weeks of combing the Geneva cards, and visiting displaced persons' camps, broken by one trip to see Natalie, Byron despaired. He was swamped. In an index book of his own he had compiled the leads under three categories:

> *Possible.*
> *Remote.*
> *Worth a Try.*

There were over seventy "possibles" alone; four-year-olds scattered over Europe, who from hair and eye color and languages understood might be his son. He had gone through some ten thousand listings of homeless children. No card showed a Louis Henry—nor a "Henry Lewis," a brainstorm which had come to him during a sleepless night and sent him running around to all the card index centers again. Following up these leads might take months. Years! He had days. Rabinovitz was not expecting Byron when he showed up in the shabby office on the Rue des Capuchins over a very ill-smelling restaurant.

"I'm going to Prague," Byron said. "Maybe it's a long shot, but I'm starting over."

"Well, all right, but you'll butt up against stone walls. The Russians are tough and uninterested, and they're in complete control."

"My father's in Potsdam. He's President Truman's naval aide."

Rabinovitz straightened up with a squeak of his swivel chair. "You didn't mention that."

"I didn't think it was relevant. He's had duty in the Soviet Union, and he speaks Russian in a fashion."

"Well, that could help you get around Prague. If the Military Governor receives word from Potsdam about you, the wheels will turn. At least you'll satisfy yourself whether he's there or not."

"Why should he be anywhere else, if he's alive?"

"He wasn't there, Byron, when I searched, though God knows I could have missed something. Go ahead, but talk to your father first."

Rabinovitz worked with an organization taking Jews into Palestine in defiance of the British immigration laws. Briefly relaxed at the first exposure of the Nazi horrors, these laws had tightened up again. He was grindingly busy. Natalie Henry was not a main concern of his. He felt compassion for her, and a wistful trace of the old hopeless love; but compared with most Jews in Europe, she was now out of danger, a convalescing cossetted American. With the arrival of Byron he put her from his mind, and did not visit her again. When a couple of weeks later the telephone rang in his Paris flat at two in the morning, waking the three men he shared it with, and the operator said, "Hold for London, please," his sleepy mind ran through many dealings he was having with London, most of them illegal and risky. He did not think of the Henrys.

"Hello. This is Byron."

"Who?"

"Byron Henry." The postwar connection to London was not good. The voice wavered. ". . . him."

"What? What did you say, Byron?"

"I said I've got him."

"What? You mean your son?"

"He's sitting here in my hotel room."

"Goddamn! He was in England?"

"I'm bringing him to Paris day after tomorrow. There's a lot of red tape still, and—"

"Byron, what's his condition?"

"Not so hot, but I've got him. Now, will you tell Natalie, please? Let her get used to the idea that he's found. Then when she sees him it won't upset her too much. Or him. I don't want him upset. Will you do that?"

"With the greatest pleasure in my life! Listen, what's the story? What shall I tell her?"

"Well, it's complicated. The RAF flew a bunch of Czech pilots back to Prague right after the war. A British rescue outfit got them to bring homeless kids back in the empty planes. I found this out last week in Prague. Pure luck. The records there are unbelievably rotten, Avram. I heard a guy in a restaurant talking about it, a Czech pilot, telling it to a British girl. It was luck. Luck or God. I followed it up and I've got him."

It was raining hard in the morning. Rabinovitz telephoned the convalescent home, and left a message for Natalie that he would come at eleven with important news. She stood waiting for him in the lobby when he arrived, shaking rain from his trench coat.

"I thought you must have gone to Palestine." Her face was taut. Her hands were clasped in front of her, the knuckles white. She was filling out; there were hints of curves under the dark dress.

"Well, I am going next week."

"What's your important news?"

"I heard from Byron."

"Yes?"

"Natalie." He held out his hands to her, and she seized them. "Natalie, he found him."

His grip on her hands was not firm enough. She grinned crazily and dropped to the floor.

The strong child brought the two little lumps together over Hiroshima that day. The new light seared more than sixty thousand people to cinders. The lone plane headed back to Tinian, radioing, *Mission successful.*

The controversy will go on while human life survives. Some of the arguments:

The Japanese would have surrendered anyway, without being bombed by radioactive lumps. They had sent out peace feelers. The American code-breakers knew from their diplomatic messages that they wanted peace.

Yet the Japanese rejected the Potsdam ultimatum.

Truman wanted to keep the Russians out of the Japanese war.

Yet at Potsdam he did not waive Stalin's commitment to attack Japan. He had Marshall's advice that the Russians could not be kept from attacking if they wanted to.

An invasion of Japan would have caused far more Japanese deaths, let alone American ones, than the Hiroshima casualties. The Japanese army leaders controlled the government, and their plan to fight invasion called for a bloody scorched-earth battle to the last like Hitler's. The bomb gave the Emperor leverage to force a decision for the peace party in his councils.

Yet the B-29 bombardments and the submarine blockade might have done so too, in time to scrub the invasion.

If not, and if the Soviet Union had materially aided an invasion, the Red Army would have occupied part of the land. Japan might have ended partitioned like Germany.

Yet whether the Japanese think the deaths at Hiroshima were an acceptable price for warding off that possibility is far from certain.

This much is certain.

The uranium weapon had been perfected barely in time for use in the war. There were two bombs available; only two, one of U-235, one of plutonium. The President, the cabinet, the scientists, the military men, all wanted the bomb rushed into combat. Harry Truman later said, "It was a bigger piece of artillery, so we used it." There were worried dissenting voices: few, and futile. The momentum of all that expenditure of money, manpower, industrial plant, and scientific genius was irresistible.

War scares nations, by murdering their people, into changing their politics. Here was the ultimate expression of war, after all, a child's handfuls murdering a city. How could it not be used? It did scare a nation into changing its politics overnight. "Greatest thing in history!" said President Truman at the news of Hiroshima.

Greatest thing since canned beer.

Byron came through the plane gate leading by the hand a pale small boy in a neat gray suit, who walked docilely beside him. Rabinovitz recognized Louis, though he was taller and thinner.

"Hello, Louis." The boy looked solemnly at him. "Byron, she's fine today, and waiting. I'll drive you there. Did you hear about the atom bomb?"

"Yes. I guess that's the end, all right."

Walking to Rabinovitz's very decrepit Citroën, they made the common talk being repeated all over the world, about the terrific news.

"Natalie says she's ready to go home, now that you've got him," Rabinovitz said as they drove. "She thinks she'll recuperate better there."

"Yes, we talked about that last time I saw her. Also she has property. Aaron's publisher has been in touch with her. There's quite a lot of money. And that villa in Siena, if it's still standing. His lawyer has the deeds. It makes sense for her to go back right now."

"She won't go with you to Germany, that I can tell you."

"I don't expect her to."

"How will you feel there yourself?"

"Well, the U-boat men are just professionals. I've got a job to do with them."

"They're murderers."

"So am I," Byron said without rancor, stroking Louis's head. The boy sat on his lap, soberly looking out of the window at the sunny flat green fields outside Paris. "They're the conquered enemy. We study their equipment and methods as soon as possible after surrender. That's standard."

Silenced for a minute or so, Rabinovitz said abruptly, "I think she'll stay in America, once she goes there."

"She doesn't know what she'll do. First she has to get well."

"Would you come with her to Palestine?"

"That's a tough one. I know nothing about Zionism."

"We Jews need a state of our own to live in, where we won't get massacred. That's all there is to Zionism."

"She won't get massacred in America."

"Can the Jews all go there?"

"What about the Arabs?" Byron asked after a pause. "The ones that are there in Palestine already?"

Rabinovitz's face as he drove became grave, almost tragic. He looked straight ahead, and his reply came slowly. "The Arabs can be grim, and they can also be noble. Christian Europe has tried to kill us. What choice have we? Palestine is our traditional home. Islam has a tradition to let the Jews live. Not in a state of our own, not as yet, that's a new thing in their history. But it will work out." He glanced toward Louis, and caressed the quiet boy's cheek. "With a hell of a lot of trouble first. That's why we need him."

"Will you need a navy?"

Rabinovitz briefly sourly smiled. "Between you and me, we have one. I helped organize it. A goddamn small one, so far."

"Well, I'll never be separated from this kid, once I'm demobilized. That much I know."

"Isn't he very quiet?"

"He doesn't talk."

"What do you mean?"

"Just that. He doesn't smile, and he doesn't talk. He hasn't said a word to me yet. I had a time getting him released. They had him classified as psychologically disabled, some such fancy category. He's fine. He eats, he dresses and cleans himself, in fact he's very neat, and he understands anything you say. He obeys. He doesn't talk."

Rabinovitz said in Yiddish, "Louis, look at me." The boy turned and faced him. "Smile, little fellow." Louis's large eyes conveyed faint dislike and contempt, and he looked out of the window again.

"Let him be," Byron said. "I had to sign more damned papers and raise more hell before I could pry him loose. It's lucky I got there when I did. They're shipping about a hundred of these so-called psychologically disabled kids to Canada next week. God knows if we could ever have traced him there."

"What's the story on him?"

"Very sparse. I can't read Czech, naturally, and the translation of the card was pretty poor. I gather he was picked up in a woods near Prague, where the Germans took a lot of Jews and Czechs and shot them. The bodies were just lying around. That's where somebody found him, among the bodies."

As they walked into the sunny garden of the convalescent home, Byron said, "Look, Louis, there's Mama."

Natalie stood near the same stone bench, in a new white frock. Louis let go of his father's hand, walked toward Natalie, then broke into a run and leaped at her.

"Oh, my God! How *big* you are! How heavy you are! Oh, Louis!"

She sat down, embracing him. The child clung, his face buried on her shoulder, and she rocked him, saying through tears, "Louis, you came back. You came back!" She looked up at Byron. "He's glad to see me."

"Sort of."

"Byron, you can do anything, can't you?"

His face still hidden, the boy was gripping his mother hard. Rocking him back and forth, she began to sing slowly in Yiddish,

> *Under Louis's cradle,*
> *Lies a little white goat.*
> *The little goat went into business—*

Louis let go of her, sat up smiling on her lap, and tried to sing along in Yiddish, in a faltering hoarse voice, a word here and there,

> *"Dos vet zein dein baruf,*
> *Rozhinkes mit mandlen—"*

Almost at the same moment, Byron and Rabinovitz each put a hand over his eyes, as though dazzled by an unbearable sudden light.

In a shallow, hastily dug grave in the wood outside Prague, Berel Jastrow's bones lie unmarked, like so many bones all over Europe. And so this story ends.

It is only a story, of course. Berel Jastrow was never born and never existed. He was a parable. In truth his bones stretch from the French coast to the Urals, dry bones of a murdered giant. And in truth a marvelous thing happens; his story does not end there, for the bones stand up and take on flesh. God breathes spirit into the bones, and Berel Jastrow turns eastward and goes home. In the glare, the great and terrible light of this happening, God seems to signal that the story of the rest of us need not end, and that the new light can prove a troubled dawn.

For the rest of us, perhaps. Not for the dead, not for the more than fifty million real dead in the world's worst catastrophe: victors and vanquished, combatants and civilians, people of so many nations, men, women, and children, all cut down. For them there can be no new earthly dawn. Yet though their bones lie in the darkness of the grave, they will not have died in vain, if their remembrance can lead us from the long, long time of war to the time for peace.

The history of the war in this romance, as in *The Winds of War,* is offered as accurate; the statistics, as reliable; the words and acts of the great personages, as either historical, or derived from accounts of their words and deeds in similar situations. Major figures of history do not appear in times and places not historically true.

World Holocaust, the military treatise by "Armin von Roon," is of course an invention from start to finish. Still, General von Roon's book is offered as a professional German view of the other side of the hill, reliable within the limits peculiar to that self-justifying literature. Except where directly challenged by Victor Henry, Roon's facts are accurate, however warped by nationalism his judgments may be.

The reliability of detail in the well-known battles, campaigns, and events of the war—Singapore, Midway, Leyte Gulf, the Tehran Conference, the sieges of Imphal and Leningrad, and the like—will, it is hoped, be evident to the informed reader. The notes that follow deal with little-known or unusual historical elements of the story, and with passages where fact and fiction are especially intertwined.

The exploits of the fictional submarines *Devilfish, Moray,* and *Barracuda* are improvisations on actual wartime submarine patrol reports. The death of Carter Aster is based on the famous self-sacrifice of Commander Howard W. Gilmore of U.S.S. *Growler,* for which he was posthumously awarded the Congressional Medal of Honor. Aster, however, is a different and fictional character.

All other Navy vessels in the novel are actual and their movements and actions follow the historical record. All admirals in the Pacific are real personages and are treated like the major political figures. The story of the heavy cruiser *Northampton,* except for the fictitious captains Hickman and Henry, follows its war diary from Pearl Harbor to its sinking at the Battle of Tassafaronga.

The names of the pilots and gunners in the three torpedo squadrons at Midway proved surprisingly difficult to recover and verify, so quickly is the record fading. The rosters printed in the novel are the result of a long search. Any reliable corrections will be welcomed for future editions.

The story of the *Izmir* is a fictionalization of actual illegal voyages of refugees from the Nazis, who reached Palestine in this way or died trying.

"The Wannsee Protocol" is a historical document, and as described in the story, only one copy out of thirty of this top-secret record was preserved, through an accident of bureaucratic overthoroughness. Disclosure of a smuggled photocopy to the American legation in Bern is fictional, as are the characters in the legation.

Americans caught in Italy by the war were interned in Siena, as narrated. Those caught in southern France were first interned in Lourdes, then moved to Baden-Baden, as in the story; and harshly bargained for by the Germans thereafter, for more than a year.

The Comte and Comtesse de Chambrun are real figures; the comte did administer the American Hospital in Paris. The German ambassador in Paris, Otto Abetz, is historical. Werner Beck is a fictional character.

The Joint Declaration of the United Nations in December 1942, which led to the Bermuda Conference, is history. Its text is given in full in the novel. Assistant Secretary of State Breckinridge Long is an actual person, whose conversation and actions are drawn largely from his own writings and his congressional testimony. Foxy Davis is fictitious.

The Bermuda Conference happened as described. The public reaction that gradually ensued, and the establishment of the War Refugee Board, are facts.

The main source for the furor in 1943 over Soviet suppression of Lend-Lease facts is Admiral William Standley's autobiography. This Soviet practice, incidentally, continues to the present day. General Yevlenko is fictional.

"The Declaration of the Three Powers Regarding Iran" (referred to in the text as "The Declaration of Iran") is a historical fact, as is the general outline of how it came about; though of course Victor Henry's conversation with the Minister of the Imperial Court, Hussein Ala—a real person—is invented. General Connolly of the Persian Gulf Command is an actual officer, and the description of Lend-Lease aid to the Soviet Union through that corridor is factual. The fictitious Granville Seaton describes true Persian history.

"The Paradise Ghetto" in Terezin, or Theresienstadt, Czechoslovakia, was known about during the war. Nothing is invented or exaggerated in this account, though the parts played by Natalie and Dr. Jastrow are fictitious. The SS officers are all real, as are the High Elders Eppstein and Murmelstein. The general history of the ghetto is true. The "Great Beautification" for the one visit of neutral Red Cross observers is a well-documented fact, in all its bizarre details, as is the visit itself. A fragment of the film "The Führer Grants the Jews a Town" survives in the Yad Vashem archive in Jerusalem. The making of the film took place as described, but the film was never exhibited.

The scenes in Oswiecim, or Auschwitz, are based on a study of the available documents and literature, as well as on consultations with survivors. These scenes have been meticulously reviewed for authenticity by eminent authorities on this terrible subject. Oswiecim may be forever beyond the grasp of the human mind, now that nothing is left of it but a dead museum. It is hoped that living survivors of Auschwitz, comparing their recollections with this fictional Remembrance, created by one who was not there, will see an honest effort to make the vanished horror live for all the world that was not there.

The march of Soviet prisoners from Lamsdorf to Oswiecim, the episodes of cannibalism, the experimental gassing of these Soviet prisoners of war with Zyklon B to test its efficacy for killing Jews en masse: all these are facts. An important source is the memoir of the Commandant himself, Rudolf Hoess, written while he was awaiting trial after the war. He was found guilty of the mass murders, which he freely admitted, and was hanged in Auschwitz.

The other SS officers are real people, except that Klinger is fictitious. The inspection visit of Himmler, and his viewing of the gassing process from beginning to end, took place as described; in July, however, not in June. The construction of the crematoriums, the general picture of the Auschwitz Interest Area with its industries and agricultural installations, the treatment of prisoners who attempted to escape, the roll calls, "Canada": all facts.

Kommando 1005, the roving German unit that exhumed and eradicated the mass graves, is a matter of history. SS Colonel Paul Blobel is an actual person. The mutiny of Mutterperl is fictitious. The mass escape of some prisoners is improvised out of accounts of such escapes from SS slave gangs.

Berel Jastrow's fictitious journey from Ternopol through the Carpathians to Prague is based on several such incredible journeys, made by Jews who escaped from the death camps with photographic and documentary evidence, and crossed all of Nazi-held Europe to bring the revelation to the outside world; only to encounter the almost universal "will not to believe." The fictitious partisan bands of Nikonov and Levine are derived from existing partisan literature. Reference is made in this passage to some actual partisan bands.

The treatment of the landing craft and atomic bomb programs is factual. There was a conflict over priorities involving a coupling. Victor Henry's part in it is of course fictitious; Dr. Oppenheimer's visit to Oak Ridge is a fictional scene; and Kirby, Peters, and Anderson are fictional characters. It is a fact that Dr. Oppenheimer recommended the very late introduction of the Navy's thermal diffusion system into Oak Ridge, to provide enriched feed for the electromagnetic separation process; and that this made possible the production of one U-235 bomb for use in the war, over Hiroshima. The Nagasaki bomb of plutonium was produced in the Hanford reactors. It is also a fact that no other bombs were available from the Manhattan Project when these two were dropped.

The account of the FM sonar, "Hell's Bells," and of its use late in the war, is factual.

To sum up: the purpose of the author in both *War and Remembrance* and *The Winds of War* was to bring the past to vivid life through the experiences, perceptions, and passions of a few people caught in the war's maelstrom. This purpose was best served by scrupulous accuracy of locale and historical fact, as the backdrop against which the invented drama would play. Such at least was the working ideal.

Herman Wouk

1962–1978